Marjorie Eccles was born in Yorkshire and spent her childhood there and on the Northumbrian coast. She has written twenty-five books and many magazine serials and short stories. In 1998 she was awarded the Agatha Christie Short Story Styles Award and in 2004 was shortlisted for the Crime Writers' Ellis Peters Historical Award. She has one son and one grandson, and lives with her husband in the Chilterns.

Also in the Gil Mayo Mystery series

MORE DEATHS THAN ONE

LATE OF THIS PARISH

THE COMPANY SHE KEPT

AN ACCIDENTAL SHROUD

A DEATH OF DISTINCTION

A SPECIES OF REVENGE

KILLING ME SOFTLY

THE SUPERINTENDENT'S DAUGHTER

A SUNSET TOUCH

UNTIMELY GRAVES

THE GIL MAYO MYSTERIES OMNIBUS

CAST A COLD EYE
DEATH OF A GOOD WOMAN
REQUIEM FOR A DOVE

Marjorie Eccles

TIME WARNER
BOOKS

TIME WARNER BOOKS

This omnibus edition first published in Great Britain in March 2006
by Time Warner Books

The Gil Mayo Mysteries Omnibus Copyright © Marjorie Eccles 2006

Previously published separately:
Cast a Cold Eye first published in Great Britain
in 1988 by Constable & Company Ltd
Copyright © Marjorie Eccles 1988

Death of a Good Woman first published in Great Britain in 1989
by William Collins Sons & Co. Ltd
Copyright © Marjorie Eccles 1989

Requiem for a Dove first published in Great Britain in 1990
by William Collins Sons & Co. Ltd
Copyright © Marjorie Eccles 1990

The moral right of the author has been asserted.

A CIP catalogue record for this book
is available from the British Library.

ISBN-13: 978-0-7515-3861-8
ISBN-10: 0-7515-3861-2

Typeset in Plantin by M Rules
Printed and bound in Great Britain
by Clays Ltd, St Ives plc

Time Warner Books
An imprint of
Time Warner Book Group UK
Brettenham House
Lancaster Place
London WC2E 7EN

www.twbg.co.uk

CAST A
COLD EYE

CHAPTER 1

The party was still in full swing, but it had been over for a long time as far as the pair from the *Advertiser* was concerned, Matt could see.

The young reporter, bored out of his mind, accepted his third glass of champagne, or maybe his fourth, shot his cuff to look at his watch yet again, and rolled up his eyes at the photographer.

Well, it wouldn't be his kind of party, would it? No music, no dancing. Not even outside in the spacious gardens as it would have been a few weeks earlier, before October set in. Instead, polite chat and restrained laughter in the elegant surroundings of the Lethbridge drawing room here at Brome House, all rich, deep colours, dark panelling and antique furniture. Not his scene at all. Experience told Matt what it felt like to wait like this, wishing your host would get on with the knitting – the speeches, the toasts, whatever – so that you could get your story and get the hell out of it, and back to civilisation. In this case, on the road from Brome to Lavenstock. Matt grinned in sympathy, and then, as Caroline came up to him, he forgot all about the pair.

Clive Lethbridge wasn't anywhere near ready yet to wind up his party. He was very obviously enjoying it, basking in the congratulations which fell upon him like manna as he circulated among one group and another. Expansive, flushed with the triumph of his success, having his hand pumped and his back slapped, Clive was a man on the crest of a wave.

A telephone rang somewhere in the recesses of the house and presently Clive's secretary, a mousy girl with round thick-lensed spectacles, sought him out, catching him between groups. Briefly, as she spoke to him, Clive stood very still. Then with his heavy, purposeful stride, he left the room.

It was some time before he came back, and it was perhaps only his wife, Caroline – and Matt, who was as usual watching her reactions – who noticed the difference in him.

'Excuse me a minute, Matt.' Pushing back the smooth wing of dark hair that fell across her cheek, giving Matt a glimpse of her slow, sweet smile, Caroline left him with only the faint drift of her elusive scent and the touch of cool fingers on his wrist. He watched her walk, graceful and unhurried, her dress a drift of soft dove colour, to the table by the window, where Clive was pouring himself a stiff scotch, downing it in one go and then pouring another.

Matt caught a sideways view of their reflections in the dark window. Standing beside Clive, completing the picture of the pair they presented to the world, Caroline's petite slenderness was a piquant contrast to Clive's big, heavyset frame. An unusual, intriguing couple. With a sharp twist of irony Matt thought, not for the first time, that the coarse-grained Lethbridge had at least shown a redeeming streak of sensitivity in choosing Caroline for a wife. Her money, of course, could not have been a disadvantage, either.

All right, one had to respect the man, professionally at any rate. He was a demon for work and extremely competent – in a fairly run-of-the-mill way, yet with occasional flashes of something like inspiration, now flowered into the astonishing, soaring vision personified in the architectural model set on the table in the centre of the room, together with the photographs of its final realisation, humbling Matt as he looked at them yet again. What standards was a man judged by, after all?

With more force than was necessary, Matt ground out the stub of the cigarette he shouldn't have been smoking. If he'd any sense, he would pack the job in, shake the dust off his feet here and now, tell Conti that he'd either have to find another architect than Clive to collaborate on the production of the book, or find another writer. But he knew he was only making noises. It was too late; he had long since gone beyond the point of no return.

Often lately, in the sleepless reaches of the night, Matt regretted having allowed Conti to persuade him into accepting the commission, but he was well aware that, given the chance again, he'd make the same decision. The work had brought him into touch with Caroline, who, besides being Clive's wife, worked as a publisher's reader for Conti. And for the second time in a year, he found his life and its direction turned upside down.

Clive, whatever his other faults, had been only a moderate drinker since his doctor had told him to lay off if he wanted to keep his weight and his blood pressure down, and he'd already consumed what he regarded as his quota. Caroline felt a prickle of unease as she saw the speed with which he now drank this, then another whisky. He was drinking automatically, staring at his own distorted reflection in the rain-spattered lattice of the darkened window behind the drinks table, his face drained of its ruddy glow of self-congratulation. That telephone call. Maybe it wasn't his reflection he was staring at; maybe he was looking beyond the darkness, to the house on the slope of the far side of the valley, where the Dymonds lived.

'Clive? What's wrong?'

He broke his stare, turning to face her. 'What do you mean, wrong?' His voice would have sounded normal to anyone else, but she was too used to his moods not to notice the edge to it, to know that his euphoria had left him. A prominent vein pulsed in his temple, as it always did when he was upset, a dead giveaway. A storm signal for rough weather ahead.

She took a steadying breath. 'I meant the phone call. Was it another one of – of *those*? You look . . .' 'Desperate' was the word, but not to be used now, with controlled violence just below the surface of his calm.

'It's nothing,' he replied with an effort. 'I've just had enough of this bloody lot, that's all.' He half turned as he spoke, pinning a social smile on to his face, and nodding to someone who caught his eye. 'Clear them out, Caro.'

It was a command rather than a request, and she bit her lip at the arbitrary tone but deliberately stifled her resentment.

'All right, but you *are* supposed to be celebrating, don't forget. People aren't expecting to go just yet. And Harry's waiting to say a few words.'

'Oh God, yes, Harry.' His strong, blunt fingers had tightened round his glass until the knuckles were white. 'Harry, by all means. Tell him to get on with it, then.'

Harry Waring, Clive's senior partner, smooth and late-fiftyish, rosy with good living, was standing beside the table that held the model, cigar in one hand, glass in the other, having just escaped Clive's new secretary. He took a revivifying sip. God, but she was hard work, no conversation, that one, that Susan – no, Sylvia, Sylvia Johnson, never could remember her name. Difficult to remember *her*, sometimes – a personality as drab as that potato-coloured dress which did even less for her than her usual dreary skirts and jumpers.

Thoughtfully, he contemplated the model. 'Astonishing, isn't it?' he remarked to Matt, who had just joined him.

Astonishing. The very word Matt himself had chosen earlier. 'Sure,' he agreed, though not altogether certain what Waring had intended by the word. Astonishing as an architectural concept, or merely astonishing for Clive Lethbridge?

Waring said suddenly, 'I'd like a word, Royston. Can we fix a time?'

Matt nodded, surprised. 'I shall be away for the next week, but when I get back I'll give you a ring. Will that do?'

'Yes, do that if you would. Ah, Caroline.' At the sound of her low, slightly husky voice, Harry turned affectionately towards Caroline, who was in his opinion everything a woman should be –

pretty and feminine, socially adept, clever, too. Just the right wife for a man in Clive's position – though Clive needed a kick up the pants for how he treated her sometimes.

Caroline smiled at him, the luminous blue of her eyes lighting the habitual gravity of her expression. 'Are you ready, Harry?'

Harry had expected, indeed asked for, the opportunity to make a small speech on this occasion, and he would perform with his usual urbanity, Caroline knew, so that when he began she was surprised that it was hesitantly, without his usual fluent composure. After a moment or two, however, he was into his stride, making a polished and graceful performance of it, conceding the honours for the success that had lately fallen on to the firm justly to Clive's brilliant, award-winning design, following its success in a world-wide competition.

There were handclaps for him as well as Clive when he paused appropriately so that Clive, who had by now taken a grip on himself, could acknowledge the accolade, and murmur something deprecating about it all being a team effort. Harry resumed, smiling. Yet Caroline, accustomed to his witty and humorous deliveries, again detected something a trifle forced, almost as if, she thought, he were trying to convince himself as well as his audience of the value of the splendid design, which of course was nonsense, an aberration on her part; no one else appeared to have noticed. Her eyes unconsciously searched the room for Matt, but if she had expected to be able to read on his face confirmation of what he was thinking, she was disappointed.

He was leaning negligently against the wall, a little apart from the rest, a tall, rangy man with a fading tan, straight, grey-threaded fair hair and contrastingly marked dark brows. A strong, mature face, experienced and knowledgeable. He was thirty-six and looked older, and there was a wry quality about him, a way of looking at himself as well as others, that might just, one day, turn to cynicism. At that moment, as if at some prearranged signal, he turned his head and their eyes met, and things carefully unspoken

7

between them ever since they had been introduced were suddenly and silently said.

Caroline felt a wave of actual faintness. It was as though some support to which she had been desperately trying to cling for weeks had given way, and she was adrift, fighting breathlessly against a tide that was inevitably going to carry her away, into forbidden waters. Desperately, with an almost physical effort, she forced herself and her attention back to what was going on.

Harry had finally finished. Glasses were being raised, the photographer's bulbs flashing. The young reporter's usually laboured shorthand flowed under the influence of the champagne. Caroline was asked to pose with Clive for a photograph which would be on the front page of next week's *Advertiser*. Clive was asked for a quote. And then the party was really over.

CHAPTER 2

Clive was in the habit of working at home one day per week, more if he happened to be pressed. It gave him personal space, time to catch up on the backlog of correspondence which accumulated during the week, and to review his plans without constant interruption. There was peace here, unlike his main offices in the centre of Birmingham, where everyone was on top of everyone else and there was no room to swing a cat. He had to have this mid-week change of gear; he *needed* it – especially today, the morning after the celebration party.

For by God, he thought savagely, simmering with controlled rage as he remembered yet again, no slimy-tongued anonymous telephone caller was going to mess up his life! He'd managed so far to ignore the insinuations and threats – well, let them get on with it and see how far they were prepared to go. Nobody was better at brinksmanship than he was. He'd had plenty of practice.

So. He sat quite still for a moment, taking a deliberate hold on himself, then opened his diary, without which he swore he couldn't function. His secretary noted down his appointments and sometimes also reminders of Caroline's social commitments so that they shouldn't clash. He had the habit of using the book almost like a scratch pad, jotting down the odd thought or calculation, sometimes making a quick sketch as an idea occurred to him, as well as making his own notes of things to be done each day. On principle, he always made this list longer than he could reasonably be expected to accomplish ... yet rarely was it left unfinished at the end of the day. It was his way of driving himself, of going that bit further and therefore getting one up on the next man, which was, he figured, the way any thrusting, successful man should operate.

At length, he shut the book with a decisive snap and leaned back in his chair.

He saw with satisfaction that today the weather at least was in league with him, the morning very warm for early October, after the previous day's rain. There were still roses on the bushes outside the open french window, the perfume drifting in. MacAllister would see Brome House at its best, and not need too much persuasion to put his money into financing the project. Because now, *now* was the time to do it, to approach MacAllister with this latest success behind him. His gaze rested on the Svensen Centre model, now standing on a small table beside the window, and he smiled.

Situated out here, midway between Lavenstock and Birmingham, the location of Brome House was convenient, the setting idyllic. He had cultivated the habit of bringing business associates and prospective clients here, so that they could meet and discuss their business in a leisurely manner. A walk round the garden, drinks on the terrace, lunch afterwards in the gracious dining room – no need to take anyone out to lunch when

Caroline, with the help of Janice Wharton, could provide better food than any local restaurant, and act as hostess at the same time. It was all part of the softening up process, which almost always worked.

Clive smiled again, hitched his chair forward and began work on a pile of routine papers, but his mind still circled round his cherished plan. She would come round, he told himself – he'd find a way to *make* her see his point of view. He was confident of his ability to find some means of putting pressure on her, making her agree to do as he wished. He fully intended anyway, Caroline or no Caroline, one way or another, to go ahead, but it would be easier with her support.

The plan, like a rich fruit-cake, had improved with keeping. He would do a first-class conversion job on Brome House here, turning the whole place into a set of prestigious offices – without, of course, spoiling the leisured country-house atmosphere. Clients liked that sort of thing – and the conversion would be an advertisement in itself. He and Caroline and Pippa would then move to the new house he planned to build on the site he had acquired lower down the valley. It was time Caroline's ideas were changed; it was ridiculous and outmoded these days to think of the three of them rattling around in a house this size, just because her family had inhabited it for generations. A pity the house was still in his wife's name; it had been the only thing he hadn't been able to persuade her to make over when her father's estate had been settled. Caroline could be very stubborn about some things.

He could hear Sylvia Johnson already moving about in the room next door, which she used as an office. It was only twenty to nine, twenty minutes before her starting time. Sylvia, too, worked here on Clive's non-city days, but she was so unobtrusive she never got in the way, and so capable he was beginning to wonder after only six weeks how he had ever doubted anyone could replace Amanda, that hitherto irreplaceable paragon of efficiency.

He reached for a blue file marked 'Oddings Cottage.' As he did so, the stutter of a motorbike starting up broke the silence of the morning, then roared away.

Clive sprang up and leaped through the open french windows, shading his eyes against the bright sunlight as he reached the gravel drive outside, which completely encircled the house. He was just in time to see the bike disappearing through the main gates. Without stopping to think, he charged across the lawn towards the lodge.

The back door was open. A young woman was standing by the scullery door, taking an overall from a peg.

'Where's Terry gone?' Clive demanded, stepping in uninvited, panting only slightly from his sprint. Though heavily built, a daily stint of jogging was part of his programme for keeping himself fit.

The woman spun round, paused when she saw who it was and what mood he was in, then answered calmly, beginning to roll up the overall, 'Up to the university, Mr Lethbridge. He has a seminar this morning.'

'Seminar? Why didn't he tell me that yesterday? I told him then I should want him to mow the lawns if it was fine.'

Janice Wharton tucked a strand of escaping hair more firmly behind her ears, a neat, brown-haired woman in her late twenties or early thirties. 'I expect he forgot. It was only Saturday when he did them, wasn't it? His usual day.'

'He's not damn well paid to forget! And whether he cut them then or not's immaterial. When I say I want something done, I want it done. All that rain's made the grass shoot up, and I particularly wanted the grounds to look their best today. He knew that – why the hell didn't he tell me yesterday he wouldn't be here?' Clive demanded, thrusting a pugnacious face close to hers, the prominent vein throbbing in his temple.

You know very well why, Janice thought, endeavouring to step unobtrusively back. If Terry *had* mentioned the seminar, Clive would have kicked up an almighty fuss, no doubt about that. All right, in the end he would probably have conceded the point

11

because, to give him his due, he never went back on his word, and he'd promised when they came here that Terry could run his studies alongside the job – but the concession wouldn't have been given before he'd left Terry abject and humiliated. And humiliation wasn't something her husband swallowed easily. He'd learned to keep more of a rein on his temper lately, but he'd only stand so much.

Janice's hands were clenched into fists at her side. She wished fervently that Terry would at least try to be diplomatic with Clive – why wouldn't he see that he *mustn't* throw away this chance which had been given them like another life?

It was still something so wonderful she couldn't quite believe it, an opportunity for Terry to get himself qualified for a decent job, to work for a degree, and at the same time have somewhere as incredible as this to live.

'I'll see if I can find time to do the grass,' she told Clive. After all, it was only time that it took. There wasn't much effort needed. You sat on the mower seat and steered the machine round, and the motor did the rest. She'd done it before once or twice, when Terry had an essay due.

'Mrs Lethbridge will need your help in the house this morning,' Clive returned shortly, suddenly coldly formal. 'Do I have to remind you that's what we employ you for?'

Quick colour stained Janice's cheeks, but all she said was, 'We're well ahead with preparations for the lunch, and if I hurry with the cleaning, I'll get through.' She reached for the overall and tucked it under her arm.

He said nastily, 'I sometimes wonder whose benefit this arrangement we have is for,' and left her without another word.

Janice glanced at the clock, saw she still had a few minutes in hand and took the time to get herself together. She found she was shivering and stood by the sink, her arms crossed, holding herself tight, looking round at every detail of the bright kitchen.

This little house, Brome Lodge, was part of the remuneration for their husband-and-wife services as home help and handyman in the house and garden. She was so proud of it; they had made it so nice, she and Terry, painting and papering and doing up the old furniture Caroline had found for them in the attics of the big house – really good stuff, some of it had turned out to be. After the appalling years of trying to bring up two children in terrible rented rooms, or even squats, it was very nearly paradise to her. There wasn't much she wouldn't do to keep it.

Meanwhile, letting Clive Lethbridge's barbs get under her skin was a luxury she couldn't afford. She had better get on if she wanted to get that grass cut before that client of his arrived. Locking the door and pocketing the key of her little kingdom, she began to walk up to the house and thought, as she did every day of her life, I wonder what he'd do if he *knew*.

A few minutes ahead of her Clive, as he went back, again taking the short cut across the unmown lawn, debated whether he shouldn't get rid of the Whartons. It had been a mistake to let Caroline persuade him with a hard-luck story when old Ganson had died and the lodge had become vacant. He wasn't averse to being regarded as a benefactor, and Janice, according to Caroline, had become indispensable, but Terry, besides being unreliable, wasn't much cop, not as a gardener anyway. He did what he was told to do – when he felt like it – but he was no substitute for Ganson. It was only the fact that he was extremely handy with the cars and odd jobs around the house that had saved him so far. All the same, he was also employed to cut the lawns, and cut them he had not. Still fuming, Clive went through the french windows into his study.

Sylvia had put the post on his desk while he had been out, unopened. Mail that came here was usually of a personal nature; anything else waited at the office until the following day, unless it was urgent, when he would be contacted. He had picked the pile up and was beginning to throw out the unsolicited junk when Sylvia walked in, drawing back in a startled manner when she saw him.

'Oh, excuse me! I didn't hear you come back in.'

'Did you want something?' He spoke curtly; it would take some time for him to recover his composure.

'Oh well, only that file, with those notes of Matt Royston's you promised to check. I put it out yesterday for you to bring over; it needs tidying up.'

He gestured towards his briefcase, not raising his eyes, putting an electricity bill to one side. She took the file out of the briefcase, made for the door and paused. 'Mr Lethbridge?'

'Yes?'

'There's something I'd like to have a word with you about – but it doesn't matter, it can wait,' she added hastily as she watched him pick up another envelope and draw in a sharp, audible breath.

'Yes, later,' he said roughly, not looking at her.

She didn't move for a moment, still watching him. 'When you can spare a moment,' she said at last, and went out so silently he never heard her.

Clive knew what he ought to do with the thing. Tear it into bits and flush it down the loo, as he had with the others. But just for a moment, he was scared. Frightened as he hadn't been since he was a kid, waiting for the results of the exam that could take him away from the aunt who had brought him up, and the stuffy respectability of working-class Nottingham, never to return.

Then the model caught his eye again, reassuring him.

The whole project had been envisaged and financed by a health-conscious Norwegian millionaire. Having recently visited Epidaurus, he had returned home fired with the rediscovered beliefs of ancient Greece, that the mind and body are so interdependent it is futile to treat one without the other, determined to reproduce another healing centre such as Epidaurus, though better, in Norway. The brief for the competition thus launched had included a hospital, theatre, library, and a gallery to house the millionaire's art collection. Peace and tranquility were paramount requirements; music, books and theatre were to be freely available, patients would be surrounded by paintings and sculpture, and other works of art, inside and outdoors. The whole – view, ambience, art treasures – was calculated to free the mind so that the body could be treated, or vice-versa. To be, in the jargon, a total and enriching experience.

The basic design was good – all right, outstanding, a complex of glass and steel so radical there'd been doubts about its viability – but the brilliance lay in the use to which it had been adapted, in the marriage of the site with the buildings themselves, in producing a solution so perfect to the requirements. Chosen from hundreds submitted from around the world, now finished and in use, it was set in the mountains, amongst bracing air and the dappled shade of light woodland, with breathtaking views from the windows. It was to be known as the Svensen Centre.

Clive walked across to the window and stared out.

A couple of miles away was the opposite slope of the valley with, almost directly facing Brome House, the house where *they* lived. Mr Marcus bloody Dymond and his wife. Built sometime during the 1930s, it was pleasant, largish, mock-Tudor style with a garden which had been something of a showpiece until Enid had at last been forced to succumb to her illness and take to a wheelchair. The garden had been her sole interest in life, and she still managed, with the aid of special long-handled tools, to do a very small amount from her chair, but this was limited, owing to the sloping site of the garden, and as far as Clive could gather, the whole thing was becoming a burden. That husband of hers apparently had neither the knowledge nor an enthusiasm equal to hers to cope with it.

So she had nothing to do all day except sit at her window staring through those damned binoculars. Bird watching, she called it, which was another way of saying spying. Spying on the occupants of Brome House and setting her sights on Oddings Cottage, nestling beneath the shelter of the big house. For a moment

15

remorse touched Clive, then a puzzled fury drove it away. How could Dymond have found out? How could he *possibly* have found out?

There was, of course, the boy – though he wouldn't have thought . . . But it must be so; it had to be.

It was Dymond who had sent the letter, of that he was sure, just as he was certain Dymond had sent the others – *and* been the instigator of the telephone calls. Savage thoughts churned in Clive's breast. To hell with him! No way was he going to be intimidated by a jumped-up schoolmaster, or anyone else! Survival of the fittest was what it was all about.

Scrunching up the letter in his fist, the tell-tale vein beginning to jump again at his temple, Clive reached deliberately for the telephone and dialled the number of the Lavenstock Police. Then, before it was answered, he changed his mind and put the receiver back.

Damn Dymond! Damn, damn, damn him.

CHAPTER 3

After lunch had been cleared away and MacAllister had left, Caroline thrust a letter into her pocket for posting to Pippa, her nine-year-old daughter, who was in Brittany, convalescing after chicken pox, staying with family friends.

She went down the drive, a slim figure in her cream linen suit, walking alongside the front lawn Janice had mown into immaculate stripes. A pile of manuscripts waited her attention, but she needed a breath of air after her busy morning, and moreover to be alone to be able to think over what was to be done. There had been no chance this morning, and last night, after the party, she had been so exhausted she had sunk immediately into oblivion, almost as soon as her head touched the pillow. An oblivion perhaps self-induced, so that she could postpone facing up to the dizzying realisation of what had been admitted, albeit unspokenly, between herself and Matt.

But whether she wanted to think about it or not, it had been there, with her all morning, worrying her, yet making her alive to a new awareness of herself, as if all her life she'd been asleep and untouched until now. Moments of near-panic intervened. Perhaps he didn't after all feel the same way; maybe she'd been imagining . . . But the doubts didn't last long. She knew with certainty that he did. The recognition had been total and mutual.

She shouldn't be allowing herself to think this way – it wasn't playing the game. A phrase of Clive's came to her. 'It's only a game, you know,' he was wont to say, having done something that had gone too far. Which was all very well, if everyone knew the rules, and stuck to them. Like playing hostess for Clive as part of the game of keeping up appearances, of pretending there was nothing wrong with a marriage that was a blank, a façade, an as yet unvocalised failure.

Why, she asked herself despairingly, had she ever married Clive?

Her mother had died when Caroline was a very young child, leaving her to the tender mercies of her father, a cold and domineering man, under whose influence her own identity as she grew up had struggled to survive. He had taken an instant dislike to Clive as soon as she brought him home – was this why she had uncharacteristically rushed headlong into the marriage? Because she had known that if she didn't make this stand, she herself might sink without trace under the weight of her father's overweening personality? A bid for independence? Or because *Clive* wanted to marry *her* – and Clive always got what he wanted?

Certainly he had warmed her with the energy and fire of his ambition; his vitality had excited her – but love? It was hard to tell, now. When the fire had died down, the gulf between them had gradually widened, and for years they had had nothing in common, except Pippa, the child they both loved so deeply.

Her mind veered away from that old, painful problem, only to be faced with another, newer one.

Lunch, after all, had passed off successfully and pleasantly, which should have pleased Clive, but she wasn't so sure that it had. During the meal, through his favourite pork tenderloin cooked with apples, cream and calvados, to the dark, fragrant coffee and cognac, she had sensed an unusual preoccupation in him. He hadn't been turning the whole battery of his charm – which was considerable when he wanted it to be – on MacAllister, even though he had told her beforehand how important this meeting was to be.

With a sense of foreboding, she had guessed the reasons for its importance. It was all to do with this brash scheme of Clive's to turn Brome House – her home! – into offices. No! She clenched her fists in the pockets of her skirt. It was out of the question, so wholly unacceptable that it couldn't be thought about. How could Clive even contemplate such a thing? But that was symptomatic of their relationship, that he didn't know how he was hurting her. He should have known, and cared – but it had been a long time since Clive had known what she was thinking, if he ever had. Well, this was something he wasn't going to get his hands on. She was rather shocked at her own way of expressing that – she had, after all, quite willingly surrendered everything else. That she now regretted doing so was another matter – but so was Brome.

Halfway down the drive she turned along a narrow gravel path between clipped yew hedges and into the small, circular walled garden with a cool green pool in the centre, which was her special retreat. The wide stone parapet of the pool, on which she sat, was warm in the sun, roses and clematis clothed the brickwork, a golden carp occasionally flashed from under a lily pad, and through the opening in the wall she could see the house stretched before her in the sunlight.

Maybe it hadn't all that much architectural merit – too many generations of Baddesbys had added or subtracted a wing here, a storey there, changed a window or two according to their own personal idiosyncracies and the fashion of the time – nevertheless it had somehow settled into an unusually charming and attractive whole. Visitors were apt to enthuse about it, and with its mellow red brick and its sweeping pantiled roofs enclosed in the shelter of dark yews, it was photogenic enough to have warranted a recent colour feature in the county magazine. Caroline loved it uncritically; it was her home and she would be quite ruthless in defending it to her last breath.

The sun in the warm enclosed space brought out the incense smell of the thyme, crushed underfoot. It reminded her of being in church, and gradually the same sort of peace stole over her. She didn't have to make a decision about Matt, not yet. He was going away today and she had a whole week to come to terms with herself, so that when they next met, she would surely know how to act.

As she came out of the main gates and set off towards the village post office, she almost bumped into a man who was just emerging from the narrow lane which ran alongside the house.

'Marcus, well, what a surprise!'

As a child, Caroline had often been afraid of this dark, sardonic man with the caustic tongue, and even now she was never quite at ease in his company. Marcus Dymond had been a regular visitor to the house many years ago, in the days when he and her father had played chess together twice a week, a lean, aloof and austere figure. Recently, however, she had scarcely seen him at all. When she visited his invalid wife, he was invariably, and purposely, she fancied, otherwise occupied. Why he didn't want to see her was all too understandable, but what, she wondered, was he doing here now? Coming from the lane that led to Oddings Cottage?

He didn't look particularly pleased to see her, but neither did he seem discomfited. Indeed, he was uncharacteristically forthcoming.

'In the interests of what my doctor is pleased to call fighting the flab, I walk a good deal since my retirement,' he remarked with a faintly mocking smile, forestalling any question. 'I came down the valley and found myself faced with either a long walk round or, after a somewhat undignified scramble over a fence, the necessity of trespass. I'm afraid I chose the latter.'

His spare frame held not an ounce of flab, and he knew as well as she did about the fence. As for trespassing . . . accusing Marcus Dymond of it would be somewhat like forbidding the Pope the freedom of the Vatican.

'I thought of taking a look in at your garden while I was up here and reporting back to Enid,' he added. 'She still takes an interest, you know.'

'You're very welcome. I'll come round with you.'

He waved the suggestion away. 'No, no, don't bother. A peep through the gates will suffice.'

'Why don't you bring Enid up in the car one day? I'm sure she'd love to see the garden again,' Caroline said impulsively. 'Bring her before the maples are past their best.'

'In the highly unlikely event of my ever not being persona non grata at Brome, my dear Caroline, I would willingly do so. As it is . . .'

He left the sentence unfinished, but Caroline could supply the rest.

The last time he had come to the house, he had told Clive exactly what he had thought of him, using such biting sarcasm that even Clive had flinched. She knew that Clive believed Marcus was the one who had been harassing him, and she thought he might have every reason to be afraid of what this man might do, but not in that way. He was capable of malice, certainly, but making anonymous telephone calls – no. His weapons would be more direct – or more subtle.

She looked at him with a troubled face. 'I – I'm so terribly sorry.'

'You always did have a tender conscience if I mistake not, but I imagine Brome will continue to get on well enough without me, if that's what you meant,' Marcus answered dryly.

'I was thinking more of Oddings Cottage. I know you'd set your mind on buying it.'

'Not,' he replied, lifting a sardonic eyebrow, 'at nearly double the price it's worth.'

There was very little Caroline felt she could say to mitigate what, after all, had been one of the most indefensible things Clive had ever done. He had *known* the Dymonds were hoping to buy the old cottage when it came on the market. It was really two small one-storey cottages which had been knocked together at some time, and all the rooms being on one level, it would have been ideal for Enid, incapacitated as she now was. Clive, however, had offered way above the asking price, which not unnaturally was promptly accepted, and now Enid must look at it from her window, disappointed, while Clive . . .

Dymond, who had been intently watching her expressive, revealing face, remarked ironically, 'One of our more enlightened architects, we must expect to see great things arising from this determination to have the property. Anything less would be quite disgraceful – would it not?'

Before his retirement, Marcus had taught maths at what had once been the old endowed grammar school in Lavenstock and was now, to his deep disapprobation, a comprehensive school. Caroline at this moment saw why his pupils had been reputed to go in such terror of him: she was afraid he was looking right into her mind and reading there just what Clive intended – not to renovate the cottage at all, but to knock it down and rebuild his new modern-style house there, where he hoped to take Pippa and herself to live, so that he could carry out his plans for the big house. The cottage wasn't worth restoring, or so he said; at its best it could only ever have been an Elizabethan slum. Some interfering busybody had got a preservation order put on it, but there were ways and means, he asserted with a laugh, of circumventing that, if you knew what you were about.

'And what if you can't?'

'I don't budget for failure,' he'd answered forcibly. 'I budget for success, and what's more, I make bloody sure I've got my sums right, so there's no possibility of anything else.'

Hurriedly now, she asked Marcus, 'How is Enid?'

'A little better, I fancy.' He added abruptly, 'No, that's not true. She'll never be better; we all know that, don't we? But some days are less worse than others.' He paused. 'I'll tell her I've seen you, and that you've asked after her. Au revoir, Caroline.'

One might have thought Marcus Dymond a man incapable of affection; in reality, Caroline knew his devotion to his wife was utter and complete. This had been especially evident since her illness, something that gave a more sympathetic insight into his difficult character.

'Give her my love, will you? And tell her I'll be down to see her early next week.'

Dymond raised his deerstalker and left her.

The silvery chimes of the bracket clock in the dining room were sounding a quarter to four just as Caroline eventually stepped back into the dim coolness of the house. She would have to stir herself if there was any work to be done that afternoon – but first, some tea. She found the kitchen empty and was just about to pick up the kettle when Sylvia Johnson came in, moving in that noiseless way she had, startling Caroline. She carried a tray with used cups and teapot and, when she saw Caroline, exclaimed, 'Oh, Mrs Lethbridge, what a pity, you've just missed tea! But I can soon make some more.'

Slightly irritated by the implication that she wasn't prepared to make her own, Caroline felt all the same, glancing at the righteous expression on the girl's face, that she'd better not offer. Sylvia peered into the kettle, saw there was enough water left in it and plugged it in, then reached another blue and white china cup and saucer from the dark oak dresser ranged along one wall. Caroline was surprised to see her hand trembling, enough to make the cup rattle on the saucer.

'Are you all right, Sylvia?'

'Oh yes, quite all right, thank you, Mrs Lethbridge.' In a tone that quite clearly indicated she was not. She began to fuss with preparing the fresh pot of tea.

Oh dear. Sylvia was not a young woman with whom Caroline felt instant rapport – indeed, she found her tiresomely uncommunicative – and though she had tried on the few occasions they'd been alone to find some common ground, she'd so far failed. But clearly now she couldn't, however much she might wish, leave her to her troubles.

'Come on, something's bothering you – what is it, has Mr Lethbridge been getting at you? He can be a bit sharp sometimes, but he thinks very highly of you, you know –'

'Oh goodness, no, it's not Mr Lethbridge!' Sylvia answered with such fervour that Caroline looked sharply at her. Heavens, she couldn't be getting some sort of crush on Clive, could she? She wasn't all that young – old enough to have passed that stage, certainly, Caroline would have thought. 'He's never like that with me . . . not unless I've done something really stupid.'

'And from what I gather, you don't usually do that, do you?' Caroline smiled, causing a small gleam of self-satisfaction to flash across the other's face. 'So what's the trouble?' she repeated, watching Sylvia pour boiling water on to the leaves in the teapot. 'Anything I can do to help?'

'It's – it's only – well, the thing is, I can't make my mind up.' Sylvia adjusted her slipping spectacles with an ungainly gesture, sliding her forefinger along her nose. Caroline perched on the edge of the table, prepared to listen. 'You see, I've had the chance to go to America.'

23

'Well, lucky you!'

'Oh, I don't know about that. But it *was* only temporary, my coming here to work for Mr Lethbridge, as you know –'

'While Amanda has her baby.'

'Yes, but I was beginning to hope – think it might be more permanent, that Amanda might change her mind about coming back after the baby comes.' Sylvia fiddled with a spoon, trying to hide her embarrassment.

'That's always a possibility, of course, but if you've had another chance, I should take it. Amanda's very career-minded.'

'I know, and my aunt who lives in Boston has got me the promise of this marvellous job there, knowing I only had a temporary position here – and she's sent me my plane ticket and everything.' Her plain, sallow face was doleful, her eyes owlish behind the thick spectacles.

'Maybe I'm being obtuse – but what's the problem?'

'I – it's just that I – I don't like leaving Mr Lethbridge in the lurch.'

'Goodness, he'll find someone else easily enough,' Caroline said gently. 'Jobs like this aren't easy to find; there'll be a queue.'

'Ye-es.'

'So why the hesitation?'

'I'd rather not say,' Sylvia answered primly in a voice little more than a whisper, casting her eyes modestly down.

Caroline looked at the bent head and the lank, mousy hair dragged back into an unbecoming sort of pony-tail. She'd been right in her earlier supposition; Sylvia did have a thing about Clive. Well, it shouldn't be all that surprising. Clive had considerable physical voltage and could be infinitely charming when it suited him, when anything pleased him, and Sylvia had undoubtedly done that, with her ability to smooth his path efficiently. Caroline felt very sorry for her; unrequited love was extremely painful at any age, while it lasted. She didn't feel it could be serious, but one never knew, and Sylvia struck her as being deep. Surely she didn't really mean it, about not going to America?

'Well, I know if I were you, I wouldn't refuse. Opportunities like this don't happen every day, do they? And you say your aunt's sent you your ticket? When is it for?'

'Next Friday, twelve-fifty from Heathrow,' was the prompt reply, indicating that perhaps the idea hadn't been dismissed out of hand after all.

'So soon! Friday, that's the fifteenth, isn't it? You're in luck, as it happens. I have an engagement for lunch not too far away from the airport. Would you like me to drive you there?'

For a moment Sylvia looked nonplussed, as if such kindness didn't often come her way, or perhaps at having her mind made up for her, but she quickly recovered herself and all of a sudden said, yes, it would all be for the best, wouldn't it, and yes, she would appreciate a lift.

Clive wasn't going to be pleased. It would mean finding another replacement, and not just any old temp either, until such time as Amanda came back. Caroline decided she would have to do something herself about this. It might make up for encouraging Sylvia to leave at such short notice. Though on reflection she had a strange sort of feeling, that the boot was on the other foot, that it was she who had been manoeuvred, especially when she remembered that she had asked Sylvia some time ago to make a note in Clive's diary about her lunch appointment in Maidenhead.

CHAPTER 4

Deep in the intricacies firstly of Baillie-Scott domestic architecture way up on the west coast of Scotland, then Mackintosh's School of Art in Glasgow, Matt had had reason to appreciate the breathing space the last ten days had given him, and the work which necessarily had to occupy the forefront of his mind.

Hitherto, his work as a newspaper and television journalist had taken him to remote and troubled places of the world, where danger and risk were parts of the business he took for granted. He thought he'd learned to put a glass wall between his emotions and that which had to be met and faced in earning his bread and butter. Last year, however, spent in the unspeakable horrors of famine refugee camps in the third world, had put paid to that theory. But only because that damnable recurring dysentery had laid him low, he told himself, debilitating him mentally and physically, leaving him with nothing to fight an almost suicidal despair and anger at the blindness and stupidity of human beings, and bringing him as near a nervous breakdown as ever a man of his sort and condition could come. It had been not only sensible, but necessary, to accept medical advice and opt out for a while, go home and let his mind and body heal.

He had in the early days of his career worked for the architectural press – a long time since now, but a good newspaperman should be able to cover anything, he'd been told when he was a cub reporter still wet behind the ears. So he'd accepted the offer to work in collaboration with Clive on this book, which was concerned with the influence of British architects during the last hundred years on modern European architectural development, the final achievement chosen to illustrate the theme being this greatly acclaimed design of Clive's.

Working with Clive hadn't been easy. Matt was also pretty damn sure Clive was hell to live with, and that was why Caroline was near to breaking point.

Or was she? He had immediately sensed the strains of her marriage when they first met, but he couldn't be sure of her yet, of her strengths and weaknesses – and he would never make the mistake of underrating her capacity for loyalty, or the depth of her love for her daughter. And maybe being on the edge of tension was naturally part of her, a necessary part of her marriage, too – and if it wasn't, what reason had he to think that he, Matt, had anything to do with it?

He'd never experienced anything like this before: up to now, his sex life had been taken care of by transient affairs, unmemorable for anything more than a passing attraction and perhaps a mild affection. He'd believed anything else unnecessary to him and his chosen way of life. Then, this shattering realisation that with Caroline, his needs took on another dimension entirely: a tenderness, a need for her, permanently and totally committed, as he himself already was.

He could be mistaken about her in every way, though on the strength of an answering look, that night of the party, across a crowded room, cornier than corny, he was prepared to believe not. But he sensed there were frontiers she wasn't yet ready to cross, and he had no intention of forcing the pace, of ruining the relationship before it began. The first move might have to come from him, but the final choice must ultimately be hers.

Accordingly, he made himself stay away from Brome for another couple of days after he got back, working in the privacy of his hotel room on the material he had collected. He'd asked for accommodation where the noise of his typewriter and tape-recorder wouldn't be likely to disturb the other guests, and had been given a room in the annexe, which turned out to be pleasanter than in the main building, less overheated and with easier access to the car park and the extensive grounds, where he could stretch his long legs occasionally.

By late afternoon he'd almost finished the final draft of his last night's notes when the telephone rang. It was Caroline.

The full-blooded screams ringing out down the corridor would have done credit to a prima donna, a role for which Mrs Peach undoubtedly had the physique to qualify, and sometimes the temperament, too. This time she wasn't acting. Her face under her

27

careful make-up drained of colour; then, with no more breath for screaming, she made for the kitchen.

'In the study,' was all she could get out at first. 'I went in for his tea tray and there he was – oh my God!'

Janice Wharton switched off the chicken soup whizzing round in the food processor, whose noise had prevented her from hearing the screams, and looked up as Mrs Peach rushed in, a sense of dread clutching her. Her hands reached out to grab the table for support as the meaning sank in. She stood rigid, her blue-overalled figure silhouetted against the cheerful red Aga.

'Is he – he isn't –?' she began, in a dry, hurting whisper.

'I think,' announced Mrs Peach, 'I'm going to faint – or be sick.'

Torn between necessities, Janice took a few jerky, uncoordinated steps, hesitating between Mrs Peach and the door.

'Don't!' The older woman recovered with speed as Janice's hand finally reached for the knob. 'Don't you go into that there study, Janice, for God's sake. There isn't nothing you can do, anyway.'

Caroline was aware of something out of the ordinary as soon as she had parked her car in the garage, formerly one of the old stables. For one thing, Mrs Peach's orange Volkswagen Beetle was still there, K registration and looking as if it had emerged from the showroom yesterday. One careful lady owner, in this case no contradiction in terms, as Clive had once remarked with a rare spark of humour.

The sense persisted as she opened the kitchen door, where an unnatural silence reigned, rather than the activity usual at this hour, when the evening meal was normally well under way. Also very oddly, Mrs Peach was sitting at the old-fashioned scrubbed-top table, leaning back ostentatiously with her eyes closed, the teapot and the brandy bottle in front of her. Janice was crouched against the Aga, as if, despite the warmth of the evening, she needed all the heat she could extract from its slow-ticking oven.

'Still here, Mrs Peach? Shouldn't you be at home by now?'

The older woman sprang to her feet. 'Oh, Caroline!'

Mrs Peach had known Caroline since she was a little girl, and she was the last person in the world to be deliberately cruel, but now that she was recovering somewhat from the initial shock, her natural sense of drama was returning fast. She clutched her hands in front of her imposing bosom. 'There's been a terrible accident!'

Caroline stopped abruptly, halfway across the kitchen. She forced herself to say it. 'It's Pippa. It's Pippa, isn't it?'

'No, no, m'duck, thank God it's not her!'

'I think you'd better sit down.' Janice threw a look at Mrs Peach, pulled herself together, and since 'accident' wasn't to her an acceptable euphemism for murder, told Caroline straightly what had happened.

Then, as Caroline stood transfixed, they heard the sound of the first of the cars arriving.

'Who found him?'

By the time the investigating officer arrived, Detective Chief Inspector Gil Mayo from Divisional Headquarters in Lavenstock, ten minutes behind his sergeant, the sombre routine machinery of violent death was already rolling smoothly into action. The room was thick with photographers, the scenes-of-crime team, and the grey dust of fingerprint powder. The police surgeon arrived, pronounced life extinct, and now that the photographer had finished with his stills and his video camera, was ready to examine the body further.

'Mrs Peach,' answered Sergeant Kite, who'd already been gleaning information from P.C. Trenchard, the local man. 'Lady from the village who helps to clean two or three times a week.'

'Hm.' Mayo stood in the centre of the room, being careful not to move about too much, so as not to disturb the evidence, looking impassive, even bored. A tall, solidly built Yorkshireman, just the wrong side of forty, with thick, strong hair, disciplined from its inclination to curl by a short haircut, deep-set eyes that could disconcert by their concentrated observation, he was by nature not inclined to speak overmuch. Now he stood silently, taking it all in, absorbing all-important first impressions of his surroundings, getting a gut feeling about the case. His trained eye ranged round the room, noting each feature and filing it for further use.

The room was a shambles, but that couldn't disguise dark oak panelling, good, solid furniture with the sort of patina that only came from years of dedicated polishing, several very good modern paintings and some old oriental rugs, their blues and reds softened by time. One wall was devoted to framed photographs of what was presumably the work of the dead man – municipal buildings, an art gallery, dozens of houses, a factory or two. Some had been knocked askew in the violent attack on the room, but none had been broken. His glance passed on, coming back to the body.

Mayo was necessarily familiar with death in its more horrific manifestations, but appearances to the contrary, he hadn't yet come to regard it with indifference, become case-hardened as some of his colleagues were – or allegedly so. Well, everybody had to learn to cope in their own way, and his was total detachment, as far as this was possible. Shut your mind off from everything but the hard facts, the input that fed the computer called the brain, and don't cloud the issue by being squeamish, or emotional. Difficult. Nearly impossible, but you'd damn well better do it. It was there, a crime to be solved. Violent death, the ultimate silencer, the irrevocable end, somebody's answer to jealousy, greed, revenge, fear. Always shocking, and evil hanging wherever it had occurred, like a miasma. In this room now, like the smell of blood, and of death itself.

Clive Lethbridge was still in the position he had been found, slumped forward over his desk, arms outspread, his head slightly to one side, the back of it brutally smashed in. Dark, sticky blood, greyish brain tissue and fragments of white bone were matted in with the thick, wiry hair.

There was blood all over. It had spattered the walls and the curtains and the windows and the back and sleeves of the cream silk shirt the victim was wearing, and run down behind his left ear to soak his collar, and spread out on to the papers beneath his head and body. God, a right old mess.

'Probably stunned with one blow from behind, then killed by further blows,' the doctor pronounced, straightening up. 'All that blood. Indicates the heart went on pumping for some time after the first blow. Which was made with something heavy, with a sharp edge and used with considerable force, I might say.'

'With something like that, for instance.'

Ison followed Mayo's pointing finger to where an extremely handsome and heavy cut-glass inkwell lay rolled on its side on the carpet, its brilliant refractions winking in the evening sun which streamed through the open french window. Surmounted by a domed, cut and faceted lid mounted in silver and hinged to the base, it was a half-sphere, about the size and shape of half a coconut, with a small hollow designed for ink, when being put to its original use. A deeply cut pattern of vertical incisions segmented it, continuing underneath the base to repeat and catch prismatic reflections from each other. The glittering ruby highlights, so pretty in the sun, came from the dried blood on the serrations at the edge of the base, which, Mayo had no doubt, would match exactly the jagged edges of the wounds in the smashed skull.

'Probably.' Ison in fact had no doubts either, but caution was second nature to him. 'The P.M. will make certain.'

'How long's he been dead?'

'Not all that long. According to the body temperature, and the temperature in here, which is warm, about an hour, I'd say.'

'Four twenty-five?'

'Give or take.'

Ison rolled down his sleeves and side-stepped the scenes-of-crime officer, D.C. Dexter, who knelt on the floor, hands encased

31

in thinly stretched, transparent protective gloves. At that moment he was lifting the inkwell with extreme care, preparatory to packing it in a sterile container. Besides the blood adhering to it, there would almost certainly be minute traces of skin and hair and brain tissue . . . though probably, unless the murderer had been particularly careless, no fingerprints. Villains nowadays saw too many TV cop shows.

'Strewth, heavier than it looks, this, must weigh all of four or five pounds, I reckon,' Dexter grunted.

'Lead crystal, by the look of it. Victorian, at a guess, wouldn't you say, Kite?'

'I wouldn't know.' The tall, lanky sergeant eyed the ornate piece of craftsmanship disparagingly. 'Not the sort of thing I go for myself . . . even supposing I could afford it.' The expression on his slightly ingenuous, normally cheerful face endorsed his opinion of the richly comfortable circumstances that the deceased had apparently enjoyed. 'Easy enough to handle, though, I should think. Get a good grip on the silver mounting, with the lid in your palm, and bingo!'

'A man's hand, yes. Or both of a woman's.'

'Hardly a woman's crime, though, is it?' the doctor commented, snapping his case shut. 'Nasty, brutal.'

Mayo said, 'You'd be surprised, some of the women I've known.'

Ison, packing his instruments, conceded the point with a wry smile. 'As you say.'

But male or female, one-handed or two-handed, the murderer had operated from behind. The desk over which Lethbridge slumped was a very large one, almost square, the kind known as a partners' desk, with drawers back and front, and was set towards the centre of the room, and at an oblique angle to the window. When he was attacked, he had been sitting facing the room, his back to the garden. The french windows were wide open, and fastened back.

'So he either knew his murderer, and therefore was unsuspecting when he moved behind him for some reason – or somebody crept up from outside and did for him,' said Kite.

Ison nodded. 'Either way, the first blow would have knocked him out sufficient to quieten him, if that was all that was wanted, even if it didn't actually kill him. The rest was either making sure or just being vindictive.'

'Whichever, he was disturbed in the middle of what he was doing, wasn't he?' Kite leaned gingerly forward, peering over the dead man's shoulder. A pencil was still gripped between the fingers of his right hand, and a long, deep line from where the large, confident handwriting stopped had scored the only visible page, most of which, however, was obscured by the rusty stain of dried blood.

'As soon as you can,' Mayo remarked to Dexter, with a nod at the mess on the desk, 'get me the lab report on that. I'd like to know what he was working on.'

Things moved with speed and efficiency when Mayo was around, but he was inclined to expect results the day before yesterday. 'Do my best, sir, but you know how it is. We're up to our eyes as usual.' He met Mayo's grey stare. 'Yes, right. Right, sir.'

'We all have our problems,' said Ison, and left.

Mayo walked to the window, thinking about the layout of the house. The study was a double-aspected room, set on the corner of the house, with long views of the gardens and the gravelled main drive, which divided outside the study to sweep round, encircling the entire house. Flanking the drive were rose beds and herbaceous borders. There was a yew hedge at some distance, and a shrubbery alongside the road. At the back were extensive lawns, beyond which lay an orchard.

'Any idea where that leads?' he asked Kite, pointing to a path crossing the lawn, apparently opening on to a lane which separated the property from the adjoining one.

'According to Trenchard, eventually up on to the Lavenstock

road. A bit of a scramble, and private property anyway, though apparently that doesn't stop anybody. It's a favourite picnic spot down by the stream.'

'Did he say who owns the place next door?'

'Chap called Comstock – runs a stud farm. He uses the lane for access, but it belongs to Brome House. They seem to use it mostly for delivery of heating oil and stuff for the garden.'

A wide area just outside the french window had already been cordoned off. Some of the gravel from the drive was on the carpet just inside the window, not necessarily brought in by the murderer since there was also a small gritty patch of it under the pedestal of the desk, near the dead man's feet in their highly polished tan slip-on shoes.

'Terrible stuff, gravel, for treading indoors,' Kite said feelingly, watching Dexter, who was still crawling about on the floor, scoop the two separate lots into plastic bags, seal and label them. His wife had briskly refused to have it laid on the drive of their new house, especially with the kids running in and out and herself busy with her new career. She'd opted for mock-stone slabs instead. You wouldn't have thought it could do much harm to the rugs in here, though. Tatty old specimens, Sheila wouldn't give them house room. Spoiled the look of the good fitted carpet they were spread on.

'Not quiet, either,' added Mayo absently, staring down at the Georgian console table which stood between the window and the bookcase, its bare top greyish now with fingerprint powder. Was that where the inkwell had stood, conveniently to hand for any intruder? It was the only flat surface of its kind in the room that had not apparently been holding some bibelot or objet d'art, though it was difficult to tell in the chaos of the room.

'Anything strike you as odd about this lot, Martin?'

Kite looked at the cushions thrown on the floor, the pictures knocked off the straight, books swept to the floor. 'Not very convincing, is it?' he said, after a moment's thought.

'Right. As if somebody in too big a hurry to take much trouble wanted to suggest robbery as a motive for the killing. Or,' he added thoughtfully, 'as a cover-up for destroying this thing here – the only thing that *has* actually suffered any damage, you'll notice.'

'What is it?'

Mayo was peering down at the baize-covered table on which remained all that was left of the Svensen Centre model, a heap of Perspex and balsa, recognisable for what it had once been only by the metal label which had been fixed to the base. 'Model of some sort. Must have been that hospital or whatever he won that prize with. Wasn't there a picture in last week's *Advertiser*?'

'And a big write-up. I remember. Clever bloke.'

'Well paid for it, any road,' remarked Mayo, beginning to prowl around the room, carefully avoiding touching anything, 'if this house and what's in it's anything to go by.'

'Well, likely this is all family stuff. Wife's family,' Kite added, having forgotten for the moment that Mayo, being newish to the division, might not know this. 'The Baddesbys, been grinding the faces of the poor around here since Adam was a lad, and not short of a bob or two, neither.'

Mayo made no answer to this beyond a swift, sharp glance at Kite. He twisted his head sideways to look closer at a modern painting hanging wildly askew. 'This wasn't handed down, though.' If it was indeed an original Hockney, it hadn't been given away with cornflake tops, either.

Kite did his best not to avert his eyes from it. 'Well, it takes all sorts,' he said at last, not being able to think of anything else to say and uncertain as to whether his gaffer might actually be admiring the painting.

Kite hadn't quite got the measure of Mayo yet, what really made him tick; they'd only worked together on a few cases so far. Despite that blunt Yorkshire façade, he seemed easy enough, yet Kite had the feeling it wouldn't do to push your luck with him.

Wasn't married, though he had been once; whether widowed or divorced was still a matter of speculation in the division. He had a daughter, but he didn't invite questions about his personal life. Truth to tell, he seemed to be something of a loner, a mite austere. He didn't smoke, play games or even follow them, not even cricket, which for a Yorkshireman must be tantamount to treason. It was rumoured that he liked music, the heavy stuff, symphonies and that. He read a lot.

But Kite wasn't going to hold that against him. He was disposed to like Mayo. He was a damned good policeman, with a steady record of success behind him, and a seemingly predictable future ahead in the way of promotion prospects. He was fair, and didn't hog the limelight. Kite wouldn't have resented this last anyway. Having sweated to reach sergeant early, his own desire for promotion had received an unexpected check. Give it time, he told himself; it takes time to adjust to the idea and circumstances of two ambitious parents in one happy family.

Happy, he repeated. That's right. They'd work it out, sure they would.

A scrunch of gravel under tyres announced the arrival of the mortuary van. They watched, soberly, as Clive Lethbridge's body, plastic-sheeted, was carried out.

'Right, then,' Mayo said abruptly, 'let's get moving. Can't afford to waste time.' He moved across to the small room adjoining the study and peered in. Little more than a cubbyhole with a desk occupying one wall and an electronic typewriter standing on it, plus a filing cabinet, a plan chest and a photocopier. The room at present was crammed to capacity with a large fingerprint man and the photographer. 'We'll make a start on that lot when the lads have finished, see what turns up. Farrar can give me a hand. The rest of the house I'll leave you to organise.'

Kite looked gloomy. 'Not exactly a semi, is it?' He thought of attics and cellars, the kitchen, a vast room so old-fashioned it was trendy again, and a bathroom which still had its original mahogany seat. God knew how many bedrooms. Folks with so much room they never threw anything away.

'Take you a bit longer, that's all. I'll see you're not short-handed. You can have Deeley.'

Kite rolled up his eyes.

Despite a regrettable tendency to flippancy, Mayo knew Kite was conscientious and thorough, often acute, and that he could rely on him. He thought that given time, they'd make a good team. 'Cheer up, son. There's none of us here for a good night's kip. Meanwhile, let's get the day's pattern established – who came and went, where he'd been, who he'd been seeing and so on.'

Kite pulled out his notebook. 'According to Mrs Wharton, he didn't go out, had no visitors. He was working alone here all day, had lunch alone, and tea.'

'That simplifies things – who's Mrs Wharton?'

'Yet another of the helpers in the house . . . Gawd, how the other half lives!'

Hands in pockets, Mayo surveyed his sergeant. 'Pack it in, lad.'

Kite's round, candid face assumed innocence.

'Now you've got it out of your system, can we contrive to manage without the snide socialism, and get on with the business?'

'Yes, sir; sorry, sir.' Kite, whose leftist sympathies had long been little more a habit, had merely been firing token shots, more as a gesture of independence than anything else. He looked sheepish and consulted his notes. 'Tea was brought in about half-three by Mrs Peach, give or take a few minutes. At five to five, when she came in to collect the tray before going home, he was dead. Which more or less squares with what Doc Ison tells us.'

'An hour and a half, during which he wasn't entirely alone. Somebody must have heard or seen something. What about his wife?'

'She's been out all day.'

'Oh, where?'

'I don't know yet. Shall we have her in and ask her?'

Mayo thought about it. 'Yes.'

Kite poked his head round the door and spoke to the detective constable, Deeley, on duty in the corridor outside. Mayo heard a muffled altercation, and then Kite was back in the room, with Deeley in front of him and the door closed behind him. 'It seems,' he announced, 'that Mrs Lethbridge has gone out again.'

CHAPTER 5

'Gone out? *Out?*' Although Mayo addressed Deeley quietly enough, Kite felt the draught from where he stood. 'I thought you said she came home just before we arrived?'

'Yes, sir, she did, but she went out again. By the back door, sir,' answered Deeley, a beefy young man who occasionally, like now, wondered if he was in the right job, detecting criminals. Maybe he should have stayed on the beat, rather than going through all that grief to get into C.I.D. He'd give a week's pay to be back there right now. 'I understand she's gone to see a Mr Waring, sir. He only lives in the next village.'

A look passed between Mayo and Kite. Mayo turned back to Deeley, the cross he'd had to bear since coming to Lavenstock. 'Then it shouldn't take you long to get over there and fetch her back, should it?' he asked, more mildly. Deeley was heavy weather, with no imagination whatsoever, but there was room for the plodders as well as the high-flyers. So they said. 'What's keeping you?'

'Nothing, sir, only there's Mrs Peach, the cleaning lady. She's waiting to be off home. Says her husband'll be shouting for his tea.'

Mayo thought for a moment. 'All right. I'll see her now.' He stood up and followed Kite and Deeley out of the room. 'Mrs Peach?' he said to the woman waiting outside. 'Sorry if we've kept you hanging about, but we shouldn't be much longer now. Is there somewhere we can talk for a few minutes?'

'I suppose,' Mrs Peach answered stiffly, unappeased, 'we could go into the garden room.'

'That would be useful, thank you.'

She marched along the thickly carpeted corridor and led the way into a room farther along, filled with evening sunlight and furnished with a haphazard selection of cushioned armchairs slip-covered in faded cretonne, together with a rubbed yellow velvet sofa and one or two bookcases and occasional tables, on one of which stood a huge bowl of old-fashioned cream Provence roses, deeply scented. Photographs in profusion lined the walls, a television set stood in one corner, and two latticed french windows led out on to a paved terrace overlooking another aspect of the main garden. An unpretentious, slightly shabby room, it had a comfortable air of being much used.

Mrs Peach removed the roses to a corner bookcase, very pointedly, and only then indicated to Mayo that he might now be permitted to use the table.

'Thank you; please sit down.' Mayo waved her to an armchair and sat down himself in an elderly one with a sagging seat facing her, which turned out to be surprisingly comfortable. 'Now, Mrs Peach, let's have a few details.'

He leaned back, leaving the note-taking to Kite, ready to concentrate on the answers to his questions, trying to pick up the hesitancies and nuances of conversation, as well as the apparent irrelevancies which interviewees were apt to pursue, and which could be so revealing about the person being questioned.

In this case Beryl Peach, a spritely, full-bosomed lady, fifty-three years old, with a strong Midlands accent. Worked here since Mrs Lethbridge was a little girl, she had, before her mother – Caroline's mother, that was, Mrs Baddesby – died. Came every morning except Friday, when she came in the afternoon.

'That's my afternoon for the silver, and odd jobs like that. It's not convenient for me to come here of a Friday morning, see,' she added independently. 'It's when I do my weekend shopping up in Lavenstock and then go on to have my hair done after.' She patted her Silver Pearl-rinsed curls.

'Very nice,' remarked Mayo, seeing some comment was called for, and feeling the effort was worthwhile when she unbent so far as to look faintly mollified, though she never took her round, somewhat beady eyes from his face for a minute. The stare unnerved him a little.

'So you saw Mr Lethbridge when you took his tea in to him. What time was that?'

'Just before half past three.'

'Did he have anything to eat with it?'

'A couple of my buttered scones, that I always make a batch of on Fridays. I don't usually do the cooking, but Janice hasn't got such a light hand with scones, and he did enjoy one or two with his tea.'

'How did he seem when you went in? As usual?'

'He was standing in front of the window, and he didn't turn round, just told me to put the tray down. And the next time I saw him, when I come back for the tray, soon as I opened the door, there he was, dead!' She lifted a handkerchief to her eyes.

'How did you know that?

The handkerchief was lowered abruptly. 'Well, he didn't hit his-self on the head, did he, and he looked dead enough to me, dead as mutton!'

'What I mean is, you must have walked right into the room in order to see the condition he was in.'

'I did; I thought at first, before I got near to him, he'd just been took bad, but I didn't touch him, if that's what you mean! I told Janice – Mrs Wharton – you should never touch the body. However, she said we ought to make sure – what if he was still alive? You wouldn't have got me back into that study, not for King

40

Dick. But she would have it. However, I was right, wasn't I?' On a much more subdued note. He saw she was much upset underneath the histrionics.

'Yes, Mrs Peach, I'm afraid you were. I do realise this has been a very nasty experience for you, but you've been very helpful so far. What time did you fetch the tray back?'

'About five to five, just before I was ready to go home, like I always do.'

By which time Lethbridge had probably been dead just over half an hour. 'Now – this Mr Waring, this gentleman Mrs Lethbridge has rushed off to see ... Very good friend of the family, is he?'

'Yes, he is, but there's no hanky-panky going on there, so don't you go insinuating there is!' Mrs Peach retorted with spirit. 'Mr Waring must be sixty if he's a day, I'll have you know.'

Mayo reckoned he hardly had a good twenty years left to him, on that basis. He avoided Kite's eye and said mildly, 'I was only wondering, why him? Why Mr Waring in particular? And why Mrs Lethbridge didn't simply telephone?'

'Oh, the telephone! Not much sympathy from a telephone, is there? Besides, I've told you – he's a close friend. Mr Lethbridge's partner and ever such a nice gentleman, he is. He only lives over at Addencote, anyway, not more than five minutes in the car.'

'I see. Well, let's get back to Mr Lethbridge. As an employer, what was he like?'

'I've no complaints. He was always all right with me. It was only with them as give him old buck that he got a bit nas – a bit worked up.'

Here we go again, thought Mayo, the old speak-no-ill-of-the-dead syndrome that was, however, often more revealing than the truth. 'Short-tempered, was he? The sort to make enemies?'

'I wouldn't know about that,' Mrs Peach answered primly.

'Hm. Were you responsible for cleaning the study?'

'Only on Thursday. Janice saw it had a once-over every day,

41

then I always give it a real good do of a Thursday, because he worked at home most Fridays and he was very particular about everything being kept nice and polished.'

'As soon as we can, we'll get you to have a look and see if there's anything missing. You'd know, of course?'

'Oh, definitely!'

'I suppose I can rely on Mrs Wharton for the same thing?'

'You can rely on Janice for anything; good as gold, she is, not like that husband of hers.' She bit her lip and stood up hurriedly, aware that the brandy she'd consumed had loosened her tongue. 'If that's all, I'd like to get off.'

But Mayo, realising he had before him God's gift to policemen, a loquacious witness, was not prepared to let her go just yet. 'Another minute or two, if you don't mind.' With a heavy, resigned sigh, Mrs Peach sat down again. 'I'm sorry to keep you, but you see, in a case like this,' Mayo went on, using unashamed flattery, 'it's important to talk to people who are observant and keep their eyes and ears open. Somebody like you, who'd know for instance if Mr and Mrs Lethbridge didn't get on well together.'

'Oh no, there was nothing like that! What I mean is, they got on as well as most.'

'I suppose they had their differences, like most married couples?'

'Not in front of me, they didn't,' she answered firmly.

He saw that her loyalty to Caroline Lethbridge was paramount, and decided to press the advantage. 'You've known Mrs Lethbridge since she was a little girl, you say, so it must have pleased you to see her happy.'

'Happy?' The exclamation was out before she could stop it. She bit her lip, then said soberly, 'I never said she was happy.' There was a longer silence, then suddenly, with another sigh, she gave up pretending. 'I only wish she was. I don't know what it is, but it seems to me something's been wrong for quite a while now.'

'Money troubles?'

'Oh, I wouldn't say that . . . but I don't know, a house like this doesn't run on fresh air, does it? They didn't seem short to me, but that's all according. All I can say is, things weren't as they should be.'

Mayo thought that she was almost certainly telling the truth, and that she knew no more than she had told him. He questioned her a little more about the day-to-day routine of the house, then said, 'That's about it, Mrs Peach, for now. As you found the body, we'll need you to make a signed statement, but it'll do later, when we've finished with the room. I take it you'd have no objection?'

Clearly, Mrs Peach had not. It didn't often come her way to play the leading lady. All in all, it was quite a red-letter day in her life.

'I thought we'd ruled out thieving as a motive.' Kite asked when she'd gone.

'We haven't ruled anything out yet, lad.'

Mayo stood looking out of the window, which faced directly on to a great cedar of Lebanon, possibly two hundred years old, its wide arms sweeping the lawn beneath the terrace. He hated the disorientated feeling at the beginning of investigations of this sort, before you could see the shape of the case and you were still fumbling around, seeking which direction to go in to find the answer. 'We both know murderers who've killed for reasons neither you nor I would recognise as a motive at all – but motive of some sort we've got to look for. Unless we're faced with a psychopath, who just happened along and clobbered him to death for the hell of it . . . which is possible, all right, but I think we'll stick with the other . . . that's what we're looking for. And having seen that lot in there, I think it more than likely somebody must have finished up looking like an assistant in a ritual slaughterhouse.'

'So how'd they get away, looking like that? They'd be taking a hell of a risk.'

'Maybe it was someone who didn't need to get away. Maybe

43

they were here already.' Mayo stepped out of the french window, fastened back with a hook to the wall. 'With this open, I doubt if he'd be taken by surprise,' he said, crunching his feet on the gravel to make his point.

CHAPTER 6

Mrs Peach, her coat on and handbag over her arm like the Queen Mother, found Caroline, brought back from Addencote, with Harry Waring in the shadowed drawing room. The sun had gone from this side of the house, where the oak-panelled walls and the huge, sombre pictures absorbed even more light. Caroline looked very small, curled in the corner of the Knole settee, as if she wanted to hide in its high-backed depths, her face a white blur against the dark blue brocade.

She had felt numb ever since she had been told of Clive's death, she didn't seem able to take it in yet, she was frozen inside, white-faced and withdrawn behind a wall of silence.

'They say they'll see you now, seeing as you're here, Mr Waring,' Mrs Peach announced, as if she'd personally arranged it, and to Caroline, 'What's-his-name, that there inspector, says I can go now, so if it's all the same to you, I ought to be off.'

Harry stubbed out his cigar, reduced the level of whisky in the heavy Waterford crystal by half an inch, stood up, gave Caroline's shoulder a rather helpless squeeze, and said to Mrs Peach, 'Can't you stay with her until I get back?'

'Oh, for heaven's sake, Harry, I'm not a child! Don't you see, that's just what I *want*, to be alone.' Caroline was roused enough from her lethargy to protest, in a sharp way so uncharacteristic of her they both looked at her in surprise. 'I'm sorry,' she said. 'You've been so kind, you've all been so kind . . .'

'It doesn't matter.' Harry patted her shoulder again and went out.

Mrs Peach said matter-of-factly, 'With all them policemen trampling all over the house with their big feet and drinking us out of tea and coffee, we're likely to run a bit short – shall I bring some more instant when I come tomorrow? No point in giving that lot fresh.'

'If you think so,' Caroline answered colourlessly, but that didn't satisfy Mrs Peach.

'What I *do* think is, you should have something to eat. Why don't you try just a drop of that chicken soup Janice made? You won't do no good starving yourself. And what are you doing sitting in the dark?' She reached out and bossily switched on a lamp.

Caroline blinked, defenceless in the sudden radiance. 'I might have some later,' she answered evasively, though the last thing she wanted was food.

'I know how you feel, m'duck,' the older woman said unexpectedly, and hesitated, as if about to offer more sympathy, then evidently thought better of the idea. 'However, I should have a try to eat something. It'll do you good.'

'I'll try, I promise.'

Mrs Peach was clearly unconvinced, but she gave a nod. 'Well, see you do. I'd better love you and leave you now, and go and get Arthur his tea – his supper by now, I suppose it'll be. He'll be hopping mad, he will, but he'd starve to death before he'd lift a finger to get cracking hisself.' Yet unexpectedly she felt an affection for Arthur that hadn't been expressed for a long time. After all, even a husband like Arthur was better than none at all.

At last she took her departure, leaving Caroline staring at the smoke from Harry's abandoned cigar spiralling in the lamplight, wrestling with the guilt that was the uppermost emotion in her mind.

'I suppose they want to see me next,' she said when Harry came back, making a beeline for the drink he had left. 'Oh God.'

'They haven't said so – but there's nothing to be nervous about. That chief inspector chap seems pretty decent – just tell the truth, and you'll be all right.'

'The truth, yes,' Caroline murmured, her pulses jerking. Harry was contemplating what was left of his cigar as if wondering whether it was worth re-lighting. 'Why did you ask to see them, Harry? What have they been asking you? You've been in the office all day, haven't you? You couldn't have had anything to do with it.'

'Presumably I could tell them something about those who could have,' Harry replied selectively. 'They did ask me a lot of questions.'

'Such as?'

'Oh, the usual sort of stuff, I suppose, when they're looking for – well, you know, in a case like this – the people he had contact with, both here and in the office – whether Clive had any enemies and such like. They seemed very interested,' he added carefully, 'in the letters, and the calls.'

Caroline stiffened. 'The anonymous letters? How did you know about them?'

'Why, Clive. Clive told me. Does that surprise you?'

'Since he told me not to say a word to anyone, and vowed he wouldn't either, yes, it does. He was quite adamant that the only thing to do with poison like that was to ignore it.'

'And he was right, of course. All the same, he did mention them to me.'

Caroline's nervous fingers twisted the decorative fringe on the high side of the settee. A strand of it came loose.

'Did he tell you who he thought was sending them?'

'As a matter of fact, he did.'

'And you told the detective? So that was why you asked to see him!'

'I had to, Caroline. We can't any of us have any secrets now.'

Caroline felt the colour rising in her cheeks, but if Harry noticed, he apparently mistook the cause. 'I can understand your

46

reluctance to name names, but Marcus Dymond,' he said gently, 'is already implicated. He was here this morning – and they had a blazing row, he and Clive.'

'Marcus? *Here?*'

'Unfortunately for him, yes.' Her patent incredulity prompted him to add, 'Marcus told me so himself, on the telephone, after he'd been here. He rang me, demanding information, which I naturally refused to give him.'

'About what?'

'I could only infer,' Harry said cautiously, 'that he must have learned about Clive's plans for Oddings Cottage.'

Another shock. She hadn't known this, either, that Harry was a party to those particular proposals . . . though of course she ought to have realised, as Clive's partner, it was on the cards he would be. As though he felt her unspoken censure, as if in his own defence, Harry added, 'I didn't feel it necessary to tell the police what I believed the row with Clive was about, because I may be totally wrong. I only know Dymond was absolutely livid about something.'

'But he didn't murder Clive!'

'How do you know?' he asked, rather quickly.

'I – well, I just do. Marcus would *never* do anything like that; it's not his style.' Whatever his faults, one had to be fair to him. 'Oh, I know what he's like, and what the situation was between him and Clive, but he's simply not capable of murder.'

'We're all capable of it,' Harry said heavily. 'We all have the seeds of violence in us. All it needs is enough provocation.'

She gave him a frightened look. But yes – no one could deny that Clive had annoyed and upset so many people, not only Marcus.

It was always possible, of course, that Marcus had on this occasion found it too much and had acted irrevocably, but could anyone truly believe this? 'Harry, do you know exactly what those letters said? Clive never actually showed me one.'

47

Harry paused. 'He never showed me, either.' He stood up, finally discarding the cigar. 'My dear, won't you change your mind and come back home with me? Cynthia will never forgive me if I leave you alone tonight. She'd have been here if she hadn't been staying in town until tomorrow . . . She'll be kicking herself as it is.'

Caroline was sure she would. The thought at this moment of Harry's divorced sister, Cynthia, with whom he had shared a house since his wife's death . . . Cynthia, immaculate, organised, her tireless advice and her ceaselessly jangling bracelets, was insupportable.

'Thank you; it's thoughtful of you, Harry, but I'd rather be here – and I shall hardly be alone, shall I, with half the Lavenstock police force on the premises? There is something you can do for me, though, if you want to help . . . If – if you could phone the Pelhams in Brittany . . . and tell them what's happened. There's no need for Pippa –' She swallowed hard. '– there's no need for Pippa to come home just now. And I'd be grateful if they can keep it from her until I can tell her myself . . .'

'Pippa, oh God, yes, I'd forgotten her, poor child!' Harry exclaimed, with more feeling than tact. For a moment, as his eyes rested on Caroline's pinched, withdrawn face, he fell silent, then he said briskly, 'Yes, I can at least do that for you, my dear. And if it's really what you want, to be left alone, then I won't press you.' She thought she detected a faint relief on his face, and was glad she'd refused. 'Good night, and I'll see you in the morning.' His kiss on her cheek was awkwardly kind as he parted from her at the door, leaving her blessedly alone.

Alone, yes. But what she really wanted was Matt, strong and comforting, able to cut through the tangled knot of her fears, here beside her when, she thought with a kind of terror, he was the very last person who must be brought into it.

The soft scents and sounds of the evening garden surrounded her as she stepped outside a minute or two after Harry's car had disappeared down the drive. The sky was a pale green, deepening to orange, with a single star. It was very quiet, her own footsteps on the gravel the only sound, save for the more distant drone of an aircraft and a dog's sudden, sharp bark, the soft whinny of the horses in the Comstocks' paddock.

In contrast, the house itself, usually silent and peaceful at this hour of a summer evening, or perhaps with music coming softly from one of its rooms, was restless with the movement of police. Lights were on everywhere, in unaccustomed places, in unused rooms, and suddenly everything familiar was bewildering; even the garden where she stood was alien territory, the deepening shadows under the cedar held terror, and for the first time, the absolute reality of Clive's death hit her.

Clive was dead. Clive, so overwhelmingly full of life, so sure of himself. Uncontrollably, she shivered.

An owl swooped silently, like a great grey moth against the sky. Gravel scrunched, and the detective chief inspector, tall and broad in the dusk, drew level with her.

Facing him later, across the table in the garden room, it struck her that she had never encountered a detective before, other than on the TV screen. This one wouldn't have stood a chance for a role on the box, being neither outstandingly handsome nor outstandingly tough, though he was a little bit of both. He had an air of quiet authority, his questions were polite but direct; there was nothing soft about him. You wouldn't be wise to play around with him. Her heart began to beat a little faster.

The lanky sergeant came in and sat down, taking out his notebook.

Routinely, she was asked her full name, her age, how long she had been married. 'Ten years,' said Caroline, 'nearly eleven.'

Mayo studied her, taking her measure while she answered him, deciding which approach to use in questioning her. A soft sweep of dark hair, limpid, troubled blue eyes, a formal and elegant silk dress, the colour of autumn beech leaves, soft bronze leather shoes. He would have put her at less than thirty-three, perhaps because initially that vulnerable look was one you normally didn't see much, beyond youth. She had an indefinable air of having been sheltered all her life, accustomed to luxury and soft living, with her expensive clothes and perfume, her pampered skin and shining hair; but her luminous eyes were steady and intelligent, and her responses quick.

'Have you any children?'

'One. Philippa, we call her Pippa; she's nine. Luckily, she's staying with friends.' For the first time, Caroline faltered. Mayo watched her eyes turn involuntarily towards one of the photographs on the wall, a snapshot of a small child on a beach, with a large, chunky man crouched beside her, father and daughter laughing into the camera.

This was something he was never easy about, the pressing for advantage when a witness was most defenceless, though he didn't shirk the duty, and at once began to question her closely about her movements during the day, pausing after a while to recap. 'So you drove straight from here to Heathrow this morning, deposited Miss – Johnson, that's right, isn't it, yes, Johnson, to catch her flight to Boston, and then on to Maidenhead for lunch. What time did you leave there?'

'Just after two, about five past, I think. We had lunch early because Mr Conti and his wife had another appointment. That's why I saw him at home, rather than at his London office, as I usually do . . . Besides, I know them as old family friends, as well as in business, you see.'

'What business is that?'

'Mr Conti is a publisher, and I work for him as a reader – that is, I read manuscripts and make recommendations about publishing. Or not, as the case may be.' She immediately wished she had not added the explanation; it appeared patronising, as though a mere policeman couldn't be expected to know what a publisher's reader did. The concentrated regard didn't waver, however. He merely remarked that it sounded interesting work.

'I find it so.'

'And you left at five past two then, and got home at what time?'

'Twenty past five,' Caroline replied, her eyes darkening at the memory of that awful moment when she had walked into the kitchen, every detail of which would be implanted in her mind forever.

Kite cleared his throat and, over her bent head, exchanged glances with his chief. Mayo answered the sergeant's unspoken request to take up the questioning with a barely perceptible nod. Kite hitched himself a little nearer Caroline's chair.

'Three hours – that's a long time, isn't it, from Maidenhead? I believe you drive a Fiat Bertone? White, isn't it? Nippy little car.'

'Yes,' said Caroline, 'but there was a fair amount of traffic, and you know what it's like along the A34 out of Oxford.'

'Right. Not many opportunities for passing, especially if you're in a line with something slow in front. Not until you're through Stratford, that is. Traffic heavy there, as usual?'

'As usual, yes, thronged with tourists.'

'I know.' Kite was sympathetic. 'Took me the age of a duck to get through the other day. Which way did you take?'

'Straight through. Up the main street, and on to the Evesham road.'

'Busy, was it?'

'Wood Street was chock-a-block.'

'Wood Street?' repeated Kite, keenly.

'Yes, going towards the market square.' She gave him a puzzled look. 'It was terrible, but I wasn't in any hurry, I took my time. Then when I got to Lavenstock . . . I had a call to make.'

'Where was that?' Mayo intervened.

'I called at the Pearson Secretarial Agency to see if there was any chance of them getting a quick replacement for Miss Johnson.'

'What time did you get there?'

'It must have been about ten to five, I suppose. Mrs Pearson was just packing up to go home, I remember, and I didn't stay long, certainly not more than ten minutes.'

It was at times like this Caroline wished she smoked. Her hands tightened together in her lap, then consciously relaxed as she remembered the two trained observers watching her. He had grey eyes, the chief inspector, grey and steady and searching, as if he read her mind. She hoped they would put her tension down to the awful realisation that Clive would now no longer be needing another secretary, just another of the things that would now be superfluous . . . his secretary, his car, his wife . . .

'And then?'

'I had to queue to get out of the multi-storey car park – it's always busy at that time – but then I drove straight home.'

'Reaching here at five-twenty.' She nodded. 'Mrs Lethbridge, why did you go straight out again when you heard what had happened? I believe Constable Trenchard had requested you not to.'

'Did he? I don't remember,' she said vaguely. 'I don't really think I knew what I was doing. I just wanted to talk to someone, and Harry is very understanding.' It had been an impulse, quickly regretted; it was far better in the long run to face things alone.

'You expected him to be home at that time, before six o'clock?'

'Harry doesn't keep late office hours. It was something he and Clive disagreed about. Clive often didn't get home until eight, or even later.'

While Kite noted the times, Mayo said, 'Mrs Lethbridge, this is very distressing for you, I know, but I have to ask you some rather personal questions.'

'Go ahead,' she said steadily.

'This house? It comes to you, now your husband is dead?'

'Brome already belongs to me. It's been in my family for generations.'

'So it's unlikely you would want to sell it?'

'Sell Brome?' She looked almost insulted, making him feel as though he'd been impertinent. But then she said quietly, and more decisively than he'd yet heard her speak, 'No. I would never do that.'

'Do you have any private income?'

'A little, enough for my personal needs.'

'Your husband was a partner in a successful architectural practice. Presumably you'll inherit his share, and that will enable you to keep the house going?' He didn't tell her, at this juncture, that amongst Lethbridge's neatly documented papers, he had already found a copy of the will, and that he knew she would come in for everything Clive had possessed.

'Yes. But a good deal of it's money that was originally my own. When we married, I made everything over to him, to buy his partnership, you know how it is.' What was he getting at?

'Was your relationship with your husband a happy one, Mrs Lethbridge?'

With both men watching her, Caroline felt her nerves exposed. It took a long time to find the courage to answer honestly, which she had to do, because others would tell him if she didn't. 'Lately, we hadn't been too happy, no. There was nothing openly antagonistic, though; it was more that we became – mutually disinterested.'

'You both went your own ways?'

'Clive did. I don't know that I went any way at all. For years I'd just been drifting –' She stopped, her colour heightened, and Mayo wondered whether he could have supplied the word she had bitten off. Until? Until something, or somebody, had happened to make her change her mind, and precipitate a crisis?

'There was no question of divorce?'

'We have a child, Chief Inspector, as you know . . .'

'Yes?'

'They adored each other – not that I'd have wanted it any other way. It was the best thing about Clive.' Her voice shook a little. She looked down at her hands, then went on more steadily,

53

'I sometimes thought he was in danger of spoiling her with too many expensive presents, but that was another matter. She loves us both, and it would have broken her heart if we had split up, and anyway, Clive wouldn't have given her up without a fight, and . . .' She stopped again, then said unexpectedly, 'My father used to say I was by nature too disposed towards a peaceful existence, and I'm afraid he was right. Perhaps, if I'd been more positive, things might have been different.'

'We all tend to blame ourselves after the event, Mrs Lethbridge. And death especially leaves a legacy of guilt.' He paused to look down at his papers, then said in quite a different tone of voice, 'Do you know of anyone with reason to want your husband out of the way?'

Surprised both by the insight and the hint of something personal which had very briefly crept into his voice, the abrupt switch of direction made her blink. 'Of course not!'

'No one with a grudge, an ex-employee for instance, no enemies?'

'My husband was not a very easy man, and I suspect very few people can go through life without anyone disliking them – but,' she replied in a low voice, 'not enough to *kill*.'

'Mr Lethbridge had been receiving threats, however.'

'Threats? I didn't know that!'

Mayo became alert. 'You didn't know?'

'I mean,' she explained awkwardly, 'I knew he'd had anonymous letters, and calls, but I didn't know they were threatening.' Yet Harry had known. Clive had told Harry – he must have done – who'd told the police. 'He wouldn't talk about them. I just assumed they were the poison-pen type, you know.'

'Could you say when he received the last one?'

'I don't know about the letters, but I suspect he may have received one of the calls at a party we had last week; at least he took a call which seemed to upset him.'

'Was the caller a man or a woman?'

'I've no idea; I've told you he didn't discuss the matter with me.'

'Except to say who he thought was behind them, of course.'

'Yes. Yes, he did say that,' she admitted reluctantly.

'Did you agree with him that it might be Mr Marcus Dymond?'

'No, that was absurd. I've known him all my life, and he's not that type.'

'Yet they did have a major disagreement, which apparently flared up this morning. Would you like to give me the substance of their differences?'

There was nothing she would like less, and telling of the quarrel about Oddings Cottage didn't make it any more edifying, but she made herself relate it as factually and unemotionally as possible. Like Harry, she didn't feel the need to elaborate on the fact that Clive had intended to pull down the cottage, once bought, because this would involve explanations of his plans for Brome itself, and these were, she realised with a tingle of shock that was not unpleasant, now irrelevant.

Mayo listened attentively but made no comment. 'Tell me about this party, will you, please? Was it a dinner party?'

'No, no, a cocktail party, for about seventy people. It was a business arrangement, really. Clive had recently won an award, for designing a rather special holistic healing centre that's just been built in Norway, and it seemed appropriate to celebrate it that way.'

'The person who killed your husband smashed the model of it, did you know?'

She looked blank. 'Why should anyone do that?'

'I hoped you might be able to tell me.'

'It seems a sick sort of thing to do. No one I know would do such a thing!'

'That, I'm afraid, remains to be seen. I wonder if you could let me have a list of the names and addresses of the guests at the party.'

'Yes, I suppose there still is one, sòmewhere.'

'Good. Then that's it for the moment, Mrs Lethbridge. We'll need to check your car over, by the way. Perhaps you'd let me have the keys? A matter of routine,' he assured her, seeing her frown.

'I'll let you have them right away.' She stood up to go, still frowning. 'That's it!' she exclaimed suddenly, 'My car! When I put it in the garage tonight, I noticed something odd, but I couldn't think what it was. Clive's car wasn't there – it was being serviced today, and it should have been back.'

'You garage your cars round the back of the house, don't you?'

'Yes, in the old stables. But perhaps they've brought it back since,' she suggested vaguely.

Mayo raised an eyebrow at Kite, but Kite shook his head. 'Hasn't been brought back since we got here.'

'Was that the usual thing? For the garage to return it?' Mayo asked.

'Yes; when it needed servicing, Clive always took it in the evening before, usually on Thursdays, on his way home from work. Harry went along, too, in his own car, to drive Clive on here. It's on his way home. Then the garage would bring the car back when it was ready.'

'They've probably found something that needs attention. What kind of car was it, and what garage did he use?'

'A BMW. Sanderson's, the BMW agents on Queen's Road in Lavenstock.'

'We'll check it tomorrow. All right, Mrs Lethbridge. We shall want to see you again, of course, but for the moment,' he added with an unexpected kindness that nearly unmanned her, and a smile that totally changed the serious caste of his features, 'try to get a good night's sleep. I'll see that my men don't disturb you.'

'You're very kind,' she said for what felt like the thousandth time that day.

CHAPTER 7

'What was all that in aid of?' Mayo asked, as soon as the door had closed behind Caroline. 'All that about Stratford?'

'She's lying.'

Kite was looking so pleased with himself that Mayo restrained himself from saying that a child could have seen that, and waited for him to explain.

'Well, it's Stratford Mop, isn't it, this week-end?'

'It's what?'

'The Mop Fair, held every year, a big tradition. The fairground stalls and vehicles park all along the main streets while it's on, and through traffic's normally diverted. It's a right dog's breakfast, and not possible she could have come through as she said, not without being aware of it.'

'Sure you've got the dates right?'

'I'm sure. We've promised to take the kids down this weekend,' Kite told him, on a note of hopeful pessimism.

'Hazards of the job, lad.' Apparently unmoved, Mayo was sorry for Kite's sake that a murder investigation had cropped up to spoil his plans. Letting down the family, or the wife, was an occupational hazard for policemen. He, more than most people, was aware of how much of a contributory factor this was to the breakup of a marriage. Depending on the marriage, of course. But he had no intention of rushing things at this stage – or letting Kite do so. The beginning of a case was the time to hold your horses, take things slowly and patiently, until it began to gather its own momentum.

'It might be the last chance we'll get for some time, for a family outing, I mean. It's Sheila, see. She's been accepted for that job.'

Kite's wife had returned to work when their youngest had started school, considering herself lucky to be able to augment the family income by finding part-time work as a shorthand typist in the personnel department of a large engineeering works. How it had come about, Kite wasn't quite sure, but before long she was working full-time, the firm was realising her potential and Sheila was enlarging her ambitions. She was sent on courses, and began to progress so fast up the ladder that she had now been appointed assistant personnel manager.

'Great news; give her my congratulations. You must both be chuffed.'

'Oh, sure, over the moon.' And he was, really. 'It's going to make a hole in her spare time, though. I can see us making appointments to see each other before long.' Kite stuck his hands into his pockets, frowned, then shrugged. 'Anyhow, that's how I'm certain about Stratford.'

'It's worth following up,' Mayo told him, taking the hint and not pursuing the subject of the promotion. Obviously Kite didn't know quite what had hit him yet. 'Dig around and see what you can come up with, about this time Mrs L has unaccounted for . . . unaccounted unless she *is* a very slow driver, that is.'

'No way. She's been copped for speeding a couple of times to my knowledge.'

'Has she, by gum? I wouldn't have thought she was the speeding type.'

'Well, a car like that . . .' There was a wistful note in Kite's voice that many men would have recognised.

'Presuming she came up the motorway and got here earlier than she said, then. Could have parked in the back lane behind the orchard, nipped in and done her husband in, then driven off again – cleaned herself and her car up and come back, all innocent-like?' It could be established. There were tyre-tracks in the lane, going as far as the gate, then reversing out again, fresh after the rain of the previous night, from which casts were even now being taken.

'But is she capable of killing at all, much less bludgeoning anyone to death?' Caroline Lethbridge looked an unlikely candidate for the role of murderess, though experience taught any policeman that signified nothing. 'It's my guess she's a bit of a martyr, the sort who could go on agonising for years rather than take a positive step that's likely to be painful – though we have to remember she wasn't happy with her husband, there were problems, she may even have met someone else, which could change a lot of things.'

'If she was against divorce because it would upset the child so much,' Kite objected, 'it's hardly credible she'd choose murder as the other alternative to gaining her freedom.'

'True.' Yet Mayo had watched the expressions crossing her face while they spoke of Clive's death. Shocked, as anyone would have expected, by sudden death. Distressed at its violence, yes . . . worried, certainly . . . yet a real sense of loss, true sorrow, grief, or pain – where were they? Their lack lent weight to Mrs Peach's hints about the state of the relationship between Lethbridge and his wife, but if every marriage that fell short of the ideal led to murder, Mayo thought wryly, he'd be a busy man. He needed to know more about the background before assuming that. What had he been like, Lethbridge? What manner of man had that shell of a body contained? Death had wiped the face clean – of humour, intelligence, strength or weakness, indeed, anything of the man who had in life been loved, feared, or hated.

'Have all her movements checked – what time she left these people she had lunch with . . . when she arrived at this agency, what time she left.'

He sat still for a moment, frowning. 'What did you make of Waring?'

'Seemed straight enough to me. Bit of a smoothie, though.'

'Right. And more than a bit anxious to tell us about this row between the deceased and Dymond, wasn't he? Not like Mrs Wharton, who seems to have seen fit to put it about there was no one here all day. I think we'd better have a word with her, and see why, before we see Marcus Dymond.' It was getting very late, and he decided Dymond must wait until tomorrow morning. A devoted husband with an invalid wife, as Dymond was, according to Waring, wasn't likely to push off. 'What's the set-up there?'

'With the Whartons? Both work here, as housekeeper and general handyman, with the Lodge as tied accommodation. It suits them because the husband's reading for an external degree at the university. One of those mature students.' Kite paused, personal analogies intruding. Then he said, 'It's my bet it was him who told Mrs Wharton to say nothing about Dymond being here.'

'Why?'

'General bloody-mindedness, I imagine. Cocky little sod, he is. The sort who's anti-police on principle. Police, and all the world agin him besides. I only saw him for a minute or two in the kitchen with his wife, but it stood out a mile that he's carrying a thumping great chip on his shoulder . . . Can't see why; he's got a pretty cushy number here, easy job, nice house. There's a lot would be grateful.'

'Depends. On what price you're prepared to pay for being constantly beholden.' Mayo consulted the list of names Kite had given him. 'I see we've got the Whartons lined up to see next. Let's move.'

Brome Lodge, just inside the main gates of Brome House, was a small house of Victorian construction, of the *cottage orné* variety, a highly desirable residence in these over-priced times, despite the pigmy-sized rooms and lack of light, which the Victorian Baddesbys had evidently considered less important than overall picturesqueness.

'Quaint, isn't it?' Kite remarked.

With its curly eaves and Gothic windows, it reminded Mayo of a Victorian money box he'd had handed down as a child, where you put your pennies down the chimney, though he'd soon found you could get them out by removing the doorstep with a knife.

Inside, laudable efforts had been made to counteract the

general subfusc claustrophobia by way of shining paintwork and light, sprigged wallpapers, with much success. Not an interior decorator's tour de force, certainly, but the effect was charming, that of a spotless doll's house. And a home for all that, where comfort wasn't sacrificed for appearances. Toys and books were scattered around, a child's drawing pinned to the wall. Janice Wharton gently smoothed into place the loose cover on the arm of her chair as she sat down, almost as if she stroked the hair of a beloved child.

After what his sergeant had said, Mayo had been half-expecting a little woman, meek and mild, but Mrs Wharton was of average height, with strong features and heavy brows, saved from plainness by a pair of clear and beautiful hazel eyes. Her smooth, dark hair was caught back, simply, with combs. He could imagine her being under no one's thumb, though she was exceedingly pale and, at the moment, he would have sworn, under some stress. Her large, capable hands, which she endeavoured to keep folded calmly in her lap, occasionally betrayed her. Watching them unconsciously tighten, Mayo thought she was as tense as an overstrung guitar.

She answered his questions about her circumstances and the general routine of the house clearly and briefly, without adding comments of her own. As far as today went she could, she said, tell them no more than they already knew, that Clive had worked alone all day, had his meals taken to him in his study, seen no one.

'Except Mr Marcus Dymond.'

Janice Wharton did not meet his eye. A very faint colour rose in her cheeks, but she said nothing.

'Come on, Mrs Wharton, you're not going to gain anything by not telling us everything you know. It's only going to hold things up.'

'How did you find out?' she asked at last, her voice very low.

'Never mind that. Were you aware that they had a quarrel?'

'No.'

Mayo knew she was lying. He said rather sharply, 'We are investigating a murder, and I think we may reasonably expect a little co-operation. Think again, please.'

'It was this morning when Mr Dymond was here,' she admitted at last, but still avoiding a direct answer. 'Mr Lethbridge was alive until after tea, so how could he have killed him?'

Mayo resisted the impulse to tell her it was the job of the police to make the deductions, and pointed out that Dymond could have come back later. 'But of course, you would have known if he did, wouldn't you? You would have heard him and let him in, even if Mrs Peach didn't. She's slightly deaf, isn't she?'

This long shot, based on what he'd deduced from the unnerving fixity of Mrs Peach's stare, and her scorn of the telephone, came off.

'She is a bit, though she won't admit it. But I wasn't there this afternoon.' Perhaps on surer ground now, she loosened up, became more talkative. 'The arrangement is that I have the afternoons free, then go back to help with the dinner after I've picked up Nicky and Jane from school and given them their tea. Terry's usually home by then. I was able to get off early today because Mr Lethbridge said he wanted only a light lunch, so I left him some salad and cold salmon, and a half-bottle of Montrachet in the fridge.' She added, with what might have been a smile in other circumstances, 'It was left-overs from dinner last night. He said he had a very busy afternoon and didn't want to be disturbed, on any account, until he rang for his tea.'

'There's an internal telephone system, isn't there?'

'There has to be, in a house that size.'

'And it was Mrs Peach who made his tea?'

'She always does when she's here. Otherwise Mrs Lethbridge, or the secretary, does it.

'Oh yes, the secretary who's just left.'

'That's right,' she agreed, without noticeable enthusiasm, 'Miss Johnson.'

'So you couldn't swear that no one visited the house this afternoon?'

She didn't reply for so long that Mayo, bringing official jargon to bear, added sternly, 'Don't you want to see the culprit brought to justice?'

At that she looked up, regarding him steadily with those wide, clear hazel eyes before speaking. 'Whoever killed that bastard,' she said deliberately, 'deserves to go free. Society should be grateful to him.'

Kite looked decidedly taken aback, and even Mayo, who had become increasingly aware of a strong will, needing to be met, had hardly expected such a vehement answer.

'I'd like you to explain what you mean by that remark.'

'She means,' came a voice from the door, 'that Mr Clive Lethbridge was bad news, and not only for some. It'd be a lot easier to find somebody who didn't want him out the way than somebody who did.'

Terry Wharton swaggered into the room, his fists deep in his pockets, and Mayo saw what Kite had meant. Wharton was a short young man in his early thirties with a mop of blond, over-long, wavy hair, and very blue eyes. There was, however, nothing in the least effeminate about him. He was wearing jeans and a black T-shirt that revealed the wide, muscular shoulders, deep chest and narrow hips of the athlete. He stood before Mayo, shifting his weight on the balls of his feet, leading with his chin, like a bantam-weight boxer waiting for the next round.

'Mr Wharton? I'm Detective Chief Inspector Mayo, Lavenstock C.I.D., and this is Detective Sergeant Kite. We'd like to talk to you about this afternoon's events. Please sit down.'

Wharton ignored the outstretched hand, declined the request. 'I'll stand.'

'Please sit down, Mr Wharton, and be prepared to answer our questions,' Mayo repeated, without undue emphasis, but fixing him with a look that caused Wharton to comply, and lounge into a chair with ill grace.

Mayo continued amiably, conversationally, 'Don't come from round here, do you? I think I detect a fellow northerner.'

'Manchester.'

'Thought so. I'm from the other side of the Pennines, myself.'

'Yeah?' answered Wharton, with enormous disinterest.

Mayo surveyed him thoughtfully. He probably needed all this aggression to add a few inches to his height. He said, smiling and not raising his voice, 'And we don't stand for being buggered about, us Yorkshiremen, Wharton. So watch it!' Wharton blinked and sat up straighter, and Kite, who had never heard Mayo swear at a witness, thought, by God, he'd better, and hid his grin in his notebook.

'Let's have a few personal details first.' They went through the business of taking name, address, age, etc. Then Mayo asked, 'How long have you lived here?'

'Eighteen months, give or take a bit,' Wharton said, glancing at his wife for confirmation.

'Eighteen months exactly. On the fourth of last month.'

'Nice house you have.'

'We've worked at it.'

'It's a credit to you. You can't have much spare time. Your wife has told us of the conditions of your employment, and that you're working for an engineering degree as well.'

'I manage to fit things in.'

'Where were you this afternoon, Mr Wharton?'

'Shut up in the bedroom, trying to work on an assignment.'

'All afternoon? You never went out?'

'No.'

Something had crept into the room, something tangible. Fear. Someone was holding their breath.

'And you never heard anything? Deep in your books, were you?'

Wharton said through his teeth, 'Maybe that strikes you as funny –'

'Not in the least. Why should it?'

Mayo might have saved his breath. 'It doesn't come easy to me, you know, theory. I'm all right with the practical stuff, but theory – that's another ball game. But I'm prepared to work at it, see, slave my guts out if it means a better job at the end. I took this on because I want my kids to have a better future than I had. I couldn't do what I'm doing without this job to keep me going, and this house. And my family are happy here. So if you think I murdered Lethbridge, you'd better come up with a damn good reason for me to do it.'

Kite looked up from his notebook as Mayo said, 'One reason could be that you had a row with Mr Lethbridge, and lost control. It wouldn't be the first time, would it?'

There was a small sound from Wharton's wife.

'Christ, you're all alike, aren't you, you lot?' Wharton burst out. 'You don't care who you pin summat like this on, as long as you get some poor bugger! Where'd you get hold of that?'

'From Mrs Peach,' said Mayo mildly.

'Mrs –?' An odd expression crossed Wharton's face; a look passed between him and his wife, who, Mayo noted, was white as paper. Wharton gave a sudden short laugh and said, more easily, 'Oh, old Peachey! You don't want to take no notice of her; she blows everything up into a big production.'

Mayo went back to his original theme. 'You didn't get on with your boss, though, did you?' He used the term in a deliberately provocative way, but Wharton didn't take the bait. For some reason, perhaps because he'd got something off his chest, his aggression had left him.

'No, I didn't, and I'll tell you why. Lethbridge was like a lot more, chucking his weight around because he had the upper hand, thought we should lick his boots because he'd given us this job, and he got up my nose with it, right! I've had my rows with him, and I'll admit it, but the last thing I'd be likely to do would be to cut off my bread-and-butter supply.'

As they left the cottage, Mayo said, 'A right one, he is. And he read into my words more than I meant, when I spoke about losing control? If he hasn't got form, I'm a monkey's uncle. Get on to it, will you?'

'All the same, she's the one who wears the pants.'

And there Kite had put his finger right on the button. For all his macho image, Terry Wharton wasn't the only one to watch there. His wife was far deeper. Her attitude throughout the interview had shown she was well aware that he, Mayo, was thinking she had not only had ample opportunity, but also the capability, to commit this crime. He wondered if that was what she was afraid of, and thought again of her hands, large and strong. Her will, he suspected, was equally so. Yet all the indications were as Wharton had said, that the two of them stood to lose everything, and gain nothing, by Lethbridge's death.

CHAPTER 8

Mayo arrived at the office by eight the following morning, ready for the briefing session with his team, culled from the Regional Crime Squad, which would begin the day. He found Kite already there, a large bacon sandwich in his fist, and a pint mug of coffee steaming on the desk beside him.

'Didn't your mother ever tell you all that coffee'll rot your socks?'

'Give over, got to have something to bring me to the surface! We didn't get much sleep last night, remember – besides, I don't drink all that much, do I?'

'I suppose we should be thankful it's not beer.'

'What, on my salary?'

'Stir yourself and let's be having some evidence you're worth that much.'

But Kite, despite not having rolled into bed until dawn, must have been in the office for some time. He'd already submitted his reports, in his execrable typing. Before the session, he and Mayo went through the case with Garvey, the allocating sergeant, and Backhouse, the detective inspector in charge of the incident room, which was already alive with both plain-clothes and uniformed men and women, video screens flashing, telephones and type-writers going. Whenever possible, Mayo set his incident room where such facilities were easily accessible, as in this case, with the murder location within striking distance.

'Detail somebody to go through Lethbridge's office in Birmingham this morning, will you, Sergeant?' he asked Garvey.

'Inspector Atkins?' Mayo nodded. Atkins, an inspector for twelve years and aspiring to nothing higher, preferring to work under instruction rather than use his own initiative, was tireless over humdrum, routine work. Phenomenal in his local knowledge, stubborn as a mule, therein lay his strength.

Before he left, Mayo buttonholed Kite. 'I've got the P.M. at eleven, so that leaves me just about time to see Dymond first, but I want you over at Brome. You know the drill. Get the door-to-door finished, see whether anybody noticed a car parked in the lane, or anything unusual. If they've finished with the study, get Mrs Peach to take a look and see if anything's missing – Mrs Lethbridge as well, of course, though I'll be surprised if it is. And don't forget her car. Looks like I'm lumbered with Deeley this morning. Ah well, I reckon it's time he was made to justify his existence.'

'Better get off right away, then. I'll see you back here?'

'No, wait, we'll drop you at the house on the way to Dymond's. No sense in taking two cars, even if you're not paying for the petrol. Come back when you're ready in one of the squad cars; they'll be to-ing and fro-ing all morning.'

Spoken like a true Yorkshireman, Kite thought, but didn't quite dare say it.

Earlier that morning the bright sun, concentrated through a chink in the drawn curtains, shone on to Matt Royston's face, waking him five minutes before the telephone at the bedside rang. He had worked late the previous night, successfully shutting out everything else, but his thoughts this morning could not be so easily controlled. Clive had promised him free access to all sketches, plans and notes which had charted the progress of the Svensen Centre, but now . . . Matt faced his own attitudes with some ambivalence.

The telephone rang, startling him. Looking at his watch as he reached out for it, he saw it wasn't yet seven.

'Waring here,' announced the caller. 'Harry Waring.'

Waring? 'I was about to ring you today to fix that appointment we spoke about. Looks as though you've beaten me to it.'

'Oh, that!' Waring gave a short, nervous laugh. 'Better forget it; it doesn't matter now. Look, I'm sorry to disturb you at this hour, but I know you were due to meet my partner over this book of yours this morning . . .' Waring paused. 'I have to tell you that something very shocking has happened . . .'

Matt sat on the bed, his hand still resting on the receiver after Waring had rung off, staring at the shaft of sunlight on the carpet. Lethbridge, dead. Irrevocably, incontrovertibly dead. He found to his surprise that he was sweating, and his hands were not quite steady. Caroline. He must see Caroline. Immediately.

He showered, dressed, then took time to have breakfast in the dining room when he realised she might not be ready to see him just yet – Waring had spoken of sleeping pills – if indeed she was willing to see him at all. He would have understood that, in the circumstances.

Yet the bizarreness of what had happened only really hit him when he was let though the gates by a uniformed constable, and then given the once-over by a plain-c!othes man in the house before being allowed to see Caroline, who was, he was told, in the drawing room.

They faced each other, awkwardly, divided more by Clive dead than Clive living. Matt felt that anything he said was likely to be wrong, and he guessed Caroline probably had similar hesitations. There were shadows like bruises under her eyes. She took refuge in offering him coffee from a heated jug that was standing plugged in on a side table, coffee that had stood too long and was bitter and black. He noticed that though she had poured one for herself, she forgot it and left it on the table. She walked to the fireplace, where she stood leaning her elbow on the stone mantel and looking down into a copper urn massed with dahlias in fiery tones of orange and red that had been set into the empty grate.

'Caroline, I –'

'Don't, please. There's nothing to say now, is there?' Her voice was cold and formal. 'It was kind of you to come,' she added, as though he was the vicar offering routine condolences, as though yesterday afternoon, and what they had planned together, had never happened, or meant nothing to her.

Oh, Christ! This wasn't going to get them anywhere. He could understand the awkwardness of the moment, that physical contact between them might seem inappropriate to her at this moment, distasteful, even an obscenity; he could understand that she might be feeling guilty by association, because he was in fact busy coping with a fair-sized portion of self-disgust on his own behalf. His first thought on hearing that Clive was actually *dead* had been, well, whatever comes of it, that's one problem solved.

Caroline spoke unexpectedly, on a soft, prolonged sigh, as if she had tuned in to his wavelength, and seen the futility of trying to keep up a barrier between them. 'Do you believe that if you want something passionately enough, you can make it happen, Matt? If I hadn't wanted so desperately to be free of Clive –'

'No,' he interrupted roughly, 'I don't.'

'No. I don't know why I said that, I don't believe it either, not really; that sort of thinking is just being self-indulgent . . .' She stopped herself abruptly, her eyes huge. 'It was such a pointless thing to have done, after all.'

'Whatever else, murder isn't often pointless. Is it, Caroline?'

'Oh, Matt!'

They stood looking at one another, facing the enormity of what had been done.

'The police think it was somebody who knew him,' she said at last, 'maybe somebody connected with this house, and . . . oh God, I've done such a stupid thing; I told them a lie, and I think that sergeant spotted it. I'd forgotten about the Mop Fair . . .'

When she had finished telling him what she had said to the police, he looked at her steadily, saying quietly, 'You didn't want them to know you'd spent an hour with me. Why?'

'Why? Don't you see? Won't that make them realise we might have had a reason, an opportunity – for, for murdering Clive?'

The silence didn't last very long, but to Caroline it seemed to stretch out between them like an elastic band being pulled to its limits.

'But we didn't,' he said at last, deliberately, 'did we?' And crossed the space between them in one stride.

'There's also the question of the book,' he said later. 'Do you still want to go ahead with it?'

'Why not? If it's possible, that is. Clive was so – *triumphant* at being included, you know. It would seem the least we can do.'

'Then I will, if *you* want it. I know he'd finished getting together all his notes and sketches, and he had my main outline, which he'd commented on and was going to return to me this morning when he handed over his notes. I must have both sets of papers, but otherwise there's no problem.'

'You'll have to ask the police. I daresay they'll be with all his other papers, in the study, but they've locked it up.'

The senior detectives in charge of the case wouldn't be here until later, the young plain-clothes man he'd spoken to before told him, and he was sorry, it was outwith his responsibility to let Matt into the study, or the secretary's room.

'I don't need to go in. It's only a file I need.'

The detective constable was an urbanely smiling young man called Farrar, a neat dresser, with smooth, fair hair and sharp blue eyes. Forensic had finished with both rooms, and last night he and the chief inspector had spent a couple of hours going through the desk and filing cabinets. Mayo had taken away anything he considered important, but it was more than Farrar cared to risk, letting anyone in without the gaffer's say-so. 'I'm sorry, sir, I can't let you have it, not without Mr Mayo gives permission. He or Sergeant Kite. Either of them should be here shortly.'

'It's my own property, a blue manilla file, clearly marked with my own name.'

'Makes no difference, sir, and in any case, I don't recall such a file – and I was the one who listed the contents of the desks and filing cabinets.'

'You must be mistaken.'

'No, sir.' Detective Constable Farrar was no longer smiling. And he was quite evidently not to be moved from his position.

'Maybe it's up at the office,' Caroline suggested. 'It's not likely to be anywhere else in the house. Clive was always very careful not to leave anything to do with his work lying around, but I'll have a look, if you like.'

She seemed glad to have even this small thing to occupy her, and left Matt to try his luck on the telephone to Waring & Lethbridge. There was, as he'd hoped, someone there. A Mrs

Endicott, Harry Waring's secretary, a woman speaking in a consciously modulated voice, albeit with iron-grey overtones, who made the conventional shocked noises about the death, then told him that a police inspector called Atkins was already there, going through Lethbridge's office. 'As if all this wasn't upsetting enough,' she said, touchily, 'they want to lock up all his papers and files; it's really very inconvenient for Mr Waring.'

She had been with the inspector, showing him where any relevant material was kept, she said, managing to convey that she held him directly responsible for her interrupted weekend, and she was absolutely certain that neither Matt's own manuscript, nor Clive's notes on it, had been there, in a blue manilla folder or anywhere else. Matt believed her.

'Miss Johnson would have known where they were, but of course, she's in America now, isn't she?'

'Yes, I believe so, but that's a thought, all the same. It might be worth a telephone call,' said Matt, to whom telephone calls halfway across the world were routine. 'Would it be too much trouble to ask you for her address there?'

'Not at all. Give me a few minutes and I'll ring you back.'

She was back within five minutes, sounding flustered. 'I'm sorry, but it doesn't appear that she left a forwarding address. There's no reason why she should, of course, officially, and she wasn't personally on terms with any of the girls to correspond with them.'

Matt thought for a moment, then said, 'Let me have her home address, here, if you will. They'll be sure to know.'

There was a small silence at the other end. 'The thing is,' announced Mrs Endicott unhappily, 'we don't appear to have that, either.'

'Isn't that rather unusual?'

'It's unheard of, I assure you, in *this* office! However, Miss Johnson wasn't set on through the usual channels – Mr Lethbridge himself engaged her, quite irregularly, only five or six weeks since, presumably through some employment agency, though we haven't had any invoices for her services as yet.'

And that was what came of bypassing the official channels, her voice said. Matt thanked her for her trouble and rang off.

Caroline had had no luck, either, but when he told her of his conversation with Mrs Endicott, she said immediately, 'It wasn't through an agency that Clive got hold of Sylvia; it was through Amanda.'

'Amanda?'

'Amanda Bradford, his previous secretary – his permanent one, really. She's on maternity leave at the moment, and recommended Sylvia as a temporary replacement.'

'Bradford? I remember the name . . . She was the one I dealt with when we made the first approaches to Clive about the book. Okay,' Matt said, 'what's her number?'

It seemed inevitable, given the other frustrations of the morning, that the number should be out of order.

'I suppose nobody knows her address, either?' he asked Caroline with resignation.

'Of course I do; she lives over at Hinton.'

CHAPTER 9

Detective Constable Pete Deeley turned the police car left, off the Lavenstock road, conscious of the chief inspector's eyes on the back of his neck, and therefore mindful of police driving school techniques. Sergeant Kite, announcing that Deeley's driving made him seasick if he sat in the back, had opted for the passenger seat beside Deeley, but the gaffer was in an unusually talkative mood. Consequently, Kite's seat-belt making it difficult for him to carry on the conversation without turning round, he had to twist his neck every time an answer was required. Deeley grinned to himself.

'What do we know about Dymond,' Mayo wondered aloud, 'other than this feud that seems to have existed between him and Lethbridge? Didn't he used to be a maths master at the old grammar school?'

'Search me,' Kite said.

'I know him a bit, sir,' Deeley put in diffidently. 'Or I used to – he taught me at one time.'

'*You?*' Kite uttered with unflattering amazement, which the other two rightly ignored, Mayo because he knew there must, contrary to all appearances, be more to Deeley than appeared on the surface. The powers that be who'd selected him for C.I.D. couldn't be complete fools.

'What did you think of him, Deeley?' he asked the constable, with interest.

'We hated him – sadistic bastard, he was, sir. Most of us, anyway. Some swore by him – the high-flyers, the ones he got through to Oxbridge. I believe,' Deeley said, struggling to be fair, 'he was reckoned a good teacher, for such as them. He'd no patience with the hoi polloi, only spoke to us to put us down. No wonder Lethbridge hated him.'

'Your prejudices are showing,' Mayo commented, mildly amused but interested in this, the longest speech he'd ever heard from the inarticulate Deeley, who played a formidable wing three-quarter in the divisional rugby team, but was not otherwise noted for his prowess. 'Let's see what you make of him now.'

'You won't want me to come in with you, will you, sir?' Deeley's agony was acute.

'You'll learn nothing sitting in the car with your nose in page three, lad.'

'He won't remember you, now you've grown your feathers,' Kite grinned.

Deeley's hand went defensively to the full, silky moustache he'd recently begun to sprout. His face assumed a look of martyred endurance, and he said nothing more.

They dropped Kite at the entrance gates of Brome, where a uniformed constable stood on guard. Mayo leaned out of the car and called after Kite, 'If they haven't already done so, get this lane checked out as far as the Lavenstock road, okay?'

Kite stuck up a thumb. 'Will do.'

They drove back through Brome village, on to the Lavenstock road and up the further slope of the valley. Russell Road, when they eventually found it, was an unmade road, and the house they sought was one of half a dozen largish properties, mostly mock-Tudor style with steeply sloping roofs and gables. All of them were fronted with well-kept gardens, not least the one they were interested in, which had a sweep of velvet lawn setting off a profusion of unusual plants and flowers, beautifully tended and perfectly grown.

A woman in a wheelchair was very slowly and with evident difficulty clipping a too enthusiastic spray from a luxuriously rampant climbing rose, using long-handled secateurs. Difficult as it was, she appeared to be coping admirably. When she saw them approaching, she abandoned the task and leaned the secateurs against the wall, removing her gardening gloves.

'Good morning. You must be the police; I'm Enid Dymond,' she greeted them composedly when they reached her, extending a hand which Mayo found as light and insubstantial as a bird's claw. 'Lovely weather, isn't it?' Mayo introduced himself and Deeley. 'My husband is expecting you, Chief Inspector,' she went on, as calmly as if they had called to read the gas meter. 'Just ring, will you? Marcus is out at the back, but we have a garden extension bell, so he'll hear you.'

Deeley stepped forward and pressed the bell, while Mayo remarked, 'He's expecting us?'

'Well, yes. It's about poor Caroline's husband, isn't it? Dr Ison made his usual visit to me just after he'd been called out there to

Brome – what dreadful things our doctors have to do! And since Marcus was there at Brome yesterday also, we assumed you'd wish to see him. Poor Caroline, and poor little Pippa!'

Mayo noted that Mrs Dymond gave no evidence of being unduly worried about her husband's involvement in a murder enquiry. The confidence of innocence? And though apparently a compassionate woman, her regrets were for Caroline Lethbridge and the child only. He wondered briefly whether anyone at all was sorry for the poor devil whose life had been so suddenly terminated.

Marcus Dymond appeared to be in no hurry to receive them, and to bridge an awkward gap while they waited, Mayo commented on the garden, asking the name of the climber Mrs Dymond had been snipping at. Her face came alight; she touched one of the white petals lovingly. 'Ah, isn't it a beauty? It's Kiftsgate – its only fault is that it's so exuberant. It must never be allowed to get out of hand, otherwise it takes over, and then tends to grow very shapeless as it grows older – rather like the rest of us, hm?'

Mayo had expected to be hampered by interviewing a probable murder suspect in front of his frail, white-faced invalid wife, had indeed been half-prepared to insist that the interview be conducted privately, so that he was now greatly relieved to see that this would most probably not be necessary. Enid Dymond might indeed be frail in body, but he was prepared to believe her mind and intelligence as robust as the next. She somehow still contrived to look elegant rather than thin; the gauntness of her face was mitigated by a discreet and careful make-up, her hair was neatly arranged and her clothes becoming. Her mouth was humorous; only her eyes gave her away. Mayo had seen that look before; with pity, he recognised what it meant.

At that moment, Marcus Dymond came to the door. A tall, lean man with a bitter face, hollowed cheeks and an unyielding mouth, a face straight from the illustrations in a medieval history book, the closed face of a monk or a martyr. Once more introductions were made. 'Deeley,' the man repeated, dry and precise, when it came to the young constable's turn. 'Peter Deeley. How many years since I taught, or attempted to teach, you?' His eyes rested unerringly on Deeley's sunset-hued tie and tightly-filled suit.

'Nine or ten, sir.'

'All was not lost, it seems. One's faith in the value of our education system is restored to see Deeley upholding the forces of law and order.'

'Yes, sir,' answered Deeley, his face wooden.

'I think you know why we're here, sir; shall we go inside?' Mayo intervened, somewhat shortly.

Marcus Dymond turned and, pushing his wife's wheelchair ahead of him, led the way through the hall into a room at the back, where a wide window with a french door overlooked the garden at the rear. Even Mayo, who was no gardener, felt the sheer delight of the subtle blending of plants and shrubs, colour and form. Near the house, where the ground was level, not a weed was visible, every plant and flower flourished voluptuously; it was only farther away, where the ground began to slope, gently at first, then more steeply away from the house, apparently in a series of terraces, that traces of neglect could be discerned in the plumes of uncut grass and unstaked plants.

'It's large,' the other man remarked, seeing his interest. 'Over an acre in all. Fortunately, we can close our eyes to its present shortcomings, since one can in fact see comparatively little of it from here. But it really needs someone younger to take it over.'

In the look that he exchanged with his wife, Mayo saw that Dymond had not yet accepted that his wife had passed beyond the point at which it mattered greatly, but that she allowed the fiction to continue. To admit otherwise would be to admit that she had given up hope.

'You'll have some coffee?' Mrs Dymond asked. 'It won't take long to make.'

'Thank you, no, we've just had some.' They seated themselves in the chairs Dymond waved them to. A comfortable room, its furnishings obviously unchanged for many years, its design, like the house itself, popular in the 1930s – mock-oak ceiling beams, oak studding on the white plastered walls, a mirrored overmantel and a plate rack bearing a fine collection of blue and white Delft. Polished boards surrounded a carpet square, and in the ingle-nook were two deeply comfortable leather club armchairs, rather the worse for wear, which Mayo, sitting in one of them, irrationally and immediately coveted.

Deeley's interest, however, was concentrated only on one part of the room, where on an upright piano a group of signed photographs was arranged. Ex-pupils at degree ceremonies, self-conscious in new academic regalia, groups taken at school functions. In none of them did Deeley himself feature. But he could recognise a few of his fellow pupils – Anderson, captain of games in his own last year . . . and that one, what was his name, the boy wonder, Simon something or other . . . and the Davenport twins . . .

The chief inspector's voice brought Deeley back to now. Hastily he sought notebook and biro. He was going to need all his concentration.

'Mr Dymond, we're here to make enquiries about the sudden death of Mr Clive Lethbridge, and I'd like to start by asking you what the purpose of your visit to him yesterday was, at his home.'

Dymond laughed shortly. 'It wasn't simply a friendly call, as I suppose you've gathered.'

'I understand you had high words.'

'We did indeed. Alas, it's no secret that I was on bad terms with Lethbridge. It goes back a long way –'

'Marcus, please don't upset yourself.'

'My dear, I've long since ceased to allow it to do that!' The harsh lines of Dymond's face relaxed as he smiled at his wife. 'Though I never could stand the fellow – and the feeling was mutual. To be frank, we couldn't meet for five minutes without putting each other's backs up, so I kept out of his way.'

'On this occasion, however, you sought him out, and the ensuing quarrel was quite violent.'

'On this occasion, Chief Inspector, he had gone too far, even for Clive Lethbridge.'

'In what connection?'

Dymond stood up and walked to the mantel, picked up the pipe that was lying there and shoved it in his mouth. He didn't light it, however, and after a moment he took it out, gesturing towards the window with the stem. 'Observe the bone of contention.'

Mayo raised his eyebrows questioningly.

'The cottage straight across from here, standing on that small plateau just below Brome House on the crest of the opposite hill.'

Just visible was a long, low building, black and white, with a red pantiled roof, backed by trees. On the skyline, the upper half of Brome House and its red roofs and tall, twisted chimneys could be seen.

'Oddings Cottage,' went on Dymond, 'for which, some months ago, Lethbridge severely overbid. He paid a quite ridiculous sum for it, but the general opinion was that even after restoring it, he could expect to resell and still make a fairly substantial profit. Odious, but understandable in a man of Lethbridge's type. I learned yesterday, however, that he had applied for a contravention of the preservation order, intending to pull the whole thing down and build a new, modern-style house.'

'Use those binoculars and you'll see why we were so angry,' Mrs Dymond added.

Mayo put the binoculars lying on the window sill to his eyes and focused the powerful lenses. The cottage then sprang into sharp relief, but without the glasses, it had been unobtrusive enough. A modern house equally, however avant-garde, would surely be unobjectionable at this distance, but in such cases, between the conservationist lobby and the modernists, feelings were apt to run high . . . In this case, there was added provocation. 'I believe you also made a bid for the cottage when it was put on the market?'

'If you know that, then you'll know what my principal differences with Lethbridge were. Yesterday I made my position quite clear, which was that I would stop him with any means in my power. Then, since I had no more to say, I left, and,' he added dryly, 'I didn't go back again.'

Mayo said blandly, 'I take it that means you can substantiate your whereabouts during the late afternoon.'

Dymond took the pipe, which he had neither filled nor lit yet, from his mouth and knocked it against the brick of the fireplace. 'Actually, no. I was here, pottering about the garden, but I've no witnesses to the fact.'

Enid Dymond said, 'But don't you remember, Marcus? I was resting,' she told Mayo, 'and he brought me a cup of tea up at four.'

Mayo intercepted their quick exchange of glances . . . thanks on his part? On hers, a kind of defiance? Certainly a barely perceptible shake of Dymond's head as he smiled at his wife. A transforming, almost boyish smile, wiping his features clean of their sardonic expression for a brief moment. Then he said, 'More to the point, I made a telephone call, which I assume could be verified.'

'At what time?'

'Half past four, after I'd had my own tea.'

'The call was made to –?'

'Waring. Mr Harry Waring, Lethbridge's partner.'

This confirmed Waring's statement, and assuming both were telling the truth, it put both of them in the clear at the time of the murder. 'What did you speak to him about?'

'I wanted to know what Lethbridge was up to. If he was going to take Caroline and young Pippa to live in this monstrosity he planned to build on the Oddings Cottage site, which was what he told me he intended, what was going to happen to Brome House? I quite violently disliked the thought of a modern housing estate up there on the hill in its place.'

'So that was what he was planning?'

'No. It wasn't, as it happens, but something equally barbaric was being mooted, from any thinking person's point of view. Nevertheless, I was actually quite relieved when I learned from Waring what it was, simply because I could not see Caroline ever being a party to such absolute desecration. He was actually planning to turn that beautiful house into what he called a suite of prestige offices. Sheer vandalism! Not, of course, that that would have worried him.'

But who else might it have worried? Dymond himself? Yes. Caroline Lethbridge, perhaps. Hm. Mayo put the question aside for the moment. 'What kind of car do you drive, Mr Dymond?'

'A Mini.' So that was out; the tyre-tracks found in the lane indicated a wider wheelbase. He stood up. 'Before I go, I'd like a specimen of your handwriting, please.' Dymond wasn't to know that they possessed no copies of the anonymous letters, that they didn't even know whether they'd been handwritten or not. Mayo thought it unlikely, given the sort of man Dymond was, that the request would provoke a reaction; he was too intelligent for that. All the same, it was worth a try.

'My *handwriting*? Don't you mean my fingerprints?'

'Those, too,' Mayo said.

'May I ask why – why the handwriting?'

Dymond seemed to be suppressing some inner amusement as he reached for a biro off the mantelshelf, but the look changed when Mayo said, 'You didn't know Mr Lethbridge had been receiving anonymous letters?'

The other's astonishment at this appeared genuine, but it was momentary. 'That's a most offensive accusation.'

'I made no accusation, sir, offensive or otherwise.'

'Not offensive, to suggest that I would stoop to such juvenile behaviour?'

Mayo thought, God, he's actually less concerned about being accused of murder than writing anonymous letters! Or maybe – that's what he meant Mayo to think. A complicated man, Marcus Dymond, a man of secret thoughts.

CHAPTER 10

Wykefield Close, Hinton, was a desirable address by Lavenstock standards, whose citizens were of the general opinion that the houses must be good if they cost that much. Hinton itself was a village recently expanded by the building of a large private housing estate and a shopping precinct, until it now touched the edges of the town. There were three main varieties of house: the 'Regent,' a four-bedroom Georgian style; the 'California,' a three-bedroom bungalow; and the 'Lausanne,' a four-bedroom chalet style. All were detached, if only just.

The Bradfords occupied a Californian bungalow on a corner plot, and though it couldn't have been more than two or three years old, the garden that encircled it already looked thoroughly well established. Instant gardening by means of pot-grown shrubs and trees bought at one of the new garden centres, Matt thought as he rang the bell.

A young woman in late pregnancy opened the door, and Matt introduced himself, apologising for not making an appointment, explaining that her telephone was out of order.

Amanda Bradford told him that she had already reported it. 'I thought, in fact, you were the repairman.'

She remembered his name and, recalling the correspondence about Clive's collaboration on the book, had no hesitation about asking him in, showing him into a large, specklessly tidy L-shaped room, which reminded him of the faultless letters she had sent him . . . she herself, for she had been that kind of secretary.

She offered him coffee, and while she was preparing it, he looked round the large room, furnished pleasantly, though without much originality, like something lifted from the Ideal Homes Exhibition. Ruffled Austrian blinds at the windows, oyster-coloured velvet three-piece suite, expensive wallpaper and a reproduction Regency dining set occupying the foot of the L. An imitation gas coal fire whose contours never changed, nor fell into troublesome ash, was set in the Adam-style grate. All organised to a T, the housework already done and Ms Bradford, used to the rush and bustle of a busy office, bored enough to be pleased to have someone to talk to.

Matt, who knew nothing of pregnant women's susceptibilities, was just realising that he was going to have to be the imparter of some shocking news, and he waited until he had taken the coffee tray from her and placed it on a table before he told her, somewhat warily, what had happened. She was visibly shaken. 'Clive Lethbridge? Murdered? But that's terrible!'

'You liked Mr Lethbridge?' Matt was surprised to see her feel for a chair as though her legs would no longer hold her. Nice legs, with ankles still slim and neat, despite her advanced pregnancy. She was very attractive altogether, in fact, her make-up immaculate, her hair a silken bell of light brown. She was well into her thirties, Matt surmised, recognising the now familiar phenomenon of the career woman whose child-bearing was briskly fitted into her schedule.

'I worked for him for nearly eight years. No, I wouldn't say I was over-fond of him; he could be very difficult indeed to work for, but still . . . I had hoped to go back, after the baby . . . His present secretary was only temporary, you know.'

'Sylvia Johnson,' Matt said, wondering which had jolted her most, the fact of Clive's murder or the sudden termination of her career prospects.

'That's right. You'll have met her, of course.'

'Actually, she's the reason I'm here . . . I'm trying to find the address she's gone to in Boston.'

'Boston, America? Sylvia's in America? I didn't know that! What's she doing there?' Amanda was plainly astonished. 'Has someone else replaced her?' she added rather quickly.

'No, not yet,' Matt told her, answering the last question first. 'Sylvia has an aunt in Boston, who's found her a job. She flew there only yesterday, and since some papers I need can't be found, I had the idea a telephone call to her might establish their where-abouts. But if you don't know her address in the States, perhaps her people here can give it me – if I can contact them. The office don't seem to have had her home address, however.'

Amanda frowned. 'They don't? How very odd. Well, I'm sorry, but I don't know it, either.'

'Hm, that's awkward. I assumed, when Mrs Lethbridge said you were a friend of hers, that you would. You were the one who recommended her to work for her husband?'

'Yes, I was, and I believe he was very satisfied.'

'So I've gathered.'

Amanda busied herself for a while by pouring more coffee for them both. 'Mind you, once or twice at the beginning, I had a few doubts about that, so I rang and asked him how she was getting on, but he spoke so glowingly about her, I knew it was all right, after all.'

'Why should you have doubts?'

'Well, you see, I didn't actually know her very well at all.' She bit her lip. 'It was funny, really, how I met her. It was one evening last winter, I'd called at Sainsbury's on my way home from work, on their late shopping night; there's one in the new shopping precinct here . . . Anyway, just as I came out of the door, we collided with one another, one of my shopping bags was knocked from my hand and everything went all over the place. She was terribly embarrassed and helped me to pick them up and carry them to the car. We were ages getting things sorted out – a jar of jam had broken and a flour bag burst; you can imagine what a mess there was. It took us so long she missed her bus, so the least I could do was to offer to run her home, but she wouldn't hear of it. Her next bus wasn't for nearly half an hour, so I suggested she came home and had a cup of coffee with me while she waited. And that's how it was.'

'You struck up a rapport?'

Amanda hesitated. 'Not exactly. Sylvia was a bit of a funny girl, really. At first I thought she might just have been lonely. I told her to pop around any time she felt like it, and she took me up on that . . . People don't always, do they?'

Matt had the impression Amanda had not been altogether too thrilled about it, either, but it was an impression she sought to dispel very quickly. 'I mean, I didn't mind, as long as she gave me a ring first. My husband's job takes him away quite a bit, so I'm often on my own, but I do have other friends I like to see regularly.'

Matt nodded, mildly amused at the thought of Amanda's friends being allowed their allotted time. 'What do you mean, a funny girl? Did she make a nuisance of herself?'

'Oh gosh, no, but she was – well, secretive. She never invited me back to her place; I don't even know where it was, except that she always got a number ten bus . . . To tell you the truth, we hadn't an awful lot in common, but I felt sorry for her; she didn't seem to have any family or friends. I knew her qualifications were excellent, though, and I thought I could help her a bit by mentioning her name when I was ready to leave.'

She glanced quickly at Matt and must have thought she hadn't impressed him very much with her reasons for thinking Sylvia slightly odd, because she said, 'Another thing, she was a member of one of those queer sects. I don't remember the name . . . She only mentioned it once, because I think she saw I hadn't got much time for that sort of thing. She didn't push it down your throat, like some of them do, I'll give her that . . . Oh, hang on a minute.'

She raised herself awkwardly from her low chair and went to a drawer set in a large wall fitment, returning with something which she held out on her palm. It was a small gilded brooch, or rather a badge, apparently made up of intertwined initials, though what they were, it was impossible to tell at first glance.

'I think this may have been something to do with her religion; at any rate, she always wore it, and she wasn't one for jewellery or anything like that, not even make-up, though she could have been quite attractive – as it was, she couldn't have made herself look worse if she'd tried.'

Sylvia Johnson had been so neglible, so nondescript, without a modicum of originality, that Matt found it almost impossible to recall what she'd looked like.

'I did try to get her to take an interest in herself, but she just didn't want to know; perhaps it was against her principles or something.' Amanda shrugged. 'Anyway, if you look at the back of this, you'll see the pin's broken. I found it the last time she'd been here.'

'Do you mind if I borrow it?'

'Keep it, if you want,' Amanda said indifferently. 'It's no good to me; then when you do contact Sylvia, she can have it back.'

Matt drove back to Brome House in a very thoughtful frame of mind.

CHAPTER 11

Post-mortems were ordeals with which familiarity bred neither contempt nor congeniality. Mayo got through by regarding them as a necessary evil, occasions to endure. They were always over, eventually. The pathologist, Timpson-Ludgate, confirmed Ison's findings, that death was due to the injuries resulting from multiple blows to the skull. Examination of the stomach contents indicated that death had occurred between four and four-thirty.

Mayo left his car parked in the forecourt of the new building that was the divisional headquarters in Lavenstock. He'd never before looked at the building objectively: only now did he realise, with a shock, how ugly its brick and concrete structure was and, though he was no judge, how far from any architectural merit it must be. He wondered why – why couldn't function equate with agreeableness, as it apparently had in the Centre Lethbridge had designed? The photographs he'd seen had shown a pleasing, harmonious group – different, unexpected, but not jarring, even to untutored eyes. Yet someone had disliked it enough to perpetrate a senseless act of vandalism on the model. Or had that simply been a further extension of the hatred vented on Lethbridge himself?

As he walked into the entrance Evans, the sergeant who'd tyrannised over the desk for the last twelve years, a law unto himself, called him over. 'The man everybody's looking for! Press wanting a statement, TV after you to be on the box tonight, and the super wanting to see you about it when you've a minute.' His lugubrious face split into a faint grin. 'I dunno, just like a bloomin' pop star! You want an agent, just let me know; I'm available from next week.'

'Oh aye, sitting with your feet up, lucky devil, pitying us poor slobs who still have to work.'

'Don't know so much about that, with all the jobs our Iris has lined up.' Evans' face looked more like a bloodhound than ever. 'Retirement! Sooner be working, I would.'

'Get away with you! We'll miss your smiling face, though. Seeing Mallin there won't be the same. Okay, tell the super I'm on my way – and get them to send some sandwiches and coffee up to my office in about half an hour, will you, Taff? Owt'll do – cheese for preference.'

'By the way,' Evans called after him, 'we've got a replacement coming down from your old division, name of Jones. Sergeant Jones.'

'Jones? Must have been after my time; I don't recall any Sergeant Jones.'

'Case of promotion, I think.' Evans licked his thumb and turned a page. 'Sergeant Jones was a W.P.C. before. Wonder if she's Welsh.'

'What's her first name?'

'Alexandra Elizabeth,' Evans read from the notes, pulling his mouth down. 'There's posh! Let's hope she gets Sandra, or Liz.'

'Wrong on all counts. She's not Welsh, but she's a nice girl in spite of it, and no side to her, either. And she's called Alex.'

Eschewing the lifts, Mayo began to climb the stairs, a small daily discipline he imposed on himself, never quite sure whether he did so because Doc Ison maintained it was good for the heart, or because of the sense of virtue thus accrued. Alex, eh? Now, there was a turn-up for the book, sergeant and all, though nobody deserved promotion more. Thoroughly reliable, cheerful, sensible, and a good-looker into the bargain. He wondered why she'd transferred here.

'Come in, Gil, sit you down.'

Superintendent Howard Cherry and Mayo were old friends. They had started together many years ago, round about the same time, in the old West Riding Constabulary, and when Mayo had made his application for a transfer and been offered Lavenstock, the fact that Cherry would be his superintendent had been a deciding factor in his acceptance. He was a man comfortable to work with, who didn't breathe down your neck too heavily, as long as you kept him fed with the necessary information.

They discussed the press release, decided Cherry would do the TV bit, then Cherry asked, 'Any leads yet?'

Mayo said cautiously, 'Not the usual domestic squabble, I can tell you that.'

Cherry raised disciplined eyebrows. He looked like a well-brushed civil servant, a tall, impeccable man whose urbanity concealed an open, shrewd and agile mind. He knew, as well as Mayo, that the majority of murders were solved before the corpse was cold, the weapon practically still in the hands of the murderer, someone pushed beyond the limits of endurance, stunned and appalled at a situation that had run so suddenly out of control. 'No suspects?'

'Trouble is, *everybody* seemed to hate his guts. Nearest suspect we've got at the moment's a chap I interviewed this morning, name of Marcus Dymond, and he's debatable.'

'Marcus Dymond?' Cherry echoed. 'Retired schoolmaster? But he taught my eldest lad!' He registered Mayo's expression and grinned ruefully. 'All right, carry on.'

As succinctly as he could, Mayo reviewed the case so far. Cherry listened attentively. He made no notes, but Mayo knew he would remember everything, right down to the fine details. When he'd finished, Cherry said, 'Well, see how you go – but stick to the book with this one, Gil. Play it carefully. These aren't the sort of people we can afford to upset.'

Mayo had time to make a few telephone calls and a quick scan of the papers he'd gathered up on his way in before his sandwiches arrived. They were very good, wholemeal bread and not too much pickle. Kite came in just as he wiped the last crumbs from his mouth.

Atkins had apparently found nothing of any relevance in Lethbridge's office. Nor had the house-to-house enquiries in Brome village revealed anything, though they were still incomplete, Saturday morning being the worst possible time to catch people at home. Half the village seemed to have taken themselves over to Lavenstock, to shop or pursue various weekend activities. Kite's investigations into the non-return of the BMW, however, had opened up a new line of enquiry.

'The garage people did take it back to Brome House on

Thursday afternoon, about half past three, as arranged. One of the lads drove it, with another behind him in the garage runabout to take him back. Lethbridge apparently saw them coming up the drive and stopped them outside the study as they were driving it towards the back. Told them to leave it where it was with the keys in, as he might need it shortly. And that's the last anybody's seen of it. Mrs Peach confirms seeing it there, though she didn't hear it arrive, or hear it being driven away, though she probably wouldn't, being hard of hearing.'

'What about the Whartons? They're not deaf – either of them see or hear the car go past?'

'Apparently not, but both the bedroom, where Wharton was working, and the kitchen, where Mrs W was doing some ironing, are at the back of the Lodge. Maybe Lethbridge actually did take his car out, and left it somewhere, though it seems unlikely, and it wouldn't give him time to get far – and to come back – in time to get himself murdered by half past four. Seems a fair bet the murderer used the BMW to get away.'

'Widens the field of suspects, and lends weight to the idea it wasn't premeditated. I must say, I find the idea of anybody planning a murder and not providing the means to get the hell out of it as fast as possible very hard to take.' Mayo tapped his teeth reflectively. 'Any results on the tyre-tracks?'

'They've taken casts, and promised to get a move on with the results. Oh, and Terry Wharton . . . You were right, he does have form. Seems he nearly killed a bloke once; there was a row with a mate he was working with, and he upped and hit him with a spanner. Lucky it wasn't manslaughter. Four years with remission, and while he was inside he took O and A levels.'

'And got himself accepted for college when he came out?'

'Some of these universities are very liberal,' Kite said.

Mayo pushed his tray aside. 'You've had a busy morning, lad.'

'There's more. Wait till you hear this. It looks like there's a boy-friend in Mrs Lethbridge's life – a bloke I met this morning at the house, journalist by the name of Matt Royston.' The name didn't have the effect Kite had hoped, so he repeated it. 'Matthew Royston. *The* Matthew Royston. "News at Ten."'

'My God,' said Mayo, 'that's all we need.'

'Maybe it's not so bad. He's been taking time off from journalism, to collaborate in writing a book with Lethbridge, and he's no intention, or interest, in getting involved with covering the murder. Or so he says.'

Mayo regarded this with even more scepticism than Kite, his opinion of the press in general not being very high, though he took care to keep his relationships with them as amicable as possible, working on a tit-for-tat basis: information on his side, discretion on theirs.

'That's probably where she was yesterday afternoon. I'll tell you what, though, he's in a sweat about a file of his that's gone missing. It's not in the house nor, according to Waring's secretary, at the Birmingham office.'

'What was in it?'

'Notes for this book of his, as far as I can gather.'

The telephone on the desk rang, and Mayo reached for it, pushing across the desk to Kite the path lab transcripts of the bloodstained papers on which Lethbridge's head had been resting. 'Yes, put him on.'

Kite skimmed through the reports while Mayo spoke. The document Lethbridge had apparently been working on when he was killed seemed to be the rough draft of a letter, in answer to one from a firm of merchant bankers in the City of London, called MacAllister Associates. It was signed with a large scrawl which after some difficulty it was possible to identify with the name of the chairman and chief executive, printed at the head of the letter, Leonard M. G. MacAllister. The letter comprised two sheets of A4, closely typed and long-winded. Boiled down, it came to the fact that MacAllister Associates would in the main be happy to consider giving Clive Lethbridge the backing he needed for his projected conversion of Brome House into a suite of prestige offices, with weekend conference facilities included, in return for a controlling interest in the public liability company thus formed.

Mayo, whose conversation with Waring had been brief, put the receiver back thoughtfully and waited until Kite had finished his reading. 'That was Waring – he wants to talk to us. I've arranged to be at his Birmingham office at three o'clock. You'd better come with me.' He looked at his watch. 'Whereabouts can we get hold of this Royston? I think we should see him as well. Can we fit him in before then?'

'He said he'd be working this afternoon, back at the hotel where he's living at the moment. The Brandon Hall; it's on our way.'

In the car Mayo brought Kite up to date on the interview with Dymond. 'So,' he concluded. 'You've read the path reports – that letter seems to confirm what Dymond believed Lethbridge was hoping to do with Brome House.'

'Think he's our man, then?' asked Kite.

'I'm not sure I'd go as far as that, not yet. He has pretty strong views on what he thinks of as Lethbridge's vandalism, but I wouldn't like to bet on anything with him, except that I doubt he'd ever do anything without thinking it through first. And this doesn't have the smell of that sort of killing to me.'

'Maybe he didn't intend to kill, just seized his chance.'

Mayo thought of that secret, contained face. Dymond was a man who would do anything for his wife, and he had hated Lethbridge, who had put paid to the plans for his wife's last years. But Mayo was uneasy with the theory on several counts. 'If he went back to Brome House in the afternoon and killed Lethbridge, it would have been with deliberate intent, I'd swear it. He'd have had every move planned, including how he was going to get away quickly afterwards. Which means that he'd have had to know that Lethbridge would be alone. And if so, we'd better find another theory for the disappearance of the BMW. Besides, he has an alibi, if he and Waring spoke together at four-thirty.'

'Assuming he rang from home. He could have rung from somewhere nearer to Brome House.'

'And the cup of tea he took his wife at four?'

'If he did take her one. Which you seem to doubt,' Kite said, warming to the theory.

'A spot of misplaced loyalty on Mrs Dymond's part.'

'He could have walked up through the valley, killed Lethbridge, got away in Lethbridge's car, stopped to ring Waring to establish an alibi . . .'

'Or even rung from the house – he's cool enough. But he couldn't have dumped the car very far away in that case . . . Doc Ison called to see Mrs Dymond on his way home from here, and he confirms that Dymond was at home then.' Mayo was silent, lost in thought. 'It's a theory, but there's not a shred of evidence to support it. We've got to do better than that, Martin.'

The receptionist at the Brandon Hall Hotel, a magisterial middle-aged lady, who was also the owner, was inclined to raise objections when Mayo asked for Matt Royston's room number, refusing with some justification to give it. She quickly gave way, however, when Mayo produced his identification, ushering them out with some speed, as though their presence might contaminate any guest who might happen to come along. 'His room's in the annexe. You can go through the hotel, but it's quicker to go outside and through the car park.'

Following her directions, they made their way towards a separate building stretching at right angles to the main hotel. Mayo paused before pushing open the annexe door. 'Take a look at that. Direct access to the car park. Easy as falling off a log to slip out of here without being seen. How long would it take to get from here to Brome and back?'

'Not too long. Half an hour, including time to kill Lethbridge.'

They found Matt Royston working in shirt sleeves amidst a welter of papers that overflowed from the small writing desk on to the bed. He began to clear a velvet-covered tub armchair, apologising for the clutter. 'Don't bother,' Mayo said, looking at the size of the chair. 'I take it there's somewhere where we can go and talk? Later we may want to go through your things. You've no objection to your room being searched, of course? Just routine.'

'Would it matter if I had?'

'You could always refuse,' Mayo replied blandly.

Matt laughed shortly and led the two policemen back through the reception area. The hotel had been converted from a large early-nineteenth-century house and still retained a romantic if gloomy grotto, complete with dripping rocks, pools and forests of ferns, built on to the north-facing side of the house. Even with central heating installed, it could be piercingly cold on sunless days; today, warm as it was, it held a welcome coolness, and had the added advantage, at this time of day, with lunch in progress, of being practically deserted. A couple of businessmen, expansive at the coffee and brandy stage, cigars well alight, were far enough away not to bother them.

Mayo waved aside the suggestion of drinks, and when they were seated on a comfortably cushioned cane settee, Matt on a similar chair opposite, he remarked, 'It can't be very convenient, working here, can it?'

'No, but more so than trekking up from London every time I wanted to consult Lethbridge.'

'Fair enough.' He need waste no time coming to the point with Royston. He was a professional like himself and understood the necessity for obtaining information in the most direct way possible. He, too, was a trained observer, and those level grey eyes wouldn't miss anything much, nor that sharp intelligence fail to digest it. But he was not an impartial observer in this case, and it would be as well to remember that. And that the easy, laconic manner could well be a cover for a certain ruthlessness. Mayo understood and respected this. When the occasion demanded it, he could be ruthless himself. He found himself liking Royston more than he had expected.

'Okay, this book you were working on, now. What sort of book was it? Tell me about it, will you? I'm not altogether quite clear.'

Matt explained, succinctly, a lifetime of cutting his prose to the bone standing him in good stead. The book was concerned with the major innovative British architects of the present century, those who had broken new ground, and their influence upon present-day architecture, with at least one of their major buildings, its inspiration, inception and final realisation, discussed in fine detail whenever possible – an analysis of the whole creative process, in fact. Lethbridge's own prizewinning scheme was to be the last in the book, and he'd agreed to make all his notes, sketches and plans available, charting its progress from beginning to end.

Mayo listened intently, without interrupting.

'Was he that brilliant?'

Matt took his time about answering. 'To be honest, he was only fair most of the time, but occasionally he was outstanding. This Centre, for instance, was beyond anything he'd ever done; it was so innovative there was some doubt as to whether it could in fact be built at all . . . You know about it, you've seen the model?'

'I've seen it,' Mayo said, 'smashed into a thousand pieces.'

'Smashed? God.' There was a silence, punctuated by the steady drip, drip of water from the rocks into one of the little stone basins of the grotto, and the tiny throb of the pump which worked the flow. Matt fished a battered pack of cigarettes from his pocket, holding it out to Mayo, who shook his head. 'You're right,' Matt said, putting it back. 'I've had those five in there for over a week. No point in spoiling the record now.'

'Let's get back to this file of yours that's missing. Why is it so important? Don't you have a copy?'

'Sure I've a copy. I'm just bloody furious at the idea of a nearly completed manuscript of mine sculling around, for anyone to get their hands on. But it's not only my manuscript; Lethbridge's notes are with it. I've been trying to get in touch with Miss Johnson, his secretary who's just left, to see if she's any idea where it might be, but she's a very elusive lady. So elusive that nobody, but nobody, seems to have a clue as to her whereabouts, past or present. And that, Chief Inspector, is something I'm beginning to find highly suspicious.'

'Are you? Why?'

Matt recounted his visit to Amanda Bradford, and what he had learned about Sylvia Johnson. 'It looks to me as if she infiltrated herself very nicely into that job, and left for America, where she couldn't be contacted, very conveniently. Though just because Mrs Lethbridge left her at Terminal Three doesn't mean to say she actually boarded the plane for Boston.'

'She did, though,' said Mayo.

'What?'

'Sylvia Johnson was a passenger on board the twelve-fifty flight 746 on Thursday the fifteenth to Boston. We already had that checked out by eleven last night.'

Matt leaned back in his chair. 'One up to you!'

'We'd have to have a bit more to go on anyway before suspecting her of murder. What could her motive have been, for instance?'

'I'm not saying she killed Lethbridge. But maybe she was planted there to suss something out for the person who did.'

'Your manuscript, for instance?' Mayo remarked dryly.

'Don't be snide, Chief Inspector. It's a damned good manuscript; it just happens to be very much on my mind because I can't finish it – not as it was originally planned, anyway – without Lethbridge's notes.'

Mayo had a feeling they may be getting away from the point – that Royston's concern about a missing manuscript could be a cover-up, an implication that he'd hardly be so bothered about such a trivial occurrence if he had murder on his conscience.

Matt said suddenly, 'There was a party last week, to celebrate Clive winning the award.'

'I've heard something about it already. Let's hear your version.'

Matt described the party, briefly. 'I had an undefined but very strong feeling of something wrong. Nothing I could put a finger on, but I think Harry Waring was aware of it as well. I've been away for a week, and he asked to see me when I came back, but he changed his mind and said it didn't matter, now Clive was dead.'

'That's interesting. What do you think made him say that?'

'I think he suspected Clive was up to something. He'd been trying – Clive, I mean – to put pressure on Caroline, about Brome, you know. She's been offered a permanent, full-time editorial job by the publisher she reads for. It would possibly mean living in London for most of the time. She was worried that if she accepted, Clive might have tried to use Pippa as a lever.'

'The child to live with her, in return for permission to convert Brome House?'

'So you know about that? Yes, well, it was something of the sort.'

'You're remarkably conversant with Mrs Lethbridge's affairs,' Mayo said bluntly. 'How well do you know her?' Their eyes met.

'I'm hoping to know her a great deal better very soon,' Matt answered steadily, but shortly. He wasn't such a fool as to think by admitting this he was telling the detective anything he didn't already know, or suspect, or would find out, but he wasn't going to give away more than he had to.

'She was with you here, yesterday afternoon?'

After a pause, Matt said, 'Yes.'

'She didn't tell us that, when we questioned her. Might that have been because she didn't want to alert us to the fact that you had both motive and opportunity to put her husband out of the way?'

'She panicked, that's all. God, you don't really think that Caroline . . .!' Matt stopped abruptly. 'There's been nothing between us, nothing like that. We've hardly been alone. Even yesterday, we met in reception and came in here for tea; and there were witnesses – the waiter, and another resident, an old lady with a poodle.'

'And the reason for your meeting?'

'Conti, the publisher she reads for, was wanting her to make up her mind about the job, and she wanted my advice. There was nothing more to it than that.'

But when they'd gone, Matt remembered that he'd said to her, 'I'll think of something we can do.' Her troubles hadn't seemed to him beyond what could soon be put right.

She'd replied, unexpectedly, 'I don't go in much for compromise, you know,' and he was reminded of how he'd warned himself not to underestimate her.

'Compromise was hardly what I had in mind – but he mustn't be allowed to trample over you – over anyone. Never fear, we'll sort him.'

He'd forced himself to speak mildly, but he knew his expression was grim when he'd seen that, for a moment, Caroline had been just a little afraid.

He went back to his room and poured himself a stiff scotch from the bottle he kept there, annoyed to find how much he needed it. Taking a deep gulp, he leaned back, tipping his chair dangerously, his hands thrust deep into his pockets, jingling a fistful of loose change – and felt a small alien shape amongst the coins. The badge Amanda Bradford had given him, which he had forgotten about until now. Turning it round, he examined it more closely. The initials of which it appeared to be composed were twisted together into a circular, vaguely art nouveau-ish ornament of the kind derived from Celtic forms. The letters may have been A, M or W, encircled by a C, but in any case conveyed nothing to him. He tossed it up several times as he finished his drink, then, making a decision, reached for his jacket and made for the car-park.

CHAPTER 12

The shop was seedy, no doubt suffering from its situation alongside the new ring road, where no cars could stop and few would bother to park and return for the poor selection of goods to be seen through the mud-splashed windows of V. Aikerman, high-class jeweller. The tarnished gilded sign above the shop seemed founded on hope rather than fact, since the goods in the window consisted of cheap watches, imitation jewellery and a depressing display of china and glass giftware. Felt-penned notices stuck on a glazed door fortified with a stout metal grating, not so much a safeguard as a prop to self-esteem, proclaimed: 'Best prices for old gold' and 'Ears pierced while U wait.'

Matt grinned and not too hopefully pushed the door open, the last try in Lavenstock. Summoned by the ring of the bell, a small man as depressed-looking as his stock emerged, shirt sleeves rolled up and running his tongue round his teeth. A strong smell of hamburger followed him from the back premises.

'What can I do for you, squire?'

Matt, putting aside his aversion equally to the form of address and the smell of onion breathed in his face, leaned forward to place the badge on the counter, but before he could open his mouth, the other exclaimed, 'Strewth, not again! What you do with 'em, eh?'

Bingo! Matt hid his jubilation with a non-committal shrug.

'You should send them back, why don't you? Them pins was never put on right in the first place. Costing you more to keep having 'em mended than they're worth. Okay, about a fortnight.' He reached for a receipt pad.

'Hold on,' Matt began. 'I don't want it repaired; it's not mine, in fact. I'm only trying to trace the owner.'

'What for?' The shopkeeper eyed him suspiciously. 'Not worth the trouble, thing like this.'

'Well, as a matter of fact, it's the lady herself I'm hoping to trace.' Matt, whose success had often depended on his quick summing up of a character, assumed what he hoped was a meaningful expression, and was rewarded when the man behind the counter gave an unexpected cackle.

'That so? Well, I'll tell you something, squire – and for free – you're wasting your time on that lot of Jesus freaks; you'll get no joy from any of them wenches up there. Very clannish, they are, if you get my meaning.'

'I thought it was some sort of religious society.'

'What's that got to do with it? They're the worst of the lot, they are, all brown rice and free love, no husbands and no bras. Okay for some, I suppose, but not the sort of birds you or I'd fancy. Hari Krishnas or summat I reckon; put you off your dinner, they would.'

'Live around here, do they?' Matt asked, not attempting to sort out this somewhat confused philosophy.

'Not far off, up at Branxmore. Taken over them houses that are still left up on Amelia Road, they have. Only till the council pulls them down to build some more flats, I reckon. D'you want this mending, or not?'

'No, I'll take it with me, but thanks for your information, Mr – Aikerman?'

'S'right.'

Money changed hands, and as Matt went towards the door, Aikerman called, 'Good luck, squire, you're going to need it.'

Amelia Road was on the very edge of what was left of Victorian Lavenstock. Its right-hand side had given place to blocks of flats, not unpleasing in appearance, a big improvement on the left side, where most of the houses had already suffered the mayhem and mutilation of the bulldozer, and obscenely indestructible polythene flapped greyly over heaps of fenced-in builder's rubble and the reeking remains of a bonfire. Sodden crisp packets and lolly wrappers impaled themselves against the sagging chain-link. Behind it used beer cans and rusty petrol tins lay where they had been tossed; an old vinyl-covered armchair sprawled with its springs and stuffing wantonly exposed.

Less than a dozen of the original houses were still standing, largish, three-storey red brick, of the more restrained type of early Victorian. Agreeable houses in their heyday, the last bastions of a more graceful age, they held possibilities even yet, though given the fate of the opposite side of the road, little hope of surviving to prove it. The short front gardens were denuded of flowers and bounded by untrimmed hedges.

The paintwork at number twenty-five, like that of all the houses, was greyish and peeling. Here someone had planted a few Michaelmas daisies, but they didn't look enthusiastic about it. Walking up the steps, Matt saw a small ceramic plaque, decorated with a replica of the intertwined initials on the badge in his pocket, and beneath it the legend: 'Church of the Assembly of Alternative Witnesses.'

Some privacy from the road had been provided by untidy net curtains on sagging wires, and he thought he had probably been observed walking up the steps by the speed with which the door was opened after his ring. The girl answering the door was a surprise on all counts. For a start, she was pretty, damn pretty, and was wearing provocatively tight jeans and china doll make-up. Her abundant dark red hair tumbled deliciously round her shoulders in a mass of shining waves, reminiscent of some forties starlet. She had clear, green, almond-shaped eyes, like those of a cat. He felt he'd seen her a thousand times, advertising toothpaste, or shampoo, or After Eight mints. 'Hi!' she said. 'Can I help you?' Her smile was slow and ravishing.

Speedily adjusting his preconceived ideas, and deciding sober caution was the watchword with this one, he rejected various interesting responses to her question. 'I'm enquiring,' he said, 'about Miss Sylvia Johnson. I believe she used to live here?'

The girl's expression changed only in one degree, in a slight, almost illusory flicker of the green eyes.

'Sylvia? Oh yes, she did live here, but she's left. She's gone to America, lucky thing.'

'I know. And it's really her address there I want. Do you happen to have it?'

'Not at my fingertips. What do you want it for?'

'She may know the whereabouts of some property of mine.'

'Now look here –'

'I'm not suggesting anything untoward, Miss –'

'Morrow, Elaine to my friends. I should hope not, but, well . . . Look, you must see I can't go giving people's addresses away to strangers. It's more than my job's worth.'

'Your job? You mean you work here? You're not one of the community, then?'

'Do I look as though I am?' asked Miss Morrow, arranging herself more attractively against the doorpost.

He had to admit that she didn't. As a personification of the religious life, she defied preconceptions. She was evidently not sworn to poverty, unlikely to chastity either, and hopefully not to obedience. 'Come on,' he said, 'I'm sure you could get me that address. Perhaps we could go inside and I'll explain why I want it.'

'That wouldn't be terribly convenient at the moment.' She threw a quick glance over her shoulder into what appeared to be a bare hallway, with a floor of coloured Minton tiles. 'And anyway, I'm pretty sure she didn't leave an address. If she wants anybody to know where she is, she'll write, won't she? What have you lost, anyway?'

He saw no point in going into detailed explanations, so he merely told her that a file of his containing his notes had been lost, and he wanted to track Sylvia to see if she knew of its whereabouts.

She listened with no show of impatience, watching him indeed with a look of secret enjoyment, evidently nothing loath to extend her conversation with him. 'I'll tell you what,' she said when he'd finished, fluttering long, patently false, eyelashes at him, 'if *I* had a gorgeous man like you looking for me, I'd be wild if nobody helped you to find me.' Once again, she cast a glance backwards, but if it was meant to imply nervousness, it singularly failed. 'He'd kill me if he knew – but, I like you, so –'

'Who?' Matt intervened. 'Who'd kill you?'

But she merely smiled and continued. 'If she does happen to have left an address, it'll be in the office.' She pointed towards a building at the end of the road.

'The church?'

'Sure. It belongs to the Assembly. It's where all the records are kept. So just you leave it with me, and I'll see what I can do, all right?'

There was nothing he could do but accept her offer. He thanked her and handed her his card and left, with no very great hope that she'd remember to do anything at all. Or would she? he wondered.

It was a rum set-up there, whichever way you looked at it. He'd have given much to get inside the house, or more preferably the church, and find out more of this so-called sect, and what its aims were. What were they doing employing outside help, which he'd have sworn didn't come cheap? Come to that, what was a girl like Elaine Morrow doing working for an outfit like that, unless she was religiously committed, which unlikely contingency he would-n't be prepared to bet on? All right, jobs were scarce, but with her looks she could surely do better than that. There had been something in that young woman's amazing green eyes that told him she was neither as ingenuous nor as disinterested as she might have made believe, either.

CHAPTER 13

Harry Waring had had a busy morning.

In the next room the police had been turning Clive's office upside down, while in his own blandly tasteful private office the bright sun, filtered through champagne net, had fallen on to the rosy face and corpulent figure of Harry Waring, being unusually brisk. Mrs Endicott, pressed but not one to hang about doing nothing, had, besides getting on with some routine work and dealing with the police – not to mention that time-wasting telephone call from Matthew Royston – trotted between the outer office and the inner sanctum with files, obtained telephone numbers direct for her employer so that they shouldn't go through the switchboard records, and then retreated discreetly into her own office. Harry thought she hadn't noticed anything odd about his morning's work, or that she wouldn't know why, anyway. She had, and she did.

By one o'clock her employer had relaxed and was looking his usual expansive self when he broke for what he considered a couple of well-deserved gin and tonics and a good lunch, indicating he'd be glad if she could stay on. Mrs Endicott tidied up his office, emptied his overflowing waste basket into the incinerator, took out her cottage cheese and crispbread and sat back in her typing chair to reflect, resignedly abandoning the visit she'd planned for that afternoon to a stately home. It didn't take her long to come to the conclusion that what the C.I.D. didn't know, they wouldn't worry about. She was a widow, not far off retiring on a comfortable pension, and she saw no point in putting her job in jeopardy at this stage.

Osnabruck Road was a pleasant street of early-nineteenth-century houses, now for the most part offices, occupied by professional people – quantity surveyors, architects, solicitors and the like. The offices of Waring & Lethbridge were superior, commanding a corner position, and were carefully decorated in period style, as white as a wedding cake, the upper windows decorated with lacy wrought-iron balconies. Drawing boards and anglepoise lamps could, however, be seen through the downstairs windows. Inside there were too many people and not enough room. The light couldn't always be good enough for working.

Waring's private office was upstairs, and into this Mrs Endicott, a small and neat, smiling, yet formidable lady with smoothly arranged steely hair, admitted the chief inspector and his sergeant. This, unlike the rooms downstairs, was not the office of a working architect, more like a sitting room which happened to be equipped with a desk, designed to give an impression of efficiency so unobtrusive that it was invisible. Though not over-large, the room was gracefully proportioned, the panelled walls painted a soft Georgian green picked out in white; velvet curtains were in deeper green, and armchairs covered in muted floral pinks and greens stood on a mushroom-pink velvet pile carpet. There were several good watercolours framed in gold on the walls.

Waring obviously liked comfort. His handshake was warm and flabby.

The chief inspector and his sergeant sat back in well-sprung armchairs facing him across the shining expanse of a mahogany desk, while Mrs Endicott poured Earl Grey from a silver pot into rose-patterned Wedgwood china cups.

'Thank you, Milly. See we're not disturbed, won't you?'

Mrs Endicott nodded acquiescence and offered Shrewsbury biscuits before leaving them.

Waring sat back and sipped his tea and, when the door had closed, said, 'I expect you're wondering why I wanted to see you, Chief Inspector.'

On the contrary, Mayo thought he had a pretty good idea of what was to come. A confession of some sort, though hardly to murder. Waring, unless Mrs Endicott and the rest of the staff, and

Marcus Dymond, too, were lying in their teeth, had a cast-iron alibi. He looked, however, like a man who had slept on his original statement and decided that honesty was the most expedient policy. Why the delay? Ten to one he'd been up to some fancy footwork somewhere along the line, and had needed time to cover his tracks before enquiries into the murder led to suspicions in other directions. Nothing too black. Waring, he would guess, was too careful of himself to risk anything much deeper than a pale shade of grey . . . But now he had nothing to hide, he could not afford anything but sweet co-operation.

'Chief Inspector, I've been thinking about what I said to you yesterday, and wondering if maybe I gave the wrong impression.'

Dear oh dear, thought Mayo. 'In what connection?' he asked neutrally.

'About those anonymous letters. Clive never showed them to me, as I told you. I knew he'd been getting them, and some nasty telephone calls, too. He once took one when I was with him here in the office, and I suppose he felt he had to explain – to a point. When I told you I didn't know the contents of the letters, that was true. But – thinking about it . . . I'll be honest with you and tell you I also had one myself.' Relief shining on his face at having got that off his chest, he allowed himself a hasty sip of tea. 'I suppose you'll think it rather reprehensible of me not to have told you about it last night.'

'We're not paid to make moral judgements, Mr Waring, we're paid to get the facts, and hope they add up to the truth, but it certainly helps if people are frank with us. As a matter of interest, why weren't you?'

Waring spread his hands wide. 'I just couldn't see my letter – or even Clive's for that matter – could have anything at all to do with the murder. After all, blackmailers don't usually kill off their victims, do they?'

'Blackmail? I thought you said they were threatening letters.'

'What else is blackmail? Threatening exposure if you don't pay up.'

Kite cleared his throat. Mayo said shortly, 'We're wasting time, Mr Waring. Blackmail presupposes something to hide. What was it?'

'I don't actually *know*. Clive was very cagey, and the letter I had wasn't specific –'

'It's too much to hope that you've kept it?'

Waring was regretful. 'Ought to have done, I suppose. But the damn thing was so offensive – implying I knew what Clive had been up to, and that I could persuade him to cough up in order to have it covered up. Chucked it on the fire. Sorry about that.'

'Well, it's a pity, but never mind that now. You say you don't actually know what the threats were all about. But I take it you can make an educated guess?'

Waring dabbed at a biscuit crumb on his plate and transferred it to his mouth. 'I may well be wrong.'

'Let's take a chance on that, shall we?' said Mayo, drawing on his patience.

'Reading between the lines, I think that somebody was hinting there was something – well, not quite all above-board about this splendid design of Clive's – you no doubt know of it, the Svensen Centre, the one that won the prize?'

'Yes, I do. What kind of irregularity?'

'I'm guessing,' answered Waring after a pause. 'But the accusation seemed to me to be implying that Clive had been seeing someone all right so that he'd be assured of the prize.'

'You mean that he'd been using bribery.'

Waring looked pained. 'Well, yes. But I can assure you allegations of that sort were totally unjustified. One of the unsuccessful candidates just slinging mud, was what I thought. Nevertheless, mud sticks. If anything like that got out, it wouldn't do the firm much good.'

'Was it in that connection you wanted to see Matt Royston?'

'Oh, so he mentioned that, did he?' Waring said, guileless, but not enough. So this, after due reflection, was why he'd decided to

107

come clean? 'Yes, it was. I was beginning to think the idea of this proposed book wasn't very sound, in view of those letters. Whoever was blackmailing him didn't know Clive very well. He wasn't a man to submit to threats of any kind – he'd simply have brazened it out. It certainly wouldn't have stopped him going ahead with the book – and the result would have done nothing but bring notoriety to everyone concerned. Royston was involved in writing the book with Clive, and I thought he had a right to know about the accusations. He might not have wanted to go along in the circumstances.'

'What made you change your mind?'

'Simply because the whole thing's no longer relevant. I assume the book will be abandoned – or at least Clive's part in it.'

Mayo let this unjustified assumption pass, and changed gear. 'What did you think of this proposed scheme for the conversion of Brome House?'

'More tea, Chief Inspector – Sergeant?' Kite brought his cup over to the desk, hoping the pale liquid would be stronger now that it had stood. It wasn't, but Mayo, too, accepted another cup. Waring said eventually, 'I was against it. It called for an investment from the firm I wasn't prepared to go along with. Besides, the whole idea's unpalatable to me.'

'Was that why your partner was negotiating with MacAllister Associates?'

This time, Waring's astonishment was genuine. He looked blankly at Mayo as he produced a copy of the letter, and read it through carefully when it was handed to him, obviously struggling with his feelings. When he'd finished, he passed the document back. 'I knew nothing of this, nothing at all.'

'I understand Mrs Lethbridge is the owner of Brome House. This letter seems to indicate she might have agreed to the conversion.'

'Caroline? Not a chance! But this was just the sort of thing Clive was wont to do, you know. He'd go ahead with something he'd put his mind to, and then bulldoze everyone into agreeing with him. I should think he'd overstepped the mark in this case.'

Mayo said, 'You told me yesterday you'd no knowledge of anybody who might have had a grudge against your partner. In view of what you've just told me, I'd like a list of all your ex-employees, please. The number of your staff must be relatively small, so I don't suppose it'll be too difficult, unless you have a very large turnover.'

'On the contrary, we've a loyal staff, who stay with us because we pay good rates, but *none* of them – oh, very well, Mrs Endicott will know.' He spoke into the intercom on his desk. The crisp reply came audibly into the office.

'Certainly I can do that, Mr Waring. How far back do you wish me to go?'

Waring raised his eyebrows at Mayo, who said, 'Five years should do, for a start.'

'Including all the temps?' enquired the secretary. 'We do employ quite a few from time to time.'

'Only permanent staff for the time being – we may need the others later.'

'No problem. I'll be as quick as I can.'

A small silence fell while they waited, which Waring, staring out of the window, broke. 'This is going to mean the end of Waring & Lethbridge, you know, Chief Inspector.'

'It is? And that's something you mind very much?'

'In a way, yes. My father's firm originally, you know. But in another way, frankly, no. I'd been thinking about pulling out anyway, since my wife died. I'm fifty-eight and there's a lot I haven't done yet . . . daughter in Canada, and grandchildren I've never seen. And to be honest, I haven't liked the way things were going in the firm recently – this damnfool conversion scheme of Clive's, for one thing.'

So there'd been disagreements – and that news about the MacAllister negotiations had come as an unpleasant shock. Mayo speculated on the nature of their partnership clause. If Waring had tied himself up contractually to the firm for X number of years, say, and Lethbridge hadn't agreed to him breaking the contract, that could have provided more resentment. Almost certainly, Waring hadn't killed his partner, but equally certainly, he wasn't sorry to have him removed, either.

At that moment Mrs Endicott came in and left a neatly typed list on the desk, not a long one, about twenty-five names, and beside each, the date of their departure and a small note giving the reasons for it. Most of those who'd left seemed to be women, for domestic reasons was how Mrs Endicott phrased this. Of the five men, two had retired, one had gone to the architect's department of a local council, another as chief draughtsman to a firm of speculative builders.

Mayo's finger stopped beside the fifth name, one minus any accompanying comment. 'This one? What happened to him?' He turned the paper round so that Waring could see.

'Murfitt,' read Waring, 'Donald Murfitt. Murfitt, Murfitt? I remember the name, but who the hell was he?' He sat thinking for a moment, frowning, then his face cleared. 'Yes, I do remember him now, a draughtsman – not a very satisfactory type, as I recall. God yes, I do remember now! Clive sacked him – work not up to scratch or something. Do you think he could have anything to do with the letters?'

'Anything's possible,' said Mayo. 'The question is, where can we find him now?'

'Mrs Endicott will help,' Waring said with confidence, but before he could summon that long-suffering lady again, Mayo told him that he would speak to her on his way out.

'I've really no idea at all where he is now, Chief Inspector. Nor do I know why he left. He went in a hurry, but I was never told why.'

'Mr Waring thinks Mr Lethbridge dismissed him for unsatisfactory work.'

'Then maybe he did, though it would surprise me. He was generally very competent, though I have to say, really rather an odd person. He did used to infuriate Mr Lethbridge, I remember, because he was an extremely poor timekeeper. Invariably late, and always one of the first to leave, though he only lived in Moseley. A distinct clash of personalities there, if you understand me.'

'Do you have the address where he lived in Moseley?'

'I could get it for you, but I don't think it would do you much good.' She hesitated. 'There was nothing exactly *wrong* with him, you know – but, well, I wasn't entirely surprised to hear that shortly after he left here, he packed up and went off to join one of those peculiar sects.'

'A religious sect?'

She nodded. 'One of those crackpot religions . . . brought over from California or somewhere, I suppose. Like the Moonies, you know.' Mrs Endicott was herself very High Church.

'You don't happen to know its name?'

'I'm sorry, I don't – but I think they were based somewhere over in Lavenstock.'

'Lavenstock?' Mayo stood up and held out his hand. 'You've been most helpful, Mrs Endicott. There can't be all that many religious sects in Lavenstock, so I don't expect we shall have much trouble in tracing it.'

CHAPTER 14

In fact, Mayo had a pretty fair idea where to look. 'That odd lot of bods up at Branxmore,' he asked Kite as they drove back towards Lavenstock. 'What the devil was their name?'

'The Assembly of the Latter-Day Prophets? The Gathering of God?' Kite being facetious again, but the name was probably something equally meaningless, or they wouldn't both have forgotten it so easily.

The assorted members of the community had been harmless enough, as Mayo remembered them, if way-out by his own standards. A handful of earnest seekers after truth, some ageing remnants of flower power and the Me generation still finding themselves, one or two bone idle layabouts, plus a small minority on the lunatic side of extreme religious belief. An eye had been kept on them since, however. You never knew: these sorts of groups were a magnet for the oddballs and misfits of society.

'I don't recall meeting any Donald Murfitt when we were there,' Kite said.

'Doesn't ring a bell with me, either.'

But it had been Atkins' case mainly, one quickly over because the missing teenager, Mayo recalled, had returned home, penitent and disillusioned with the so-called freedom she had found in London, before there'd been need to question all the members of whatever it was they called themselves.

It began to rain as they left first the concrete canyons of the developed city centre behind them, then the polyglot areas of the inner city, the Asian shops and Irish banks and Chinese takeaways, where bus tickets and fish-and-chip papers and inexplicable drifts of polystyrene packing beads blew along the pavements. Perhaps the Indian summer was over. Now the windscreen wipers flicked steadily and the tyres hissed on the wet roads with barbered verges of the more affluent suburbs and occasional villages which stretched between here and Lavenstock. Kite glanced at Mayo, sitting silently beside him in the steamy car, and settled his length back in his own seat, relaxing at the wheel, Mayo's concentrated absorption telling him his attempts at conversation weren't likely to be appreciated.

Within half an hour Kite was parking the car at the end of Amelia Road in Branxmore. The rain had lessened to a mere drizzle, but it was a miserable end to the afternoon. Mayo stepped out, hunching his shoulders, and began walking towards the church, which he had an idea was the headquarters of the sect. A sombre red-brick edifice standing at the end of the road, with a low roof sloping down over its windows, like a scowl. The tall figure of a man was leaving it, striding towards the block of new flats at the corner, a figure that Mayo didn't for the moment recognise. Then he realised the man was Matt Royston. Without making a conscious decision, he set off at a sprint.

Matt, bending to put his key in the lock of his Renault, heard pounding footsteps rounding the corner. Before he could straighten, he felt a heavy hand on his shoulder. In a quick reflex action he spun round, and recognition came only just in time to save his fist from making contact with the jaw of the chief inspector. 'Hell's teeth!' he muttered, feeling a fool, letting his hand fall limply to his side. 'I thought I was being mugged.' It took him only a moment, however, to size up the situation. 'Well, well, so you didn't find my theory so cock-eyed, on reflection?' He could after all only conclude that the chief inspector had been more open to suggestion than he, Matt, had given him credit for, and that they had arrived at the same destination by different routes.

'What are you talking about?'

'Don't tell me you're not here looking for Sylvia Johnson as well.'

Mayo fixed Matt with a steady look, showing none of the sudden alertness he felt. 'We'd better talk, but somewhere else if we don't want to attract an audience. This may take some time.' Already a window cleaner, setting up his ladders despite the drizzle, and two mothers with prams and plastic-macked toddlers, were showing a decided interest in the proceedings. Mayo jerked his head, and Kite, who had arrived only a few steps behind Mayo, led the way back towards the C.I.D. car.

The sergeant opened the back door for Matt whilst Mayo walked round to the other side and slid into the seat beside him. 'Now then, you were saying. About Sylvia Johnson.'

Kite, in the front seat, gave them a quick glance, then took out his notebook.

Matt pulled the broken badge from his pocket and held it out on the palm of his hand. 'Ever seen one of these before?'

Mayo looked at it without attempting to touch it. He recognised it immediately as the logo of the Church of the Assembly of Alternative Witnesses. The name came back to him in full, without even trying. Kite hadn't been so far out after all. 'Where did you get that?'

'It belonged to Sylvia Johnson. Amanda Bradford gave it to me when I saw her this morning. I'd forgotten all about it until after you left this afternoon.'

'Forgotten?'

'Completely, I'm afraid, until I came across it amongst my small change.'

Mayo gave him a swift glance and decided to give him the benefit of the doubt. He nodded to him to continue, and listened with a sharpened attention. Matt told how he had tracked Sylvia's address down by means of the badge, and of meeting Elaine Morrow, wondering as he did so how the devil Mayo had found out that Sylvia Johnson was living here. Mayo, however, wasn't about to indicate that he'd had no idea she was, until Matt had spoken. Whether Royston had really forgotten the badge or not, his tracing it here had probably saved the C.I.D. a certain amount of leg work, so he was less inclined to tear him off a strip than he might have been for not turning it over to them. 'All right, leave this with us now. Thanks for the information, but in future, leave the detecting to us, hm?'

Matt slid out of the car, walked a few steps, then turned back. 'The church is locked,' he said. 'I've tried it.'

'He's bloomin' anxious to find that file,' Kite remarked suspiciously, twisting round in his seat to stare after Matt's striding figure.

'You know journalists. Like bull-terriers, they are. Never let go once they get their teeth into something.'

'More like an excuse to get on to a story.'

Mayo grunted. 'Never mind Royston; we've more important things to occupy us, this young woman for one. Why should Royston have all the perks?'

They were doomed to disappointment. The door of number twenty-three was answered after some time by a thin, tense woman who wouldn't have been a perk for anyone. Wispy, fair hair, rimless spectacles, without joy. A tight, buttoned-up mouth that barely opened enough to admit that she was Mrs Murfitt and her husband was not at home. No, she didn't know where he was; no, she had no idea when he'd be back. She was the type who gave nothing away, on principle. Mayo didn't waste time on her, bade her good day, and left.

'Let's have a look at the church anyway.'

It had seen better days. In its prime it had served a congregation of well-heeled Victorian industrialists and their lawyers and bank managers, for whom it had largely been built. Lavenstock had grown on the foundations of its light metal industry, and its aristocracy had grown with it. They had lived in the houses making up the tree-lined roads around the church for nearly a hundred years, until the houses with their cellars and attics and their lack of central heating and garage space had come to be looked upon as anachronisms, whereupon the planners were let in to begin their wholesale destruction. Here and there in Branxmore, odd houses, in some cases whole streets, had survived and were now being gentrified and lived in again as discrimination and common sense took over. This street, this church, was not so fortunate.

A few feet of path stretched between the gate and the main door, which was led up to by a flight of steps, at the base of which were two short pillars. One was surmounted by a stone ball, complete; the companion ball on the other pillar was lying newly broken on the ground. Mayo noticed, as they walked up the path, that there were several tiles missing on the long, sloping roof, stained glass had been damaged and not repaired, but on the whole the building was in better condition than he had expected. The main door *was* locked. The two detectives began to walk round the church to the back.

'Hello there! Are you looking for someone?'

A cheerful-looking man was advancing through the churchyard towards them, walking with a limp and leaning on a stick. A man with a handsome young-old face and curly hair that was receding slightly. On one side of his jaw was a large and ugly bruise.

'A Mr Murfitt,' Kite answered. 'Know where we can find him?'

'I'm Donald Murfitt. What can I do for you?'

The hand not holding the stick gripped each of theirs firmly in turn after Mayo had announced their identity and requested a little of Murfitt's time. 'We shan't need to keep you very long, I daresay.'

'I'm in no hurry. Anything I can do. Come along, come along.'

Murfitt led them along the north side of the church, limping heavily. 'Sorry about the stick, and the bedroom slippers. Had a fall the other day, down the front steps of the church. Sprained my ankle, not to mention bruising myself head to foot. I didn't do the pillar at the bottom much good, either!' His laugh rang out.

'We noticed it was broken,' Kite remarked.

'Oh, did you? You're very observant – but then, I suppose you have to be. Here we are.'

Mayo and his sergeant exchanged looks as they followed him. They had long since passed the stage of allowing themselves to prejudge anyone, or being surprised when people didn't fit into accepted categories, but both had subconsciously been prepared for something very different, certainly not this projection of muscular Christianity, which the man radiated from his cheerful smile right down to his old tweed jacket with its leather-patched elbows.

He pushed open a small door set into the angle between the nave and transept of the church. Following him inside, Mayo saw that they were in what he took to be the former vestry. A smell peculiar to churches everywhere pervaded it, defying description but bringing to mind old hymn books and starched surplices, a residue of incense, a general odour of sanctity remembered from long-ago days as a choirboy.

The vestry had been transformed into an office of sorts by the addition of a green metal filing cabinet, an electronic typewriter, a large desk facing a small window, a couple of chairs and an old gas fire, leaving the occupants to fit in as best they could. The first thing Murfitt did was to light the fire, so unnecessarily that Mayo wondered why he did it. Kite perched on the far edge of the desk, folding his long legs out of reach, and when Murfitt pulled out one of the chairs for Mayo and took the other himself, resting his arm along the side of the desk, they were sitting almost knee to knee.

Mayo hitched his chair back as far as he could and went straight into the subject of Lethbridge's murder, which didn't come as any surprise to Murfitt. 'Heard it on the local radio this morning,' he said, suitably grave. 'I thought that was why you were here. You must've learned that I worked for him once.'

'And left rather suddenly, with bad feeling.'

'Not to put too fine a point on it, I was sacked, as you must certainly have been told.' He had a rather loose-lipped mouth, now turned down at the corners. 'But you're wrong – there was no bad feeling. At least, not on my part.'

'Really, Mr Murfitt? You were sacked, and felt no resentment?'

'Correction. There *is* no bad feeling, not now,' the other man said, doodling on a scratch pad with heavy downward strokes. It could have been a church steeple he drew, or a dagger. He looked up, smiling with benign forgiveness. 'Oh, at the time, yes, I'll admit it, I felt a bit aggrieved, but the ways of the Lord truly are mysterious.' He had a faint Scottish accent, which seemed to emphasise his pompous diction. 'If that hadn't happened, I shouldn't be here now, doing His work, leading His flock. We all come to God in different ways.'

'Is that so? And what is this work? What exactly do you do?'

'Do?' Murfitt leaned back, and his shoulders relaxed. Despite the frankness of his admissions about his leaving Waring & Lethbridge, he was undoubtedly relieved to have the subject changed, Mayo noticed. 'You could describe it as learning to love one another.'

'And are you paid a salary while you learn, Mr Murfitt?'

'A token.'

'Paid by whom? Who supports you?'

Mayo prepared to hear that it was the Lord who provided, and braced himself not to wince, but Murfitt shrugged and said, 'We live very simply, and all our money goes into a common pool. Those who are able to work contribute towards those who for some reason can't. And many, many people are very sympathetic to our work.'

Which amounted to much the same thing as Divine Providence, Mayo thought. He said, 'But you must have had some capital – to buy this church, and the houses you live in?'

Murfitt smiled. 'We have a Founder. A very dear and wonderful lady, an American, who came over here and started this branch of our faith.'

Mayo gave him a judicial look. 'You still haven't explained what your religion is exactly, nor its philosophy.'

'We have no dogma. We simply offer an alternative to all forms of organised religion. We are just what our name implies – an Assembly of Alternative Witnesses, those who have been born again into a new life. You'll be surprised to learn we number former Buddhists, Jews, Hindus and even one Chinese among our followers.'

With a look at Mayo's face, he added gently, 'I sense your scepticism – but no one is forced to join us. We don't, Chief Inspector, entice children away from their parents, or milk people of their money, or anything at all like that. As for our philosophy – we are dedicated to Love as a principle, without commitment to any special faith. Everyone here leaves their past behind them when they come. We are all spiritually born again.'

Mayo was becoming increasingly aware of a growing dislike of this very worthy young man. This was a luxury which, as a policeman, he couldn't afford. He was, however, paid for being suspicious, and suspicions were gathering fast in his mind: paramount, that he was listening to the biggest load of old codswallop he'd heard in many a long year, and that this man was getting paid for uttering such, and probably for little else. Unless, he wondered briefly, the organisation could possibly be a cover-up for something else. He'd get Atkins on to that, but he thought not. He thought it much more likely that Murfitt had simply settled for an effortless way of getting a living, a soft option that cost him nothing but the trouble of keeping his tongue firmly in his cheek. Possibly the loyalty of his followers stemmed from a similar willing suspension of disbelief.

Or maybe Murfitt, who in real life had been a nonentity, had simply found himself a role, and maybe his own suspicions were unworthy. Maybe. On the other hand, his instincts were invariably sound. He looked up and caught his sense of outrage reflected on Kite's face and felt justified. 'How long was Miss Sylvia Johnson with you?' he asked abruptly.

Murfitt's reply came glibly, as if he'd prepared it. 'Two years. Sylvia was with us from the beginning, when she came here with her aunt, our Founder. We shall miss her sadly; she was one of our most dedicated members.'

'Quite a coincidence, her, too, going to work for Clive Lethbridge, wasn't it?'

'In a way. To tell you the truth, I tried to dissuade her from taking the job. He wasn't a man I felt it desirable to associate with, but it was only to be for a short time, and the salary was excellent. We are prepared to swallow our pride for the general good, and what had gone had gone.'

Was this what was called turning the other cheek? He would

119

have been prepared to swear that Murfitt still harboured a load of resentment against Clive Lethbridge, understandably so. Getting the chop so summarily was something even a born-again Christian might find hard to forgive. It was at that point that Mayo had a sudden, unshakable conviction that Murfitt was the anonymous letter writer. He had a grievance, had possibly at one time had access to some knowledge about Lethbridge and his alleged corruption. Mayo was convinced Murfitt was the type who could and would bide his time and wait for the opportunity for revenge. This could well have come with the winning of the competition by Lethbridge, bringing with it a golden opportunity to discredit him in a spectacular way. But as for killing Lethbridge . . . that was a different proposition entirely. Why should Murfitt cut off the potential source of a very profitable little income? Unless he had found out too late that he had misjudged his victim and that there was no way that Lethbridge was ever going to pay out blackmail money. And that he himself could be in danger if Lethbridge chose to expose his threats.

'Well, if that's all, Chief Inspector –?' Murfitt looked at his watch.

'I'm afraid it isn't, not by a long chalk. I've quite a few questions I want to ask yet. Miss Johnson, I understand, has gone to stay with an aunt in the States – would she be the same aunt you spoke of, the one who is your founder?'

'Yes, that's right. Mrs Carlene Winthrop.' It was an unsolicited offer which came just a little too readily, a little too pat, offered with the nervousness of a man who has something to hide.

'And perhaps also you wouldn't mind telling me why you were dismissed by Clive Lethbridge?'

Bending to pick up the biro which slipped off the desk, Murfitt made a clumsy movement which caused his bandaged foot to come into contact with the table leg. An exclamation escaped him, and when he straightened, his face was screwed up, tight with pain. 'Must learn to be more careful,' he muttered.

'Well, Mr Murfitt? I asked you a question.'

'Oh – yes. Didn't they tell you why?'

'I'm asking you.'

'Why I lost my job? I'm sorry to say, it was too petty for words, pure spite on Lethbridge's part. A complete nonsense because I came in late once or twice in the mornings. Anyone else might have taken him to an industrial tribunal for unfair dismissal, but it would have been against all my principles to have argued over it, as well he knew. Dismissing me for such a triviality was just an excuse because my face didn't fit.'

'And there was nothing else? No other reason?'

'No. Why? Should there have been?' He was on the defensive again, palpably nervous. His cheery bonhomie had slipped from his grasp. That the poor timekeeping was simply an excuse for dismissal, Mayo was inclined to believe, but the real reason? He'd known too much. Possibly he'd even tried a spot of blackmail then.

'You're a trained architectural draughtsman, Mr Murfitt. Presumably you know of this award recently given to Lethbridge? What did you think of that?'

Murfitt took his time in answering and Mayo let him, watching him carefully. Murfitt, however, didn't even blink.

'It was controversial, but I believe it was worthy of the prize.'

Mayo nodded, and left it. Murfitt's feelings on that subject would certainly be worth pursuing, but perhaps not now. He told him he would like Sergeant Kite to take a specimen of the typeface on the machine in the corner. 'Be my guest,' Murfitt said, easily.

'And a specimen of your handwriting, please.'

Murfitt reached for a scratch pad, wrote his name and address, handed it over with a flourish. Unless he was a fool, which Mayo didn't think he was, not even a well-meaning fool, he knew he had nothing to fear in that direction. 'But is one allowed to ask what all this is about?' he asked.

'It's about murder. Clive Lethbridge has been murdered, in

121

case you'd forgotten. And apropos of that – what were you doing yesterday afternoon?'

Murfitt closed his eyes, briefly, as if in prayer. Then opening them and fixing them on Mayo, he said, 'I feel your suspicions, Chief Inspector. Are you suggesting I murdered him?'

'Someone did,' Mayo said dryly. 'Someone sent a series of blackmailing letters to him and then, because he refused to pay up, went to his house and killed him.'

'I wasn't that person, and I may say, your accusations are unworthy.'

'Oh, I'm accusing you of nothing – yet. I'm merely asking, where were you yesterday afternoon?'

Murfitt was sweating now, perhaps because of the heat in the room, and the hand holding the biro wasn't altogether steady, but there was no panic in his voice. 'As a matter of fact,' he began, 'as a matter of fact, I was here, in the church.'

'Alone?'

'I was meditating. You should try it sometime, towards the salvation of the soul.'

'I'll take your word for it, but you'd have been wiser to have had someone with you.'

Mayo became aware of a welcome draught and saw that Kite, who had been listening to all this with incredulity, had turned towards a door, presumably opening into the body of the church, which had been quietly opened. A young woman was standing watching them. How long she had been there was anybody's guess. She moved forward with a sinuous movement that reminded Mayo of a cat. Elaine Morrow, Miss World herself. From Matt Royston's eloquent description, she could be no one else. The room, already overpowering, became suddenly charged. 'Tell them, Donald, why don't you? After all, the police must hear worse things every day of the week, and I'm sure they won't tell Isobel.' She laughed, and Murfitt looked as though his collar had suddenly become too tight. 'As a matter of fact, I was with

122

Donald. Meditating,' she added reflectively. Her eyes, clear and green, were sparkling; a feline smile curved her lips. She evidently liked making an entrance, enjoyed an audience.

Murfitt's hand went to the bruise on the side of his face; he licked his loose lips and gave a barely perceptible nod of acquiescence. As an alibi, it was so flimsy, it might well be true. There's an explanation for everything, Mayo thought. Murfitt's wife had looked as though she could enjoy making his life a misery. No wonder he looked scared out of his wits.

The electronic typewriter with which Kite had been fiddling in the corner, trying to make it start, suddenly whirred into life. 'Oh goodness,' exclaimed Miss Morrow, 'what *are* you doing?'

'Not coping very well,' Kite said. 'I'm not used to these electronic things, only the steam kind.'

'Let me show you.'

Sitting down on Kite's vacated seat in front of the machine, she rapidly and expertly produced a piece of copy, which she handed to Kite. As he read it through, his eyebrows raised and he grinned. She smiled back. 'There you are! I'm not just a pretty face, Sergeant.'

Kite spread his hands in acknowledgement, and now that the theatrical pantomime was over, Mayo stood up. 'Just one more thing, Mr Murfitt. What kind of car do you drive?'

'I don't. From social awareness, and also because the money I should spend on maintaining one can be put to better use.'

'Very admirable sentiments; wish I could afford them. We shall have to see you again, sir, so keep us informed of your movements. Don't go further than you have to, without letting us know.' Kite handed Murfitt the Lavenstock Division number, written on a page torn from his notebook, snapped the elastic band back. 'Good day to you.'

'May God bless you.'

Outside in the car, Kite rolled the window down. 'Phew! With a combination of those two, we need fresh air. What do you make of all that? He wrote the letters all right, didn't he? No wonder he was sweating on the top line. Easy to see why he was sacked . . . He found the skeleton in the cupboard – about Lethbridge and the bribery, I mean. I'll get on to that.'

'Let's shelve that for a while,' Mayo said, to Kite's surprise. 'We can't do anything until Monday morning anyway.' The idea of influencing what must surely have been a panel of international judges sounded improbable. He had a distinct feeling that Waring was grinding some axe of his own there. 'All the same, I think we're basically on the right lines – dig out the dirt on the blackmail, and we'll have our motive for the murder.'

'Always assuming they're connected.'

For a moment Mayo looked uncertain, then his jaw set. 'They are. I know they damn well are. It's just that we can't see how at the moment.'

Kite was silent. 'Well, what now?'

Mayo looked at his watch. 'Back to the office for an hour's paper work, then shove off home to catch up with some sleep. I suggest you do the same.'

Kite would go home to his semi and, while Sheila got on with her housework, put his two kids to bed, or maybe vice-versa; there was no telling these days. He'd go home himself, to the flat. A drink, a meal, some music – and Julie. The last thought warmed him like a double whisky.

As Kite was about to start up the car, Mayo asked, 'By the way, what was that the delectable Miss Morrow typed?'

Kite extracted the sheet of paper from his pocket book and began, aloud: '"When I consider how my light is spent . . ."' He finished: '"They also serve who only stand and wait",' grinned and handed it over to Mayo. Fourteen lines of Milton, with no mistakes in the impeccable typing and no reason to think there were any in the text. 'As the lady said, "not just a pretty face." And not exactly an unprejudiced witness, either – if they *are* having it off.'

'If?'

'All that's a load of baloney,' Kite asserted confidently. 'They didn't even like each other.'

'What's that got to do with anything?' asked Mayo.

Sifting through the day's information took Kite and himself a further hour and a half. So far, the tyre marks in the lane didn't fit any car belonging to anyone so far involved in the case, and no one admitted to any vehicle having been parked there . . .

'What do you think of this?' Kite passed over the details of the search of the lane running alongside Brome House, and the woods beyond. A bicycle, not new but in too good a condition to warrant the assumption of it having been abandoned, had been found in some bushes by the stream at the bottom. Well concealed, according to the man who had found it. 'It's being checked out, but nothing's come of it as yet. Are you thinking what I'm thinking?'

'You think the killer cycled as far as the stream, hid the bike ready for his return, but took his chance to get away quick when he saw the BMW? It's a thought. Looking like a butcher's apprentice, he wouldn't want to risk being seen any more than he had to.'

'Which clears friend Murfitt,' Kite said. 'He couldn't ride a bike with that leg of his – and the limp seems genuine. It fairly creased him when he knocked it.'

'I once knew a chap with a stiff leg rode a bike,' Mayo said absently. 'And I suppose Murfitt could have hurt his ankle *after* the murder. I'll feel happier with the theory when the BMW turns up. Hope to God it won't be long.' The protective polythene seat covers the garage used while repairing cars had been left on, according to the mechanics. Nevertheless, there would almost certainly be traces, of blood at least, left behind. If the murderer had used it. If . . .

He yawned hugely and saw Kite looking as immensely weary as he himself felt. 'Time for your Horlicks by the look of you, lad. Let's pack it in until tomorrow.'

CHAPTER 15

'Hi, Dad!' Julie called.

A mouth-watering smell wafted from the kitchen. Mayo's daughter was sixteen, and when she had her A levels, she would be leaving him for a catering course in Birmingham, and a flat shared with two other girls. He didn't want to spoil things for her, or burden her with the knowledge of how much he would miss her, so he joked that her going would give him a chance to lose weight: he ate like a king when she was experimenting with her cooking. But he avoided as much as possible thinking about the time when she wouldn't be here, her presence a reassurance that not everything in his life had gone sour.

When Lynne died, Julie had elected to stay with him rather than be taken into the bosom of her Aunt Laura's large and boisterous family, a joy he couldn't believe he deserved, and ought to thank God every day on his knees for. He'd been so damned scared that Lynne's sister would be proved right, that neither he nor his career would be equal to the demands of looking after a fifteen-year-old, as Julie had been then, and he'd been more afraid than ever he'd let on to Laura of all the female teenage emotional traumas to come.

But Julie had always been a sensible child, and the last two years, thank God, had brought few problems. She was remarkably well balanced. Physically resembling her mother, heart-breakingly so at times in her slender fairness, she had inherited something of his own phlegmatic nature. Not often down in the dumps, but not, he sometimes thought with a grim sense of having missed out, often on the heights, either. Lynne had had enough of that for both of them.

Life hadn't always been easy with Lynne, and they'd had more than their share of disagreements, now bitterly regretted, about

126

the amount of time given to his work, but God help him, he had loved her. His only other regret, now that she was dead, was that he had never told her how much, yet another dimension of guilt laid on him.

Julie had made what she said was a cassoulet, with pork and haricot beans and plenty of garlic, and bits of duck, and he decided to open a bottle of claret.

'Wow, what's this then, are we celebrating, or drowning some secret sorrow?'

'A dish like this deserves better than a glass of beer to go with it.'

He had avoided a direct answer, but he knew she wouldn't press him. It had always been an unwritten family law that unless he broached the subject of the case he was working on, which was rare indeed, no one else should. 'Cheers, love!'

'Cheers, Dad. Only a glass for me, otherwise I'll never get through my homework.'

'I daresay I can manage the rest on my own. Not going out tonight, then?'

He was relieved when she said she wasn't, and not only because it meant he wouldn't have to turn out again to ferry her there or back from wherever. It was something he couldn't get used to, the fact that she was old enough to have her own life, though she obeyed his injunctions about being brought home on time and letting him know where she was. She might pooh-pooh the arrangements he had with the Brownlows, the married couple downstairs, to keep an eye out for her when he wasn't able to be home at nights, but she respected it, perhaps an admission that he, more than most, had reason to know what might happen if she wasn't careful.

They chatted about this and that while they ate their meal. He told her about Kite's wife's good news, which pleased Julie no end. They were all alike, today's women, supporting each other in this new sisterhood they had. Or maybe they talked about it more

127

nowadays. As they cleared up, he was reminded of Alex's transfer, and told Julie what he'd heard. 'You remember Alex Jones?'

'Of course I remember her!' Julie's face had lit up, hearing the name. 'She was so super when Mum died, wasn't she?'

Ashamed, he had to admit he'd almost forgotten that, as he'd pushed to the back of his mind much of what had happened in those dark days. Alex had been at school with Lynne, and they'd kept up the friendship, not all that close, but steady and continuing. Yet he recalled now casseroles left in the oven, the fridge being kept unobtrusively stocked up . . . Julie being taken out of the house to the pictures or somewhere from time to time. He was very much afraid that he had never remembered even to thank Alex. The need over, she had left them alone, and he'd never even noticed that she'd gone.

Yet she wasn't that sort of woman, not the sort you didn't notice. A real smasher, in fact, the sort who turned heads, even in the anonymity of a uniform. He decided he'd have to find some way of making a tacit apology for his boorishness.

The domestic chores over, he settled himself down with his notes and the rest of the claret, with the record player set at a restful volume.

'I'll go straight to bed when I've finished, so I won't disturb you,' Julie said, kissing him good night.

'Good night, love.'

He sat staring into the gas fire with its simulated leaping coals, a pale reflection of the real thing, an anodyne substitute, but adequate, trouble-free and sensible. Like his present lifestyle. Comfort in a bottle of claret, the 'Laudate Dominum' on the turntable, the serene mezzo-soprano voice rising and falling, climaxing, dying. Sublime, unbearable. Emotion at second hand. Mayo got up and changed Mozart for Mahler, extracted his file of notes from his briefcase and shook off his moment of self-pity.

At first he read quickly, then again more thoroughly, going through every piece of evidence connected with the case with the concentrated patience that had earned him his reputation. Rain paffered on the window outside, Lavenstock went on with its supper and watched. 'Dynasty' on TV. He picked up Lethbridge's large foolscap-size desk diary and, starting at the beginning of the year, began to work through the closely covered pages.

Clive Lethbridge had had a large, confident hand, with loopy downstrokes and firmly crossed t's. Every page was full. There were notes and scribbled calculations, jostling thumbnail sketches of architectural details and fanciful doodles by the dozen, and each page held, as well as the day's appointments, memos to himself and lists of other things to be dealt with, mostly crossed off. Mayo went methodically through, from January the first, and it told him virtually nothing, apart from one interesting fact on the day before Lethbridge was killed.

The following day, the actual day of the murder, was curiously blank after all this wealth of detail. Lethbridge had particularly asked not to be disturbed on Thursday afternoon. Had that meant he was expecting someone? His blackmailer, his murderer? Murfitt? There was no appointment noted, but there were several doodles, small, rapid sketches which Mayo recognised from the photographs he'd seen as various elevations of the spectacular art gallery in the Svensen Centre.

He leaned back, overcome with amazement, and not a little admiration, at the sheer volume of writing in the closely packed, informative diary, the record of a busy life, only one of a pile going back more than fifteen years. With days and weeks, possibly months of investigation ahead, already his own paper work seemed formidable, although he did his best to keep it in check. He'd never been one for too many written notes. As far as he was concerned, they tended to fog the outline of the unique pattern that, sooner or later, every case assumed in his mind.

As yet this one was formless and shifting. The hell of it was, he had a feeling it shouldn't be. Something was eluding him, something he should have latched on to, and hadn't. *Elimination is the essence.* The phrase sprang to his mind like a quotation. Perhaps it was.

The telephone rang.

'Deeley? Yes, what is it? Something cropped up?'

'Not exactly – well, I don't know, sir. Sorry to disturb you, sir; it's just that I've remembered.'

'What have you remembered, Deeley?' He could imagine the constable, red-faced and twiddling the ends of his moustache in his embarrassment. 'Spit it out.'

'Those photos, sir.'

Patiently, Mayo asked, 'Which photos?'

'When I went with you to interview Marcus Dymond, he had some photos on the piano – school photos.'

'And? Go on, just carry on from there, lad.' He really didn't feel in the mood for Deeley tonight.

Deep, laboured breathing came over the line. 'Sir, there was one photo there and I thought, well, they didn't *all* turn out to be blue-eyed boys. That particular bloke, for instance, got himself into some bad trouble, though I don't remember what. I couldn't put a name to him; we used to call him Brains, like in "Thunderbirds" – he was one of those intelligent types, you know, that wear big horn-rims, hardly knew what time of day it was, but his name came back to me now, just as I was dropping off to sleep.'

'Yes? And what was it?'

'Well, I know it's not uncommon, but I thought maybe there could be some connection.' There was a long pause after he had told Mayo what it was. 'Sir?'

'All right, I'm still here. Was there anything else you noticed?'

'The photo looked to have been taken at a college graduation. Brains was standing with Mr and Mrs Dymond; must have been before she took to her wheelchair. He had his arm round her, as if he'd known them pretty well. Could there be a connection with the enquiry, do you think, sir?'

'It could be a coincidence, I suppose, but I'd think it's more than likely there's a link. All right, leave it with me, and get back to your beauty sleep. Well done, lad, and thanks. I'll see you in the morning.'

Mayo stood with his hand on the receiver. What the hell did this mean? He stood, deep in thought for several minutes, then went back to his notes, to begin all over again. Back to square one. After a while, he crossed to the turntable, changed over to the Mozart again and went back to his chair, poured the last of the wine into his glass and let his mind dwell on remote possibilities and hard facts.

The facts: The boy in the photo and Sylvia Johnson shared the same surname. Sylvia had wangled the job with Lethbridge. Possibilities: If Dymond had connections with the boy, why not Sylvia, also?

Slowly, in the quiet room, a nebulous idea took shape, but the other thing that was persistently eluding him remained as fugitive as a thread of smoke.

Detective Constable Farrar, under his smooth and sharp-eyed exterior, was feeling fed-up and miserable, and mad at himself into the bargain, despite the return of the incredible weather, already hot on this Sunday morning, all on account of a two-day-old quarrel with his fiancée. They were going to be married in two months' time, and since Friday had been his afternoon off, he'd allowed himself to be taken up to Birmingham to do some shopping for their new home, an occasion which as always ended up with a tour round Rackham's furniture department. There, Sandra had seen and coveted a three-piece suite. 'Oh, Keith, it's lovely! It's *exactly* the colour I've been looking for!' Jigging up and down on the settee, stroking its softness, she breathed, 'Can't you just see it in our lounge?'

'Not really.' Sandra was quite right when she said he wasn't colour-conscious; as for envisaging how a room might look, furnished and decorated, that was altogether beyond him.

'Try,' Sandra said, sharply. 'Wouldn't it look super with a gold carpet?'

He tried, without much success, but he was lukewarm, until he saw the price tag, whereupon he'd taken against the suite quite violently, reminding Sandra that they hadn't even bought the basic necessities, including a bed, yet, and that it was bad enough having half his salary earmarked for mortgage repayments, never mind shelling out the other half for cut-velvet three-piece suites that ran into four figures. Further words were exchanged, until at last Sandra had instructed him coldly to take her straight home and not to bother coming to see her again until he was in a better frame of mind.

D.C. Farrar sighed. He'd fully intended to go round that night at the usual time and apologise for flipping his lid. By that time Sandra would have come round and would admit she'd got carried away. She was a sensible girl and ready enough as a rule to concede that they couldn't afford fancy prices like that – later maybe, because he wouldn't be a D.C. all his life. But fat chance there'd been of getting off to see her in the middle of a murder enquiry. He'd been called in to the station that night and didn't get home until the small hours. Then last night when he'd called, he found Sandra had taken her dad's car and driven her mother over to visit her sister.

He felt resentful at being left out here on a limb when he ought to have been put on to some real detecting, at a loose end, waiting for nine o'clock, when he was due to continue the house-to-house with P.C. Trenchard. Nothing better occurring to him, he decided to check whether the scene-of-crime boys had missed anything in the lane where the tyre-tracks had been found. Farrar, who was keen to get on, didn't believe in leaving things to chance, or people, whoever they were, to do what they were supposed to do, without checking.

The light rain of yesterday afternoon hadn't yet obscured the tracks, though the earth around them was trodden where the men had walked to make the casts.

'Officer!'

Caught squatting on his haunches like an amateur Sherlock Holmes, Farrar straightened up in some embarrassment as a confident, well-bred female voice accosted him. He had a feeling of recognition, but on reflection realised this was only because she was the umpteenth lady he had seen wearing green wellies and walking a golden Labrador, both of which seemed mandatory for residents of Brome.

'You *are* the police, aren't you?' Expressing a belated, if reasonable, doubt.

Farrar, who did not lack a sense of humour, made a gesture equivalent to touching his forelock. 'Yes, ma'am.'

'I understand you were questioning people in the village – about this dreadful happening on Friday.'

'That's right. We're hoping this morning to catch those who were out yesterday.'

'I wasn't at home yesterday. W.I. outing. To a micro-wave cookery demonstration. Frightfully inconvenient day, and not really my cup of tea – new technology they call it, though I call it laziness. But I'm chairman, so it's my responsibility to go, d'you see?'

'Popular outing it was; half the village ladies seemed to have gone along there with you, Mrs –?'

'Mildmay, Virginia Mildmay, from "Redroofs," just along the road. I *was* at home on Friday, however. Brought Heatherington out for his usual run – and I saw a car parked here.'

'You did? What time?' asked Farrar sharply, endeavouring to push away the Labrador, who, on hearing his name, had loped up and was nudging the detective with its huge golden head, and trying enthusiastically to embrace him with its filthy paws on his shoulders. Farrar backed away, fearful of his nice grey suit. The damn dog must have been in the stream in the valley, or worse. If the man existed who could patent a deodorant for wet Labradors, he would make his fortune.

'Four o'clock. Down, Heatherington!'

'You're sure of that?'

Mrs Mildmay regarded Farrar sternly. 'I *always* take him out at four, when I'm here, just as I always take him out at eight-thirty in the morning, too. He wouldn't like it if I didn't. Anyway, Mrs Wharton at the Lodge could confirm it. She was just by her back door, and I passed the time of day with her as I went by. Couldn't have missed seeing a car parked from there, could she?'

Farrar, following the line of her pointing finger, and noting that only a low hedge bounded the Lodge garden at the back, agreed thoughtfully that she couldn't. 'Did you notice what kind of car it was?'

A little of the lady's certainty left her, but not for long. 'Oh, these cars all look alike to me, but it wasn't a small car – and I do remember the colour! I've an excellent colour sense.'

'Have you?' Farrar said gloomily. You and Sandra and everybody else bar me.

'Yes, indeed. And I took a particularly good look at this car. It was parked in a very slovenly manner,' she added disapprovingly, 'and I remember thinking old Comstock wouldn't be best pleased if he wanted to get his horse-box out. People have blocked *me* in before now, parking on my verge, picnickers down by the stream, you know.' She pointed down the lane where it sloped through the woods to the valley bottom. 'Until I had the staddle stones put there, that is.'

Farrar knew the house now. He'd sympathised with the gardener yesterday, swearing as he tried to manoeuvre his mower between the mushroom-shaped stones. 'What colour would you say this car was, Mrs Mildmay?'

'Well now, I'd call it – aubergine. Yes. A sort of cross between a maroon and a true purple. Yes, definitely – aubergine. But what's more,' she added triumphantly, 'I remember the number!'

Farrar barely controlled his yelp of excitement. 'The number?'

'It was a C registration, and the prefix was GOM.'

'Birmingham.'

'The other numbers were, let me see, a nine and an oh, and a six, I'm afraid I can't remember in what order.'

'Never mind; new technology does have its uses. The computer will spit the answer out in two minutes flat. You've done marvellously, Mrs Mildmay.'

'Oh, have I? Have I really?'

Farrar assured her that she had, thanked her once more for her help, reminding her that they would need an official statement, to which she public-spiritedly agreed, whereupon they parted amicably, Mrs Mildmay to stride off in her wellies towards the road, Farrar to intercept the chief inspector's car, which was just arriving.

Terry Wharton wasn't available for interview, having taken his two children to the Lavenstock Sports Centre for swimming lessons, but Mayo was not displeased on the whole to find Janice Wharton alone, peeling onions in the large, quiet kitchen of the big house.

'So you didn't see the car, Mrs Wharton?'

'I may have done. We get quite a few cars parking down that lane there. They drive until the road gets too bad, then they leave their cars and walk down to the woods.' Not looking at him, she swept the skins rapidly into a waste bin and began to slice the onions at an alarming rate. He took the knife gently from her. It looked sharp as a scalpel, and one fatality on their hands was quite enough.

'Sit down and let's talk this over calmly.' He hitched himself on to the corner of the table. Obediently, she perched on the very edge of a straight, rush-seated chair. There was something in her submission, an obstinacy which boded the same lack of co-operation as before. Kite wanted to tell her to be careful. He was keeping a low profile this morning, himself. Already he'd had his head snapped off for no apparent reason, though Mayo was so preoccupied he was probably unaware of it, Kite thought, deciding to be charitable.

'Now, let's be sensible about this,' Mayo was going on. 'It's no use prevaricating. We've a witness who waved to you from the lane, and was standing by the car at the time.'

'Oh.' The colour suddenly flared in Janice's face. She bit her lip. 'Mrs Mildmay. Yes, I do remember her waving now, but if I noticed the car, I've forgotten it.'

'I don't think you have, you know. I think the reason you've "forgotten" is because you knew who the car belonged to, isn't that so?'

Her head jerked up, and her frightened eyes met his.

'Who are you protecting?'

'I'm protecting nobody. I tell you I don't remember seeing a car there.'

Mayo gave her a hard, bright look. 'Did you think it was Mr Dymond's?'

'Mr Dymond's?' She appeared honestly bewildered by the suggestion. 'I wouldn't have any idea what kind of car he has! He doesn't visit here regularly, not since we came. I've only ever seen the man once, and that was on Thursday morning when I let him in to see Mr Lethbridge.'

Mayo sighed. 'All right, we have the car's number. It won't be long before we trace it.' He waited.

The clock on the wall, a big, old-fashioned country-made affair with wooden weights and a big pendulum hanging down, clacked out the seconds noisily. 'Oh God.' She was suddenly shaking. 'D'you mind if I smoke? I don't usually, not here in the kitchen, but –'

He did mind, strongly, with all the fanaticism of a reformed smoker, but if it would help her . . . He shrugged and gestured acquiescence. While she pulled a packet from the pocket of her overall and lit one, he signalled to Kite, who filled the kettle and plugged it in. 'Coffee or tea?'

'What? Oh, coffee, please, black.'

Kite found instant coffee and spooned it into three mugs.

'His name's Wisden,' Janice Wharton said all at once. 'The man who owns the car, Bert Wisden. He's supposed to be a car dealer, amongst other things. He's not – not a very nice type. Terry met him . . .' She broke off, her brown eyes wide, as if afraid to go on with what she'd begun.

'When he was in prison,' Mayo supplied.

'Yes . . .' And she gave a kind of released sigh that was very nearly a sob, that caught the next words in her throat. 'He said you were bound to find out.'

'It won't be held against him – not if he's done nothing wrong.'

'Try telling Terry that!'

'They never believe it.' Kite placed three mugs on the table and pushed the sugar across. Mayo said nothing, and Kite, watching him stirring and stirring his coffee though he didn't take sugar, knew he wasn't hearing what he'd hoped to hear.

'What can you tell us about Wisden?'

'Not much. He came to see Terry on Thursday afternoon. Why did it have to be *then*? He said he had a proposition, a chance for Terry to make some big money. I knew it couldn't be anything straight, and I told him I didn't want him in my house. Terry was mad at me and said they'd better go and discuss it somewhere else then.' She closed her eyes. 'Oh God, when I knew he'd been murdered, I was so *frightened*.'

'You thought Wisden had something to do with it, and that your husband had been persuaded to lend a hand?'

'No! Yes – no, not at the bottom of me, but at first, I just didn't know. But he's sworn he hadn't, and he doesn't lie, not to me. He said he'd told Wisden to push off and get someone else to do whatever dirty work it was he'd wanted him to do, but it would be better for us to keep quiet and not mention his visit.'

'Why were you frightened?' Mayo pressed.

'Like Terry said – you'd never have believed him.'

'No, why were you so frightened when Lethbridge was found murdered?'

137

Abruptly she went to lift the lid of the Aga and threw in her half-smoked cigarette, taking her time about it. He waited until she turned round before going on. 'It wasn't only because the sole alibi for your husband could only be provided by a professional villain, was it? There was another reason. You knew that Terry also had a motive for killing Lethbridge.'

She stood rooted to the spot, staring at him, her eyes wide in mute appeal.

'Because the day before, Lethbridge had given you notice of dismissal.'

It was Kite's turn to stare. Janice Wharton whispered, 'I suppose Mrs Lethbridge told you?'

'No.' He didn't have to tell her why he knew, but he saw no reason why he shouldn't. 'There happened to be a note about it in Clive Lethbridge's diary. You'd been told, the day before he died, to leave the house and job within the month, that's right? Had he found about your husband's record?'

Slowly she shook her head. 'It wasn't that. They'd been having a silly argument about Terry cleaning the outside windows. Terry said that wasn't what he was paid for, and all of a sudden Mr Lethbridge flew off the handle. He said he was fed up with Terry's attitude, and he could easily get us replaced. So Terry said okay by him, he could stuff the job.' She said wryly, 'You can guess the answer to that – if that was how he wanted it, he could go. It was stupid of Terry, and irresponsible, I know – but he didn't kill him, he didn't! You get hold of Bert Wisden, and he'll be able to prove Terry couldn't have. He's staying at the Prince of Wales in Lavenstock . . . Nothing but the best for him.'

'Don't worry, we'll do just that.' Mayo hadn't the heart to tell her that Wisden might well deny the meeting, out of spite, that he might very well take the greatest pleasure in seeing Terry Wharton in it right up to the chin. Not that it mattered all that much anyway, not now.

'All right,' he said, finishing his coffee, 'we'll leave it for now. Where can we find Mrs Lethbridge?'

'Mrs Lethbridge?' Janice blinked as if it were an enormous effort to bring her mind back. 'Oh. I think she's doing some gardening. Shall I tell her you want to see her?'

'Don't bother, we'll find her.'

She said, as they reached the door, '*She* knew right from the start, about Terry – Mrs Lethbridge, I mean – but she said there was no need to tell her husband. She was prepared to help him to a new start . . . She'd never have let him sack Terry.'

'But did Terry believe that?' asked Kite, as they closed the kitchen door behind them.

CHAPTER 16

'I think I know what you want to see me about,' Caroline Lethbridge greeted them soberly as they came through the arch in the yew hedge and into the walled garden, heat-enclosed on this brilliant day, October borrowed from August. She had been tidying up the roses, as if keeping up with normal tasks could deny the abnormality that had struck Brome. A trug full of late blooms lay on the stone flags near a wheelbarrow almost full of prickly stems. She drew a deep breath. 'I can only say that I'm sorry I misled you.'

Why couldn't anybody ever bring themselves to say, 'I lied?' Moreover, she seemed to think now that she'd made this brief apology that everything was hunky-dory, that he should doff his cap and say, 'Quite all right, ma'am,' and that would be the end of it, when by rights he ought to give her a dressing down for obstructing the course of justice. Mayo said, brusquely, 'I saw you'd changed your mind when it came to signing your statement, but we've more important things to dwell on for the moment.' He almost, but not quite, regretted his tone when he saw her expression. Dammit, what right had she to shrink from him, as if he frightened her, but making him suddenly aware of his own irritability, and pulling him up short? You haven't the finesse, lad, for dealing with such tender hot-house plants, he told himself wryly. Accepting his limitations, he pressed on, however, in the only way he knew how.

'We've traced your husband's BMW,' he told her, 'found in the long-stay car park at Birmingham Airport.'

'Birmingham Airport? For goodness' sake!'

'As good a place as any for ditching a stolen car,' Kite said.

'And Mr Royston will be glad to know his file was in it. Under the driving seat – probably slipped off the back seat.'

'Well, I suppose that's very probable. Clive always brought an armful of work home on Wednesdays, for the following day, usually dumped on the back seat. Matt will be so relieved; he'll be able to meet the deadline for the book now.' She pushed back the soft wing of dark hair from her face with the back of her gloved hand. Mayo noticed her pallor had been improved by judicious make-up, but her eyes still had a bruised look, their blue deepened by the dark heather colours of her simple Liberty print cotton frock. She looked as though she hadn't slept much since Friday. Well, he hadn't slept a lot, himself.

'He won't be able to have it just yet,' he said. 'Not until we've had a chance to examine it.' Flipping through the file, he'd been inclined to regard the contents as harmless as Royston had claimed, but it would of course have to be subjected to the usual rigorous tests before he could authorise its release.

'And the car – you've been able to discover who took it – and why? Are there any indications –?' she asked, and then stopped, halted by his impassive look.

He wouldn't tell her that, of course. She couldn't expect him to. 'We've not had the final results of the tests yet. It'll be in a mess. Everybody's fingerprints all over the place – but that's not what I wanted to talk to you about.'

'No?'

'We need to know a bit more of the background, if you can give it, about this animosity that existed between your husband and Mr Dymond. As I understand it, it went back much further than the sale of Oddings Cottage.'

He watched her carefully, saw the surprise spring to her face, surprise and what else? Relief? A kind of guarded watchfulness, perhaps, but she answered readily enough. 'Yes, that's true, they never seemed to get along, from the very beginning; I suppose they just weren't the same type. You know how it is with some people, oil and water.'

'I was thinking of some more specific cause – something must have brought their dislike into the open.'

'No, I don't think –' She stopped and said softly, 'Of course.'

She stood on the path, staring across the garden, opening and shutting the secateurs in her gloved hand, silent for so long that he was compelled to prompt her. 'Mrs Lethbridge –'

'I'm sorry,' she said, blinking. 'Yes, you're quite right. They were never good friends, just distantly polite to each other whenever they met, but there was nothing actually in the open – until that awful business of young Simon.'

She walked a few paces along the flagged path, pulling off the gardening gloves and flapping them in her hands, until at last she stopped, looking down into the lily pool.

Mayo followed her, feeling the heat of the sun on his back, the green depths of the pool offering a grateful coolness to the eyes. It was going to be a scorcher today; he could already feel a trickle of sweat beginning to run between his shoulder blades. 'Simon –?' he prompted.

'I can't really tell you much about it; I only ever knew the bare facts.'

'Tell me what you do know.'

She lifted her shoulders. 'That Clive refused to give a job to the boy, who was a protégé of Marcus's. And the upshot of it, which

141

was really quite terrible . . .' Her voice had become so low he had to strain to hear. 'He was so shattered at not getting the job, he actually took his own life.'

There was a silence while her listeners absorbed the implications of this. We're getting somewhere, thought Kite with a sudden surge of excitement, infected with the tension that he knew was building up inside the chief inspector, who looked taut, as though poised on the edge of discovery, and the effort of holding himself back was hurting him, physically.

Mayo forced himself to tread cautiously. 'Wasn't that an excessive reaction, to kill yourself for not getting a job?'

'To most people it would seem so, but apparently Simon always was – rather over the top, or so I believe. I only knew him very slightly, myself. In this instance, it was all made very much worse because Marcus accused Clive, saying it was all his fault. Clive of course claimed he'd a perfect right to refuse to employ Simon . . . Well, his actual words were that Waring & Lethbridge weren't a philanthropic society.'

'Meaning what?

'Meaning, I'm afraid, that he'd reason to believe Simon was taking drugs, hard drugs, and he was in fact addicted. It was probably true. The cause of his death *was* from an overdose.'

'How long ago did this happen?'

'Four or five years, at a guess.'

'It would rankle with Dymond, a thing like that? He wouldn't be able to forget?'

She was very distressed. 'Forget? Oh no, never that. Simon was much more than a pupil, you see. He was very close to Marcus, and Enid; in fact, he lived with them for some time after his parents were divorced. I don't believe Marcus would forget, and he'd never forgive, either, but if you're asking me if he would kill Clive for it, especially after all this time, then I'd never believe that, either.'

*

Marcus Dymond viewed death dispassionately, a necessary view-point he had cultivated over the last few years, occasioned by the events that had overtaken him. Enid's painful and progressive ill-ness he saw as one from which death would be a blessing. He believed the only pain that death itself – not its ugly preliminaries – brought was to others, and the single, solitary regret about Clive Lethbridge's demise was the sorrow it would bring to the bereaved. Even in death, Lethbridge was capable of making others suffer. He himself knew that agony intimately; he had been there already, projecting himself into the future, when Enid would leave him behind, and back into the past, when Simon had died.

He waited, watching the daily woman, Mrs Chisholm, point the way to the two men who had rung the bell, waiting for them to reach the path to the summerhouse, the chief inspector and another policeman whom he hadn't met before, a tall, rangy man with a cheerful, youthful face.

'Enid,' he began, 'leave it all to me this time, won't you?'

'If you wish it, of course – but don't worry, my dear. Everything's going to be all right. There's nothing bad enough to hurt either of us.'

Her calm serenity shamed him twenty times a day.

The summerhouse reminded Mayo of a Tunisian birdcage. The lacy woodwork of its octagonal frame was painted blue and white, but inside it was roomy and very English, with creaking, com-fortable old basketwork furniture, and a small picnic stove. It smelled like a cricket pavilion, of dry old wood, and tea. A table was laid with cups and saucers and a teapot under a knitted cosy. The view from each side of the summerhouse was different: wind-ing paths; a small coppice of elegant silver birch; flower beds and lawns, smooth where they faced the house; a still, natural pool. Beyond this the land dropped steeply, levelling out into ploughed fields parallel with the main road, which was far enough away not to be troublesome, before rising again to Brome House on the skyline, with Oddings Cottage in the middle distance. Church bells sounded distantly, a maple flamed against a duck-egg-blue sky, the occasional leaf fluttered to the ground, and Mayo had to make an effort not to be beguiled. He waved away the offer of one of the basket chairs which Dymond indicated, and refused tea. 'Thank you, but time is pressing. Sergeant Kite and I would like to have a further word with you please, Mr Dymond. I suggest you might prefer it to be in private.'

'I've already told you all I know, and I can't see any possible reason for your questioning me further.'

'That's for us to say, sir. Shall we go into the house?'

'There's nothing you can't say in front of my wife.'

'I don't think you're in a position to judge that until you know what it is,' Mayo insisted stolidly.

The air inside the summerhouse seemed suddenly used up. Mayo had the feeling that Dymond knew what was coming. He made a gesture that seemed oddly uncharacteristic of him, a half-sketched indecisive turn, then his wife said, 'Go along with them, Marcus. I shall be quite happy here. We were watching a heron on the pond before you came, Mr Mayo; perhaps he'll come back.' She spoke tranquilly, and had already turned her wheelchair towards one of the windows. He saw that the binoculars he'd used yesterday were on her knee.

'Thank you, Mrs Dymond.' He turned abruptly, to begin the walk back to the house.

'Goodbye to you both.' She was already lifting the binoculars to her eyes when they left.

Dymond showed them into the same room as before. 'When we spoke to you last,' Mayo began, immediately he was seated in that enviable armchair, 'you mentioned that your quarrel with Clive Lethbridge went back a long way. You neglected to mention, however, the very specific event which started it, over something – or someone – who was very important to you, and to your wife. I'd like to know more of the details, as much as you can remember.'

'It appears to me you're already very well informed on the subject, which I assure you can have no possible connection with your enquiries.'

'We'll be the judge of that. Please don't evade the issue, sir.'

'I can only presume you are referring to the death of Simon Johnson.'

'I am.'

'Which you must know I held Lethbridge directly responsible for. If he hadn't refused to employ Simon, that young man would still be alive.'

'Isn't that assuming a good deal? Most people can cope with being turned down for a job without resorting to such lengths.'

'Most people, Chief Inspector, would not have had his problems.'

'Supposing we go back to the beginning. For a start, how you came to be personally involved with him – apart from teaching him at school, I mean.'

Dymond stood with his back to the fireplace, his hands clasped behind his back, as if resigned to facing a recalcitrant fourth form with a lecture in which, if he was lucky, they would appreciate about one word in ten. 'Very well.' Gazing into the middle distance, he began, speaking fluently, dryly and without emotion.

'One can say of very few boys that they are a pleasure to teach, but Simon was – not only clever, but receptive. But he was a product of our so-called civilised society, of divorced parents who took off to the ends of the earth with their respective partners, his father to Bahrein, his mother back to the United States. Fortunately, they still had enough sense to realise that Simon, who was in his last year at school, needed to continue his education here, and they decided to leave him. There was a problem as to where he should live, and since we had plenty of space, it was decided he should stay here with us for a year before going on to college.' Dymond paused to clear his throat. 'My wife and I have

145

never had children of our own, but Simon was – well, let's just say we had no cause to regret what we did.'

'May I see the photograph you have of him?'

'How –?' Raised eyebrows, followed by cynical recognition. 'Oh yes, the inestimable Deeley, I take it? One should never be surprised at anything.'

'Detective Constable Deeley was observant enough to notice it, when we were last here, yes,' Mayo replied curtly, annoyed by the man's unnecessary sarcasm, which was effectively quenching the thought that he might after all be human.

Dymond stepped over to the piano and, selecting the photograph which Mayo assumed to be the one that had attracted Deeley's attention, handed it over. Mayo saw a tall, good-looking boy with large, round spectacles, a defenceless face. Mrs Dymond looking not five, but ten years younger. Marcus Dymond looking much the same.

'Carry on, please.'

'Yes. Well then, Simon had been determined to become an architect since he was a very small boy. Buildings fascinated him, and he happened to have the required difficult combination of talents – a certain artistic ability, and a complete grasp of mathematical principles. He took a preliminary course at art college, and then won a place at the Architectural Association. He was confidently expected to become a star pupil, but something went seriously wrong. Though he continued to win commendations from time to time for his outstanding work, his day-to-day progress was so erratic, in the end he left without much honour.' He stopped, gazing unseeingly out of the window. 'We know now, of course, that someone had already introduced him to drugs. I would like nothing better,' he added, unemotionally, 'than to see such persons on the end of a rope.'

Poor devil, thought Mayo, exchanging glances with Kite. They knew all about those who sold misery and death to the young, the bored, the desperate. But he kept his opinions to himself. 'I take it you tried to get him to accept professional help?'

'When we found out, of course we did, but there's nothing to be done if the will isn't there.' Dymond contemplated the empty pipe he'd again picked up. 'Naturally, he couldn't keep a job, and it became evident he was becoming more and more dependent, losing his hold. He began to look like a – a derelict. And then, quite suddenly, he seemed to find the motivation from somewhere, God knows where. He told us he'd agreed to have treatment to help him to "kick the habit," as he put it. Later he came to see us, and he was apparently completely cured. It seemed like – it *was* – a miracle.'

'And that was when he applied for the job with Lethbridge?'

'Not then,' Dymond said. 'Not until he'd tried every other avenue open to him. But with his record, no formal qualifications, what could one expect? Not one person was willing to take him on, give him a new start.'

'But you thought Lethbridge might have done so?'

'Not I. But Simon did. He knew someone who worked for Lethbridge, who told him of a vacancy in the firm. He was quite sure they would be prepared to take him. Simon went along, full of hope, and sure enough, he was offered the job. To say he was jubilant would be an understatement. Then a letter arrived, not confirming the offer, but curtly stating that the position had been filled. That night he took an overdose and died. It doesn't take much, as I'm sure I've no need to remind you, to push a reformed addict back over the edge.' An aircraft, flying low, filled the room with its roar. Dymond waited until it had ceased. 'Well, now that you have succeeded in wringing that out of me, and seen that it has nothing to do with the case, as I said, I must ask you to leave. I can't help you any more, and I'm not sure that I want to. No doubt our present namby-pamby laws will allow whoever killed Lethbridge – if by some chance you manage to catch him – to walk free in a few years, but in this case I say good luck to him.'

It was possible to feel sorry for Dymond, in the hell he'd been through, quite impossible to like him. Mayo said, apparently at random, 'What happened to Simon Johnson's sister when the parents divorced?'

Dymond raised his head, and blinked. 'Sylvia? Why, she finally stayed with her mother. As far as I know, she's still there. We are not, and never have been, in regular correspondence.'

'She hasn't visited you recently?'

'Certainly not. Not since she was a child.'

'You didn't know, then, that she had recently been employed as Clive Lethbridge's secretary?'

Dymond looked astounded. 'That's preposterous! She would never have worked for that man after what he did to her brother.'

'She did, however, for the last six weeks. Are you sure you didn't know?'

'I've said so. And how should I have known?'

'Perhaps she told you. Perhaps she took the job at your request. Perhaps the two of you cooked up a scheme to find some way to make Clive Lethbridge pay for what he had done to Simon. Did it start with blackmailing letters and phone calls, and end up with murder? Did it, Mr Dymond?'

'You are talking utter rubbish!'

'I put it you that you could have walked from here on Friday afternoon to Brome House, knowing through Sylvia Johnson that Lethbridge would be alone in the house except for Mrs Peach, who is somewhat deaf, and killed him. You could have established an alibi by telephoning Mr Waring as if you were ringing from your own home, and then calmly walked back.'

'That's neither true nor feasible, and you know it.' Dymond had gone very pale, but he met Mayo's gaze without flinching. 'It's pure supposition.'

'Is it? It might be up to you, Mr Dymond, to prove otherwise.' He stood up, preparing to go. 'By the way, what was the date of Simon Johnson's death?'

'June the fifteenth, three years ago.'

'And the name of the friend who recommended him to Waring & Lethbridge?'

'Murfitt, his name was, Donald Murfitt – though he was Sylvia's friend rather than Simon's. I believe,' Dymond added with some distaste, 'they were both involved in some kind of freakish religion. She was, I'm afraid, that kind of girl.'

'Do you mean the sort whose religious principles might state a life for a life?'

'Not at all. I mean she was just the type to take up some extreme religion. She was unfortunately rather plain, not very clever, and without even an attractive nature to compensate. Even my wife could find very little likeable about her, and I can't say that for many people.'

'What sort of man is Murfitt?'

'I've never met him, only heard of him. But I thought him – misguided, to say the least, sending Simon to Lethbridge.'

'Do you think it might have been through his sister's influence that Simon was persuaded to come off drugs?'

'Unlikely. He was inclined to be scathing about what he called her nutty religion, her "do-gooding."'

'Yet she did try to get him a job.'

'That's true. She was very fond of him, and in any case, she would have considered it her duty. As I've said, whatever else, she was a very worthy sort of young woman.'

CHAPTER 17

'We're never going to make that one stick.' Kite wound down the car window, letting in air that was no cooler than inside the car.

'You reckon?' Mayo still sounded somewhat short, due, had Kite known it, solely to his own inability to grasp and hold that something he still felt was there just beyond his reach. Last night he'd been gripped with that surge of tension and excitement that told him he was on the verge of a breakthrough, and now . . . He looked at the seat belt buckle in his hand as if wondering what it was doing there, then clicked it fastened. What he needed was time for a rethink, a reappraisal.

Loosening his tie, he relaxed suddenly. 'Well, whatever, it won't do Dymond any harm to sweat for a bit. He owes us one, for Deeley if nothing else. Patronising buggers like him get on my wick. Come on, take that grin off your face and let's be having you.'

They drove back to the station. Mayo spent some time in the busy incident room, where every item of information about the murder was being fed into the computer, indexed, cross-referenced. He picked up fresh information which had come in during the course of the morning. Amongst this was a preliminary report on Lethbridge's BMW, mainly to confirm what Mayo already suspected, that the car was going to need a lot of working on. Several of the garage staff had handled it during the course of its servicing, leaving prints which would have to be eliminated. Hairs and clothing fibres would be more difficult, because of the protective polythene, still on the front seats. But . . . blood had been found on the driving seat covers and the carpet, quickly tested and found to be group O, Lethbridge's own, though further exhaustive tests by the experts would split it up more precisely. It was the first piece of solid evidence that had been found.

Albert George Wisden, fifty-one, of Finchley, had, it seemed, been contacted, with the result that Wharton was now apparently in the clear. A report from Deeley, who'd been sent to make the enquiry, stated that after Mrs Wharton had thrown the two men out, they had gone on to the Prince of Wales, where they could get drinks, since Wisden was staying there. The girl who served them remembered them because she was annoyed at having to open the bar up specially at that time in the afternoon, the time when Lethbridge was being murdered.

He'd just finished reading this when Kite brought in the report of the D.C. who'd talked to the waiter at the Brandon Hall. 'Odell's just confirmed that the waiter at the Brandon Hall served Mrs Lethbridge and Royston with tea at about quarter to four. There was this other witness Royston mentioned as well. She was in the grotto having tea when they had theirs, then saw Royston seeing Caroline Lethbridge off in the car park at ten past four, after they'd finished. It's unlikely she's wrong; she's an old lady living there in the hotel on her own with nothing to do but watch other folk, and she scented romance.'

Mayo said, 'So that's two we can cross off definitely, three if we count Mrs Wharton, which I'm inclined to do, barring some hitherto undiscovered motive turning up, four with Caroline Lethbridge now that the employment agency have confirmed the times she gave us. But what about Royston? What about him, Martin? D'you see him as a murderer?'

Kite thought for a moment or two. 'He's capable of taking decisions into his own hands, and if he saw murder as the only solution, he might not hesitate, but I'd bet he'd look for a more civilised way out first. Though there was time for him to have done it, just.'

'He'd have had to get a move on, but it's just possible.' Mayo pushed his papers away. He was back on an even keel. He never despised instinct, that other name for gut feeling or whether or not something smelled right, but this last hour was what it was all about as well, routine procedures, weeks and months of patient, even boring sifting of information, slowly piecing a case together. Police work was mostly based on common sense and what you'd learned about human nature. You could expect a lot of reverses and disappointments, and a few breaks, and in the end, if you were lucky, you came up with the right answers. If not, your career could be blighted with one of the unsolved cases. This hadn't yet happened to Mayo, but it was one of his nightmares that one day it might. Apart from a few back-handed comments coming your way, if you'd done your job right, nobody in the force . . . there but for the grace of God . . . would really blame you for it. But you would. He pushed the possibility far into the back of his mind and went out with Kite to find somewhere cool and quiet for lunch, where they could talk, relax and bounce a few more ideas off each other.

He couldn't have faced goulash himself on a sweltering day like today, but Kite was doing so with every appearance of anticipatory enjoyment. The pub they'd chosen, in a small, otherwise undistinguished village about four miles out of Lavenstock, was famed for its ample, tasty bar snacks, with good reason. Mayo. surveyed his own quarter pound of Cheddar, the warm, crusty bread, the liberal garnish, almost constituting a meal in itself, with approval, drank deep of his cool bitter and leaned back to see if there were any new pictures. The walls were lined with them, mostly painted by a local lady who helped out in the bar, she of the generous hand with the cheese, and some occasionally were for sale. A good deal of her liberality appeared in the paintings, which were colourful and exuberant and full of life. Mayo's brother-in-law, who was the finance director in a firm specialising in signwriting and liked to think himself an authority on art – on most things, come to that – had pronounced them the work of a talented amateur. And what was wrong with that? Mayo wondered. He liked them, and had recently bought one, a Lavenstock market-day scene, and hung it in the flat in defiance of Lynne's brother, whom he was sorry he'd introduced to the White Boar.

'Great stuff, Dolly,' Kite said, craning his head back towards the bar counter, indicating the goulash and raising his glass.

Dolly smiled and cocked a thumb in acknowledgement, a cheerful, opulent woman with a lot of black hair and a gipsy appearance fostered with big gold earrings and a king's ransom of chains and bracelets.

'You're very chipper today,' Mayo remarked, noticing the fact for the first time.

'Every reason to be. We've got things sorted, about Sheila's new job and that. We've been having problems because it's going to mean her working nine to five, no flexi-time, fitting her hours in as and when, like now.'

'That's a pity. Used to work out pretty well for you, didn't it?'

'Right, with my peculiar hours, and with Sheila's mum living in the next road. I mean, if neither of us were there, the kids could always go round to their gran – which they'd rather do than come home, in view of the way she spoils 'em rotten!' Kite grinned and took a pull at his beer. 'No, really, they think the world of her and she's marvellous with them, and I don't know how we'd have managed without her. But thing is, she's been half-inclined, recently, towards selling her house and buying one of those new flats in Hinton, all fitted up and easy to run. So naturally we couldn't spoil it by telling her about Sheila's promotion.'

'She'd have abandoned the idea of the new flat, you mean?' The masochism of grandmas never ceased to amaze Mayo.

'Without a second thought, I can tell you. Obviously, we didn't want any comeback about influencing her, but I didn't much like the idea of my kids left to their own devices after school. Anyway, it's worked out after all. Mother-in-law's decided she can't bear the thought of losing her garden – and between you and me, not seeing the boys so much as well – so she's decided to stay put and have a new kitchen installed where she is. Relief all round.'

Rather Mrs Temple than me, thought Mayo, the few occasions when he'd encountered Kite's children being indelibly imprinted on his mind. A right couple of young tearaways, you needed four pairs of eyes and twenty hands when they were around. He heartily endorsed Kite's misgivings about leaving those two unsupervised after school hours.

The unrelenting heat had taken most of the Sunday-morning customers outside to eat and drink and sweat in the paved garden at the back, on the British premise of taking whatever sun you could get, though it was much more pleasant here, unpretentious, stone-flagged and cool . . . and quiet. While Kite had ordered their meal at the bar, Mayo had managed to secure a secluded corner where they could talk in private. He picked up a copy of this week's *Advertiser* someone had left, but the news of Lethbridge's murder had broken too late for him to be featured for the second week running, for even the brief official handout in the 'Stop Press.' He commented idly on this to Kite.

After a moment or two Kite said thoughtfully, 'This business of Simon Johnson. It's bound to make a difference, give us a new angle – could even provide an alternative motive for the blackmail. A threat to expose Lethbridge for what he'd done to Simon Johnson – it wouldn't have looked too good for a man in his position, would it, refusing to give a helping hand?'

Mayo shook his head. 'Doubtful, to say the least. Morally, of course, you could say the way Lethbridge acted was unpardonable, but from a pragmatic point of view – well, I'm afraid there's a lot of people would agree with what he did, with some justification. Taking on somebody with problems like that isn't something most firms can afford. All right, he could have approached the whole thing in a more positive way, offered to do what he could in other directions or something of the kind, but he wasn't that sort, and he didn't. And from what we've learned of Lethbridge's character, I can't see revelations like that disturbing him too much, anyway. Especially three years later.'

'People have long memories. And it *might*, as you said, account for Dymond – him and the girl, not forgetting Murfitt. They'd all good reason to hate Lethbridge.'

Yes, it had been a vicious killing. A vision of the blood-spattered room, and the savagely smashed model, recurred time and again.

'Maybe Sylvia Johnson especially,' Kite continued, 'depending on how fond she was of her brother.'

'And who was on her way to America when Lethbridge died.'

'That doesn't rule her out. She *must* have been in it, some way or other,' Kite averred stubbornly. He forked up the last of his goulash and settled his length in the Windsor chair.

A three-cornered plot, involving Murfitt, Sylvia Johnson – and *Dymond*? It wasn't on, it didn't ring true, those three, not to Mayo. Yet there *was* Simon Johnson. Linked to all three. 'You noticed the date Simon Johnson died?' he asked. 'And only a few weeks later, Murfitt was sacked.'

'That's it; the connections are too obvious to ignore! It's pretty clear the girl wormed her way into the job, possibly in order to find some way of getting back at Lethbridge for what he'd done to her brother. She found something nasty in the woodshed that they could blackmail him about – this business of the judges being bought, for instance, and Bob's your uncle.'

'Too pat by far. And why wait until now?'

'Because she'd been living in America, and had only just come back home.'

Mayo was shifting restlessly in his seat, but suddenly he sat up straighter. 'What did you say?'

'I said she'd just come back from America.'

'No, you said she'd come back home.'

'Same difference.'

'Not from where I sit.'

Mayo's face was a study. He had finally caught the slippery fact/thing which had been eluding him for two days. He stared through the flung-back lattice window, watching a dog making a pest of itself chasing between the tables and annoying the customers, and saw the case beginning to take on a new shape. He thought, it's all a matter of perception. Like that picture: one way you saw a classical black vase on a white background; adjust your perception and two female profiles faced each other.

Or put it another way. Shuffle the cards so that they began to take on different relationships to each other. And hitherto unregarded factors became the key upon which the whole crime turned. 'Waring,' he said softly, suddenly. 'Yes, by God. What's become of Waring since he gave us all the slip?'

'Gave us all the slip?'

Kite had failed to recognise the quotation, but Mayo was too preoccupied to bother to elucidate. 'What exactly did he say, when we interviewed him at his office, about the anonymous letter he said he'd received? Got your notebook?'

Kite thumbed through the pages until he came to the relevant one. 'He said the letter wasn't specific but hinted at something not being all above-board about the competition for the Svensen Centre.'

'And he translated this to mean Lethbridge was being accused of offering bribes?'

'Which he denied was possible, of course.'

'Of course he would. There could never be any proof, any stink, because there never were any bribes. Whereas, if the truth's what I think it might be . . . Drink up; it's time we renewed our acquaintance with friend Waring.'

Kite gave up. Like Dr Watson before him, he had heard all that the master had heard but was no nearer the solution. Whereas Mayo, the superior sod, evidently had it all sewn up bar the shouting. He wouldn't have opened his trap otherwise. Kite grinned wryly and lifted philosophic eyebrows, drained his tankard and, with a glance at the families sunning themselves in the garden as they went out, and a passing regret for his lost weekend, followed him into the blanketing heat of the afternoon.

CHAPTER 18

Addencote was seven minutes' drive the other side of Brome, and the house Harry Waring shared with his sister lay about another half a mile farther on. Its name, chased in pokerwork on a varnished plaque swinging from a kind of gibbet near the gate, was 'Silver Birches,' though evidence of birches, silver or otherwise, there was none. Standing on a slight rise, it was a large neo-Georgian structure of rather aggressive red bricks, approached by a short tarmac drive. Ding-dong chimes sounded when the bell was pressed, and presently the door was opened by a woman, fair, fat and nearer fifty than forty, swinging a pair of sunglasses in her hand and wearing a yellow sundress that revealed too much abundant flesh, prawn-pink.

'Yes?'

She was not too pleased at having her sunbathing interrupted and was ready with the brush-off until she saw their warrant cards, when her manner underwent a rapid change. Funny, this nervous reaction people had to the police, even when totally innocent. They talked too much, as if aware of some secret guilt that might otherwise come to light with the mere presence of the law. She introduced herself as Cynthia Jenner and said how awful it all was, wasn't it, and poor Caroline, and that her brother was out on the terrace, they'd just finished lunch, if they'd come with her . . .

She kept it up, her heavy gold charm bracelet a jangling accompaniment, as they followed her through a wide parquet-floored hall furnished in a curious medley of styles. A low-arched briquette fireplace was built into an end wall; an open-tread staircase rose from the centre. An enormous cut-glass chandelier, suspended from the upper regions and reflected in the various gilt-framed mirrors with which the hall was equipped, hung so low that Kite automatically ducked his head in passing. Ye Gods! thought Mayo, remembering the bland good taste of Waring's office, and wondering whether the house belonged to his sister, or if he'd merely allowed her her head with the decorations. They emerged through a door set into an arch, opening on to a flagged terrace furnished with a classical-style stone balustrade, Spanish flower-pots, and cushioned chairs set round a table. A swimming pool of dazzling turquoise blue and a hacienda-type changing room took up most of the garden.

'It's the police, Harry.' As Waring, clad in leisure wear that wasn't as kind to his well-fleshed torso as was a business suit, rose to greet them from the lounger where he'd been stretched, Cynthia Jenner went on with scarcely a pause for breath, 'Sorry about the clutter; if you'll excuse me, I'll just clear it . . . Would you like some lemonade? It's homemade,' she offered, waving a giant insulated pitcher.

If Waring was surprised to see them, the sunglasses he wore effectively concealed it. He gave them his flabby handshake, waved them to chairs and said, smiling, 'Oh, something stronger than lemonade, surely!' His own glass indicated red wine. 'No? Well, we can rustle up some coffee if you like.'

'Lemonade will be fine, thanks.'

Cynthia poured the icy fruit juice into tall glasses and then made a great business of clearing the table of what was evidently the remains of lunch. Waring padded across to her on bare feet and picked up the piled tray when she'd finished, and with an adroit manoeuvre, shepherded her in front of him into the house. In a moment or two he was back, saying affably, 'I assume it's only me you want to see. I'm sure you'll excuse my sister; she has things to attend to . . . people coming in this evening for drinks.' His voice was gravely lowered. 'Caro and Clive would have been here, of course. We did think of cancelling, but life, as they say, must go on . . .'

'Quite.' Caro and Clive, Mayo thought. 'You saw a good deal of them, socially as well as in business, then?'

'Lord, yes. Known Caroline all her life – and always been very fond of her.'

'And Lethbridge?'

'We became partners shortly after they married.' Mayo noted the different shading of the response.

'A man of integrity, would you say?'

'No question.' This answer came blandly, readily; the mouth smiled, the eyes were hidden behind dark glass. 'But we went over all this yesterday. I fancy it isn't what you came to talk to me about.'

Mayo leaned forward, lifted his lemonade glass from the table and sipped it as if it were the finest malt. 'Professionally, and as far as that's possible without personal bias, what was your considered judgement on the design for the Svensen Centre?'

Waring's sunglasses might conceal his expression, but his bare feet gave him away. The toes curled sharply, involuntarily, then slowly relaxed. 'The Svensen Centre? There's no other word for it, in my opinion, but spectacular.'

'And didn't you find that surprising?'

Waring suddenly sat up and took off his sunspecs, reached for the packet of cigars on the table beside him, waved it questioningly at the other two and then, as they shook their heads, cut and lit one himself. 'I'm not sure that I follow you,' he said carefully.

Mayo said, 'I'm told that Lethbridge was a good, competent architect. That he'd never designed anything on this level before.'

'That doesn't mean to say he never could. We're all of us, at times, capable of expanding our reach beyond what anyone imagined of us.'

Indeed, indeed, and here was Waring, capable of surprising him, but already halfway to admission. The slightest tremor of his hand as the lighter flickered showed the hesitation in his mind. Mayo waited patiently. Waring wasn't a man to hold out; he would always take the easy way. As he had before. 'In that, I echo your sentiments. All the same,' Mayo said, making it easier, 'I believe you may have had doubts.'

'Doubts? Not in the least. As I told you yesterday, there was no question of undue influence. No one in my firm has ever gone in for that sort of thing, not even pre-Poulsen.' Waring gave his urbane smile, drew on his cigar and observed the glowing tip.

'I'm not talking about bribery. I'm talking about the design itself. I think you knew it wasn't Lethbridge's.'

From the direction of the kitchen came the whirr of some electrical appliance, a mixer or some such, working in sporadic bursts. Waring said nothing. Neither did Mayo, letting the silence draw out until Waring would have to break it. He did so sooner than Mayo had hoped. He seemed relieved as he began to speak.

'Well,' he said, 'I'd hoped . . . But never mind. All right, what do you want to know?'

'The truth about the design, Mr Waring, that's all.'

The other man drew on his cigar and then said, 'It wasn't the brilliance that surprised me, you know. Clive always had more potential than he realised, but he'd always seemed too intent on success to risk the failure or ridicule of stepping too far out of the mould . . . Do you understand me?' Mayo nodded, and Waring went on, 'It was the style. Simply, it wasn't his. It didn't have his signature; it had none of the personal idiosyncrasies and repetitive themes every architect of any pretensions at all subconsciously develops. But . . . I was out of the country for most of the time the designs were being prepared for submission, working on one of our projects in Australia – and to be frank, I didn't let it bother me too much because I thought it was in any case far too avant-garde to stand much chance in a competition of that nature. When I heard it had won, I was amazed.'

'And because of the kudos it brought to the firm, you smothered any misgivings you might have had?' Waring shrugged, spread his hands, avoided looking directly at either of them. 'You must have had a shock when the blackmail threats began to come in. That's what they were about, weren't they? Not accusing Lethbridge of trying to influence the judges, but of appropriating someone else's design.'

'What could I do? I tackled Clive about it, and he denied it, absolutely. I'd no alternative but to believe him.' Waring's voice was loaded with self-justification.

'Did you know, or suspect, whose the design was?'

'I had no idea, none at all.'

'What does the name Simon Johnson mean to you?'

'Nothing whatsoever.' The response was genuine, Mayo would have sworn.

'An extremely talented young man who applied for a job with your firm three years ago?'

Waring shook his head. 'Is that who –?'

'Yes,' Mayo said, with conviction. He stood up. 'Have you got all that, sergeant? Right, sir, we'll be on our way now. Thank you for your co-operation.'

'Just a minute,' Waring said. 'What's going to happen?'

'I can't tell you that. All I can say is, Simon Johnson won't be claiming anything from you; he's dead.'

Waring also got to his feet, in an ungainly scramble. His rosy affability had abruptly gone, leaving him shaking. Varying degrees of shock and alarm chased each other across his face as new probabilities occurred to him. 'Dead? Dead, when? You can't go yet! I've a right to know what's it all about, surely. My God, this is more than I bargained for!'

'I'm sure it is – but I'm sorry, that's all I'm prepared to say at the moment. If there's anything you need to know, you'll be informed in due course. There's one thing you can tell me, though,' Mayo said as he reached the door into the hall. 'Was Sylvia Johnson American?'

Waring's frantic alarm was stilled. 'Sylvia – Johnson? Clive's secretary? *Johnson?* My God.'

'Was she? American?'

'No. No – I don't know. She didn't have an American accent, not so's you'd notice.'

'Thank you, Mr Waring. Make the most of this weather; it can't last.'

They left him to sweat, on the Spanish patio beside the pool, though clouds were already beginning to obscure the sun.

161

CHAPTER 19

The golden morning had dulled by the late afternoon into a heavy, leaden humidity. A wind got up, blowing up for rain, but hadn't yet brought coolness. It had grown so dark that the lights had had to be switched on in the interview room, and so stuffy that all the windows were thrown wide open. Caroline and Matt, brought there by Mayo for purposes of his own, sat uncomfortably on hard chairs under the stark fluorescent lights. A stolid-looking policewoman sat in the corner, the short sleeves of her uniform shirt strained around her fat, freckled arms, her freckled nose shining with perspiration.

Mayo didn't keep them waiting overlong. He had plenty of reasons for not wanting to draw out the proceedings. He came in, followed by a man leaning on a stick, a woman and Sergeant Kite. There scarcely seemed enough air for all of them; there were too many people in the small room, seated round the centre table, with Mayo at the head – though not centre stage. The focus of attention was on the young woman, a focus drawn to herself without words, by the sheer force of her personality.

'Mrs Lethbridge first,' began Mayo, turning to her. 'All I want you to do is tell me if you recognise either of these people. Take your time.'

Caroline knew she'd never seen the man in her life before. Receding curly hair, petulant expression. Dejected, a superannuated, fallen boy scout. An impression reinforced by the tweed jacket with leather patches he was wearing . . . in this heat?

But the girl.

For a long time Caroline looked at her, knowing immediately and intuitively, as women often do, but needing to be absolutely sure. She was met with a defiant stare from green eyes, a toss of luxuriant coppery hair. She looked away, and the image of another girl superimposed itself on her mind. Take away thick-lensed

spectacles, drab, shapeless, figure-disguising clothes, a self-effac-
ing manner. Substitute contact lenses, skilful make-up, a new style
and different colour of hair, clothes designed to draw attention.
Above all, replace the habit of fading into the background with the
confident projection of self . . .

Caroline turned her gaze back to the girl in front of her. 'I do
know her. She's Sylvia Johnson.'

'Mr Royston?'

'She told me her name was Elaine Morrow.'

'Her name is Elaine Morrow, but she's the woman you knew as
Sylvia Johnson, Mrs Lethbridge,' Mayo said, 'and she's being held
for questioning in connection with the murder of your husband.'

The relationship between Murfitt and the girl was a fragile one.
Not one to stand up to the pressures being put on it. Mayo knew
it, and Elaine Morrow knew it, too. Mayo could see it in her face
as she looked at her erstwhile – friend, lover, accomplice? The
knowledge that he was going to save his own skin, whatever the
cost to her.

He thought he could sense the struggle going on in her, a conflict between her innate need to dramatise herself, to tell the story
in her own flamboyant way before an impressed audience, and the
innate secrecy of a nature that precluded her from admitting anything. For the moment, she was refusing to answer questions, to
talk at all. Mayo left her with W.P.C. Sutton, a stolid young woman
who wasn't impressed by much, presently let the others go, then
went to concentrate on Murfitt.

Murfitt was closeted in the small interview room with Mayo,
Inspector Atkins between them like the Rock of Gibraltar, all of
them wilting in the heat. His lips were stubbornly set, but his thick,
pale skin was glistening with fear and perspiration.

'Why don't you take your jacket off?'

Murfitt clutched his lapels, then removed it. An acrid stench of
stale sweat pervaded the room. He might have done better to leave

it on, anyway. Without it, in his shirt sleeves, his confident self-image seemed to dissolve. He looked defeated, without the air of being set apart from those who could do wrong.

He licked his lips. 'What'll happen to me if I tell you the truth?'

'It's more what'll happen if you don't.' Mayo wasn't prepared to start trading with Murfitt. 'Like being charged with being an accessory to murder.'

'You can't do that!'

'Can't I?' Mayo asked nastily.

Murfitt was very badly shaken. He'd give in and admit what he knew sooner or later, sooner at any rate than Mayo's patience, endless in such situations, would give out. 'She's been using you, Murfitt. Think about it.'

You could see him doing just that as the questioning went on, and finally he broke at the same time as the storm, at the first clap of thunder. The words came forth just as the rain did, large, heavy drops at first, then a torrent, and afterwards relentlessly, monotonously, falling on and on.

It promised to be a very long night.

It had all seemed so simple at first, Murfitt began, an opportunity to avenge himself for that humiliating dismissal from Waring & Lethbridge. Dismissal, not for being late a few times, but because he'd stuck his neck out, feeling it his duty to inform Lethbridge what had happened when Simon Johnson had received his letter. A high moral tone entered, bolstering the self-justification. Lethbridge's rash and ill-considered promises, cruelly raising Simon's hopes only to dash them again, had certainly sent him to his death. Clive Lethbridge was a murderer. Murder was a mortal sin. Sinners should be given the opportunity to repent –

'Or accept the wages of sin?'

'No, no!' Murfitt's eyes rolled. He looked like a terrified horse. 'I didn't mean that!'

He meant that Lethbridge couldn't have been allowed to

remain in ignorance of the consequences of his action; he meant that he, Donald Murfitt, had felt it his duty to inform him of what had happened. It was only right that such a one should feel remorse. He *deserved* to have it on his conscience . . .

Self-righteous, Lethbridge had called him. To be more precise, a bloody self-righteous hypocrite. A busy-body. And much worse. 'And what do you propose to do about it?' he had demanded. Knowing there was nothing at all to be done, that he would as usual ride over any accusations of moral turpitude, merely laugh or more likely counter-attack, as he had in actual fact done, by finding the first opportunity he could to get rid of Murfitt. The bad timekeeping was an excuse Murfitt wasn't prepared to fight, Mrs Carlene Winthrop and her Assembly of Alternative Witnesses having by then arrived timely on the scene. All this was what Murfitt said. He mentioned nothing of the slow-burning resentment Mayo sensed in him. Perhaps it was hidden even from himself.

'And then?'

It wasn't until two years later that Murfitt had opened his newspaper and read the news that an international award had been given to a local architect, and seen before him the artist's impression of the group of buildings that would shortly be the completed Svensen Centre.

He would never forget that moment of choking disbelief. He knew those designs, intimately, and the last time he'd seen them had been the night when Simon Johnson was getting his portfolio ready to take with him to the interview the following day with Clive Lethbridge.

Faced with the sketches in the newspaper, hardly able to credit the direction his thoughts were taking, Murfitt poured himself a stiff glass of brandy and then went along to the reference library and looked up several of the most recent issues of magazines devoted to the interests of the architectual profession. Sure enough, he found there what he wanted, a laudatory article discussing the Svensen Centre, spread over several pages, together with photographs and detailed plans.

He sat there, staring into space, and then went home and wrote a letter to Elaine Morrow. She was on his doorstep within a few hours of receiving it.

'Tell me about Elaine Morrow. What you know about her.'

Elaine, Murfitt said, was the woman with whom Simon Johnson had lived for nearly six months before he died, an influence on him as strong as the pull of the moon on the tides. She had virtually dragged him from disaster . . . though in retrospect there had always been something several degrees less than normal in the fierce, intense possessiveness she showed towards him. A power which, had Murfitt stopped to analyse it earlier, might very possibly have prevented him from acting as he had.

He had had no doubts that she would have kept all Simon's work, and indeed, when she arrived back in Lavenstock, she brought with her everything Simon had ever done, including the portfolio he had taken with him to the interview . . . and the Svensen Centre designs were not there. She remembered them, as clearly as Murfitt did, even though she hadn't been able to bring herself to look through Simon's work since he had died, and so hadn't noticed their absence. The conclusion they reached was that Simon, on the day of his interview, excited and euphoric at being offered the job, had accidentally overlooked them when gathering his things together before leaving Lethbridge's office.

And that Lethbridge, learning of Simon's death, hadn't bothered to return them. He'd kept them and then, certain no one was going to claim them, had made use of them.

'I'll make him pay,' Elaine said. And that was when she'd contrived a friendship with Amanda Bradford in order to get nearer to her objective, to find out how she might best get her revenge, and grasped the opportunity, when Amanda left, to take her place as Clive's secretary.

And that was it, Murfitt shrugged.

Not by a long chalk it wasn't, Mayo said. 'That's when it all began, when you began to blackmail Lethbridge, threatening him with exposure – making out you'd some proof the drawings weren't his. A serious crime, attempted blackmail.'

'Money was never asked for! Only an admission – to see Simon get his rightful due.'

'Oh, right, nothing but the purest of motives! And vengeance? Revenge? They didn't enter into it, I suppose. Give over, Murfitt.'

Murfitt said at last, sulkily, 'Oh, if you like.'

But that was *all* he'd done, he insisted, gone along with Elaine, made a few telephone calls for her, to put the wind up Lethbridge good and proper – which they'd succeeded in doing. Elaine had been there and seen the effects of the calls Murfitt had made, the letters she herself had written. 'And that's the truth.' He leaned back and wiped his damp forehead; the rain drummed on the flat roof and poured down the gutters.

'Why did she pass herself off as Sylvia Johnson?' Mayo asked at this point, Murfitt evidently believing he'd come to the end of his statement.

'I don't know.'

'*You don't know?* Come on, try again.'

'I *don't* know. She's the sort who likes to play games. There's no telling what goes on in her mind, and no stopping her either, once she's set on course.'

'Playing games in the church Friday afternoon, weren't you? Both of you?'

Dull, furious colour stained Murfitt's cheeks; a hunted look came into his eyes.

'Or were you cycling towards Brome House to keep an appointment with Lethbridge? Hiding your bike in the bushes, and leaving it there after you'd murdered him, using his own car to get away instead?'

'You're making a lot of assumptions, without any proof,' Murfitt said, trying to summon some spirit.

167

'Except your dabs all over the bike.'

'Not surprising, if, as you say, it's my bike! And aren't you forgetting something – how could I drive a car, let alone ride a bike, with my leg like this?'

His protests were token. He was backing down, now that they were getting down to the dangerous nitty-gritty. Now that suspicion was pointing its finger at him.

'Let's take it again, shall we?' Mayo asked. 'Starting with Friday afternoon . . .'

CHAPTER 20

'It's all wrapped up,' Mayo said. 'Elaine Morrow's been charged with wilful murder and will be committed for trial.'

'She's confessed then?' asked Woman Police Sergeant Alex Jones.

'As much as she ever will. There'll be no difficulty in assembling the evidence against her, anyway. Forensic have come up with hairs and prints in the car – fibres, too, though she burned every stitch she was wearing that day, threw them on the demolition site bonfire at Amelia Road. Her plea that she killed Lethbridge under provocation's hardly likely to stand up, in view of the elaborate charade she set up beforehand.'

'By that you mean her impersonation of Sylvia Johnson?'

'And the pretence of taking the flight to Boston.'

They were sitting together amidst the self-consciously fashionable green and gold neo-classical decor in her sister's flat, above the shop, where Alex was staying until she found somewhere of her own to live. Mayo had been unaware that she had a sister, let alone that she was Lois Fielding, Interiors, owner of the small but expensive boutique just off the Cornmarket, here in Lavenstock.

Half an hour after ringing the bell and being persuaded into coffee and ham sandwiches, he was still surprised to find himself there at all, to find that he'd so quickly taken up her invitation to drop in any time, when he and Alex had renewed their acquaintance at the station. Never before had he felt the need to discuss a case, other than with those directly involved – but then, never before had he had a case quite like this . . . and Alex, after all, was on the inside, so to speak.

She was wearing gold studs in her ears and a suede skirt with a perfectly matching striped silk blouse that reminded him of mint humbugs, but nevertheless met with his approval. Feminine, but not fussy. In uniform, she tended to appear rather prim and severe, with her pale complexion and black hair, shining and cut in a sharply defined style. Out of it, she smiled more, the vividly blue, thickly lashed eyes danced, in tune with a cheerful, optimistic outlook on life. He speculated on the possibility of a bit of Irish in her ancestry.

'So why did she do it?' she asked, extricating the coffee-pot from a table crammed with miniature obelisks, statuettes and a malachite spillholder.

'Take on Sylvia Johnson's identity? Because if Elaine, as Sylvia, came under suspicion of any kind, she'd have an alibi, since Sylvia was three thousand miles across the Atlantic when the murder occurred.'

'What I meant was, how the dickens did she expect to get away with it?'

'I don't think it ever entered her head she'd be caught. She lives in a fantasy world where anything's possible if she wants it to be so. The flaws in the plan she simply shut her mind to, and maybe because failure was unthinkable to her, the whole thing might just have come off.' When logic ceased, that was when the difficulties of detection began, sometimes defeating careful, inexorable step-by-step police procedures. 'And you know, there was more than a sporting chance Elaine Morrow might never have come into the investigation, if she'd had the sense to take herself off back to London and disappear, immediately after the murder, instead of believing herself invulnerable.'

Mayo had asked that question of himself – why hadn't she put as much distance between herself and the crime as possible? But that was before he'd begun to assess the depth of her obsession with herself and the effect she was producing. The answer emerged clearly enough during his interrogation, and was simply that she could not have borne to be absent, never to see the drama she had created unfolding.

'Is she mad, do you think?' Alex asked, following the direction of his thoughts.

'That's for the shrinks to say, not us, thank God, but I don't think so, not within the clinical definition. Unbalanced, yes. Over the top to the point of outrageousness, sure. She just has to see herself in some kind of role, in this case first as Simon's saviour, then his avenger. She's an exhibitionist, she exists at a permanent remove from reality, and I think Murfitt was right when he said to me that living on the edge of danger was necessary to her. It gives her the stimulus and the spice she needs.'

And so the temptation to remain on stage had been too great, even though she must, by then, have known how perilously close she was to discovery. 'What's more, if she'd gone back the way she came, by bicycle, and left Lethbridge's car alone, there'd have been precious little evidence to connect her with the case.'

Why *had* she taken Lethbridge's car?

'I didn't know there'd be so much blood,' she'd admitted when he questioned her about it, and he'd sensed her first and only moment of natural panic. 'I was in a terrible mess, and I couldn't risk anybody seeing me. And then I saw the BMW outside the window and I thought, why not?' A sparkle in the eyes at that reckless moment remembered, giving a charge of excitement that banished any fear. 'I drove back to Amelia Road, changed and then dumped the car.'

About certain aspects, she had talked quite freely to him, the parts in which she thought to appear clever. Not knowing that the chief thing which invariably impressed Mayo about the criminal mind was its ultimate stupidity. But then, her whole confession had been a self-regarding presentation, her green eyes brilliant as she made it. She showed no shame, no remorse. Yet all through, she kept up the fiction that she hadn't planned to kill Lethbridge. Which perhaps indicated, after all, a subconscious admission that she was not so entirely unworried about the consequences as she made out.

'What was the reason you went to Brome House, if not with that intention?'

She shrugged. 'He'd ignored the letters, the calls. He had to be made to understand there was no bluff involved. Never mind waving it aside.'

'So you made an appointment to see him?'

'Appointment?' She laughed. 'Why did I need an appointment? I knew he'd be there, working on his precious conversion scheme, most likely. He had probably given orders not to be disturbed – he often did on Thursdays – so I went in through the french windows. I wasn't going to give him the chance to refuse to see me. He didn't recognise me, of course.'

'I'd like you to tell me exactly what happened.'

'I told him who I was, and what I wanted, and he just sat there, sneering. He told me to go ahead, prosecute, try to blacken his name, whatever, he couldn't care less. There was no proof he'd stolen Simon's drawings, and he'd just deny everything if necessary, and we could do what we liked. Nobody would believe, or even care, what he'd done, he said. He didn't even bother to deny it, as if I was of so little account that my knowing about it was almost beside the point.'

It was the worst insult he could have offered her; Mayo could see that. Remembering it, she seemed to metamorphose before his eyes into a different being. Her lips tightened, the face became pinched and bitter, plain, and it was possible to envisage the young woman everyone had known as Sylvia Johnson. The change was brief, a mere moment before she laughed and was again Elaine Morrow. 'He said if he heard any more, he'd go to the police. He actually jerked his thumb and told me to get out the way I'd come, through the garden. And then he simply ignored me. He picked a pencil up and began writing, just as if I wasn't there. I went behind him and I picked the inkwell up and hit him. He fell forward without a sound, and I hit him again, several times, to make sure.'

It wasn't, whatever she said, as spontaneous a response as that. She must have gone prepared with some sort of weapon, but there was no way she was going to admit it. The inkwell had been there to hand, she'd used it, and it added veracity to her insistence on unpremeditation.

'And then, before you left, you smashed the model.'

'The model,' she said casually. 'Oh yes, I smashed that. With my shoe. And then I thought perhaps I'd better muss the place up a bit, to make it look as though there'd been a break-in.'

'It was much the same sort of thing,' Mayo said, shifting his backside on the slippery silk of an elegant but damnably uncomfortable sofa, 'as using the coincidence of Mrs Lethbridge's appointment and actually going down to Heathrow – which she'd no need to have done. But it added authenticity, and automatically diverted suspicion from Sylvia. A bit more embroidery . . . like hinting to Caroline Lethbridge that the reason behind her going to America was that she'd fallen for Lethbridge, which might well have been the sort of thing which could happen to the real Sylvia.'

'What *about* the real Sylvia Johnson?' Alex asked. 'She must have known what was going on, surely.'

'Apparently not. It's not inconceivable that she closed her eyes to it – she loved her brother deeply, and mightn't have been averse to a little revenge on her own part, but that's a point that might never be cleared up. She'd been staying with a friend in Brighton for the last couple of months. Elaine was in touch with her, learned her flight time and planned accordingly. All she had to do was to walk away when Mrs Lethbridge left her, catch a train back to Lavenstock and become Elaine Morrow again, do what she had to do. I wouldn't put it past her to have arranged to see Sylvia off.'

'Some people are like that, they enjoy manipulating others for the sake of it; it gives them a sense of power.' An unexpected sharpness in her tone caused Mayo to look quickly at Alex, but her expression remained cool, if analytical. 'After all, what she did for Simon was manipulation, of a kind.'

'She called it love.'

'That's not love, Gil,' Alex said. 'That's just an extension of the ego.'

There was something off-key here, a personal intrusion that needed exploring. The chi-chi apartment wasn't conducive to thought. He tried concentrating his vision. A bust of Napoleon, brooding on top of a marble column, gave him no help.

Alex, perhaps aware by his silence that she'd revealed more than she wished, returned to the safer subject of the murder. 'Wasn't it unnecessarily risky, pretending to be Simon's sister?'

'The name's common enough not to arouse suspicion, even if Lethbridge or anyone else had known Simon had had a sister. And if they had known, it wouldn't have mattered. Because that Sylvia was American, as Simon had been.'

He ought to have realised this when Murfitt had mentioned the American aunt, and that Sylvia had come over with her to found the English branch of the sect. When Marcus Dymond had spoken about the parents' divorce and the mother returning to America. The fact *had* registered subconsciously, but only surfaced when Kite had spoken, in the White Boar, about Sylvia coming 'home.' It had sounded wrong, it was wrong. Home to Sylvia was America. No one connected with the case had mentioned her being American, for the simple reason that the Sylvia Johnson they knew wasn't. It was this that had set

173

his mind working, pointed the way to the successful solution of the case.

Solution? What was ever solved by murder? And what was success?

He drained the last of his coffee and stood up, ready to go. Alex stood up, too. Frowning slightly, she stepped across to the fireplace and adjusted a small picture that was a fraction out of line. A thought that had been lying submerged in Mayo's consciousness chose this moment to rear its head.

Cautiously he examined it, considered it, but it was too new and untried. It involved too many assumptions, too little knowledge. About himself perhaps, mainly about Alex and, despite the cheerfully tolerant façade, the something in her that spoke of the perfectionist who might expect too much of anyone. Maybe that's why she'd never married. Perhaps not many men would care to subject themselves to the test.

He asked abruptly, 'Why'd you come here, Alex?'

And was sorry he'd asked, although she smiled as she answered, and gave a reply he knew she'd prepared. 'I'll tell you about it sometime. When we know each other better.'

He didn't know what to think about that. He was all at once very tired of thinking at all. He felt middle-aged. A knackered, middle-aged copper – in need of a good night's sleep, he thought wryly, to clear his head and rid himself of fantasies.

'Thanks for the coffee. Good night. Until tomorrow morning.' And the next case.

She smiled and touched him lightly on the arm, and suddenly he felt heartened by what she'd said. Sometime they'd know each other better. And the thought entered his mind that the day might well be worth waiting for.

CHAPTER 21

The best view of the drive was from the room they called the library, named so because it contained marginally more books than any other room in the house, and predominantly those of the greatest dullness. At Brome, books were meant to be read, and the more interesting ones had long since been dispersed comfortably amongst most of the other rooms. One day, Caroline promised herself, one day she would catalogue them all . . .

It was a masculine room of crimsons and browns that was welcoming on a lamplit winter evening with the curtains drawn and a cheerful fire blazing in the grate. Today it was sombre, the thick, stuffy draperies and heavily patterned carpet emphasising a dull and weighty day, with dying leaves floating listlessly to earth.

Waiting for Matt's car, her bag packed, ready for the journey to Brittany to fetch Pippa home, she sat on the cushioned seat by the open window, in the aimless state that had lately characterised her.

There was so much that would have to be done, but not yet, presently, when all this was over. Now was a kind of limbo, between one life and the next, with nothing to do but think. And her thoughts sometimes frightened her. Things were never going to be the same again. A family in which murder has occurred never could be the same again. A murderer had entered and would remain as a presence among them, first companion to the victim, marked and remembered by his terrible end.

And for the first time in her life she would have to make decisions.

It seemed to Caroline now that she had moved straight from the dominion of her father to that of Clive. I shall have to learn to be myself, she thought, trembling.

The decision uppermost in her mind, needing resolution, was that involving the future of Brome. The new offices Clive had envisaged would no longer be needed now that Harry was retiring and Waring & Lethbridge would shortly cease to exist. Perhaps she and Pippa could occupy the part of the house destined for such, and the rest could be converted . . .

The irony of it did not escape her. She wondered from time to time if she had opposed the conversion plans just because they had been Clive's – looked at dispassionately and not swayed by remorse, modified to some extent, the idea might be a workable solution to her problems. Matt thought so, but she knew the decision had to be hers alone. That, at least, she could do for Clive. Accept the best of what he had left, forgive the man he'd been, smaller than he need be.

Matt's car was coming up the drive. Caroline stood up, closed the window and went outside to meet him.

DEATH OF A
GOOD WOMAN

CHAPTER 1

The Saturday before Christmas, with only one more shopping day to go, had been no busier than any other Saturday. The majority of the population of Lavenstock, it seemed, was no more inclined to buy antiquarian books, even at Christmas, than it ever had been, but since he hadn't expected anything else, Edwin wasn't unduly disappointed. One or two small transactions, an old map and a few orders sent by post had, in fact, been the total extent of his business that week.

Maybe he should have listened to Fleur's suggestions. Her flair for making money was, like her imagination, never in short supply.

For as long as he could remember, the business had only barely paid its way, but as even the least discerning customer was bound to realise some time, that wasn't what Edwin Saville was in it for. His pleasure and passion was to obtain, handle, and only as a last resort to sell, rare and beautiful old books.

It was nearly half past four, dark and bitterly raw, and today – this turbulent, calamitous day – unable to shake off that plunging sense of disaster, he couldn't bring himself to hang about any longer, not just on the unlikely chance that the odd customer might conceivably drop in during the next hour. He'd had more than enough for anyone. And he had, after all, a compelling reason for being home early tonight.

Pulling the shop door behind him, he stepped out into the cobblestoned alley half hidden behind the Cornmarket. Strains of 'O Come all ye Faithful' drifted across to him from the Salvation Army band. A street lamp fifty yards away cast a glancing light on the old bow window and the faded sign, Edwin Saville, Antiquarian Books, Maps, Prints, the sign that hadn't needed to

179

be changed since his father's time, because he bore the same name.

'Straight out of Dickens, darling!' Fleur would tease, gently smiling, and wasn't he lucky, because that was just what people went for nowadays. He really ought to have the shopfront repainted, though: shiny black, or dark green, and the signboard relettered in gold copperplate, or Gothic script. She urged him to leave the blinds up at night as well, with one of his old maps displayed on an easel, lit by a lamp left burning in the window, like the fashionable interior decorator's which had opened on the corner. And while he was at it, why not diversify?

Edwin, seeing another colourful flight of fancy beginning to take wing, and already bored with a proposition he found irrelevant, had pointed out that his father had diversified when he went in for selling prints and maps. He considered he himself had gone far enough by starting a sideline in books on criminology among the first editions and other rareties, after his father had died.

'Darling Edwin, the world's changed in twenty-five years!'

And not for the better, he thought, as she went on – about selling new books, as well as old – and what about those mass-produced prints, already framed? Victorian style for choice, though Art Nouveau, and even Art Deco, were popular in some quarters. They were going like a bomb, the fashion had gone back to having pictures and knick-knacks about the place . . . 'You're not listening, are you, Edwin?'

He knew, with an obscure feeling of guilt, that he sometimes got on her nerves, though she'd never actually said so. He wasn't quick or interesting enough for her. But on that occasion he had been listening, and prepared to believe what she was saying, though quite unaware himself of this or any other fashion. If people *wanted* reproductions – her short, blunt-tipped little fingers lovingly stroked her own genuine seventeenth-century Pembroke table – what was wrong with supplying them? She was sweet and reasonable, as always, in the way that so few people could resist, certainly not Edwin.

Only this particular idea he'd pushed away, refusing to think of it. Himself, he would rather do without than go for second best, and he couldn't begin to understand how anyone else should feel differently. He'd held this point of view since it had been inculcated into him by his father, and Edwin rarely changed his opinions, once formed. Though to be strictly honest, denial of anything, the pictures and books he loved, not to mention other material comforts, had never needed to feature much in his calculations. He sometimes felt vaguely guilty about this, though not enough to compel him to do anything about it.

As he turned the key in the lock, the half-forgotten conversation with his wife came back to him with sudden, vivid clarity, and he stood for a moment in the lamplight, his long serious face gaunt. Then he turned away, a tall man in his fifties, raincoated, stoop-shouldered and thin, his greying, curly hair brushed into the sideways quiff he'd always worn. Carrying the bulky parcel under his arm, he made his way through the square, past the carol-playing band and alongside the market stalls, moving with the absent-minded, sloping stride of a man whose thoughts are habitually turned inwards. Intermittently throughout the afternoon it had sleeted, and the light spilling from the surrounding shops and stalls shone on the layer of thin black mud trampled on to the pavements by the shopping crowds. The big decorated Christmas tree stood, as it did every year, in front of the horse-trough in the centre of the Cornmarket, glowing with coloured lights. There was a strong smell of celery and sprouts and oranges from the greengrocery stalls, and hamburgers and onion from McDonald's across the way.

'Yoo-hoo, Mr Saville!'

Someone was rattling a collecting tin under his nose. He blinked and saw a familiar face in an unfamiliar frame. Lola Tennyson in her Army bonnet. The bleached, ragged hair was more or less concealed by the hard straw hat, her meagre figure was encased to the neck in blue serge, but even on Christian duty bent, Lola hadn't been able to resist hitching up her skirt above the knee, a length still mistakenly favoured by her at forty, though why was not easy to understand. Her legs were regrettable, knobbly and sparrow-like. The bonnet was unkind to her thin little face, perky and streetwise, looking always starved and ill-nourished, stamped by generations of underprivilege.

She sounded breathless. 'Oh, I'm really glad to see you!'

Edwin's expression registered no reciprocal pleasure at this unexpected and unwanted declaration. 'Oh?'

'I left my money on the kitchen table this morning, see, after Mrs Saville gave it me, did you find it? I tried to get in touch, but –'

'How much?' he interrupted, reaching for his wallet.

'She did give me fifteen, seeing as how I come in special. Oh, that's good of you, save me a lot of trouble that will, I'd have come up to the house tonight for it, but now – oh, thanks ever so!' The notes he gave her disappeared with a conjuror's dexterity into her pocket. 'And I'm sure you'll be pleased to give generously to the Lord's work at this festive season.'

She was incredible. Affronted both by the glibness of the spiel and the extremeness of her sudden commitment to yet another craze – Lola could never do anything by halves – only surprised that she wasn't actually clashing cymbals in the band, he tried to tell himself that she probably meant well, that her intentions were as good and genuine as those of her companions. That it was ridiculous to feel a hidden threat under the request, that the gooseberry eyes were looking at him with secret knowledge. Feeling hunted, he thrust another five-pound note into her tin, buying his escape. 'God bless you!' followed him, mocking and derisive to his ears.

'Here, watch it, mate!'

Edwin, whose preoccupations quite often made him clumsy

182

and unheeding, had this time blundered against a hardware stall, knocking into a precarious pile of plastic washing-up bowls and baking tins, which the stallholder only just saved with an adroit movement. Stepping back with a muffled apology, his face came into unpleasing contact with the warm and sticky, chocolate-coated hand of a baby being carried in its mother's arms. He fled.

A few minutes' rapid walk and it was all, thank God, left behind, everything he hated – the noise, the crowds, the relentless jollity of these commercialised Christmases. Quiet engulfed him. He strode on in the cold, intense dark, down the hill past the parish church and the park entrance and into Kelsey Road, sheltered and tree-lined, presently reaching the peaceful refuge of his own house, comfortably detached from its neighbours. By then, it had begun to snow in earnest, and looked likely to stick.

The house was in darkness. No welcoming light in the porch to help him with his key in the latch, no curtains drawn back to reveal the warm lamplight of Fleur's tasteful interior, with its Sanderson chintz covers and copper bowls of chrysanthemums, silver photo frames and the rest. He tried to remember whether she'd said she would be out – she often was, on one of her charitable occasions, though rarely on a Saturday evening. He recalled belatedly it had been the Buttercup Club Christmas party for the children today. That was something he oughtn't to have allowed himself to forget. He stared round dully.

Nothing was left ready – neither his slippers warming nor the usual daintily-laid tray on the working surface, with a note to say that there was a casserole on low, salad in the fridge or a meal he might heat up in the microwave oven. She'd never been forgetful of things like that . . . but then, everyone who knew her agreed what a caring person she was.

He hadn't been able to eat any lunch at all, and now, suddenly, he was ravenously hungry. He felt a need for something filling, satisfying and soothing. The large fridge was even better stocked than usual in preparation for Christmas, but mostly with raw ingredients as yet, and he was very much afraid he was going to have to cook for himself. Poking about, he came across a bowl of pork dripping on a shelf, poured off from the joint they'd had on Sunday – ready to give to Lola Tennyson, no doubt, who couldn't afford to be as fussy as Fleur about not eating animal fats.

For a moment he hesitated. Well, Fleur wasn't here to see. Experiencing a guilty kind of freedom, Edwin softened the dripping slightly with a quick go in the microwave, then spread it liberally on to several thick, unhandily-cut slices of Fleur's home-made wholemeal bread, garnishing it with beads of salty brown jelly from the bottom of the bowl. He softened the dripping further, so that when it set it would be level again, then carried the food on a tray with a large pot of strong tea and one of the kitchen mugs into the sitting-room.

With the coals in the grate well alight, easy with his jacket off and his old pullover on, settled in his comfortable wing chair with the firelight flickering on silver and gilt and flowers, on his pictures and the soft leather bindings of his books, Edwin settled down to enjoy the illicit schoolboy snack, nostalgically reminiscent of wartime prep-school suppers, bath nights and his Nana. All that was missing was the cocoa.

'That's incredible!' Nell Fennimore burst out, replacing the telephone before joining her husband in the living-room. 'I don't believe it – he says she's gone to the cottage, to try and finish her book! *I* didn't know her book was anywhere near finished.'

'Fleur Saville's whole life doesn't have to be an open record, not even to you, darling,' Gerald answered absently, in the middle of two down and nine across in *The Times*.

'Well, I know, but she *is* my best friend.' Nell flushed a little at Gerald's quizzically-raised eyebrow, suddenly aware of sounding exactly as she had when she and Fleur had been in the sixth form together at Princess Mary's, when Fleur had already become as graceful and beautiful as she was now, and Nell had been so proud of being her chosen friend. 'But he sounded really funny.'

'Funny, how?' Gerald abandoned his crossword with resignation. When Nell got these premonitions, there was no shrugging the matter off. She'd go on worrying until everything was settled to her satisfaction. Gerald sighed, but without rancour. Her energetic concern for other people's welfare was, after all, one of the chief reasons he loved her.

'I don't know,' she answered, frowning, 'just – off. Rather sharp. Not a bit like Edwin, really.'

'Probably not very keen at being left to fend for himself. You know how fond of his creature comforts he is.'

'That's just it – I've always said Fleur spoils him, and now – it's perfectly ridiculous, he says she may even be away over Christmas!' The last words were uttered with mounting disbelief.

'Good Lord.' Even Gerald was surprised at that – but not prepared to let it spoil their Saturday evening. 'Come and have a drink, my love,' he said, 'and forget Fleur for once.' Nell hesitated, then smiled faintly.

'I expect you're right. All the same, I think she might have let me know, at least. I had all the organising and most of the clearing up to see to at the party this afternoon. It's not like her, she's so efficient, and I'd have thought she couldn't have borne not to see how things turned out . . . considering how much it means to her . . . and she's worked so *hard* to make sure everything went smoothly.'

'You haven't done so badly yourself, love.' Fleur couldn't have had all that much to do, not with the amount of work Nell had put in. She looked worn out this evening.

'She did have that bad attack a few days ago, remember – somebody had to take over.'

'Quite.' The subject of Fleur's asthma was one Gerald was liable to grow tired of very easily.

'We shall have to see what we can do about having him here

185

over Christmas as much as possible if she persists in this mad idea of staying up there at the cottage,' Nell went on, still troubled.

Gerald suppressed a groan. Edwin was all very well, a good chap, one of the best, really, but so damned – distant. Quite out of this world, sometimes. And Christmas was Christmas, after all. The grandchildren would be staying, and Edwin was hardly likely to be a wow with the tinies.

The trouble with Nell was that she was too good-natured.

She came behind his chair and, leaning over his shoulder, put her cheek against his. 'Methuselah,' she said, pointing. '"The mule has thrown the old man."'

The trouble with her also, you forgot how clever she could be.

By seven o'clock, stamping snow off his boots and closing the door for the last time, Edwin's euphoria had left him. The sad, bitter unease had settled on him again. No Fleur, and the anticipated joy in opening his parcel of books and savouring the contents quite gone. And perhaps the bread-and-dripping had been a mistake. The fire was almost out and after he'd mended it from the replenished coal scuttle, feeling stiff and cold, he crossed to draw the heavy velvet curtains against the snow-filled darkness outside. He stood looking out, his hand still on the curtain, mesmerised by the steadily-falling flakes, which had already covered the tracks he'd made and settled a thick layer on the garden, and was beginning to drift against the garage door. Then he walked upstairs to pull the curtains in the bedroom. It was only when he had finished doing so, at the window nearest the dressing-table, that what was on there registered with him.

Her wedding ring, her engagement ring and the Victorian garnet bracelet he'd bought her last birthday, ranged neatly together on the polished surface.

And in that moment he realised that, since that incredible half-hour after breakfast, he had been existing in a sort of limbo, performing actions mechanically, shutting his mind off from what

186

had actually happened. But that now he was going to have to face it, and decide what to do about it.

At that moment, Nell Fennimore rang, and the lies began.

CHAPTER 2

Time was, mused Detective Chief Inspector Mayo, when the Christmas holiday meant Christmas Day and Boxing Day and if either happened at the weekend, hard luck. Whereas nowadays, what with New Year included, days in lieu, and it hardly being worth opening up for two or three days et cetera, et cetera, Christmas had become an indefinite extension. Never mind the crashing boredom that descended like a pall upon the nation, and anybody you needed being incommunicado for a fortnight.

This year, making matters worse, repeated falls of snow and freezing temperatures surpassing all records had further disrupted communications all over Britain, blocked roads and several times brought motorway and city traffic to a standstill. In Lavenstock, even the normally lively little Stockwell, cheerfully bubbling along to join the Avon, had frozen. Traffic Division, who were still having it rough, cursed the white Christmas and envied the rest of the strength with their lesser problems, confined mostly at the moment to minor incidents of a domestic nature – largely fights and squabbles due to too much alcohol and the unaccustomed and prolonged proximity of the nearest and dearest.

Mayo wasn't grumbling. Just before Christmas the worrying, several months' old investigation into the disappearance of a young girl called Sharon Nicholson had been resolved. A depressing outcome, to an extent, in the sense that even though the girl had turned up safe and well, it had not been through police efforts. Sharon herself, who prior to her disappearance had shown no signs of emotional disturbance had, it turned out, been finding her home pressures so intolerable she had eventually run away and been taken in by a conniving aunt. In the end, miserable and unhappy, wanting to go home but not knowing how, she'd pre-empted her own discovery by sending a Christmas card, easily traced by the postmark, to her mother.

The comparative lull after Christmas had given Mayo no choice but to plunge into the backlog of computer information about the enquiry which had avalanched on him and had to be dealt with in closing the case, and not least in finding answers to the sharp questions that were being asked. He thought it more than likely he might disappear and never be seen again under the weight of it. He was just easing the crick in his neck, in a moment of uncharacteristic depression, when the telephone rang in his upstairs office.

'Mayo here.'

The voice of the woman police sergeant behind the desk came crisply, 'There's a lady here would like a word with you, Chief Inspector, if it's convenient, a Mrs Fennimore. She says you met last month when you gave a talk to her Women's Guild. Are you free, sir? She says it's important.'

'Fennimore?' A vague recollection of a friendly person came back to Mayo. A further prod at his memory brought the realisation that she was the wife of the Fennimore who was the dentist up on Quarry Hill, a man with a successful practice and active in local affairs. He glanced at his watch. 'All right, yes, I'll see her, Sergeant Jones. Send her up, will you – or, no, tell her I'll be down in a minute.'

'Right, sir.'

'Thank you, Sergeant.'

Mayo straightened his tie and ran a comb through the thick, short pelt of his dark hair: an ordinary man, with a serious, anony-mous face, which you wouldn't easily remember, except for the eyes, watchful and alert, and the sudden smile that totally changed his face. He smiled a little now as he shrugged his shoulders into a jacket that had seen better days. They hadn't been so formal the night before last, he and the sergeant, seeing the New Year in, raising their glasses in the uncarpeted sitting-room of Alex's newly-acquired flat that still smelled of the emulsion they'd put on over the weekend. A toast to the New Year, and perhaps to other things. Perhaps. Caution had become a key word in their still-tenuous relationship, and not only for reasons of circumspection Time will tell, thought Mayo, deliberately smothering his impatience and fondly imagining he was past the age to rush things.

Crisp as her voice, her dark hair a sleek cap, Alex Jones gave him only a cool, blue-eyed professional glance and a general sort of smile as she introduced the woman waiting for him.

He remembered Nell Fennimore as soon as he saw her, a sensible-looking woman with dark curly hair touched with grey, warm brown eyes that were worried now as she asked if she could speak with him privately. She wasn't the sort, he decided, quickly summing her up, to waste time, her own or anyone else's, and took her back up to his office, requesting some tea to be sent up.

Right away she told him why she'd come, that she was worried about the inexplicable absence over Christmas of her friend, Fleur Saville. The story was so well put together he knew she must have gone over it many times in her own mind previously, and looking at her kind, sensible face, guessed it had taken a good deal of soul-searching before she'd taken matters as far as this. He listened patiently to the run-up, about the preparations for the annual Christmas party given for disabled children, by members of something called the Buttercup Club, on the Saturday before Christmas.

'We'd hired the church hall,' she explained, 'and spent most of the morning getting it ready for the party in the afternoon. Fleur had decided – that is, the committee had decided – not to have caterers, rather to get as many people as possible to contribute something in the way of food, so Fleur and I and one or two

189

others were very busy arranging the tables and so on as the stuff came in – and getting the games ready, of course. We worked until lunch-time . . . the last thing we said was that we'd be back at the hall at half past two. And that was it. Fleur just never turned up, and nobody's heard a word since. It's unbelievable! I know she wouldn't just go off like that, with never a word to me – or at least without some sort of explanation or apology, I'm closer to her than anyone. Except of course Edwin.'

'Edwin being the husband?'

'That's right.' She paused. 'He has the bookshop down Butter Lane – antiquarian books, and maps and things like that.'

'I know it.' Saville's specialisation in criminology had enticed Mayo to step in to the shop occasionally and treat himself to a book or two. A stiff, awkward man, he recalled, who seemed to have difficulty in smiling. 'What has he to say about it?'

'He says there was a sudden crisis with the book she's writing . . . but you know, I'm afraid I do find that hard to believe. Fleur's just not like that. She's terrifically organised, you can't write twenty-nine books without being – *and* put in the time she does for charity, especially the Buttercup Club. She just wouldn't *let* herself have a crisis.'

'A writer, is she? I don't think I know –'

Mrs Fennimore cut in, with a kind of pride, 'You'll have heard of her, though. She's Fleur Lamont.' Mayo had, somewhere or other, but he was blowed if he could think where, until she prompted him by adding, 'Historical novels.'

He'd no diffficulty then in placing her, seeing in his mind's eye the popular paperbacks with lurid covers portraying well-endowed females with revealing necklines. Not his sort of literature, but he'd have been hard put to it to count the times he'd come home in the small hours when his wife was still alive, to find her awake, reading, unable to put down the newest offering. Fleur Lamont had helped assuage more of his own personal guilt than he now cared to remember.

'Besides, to go off so suddenly, and leave Edwin on his own over Christmas, when he can't even boil an egg – it's just not on,' Nell Fennimore insisted. 'Especially not to the cottage, in this weather. It's not centrally heated, only a small open fire, and Fleur can't stand the cold. And I've rung and rung the cottage, and there's no reply.'

'Lines are down all over the country. The snow's specially bad in Shropshire.'

'I've checked, it's not a fault, there's just no reply.'

'Could be, if she's busy writing, she may simply not be answering the phone.'

In his own mind Mayo hadn't many doubts as to what had happened. Fleur Saville had pushed off, almost certainly. Ten to one, with a lover. To spend Christmas with him – or the rest of her life. Something had sparked it off, a quarrel, or maybe the thought of spending the long holiday cooped up with that dry stick Saville had caused something suddenly to snap and she'd simply walked out. People did it with monotonous regularity, walked out of lives that had, for one reason or another, become intolerable to them. Look at Sharon Nicholson. Only those closest to them couldn't accept that they left no traces because they didn't want to be found, and that in most cases they weren't. Nell Fennimore for one wasn't going to be satisfied with this explanation.

'You say her husband isn't worried?'

'He *says* not,' she answered doubtfully, 'but it's not easy to tell what Edwin's thinking or feeling. He's a very quiet man, he never says much.'

Mayo could imagine that.

'Mrs Fennimore,' he said, choosing his words carefully, 'I agree the circumstances of her going off so suddenly are unusual, and I understand how worried you must be. But I think you may have to accept the fact that Mrs Saville might very well for some reason have left her husband. This so-called crisis about her book.

Probably a bit of face-saving on his part, you know, until he can bring himself to admit it.'

She said nothing for a moment, looking down into the dregs of her tea. 'I realise that's the usual explanation, but you don't know them – how devoted they are to each other. He'd give her the top brick off the chimney if she wanted it . . . and she thinks the world of him.'

How many marriages presented this devoted front to the world, and only when something like this happened was it seen to be a façade, a sham? He said quietly, 'Then – what *are* you suggesting?'

There was another pause. Nell looked wretched. 'I don't know,' she said at last, faltering under his steady regard. 'I really don't know. I just . . . well, have this feeling that something's terribly wrong.'

'In an emergency people don't always act rationally. If Mrs Saville left in a hurry, everything else probably went out of her head, it didn't occur to her to let you know.'

Nell clasped her handbag. 'She wouldn't,' she said stubbornly, 'and another thing she certainly wouldn't forget, whatever the circumstances, was her inhaler.'

'Inhaler?'

'Fleur's asthmatic, and she'd never so much as set foot out of the house without it, it's absolutely essential to her. On the morning of the party she suddenly panicked, remembering she needed a new one. I offered to pick up her prescription at lunch-time as I was going into Boots anyway, and I've still got it, here.' She took a small blue cylindrical atomizer from her bag and held it out to him.

'If she's so dependent on it, wouldn't she keep one in hand, not to run the risk of running out?'

'I think she usually did, but this time she couldn't have, could she? She reminded me several times not to forget, otherwise she'd be in trouble.'

He sat, twisting the small tube round in his fingers, thinking.

'Mrs Fennimore, I'm sorry. There's not really anything to warrant starting an investigation at this stage, and I can only suggest you give it a few more days and see what turns up.' He was being tactful. What he really meant was that he'd more to do with his time than chase runaway wives. 'Meanwhile, though, I'll see if I can get someone from the local force out in Shropshire to check the cottage, make sure everything's all right.' That wouldn't do any harm, and he was glad he'd made the suggestion when he saw worry and disappointment change to relief on Nell Fennimore's face.

'Would you? Oh, would you? I'd be so grateful. Probably I *am* worrying unnecessarily, but Fleur . . . she's more like a sister than just a friend, you see . . .' She hesitated. 'Only, I wouldn't want Edwin to think . . .'

'We'll be tactful, Mrs Fennimore.'

She thanked him once more, seeming reassured at last by this big, solid man with his air of quiet authority, and stood up, preparing to go, then said awkwardly, flushing a little, 'I thought you might possibly want to see a picture of her, so I've brought one with me.' She opened her bag and handed him a photograph mounted inside a folder. 'This is the four of us, taken at a Rotary evening earlier this year. That's my husband Gerald, there's Edwin – and that's Fleur.'

Mayo recognised the bookdealer, his eyes fixed a little above the camera, looking uncomfortable in evening clothes, his tie slightly askew, unlike Gerald Fennimore, a very handsome man with dark wavy hair and something of a nineteen-thirties' matinee idol about him, who wore them with panache. The focal point of the picture, however, although Nell too was in the foreground, was Fleur Saville.

He thought she would always dominate any group in which she found herself. There was something about her . . . not outstanding beauty, though she was very attractive and might possibly have had that quality some actresses possess of making one think them beautiful. Small and slender, soft fair hair, winsome face, delicate

193

and appealing, though there seemed to be an unknown quality about the closed smile. And it might or might not have been the shadow that made her chin seem a trifle overlong, the jaw a shade too firmly rounded. She was wearing a dress, dark and simply cut, that made Nell's bouncy pastel taffeta look schoolgirlish and unsuitable. He had the feeling she was the sort of woman of whom you might say, "There's more to her than meets the eye.'

He handed the photograph back, but she said, 'You can keep it if you want to.'

She was indeed not going to give up easily, but he thanked her and put the photo in a drawer, then walked to the door and opened it for her. 'If I hear anything, I'll let you know, Mrs Fennimore,' he promised.

CHAPTER 3

'I'm not one to speak ill,' Lola Tennyson announced over the washing-up, giving the chopping-board a vigorous going-over with Domestos and a hard scrubbing brush, 'my Religion's taught me that – but there's somethink up with them down Kelsey Road.'

Nell wished she had the strength to say *her* religion forbade her to listen to gossip, but regrettably the mention of Kelsey Road immediately had her hooked, and after that she really couldn't have borne not to hear. She compromised by saying nothing, rescuing one of her silver eggspoons that Lola was just about to attack with a pot-scourer.

'I mean,' Lola went on, 'my Debra went back to work yesterday after the holiday, and there was no instructions nor no typing nor nothink left for her. The study was all locked up, and he wouldn't open it, sent her home he did. Not that it bothered her. She's a good girl, I'm not saying no different, but she can sit about all day, mooning, not like her Mum she isn't. Me, I just can't keep still,' she added unnecessarily, as though the constant restless movement that drove everyone else mad was a trait to be envied and admired. 'You ought to get your husband to buy you a dishwasher like Mrs Saville's why don't you? Everybody's got one nowadays.'

Nell often asked herself whether Lola was worth the trouble, but the answer was yes, on the whole, and even if she hadn't been, kind-hearted Nell would probably have kept her on. Lola divided her time erratically between cleaning jobs for several different people, her skinny little figure zipping through her chores with speed – and attention, if supervised – permanently tuned in to the local radio station on the Walkman she carried around with her. She needed the money because she was, as she frequently reminded anyone who would listen, a one-parent family. Debra, who also worked for Fleur, had been a mistake. There were two other mistakes, besides. Emotionally feckless, her capacity for dashing about was equalled only by her capacity for getting herself into some kind of trouble: another disastrous love-affair, non-payment of the HP on the latest expensive video, one of her offspring playing hookey from school. She remained unbowed, undaunted, she knew exactly what benefits she was entitled to under the Welfare State. Nell greeted Lola's twice-weekly arrival, and the next highly embroidered instalment of the serial story of her life, with a mixture of amusement, sympathy and exasperation.

'She's got all the latest gadgets, hasn't she?' she went on, undeterred by Nell's silence. 'He doesn't begrudge her nothink. Mind you . . .'

She gave Nell a sideways, encouraging glance, but you didn't gossip with Lola unless you wanted it told, with embellishments, all round the Wrekin, and Nell decided she'd listened enough. She draped the tea-towel over the radiator and said brightly, 'Looks as though I'd better brave the weather and be off to Sainsbury's this morning – amazing, isn't it, all the food you stock up with over Christmas, how soon you've to start again?'

'Yes,' Lola said, 'mind you . . . what with that row they had just before Christmas, I'm not surprised she's decided to stop away for a bit and let things cool off.'

'What was that you said?'

Lola nodded, her eyes gleaming like boiled sweets, relishing the effect of her bombshell. 'That's right, Saturday before Christmas, at breakfast-time, going at it hammer and tongs they was. I'd just got there, they must have forgotten I'd agreed to come in, just for an hour or so. I don't usually of a Saturday, as you know, but she needed a hand because of the party, see, for the kiddies, poor little mites.'

'Quarrelling? Fleur and Edwin? Oh, surely not, Lola. You must have been mistaken.'

'Oh no I wasn't. They wasn't bothering to lower their voices – and you could have knocked her down with a feather when she come into the kitchen and saw me, I can tell you.'

'Well,' Nell returned, with a briskness she certainly wasn't feeling, 'everybody has their disagreements from time to time, I dare say. And it's not something they like to have talked about – is it?'

'Of course it isn't, but you know me, I'm not one to blab. If I hadn't been a Salvationist, I'd've been a Quaker.'

The call from Shropshire had come in just before Cherry came into Mayo's office to speak about a call *he'd* had from Nell Fennimore.

The Detective-Superintendent, spruce and well-brushed, hitched himself on to the corner of the desk, carefully adjusting the crease in his trouser leg and listened to what Mayo had to say, not making any immediate comment. 'OK,' he said finally, 'I'm with you about not over-dramatising the situation, there could be a dozen reasons for what's happened – but for God's sake, don't let's tread on any toes over this. It might be best if somebody went and had a word, Gil.'

Mayo thought for a moment. 'I'll go myself.'

'You? Oh. Well, you are already in on it, I suppose.' The older man sounded apologetic, but relieved. It was a bit *infra dig*, not the sort of job he would normally have dreamed of expecting one of his senior officers to undertake, but perhaps in the circumstances . . . tact and diplomacy . . .

'Better than Kite or anybody else putting their size tens in,' Mayo said.

'Right. I'd much rather we didn't involve ourselves at all, we've had enough stick to take recently. But you know how it is.'

Both men's eyes were drawn to the Sharon Nicholson files, inches thick, lying between them on Mayo's desk. The stick the Superintendent was referring to went by various names – public accountability being the one bandied about at the moment, mostly in connection with the case of the missing girl. Stones had been thrown, the ripples went on widening. A few nights ago on television the mother, who'd been so occupied with her own life she hadn't noticed her daughter was missing for twenty-four hours, had accused the police of not having done enough to find her, backed up now by the father, who hadn't seen either his wife or his daughter for two years. The sympathy of a large part of the public, who weren't aware of this, was with the parents. If the same public had ever experienced the grim atmosphere, the sleepless dedication of the men, fathers themselves, in any police station in the country when a child went missing, they might have spared some for the police.

Mayo understood Cherry's dilemma. Though differing in the degree to which they sought advancement, they were two of a kind, able, intelligent men, colleagues of some years' standing from the same part of the country, who took their jobs seriously and responsibly. In this instance, it was implicit between them that those concerned so far in this matter of Fleur Saville were people with clout, capable of making waves. Gerald Fennimore was a member of the Police Authority, his wife and Mrs Saville headed more committees than Margaret Thatcher. They moved in circles that were important in Lavenstock – Rotary, Inner Wheel, and the rest ... Mrs Fennimore had already gone over Mayo's head in speaking to Cherry. The Chief Constable could be the next step.

The whole business was irritating and time-wasting, but the quarrel between Saville and his wife, reported by Nell Fennimore, did subtly change things, however reluctant the police might be to interfere in marital upsets. Cherry was right. They'd have to be seen going through the motions at any rate.

'He won't like it,' Sergeant Kite said. 'Police interference and all that.' His expression was uncharacteristically sour this morning, he having spent most of the previous night with his long, lanky frame crouched behind a couple of noxious dustbins outside a Chinese takeaway, acting on a tip-off, waiting for a break-in that hadn't materialised until three o'clock. They'd nabbed the villains OK, but by the time everything had been wound up it hadn't been worth going home, so he'd stayed in the office to write up his report, fortified by a couple of bacon butties and a pint of strong coffee.

'We can't win anyway, lad. We'll be accused of sitting on our backsides if we sit tight and do nowt and summat *has* happened to her.'

The Sergeant looked speculatively at Mayo. This deliberately-assumed Yorkshire persona of the DCI was always more evident when he was keeping something up his sleeve – or when he was about to pounce. Kite wondered which it was now.

They'd worked together for long enough now to have got each other's measure. Mayo knew that his sergeant's sometimes flippant manner, his inclination to jump too fast to facile conclusions, concealed a shrewd intelligence and a willingness and capacity for hard work that he liked. He was keen and took a pride in his work. On the other hand, Kite was learning that you had to be patient where Mayo was concerned, he'd tell you what he wanted, when he wanted. As when you made what you thought

198

was a brilliant deduction, and more often than not found he'd been there hours before. This apart, Kite considered he could be suffering worse fates than acting as fall-guy for a man like Mayo, who didn't stand on ceremony and didn't bite your head off all the time, as long as you went easy on the 'sirs'. All in all, Kite acknowledged, the DCI wasn't so bad.

'I'll walk across and see Saville myself now, my back's broad enough,' Mayo announced. 'Get a bit of exercise besides.' Never given to explaining himself overmuch, he said nothing about his talk with Cherry.

Kite, who'd expected to be sent himself, and hoped to be told to send DC Farrar, was relieved at not having to miss his hot lunch, but surprised, as well he might be. 'Not coming over to the Saracen's, then?'

Mayo patted his waistband. 'Three and half pounds surplus to requirements on the bathroom scales this morning, Martin.' His daughter Julie, studying at catering college, had made sure he didn't go hungry over Christmas.

He didn't explain, as he might have done, the true reason for skipping lunch. Mayo, essentially a practical policeman, had found one of the drawbacks to promotion was that unless you made damn sure otherwise, you spent more time sitting at a desk and less and less time where it mattered. Besides, he was beginning to get that tingle, that faint prickle of intuition, that there might be something about the Saville case that wasn't quite as it appeared.

The shop in Butter Lane was, as he'd half-expected, closed. Most of the smaller shops in Lavenstock still kept to half-day closing, and Saville hadn't struck him as the sort to defy tradition, so he decided to continue his therapeutic walk down Church Walk and along by the public school playing fields, across to Kelsey Road, and see if Saville was at home.

Most of the pavements in the town had now been cleared for

easy walking, though in the suburbs and across the river on the hilly slopes and in the narrow streets, among the small grimy factories and engineering shops of the old industrial part, it still lay in the dingy, inconvenient heaps where it had been shovelled, overlaid with soot. Only out in the villages, Brome and Seddon End and Grendon, was it still white, hard-packed and deep-frozen. After eleven days some of the country lanes were still impassable, even yet. Mayo thought suddenly that there might be a slight, a very slight, softening in the air, a dampness. Or was that wishful thinking, due to a definite feeling of having had enough of this lot by now, old-fashioned white Christmas and all?

It had been a good holiday though, the best since Lynne had died. Maybe because, one way and another, Alex had spent quite a bit of it with them. Alex had always been a favourite with Julie, and her stock had gone up several more points since the time she had helped so admirably and unobtrusively during Lynne's last illness. Newly independent herself, Julie had no qualms about speaking her mind. 'Why don't you two get married, Dad? she kept asking.

'Why don't you stop matchmaking, love, and get on with your cooking!'

If only it were as simple as that.

When Alex had had herself transferred to his division, shortly after his own transfer here, a new beginning after Lynne's death, he had speculated as to why, tentatively reaching a few conclusions of his own. For one thing, he didn't altogether believe that she'd come here solely to be near her sister, who'd opened the fashionable interior design business on the corner of Butter Lane. For another, she'd never married, and here *he* was, now free and unattached, still young enough . . . not all that old, anyway, not much the wrong side of forty. They got on well together. It seemed to stack.

That had been some time ago. They'd progressed since then. But the more you saw of Alex, the more you realised what you couldn't take for granted. And that was the third thing. Mayo wasn't an optimist. He'd early cottoned on that when everything seemed to be going for you, when things were just right, as like as not that was the moment when life chose to turn round and kick you in the teeth.

He gave a small grunt and turned into Kelsey Road.

It was a pleasantly mixed sort of road, houses of different styles and sizes which had grown up haphazardly since the mid-nineteenth century. No. 12 had been unpretentious but well-built when put up in the nineteen-thirties, and had now settled into a graceful and prosperous middle age with its matured garden, creeper-covered walls and a market value over a hundred per cent higher than its original cost.

Edwin Saville showed Mayo into a front sitting-room that faced the road, with a longish strip of garden between, at present hidden under billows of soot-specked snow pitted with the tiny arrows of bird footprints. The drive didn't appear to have been cleared of snow since the first fall, it lay hard-packed under the car-tracks which led to the garage.

Saville did himself well, Mayo thought. It was a roomy house without being too big, comfortably if conventionally furnished and decorated in colours that painstakingly 'picked out' the colours of the chair covers. There were some good pictures and a few choice pieces of well-waxed antique furniture, and besides the warmth from central heating, a huge fire burned in a York stone fireplace. Books filled shelves either side, the gold lettering on their spines glinting in the firelight.

Saville looked taller and thinner than Mayo remembered, and had a fearful cold. He was wearing a shapeless old pullover of the nondescript drab-green called 'lovat' over grey terylene trousers of an old-fashioned, baggy cut, and Rupert Bear slippers, the sort of clothes an eighty-year-old pensioner might have worn. Waving Mayo to a seat on the sofa, he walked across to where, on a table beside a hide-covered wing chair, stood a cut-glass whisky decanter, a jug of water and a tumbler, together with an old book, leatherbound and with thick, fuzzy-edged pages. He blew his nose and held up the decanter. 'Drink, Inspector?'

'I won't, thanks, not at the moment.'

'No? Oh, of course not.'

A short silence fell between them, while Mayo decided where to begin. When he'd introduced himself at the door, Saville had invited him in without asking his business, and made no attempt even now to do so, a thing practically unheard of in Mayo's experience. Most people couldn't wait to know what you were after them for. The impression Saville had made on Mayo on the occasions he'd been in Saville's shop was stronger than ever, an impression either of extreme reserve or complete disinterest – or maybe, thought Mayo, feeling charitable, that feverish cold was just about as much as he could cope with.

There was nothing to indicate the lack of a woman's presence in the house. Everything was neat and dusted, and a large bowl of blue hyacinths on a nearby table, giving off an overpowering scent that reminded Mayo of funeral parlours, was only one of a number of bowls of other flowering plants. But there was the cleaning woman to do the chores, the Mrs Tennyson who'd overheard the quarrel. He cleared his throat. 'I understand your wife's away from home, sir?'

'Yes, that's so.' At last there was some reaction, even if it was only a slight wariness in the way Saville raised his head.

'We've been making enquiries on behalf of a friend of hers, Mrs Fennimore –'

'*Nell?*'

'That's right. She's been trying to contact your wife, but couldn't get hold of her, so she asked our help. We've had no luck either –'

'Why should Nell do that?' Saville interrupted, now evidently quite nettled. 'Why get on to you? She'd no right. I told her Fleur was at the cottage.'

'It was only that she began to get a bit worried, what with the weather and the cottage being so isolated and all that. I'm sure you can help us sort it out, make sure your wife's all right, sir.'

'She was perfectly all right when I last spoke to her.'

'When would that be?'

'Oh, I forget, a couple of days ago. I haven't been bothering her every five minutes . . . she went away for some peace and quiet, after all.'

'She's been at the cottage some time, I believe? Since before Christmas?'

'What are you getting at, Inspector?' Saville's voice had suddenly sharpened. 'My wife happens to be a busy writer. Her American publishers have been pressing her for sight of the book she's currently working on, and she decided to take herself off and work on it until it was finished. That's all there is to it.'

'Over Christmas? Must have been miserable for you, sir.'

'Christmas doesn't mean anything to me.'

'No, it's not the same as it used to be when we were lads, is it?' In the interests of drawing people out, friendliness never hurt, and Mayo had no hesitation in aligning himself in age with Saville, in disregarding the probable ten years and more difference between them. 'Too commercialised by half. Still. It was the twenty-second she decided to go, the Saturday?'

Saville nodded, taking refuge in another bout of sneezing, so that his expression was hidden.

Mayo waited until it was over before continuing quietly, 'What would you say, Mr Saville, if I told you they had snow in Shropshire a day before we had it here – and much worse? That the lane to your cottage has been completely blocked since the twenty-first of December, the day before your wife left . . . and still is?'

The feverish colour left Saville's cheeks with alarming rapidity, leaving behind a greyish pallor, and the atmosphere in the room became uncannily still, charged like the minutes before an electric

203

storm. Suddenly he reached out and splashed a quantity of whisky into his glass, and drank. It went down without touching the sides and brought two spots of hectic colour back to his cheekbones. 'Oh my God.' He sat slumped in his chair, desolation limning his face.

'I think you'd better explain, sir, don't you?' Saville appeared not to hear. 'Mr Saville?' Mayo said, more sharply.

'She's not at the cottage,' the other man said at last. 'Never has been, as far as I know. She's – the truth is, she's left me.' This evidently distressing admission was brought out in a rush, harshly and with so much difficulty that after the effort he seemed incapable of further speech, but there were questions still to be asked and answered.

'I'm sorry about that, sir, and I realise this must be very upsetting for you, but I take it the reason she left was because of the argument you had earlier in the day?'

Saville stared at him and then smiled, or very nearly. It was the first time Mayo had seen even the faintest trace of amusement cross his face, and in the circumstances it was painful to watch, almost grotesque, like a man smiling in the face of a death sentence, and vanished as suddenly as it had happened. Nevertheless the brief flash revealed a different man and with it, astonishingly, the ghost of a hidden charm. Without further expression, Saville remarked, 'Lola Tennyson, I presume?'

'It was brought to our attention that she'd overheard you quarrelling, yes. Perhaps you'd like to tell me about it?'

They never quarrelled, he and Fleur, never. He because he rarely cared sufficiently to make an issue of anything, Fleur because somehow, in the end, she'd always get her own way anyway with that sweet gentle persistence of hers, turning the situation to her advantage or, if that failed, simply going ahead. And usually he didn't mind very much.

This time he *had* cared, and Fleur had known he would never give in . . .

In October he'd been persuaded into taking an off-season holiday and going with her on a cruise to the Greek islands, a happening Edwin had hoped to forget as quickly and completely as possible, and never, ever to repeat. Not that it hadn't been memorable in its way, they'd seen the Acropolis by moonlight and walked in the footsteps of the gods, but the company – and the food! He hadn't had a decent, simple English meal for a fortnight. So that he'd been as astounded as ever he'd been in his life when Fleur, that Saturday morning, over breakfast, put forward her proposal, all cut-and-dried and thought out, for them to buy a place on one of the islands, sell up and go there to live permanently. It wasn't as if they'd be without friends, there was quite a colony of expatriates on many of the islands, she'd gone on, gently persuasive. Of course it would mean Edwin giving up the encumbrance of the bookshop, and taking early retirement. But that didn't matter, there'd be no need for him to work, because of course she could carry on with her writing just as easily there as here. Think of the saving in taxes alone.

She'd never before objected to paying taxes, she earned more than enough – and the idea of 'retiring' at all was ridiculous to Edwin, at whatever age. His father had died at a book auction at the age of seventy-six, and Edwin could think of no better way to go himself. As for the bookshop being an encumbrance! He almost panicked. His life, his love, his refuge, gone. But no, the whole idea was so ludicrous, it had to be one of those outrageous fantasies of hers, that even she didn't really believe in. He couldn't credit she was serious.

She was, though.

But so was he. Not even the emotional blackmail of how much better it would be for her asthma could persuade him to give in.

It was deadlock, and resulted in the only quarrel they had ever had in their married lives, and because it was unique, it was monumental.

Only later did he begin to wonder why, why she had even

contemplated for one moment going to live – to *live*! – in that place – unspeakable in summer and consisting no doubt in winter of a blank half-life in a half-climate, neither one thing nor the other, thrown together, willy-nilly, with other aliens. He shuddered with horror at the mere thought, then remembered the handlebar-moustached, bridge-playing, gin-drinking Waterton, a fellow passenger on the cruise, from whom he'd always escaped faster than politeness would allow. Fleur had laughed, saying dear Bunny was at least amusing and knew how to treat a lady. He could dance, which Edwin couldn't, she was always in his company, they forever had their heads together, he'd told her of his plans to go out there and live . . . Edwin's realisations, like his regrets, came too late.

Mayo let Saville run on, spilling out his story compulsively. He wasn't sure he could have stopped him. He let him continue until at last his voice trailed away, he leaned back and closed his eyes, looking physically, as well as mentally spent with the effort.

'Well, sir. That's a lot different to the story you put about in the first place, isn't it?'

'At first, when I found she'd gone, I told myself she must be at the cottage, that she'd decided to stay there, just for a while, you know – to get over the row we'd had.'

'Did you try to get in touch with her there?'

'Yes, I did. When there was no answer, that was when I knew I'd been fooling myself. I knew she must have gone to that – fellow.'

'Forgive me, but wasn't that assuming rather a lot? A shipboard acquaintance of only a couple of weeks?'

'You think so?' Saville's mouth twisted. 'Well, I've never been much of a catch for her. I'm twelve years older than she is, and I'm not up to the sort of life she was apparently envisaging – though I never pretended I was.' He stared into the fire in a silence that stretched out drearily into the empty years ahead, a man who knew his own inadequacies but could be no other. Poor devil, Mayo thought. 'But I was sure at least she'd come back to collect her work. It means so much to her, she'd be bound to come back for it, and then I could persuade her to stay, and nobody need know she'd ever left. Well,' he ended harshly, 'she isn't going to, is she? She's never going to come back.'

'Oh, I don't know. A bit final, that, after just one quarrel, surely? You can't be certain she won't ever return. Freedom often looks different from the other side of the fence. Or did she,' Mayo asked with sudden suspicion, 'leave you a letter telling you what she intended to do?'

But Saville looked astounded, as though it were utterly incomprehensible that his wife should write to him. 'No, she left no letter.'

'And of course you've checked to see how many of her clothes have gone?'

The question was met with the same blank look. 'I'm not sure I'd know, anyway. I don't notice these things.'

'Passport? No? Money from the bank?' Another shake of the head. Mayo sighed deeply. 'Well, what about her car?'

'She didn't drive.' That was a surprise. Most women of Fleur Saville's status not only drove, but possessed their own car. 'She wasn't mechanically minded. And when I wasn't available, there was always someone else willing to ferry her around.'

'All the same, I suggest you check up on those things.'

Saville regarded him sombrely. 'I can imagine the way your mind's running. You're thinking something terrible might have happened to her?'

Mayo said cautiously, 'It's always on the cards, I'm afraid.'

'You can count it out in this case. She went of her own accord, entirely. She's no intention of coming back.'

'You sound very sure.'

'Oh, I am, I am. Because she left behind her wedding ring and her engagement ring. Even the garnet bracelet I bought her. Right there on the dressing-table, arranged in a row. You can't be more final than that.'

Mayo almost bit his tongue in an effort not to say what he

would have liked to say. If Saville had told him this in the first place, he could have been on his way twenty minutes ago. Fleur Saville had, after all, in the manner of many another bored or disillusioned wife, simply run away. It had happened just as he, Mayo, had thought it had.

All the same, he was struck by Saville's manner, which seemed to him curiously ambivalent, making him wonder what *would* happen were Fleur Saville suddenly to return. Would Saville be prepared to forgive her? Mayo was oddly certain that he would not, there would be no going back in Saville's book, that he was a man with the utmost fixity of opinion, for whom there was nothing as dead as a relationship he regarded as finished.

He left the house in a very thoughtful frame of mind.

CHAPTER 4

The thaw began slowly at first, with a barely perceptible rise in temperature, then came more swiftly when the rain began in earnest overnight. The next morning, when the hard-frozen snow had melted just sufficiently in the lane where bluebells would grow in spring and the beeches be a glory in the autumn, the body was found.

The lane had no name, being little more than a track, only just wide enough for a car, deeply rutted and with rough thickets of brambles either side. It formed the long side of a triangle of land lying in the angle of a crossroads that quartered wooded heathland, outstandingly beautiful at most other times of the year.

The woman had a name. She was Fleur Saville.

She'd been there some time. Since the Saturday before Christmas, in fact.

★

'We might be a bit off the beaten track, but that doesn't mean it's not busy out here,' said Ken Anstruther, the unfortunate young man who lived in the small, isolated cottage centred in the triangle of land, and who'd found the body. Not only found, but recognised it. He was badly shaken, and talking to reassure himself. 'That crossroad's a bloody menace – people use *that* road to bypass the Birmingham road, and *that* one from Seddon End into Lavenstock. They all go too fast.'

Several police cars were parked just inside the entrance to the lane, which debouched on to a sharp curve of the main road, a hundred yards from the crossroads' awkwardly-angled intersection. A blue revolving light on the patrol car first summoned to the scene flickered on the faces of dripping, rain-caped men moving about in the half light of early morning, beginning to rope off the area around the body.

'Are you suggesting it might be a hit-and-run, sir?' Kite asked.

'Well, it could be, couldn't it? The visibility's bad here, to say the least, and folks tend to get impatient, waiting to cross. That's why we ourselves in normal circumstances always use the back entrance from the cottage into the lane here to avoid the crossroads – saves getting held up. You can wait forever there.'

There was an edge of grievance in his tone. In another moment he'd be bringing up speed limits and roundabouts. 'It's a fairish way from the main road,' Kite pointed out, 'where she was found.'

'Perhaps she crawled here after being hit, or someone picked her up and carried her – how should I know?'

Mayo joined them in time to put an end to these hypothetical theories. 'No point in jumping to conclusions before we hear what the doctor has to say, he'll be here any minute.'

A hit-and-run accident in any case would be established by the nature and position of bruises to the body, he thought, making his own speculations. But what, in that case, had Fleur Saville been doing out here – going for a walk in the middle of December, miles from anywhere? In sleet and snow? In those shoes? *And*

209

without her handbag. In his experience, women rarely went any-where without a bag of some sort.

The rain pelted on to the treacherous surface of the lane and Mayo almost lost his footing as he turned to speak to Anstruther. 'Perhaps we could go inside and take your statement, sir, while we're waiting for the doctor.' Anstruther had found the body and whether he liked it or not, he was an important witness, even though he was innocent. If he was innocent.

'Yes, come on. I'll make some coffee,' Anstruther said abruptly. 'Real coffee.'

Kite prepared to go with him with alacrity, looking as though he didn't care what kind of coffee it was, as long as it was hot, a sentiment with which Mayo entirely agreed. The mobile police canteen should have been here by now. Where the hell was it? Theoretically, the weather must be warmer than it had been of late, since a thaw had begun, but it felt cold enough to freeze brass monkeys.

He paused briefly beside the body before following the other two, and stood looking down at it once more with the stoic expression of one who has been forced to accept the frequent sight of unnatural death but still has no stomach for it. It was a grim experience for anyone – though considering it was a two-week-old corpse, this one was less sickening than most. Sub-zero temperatures had seen to that, preserving it and arresting decay; that and a two-foot layer of deep-frozen snow which had protected it from the rats and crows. Apart from its now sodden state, the body looked much as it would have done shortly after death – the only visible injury a deeply-lacerated contusion on the left temple. She lay abandoned, face upturned to the lowering sky, fair hair dark with rain, a layer of snow still under her. Beneath the red coat she was wearing a straight black skirt and cashmere sweater, with a many-stranded pearl and gilt necklace, fine black tights and ele-gant high-heeled black patent shoes. He stared hard at the hands, small and ringless, with short, unvarnished nails, and thought of the photograph he'd seen of her, taken at that dance, the poignant contrast between it and the stillness and finality of her present state. He felt angry at the waste. There was little doubt in his mind that this was murder. He could smell evil. But these were private thoughts and personal intuitions which had better be kept to himself for the time being. It hadn't after all simply been another case of a woman leaving home, as he'd been convinced. Fleur Saville must already have been dead for eleven days when Nell Fennimore first came to see him.

'I reckon that's about it.' DC Napier began to pack up his photographic equipment with the air of one not being sorry to do so.

'Then cover her up,' Mayo said abruptly, hunching his shoulders into the turned-up collar of his raincoat. 'And get a grip on yourself, lad,' he added to the very young uniformed constable next to him, who was looking distinctly green about the gills, 'you'll see worse than that before you've done.'

'Yes, sir.'

Leaving the mackintosh-caped and booted figures to get on with their thankless task of searching, as best they could, for any least thing that might be of significance, Mayo followed his sergeant. He was glad for the young constable's sake to see the mobile canteen turning into the lane as he did so. He remembered what it was like.

In Edwardian times the cottage had been some sort of shooting lodge on the Seddon estate, a one-storey building that careful restoration and the addition of a small garden had made as charming as a toy cottage on a model railway layout. It was neat as a new pin, outside and in, a self-contained little place with a white picket fence matching the scalloped trim to the roof, small conifers and beds of winter-flowering heathers poking through the snow around the porch entrance, and more pot plants than Mayo had ever seen together in anyone's house placed in artistically arranged groups in the large through living-room. Noticing was part of his make-up, as well as his official training; he stood beside an eight-foot monstera while his quick, comprehensive glance took in the general ambience of tan leather, fashionably rag-rolled walls and understated comfort.

'People don't realise that one can practically furnish a place with pot plants,' Anstruther remarked, pleased to observe the interest of the two policemen as his neat, compact figure emerged through the jungle with a steaming pot of coffee and a bottle of Remy Martin, with which he proceeded to lace their coffee, using a lavish hand. 'If only they did! We'd be a great deal richer.'

'We? Just yourself and your wife live here, sir?'

'I'm not married,' Anstruther replied shortly. Mayo eyed him briefly. 'Myself and my partner. He shares the cottage with me – and the business.' The other man's name he gave as David Garbett, and the business they shared as the Broadfield Garden Centre just this side of Lavenstock.

'And you say you used the lane this morning for the first time since before Christmas, sir?'

'That's right. The last time was the same Saturday evening it began snowing. We were bidden to a so-called party, which I have to tell you was horrendous. One of those awful business thrashes with weak punch and warm white wine, and all the smoked salmon gone by the time we got there. The snow gave us a good excuse to escape early, but even so, by the time we reached home the lane was impassable and we had to drive in by the main gate. It always drifts along there, nothing to stop it, really. It comes, as they will insist on saying, straight from Siberia.'

'You left home at six, and you're sure the body wasn't in the lane then?'

'We'd have been bound to notice if it had been. You saw for yourself how little room there is – and we were going very care-fully. It was already a bit dicey, so much so that we debated at the time whether to stay at home or not, but in the end we decided the main roads would be clear enough.'

'What time did you get back?'

'Let's see – there was a re-run of *The Godfather* on at nine, and we were just in time to catch the beginning, so –'

So, judging by the depth of snow which had covered her, and the relatively small amount underneath her, Fleur Saville had probably lain there since just after six. Kite noted the place where the party had been held and the times, and asked, 'What about this morning?'

'We usually leave together, David and I, but today he had to pick up some cut flowers from the wholesale market in Birmingham, so he left half an hour earlier. He used the front entrance since he was going in the opposite direction.'

'Then you were alone when you came out the back way, at around eight?'

'Eight precisely, when I shut the door,' corrected Anstruther, who was evidently a very precise person, 'plus two or three minutes more to get the car out.'

'The lane's been undisturbed since the snow fell?'

'Totally, I swear. Virgin snow, until the thaw. In fact, it was a mistake to try to get out that way this morning. I should have waited.' He poured himself more coffee, added another splash of brandy. His hand was not altogether steady. 'It was her red coat I saw first . . . then her face . . . my God, it was a shock, I can tell you.'

'I'm sure it was,' Mayo said, 'especially as you knew her.'

'Well, I didn't *know* her, not in that sense. I just knew who she was. I got out to have a look, I thought something had blown into the lane, and when I saw her face I thought: Christ, I've seen her before, it's that woman who buys all those flowers, that Mrs Saville.'

Mayo recalled the scent of hyacinths, the bowls of cyclamen that had filled the Saville's sitting-room. 'You only knew her as a customer?'

'That's all. But you don't forget someone like her – she spent more money with us every week than most people spend in six months.'

'And you'd never met her socially?'

'I've told you, no. That's the only time I ever saw her, when she came into the centre. Here, just a minute, what are you getting at?' He gave a short, angry laugh. 'My God, I only *found* the body, I didn't damn well kill her!'

'No one's suggesting that, sir. Merely a matter of routine questions, that's all,' Mayo answered, neutrally official. 'But it's important we have a full signed statement from you. If it's convenient, I'd like you to accompany one of my officers down to the station now to make it.'

Anstruther opened his mouth, but one glance at Mayo's face evidently told him he'd be wiser to make sure it was convenient. He'd misread the expression, however. Mayo was thinking that Anstruther's involvement in the case was probably just what he said, and no more. He seemed truthful and the eyes, he thought, were honest. It was just his misfortune that he'd found the body.

'She's been missing since the twenty-second of December,' he told the doctor, stamping his feet. The rain had stopped, but the cold had not. 'Two weeks, and this lane's been blocked since then. That squares?'

'More than likely. Impossible to be precise under these conditions.'

Never bloomin' well hang himself, Ison wouldn't, Mayo thought, as the other man straightened up, easing the crick in his neck and taking his glasses off to rub his eyes. He'd come straight from the scene of a multiple motorway pile-up caused by the abominable road conditions, and being up half the night had done nothing to improve his temper. His eyes were bloodshot, his face unshaven. He peered out from the fur-lined hood of a parka, his breath making a cloud on the air. Scott of the Antarctic wasn't in it, poor sod.

'How? How did she die?'

'I'm only here to certify she's dead, not to pass opinions at this stage.'

'Come *on*!'

Ison grunted. 'Well, no apparent sexual interference at any rate. I'd say either her head struck some sharp object, or some sharp object struck her head.' He added irritably, as Mayo made a sound of impatience, 'I'm not joking. You'll have to wait for Timpson-Ludgate's PM before we can say for certain, but if she was hit, the injuries to the brain will be at the point of impact. On the other hand if her head struck a stationary object, a stone or something . . . Speak of the devil.'

The purr of a twenty-year-old Rover, polished and maintained in a state of pristine newness, heralded the arrival of the pathologist, Timpson-Ludgate himself, rotund, bouncy and cheerfully energetic, looking as though he'd just had a bath and a good breakfast. His pride in his motor was equalled only by the relish with which he undertook his daily examination and dissection of corpses who had arrived at their ends by various violent or unnatural means.

''Morning, 'morning, what have we here?' Broadly smiling, he approached the group assembled round the body and bent to view it with a metaphorical rubbing of hands, but as the polythene sheet was removed, a startled exclamation escaped him. 'Ye gods, you know who this is?'

Mayo said that she hadn't yet been formally identified, but they had reason to believe she was a Mrs Saville.

'It's Fleur Saville, all right. Ye gods,' he repeated, affronted, 'she's a friend of m'wife's!' As if she'd committed some unforgivable breach of good taste, being found dead in such circumstances. It was the first time Mayo had ever seen the pathologist put out at the sight of a corpse.

He left the two doctors to their consultation and walked thoughtfully back along the lane. The track emerging through the snow

215

was grass-grown, worn through to soft sand in two parallel tracks made by the few vehicles which uses it. Stones against which the victim might have fallen and fatally banged her head were in such short supply as to be virtually non-existent. The possibility of accident was in Mayo's mind remote.

'But in any case, somebody else was involved,' he said aloud. 'It's not on a bus route, she didn't drive, so somebody brought her, or put her here. Why *here*?'

One of the group of officers he was addressing coughed. Detective-Constable Deeley, a big, beefy lad. Good-tempered, slow. Works well under supervision, had been his last assessment. Is beginning to think for himself, Mayo might now have added. 'I know this lane pretty well, sir. Nobody uses it much now, except courting couples –' One of the constables at the back of the group sniggered, and Deeley stopped, reddening as he realised what he'd said, looking sideways at Kite, but Kite wasn't in his usual mickey-taking mood that morning and let it pass. 'I mean –'

Mayo said impatiently, 'I know what you mean. I haven't lost my memory.' Which wasn't what Deeley had meant. 'Get on with it.'

'Well, so maybe somebody intended to dump her body in the old gravel pits, but found the lane was blocked and had to leave her where she was found.'

'Gravel pits?'

'That's where the lane lands up, eventually. They're supposed to be very deep, and they've been abandoned for yonks, sir.'

Mayo decided he'd go along and have a look himself, but it was very likely the explanation for the body being found here. He gave Deeley a congratulatory nod. 'Well done, lad.' The young DC blushed furiously above the Lord Kitchener moustache that was his pride and joy.

'So what next?' Kite asked.

'So treat it as foul play until we know otherwise,' Mayo said.

CHAPTER 5

Lavenstock wasn't renowned for its beauty, but it had its moments, especially on days when the sun shone on the river or touched the tall spire of St Nicholas's church and the Tudor brick of Lavenstock College, the minor public school that gave a touch of class to the town. Moreover, since the bypass had arrived and a shopping precinct had been created, new vistas had opened up, revealing once more the pleasant jumble of old lanes, courtyards and buildings where Lower High Street and Sheep Street sloped down to the river from the Cornmarket. Mayo's liking for the busy little market town was growing in proportion to his increasing knowledge of it. It was beginning to have the familiar air of a shabby old friend, easy to live with mostly, sometimes exasperating, but tolerable even today, seen through the murk of the disagreeably heavy, damp mist which had succeeded the rain.

Butter Lane was one of the more venerable of its old alleyways, some of its buildings dating back to Tudor times. It had been slowly going to the dogs for years. The shops were small, inconvenient, uninteresting and out of the way. But with the soaring rents of premises in the newer part, the lane had lately been rediscovered and many of its ratty old buildings were suddenly experiencing a renaissance. The fashionable 'Lois Fielding, Interiors' on the corner, the one belonging to Alex's sister, had been one of the first. Now the lane boasted – whitewashed, blackbeamed and restored – a small, hopeful dealer in antiques, a shop devoted to selling lace, a health-food store, a home bakery – and Saville's bookshop. Here the refurbishing had stopped. Peering through the dusty bow windows of the narrow building and into the musty interior, with its low ceiling, rows of dim volumes and faded maps, it was just possible to discern an old-fashioned mahogany counter, with a pair of library steps no one could have made the mistake were there to persuade customers to linger. There appeared as usual to be no sign of life within.

Mayo stood with his hand on the door, bracing himself to face the always harrowing task of having to tell someone that a relative had been found dead, possibly murdered, even when, as in this case, the relative was likely to be the chief suspect. He had never yet found a way of doing this easily. He reminded himself sharply that his own finer feelings were not in question: it was Saville's reactions it was his job to be interested in.

'Come on, let's get it over with.' He squared his shoulders and pushed open the door.

Zoe was with him, in the back of the shop, when the bell rang.

Zoe, her pale face sharp and taut under the thick, shining copper hair that burned like a flame round her head. Comfortable old sagging chairs drawn up to the powerful gas fire. Used coffee cups and the remnants of the teacakes she had brought in from next door and toasted before the bars of the fire . . .

Edwin knew how it would look through the eyes of the two policemen as he showed them into the back: shrewd men who weren't easily deceived by anything, who must have picked up the vibrations of shared laughter and intimacy that had been there a moment or two ago, killed abruptly by the interruption of their own unwanted presence.

Zoe had already jumped up, prepared to go, sending a swift, intuitive glance from one to the other of the two men. She knew they were policemen before he told her.

'Please stay, Zoe.'

He saw with relief and gratitude that she recognised this immediately for what it was, a plea rather than the polite formality it sounded to be. Hesitating, she threw a brief enquiring glance at the Chief Inspector, and on receiving a confirmatory nod, re-seated herself.

'If I might just have your name, please?' Mayo asked her.

'Henderson.' Edwin waited stoically, questions and emotion suspended, hearing her quick, assured voice that held its own familiar ironic emphasis as she added, 'Mrs Henderson. I live across the way from Mr Saville, just off Kelsey Road.'

They wouldn't understand about his friendship with Zoe. Who would? He wasn't sure he understood it too well, himself. Except that he could talk to her with an ease he'd never experienced with anyone else. He admired the wry way she looked at life – and she could make him laugh, with a genuine deep amusement which not many people – not even Fleur, with all her vaunted sense of humour – often managed. Like a bright, clean flame, she illuminated the darker corners of his life.

Sex hadn't yet entered into the equation as far as he was concerned, partly because the difference in their ages was enough to scare him off with its overtones of a father–daughter relationship, but mainly because Edwin, married to one woman, was not the sort to entertain, however briefly, thoughts of going to bed with another.

'Don't take life so seriously,' she'd said to him, within an hour of their first meeting. Which had been a new thought to Edwin, a naturally serious, introverted man. He was still trying, several years later, to act upon the advice.

A slight cough roused him. He blinked, came back, and at the Chief Inspector's next words knew that his deepest fears were to be confirmed: the horror which he'd hidden, refused to acknowledge even to himself, was about to manifest itself.

'Mr Saville, I'm afraid I have some serious news for you . . .'

The next few minutes rushed over him like water over someone who was drowning, but some of its meaning must have penetrated the roaring in his ears. He understood that they had found her. They were asking him to go with them to identify what they called 'the body' – good God, they meant Fleur! – they talked of a post-mortem, and taking a detailed statement of his movements on the day she vanished. The implications of that had scarcely made their

219

impact before the next words struck him like a blow . . . they would need to 'take a look around' his house.

It was gone, the privacy he had always so jealously guarded. His personal life would once more be open for all the world to view . . . the quiet, bookish routine of his days that was all he ever asked for would again be disturbed and disrupted.

Saville had taken it quietly, too quietly for Mayo's liking, staring down at his feet, withdrawn into himself, letting Mayo speak without interruption. Only when he eventually raised his eyes was the torment evident, and even then Mayo wasn't sure what it was about. Nor even later when, his gaunt features a mask revealing nothing, and what little colour he'd had having fled his face, the man stood looking down at the dead body of his wife.

They left him waiting in the interview room at last, in charge of DC Farrar, while Mayo and his sergeant went to grab a sandwich and some tea. 'Couple of hours like that, God, that's what earns you your salary,' Kite remarked, straightening the tie he'd loosened as they walked down the corridor whose overheated air felt fresh in contrast to the room they'd left. Saville seemed to use up all the air around him. His negative approach had a deadening effect. But keeping to the book, holding on to your patience and your temper, being persistent without using bullying tactics . . . in the end they had a statement from him, presently being typed out. Not that it amounted to much. He was sticking stubbornly to the story he'd given Mayo when he'd originally spoken to him at his home.

'So, Mr Saville, let's go back to the beginning, starting with why you lied in the first place – all right, then, deliberately made misleading statements – about the reasons for your wife's disappearance. Why you said she'd gone to the cottage to finish her book.'

'I've already explained. I thought she'd gone away to get over the disagreement we'd had – and I couldn't think of anywhere else she'd be likely to go.'

'In weather like that? How did you suppose she'd have got there? She couldn't drive, you said.'

'She'd have hired a car with a driver. She did, when she went to the cottage alone.'

'Something she often did?'

'Not often. Sometimes.'

'But then, when you knew that story wouldn't hold water, you told a different one entirely, didn't you, that she'd left you for another man? Mr Saville, are you quite sure there isn't yet another version?'

When a suspect began to change tack, it was the first sign that he was cracking, that he might give if you leant on him. But Saville, though sweating a bit, had clearly decided the point had come when he wasn't going to be moved on the stance he'd taken.

'What I've told you is what I believed to be the truth. After the argument at breakfast, I left for business. When I came home and found she wasn't there, I knew it meant she'd taken the quarrel seriously. The cottage was where she always went when she wanted to think things over with regard to her work, and I reckoned that's where she'd gone this time. Then I found her jewellery sitting on the dressing-table.'

He stopped, and Mayo deliberately let the silence continue until at last Saville, a rising note of desperation discernible in his voice, broke it. 'You must see what it looked like to me! Leaving the things I'd given her there like that, after we'd quarrelled! Her wedding ring, her engagement ring. As if that summed up everything she felt about me and our life together – that hurt, I can tell you. Not even troubling to leave a note.'

He slumped against the back of the hard, straight chair after this barren conclusion, running his hand over his brow where the sweat had gathered, his shoulders hunched. Mayo felt the uncomfortable sense of voyeurism he often felt when witnesses, at their lowest ebb, revealed to him things they probably had never admitted even to themselves before, but he was accustomed to not liking himself very much over what he often had to do – and anyway, in Saville's last few words, he recalled, there had been more than a touch of remembered anger overlaying the evident hurt; what had started out as justification had become an accusation.

'You actually believed she'd gone for good, simply on the strength of one quarrel?'

'Yes, I did. It was typical of Fleur to make some fancy gesture like that. But what I believed was no business of anyone else's, not even Nell's. If I chose not to tell the world she'd left me, that was up to me.' Saville shut his mouth stubbornly and sat heavy and passive, possibly regretting having said as much as he had, while Mayo watched him. He didn't say anything, either.

His first impression of Saville had been of a naturally secretive, private man, that explanations or excuses for his actions would never be given freely, would indeed have to be dragged from him, and nothing he'd heard during the last hours had given him any cause to change his opinions. That uncharacteristic outburst might well be – would almost certainly be – the last. He let it go, knowing he could come back to it later.

'All right then, we'll leave that for the time being.'

He nodded to Kite, and together they began to take Saville once more in detail over the fatal Saturday.

'Tell me again, when was the last time you saw your wife?'

'At breakfast,' Saville repeated, with a weary sigh.

'You're sure of that?'

'Of course I'm sure.'

It seemed that he was accustomed to spending the greater part of his working days alone, often without speaking to a soul, apart from his wife at lunch-times, when he shut the shop at one for an hour and a half and went home. Not the lunch-time of the day she disappeared, however. That day, above all, he had chosen not to go home. Mayo asked him why. Not hungry, Saville shrugged, but when pressed, admitted that the quarrel he'd had with his wife had upset him too much.

'I'd told her I wouldn't be home. I was being rather cowardly, I suppose. Afraid the difference of opinion we'd had might start up again, that I might even be persuaded to give in to that outrageous idea of hers of selling up, going abroad, simply to put an end to the whole thing. I dislike arguments, it's so much easier as a rule to avoid them, and in the end, what does it matter? There are very few things ultimately so important that they're worth generating a fuss about.'

He'd said much the same sort of thing before, and a dark and dangerous philosophy it was, it seemed to Mayo, this kind of accidie. Taken to its extremes, one that could generate an indifference towards the importance of anything – even the value of a human life.

'But you've told me this was more than a "difference of opinion", in fact it mattered a lot to you?'

'Yes, it did. And that was precisely why I thought we both ought to have the opportunity to cool off, until we could talk the matter over rationally.'

It sounded reasonable enough. Mayo wasn't sure he believed it. 'So where did you have your lunch?'

'I shut the shop up as usual at one, made myself a cup of coffee, which was all I wanted, and stayed in the back until I opened again at half past two.'

'Did you leave the premises at all during that time?'

'No. That's what I've told you. I stayed there.'

'Alone the whole time?'

There was perhaps the faintest hesitation. 'Not if you count the woman who keeps the bakery next door. She came knocking on my back door to ask if she could park her car in my yard.' Disapproval drew down the corners of Saville's mouth. 'She's always doing it, she knows I can't very well refuse. There's never much room for parking down Butter Lane, but my yard's often free because I walk to the shop, unless I need to use the car for some reason or other.'

'What time was that?'

223

Saville shrugged. 'Possibly just before two-thirty, I don't remember. I'd no reason to keep looking at my watch.'

'And what time did you finally shut up shop?'

'I closed early, at four-thirty. I had some books I wanted to take home to look at.'

'Closed at half past four?' Kite put in. 'And went home to *read*? On one of the busiest shopping days of the year?'

Saville said remotely, 'There's not much call for old books in Lavenstock at any time.'

Especially his sort. If he'd read a tenth of his stock, he must be an expert on murder in all its ramifications, Mayo thought, reflecting that this opened up interesting avenues of speculation into other facets of Saville's character, and even possibly into aspects of the murder itself. 'Tell me, how do you manage to keep your business going if there's as little trade as that?'

'I get by. Much of my business is done by post. I advertise monthly in the literary press, and I do have my regular clients, collectors with specialist requirements and so on.'

'You had *some* customers in the course of the afternoon, presumably?' Kite asked.

'One of my regulars came in, just to browse around – Mr Howe, the headmaster at the Comprehensive, he's often in on Saturdays. And a woman who came in to pick up a map she'd bought and left to be framed. Her name doesn't immediately come to mind, but it'll be in my order book. They were the only two customers I had, but at what times, I couldn't say. Early on, I think. Oh, and about half-past three I suppose it would be, Mrs Henderson popped in.'

Mrs Henderson. Zoe. A mass of flaming hair in a fashionable uncombed tangle, a brightness about her. An enigmatic face, nevertheless. About twenty years younger than Saville, at a guess.

Mayo could tell, even before the next question came from Kite, that he'd evidently been thinking pretty much the same thing. 'Why? What was she there for?'

'Does there have to be a reason for a friend calling in? As a matter of fact, she brought in a frame she'd been repairing for me. She's an expert restorer, that's how she makes her living.'

'How long did she stay?'

'I didn't time her. Long enough for a cup of tea and a chat.'

'Fifteen minutes?'

'Possibly.'

'I see. Anyone else?'

'No. I saw no one else all afternoon. Apart from Mrs Tennyson on my way home – the person who helps my wife in the house.' Saville explained his brief encounter with Lola on her collecting round.

'And after you got home?' Mayo asked.

'I had something to eat, then fell asleep in front of the fire. I saw and spoke to no one all evening.'

'Except, of course, for speaking to Mrs Fennimore on the telephone.'

'As you say, except for her.'

They were back to square one. Mayo sat for a while, chin on his hand, watching Saville, but at last, sensing the interview had gone as far as it profitably could at this point, he stood up to indicate it was at an end. 'That's all for the moment, Mr Saville, unless my sergeant has anything –?' He raised an eyebrow at Kite, but after a glance at the hieroglyphics he called notes, Kite shook his head. 'We shall need to see you again, of course, but all we want now is for you to sign your statement, then you can go home.'

'Like you said, he can't make all that much of a living, selling those old books – yet it doesn't seem to have left him on the breadline, does it?' Kite remarked. 'House in Kelsey Road, and all.'

'In this case, probably earned by the sweat of his wife's own fair brow.'

'Oh, well, yes.'

Kite seemed to think that a matter of luck, as if he couldn't envisage writing being *work*, which, considering Fleur Lamont's highly successful career, was unlikely, but he added thoughtfully, 'It'll be interesting to see how much she's left – and who to. My guess is Saville.'

'Sure – but first things first. Which is to trace her last movements. You get along to Mrs Fennimore this afternoon, she should be able to give you a list of the helpers at that children's party. They were the people last known to have seen her, and one of them may give us some sort of a lead. Then there's this Waterton and any possible relationship with him to be established – we'll keep an open mind about that, though I'm inclined to think Saville may have blown it up. You'll have your hands full, Martin, and I've a meeting with Cherry over this Sharon Nicholson thing sometime this afternoon, but later on I'd like to get down to Kelsey Road. I'm not sure we're likely to find anything there after all this time, it'll probably be a waste of time, but it'll have to be done. As I'll be down there, I'll fit in an interview with Mrs Henderson.'

He's enjoying this, Kite thought, pushing back his chair and preparing to carry out his orders. All right for some, no wife and kids to go home to! He thought of what he'd planned for his family over the next couple of days, and cursed inwardly. Yet another lousy weekend up the spout! Incautiously, he said as much.

'If you can't stand the heat, get out of the kitchen.' Still sorting out the priorities of the enquiry, Mayo spoke idly, only half-thinking as he did so.

'Hell, it's not that!' Kite answered, stung.

Mayo threw a quick look at his sergeant. 'What's up, Martin?'

'Oh, nothing.' Kite was regretting that he'd spoken, remembering also that Mayo had mentioned tickets (in the plural . . . Kite had noticed, and speculated) for that concert at the Town Hall in Brum tonight – which he wouldn't now get to. Kite hoped whoever the second ticket was for would understand. A woman? Once or twice ideas had occurred to Kite, linking Mayo and Alex Jones, but nothing definite. Both of them were adept at playing their cards close to their chests – and a very nice chest it was, in Sergeant Jones's case. Kite wouldn't think worse of Mayo for that. But whatever the DCI had had on his mind for weeks now, it hadn't brought a smile to his face. He'd looked tired and strained, acted irritably.

Kite knew, from sources other than Mayo himself, because Mayo's private life was very much his own, that his dead wife had sometimes given him a hard time over his job, and who could blame her? Not many women could take his sort of dedication – and it wasn't easy, whichever way you looked at it, being a plainclothes copper's wife. Twice as hard if there were kids and the wife had a career, as in his own case. They had their moments occasionally, he and Sheila, over the extent of his commitment to his job, the amount of time he could devote to his family, of course they did, but it wasn't serious, though it had made him think, from time to time. Martin Kite, though not an overly-sensitive or deep-thinking man, was very far from being a fool. He was ambitious, and sufficiently clued-up to realise that frustrating himself by giving up the only job he'd ever wanted to do in all his life wasn't going to be much help to his wife and family in the long run, either. Sheila, bless her, understood.

His attention caught by the sharpness of Kite's tone, Mayo's mind was brought back to his own lost weekend. Damn, he'd forgotten that! Well, it couldn't be helped, he'd just have to hope Alex wouldn't be too put out, though she'd been looking forward to the Brahms concert, he knew. He'd have to be a bit more tactful with her than he'd been with Kite. He realised he'd unintentionally got his sergeant on the raw with his unthinking remark and tried to repair the damage. 'Sorry, lad, I know how you feel,' he apologised, 'but there ain't much we can do about it.'

'That's OK.' Mayo was relieved to see that Kite hadn't taken offence, but his was a buoyant nature, never down for long. 'Anyway, with a bit of luck we'll have this lot all sewn up by Monday –' a hopeful assumption that earned him a sardonic look from Mayo.

'We shall, shall we?'

'Why not? It's pretty open and shut, isn't it? I have this feeling Saville's having us on. He was obviously lying. He *must* have gone home at lunch-time. It'd take less than ten minutes each way. They met there and the row continued where it had left off, ending with him killing her.'

Mayo wasn't yet prepared to commit himself as far as Kite, nor waste time on theorising before they had more evidence. He had his own reservations about Saville, in that he wasn't as sure as Kite appeared to be that he was lying, merely that he was keeping something back, but he had to admit that was the most likely thing to have happened. And how blessedly simple it would be, if so. Another investigation like the last he could do without just now. Anyhow, it was something to work on, for a start. They weren't about to go looking for complications at this stage.

'Maybe it wasn't deliberate.' Kite was going on, 'maybe he just pushed her and she fell, hitting her head. He wouldn't be the first husband that's happened to. Panics when he sees she's dead, decides to get rid of her body. Goes back to the shop to establish some sort of alibi, and as soon as it's dark, shuts up and comes home, takes her rings off to give credence to the story of her having left him, and then drives the body up to Seddon End, intending to throw it in the gravel pits.'

'Then why wait till six o'clock? It was dark enough well before five, and the snow was getting worse all the time. And why leave her there in the lane when he couldn't get through? There was nothing to stop him taking her back home until he'd either thought of another way to dispose of her, or until the snow had gone sufficiently for the lane to be passable. He wasn't to know it was going to last as long as it did. And there's always the possibility that Saville had hit on the truth,' he said. 'That she had intended to leave him. That she met her lover somewhere, and *he* killed her. Waterton, maybe – Bernard Waterton, wasn't it?'

'Company director of a small builders' merchants. Known as

Bunny – but he looks like a dead duck. We telephoned him, but his housekeeper told us he's been on a safari holiday in Africa since the beginning of December.'

'Check that. Though it could just as easily have been someone else.'

'Or,' said Kite, 'the boot may have been on the other foot. It may have been Saville who had someone else in mind. And I don't think we've far to look, have we?'

Mayo thought about Zoe Henderson, her enigmatic face. She'd said nothing more that morning after giving her name and address, until Saville had been told of his wife's death, when she had jumped up and taken hold of both his hands, murmuring something which only Saville could hear. He hadn't replied, but all the same, Mayo had the impression that he had been comforted.

'No, we mustn't forget Mrs Henderson,' he said.

CHAPTER 6

Mayo's driver pulled up in Kelsey Road behind the Scenes of Crime van and a row of other police vehicles parked as near the kerb as the banked snow would allow, inviting the attentions of a small group of loiterers hopeful of some excitement. The team which had been awaiting his arrival emerged from their van as his car drew up. Other men were already busy making house-to-house enquiries down the road on the offchance that someone might remember seeing something out of the ordinary as far back as two weeks ago, with Christmas intervening, and who knew, they might be lucky.

'No need for you to hang about as well, I'll find my own way back,' Mayo instructed his driver as he got out of the car and was joined by the other officers.

229

'Right, sir.'

A uniformed constable began moving the reluctant bystanders on as the group of detectives walked towards the house. Mayo led the way, shouldering his way past two men and a young woman, sprung apparently from nowhere when they spotted him waving the three of them and their notebooks away with a brief promise of more information when it was available – his usual policy of keeping the press happy with as much truth as he could reveal, so that they didn't need to invent too much.

Saville had been allowed to go home some time earlier, and it was he who opened the door to Mayo, his hands cradled round a steaming mug of soup, looking hunted. 'Oh, it's you. I thought it was another of those reporters.'

'Been bothering you, have they?'

'They have their job to do, I suppose.'

'Take my advice and say nothing to them, they've already been given a statement,' Mayo told him, realising with grim amusement even as he did so how superfluous was his advice. They'd be lucky to get anything out of this one. When Mayo asked permission to go over the house, an indifferent shrug indicating he might go where he pleased was all the answer he received.

On his previous visit Mayo had seen only the flower-filled and booklined sitting-room, and glimpsed a formal dining-room through the open door from the hall, itself dark-oak panelled to the mock-Tudor style favoured at the time the house had been built. Now he had time to register the thick Persian-type carpeting that ran from the front door and up the stairs, the well-polished antique chest and the collection of framed embroideries and samplers on the walls, and to notice a small, inconspicuous door which, when he opened it, he found led to the garage with Saville's three-year-old blue Granada estate reposing in it. He closed the door and as he turned back into the hall, found Saville's watchful eyes upon him. The man shrugged again and drifted into the sitting-room, while Mayo went upstairs, leaving the downstairs search to be conducted as he'd directed.

In his experience, most people's lifestyle reflected their earnings, tending to over- rather than underreach. He was well aware that writers on the whole earned far less than people generally imagined; Fleur Lamont, however, had been in the top-selling class, but it wasn't reflected in the way the Savilles lived. They didn't go without anything, that was for sure, but neither could they be said to live in the lap of ostentatious luxury.

He threw a comprehensive glance around the restrained ivory and gold of her bedroom as he entered. Indubitably hers, though shared with Edwin to the extent of twin beds and his own wardrobe. An expanse of pale carpet, ivory-painted furniture, touches of gold and cut-glass on the dressing-table and turquoise silk curtains. One wall of mirror-faced cupboards. Entirely feminine, with nothing of Saville's personality at all stamped on the room.

Mayo moved carefully and methodically around, opening cupboards and drawers with hands enclosed in plastic gloves, taking time to make his own assessment. Surprisingly few clothes hung in the wardrobe, though most of them bore the kind of labels which showed they weren't bought in High Street stores. Dress bows were stuffed with tissue paper, each pair of Italian shoes had its set of trees, silk underclothes lay neatly folded on shelves. Her handbags were empty, with everything no doubt carefully transferred to the one the change of outfit demanded.

He stood thoughtfully for quite a while, before moving on to the dressing-table, where her make-up drawer was just as immaculate, with not so much as a crumpled tissue or a few hairs left in either comb or hairbrush. How many of us, he wondered, could suddenly depart this life leaving such impeccable order behind? It was unnatural.

She didn't die here, in this house, he thought suddenly. He didn't know what made him so sure. There'd been more than time to get rid of anything incriminating, and he hadn't exactly expected to find bloodstains on the carpet. But the certainty was there.

Edwin Saville's possessions, unlike his wife's, were untidily kept, not to say scruffy. His shoes were put away without being cleaned – they'd have to be taken away for examination and the mud on them compared with the mud in the lane, as would his clothes, which were mostly of the well-worn, leather-patches-on-elbows kind. Two of the drawers in the chest by his bed were devoted to clean linen, immaculately laundered, but the top one was filled with assorted junk – long-forgotten keys, pencil stubs, old diaries, an empty spectacle case, several defunct batteries, cough lozenges, not a little fluff. Mayo was reminded of a small boy's pockets.

There was nothing more that need interest him upstairs. Besides the main bedroom with its connecting bathroom, three other bedrooms and a second bathroom led off a spacious upper landing, two of which were guest-rooms decorated with Laura Ashley co-ordinated fabrics and wallpapers, their drawers and cupboards empty, and the third a boxroom, seemingly undisturbed for some time.

He went downstairs and through the dark-panelled hall again, with its dining-room on the right.

'Find anything yet?' But they seemed to have had as little success as he himself.

He could see Saville through the open door of the sitting-room, standing with his hands in his pockets staring through the window, with the lost-dog air of someone feeling like a stranger in his own home. He looked rotten, still in the throes of his cold, turning round listlessly as Mayo went into the room. 'Have you finished?' he asked dully.

'Not yet,' Mayo answered briefly. 'Where did your wife work, sir?'

'Work?' Saville repeated, as though he'd never heard of the

word. 'Why, here, at home.' Mayo suppressed his irritation and spoke patiently.

'Which room did she use as her study?'

'Oh, I'm sorry, I thought . . . sorry, through here.'

He led the way through the hall and then through a recently-modernised kitchen, designed to look as though it were in some idealised country farmhouse, with hanging copperware and strange gadgets dangling from butchers' hooks. A strong ersatz smell of the canned oxtail soup Saville had been drinking pervaded the air, but everything in here, as everywhere else throughout the house, was almost aggressively clean. Mayo was beginning to think the forensic team might as well go home. He wasn't giving much for the chances of finding anything at all in this house in the way of evidence.

'Out there.' Saville was pointing through the window to a building of timber construction, about the size of a double garage, which Mayo had seen from upstairs and thought perhaps was some sort of workshop. 'We had it put up specially, two or three years ago. You'll need the keys. It's always kept locked – hasn't been opened since she . . .' Leaving the sentence unfinished, Saville brushed a hand across his forehead, then brought a bunch of keys from his pocket, from which he selected one, preparing to lead the way.

'I'll find my own way, thank you.'

The building reminded Mayo of Doc Ison's surgery, without the waiting-room. It was divided into two, the front half being a small office equipped with the usual filing cabinets, desk and an electronic typewriter – no word processor, he noticed.

The larger half was obviously the place where Fleur Saville had worked, he surmised as he entered it. This too was workmanlike, close carpeted in brown haircord, with plain cream walls, two of which had bookshelves floor to ceiling. Several of the shelves were devoted to copies of the novels of Fleur Lamont in various English and foreign editions. There were two comfortable-looking office-type chairs and no typewriter. One of the chairs was drawn up to a plain, sturdy oak table, which she'd evidently used for writing, since the delicate little secretaire standing in front of the window, though one of the prettiest pieces of furniture Mayo had ever encountered, would have been practically useless for any real work. He walked across to take a closer look at it.

It was made of some golden wood he'd an idea was satinwood, gilded with ormolu, inlaid with marquetry, the different coloured woods worked into extravagant floral designs on the top and the drawer-fronts. He thought it might possibly be French, over-ornate for his personal taste, but its quality couldn't be denied, even to a confessed amateur such as he. It struck an incongruous and frivolous note in this unadorned room, he thought, squinting across the highly-polished surface. And what d'you know? Clear impressions of fingerprints all over it. He retraced his steps, called for Dexter.

'Here a minute, Dave.' He took the detective-constable back with him to the study. 'Get the prints off that, will you, I want to go through it. And when you've done, there's a car in the garage you'd better begin on till I give you word you can come back in here.'

Leaving Dexter to his insufflators and camel hair brushes and aluminium powders, Mayo occupied himself with an examination of the contents of the drawers and cupboards in the other room, putting aside the business correspondence and files relating to the various charities with which the dead woman had been concerned. When the main study was free again, he went back and unlocked the drawers of the secretaire with the tiny ornate brass key on the ring Saville had given him.

The drawers were as immaculately neat as he expected, with every paper in order. This seemed to be where she'd kept her personal papers, and he spent some time flipping through her cheque-book stubs, credit card flimsies, bank passbooks and statements. He also came across her passport.

It appeared that Fleur Saville had paid the bills for the running of the house, and almost every other incidental expense that occurred, including insurances, the cruise to the Greek islands they'd taken in October, repairs to Saville's car. Even with her expensive clothes and the amounts she'd spent on flowers, they'd apparently lived well within their means, within the very healthy income accounted for by her considerable earnings. He'd suspected she must have earned a tidy sum, but the actual amount made him raise his eyebrows. There was no copy of her will.

Making a mental note to ask Saville for the name of her solicitor, Mayo walked across to the window and stood looking out over the long, narrow garden bounded by a beech hedge, its leaves warmly golden brown against the snow. Beyond lay Lavenstock College playing fields, then the rosy red-brick grouping of the school buildings themselves, a quiet and agreeable outlook for a house so near the town centre, though today the buildings loomed through the darkening afternoon and the normally clear, melodious strike of the ancient clock on the chapel tower, leisurely giving out the hour across the fields, sounded muffled. By the wicket gate at the bottom of the garden a fat corgi rushed aimlessly about, yapping, while its owner, patiently waiting, stamped his feet, shot his cuff to check his watch with the clock, and yawned.

'Isn't that a lane running between the bottom of your garden and the school tennis courts?' Mayo asked Saville when he had retraced his own soggy footprints through the snow and back to the house, carrying the files and papers he wanted to take.

Saville replied that it was a track of sorts, but that it led nowhere, except back to the main road. 'It's a bit of no-man's-land, nobody uses it much except as a short cut to the park. Or sometimes it's useful if you want something delivering to the back of the garden.'

'There's access for vehicles, then?'

'With difficulty, and only when it's dry. It's too full of potholes otherwise. You could easily get bogged down.'

It hadn't been dry on the twenty-second, and there'd been several days' rain previous to that. Any car trying to park there in such conditions would run the risk of getting stuck, or at least of being noticed. All the houses had long back gardens, and neighbours from their upstairs windows would have a long view.

He said to Saville, 'I haven't come across your wife's jewellery – the things you found on her dressing-table. I'd like to borrow them if I may. You'll be given a receipt for them – and for these.'

Saville regarded the stack of files expressionlessly. 'I'll get them for you.'

He was gone only a few minutes, returning and opening his fist to drop the jewellery into the plastic bag Mayo held open. In so far as could be seen at a glance, the bracelet appeared to be a pretty example of Victoriana, a double row of garnets set in marcasite. Her wedding ring was a broad gold band, the engagement ring also gold, a conventional twist of two diamonds and a central ruby. Nothing remarkable, considering what events they might have set in train.

'Police investigations have begun into the death of Fleur Lamont, the well-known historical romance writer, whose body was found early this morning buried in a deep drift of melting snow near the village of Seddon End, and who disappeared from her home in Lavenstock on December 22nd, the Saturday before Christmas. The police are not ruling out the possibility of foul play. Miss Lamont . . .'

She snapped off the radio which had been tuned in to the local station, and whirled round, white-faced. 'Did you hear that? You'll have to tell them now, Mick, you just have to!'

'Not on your Nelly! Come on to bed, let's have an early night.'

'Listen, won't you, somebody's bound to have seen you going in and out, it'll look so *bad* if you leave them to find out. '

She was little and dark and fierce, and he loved her more than he had ever loved any human being, even his mother, but not even Jane was going to make him go to the police.

'What about your fingerprints?' she went on. 'You didn't wear gloves or anything, did you?'

'Why should I have done? Jesus, I was only taking what's mine by rights! Anyway, they'll have been dusted off by now. If I know dear Fleur, the sort of cleaning woman she'd employ wouldn't dare leave so much as a tealeaf in the sink. '

But panic screwed up his guts as he remembered his hands running all over the desk. His mother's desk. And fury scalded him again when he thought of *her* using it – one of the very few things she hadn't chucked out, as if all memory of his mother must be obliterated, as though she'd never existed. He'd stood in front of it, stroking the golden inlaid satinwood, remembering his mother telling him how it had belonged to her great-grandmother, who'd been given it by a French countess who was said to have received it – and it may even have been true – from Marie Antoinette, but anyway it was the most precious thing they had in the house. He'd tried all the drawers, and found them locked. He couldn't have forced the locks without damaging the desk, and he'd been tempted to take it, contents and all. Except that eventually having to touch *her* papers – possibly even parts of the current tripe she was writing – would have made him throw up.

'Mick, don't ruin everything, being so stupid! When we've got so much going for us, at last.' Jane twisted the brand-new, shiny wedding ring and he saw her eyes dart round the doll's house room, cosy and warm, furnished on a shoestring and now enhanced with the small treasures he'd 'rescued' from Kelsey Road: the slightly foxed Victorian watercolours, the little nursing chair that only needed re-covering, the framed family photographs and the bow-fronted mahogany chest of drawers.

'And what'll happen if I do go, hm? And they find they've already got my dabs?' D'you reckon they're going to say all right, now go home and be a good boy? With my record? No way!'

'You'll never learn, will you?' In desperation, she banged her small fists against the table. 'I've no cause to love the fuzz, God knows – I haven't yet forgotten the demos they've dragged me from by my armpits – but they're not fools. You've nothing to be afraid of. You're innocent!'

Not as innocent as you, darling Janey, not by a long, long way, for all your Cambridge degree and your clever ideas and advanced opinions.

'Mick' she said. '*Mick?*' And her lively, intelligent eyes as she looked at him grew wide and dark with fear.

CHAPTER 7

After leaving Saville's house, Mayo crossed the road to the opposite side, the as yet ungentrified, less 'desirable' side, in house agents' parlance. But house agents were not, in his experience, renowned for their sensitivity, and the appeal of Zoe Henderson's house was elusive. It lay in a tiny surprising cul-de-sac, end on to Kelsey Road, the last of a stepped terrace of three small, unremarkable artisan-type houses which some enterprising builder at the turn of the century had taken the opportunity to squeeze into a space left between the gardens of larger ones on either side. Large funereal conifers dipped sweeping branches over their high old walls to enclose the little street in a witchlike darkness where the one dim street lamp threw grotesque and slightly sinister shadows. The lowering skies of the day had brought an early dusk, moisture-laden. The thaw dripped slow and heavy.

She wasn't expecting him, but she showed no surprise, opening the front door and standing back to let him enter, drying her hands on a towel. He was invited to step straight from the darkness outside into a long, knocked-through room, vibrant with colour, furnished for comfort and use with the careless skill of someone very certain of her own taste. It had great style. He was aware of what he vaguely thought was Arts and Crafts period furniture in square, strong oak, and William Morris-style wallpaper. A pierced Gothic-type screen painted in mediaeval colours stood in one corner, some plain elegant silver with insets of coloured stones was displayed on a table. The coal fire burning in a black iron grate threw leaping shadows on to shining, polished flagstones graced with richly coloured rugs. He spoke with spontaneous admiration.

'I like your house, Mrs Henderson.'

'Do you?' She regarded him coolly through beautifully-shaped eyes, their colour the light, greenish-blue of aquamarines, slightly tilted like those of a cat. 'My husband hated it. I rather fancy it myself.' She smiled faintly, showing small, pointed teeth. 'Will you come through? I've something on the boil that I can't leave.'

He followed her, past a circular dining-table covered in floor-length red plush, through to the back, expecting, knowing the lay-out of such houses, to find himself in the kitchen, and indeed one end of the room they entered made concessions in the way of a stove and a sink, cupboards and a small pine table.

But most of the available space in this glassed-in extension was her workroom, cluttered by the paraphernalia of her trade. Saville had said she earned her living as a restorer – of anything, it seemed, from china to furniture, and Mayo looked with interest at the pieces scattered around in various stages of renovation: a chest stripped to the bare wood, an iron-framed Victorian armchair ready for re-upholstery, an elaborate picture frame with part of its moulding missing. The place was pervaded by a smell of glues and solvents, polishes and paints and whatever it was simmering on the gas burner. He hoped the latter wasn't food.

'Sorry about the smell,' she said, divining his thoughts and plugging in the electric kettle before spooning instant coffee into mugs. 'I'm used to it, but if it puts you off we can go into the other room, only I'd rather like to finish this thing first.'

'What is it you're doing?' He accepted coffee from her, which she had made without allowing the water to become quite hot enough.

She bent to the surface of the small wooden chest she was working on, her head bright under the focused beam of an Anglepoise lamp. 'Making this look old. It's called antiquing if you try to sell it as a copy, faking if you pass it off as the real thing. I assure you I don't do that – pass it off, I mean, though some of my efforts have fooled quite a few people.' She broke off to look up and give him an ironic, faintly mocking smile, and then became totally absorbed once more as she dipped a ridgy old paint brush into some kind of dark varnish and drew it quickly and expertly over the lid of the chest, then, using a rag, blurred it in.

Her hands were small, with thin, strong fingers that moved surely. With another small brush she retouched the carving and moulding round the edges. The chest was already beginning to look used, worn with time. He glanced from it to her absorbed profile, the beam of the lamp lighting the taut planes of her face. Good bones, her nose small and very straight, a narrow-lipped mouth curved up at the corners, firm chin. She moved slightly and her profile became half-obscured by the curtain of rich hair. A woman like this might easily dazzle a man like Saville. What might it be like, he wondered, with a sharp, unbidden stir, to feel the warmth of that vibrant hair through one's hands? She carefully put aside her brushes, and as she looked up, their eyes met.

'I was thinking, I have an old bracket clock,' he said, 'that has a small part of the veneer missing on the case. Could you do anything with it?'

'I'd have to see it before I could tell you.' He knew that she knew damn well what he'd been thinking, and that it hadn't been anything to do with clocks; there was a gleam in those slanted eyes that without doubt showed secret amusement. 'Why don't you bring it along and let me see?'

'I'll do that, when I've a bit of time.' Or maybe he wouldn't.

'Good. Well, now that stage's finished I'll clean myself up and

240

we can talk properly. I can come back to it later, that's one of the joys of living alone.'

'Your husband?' he asked as she washed her hands at the sink and then came back to where he was perched on a stool, and picked up her mug. 'The one who hated your house?' From the way she'd first mentioned his name, and now this further oblique reference, Mayo knew that it wasn't forbidden territory, that the question had possibly been invited.

'It wasn't really the house he hated, it was my obsession with it. He couldn't compete, so he threw in the towel. God, this coffee's horrible, I can't think why mine's always so much worse than other people's. Let's chuck it away and go and sit somewhere comfortable and have a real drink.'

He could see the husband's point of view. He handed over his undrunk coffee without reluctance. When she'd discarded the fisherman's smock she'd been working in, he saw that she wore the same flowing garments as yesterday, a full, longish printed skirt, flat-heeled Russian boots. With her pale face, the undisciplined hair, he fancied she saw herself as part of the furnishings, as a Rossetti girl, a latter-day Janey Morris perhaps, whom she resembled slightly.

Back in the glowing sitting-room, she switched on lamps, drew the curtains, stirred the fire and threw on some more coal, poured martini. When Mayo saw how she mixed it, more gin than vermouth, he was glad he had declined. 'I learned the proper way to mix a martini in America, where they sometimes *spray* on the vermouth,' she offered, seeing his attention on the way she'd fixed it. She raised her glass and took a sip, watching him over its rim, then she leaned back, the smile fading, staring deep into the fire.

He waited, time was passing, but he felt it wouldn't be good tactics to rush her. Besides, he felt reluctant to move. Despite her terrible coffee and, judging by her kitchen, her probable uninterest in all forms of cooking, she had, he thought, aware of his own tiredness, the gift of making islands of comfort and intimacy. Like now, like the cosy scene in the back of Saville's shop yesterday.

'It's all a mess, isn't it?' she said at last in a low voice. 'Horrible, and somehow – degrading. But I suppose you're used to it – murder, I mean. It was murder, wasn't it?'

'We're treating it as such,' he said carefully, interested in her use of adjectives, 'and we never get used to it, Mrs Henderson.'

'I'm sorry, I didn't mean –'

'I know what you meant.' He hadn't intended to sound pompous. 'How well did you know her?'

'Fleur? Not as well as I know Edwin.'

He waited. It was Edwin he wanted to know about, as well.

She shrugged, and said carefully, 'We often go together to the same sales – I have a small van but it's old and only about fifty per cent reliable – and he's able to put quite a bit of work in my way, one way and another. For instance, I do all his framing. Edwin's one of those people who grow on you, you know. He takes a bit of getting to know, but he's worth it when you do, an interesting man, and extremely kind and – gentle, under that reserve. *She* never saw that – but it's true. So if you're thinking he killed her, you'd much better look for someone else. And that's all there is to it.'

Oh, there was much more to it than that, he'd swear, just how much he'd have given a lot to know. He had a very strong feeling that there were undercurrents between the Savilles and Zoe Henderson which had not yet been revealed. 'Tell me about Mrs Saville, what she was like?'

'I don't think,' she answered, her mouth twisting in a funny kind of way, 'that I should be an entirely unprejudiced witness.'

'Why is that?' On surer ground now, familiar territory, his own country of interrogation and answer, he watched her steadily while still speculating on the nature of the friendship between her and Edwin Saville. An ill-assorted pair, but he had seen stranger affinities.

242

'Since you ask, I didn't like her much. She was clever, and beneath that soft, sweet manner she manipulated people for her own ends.'

'That's not the picture we have so far.'

'That's what I mean. She was clever enough for it not to be apparent that it was their emotions she was playing on, or for them not to care. They were dazzled by her glamour, and she had this sweet reasonableness, charm, I suppose, she had folks eating out of her hand . . . Edwin most of all. People were always saying how talented, how creative she was, how kind – they couldn't see the other side of the coin. Only they'd better not get tired of buttering her up. There were times when she could be a not very nice lady.'

Her chin was raised in a sort of defiance, but when she reached for her glass he saw that her hand was trembling slightly. 'See what I mean – you'd much better not take notice of me. I'm talking off the top of my head. Or maybe out of the bottom of a glass.' She raised her drink, but the level of the martini had gone down hardly at all.

'She worked very hard at fund-raising for charity, I gather,' Mayo remarked, deliberately provocative.

'That!' The firelight caught the flash of scorn in her eyes. 'That was nothing but one big ego-trip! Oh, I know, she could get blood out of a stone, how she did it's a mystery, but it was all for Fleur, wonderful Fleur, how selfless . . .' Abruptly, she stopped. 'There I go again.'

But she'd succeeded in bringing to mind a file with long lists of names and the large amount of money they'd donated. Names like Fennimore, Challis, Everard and others, all well-known locally. Also the scrapbook crammed with photographs of Fleur Saville handing over cheques, letters of thanks, laudatory newspaper clippings – and his own slight feeling of embarrassment when reading them. She added with a spurt of honesty, 'Perhaps I'm not being fair. She did do an enormous amount of good. How she did it, God knows. Emotional blackmail, I suppose.'

'And yet, despite appearances to the contrary, somebody may have had cause for a grudge against her? That's what you think? Can I ask you to be more specific?'

'You can, but I've said too much already. If I really went to town, there's no end to the people you might begin to suspect.'

'One of them may be guilty.'

'Yes. It might even be me, more than likely, on the evidence of what I've just said, mightn't it?' The look she slid him was assessing, and he wondered for a moment whether she was really clever, or just cunning, especially when she added, 'God knows, what I've just said applies to a lot of people and they don't end up murdered, do they? I don't think even Fleur was that bad.'

Despite her apparent frankness, he knew instinctively he couldn't trust her. She'd been quite right to say her opinions were not unbiased, and she'd lie without compunction if it suited her corner. She'd certainly lie to save Edwin Saville. And what about herself? How much of what she'd said was spite, how much truth? Did her dislike of Fleur amount to a willingness to get rid of her? He was quite convinced she would be morally capable of it, given the right circumstances. Physically capable, too. There were those strong, thin hands. She was slim, but used to hauling heavy furniture around. She had a van.

She also had no alibi, as it turned out. She readily confirmed Saville's statement about the time she was in his shop, though by now Mayo wasn't prepared to lay much store by that. The rest of the day she'd spent working on a small table she'd promised a client for Christmas.

'So you spent the whole of the rest of the afternoon here? Alone?'

'Alone in the afternoon, and alas, alone in the evening.' She smiled her veiled smile again. He didn't respond.

Before he left, he paused at the door to ask one more question. He knew he needn't prevaricate with her, and asked it outright.

'A *lover*?' The astounded look on her face gave him his answer, it almost, but not quite, gave way to a laugh. 'I'm sorry, but you don't know how funny that is. Fleur? A lover? The only person Fleur Saville ever loved was Fleur Saville. No, Mr Mayo, you're on the wrong tack there.'

Mayo was still thinking about Zoe Henderson and what she'd said when, ten minutes later, as he reached Milford Road and the brightly-lit car park of the police station, he spotted Alex going off duty. He waved and waited beside her car until she should reach it, the contrast between the two women, one so recently met and one so familiar, striking him forcefully. The one, malicious and having within her nature the capacity, if not the willingness, to destroy, the other so . . . but, as usual when trying to define Alex, he was brought up short, and it occurred to him that even the way she was walking towards him, tall and slim-waisted, with a dancer's grace yet ever so slightly hesitant, was symbolic of her attitude towards him: eager, yet holding back, a barrier he couldn't ever quite break through.

'Gil. How's things?' she asked with a smile.

'Hardly started yet.'

He didn't want to talk about the case. He'd had to make his apologies to her about the concert over the telephone, and as he'd expected, she'd made no fuss. She might ask her sister Lois to go with her, she'd said, take up the extra ticket. He said again now how sorry he was, still feeling he'd let her down badly. On the other hand, what could he do about it? Not a damn thing.

'It doesn't matter. Another time, hm?'

Her expression was neutral, not conveying the usual matter-of-fact acceptance of the exigencies of his job, which she understood only too well, being in a better position than most to do so. She accepted without question that in this relationship there was no place for the tears and recriminations that had eroded and worn away the fabric of his marriage.

245

She swung her long legs into the driving seat and wound down the window, and he got a closer look at her face. 'You all right, love?'

'Sure. I'm fine, why?'

'You don't look it.'

She never had a great deal of colour, her complexion was naturally clear and pale, but today she seemed drained, there were smudges under those very dark blue eyes. In fact she looked washed out. He might have put it down to the cold glare of the lighting where they stood, but it was more than that – a lassitude about her as well that was unusual. She admitted, 'I just didn't seem to sleep very well last night for some reason.'

'Have an early night tonight, then.' He added carefully, watching her, 'Wish I could do the same, but I'm likely to be here till God knows what time.'

She smiled faintly, understanding what he meant, though perhaps not fully. Julie had gone back to her flat in Birmingham earlier than was strictly needful, before the end of her Christmas vacation, either using heavy-handed tact or more likely, as Mayo suspected, because there was a boyfriend of her own in the offing. His response to this was ambivalent. He liked to think of himself as a liberal-thinking parent, but he found he didn't much care for the implications of Julie's new emancipation. On the other hand, his own private life was restricted when she was at home, since he couldn't bring himself to come out with the true nature of his association with Alex. Not to his daughter, suspect what she might. He wasn't that kind of father, either.

Alex leaned forward out of the window and plucked a tiny piece of fluff from his lapel. He was suddenly conscious of his old jacket. Alex, always pin-neat herself, could make him feel a slob. Time he went shopping for a new jacket, only Lynne had bought this one for him and somehow, getting rid of it didn't seem right. Not just yet, anyway.

'I'll take your advice,' she said.

'Think on you do.' Unexpectedly, he reached out to give her cheek the briefest of touches.

She watched him swing away and take the front steps of the building energetically, a tall man, straight and powerful, until he'd disappeared, then she slipped into gear and drove her car smoothly and expertly through the complicated one-way system of the town towards her flat. He would have been amazed if he had known what was going on inside her head, even guessed at the increasingly desperate thoughts tumbling around there. She was afraid his patience must soon run out, and she couldn't blame him. It shouldn't be like this, I'm not being fair to him, she thought. What's *wrong* with me, for heaven's sake? Why isn't it ever any good? And what am I going to do about it? Questions that never left her alone for very long these days.

Not entirely satisfied by Alex's reassurances, but unable to say why, Mayo put the niggle of worry to the back of his mind as he went inside. He paused by Atkins' desk, where the Inspector sat drinking tea. All around him, telephones rang and were intercepted, typewriters clicked busily, computer screen cursors flashed continuously, but Atkins was oblivious, frowning at his typewriter, his pipe drawing furiously.

'Still here, George? Haven't you got a home to go to?'

Atkins put his mug down patiently on the counter, rested his pipe in the ashtray, and waited. The perfunctory nod he gave Mayo was his usual, universal method of greeting, nothing personal in it.

Mayo picked up the already-typed sheets of Atkins' report lying on his desk, and scanned it as best he could, making his way through the single-spaced, barely legible print, unsullied by any paragraph separations, few full stops and no commas. He'd told George so many times to get a new ribbon in his typewriter and a dictionary and been ignored, he'd ceased to bother. He said, 'This Mrs Tennyson and her daughter – did you send somebody down to get their prints?'

'This afternoon.'

'Anything useful I should know about either of them, before I see them?'

If there was anything, Atkins would know. Unambitiously but tirelessly plodding his way through until retirement, he had unplumbed depths of information on all sorts and conditions of people living in the borough of Lavenstock. It was just as quick, and frequently more enlightening, to ask him what you wanted to know than to run the questions through the computer. He never forgot a case. His work was his life and his love. It was rumoured at the station that his wife had had twins without his being aware she was expecting, until after the event.

'Plenty,' Atkins said, 'and you'd better mind how you go. Not the size of two pennorth o' copper, she isn't, but size has nothing to do with it.'

'Like that, is it? One of our customers?'

'Not exactly, but she's been mixed up with some funny folk in her time. And that Kev of hers is a right pain. The girl's all right, though, and the youngest lad – he's at the Tech. Hear their ma's joined the Sally Army now – won't last long, few more weeks at most.'

'You reckon?'

'Nothing else has, yet.'

Mayo perched on the edge of the desk, and in the interests of encouraging Atkins to continue ignored the evilly-smouldering pipe.

'Like this, see.' Atkins proceeded to give Mayo a succinct, selective account of Lola Tennyson's varied and colourful activities: years ago, she'd been employed as a hostess at the Rose, the town's only so-called nightclub – 'and you know what that means.' That Kev of hers had been put on probation at thirteen . . . one of her live-in partners had regularly beaten her up and ended up doing time for GBH . . . she'd once kept a market stall selling second-hand clothes, toting them there in an old pram, until Kev had set fire to the shed where she'd kept them with a tossed away fag end . . . 'I won't go on. Want me to fix up a time for you to see her?'

Mayo's private opinion was that Mrs Tennyson sounded more sinned against than sinning. 'No, best leave it and I'll sort it out myself when it suits. Thanks, George.'

Atkins nodded and took up his cooling tea.

CHAPTER 8

Upstairs, Mayo found Kite ready with the information that Saville's account of his movements on the day his wife disappeared had been checked and found substantially correct. 'Not that it helps him much. All in all,' he remarked, 'less than an hour of his afternoon is accounted for.'

'Anything yet on Mrs Saville's movements?'

'Not a dickey-bird so far. Nobody seems to have seen her since she left the hall at twelve-thirty that Saturday – none of those helpers we've already seen, that is. Which is all of them, except Mrs Pound the vicar's wife, Mrs Fennimore, and Mrs Challis.'

'Mrs Challis, the JP?'

'Yes. She lives out at Lattimer Wood, so I rang first, but there's been no answer all day. And Mrs Fennimore set off this afternoon to babysit for their daughter and won't be home until late tonight. Mrs Pound was out as well, it was the vicar who gave me the names of the helpers. None of them saw her after they finished at half-twelve. There's two sisters, though, Miss Amy and Miss Violet Wood, who were a bit more helpful. They couldn't say why, exactly, but they thought she seemed a bit strange that morning. They're a couple of old ducks who obviously thought the sun shone out of her, but they're a bit vague, and the nearest either of them could come to it was that she seemed preoccupied. Not quite like her usual dear self, was how they put it.'

Kite had interviewed the two old ladies himself. Had they noticed if she was wearing her rings, he'd enquired, a point that Mayo had specifically wished to be raised.

'Her rings?' repeated Amy, the vague, sweet-faced one, shaking her head.

'Of course she was wearing her wedding ring – and I'm quite sure the pretty ruby and diamond one as well,' asserted Violet, the one who used make-up. 'I always notice people's jewellery – and their hands. Such nice hands she had.' Looking complacently at her own, still white and unblotched with the spots of age, heavily encumbered with sapphires and diamonds winking in old-fashioned gold settings.

'Not much to go on, is it?' Mayo commented.

'But it seems to confirm she went home.'

'So it would seem.' Mayo was non-committal. 'What else have we turned up?'

Kite summarised for Mayo's benefit the various reports relating to Saville's alibi collected from the DCs detailed to make the enquiries. 'First there's Mr Howe, the head of the Comprehensive. He went into the shop that Saturday just as Saville was opening up at half-two, and left about five to three without buying anything. He was watching the time, because his parking was due to run out just after the hour. Then the other customer, a girl by the name of Janet Rainbow from Branxmore, called to collect the map Saville had had framed for her. She works at Tixall's Estate Agents, and I sent Deeley to see her. She told him she dashed in to pick up the map – it was a Christmas present for her dad – but she'd no idea of the time. Mr Howe recalls her coming in as he left, though. She used to be one of his pupils and they exchanged the compliments of the season. She was in the shop only as long as it took to wrap the parcel and pay for it – probably about five or ten minutes.'

'What about the woman at the shop next door?'

'Mrs Wilson at The Baker's Dozen? I saw her myself. She went to ask Saville about parking her car in his yard a minute or two after one o'clock –'

'I thought he said it was just before two-thirty?' Mayo interrupted sharply.

'That was the second time. The first time was about five past one, but he'd already locked up – and there was no answer when she knocked. He could've been trying to pull a fast one there, saying he never went out all through lunch-time. '

'Not necessarily. He hardly strikes me as the sort to open up when he's taking his lunch-break, especially if he knew who it was. He made it plain he finds her a nuisance.'

'That makes two of them – I mean, she doesn't much care for him, either, I'd guess, though she was careful not to say so. She thought better of his wife. Lovely lady, Mrs Saville, she said. In fact, everybody we've spoken to so far seems to have had a good word for her.'

'I dare say. Sinners have a funny habit of becoming saints once they're dead, and vice-versa, haven't you noticed? It was half-past two, as Saville said, when she tried again, Mrs Wilson?'

'Just before. She wouldn't have asked him at all, she says, only she couldn't find anywhere else to park. Her own little yard only has room for the shop's delivery van. She was on about the lack of parking round there and I must agree, it's getting more chaotic by the day –'

'They'd have enough to say if they got a multi-storey car park shoved up bang in the middle of their trendy nostalgia,' Mayo remarked, intercepting the telephone on its second ring. 'Mayo here.'

'Glad I've caught you, Chief Inspector,' came Timpson-Ludgate's rich, fruity voice, equilibrium apparently restored after the shock to his social system. 'Thought you'd like to know what I've found.'

'Already! You've been quick off the mark!'

'Knew you'd be anxious to know. Besides, old son, I'm hopefully off tonight to Austria for a spot of ski-ing.' Ah, Mayo thought cynically, all was explained. But he wasn't grumbling; if it hadn't been for Timpson-Ludgate's holiday, he wouldn't have had his report this early. 'That is, if you don't find any more murders for me.'

'Murder, was it, then?'

'Let's put it this way – injuries like that are neither self-inflicted nor accidental. You'll be having my official report later, but I can tell you now that death was due to a subdural haemorrhage –'

'Keep it simple, please.'

Timpson-Ludgate gave a grunt of amusement. 'She died from a blow to the left temple.'

'Not a fall?'

'No, a single, direct blow.'

'What kind of object are we looking for? Heavy? Blunt?'

'Sharp – not necessarily heavy, but applied with considerable force. I wouldn't like to say what, but I'd say something with a sharp, right-angled corner, something with a certain thickness to it. Possibly metal, since I found no splinters or fragments of any kind. I can also tell you she may have been left curled up for some hours before she was dumped where she was found.'

'In a car boot, for instance?'

'Very likely.'

'Time of death?'

'Ah, well now. All you've got to do is find out when she had her last meal. This Arctic weather we've been having did a good job for us, preserving her like that, so it's possible to tell she died within a couple of hours of eating. Bread and cheese, practically undigested.'

Mayo's own stomach churned as he reflected for a second on the horrible aspects of the pathologist's job. 'Couple of hours, you say? That's interesting. Well, thank you for your trouble. I'm sorry it's thawing, I hope they don't have to use the snow-machines in Austria. Enjoy yourself.'

'That's what I'm paid for. The trouble, I mean. Cheers.' Mayo put the phone down.

'You heard that. All the stops out now, Martin. We've got a murder on our hands.'

Kite grunted. 'What's new? I mean, we always knew that, didn't we?'

'I've no objection to having it confirmed, all the same. There was always the outside chance of an accident.' Mayo went on to repeat the rest of the pathologist's finding to a now attentive Kite.

Kite said, 'That makes it between, say, about one o'clock and three when she died – if she went straight home from the church hall and ate her lunch.'

Quite possible, then, for Saville to have killed her. Saville, their only suspect so far, one with probable motive, and maybe opportunity. But Mayo remembered the conviction he'd had at Kelsey Road, that Fleur Saville hadn't died in her own home. With nothing to support an intuition that the reasons for Fleur Saville's death weren't that simple, an instinct that this wasn't how it had happened, he said, 'A big "if", that. We've nothing yet to show that she did in fact go home.'

'Except the jewellery she left behind.'

Mayo rubbed a hand down the length of his face. It had been a long day. Only twelve hours since the case had broken, but twelve hours on the go, with only the odd snatched sandwich in between all the work that went into setting up the machinery of an enquiry into a death in mysterious circumstances. A death that was now officially murder. Deeper investigations. Nets that would have to be spread wider.

What, for instance, about the dead woman herself? He took from his desk drawer the photo Nell Fennimore had left and studied it. Had she been the woman pictured by Zoe Henderson? Or one talented, highly thought of, the tireless worker for good causes, liked and admired by all? Leading a blameless life, with nothing to hide? He was inclined – he'd go no further than that at the moment – to reserve judgement on the latter. But anyone, for God's sake, as pathologically tidy as Fleur Saville, surely had something to hide – unless someone had deliberately tidied away all traces of her. Maybe her papers would tell them something about her? They were there, waiting to be gone through. Tonight.

He could feel himself sagging in his chair. He needed a shot in the arm: a good meal and a drink, relaxation with a book maybe – reading, as well as music, was a deep pleasure for him. He thought of Alex, alone in her flat . . . diversions and digressions . . .

'Come on, Sherlock,' he said, indicating the parcel of Fleur Saville's correspondence and files on the table in the corner. 'Sooner we get moving, sooner we see our beds.'

Kite stifled a cracking yawn and ran a hand through his hair. 'Some coffee and a couple of rounds of sandwiches before we begin, all right?' he stipulated.

Mayo agreed. 'It'll give us time to get our second wind, but for the love of Mike let's go downstairs and get something hot.' Even the canteen egg and chips – or in Mayo's own case, a boring and virtuous omelette – was preferable to another goddam sandwich.

It was past ten when Mayo got home: He showered and went straight to bed with a glass of scotch and the latest Fleur Lamont, *Salamander Fire*, said to be her best, to keep him company. He found it colourful and highly inventive, suggestive rather than explicit, and ultimately boring. He tried to persevere with it, but with limited success, managing only to get to page thirty-five before dropping off, the book sliding from his fingers.

He didn't expect to find Saville at his shop the following morning, but he made the bookshop in Butter Lane his first call and did in fact find him there, checking through a pile of catalogues in the back room in a fug of heat from the gas fire and a bubbling coffee percolator. He decided Saville was going to need that coffee, and before making the purpose of his visit known he accepted the offer to join him.

'Have you read all these?' Mayo asked while the other man poured the fierce black brew. He waved towards the piles of books that had gravitated from the shop proper into the space at the back, which, he thought with sudden insight, even more than Kelsey Road, was the place where Saville was at home, his own personal space, what he understood and maybe his solace.

'A good percentage. I find the study of the criminal mind endlessly fascinating, as you yourself must. You've bought from me occasionally, haven't you?' It was the first time Saville had acknowledged recognition. He gave a brief, bleak smile. 'But that isn't what you came to see me about, is it?'

'No, sir, I'm afraid it isn't.'

Saville sat motionless and silent after the manner of his wife's death had been imparted to him. At last he spoke. 'After the circumstances in which she was found, I can't pretend it's entirely unexpected. Nevertheless, it's a blow.' A look of bitter resignation had settled on his face. Shock, if shock there had been in the first instance, had given way to an apparently quite genuine grief, though this didn't rule out, as far as Mayo was concerned, the possibility of the man having murdered his wife. He could still have loved her deeply even if he'd done away with her, perhaps because of it. In a momentary loss of control, or at the end of his tether, perhaps through jealousy. The quarrel maybe arousing a killer instinct which had lain dormant, unsuspected, for years . . . These quiet ones, the deep sort, they were often the worst. When they flew off the handle, they did it properly.

Yes, there were all the ingredients of a classic domestic murder, except that Mayo was still having trouble believing it. It was wrong, in his head. And, usually so sure of himself, he was bothered because he didn't know why.

'Are you arresting me?' Saville asked suddenly. His face had a grey tinge, like unrisen dough.

'No, sir.' Mayo didn't enlarge. Saville must realise that they had ample grounds for suspicion, and might be fishing to know they'd yet found anything more damaging. It wouldn't do any harm to let him sweat a bit.

He sat on a high, old-fashioned stool before his cluttered table, his shoulders bowed, his face hidden. 'There was no need for it,' he said unexpectedly, looking up. 'I shall never forgive myself.'

Mayo swallowed a mouthful of coffee, burning his tongue. 'Forgive yourself?'

'Don't get me wrong, I'm not making a confession. That's not what I mean.' A corner of his mouth had lifted, seeing the effect of his words. Maybe a sense of the ironic lurked somewhere under that humourless exterior, after all. 'I mean that she had her faults, who doesn't? But she was good, a good wife, a good woman. I should-n't have entertained the thoughts I did about her – but it was the jewellery,' he said, coming to a point that troubled Mayo also, 'how to explain that? If she was killed by an intruder –' He stopped short, meeting Mayo's disbelief. 'No, that won't do either, will it? No casual intruder would have taken her away like that, or left her valuables. But it's unthinkable that anyone she knew could have done it!'

They all said that. It wasn't usually how it turned out, however, rather the opposite.

'I've asked you before, Mr Saville, but now you've had time to think I'll ask again – you know of no one who had a grudge against her, however slight?'

'She hadn't an enemy in the world.'

They often said that, too, though he wondered if this, in its strictest sense, could ever be said of anyone. Mayo said abruptly, 'You haven't been honest with me, you haven't told me everything you know about what happened the day your wife disappeared, have you?'

Saville had a prominent Adam's apple which worked convul-sively. He shook his head, denying the allegation. Mayo knew he was lying.

On the long, trestle-table under the window, among a great deal of messy, extraneous junk, were the catalogues Saville had been working on, also a small but weighty picture frame, heavily gilded and embossed, also a saucepan containing the dried-up remains of a tin of baked beans, and some burnt toast. Not a man to make out for himself, Edwin Saville. But Mayo, thinking guiltily of the state of his own kitchen on occasions, wasn't in any position to cast stones and didn't pursue the thought.

'It's not always good to be alone at times like this, sir. Isn't there anyone who could stay with you? No member of your family – a son or daughter?' The closed, shut-in look that Mayo had come to know so well returned to Saville's face.

'Fleur and I had no children.'

'I see.' Mayo stood up to leave and took the opportunity to have a better look at the picture frame. Right-angled, easily held in the hand, heavyish-looking. The sort of object Fleur Saville might have been killed with. He picked it up and brief ideas about it being the murder weapon disappeared. It was a sham, made of plastic, light and insubstantial, and no threat to anyone. He found himself wondering if this could also be true of the owner.

Saville held out his hand to take the frame back, his left hand. He'd held his coffee-mug also in his left hand, Mayo had noticed. The blow which had killed his wife had been on her left temple, and it was odds on, though by no means certain, that her killer had been right-handed.

CHAPTER 9

Nell Fennimore sat hunched on the cushioned windowseat, staring dismally through swollen eyelids at the dreary, foggy prospect outside the window. Saturday morning, and the world looking and feeling like a smudged pen-and-ink drawing done on coarse grey wrapping-paper. Her face was blotched, her handkerchief screwed into a tight, damp ball, preparations for lunch weren't even started, although it was well after midday and Gerald would soon be in. She felt she had never known such pain and misery.

Obscurely, she blamed the weather for everything that had happened. If it hadn't been for the snow, poor darling Fleur wouldn't have lain there undiscovered all that time. There were going to be questions: Why? What in the world she'd been doing out there at Seddon End at all? What had *happened* to her? Nell's mind veered away, not wanting to face the implications. Oh heavens, it was all so *awful*. And how odd of Edwin not to have let her know until today. More than that, very nearly unpardonable.

Added to which Gerald, normally so amenable, so understanding, had not, today of all days, been in the sweetest of tempers. Deprived for two weeks of his usual three daily miles of jogging, he'd unwisely attempted it this morning, seeing that the thaw was well under way, an undertaking anyone might have told him was fraught with peril. Splashed and spattered, cursed by passing motorists for impeding what was still a narrow passage between banks of traffic-blackened slush, he'd returned home disgruntled and impatient.

And when the news – the unspeakable, dreadful news about Fleur had come – he'd been horrified, yes. And lovingly supportive, as always. But his sympathy hadn't seemed *entirely* wholehearted. He was still ruffled, even a bit short at being interrupted with the news between appointments. Though on reflection, that was perhaps understandable. Saturday mornings were dedicated to private patients.

Preoccupied by her misery, she didn't hear him come in. The first intimation that he was there was when she felt his arms around her, his chin nuzzling into the back of her neck. 'Sorry, Nellie-nell, sorry if I was a bit offhand.' The silly lover's nickname made her turn a woebegone face to him, and she saw his equanimity was restored, his capacity for comfort and reassurance back in place. 'My poor darling.'

'Nothing's going to be the same again.' She felt a sob rise in her throat, the sting of fresh tears behind her eyelids.

'I know.'

He held her against him, pressing her head against his shoulder, strong and solid. But he didn't know, nobody could know, the loss. 'She was so good,' she hiccuped, 'so sweet. What am I going to do without her?'

He saw her memories were already becoming exaggerated and distorted, and might grow increasingly so, hallowed by the manner of Fleur's death, having little in common with the reality of Fleur's nature, if he didn't put a stop to it. He couldn't bring himself, however, to disillusion her. Not at this point, perhaps never.

A car drew into the drive. A man got out. 'Dry your eyes, Nellie-nell, dear. We have a visitor.'

Kite was shown into the sitting-room at the back of the house, a large and pleasant though not very tidy room, decorated for cheerfulness and comfort rather than taste, full of books and a large woolly dog of uncertain age, sex and pedigree which occupied most of the hearthrug.

'I hope I'm not interrupting your work, or your lunch,' he said politely to the Fennimores, though basically he wouldn't have allowed it to make any difference.

'Not at all, I finish surgery at twelve-thirty on Saturdays.'

'And lunch won't be much today.'

Mrs Fennimore hadn't been able to erase the signs of recent tears, but she had blown her nose and dried her eyes and generally made an effort to pull herself together, Kite could tell. He tried to show her that he wasn't about to put her through an ordeal. 'I shan't keep you long,' he told her, in a friendly manner intended to put her at her ease. 'You already gave my chief a very clear and straightforward picture up to lunch-time on the day Mrs Saville disappeared. But there are one or two other things which have cropped up.'

'Such an understanding man, your Chief Inspector.' Kite was taken aback. It wasn't the kind of compliment that often came Mayo's way. It was usually a long time before people got to know him well enough to realise there was at least a grain of truth in this. Mrs Fennimore was not quite so ingenuous as she first seemed. He coughed and opened his notebook. To begin with, did she know a Mr Kenneth Anstruther, or a Mr David Garbett?

'I've never heard of either. Who are they?'

'They're partners in the Broadfield Garden Centre, where I understand Mrs Saville was in the habit of buying flowers.'

'Oh, I know those two, yes, if they're the two men who are always around in the shop, though I don't think I've ever heard their names. I used to drive Fleur down there nearly every Friday to pick up flowers for the weekend.' Tears threatened again and she had to swallow hard before she could go on. 'But what have they to do with Fleur?'

'Her body was found quite close to the cottage where they live. It was Mr Anstruther, in fact, who found her.'

'Oh dear, poor man, how ghastly for him! But you can't mean – no, of course you don't. She didn't know them any better than I did.' She said nothing more for a moment, and then, raising clear hazel eyes to his, asked quietly, unexpectedly, 'Sergeant, how exactly did Fleur die?'

There was no reason why she shouldn't know, no way he could wrap it up. He gave it to her straight, and to his relief she didn't burst into sobs or have hysterics. 'Yes,' she answered, barely audible, 'I thought that's what you were going to say.' Her husband reached out for her hand and she held on to it as though it were a lifeline. 'Go on, please. What else do you want to know?'

'About this quarrel Mrs Tennyson overheard between Mrs Saville and her husband. It was unusual, I gather?'

'They never had a wrong word,' Nell replied with conviction, and then flushed. 'As far as I know, of course.' Kite could see the struggle she was having between her conscience and her regret that she'd been the one to bring the row to the attention of the police. 'But Lola, you know Mrs Tennyson – she has a tendency to dramatise. She *could* have been mistaken.'

Not in this case, though, Kite thought, on Saville's own admission the row had taken place. And Nell Fennimore herself had believed Mrs Tennyson to the extent of reporting it. But he held his peace, merely asking what he'd asked of all the other helpers, 'Would you say Mrs Saville behaved quite normally that morning? In no way out of the ordinary? Not obviously upset or anything?'

'Naturally, I've thought about that, over and over, since Lola told me. If Fleur and Edwin had quarrelled, Fleur would certainly have been very upset indeed, but I can't honestly say I noticed anything. We *were* very busy, though, I have to admit. They wouldn't let us have the hall before half past ten because there'd been a dance the night before and they had to clean up, so we had all our work cut out and not much time to chat.'

'I see. And when you left her, what did she say?'

'She didn't say anything, she just put her hand up and waved. I was rushing off, you see, to meet Gerald. We had a few last-minute presents to buy, and I was first out. After we'd finished the shopping and I'd picked up Fleur's prescription, we had lunch together before I went back, didn't we, darling?'

Fennimore nodded confirmation. 'At the White Cat, the café in Sheep Street.'

'So you weren't actually there when Mrs Saville left?' Nell shook her head.

'I understand she didn't have a car, but it's not far to Kelsey Road, so presumably she'd have walked?'

Nell almost smiled at that. 'Fleur hated walking anywhere. No, she wouldn't have done that. It was a foul day anyway. One of the others would be sure to have given her a lift home.'

'Did she have a handbag with her?'

'Well, of course. She wouldn't go out without one, would she?'

'Did you notice what sort?'

For a moment, Nell looked blank. 'Black patent,' she said eventually. 'I didn't notice it particularly, but it would be – to go with her shoes. She was very fussy about things like that – not like me, I tend to use this all-purpose one nearly all the time.'

The one she indicated was lying on the floor beside one of the chairs. Kite had seen them advertised as 'organiser' bags, more like a briefcase than a handbag, he thought; the way this one bulged, it didn't look very organised.

'Or it's possible,' Nell went on, 'that somebody may have asked her home to lunch. She was never short of invitations. She was that sort of person, you see – fun to have around, very popular with everybody.'

'Except young Michael,' Fennimore put in, and immediately looked as though he wished he hadn't.

'Oh Gerald, that was years ago!' What was the matter with him today? Nell bit her lip and looked apprehensively at Kite, as if he might think Gerald was implying Michael might have had something to do with Fleur dying, which was ridiculous. The Sergeant looked at first sight to be very youthful for his rank, but his bright blue eyes were shrewd and sharp when they weren't smiling, and she suspected that anybody who underestimated him might be making a big mistake.

'Who's Michael?'

'Edwin's son by his first marriage,' she got in quickly, thinking she'd put things in a better light than Gerald. 'Michael adored his mother and she died when he was very young, so it wasn't all that surprising he resented Fleur rather when Edwin married her soon after. You know what that sort of situation can be like.'

'She didn't help by packing him off to school – that was a tactical error. But I'm bound to admit,' Fennimore added, trying fairly obviously to make up for his earlier incautious remark, 'that she did try to do her best with him after he left school and came home to live, though by then it was probably too late. Michael at that age would have tried the patience of a saint. It was maybe just as well he left home, though it was a pity it happened the way it did.'

'Packed up and left after a row, did he?'

'How did you guess?' Nell asked.

'It's not unusual, you'd be surprised. What was the row about?'

Fennimore spread his hands. 'He demanded some of the money his mother had left – she came from a wealthy family – in order to go off and "do his own thing", shake the dust of Lavenstock off his feet and find enlightenment in India or wherever the young were going then. Fleur persuaded Edwin not to let him have the money, and quite right too. The phase he was going through, he'd probably have given it all to some hippie commune or other, the young fool. But a lot of bad feeling was generated.'

'Where is he now?'

Husband and wife exchanged glances. 'Blowed if I know. Haven't seen him for – oh, seven or eight years, I suppose. Nell?'

'I've no idea where he is. It was something Fleur preferred to forget, and Edwin never mentioned him. The whole thing made him very unhappy.'

'It aged him ten years, poor devil,' Fennimore said bluntly. 'And it's not hard to understand why. Michael was frankly a pain in the neck, as they often are at that age, and Fleur . . . well, old Edwin must have felt like the meat in the sandwich.'

Fennimore, out of consideration for his wife no doubt, was saying less than he might have done on the subject of Fleur Saville, Kite was sure. Otherwise it might not have occurred to Kite to ask him, too, what he'd been doing with himself that afternoon after he left his wife outside the church hall.

'Me? Oh, nothing much. I took Bismarck here out for a walk round the park and then came home and went spark out in front of the box. There was no match on because of the weather, only an old film that was so boring I fell asleep.'

263

Bismarck! thought Kite, looking at the amiable old bundle of smelly fur, which had pricked up its ears at its name and the word 'walk'. How extraordinary people are about their dogs.

Mayo allowed himself to succumb at lunch-time to the steak and kidney, when he and Kite met for lunch in the Saracen's. He was up to here with salad, and the savoury smell of their renowned dish had been too much for him – and anyway, the waistband of his trousers was already noticeably looser. 'Cheers,' he said, lifting his pint. 'How d'you get on with Mrs Fennimore?'

'She hadn't a lot more to tell me than she told you in the first place, not about the twenty-second . . . but I did find out an interesting thing or two. First, he's been married before . . .'

'Who has? Saville?' Mayo put down his glass and stared at Kite. 'Well, well. He's a bit of a dark horse, isn't he? Married twice, and with another attractive woman in tow!' He'd learned the date of Saville's marriage to Fleur, but it hadn't occurred to him to ask about a previous one for the simple but not excusable reason that Saville had to him all the appearance of a confirmed bachelor succumbing late to the married state. Yet his type was often attractive to a certain sort of woman: competent, self-motivated, often childless women who rather liked the idea of an apparently helpless man dependent on them – like Zoe Henderson, for instance. Into his mind too came the memory of that fleeting, attractive smile of Saville's. In his younger days, Mayo conceded, he could have been quite a handsome man.

'Also, he has a son by his first marriage who had a grudge against his stepmama.' Kite repeated what the Fennimores had told him, enjoying the effect on Mayo.

'The old devil! Only this morning he told me he had no children.' Or rather, he corrected himself, Saville had implied it by the manner in which he'd phrased his answer to the question, saying, quite truthfully, Mayo supposed, that he and Fleur were childless. 'Any other little gems like that, have you?'

Kite looked complacent, but shook his head. 'It all happened years ago, anyway, and Michael – the son – hasn't been seen or heard of for ten or eleven years.'

Mayo made no comment, staring at the now-brittle sprigs of holly that decorated the top of each picture set against the flock-papered walls, the tinsel draped around the bar, while talk and laughter from the Saturday lunch-time crowds rose and fell around them. It was long odds on the boy having come back after all these years to murder his stepmother, but any lead was worth following up. Especially since it was the only sniff they'd had so far of anyone other than Saville – and maybe Zoe Henderson – with even the glimmer of a motive. A large man with a shiny red face and a padded cotton jerkin cannoned into their table, spilling a few drops from the clutch of gin and tonics on Mayo's hand, blundering on without apology. Mayo wiped them off absently. 'That sounds like ours, Martin.'

The Saracen's Head had a system at lunch-times, which would have lost them Mayo's custom had it not been for the excellence of its food, of giving you a number when you ordered your meal, and calling it out when the food was ready. Kite came back from the bar bearing two steaming plates and cutlery wrapped in paper napkins.

While they consumed the pie, Mayo said, 'I managed to have a word with Mrs Saville's solicitor this morning. Those books she wrote must have been hot property in more ways than one. She was worth a mint.'

'And who benefits?'

'According to her will, Saville. Gets every penny. Plus insurances.'

'Does he, by gum? And Gerald Fennimore said his first wife was wealthy, too.'

'To lose one wife in circumstances where you're likely benefit may be regarded as a misfortune, but to lose two . . .

'Looks deliberate?'

265

'Quite. I don't know, though. Isn't it a bit too obvious?'

'You're the one who always says the obvious choice is usually the right one.'

Mayo inspected the cruet and selected more English mustard.

'Well, how many more motives do we want?' Kite demanded. 'She was trying to force him into something he didn't want to do, they quarrelled, she's left him money, *as did his first wife* . . . his time that day isn't wholly accounted for.'

Kite pushed his empty plate away, drained his glass, and got ready to leave. 'I'd give a lot to know a bit more about this first marriage of Saville's. I don't believe in coincidences.'

'Dig around. I wouldn't be averse to knowing, myself,' Mayo said mildly. 'And if I were you, I should start with Jim Sutcliffe at the *Advertiser*. Arrange for us to have a word. But at the moment it's more important to find out where – and when – Mrs Saville ate her lunch, to give us a more precise time of death. You'd better concentrate on the vicar's wife and Mrs Challis, find out if either of them gave her a lift home or whatever.'

Kite was still unable to contact Mrs Challis, but late afternoon found him waiting in the parish church for Jennifer Pound, the vicar's wife, to finish arranging the flowers on the altar for the next day.

'Hang about, shan't keep you waiting long, Mr Kite,' she said cheerfully.

The Pounds were a young couple, the subject of enjoyable speculation and controversy among the older, staider and more shockable of the parishioners of St Nicholas. He was unorthodox and didn't even wear a dog-collar, and some of them wondered sometimes if perhaps they hadn't stumbled into a country and western show by mistake for a service, what with the swinging tunes to the hymns, accompanied on occasions by the vicar's wife on the guitar. Today she was wearing jeans tucked into high leather boots, and a leather jacket. She called herself Ms and taught the Kite children at the local junior school.

'I assume it is me you want to talk to, and not my husband? Not in a hurry, are you?'

She thought he'd come to talk about Davey, who was usually in hot water of some kind.

'Finish what you're doing, Mrs Pound.'

He stood awkwardly watching her as she moved about between the altar and the vestry, substituting the fresh daffodils and tulips she'd brought for the ones already in the big brass ewers. She didn't seem to be making a very good job of it to Kite, admittedly no expert. The ones she was throwing away had appeared perfectly fresh, though perhaps they wouldn't have lasted through the following week, and they'd been artistically arranged, which hers were not. Her bottom was neat and round in the tight jeans every time she bent down, and he primly averted his eyes and stood, stiff and awkward, waiting. He didn't want to sit in one of the front pews, where he'd have to shout to make himself heard, and didn't know whether it would be taking too great a liberty to sit anywhere else. It was a long time since he'd last been in church, and that was to a wedding.

She finished what she was doing and solved his dilemma by slipping into one of the choir stalls and beckoning him to join her. 'Now, what is it you wanted to see me about?'

When he'd finished telling her, she sat silently for a moment, biting her lip. 'How crass of me. I'm so sorry, I should have known what you were here for. Such a shock it was to hear about her. She'll be a terrible loss to the whole community. How – how did she die?'

'We believe she was murdered.'

She uttered a small, shocked expression. 'Did you know her well?' Kite asked.

Mrs Pound hesitated. 'Not well. In fact I hardly knew her, only in so far as her work for the church, and charity, especially the Buttercup Club, was concerned. She'll be dreadfully missed in that direction. Aside from her work, I believe that was the one thing in her life she cared about. There was a reason for it, of course. She confided in me once that she had had a child who was born terribly disabled, and died in his first year.'

'What do you know about her husband? Is he a churchgoer?'

'No, they always seemed to lead rather separate lives. But,' she added hastily, 'you don't have to be in each other's pockets all day to be close, you know. From all I've heard they were devoted.'

'You've never heard any rumours about her – about another man?'

She looked at him, astounded. 'Fleur Saville wouldn't get up to those sort of tricks!'

Where had she been, all her thirty-five or so years, this enlightened wife of the vicarage, that she didn't know that *anybody* was likely to get up to tricks like that, even vicars' wives? She must have read his look, however, because she pulled a face and said a trifle shamefacedly, 'No, I don't really know, do I? But I honestly don't think so.'

Kite went on to ask her about the children's party. Like the rest of the women interviewed, she didn't appear to have noticed anything unusual about Fleur's behaviour that morning. She said again, 'I don't know what we're going to do without her, though I suppose Gillian Challis will be willing enough to take over the Buttercup Club, they more or less ran it together. In fact –' She broke off what she'd been going to say, as if she'd thought better of it.

'Challis?' Kite asked. 'The Mrs Challis who lives out at Lattimer Wood? We still have to see her. She was out when I rang earlier.'

'I was the last to leave that lunch-time because I had to lock up, and I'm almost certain I heard Gillian offering Fleur a lift home. They were very close friends. She's your best bet, she'll be able to help you more than I've done in every way.'

'People who are not quite so close are often better able to give a less subjective view, Mrs Pound.'

'Well, I'm not one of them, not in this case. Look, I don't mean to be uncooperative, but as I said, I didn't know her well. In fact I – never felt quite at ease with her, I don't know why. She had this beautiful speaking voice, very soft and melodious and persuasive. Somehow, you found yourself doing what she wanted, sometimes against your will. She was so good, and yet – there was something about her I didn't –' She broke off and looked at Kite with very round, very blue eyes.

'Didn't like?'

'Not – exactly. Didn't understand, I think.' She looked uneasy. For all her emancipation, he could see she still felt the old taboo about disrespect to the dead. 'She put her name to all these fund-raising efforts, but my husband, well, he used to think it was all rather well-staged to give her the limelight. He used, I'm afraid, to call her Our Star Performer.' She blushed vividly. 'I think you'd better forget I said that.'

Kite thought that Ms Pound, despite all her efforts to the contrary, hadn't succeeded in losing her natural ingenuousness.

CHAPTER 10

'And now for Mrs Justice of the Peace Challis. Got your bullet-proof vest on, Martin? The lady doesn't suffer fools gladly – though one thing's certain,' Mayo added with a short laugh, 'we'll get a straight answer.'

They were driving out together to see Mrs Challis, whom Mayo had come across several times in the course of his duty. He'd read the forceful, downright letters she wrote to the *Advertiser*, too, and respected what he'd seen of her brisk, no-nonsense manner. She could be ruthless with offenders when the occasion demanded it, largely because, he imagined, she expected everyone to have as much integrity as she undoubtedly had herself. Her trouble was that she saw everything strictly in black and white, there was never room for grey areas, and this unwavering conviction of the rightness of her judgements made her unpopular with certain sections of the community. Despite this, Mayo felt he'd rather deal with her than with some of her woolly-minded colleagues. You knew where you were with her.

The church bells were ringing from the parish church as they left and took the Birmingham road towards Lattimer Wood. Kite drove and Mayo watched people going about their business, fetching newspapers, guiding children on Christmas-present bicycles over bumpy pavements, or even – though it was still drizzling – joining the enthusiastic army of Sunday-morning car washers. In Branxmore, where there was only on-street parking, and you had to hose down your car in the street, there was much evidence of this. In the suburbs of Tannersley and Henchard, out towards Lattimer Wood, in the snooty part where town gave way to country, any such labour was discreetly hidden behind trees and shrubs in quarter-acre lots. The Challis house lay even beyond this, in open country with no visible neighbours and a sweeping drive a quarter of a mile long.

The road to Lattimer Wood led through the Seddon End crossroads. Seddon Lodge, as they passed, looked as prim and self-contained, as slightly unreal as ever, but the lane where the body had stayed undiscovered under two feet of snow had been reduced by the tramping feet of many policemen to a sea of grey slush, closed at the entrance by a red and white barrier.

Anstruther, as the unlucky finder of the body, would have to appear at the inquest, which was scheduled for Tuesday, but Mayo was fairly satisfied in his own mind that he'd had nothing to do with the murder. Both he and his partner Garbett had been provided with satisfactory alibis by their staff, with whom they'd been working the whole of that Saturday, and also for the early evening by other guests at the party they'd attended; there seemed, moreover, to be no known connections between either of them and the dead woman.

But why there? was a question Mayo had asked himself more than once. Why had that particular spot been chosen to dump the body? Not the lane – the murderer wouldn't have had any choice but to leave the body where he did, if he was making for the gravel pits. It was dangerous dumping it in full view of the headlights of any car coming from the direction of Birmingham, with that bend in the road, but on the other hand he couldn't have risked pressing on and getting stuck in a snowdrift. On the morning when the body was discovered, Mayo himself had seen how the lane degenerated when he and Kite had tramped a partly cleared path through the snow to view the deep, waterfilled pits. But why the gravel pits in the first place?

'Who'd be likely to know where that lane led, Martin?' Kite would probably know, he was a local man, born and bred in the area.

'Practically anybody . . . folks exercise their dogs on that heathland. Or anybody else could have known for that matter – it's a convenient spot to draw off the road for a break if you're driving, attractive in the summertime. And as Deeley said, courting couples. It's accessible enough at most times. Those pits aren't fenced off or anything, though they should be, even with the trespass warnings there. There was a case last year when some kids were fooling around and one of them fell in and nearly drowned. There was talk of prosecution, to make an example. Caused a lot of outrage.'

As a method of concealment, then, it lacked at least the main requirement – that of permanently disposing of the body. Sooner or later, it would have surfaced, and been spotted. Which was perhaps another point in Saville's favour. Would he, a student of criminology, have ignored this basic fact?

*

The Challis house, long and low, was of mellow stone with a red pantiled roof and lattice windows, huge stone urns beside the door lavishly planted with purple and yellow winter-flowering pansies, looking at the moment slightly battered. The only response to the hollow reverberations of the iron lion-faced knocker on the heavy oak door was the frantic, prolonged Hound-of-the-Baskervilles baying of a dog from somewhere inside the house. Somewhere a long way off. Boxwinder House had until fairly recently been a large farmhouse, with its origins in Tudor times.

'They may be away for the weekend,' Kite remarked, 'with somebody coming in to look after the dog.'

'We'll wait.'

'There's been no answer to the telephone for a couple of days.'

Mayo's only reply was a grunt, and Kite gave up and followed him back to the car, where they sat gazing out in silence. To their right, a paddock occupied by two damp and dejected ponies who were ignoring the open door of a timbered stable in the corner. In front of them, a big secluded garden, landscaped with clusters of deciduous shrubs and trees and dark, glossy rhododendrons, where a summerhouse and tennis court, and a swimming pool under a cover, lay partly obscured by the grey moisture dripping on to the slowly melting snow. Freezing conditions were forecast for the night, unfortunately likely to prolong the thaw even further.

'Ever come across Challis, Martin?' Mayo asked presently.

'Not personally. We don't move in the same circles.'

'Where's he get his money for all this?' Mayo went on, ignoring the sarcasm. 'Where does anybody, for that matter?'

'Public school and Oxford, Rugby Blue, went down without taking his degree, but straight into his father's City firm – that's Browne Moulton, the merchant bankers, very top-drawer. He commutes every day – by car, not train,' Kite recited rapidly, very pleased with himself at being able to score by having asked around, until he saw Mayo's grin and realised the questions had been rhetorical, he'd known all along.

'His public school was Ampleforth,' Mayo enlarged, infuriatingly.

'So?' Kite was casual, trying not to show his discomfiture.

'RC, that, isn't it? So they'll likely be at Mass. Not bloomin' heathens, like us lot, you know, the Catholics.' Relenting, Mayo explained, 'I was talking to the Chief Super. He's always got his nose to the ground about this sort of thing. Another thing . . .' He gazed abstractedly out of the window, while Kite waited for him to go on, until he realised he wasn't going to.

Kite sat back, feeling squashed, but resigned. When Mayo had that look on his face, you'd get nothing but monosyllables out of him until he'd worked out whatever it was that had just occurred to him.

At that moment the owner of the house, Bryan Challis, was driving his silver-grey Jaguar XJ6S, aggressively, as he did everything else, back from Mass. His wife Gillian sat in unaccustomed silence beside him.

Penny, their fifteen-year-old daughter, lolled in the back wishing her mother was driving – she did it ten times better – and debating whether or not to liven things up by saying so. In Penny's opinion, her father needed more practice at driving his own car, and more criticism when he did. Turner drove him up to the City each day, while he sat in the back and worked; otherwise, her mother almost always drove. Thinking about it, Penny decided that in the circumstances she'd better not stir things up. Her father might not, as he usually did, simply laugh and call her a precocious brat, Mummy certainly wouldn't. She wouldn't have, even if she'd been in her usual lenient Sunday mood, which she wasn't. You could tell because she wasn't boring on about old Father Flaherty's sermon and trying to involve the others in debating his arguments, as she invariably did.

273

In fact, there was a horrid feeling altogether to the weekend. The shock which had come on Friday, via the regional news on TV, had obviously shaken her mother rigid, and cut out everything else as a topic of conversation. Not that they'd talked about it much. After a brief, appalled exchange, when Mummy – Mummy! – had burst into tears and been awkwardly comforted by her father, they'd avoided further discussion, at least in front of her.

Penny could understand, though, how awful it must be for her mother. Fleur Saville had been one of her oldest chums and one of her do-gooding cronies, as well as being a famous historical novelist. Her parents thought Penny hadn't read the Fleur Lamont books. She had, though, in spite of being forbidden to do so, during the week when she was away at school, and couldn't see what all the fuss was about. There was worse on TV every night of the week.

As for her father, his mouth had tightened when they'd heard she'd been found dead, but that was all; he sat twisting his black onyx ring, looking solemn, seeming anxious to put the right expression on his face, the way he did when horrifying third world pictures came on the screen. She knew how he felt. As if it ought to have affected both of them, her father and herself, in the same way as it had Mummy.

There was a car waiting outside the house when the Jag rounded the curve in the drive, right on the spot where her father usually parked. He said a brief, forbidden word, then pulled to a stop directly in front of it, sending gravel spurting in all directions.

CHAPTER 11

While his wife and daughter went to take off their coats, Challis buttonholed Mayo: they stood facing each other in the centre of an enormous cream-washed, plastered and beamed hall, large enough to accommodate sundry weighty pieces of black oak furniture and two chintz-covered sofas, as well as several chairs and tables drawn up to a fire that could comfortably have roasted a couple of sheep. Its owner stood with feet planted apart on polished oak boards a foot wide, hands thrust deep into the pockets of his country tweeds. 'Look here, I won't have my wife bothered over this affair. She's upset enough as it is.'

Mayo's hackles rose, partly at the supercilious 'Look here', but more at the man himself, a big, handsome, dark-haired, blue-chinned man of about forty-five, with heavy dark spectacles seeking to underline his air of self-importance. Giving Challis the benefit of his own special brand of cold, grey-eyed stare, he said evenly, 'We shan't upset anybody more than we have to, sir, but that's not always avoidable when there's been a murder committed.'

'Oh well, of course, there's no question of being obstructive –' Challis was beginning with a hint of bluster, when he was interrupted by the return of his wife.

'Murder?' she repeated. 'Murder? They said on the news it was an accident. Oh God!' She seemed stunned.

'Perhaps you'd better sit down, ma'am.'

'Yes. Oh yes. And do please take a seat yourselves.'

She indicated chairs near the fire with a wave of her hand, sinking into one herself while Challis said, 'If you'll excuse me – er – telephone call to make, you know. You won't want me, I hardly knew her, and I was in Zürich that weekend, didn't get back until late Saturday.'

His wife threw him an odd, almost pleading glance, and Mayo

275

resisted the impulse to keep him anyway just because of his assumption, but in actual fact his preference was to talk to Gillian Challis alone for the moment, so he let him go. He met Kite's raised eyebrows. Yes, you'd have thought he'd have wanted to stay, if only to give his wife moral support. He hadn't even given her a word of sympathy.

Though very probably she was likely to be less in need of support than most. Evidently to Challis, big was in every way beautiful; his furniture, likewise his wife – though in fact she was not tall, but well-made in a bouncy sort of way, with hips that were beginning to spread. She was almost as fair as Fleur Saville had been, but there the resemblance between the two women ended. Fleur had been slight and pale and slender, Mrs Challis immediately brought to mind Betjeman's Olympian girl, 'standing in strong athletic pose'. An attractive woman, she still bore traces of a healthy summer tan, a subtle contrast with her fair hair and blue eyes. She was the daughter of a general, and showed it in the speed with which she gathered her forces and regained control and turned her direct gaze on Mayo.

'I'm sorry, it was a shock to hear what you said, about Fleur. We heard about it on television, and they didn't say – neither did Edwin – it's really too awful – quite unbelievable! I suppose you've come to see me because I was with her on the day she . . . How can I help you?' She was clearly very upset but her quick acceptance of the situation was wholly admirable.

Kite took up the questioning at a signal from Mayo, who chose to keep in the background when occasion demanded it, as now, observing witnesses as they answered, or when they were silent. So often what they *didn't* say was more important than what they did.

'I understand she left the hall with you at about twelve-thirty?' Kite asked.

While admiring the self-control which had taken charge, Mayo noticed Mrs Challis was not quite as together as she might wish to convey. If she went on fiddling with the winder of that expensive, emerald-set wristwatch, she'd break it. Everything about her was expensive and well-chosen: good suit, shoes that looked hand-made, the bag which she'd dropped beside her chair on coming in – square and practical but with heavy gold fittings – yet only the watch shouted it, seeming flashy against the rest of her things.

'It was about half past twelve,' she said in answer to Kite's ques-tion. 'We left the hall together in my car. I was going to drop her at home, but when she said Edwin wouldn't be there for lunch, I suggested we should drive out to the White Boar at Over Kennet and have a ploughman's lunch there, to cheer her up.'

'She told you she needed cheering up, did she?'

'Not in so many words, but poor darling, she was having diffi-culty in breathing, so I knew something was wrong. A lot of her asthma was psychosomatic – you knew she was asthmatic? Yes, well, she used to try not to allow things to get her down because of that.' Momentarily, the low, well-modulated voice faltered. 'I'm sorry, but I'm not used to the idea yet – she'd always been my clos-est friend . . . we've known each other ever since we were at school together, she and I.'

'And Mrs Fennimore as well, I believe.'

A pause. Mayo thought he detected a slight, a very slight drop in temperature. 'Oh yes, Nell too. But of course, almost immedi-ately we left school Nell got married and started having babies, which meant Fleur and I were closer together than ever. You see, I didn't have Penny until fairly late and Fleur didn't marry early. At one time it was understood that she and Gerald Fennimore . . . However, we were only eighteen then, and in the end, he chose Nell. Much more suitable choice for a dentist's wife.'

Hmm, thought Mayo, as she went on. For a long time, she went on. They had to listen to her on the subject of her friend, on her qualities as a devoted wife, fundraiser and selfless worker for char-ity, kind to those who worked for her, loved by her friends: a paragon. 'Thank you, darling, put it down there.'

This last was to the daughter, Penny, who had come in from the kitchen with coffee, which she proceeded to pour; a tall, striking-looking girl of about fifteen, her thick black hair, very like her father's, falling forward over her face as she bent over the four matt chocolate-and-white stoneware coffee cups on the tray. As soon as she'd handed round three of them, her mother said, 'Penny, would you be a darling and check up on the lunch?' It was a suggestion made gently, with a smile; nevertheless, it brooked no argument.

Her daughter gave her a look which could best be described as old-fashioned, but she picked her own cup and saucer up without demur and went out, back to the kitchen. Presently, she was seen walking past the window with an enormous prancing Airedale-type dog, which bounced along looking deceptively like an oversize stuffed toy. Mayo didn't like Airedales, they were a disagreeable sort of dog that would have your arm for lunch as soon as look at you.

'Mrs Challis,' Kite was beginning again after this interlude, 'we can assume Mrs Saville would tell you why she was depressed, seeing you were such good friends?'

She took a sip of her black sugarless coffee and said carefully, 'In the end she did. She admitted she'd had a quarrel with Edwin, which had upset her dreadfully. She didn't tell me what it was about, and I didn't ask, but it couldn't have been anything trivial, neither of them was at all that sort of person.'

'So what time did you leave the White Boar?'

'About ten past one.'

'And it's about a ten-minute drive back into Lavenstock –'

'Oh, but we didn't go straight back. It was very stuffy in the pub, and she asked me to drive somewhere where she could get a breath of fresh air. She wanted to get back to Lavenstock for a hair appointment she'd made at the new shop just round the corner from the church hall, but we'd plenty of time, so we drove back slowly by way of Kennet Edge. It's usually very bracing up there, but that day it was sleeting and altogether not very pleasant so we didn't get out of the car after all. Anyway, time was getting on by then and she seemed anxious to be off. She'd never been to this hairdresser previously and she didn't want to be late, though why she wanted to go there one can't imagine. Not our sort of place. More – well, for younger people, at any rate. When I said so, she said maybe it was time she changed her image before – before it was too late.' Her voice shook a little on the last words, and she paused, looking down at her large, capable hands, but when she resumed her voice was firm again. 'It did occur to me, with her saying that, that maybe the quarrel with Edwin had been over another woman, a younger woman perhaps – but only for a moment. If Fleur suspected that, she was very much mistaken.'

'What time was this appointment, Mrs Challis?' Kite asked.

'Quarter to two. I stopped at the corner of Peter Street to let her get out, just before the appointment was due, only for a moment, you know what the traffic's like on that corner, and that – was the last time I saw her, her red coat disappearing into the shop.'

'After you'd left her, did you go straight back to the church hall?'

'Me? Oh no, I parked my car round the back of the hall, then did a bit of shopping. I only wanted one or two bits, but everywhere was so busy I only just got back in time.'

'What did you think when Mrs Saville never turned up?'

'Frankly, I was astonished, but when I heard later from Mrs Fennimore she'd gone to the cottage, I assumed she'd taken herself off to – well, teach Edwin a lesson, or something. She was, you know, sometimes given to rather extravagant gestures.'

Kite had come to the end of his questions, and looked at Mayo for help. Mayo said, 'Mrs Challis, did you know Mr Saville's first wife?'

'Margaret?' She turned towards him, giving him a long, level look, unsurprised at the change of direction. 'Yes, though I knew her younger sister Kathleen better. I say *knew* because she – Kathleen, that is – went out to South Africa after the accident. She was dreadfully cut up about Margaret dying, and all the unpleasantness that followed.'

'The first Mrs Saville died in an accident?'

'Didn't you know? They were on a sailing holiday and she was drowned. Edwin was quite devastated, left alone with a young son to bring up. I think that's partly why he married Fleur so quickly.'

'What actually happened?'

'I don't sail, and I never understood exactly what it was, something to do with her head being struck by the boom. She fell overboard and was drowned. Edwin wasn't a very experienced sailor, the weather was rough, and the coroner had some very cogent things to say about irresponsibility.' She checked a sharp sigh, changing it to a nod of approval. It was the sort of attitude she publicly supported. 'He was quite right, of course, and I suppose Edwin deserved a certain amount of criticism. All the same,' she went on, strongly, in the voice familiar in the magistrates' court, 'I'd like you to understand that there could have been no question – no question at all – of it being anything other than an accident.'

'Was it ever suggested it wasn't?'

'There were unkind things said; there often are when money is involved, and Margaret left a good deal. It was put about that perhaps her death had been – fortuitous. Which was absolutely ridiculous, of course.'

'You seem very certain, Mrs Challis.'

'Of course I am. Because I've known Edwin Saville for many years, and I know him utterly incapable of violence, it's quite out of character.' As if that clinched the matter, she checked the time rather obviously on her watch.

'We won't keep you much longer, but I'd like to ask you a little more about the relationship between Mrs Saville and her husband. You thought it unlikely in her husband's case that there was any other – friend?' Mayo despised himself for the euphemism, but Mrs Challis had that effect on him. 'What about Mrs Saville?'

She immediately grew cold. 'Certainly not. No question of it, on either side.' She sounded, like Jennifer Pound, as though sex was confined to the lower classes. 'I can't think why I mentioned it.' Neither, for that matter, could Mayo.

'Thank you, then, I think that'll do for the present, Mrs Challis.' He'd lost her now, anyway. 'You've been very helpful. In the meantime, if there's anything else you think of, perhaps you'd let us know?'

'Of course.' She relented. 'I'm only sorry I haven't been able to help you more now. It's been such a shock. One can't – one can't imagine life without Fleur.' She looked suddenly quite wretched.

Kite took it on himself to say, 'Don't worry, Mrs Challis, we'll get whoever did it in the end.'

Her low-voiced answer was unexpected, and not only because people didn't say things like that any more. 'Yes, well, have charity. Let's not forget that whoever did this is a soul in torment.'

Kite looked as if the floor opening under his feet would be a happy alternative to having to find an answer to that one, and even Mayo, not easily outfaced, was momentarily taken aback. Though not necessarily agreeing with her, he mentally gave himself a black mark for insensitivity; he had never suspected that beneath that unwavering sense of justice there lurked compassion.

Bryan Challis stood at his study window and watched the car with the two policemen disappear down the long sweep of the drive, a worried man.

He was making mistakes these days, too many. He'd very nearly said more than he ought. He'd told a useless lie, one which the police could easily disprove. Too late, he saw that; but it had never been in his mind that they would have cause to question him, and nor had they, he reflected, relaxing visibly at the realisation. He'd nothing to worry about. After all, what was there to connect him with Fleur Saville, to arouse suspicions?

He lit a cigarette and poured himself a stiff malt whisky – the best he had handy, Laphroaig, an indulgence he felt he deserved.

Where had it all begun, the chain of cause and effect, his involvement with these women?

With Fleur? With Gillian? Or Ruth? With Candace Neale, a name from the grave after all these years? Or with his own Catholic upbringing, guilt never far from the surface, sins unconfessed and retribution ever hanging by a thread over his head?

He wore his religion more lightly than Gillian could ever wear hers; nevertheless, the sense of sin was never too far away – to be reasoned with, rationalised, excused, but never completely exorcised. It had been behind the driving ambition which had enabled him to offer Gillian a lifestyle which only he knew was an atonement.

These were thoughts not usually present in his mind. Normally, he did not allow them to surface, they were present only as a subterranean undercurrent to his life, a dark tide that could be endured only by ignoring it. Or, when that was impossible, by lavishing upon his wife and daughter expensive presents . . . the luxury cruise down the Nile, the white Audi Quattro with personalised number-plates, the new pony, and this Christmas the emerald-set watch. They said emeralds were unlucky . . .

Sometimes, when he had caught her eye resting speculatively upon him, or sensed a refusal to meet his gaze, he had wondered, with a plunge of something like fear; when she had opened the Cartier box on Christmas morning, for instance, he had caught an unprecedented glint of tears in her eyes. He had told himself it was an understandable reaction when someone was touched by an overwhelmingly extravagant gesture of affection. It couldn't possibly be that she knew, or even suspected. Gillian was incapable of that sort of complicity in her marriage.

CHAPTER 12

'You have to admit it smells to high heaven – two wives dying in suspicious circumstances, both leaving him money.'

Kite's sentiment was one with which Mayo was, rationally, bound to agree. Yet without proof, where were they? All the evidence against Saville so far was circumstantial. Moreover, since the talk with Gillian Challis, the margins had narrowed considerably. There was now, taking into consideration the findings of the post-mortem, not much more than half an hour or so after having had her hair done during which Fleur Saville could have been killed. During which time, from two-thirty to three, there were apparently unassailable witnesses to swear Edwin Saville had been serving in his shop.

They'd been trying to fit in these newest facts with what they already knew for the last fifteen minutes, over a tough roast beef sandwich at an unprepossessing and almost deserted roadside pub on the way back to Lavenstock, where they'd arranged to meet the editor of the *Advertiser*, and Kite was looking gloomy, perhaps because of the flatness of the beer, perhaps at seeing his favourite suspect being ruled out. 'It's always within the bounds of possibility that one or other of 'em, the witnesses, might discover they've been mistaken about the times,' he pressed on hopefully.

Mayo shook his head. It was possible, yes, but probable? He didn't think so. He didn't think Kite did, either, by now, although he wasn't about to give up. 'He's the best bet we've got – the *only* bet – including this hypothetical lover . . . and it'll surprise me if we find Waterton *hasn't* spent the last month chasing elephants with a camera.'

Mayo looked at his watch. Sutcliffe was late.

'OK – supposing, just for the sake of argument, she changed her mind at the last minute. Mrs Challis saw her disappearing through the door of that hairdressing place, but she could have walked out again. Supposing she went along to Butter Lane instead, and Saville killed her there. That's why he didn't answer the door to Mrs Wilson.'

'And went on serving his customers as though nothing had happened? Well, all right, yes, as far as Saville's concerned. I'd go along with that. If anybody could do it, he could.'

Kite looked interested, then frowned.

'What's on your mind, Martin? Apart from the origins of this so-called beef? Chased many a man up a tree before it got into this sandwich, I reckon.' Mayo removed a piece of gristle from his mouth and abandoned the rest of his lunch.

'I've just remembered something Gerald Fennimore said. He took his dog for a walk down to the park that afternoon . . .'

'And?'

'The quickest way from his house is via the backs of the houses along Kelsey Road. It cuts quite a corner off, and you can let your dog off the lead there.'

'Right.' He remembered the fat, bossy Corgi and its owner. 'Go on.'

'It's a long shot, I suppose – but didn't Mrs Challis say there'd been something between Mrs Saville and Fennimore once? You don't think it's possible he's been carrying a torch for her all these years?'

Mayo considered. It *was* a long shot. 'I don't see it. Or that he nipped in and did for her while taking his dog for a walk. Not without any other suspicion. Might as well suspect *Mrs* Fennimore. We'll bear it in mind, but we're not so desperate yet.'

All the same, the photograph Nell Fennimore had given him, with Gerald in evening clothes, the matinee-idol image, came to mind. But dammit, you couldn't start suspecting a man of murder just because he looked like an out-of-date film star. He looked up as the door opened. 'Here's Sutcliffe.'

★

284

'So you want to know about Fleur? Yes, of course I remember her. She worked for us at the *Advertiser* ever since she left school at eighteen – right up until she married Saville, in fact.' Jim Sutcliffe, the editor of the *Lavenstock Advertiser*, was a short, talkative man with gingery whiskers, a small round pot-belly, a permanent cigarette in his mouth and a resident cough. He was due to retire shortly – if the cough hadn't carried him off before then.

'Was she writing then – those books of hers, I mean?' Mayo asked.

'No, I don't think so – well, I know she wasn't, because I've always taken credit for starting her off on that lark. When she left to marry Saville, she said to me, "Well, Jim, that's the end of my career, he doesn't approve of women going out to work." She was laughing when she said it, though, she knew when she was on to a good thing. Saville wasn't short then, not at that time, not with all his first wife had left him. Anyway, I suggested she tried writing fiction to keep her occupied – "after all," I said, "you've been doing it for years, haven't you, dear?"'

'What did you mean by that?'

'Oh, it was just a joke.' Sutcliffe looked a bit uncomfortable and buried his face in his glass. He drank nothing but draught Guinness and was already well down his second half. 'If she thought a story wasn't interesting enough, she'd embroider it, and it used to get my goat. It's all right bringing tears to your readers' eyes occasionally by laying it on, but there's a limit. We had no end of set-to's about it. Trouble was, life was never exciting enough for her, she had to dramatise it.'

'Why d'you think she stayed in Lavenstock, then? You'd have thought she'd have gone for the big city and the bright lights,' Kite said.

Sutcliffe drew on his cigarette and coughed hollowly. 'Funny thing about Fleur. She used to talk enough about getting out, but she never did it; basically she was a small town girl, bourgeoise, as they say, by upbringing and inclination. She was pretty tough

285

behind all that feminine veneer, realistic enough anyway to know that she'd hate it like hell being a very small fish in a big, big pond. Suited her down to the ground it did, being the famous author, getting the kudos for all those fund-raising efforts, acting the Queen Bee with her retinue behind her.'

'Sycophants?' Mayo, watching the rapidity with which the Guinness level was going down, made a sign to Kite, who went to the bar to get another round in.

'Some of them, yes. But they seemed to stay around, most of them, so it must have been a bit more than that.'

'What about men?'

'She had one or two skirmishes before she met Saville, but it wasn't men turned her on.'

'What then? Women?'

'God, no, not in that way.' Sutcliffe drank up and sucked the froth from his moustache, giving the question some thought before answering more fully. 'Power, of a sort,' he said at last. 'At least, she liked to see people dancing on the end of her string, no doubt about that. It's a kind of aphrodisiac in its way. Thanks, Martin. Cheers.'

Kite resumed his seat and Mayo said, 'What d'you know about the accident to Saville's first wife, Jim?'

'Margaret? Oh, you're going back a bit now.' The journalist eyed Mayo speculatively. 'It *was* just an accident, take it from me. There was a lot of talk, which I take it you know about, but there was nothing in it. As far as I can see, the whole thing was caused simply through lack of nous. Sailing by unqualified amateurs should be banned. And Saville's a bit simple, you know, like a lot more so-called intelligent people. He might have got a first at Cambridge, but he doesn't know his arse from his elbow. I'd be willing to bet, though I've nothing to base this on, that there isn't a penny of Margaret's money left. That shop of his could be a little goldmine if he went about it the right way, but he's no idea, half the time it's not open when you want to pop in, he's off at some bloody sale or other. If you ask him to get you a book, he forgets to order it, the shop's only there for his own interest.'

Half of this Mayo agreed with, about the other half he wasn't so sure. Saville was layers deeper than Sutcliffe was giving him credit for. All this surface incompetence – Mayo was more than ready to believe it might well be an act, put on by a basically lazy man to save himself from the necessity of stirring himself to action.

'Tell you another thing about Fleur – you never knew when you had her, that one. Always something up her sleeve. Always looked as if she knew summat you didn't, know what I mean?'

Mayo did. That photograph again, that closed Gioconda smile. Was it something she had known, or done, that had caused someone to murder her?

Sutcliffe lit the last cigarette from his packet, and looked at his watch. 'Look, I don't want to rush you, but if there's nothing else you want to know I'd best be off. Vera'll give me hell if I ruin her Yorkshire pudding.'

There wasn't anything else at the moment, except for what Sutcliffe might know about Michael Saville, or Zoe Henderson, but Mayo drew a blank here. There was nothing the journalist could tell about either of them. Not one to hang about, he accepted their thanks and left, happy with a promise to be kept informed of anything further on the case of interest to his paper, and another forty fags bought at the bar.

Coming into Lavenstock from the direction of Branxmore, dominating the landscape were the tall shoddy tower blocks of the Somerville Estate, a nineteen-sixties civic mistake that strode aggressively against the skyline, as if about to stamp forward and crush the parade of small depressed shops at their feet. The shops today were all shut, with the exception of Patel's Punjabi Supermarket, We Never Close. Outside the fish and chip shop, greasy wrappers lay discarded and sodden in the gutters, yesterday's frying still lingering on the thick, damply-cold air.

They drew up outside Elizabeth House, a block of maisonettes, newer than the towers, built in their shadow, and walked to the door of No. 20.

'Oy, oy!' Kite bent down to make a closer inspection of about two thousand pounds' worth of powerful motorbike, casually propped against the wall. 'Did you say on the dole?' The door was at that moment opened, before they'd had time to knock, by Lola Tennyson, a quick, darting figure, her raggedy-blonde hair newly rinsed.

'You've found her, haven't you? Mrs Saville?' were the first words she uttered, almost before Mayo had got the introductions out of his mouth. Her clothes, he saw at once, were too young and too bright, defeating the presumed object of making her look younger than her years, her expression too eager and too avid. Mayo indicated that they had, and they followed her from the tiny hallway into the living-room, where a young girl of about seventeen or so was curled up in one of the armchairs, giving the impression of having hurriedly pushed something under the cushion as they came in. The room was warm and comfortable, and tidy, very tidy considering that there were three teenagers in the household, and apart from a blindingly patterned carpet in shades of orange and gold, plainly furnished, with a three-piece suite in mustard-coloured vinyl at one end and a light wood dining suite at the other. Heavy rock music reverberated through the floor from upstairs.

'Mr Saville rang my Debra here to tell her,' her mother went on, projecting her voice above the racket, 'she used to do Mrs Saville's typing and things like that for her, see, and he rang to say there wouldn't be no more work. What a terrible thing, she's been working for her for over two years now, haven't you, m'duck?' It was unclear whether Mrs Tennyson's outrage was for Fleur Saville's death, or her own daughter's unemployment.

Debra rose abruptly and made as if to go out of the room. 'Would you mind staying, please?' Mayo asked. She looked apprehensive, but sat down again without saying anything. She was a surprise, this Debra, a thin, grave girl, dressed in a white T-shirt and jeans, with a mass of dark hair, untidily crimped as they all seemed to wear it nowadays, and brown eyes which were wide and thoughtful behind a pair of large spectacles.

'Sorry about the noise,' their hostess apologised perfunctorily, 'it's our Kev,' as though that was both explanation and excuse. They were just in time for a cuppa, she added, she'd just brewed up, and she was sorry but our Kev had eaten all the biscuits. Tea would be fine, Mayo said, they'd stopped for a bite of lunch on the way there.

When they'd accepted cups of the fierce orange brew and Kite had settled back, notebook at the ready, Mayo said, 'I'd like to ask you one or two questions, Mrs Tennyson.' She wasn't Mrs, that much he knew, also that she never bothered to conceal it, but what else did you call a woman in her position? His mind and his tongue jibbed at Ms

'I heard them, you know, her and him, the day she disappeared, having a right old go at one another. Poor man, he must be feeling really bad now, knowing they parted in anger!' The kind of eagerness in the way she came out with the cliché was something Mayo wasn't unfamiliar with, in circumstances like this. He leaned forward to place his cup on the coffee table, and rephrased the first part of her remark.

'I understand you overheard what you thought was a quarrel on that day.'

'I didn't *think* I heard, I *did* hear.'

She was agog to tell, repeating what she'd heard, but despite her claims, there was nothing that was new. What it amounted to in total was raised voices and an assumption of the rest. Nothing had been clearly enough heard for her to be able to tell him what the quarrel had been about, she was forced to admit, but never in her life had she expected to hear Mr Saville shout like that, a real saint that man was, the way Mrs Saville only had to raise her little finger and he'd do what she wanted. 'And now she's ended up murdered, hasn't she?'

'We don't know that.' He wasn't prepared to tell her yet that they did.

'Murdered,' she repeated with relish, as if he hadn't spoken, 'Mrs Saville, fancy!'

'Mum!' interposed the hitherto silent Debra.

'Mrs Tennyson, we're trying to sort out the events on that Saturday. Mr Saville tells us that he spoke to you in the Cornmarket late in the afternoon, is that right?'

'That's right, he did.'

'I don't suppose you could give me a more precise time?'

It appeared she could. 'A minute or two after half-four, it'd be. The town hall clock had just struck when we started collecting. I told him about forgetting my money and he gave it me, and more for the box, very generous, I'll hand that to him –'

'Just a minute. What money was this?' Saville had made no mention of this part of his encounter with Lola.

'The extra that Mrs Saville had given me for going in that day to help out. Forgot it, I did, left it on the kitchen table, being in such a rush. I had to go up the town to do some Christmas shopping after I'd finished my work, and I got a real turn, I can tell you, when I found I'd forgotten to pick it up. In Marks I was. I had enough with me, but I never like the idea of money being left lying around, it don't come that easy.'

'That it doesn't.' Mayo gave her one of his sudden rare smiles, getting a never-say-die grin back in return. Life must be far from a bed of roses for her, but she was a little game 'un right enough, and she didn't seem to be making a bad job of it. He'd seen more than his share of women like her, left on their own to keep the family going on tuppence ha'penny a week. Marvellous how they did it – but then, he'd known for a long time that women were by far the tougher section of the human race. Her courage moved him. He reckoned she was entitled to her Salvation Army if it gave her a kick. 'Please go on.'

'Well, she'd put it in an old envelope, see, and I thought what if it gets thrown away? But I knew it wasn't no use calling nor ringing to find out, there wouldn't be nobody there, Mr Saville would be at the shop, and Mrs Saville was at the kiddies' party. I didn't half get a surprise when I saw his car outside when I was going home on the bus.'

'Whose car?'

'Mr Saville's, of course.'

'What time was this?'

Her eyes widened at the rapid questions. 'My bus was the twenty to three from outside the library, and it was on time for a change, so that would make it, let's see, about what, when it got to Kelsey Road –'

'Quarter to, no more than ten to at the most,' Kite supplied, unable to keep a note of excitement from his voice.

'That's right, it would.' Gratified by the interest she'd aroused, Lola settled back in her chair, curling sparrow legs under her, the tip of her snub nose turning pink with all the attention she was getting. 'So I rang straight away when I got home – that'd be about another fifteen minutes, I reckon – and there was this feller answered. I thought it was Mr Saville, but he said it wasn't.'

'What made you think it was him?' Mayo asked.

'I was expecting him to answer, I suppose,' she responded with a shrewdly-assessing glance. 'But when he said it wasn't, I could tell the difference, really. Quicker, more impatient, like. "No, there's nobody here who can help you, sorry," he said, sharpish, and put the receiver down. Well, I thought, some folk!'

If Saville had just killed his wife, it would be surprising if he hadn't sounded strange. But he couldn't have, could he?

'You're sure it was Mr Saville's car you saw?'

'Yes, of course. Leastways, if it wasn't it was one just like it. I've seen it often enough, haven't I? Sort of grey-blue it is.'

'What kind is it, what make?' Kite wanted to know.

'How should I know? I'm not well up on cars, I've never had no cause to be. But it must have been his, mustn't it?'

The thumping beat from upstairs ceased suddenly. It was followed by a loud crash, as if Kev had thrown his boot, or perhaps his stereo, against the wall. Then the music began again, louder. His mum said, 'Ooh, our Kev! We'll have her next door banging on the wall again before we know where we're at! Hang on, will you?' and rushed out.

Mayo seized the opportunity, which he suspected would be brief, to speak to Debra. 'So you'll be looking for a new job now, love?'

'Yes, I suppose so.' To his surprise Mayo heard a catch in the girl's voice as she answered. Well, it wasn't easy nowadays for any of them, poor kids. It wasn't easy to give them reassurance, either.

'A bright girl like you, you'll find something,' he told her, doing his best.

'No, I shan't. Not another job like that. Working for her was special. Like –' Tears welled, one rolled down her face. 'Oh, I don't know how I can find words to describe how it was,' she finished forlornly, looking young and lost.

'Try, Debra.'

She blew her nose, and tried.

Her lips still trembled, but gradually as she began to speak she became calmer. It turned out that she'd acted as the dead woman's secretary for getting on for three years. She hadn't been able to find work for several months after leaving school, and she'd been glad to accept the job Fleur had offered. 'I could hardly type at all when I started, never mind type manuscripts, but it was a job. That's all I thought of it at first, but in the end I got to really love it, you know? Besides –' Whatever she had been about to say, she checked herself, blinking rapidly. Her hand strayed towards the cushion and whatever she had stuffed behind it.

'You mean the job was well paid?'

'Oh no! Well, it was all right, but . . . she was good to me in other ways.'

She looked at him earnestly, stole a glance at Kite, apparently absorbed in his shorthand, and then in a burst of confidence, she told him shyly, colouring up, 'I've been trying to do a bit of writing, myself. Mum thinks it's daft, somebody like me hoping to get anything published, and if our Kev knew . . . but why not?' she added defiantly.

'Why not?' said Mayo, concealing his surprise. 'Good luck to you, lass.' He was rewarded with a smile that seemed to light the grave face from within, giving it a sheen of beauty, making him blink and feel a pang of middle-aged envy for such shining youth, such hope. 'What about Mrs Saville, did she know about your writing?'

'Oh yes!' breathed Debra. 'Ofcourse, I know I can't ever hope to write as well as she did, but she used to read my stuff and tell me I was learning all the time, show me where I'd gone wrong.' She added modestly, 'Working for her like I did, I don't suppose I could help some of it rubbing off, could I?'

A bad case of heroine worship, no doubt about it, but not perhaps entirely unjustified. A busy woman, taking time off to help an inexperienced young girl on her way – that had been a kindness. And if Fleur Saville had exacted a bit of flattery and admiration in the course of it, wasn't that only human? She had liked both, though perhaps more than most, he thought, recalling what Zoe Henderson had said about her – confirmed by Sutcliffe, and also, according to Kite, by the vicar's wife.

'There's something I'd like to ask you –' Debra was saying, her face vivid with colour, stammering in her confusion. 'I don't – I don't know if it's allowed – but if you – if you do come across it. It's well – it's a manuscript of mine, you see. Could I p-possibly have it back?'

'I should think so, if you tell me what to look for.'

'Well, I've written a book,' she said, her voice steadying, chin raised, her expression a mixture of pride and defiance, as if daring him to laugh. She threw another glance at Kite but seemed reassured. 'I didn't think it could be much good, but Mrs Saville thought it was worth sending to her publisher. Only, the thing is, she rang me that morning – the morning she disappeared, and told me she'd had it back. They'd written to her, and there were some comments in the letter about my script. They don't want to publish my story, of course, I never expected that, but she said they'd been kind about it, so – if I could have it? My book, I mean, I expect you'll want to keep the letter, and it – it d-doesn't really matter very much to me.'

She was painfully anxious not to seem anxious about what must be of the greatest importance to her. 'Deborah Shelley?' he asked, rapidly making the thinly-disguised connection. He recalled seeing the letter she was talking about among the dead woman's papers, and he particularly remembered the section in it that had referred to the book. If he'd been an aspiring author, he'd thought, he'd have been greatly encouraged by the remarks.

'You've seen it! Oh, you haven't –?' Her face suddenly paled. 'You haven't *read* it?'

Not the book, he told her gently, only the letter. He had just time to add that he would let her have her manuscript back, and a photocopy of the criticism, when he heard her mother's hand on the doorknob. He jerked his head in Kite's direction. Kite got up and walked unhurriedly to the door. Voices could be heard – Kite's, Lola's shrill tones, and then presently, the sound of heavier footsteps descending the stairs .

'Debra,' Mayo said quickly, 'you probably knew as much about Mrs Saville's affairs as anybody. Do you recall anything different that happened lately? Had she changed her routine, made any new contacts?' Debra shook her head, mystified. 'Anything at all out of the ordinary that you remember?'

'No, nothing like that, except –' She broke off, looking thoughtful. 'No, it's too long ago, and nothing ever came of it.'

'Tell me, all the same.'

'Well, it wasn't recently, it was months ago, after she'd been up to London to see her publishers. They're being taken over by an American firm, and when she came back, I could see something exciting had happened. She'd met one of the American executives, and when she came home, she was all sort of lit up. I knew there'd been some talk a while back about televising *Salamander Fire* as a serial, and I asked her if that was it. But she laughed and said something more rewarding and important than that.'

'She didn't explain any further?'

'No, never another word.'

'I don't suppose you'd remember the date?'

Debra only had to think for a second or two. 'Oh yes, I can tell you exactly. July the third it would be. I can remember because it was my birthday the following week, and when she was in London, she bought me this.' She lovingly touched the gold chain round her neck, from which hung an elegant gold letter 'D'. 'But it was funny, her saying that, wasn't it? I mean, what could be more important than a TV serial?'

'What indeed?' replied Mayo.

'That your lad's motorbike?' he asked a minute later, finding Mrs Tennyson and Kite outside with a sullen youth sporting a bright green Mohican haircut and several diamante earrings dangling from three perforations in one ear.

'That's what he's been on to me about and yes it is, and what of it?' Lola demanded militantly, jerking her head towards Kite. 'He's just got a job up the motorway construction site – nearly two hundred a week he's earning, so why shouldn't he buy a motorbike if he wants?'

'All right, love, keep your hair on,' Kite answered. 'No harm in asking.' And to Kev, 'Let's have a dekko at your licence and insurance all the same, sunshine.'

Two hundred a week for a layabout like that, a bit of a kid

who'd left school without an O-level to his name and a record to boot, I should be so lucky, he thought, reflecting on a policeman's lot.

CHAPTER 13

As usual, there had been an instant response to the appeal on radio and TV for anyone who might have seen Fleur Saville on the day she disappeared. Back at the office, Mayo found on his desk a whole clutch of reports that she'd been sighted. A woman answering to her description had bought petrol at a filling station near Cheltenham and driven away in a black Volvo (but Fleur Saville didn't drive). She'd been seen at Euston station at eleven (the time when she'd been putting out cakes and sandwiches in the church hall in Lavenstock), also in Birmingham, in Stratford-upon-Avon and in Lossiemouth, four hundred miles away in Scotland. There were more. They'd all have to be taken note of, and the possibles investigated.

Meanwhile, he'd better have another look at the dead woman's papers, after what young Debra had said. He rang for some tea and drank it while he went through them yet again. It didn't take him long to find the publishers' letter she'd spoken about, dated the sixteenth of December, which he put on one side in order to photocopy for her the section concerning her manuscript. He then went backwards through the file until he came across the carbon copy of a letter Fleur had written to them, after the London meeting on the third of July. It said thank you for the excellent lunch, and spoke of 'the matters we discussed' without specifying what these had been. It went on to say how unexpected it was to find they had mutual friends, she was sure they'd all find it very interesting to meet again here in Lavenstock, and ended very sincerely, Fleur Lamont.

Mayo noted the name of the person to whom the letter was addressed, and sat back, thinking deeply.

Fleur had learned something that day which had, in Debra's phrase, lit her up. It didn't necessarily have to be anything which had occurred at her publishers', of course, but it seemed likely.

Or what other things were capable of exciting Fleur? Being centre stage . . . she was quick to seize upon the drama of a situation, and the opportunity of basking in the limelight seemed never to have been far from her mind. She had liked power. Manipulating someone to her advantage.

He looked again at the letter. Was he imagining the veiled threat that seemed contained in that last brief paragraph? He allowed his mind to dwell on the subject of it: a mutual acquaintance – something more interesting, apparently, even than televising *Salamander Fire*. He closed his eyes, trying to remember exactly what she'd said to Debra. '*Oh no, something much more interesting than that.*' No, he hadn't quite got it . . . '*something more interesting and rewarding.*' Had that been the precise word Fleur had used? Rewarding?

He decided to search the Buttercup Club files yet again. The idea that had come to him while waiting outside the Challis house was growing in his mind. It wasn't very clear yet, but if he didn't pursue it, he knew he'd get no peace.

It was just before half past seven when Mayo finally put his key into the door of his flat. As soon as he let himself in, it hit him. Although not an unduly gregarious man, he would never have remained solitary through choice, and the bleak loneliness overwhelmed him with the feeling that his life had fallen apart, a sense of personal failure. Depression like this didn't come so often now, but it was still hard to take, and it always came when he wasn't prepared for it . . . after an unrewarding day, in a crowded room, coming unexpectedly on something that had belonged to Lynne . . .

He'd worked out his routines to combat it. Doggedly, now, he brought them into play, upping the thermostat of the central heating, then taking a shower. Later, in his dressing-gown, he began to potter about until he should feel like getting himself something to eat. A beer, some Dvorak going, vigorous rhythms suggesting strong forward movement and controlled energy which rarely failed to help him sooner or later to shrug off his mood.

He tried to settle down with the Sunday papers and his book, but the papers were too full of the usual post-Christmas features on glamorous holidays in far-flung places, and Henry James's Maisie suddenly seemed a tiresome, precocious little perisher who knew too much and whose neck he could cheerfully have wrung. The TV offered nothing but a soap opera about sailing, and a comedy show repeat which hadn't amused him the first time round. The appeal of *Salamander Fire* was nil. On an impulse he fetched out the clock he had mentioned to Zoe Henderson. Tinkering with some form of machinery, preferably a clock or a watch, had always been a form of mind release for him. There was something soothing about letting his hands perform the mechanistic exercise of cleaning and oiling the beautifully machined springs and wheels, fitting them together again in their interdependent, logical pattern, shifting his mind on to automatic pilot.

A small Edwardian bracket clock this was, about six inches high, a pretty thing veneered in walnut, inlaid with ebony, with only a small part of the veneer missing, a corner of the base. That wasn't why it had been put to the back of the cupboard, but because it had stopped at ten to four and refused to go again, and he couldn't abide a clock that wasn't in working order. They spoke too eloquently of empty houses, lives that had stopped. He began to fiddle with it, and before he knew where he was, had the parts spread out over the table.

The idea that had come to him had been sparked off by something that had been said during the course of the day, and it was frustrating him because he couldn't remember what it was. Usually when this happened, he ignored it, knowing that it was likely to come back to him when he least expected it, when it might or might not turn out to be of importance. But tonight it nagged, as if it were the missing key piece in a Chinese puzzle that he must find. He hated unanswered questions; he liked things to fit into a pattern, perhaps that's why he'd become a detective, trying to replace unrelated parts into his own idea of an ordered scheme of things, though Lynne used to tease him – saying it was because he was just a Nosey Parker with a talent for sniffing things out that people would often rather have kept hidden. That had been at the beginning of their marriage, when the inconvenient demands of his job could still be made light of with a joke.

Hell, this was getting him nowhere. What was all this with Lynne tonight? She was gone, nothing would bring her back, unsay the things that had been said, and not said; nothing could tidy up and smooth out the past.

He reassembled the clock, setting it down carefully and watching it for a while. The music stopped and he went to start the record again from the beginning. The clock went on ticking, quietly, steadily, and he sat back, pleased at last with his efforts. Was it something Mrs Tennyson had said, or perhaps the girl, Debra? Or was it simply that unexpected remark of Gillian Challis's – 'Have charity –' that had lodged in his head because of its unexpectedness? No, not that, but –

The doorbell rang.

It was Alex, with a brown paper carrier bag in her hands. 'All right if I come in, Gil? I know it's late, but –'

'All *right*? You can't know how all right it is.' But he had a moment of dismay. No way would Alex fail to notice the untidiness of the flat. Very particular, she was. He kept it clean enough, but the niceties of plumped-up cushions and fresh flowers and washing up his breakfast coffee cup every time before he went out was something he just couldn't be bothered with . . . he hoped she wouldn't insist on washing up before she sat down, as she had the last time.

But there was a smile in her eyes, the cold air had brought a flare of colour to her pale cheeks, she looked luminously pretty in a softly-wrapped mole-coloured tweed coat with the collar turned up to frame her face and a Gitane-blue scarf that echoed the blue of her eyes tucked in at the neck. He drew her inside, circling her lightly with his arms.

'You've not eaten?' she asked. 'Good. Just put this in the oven then, to keep hot, plates in, too. It's only Chinese takeaway, not one of your Julie's Cordon Bleu efforts, but I'd been to the pictures and saw your light on as I passed and decided to take a chance.'

That sounded like a lonely Sunday evening, a clutch at his heart, but he knew he was on shaky ground, saying a thing like that to Alex. Don't push your luck, when she's doing the running. 'I'll just clear the table,' he said instead.

Her glance followed the wave of his hand. 'Another clock!'

'What d'you mean, another?'

'How many is it? Six, at least. In a flat this size?'

'Seven, actually.' He laughed at her expression. 'Runs in the family, you should see the number my father had. He used to fiddle with them as well, till his eyesight got too bad, so did my grandad. I'd forgotten what good therapy it is, even if you don't get it right first time.' He stared at the clock, frowning. It had stopped again. 'Give me a minute and I'll have it all away.'

'Don't bother, we'll have it on trays by the fire – and leave the music on, as well.'

'Sure you don't object?'

'Love it.'

The Seventh Symphony swept gloriously through the room with great melodic surges while they ate. His tiredness had left him. This was how it could be, he thought, not just occasionally, but every night, if they were married. How many times had he asked her? How many times had she put him off – they were all right as they were, weren't they? Why spoil things? *Spoil?* He couldn't understand her, and was beginning to feel he was entitled to demand more explanation than that, but he was more afraid than he liked to admit that if he did he might lose her altogether.

He awoke, as he always did, at the dawn light, but Alex was awake before him. And up, out of bed, even dressed, sitting by the window where the curtain had been left half drawn. The view outside was worth looking at, a still predominantly white landscape with a necklace of lights stringing the road down the tree-lined hill, sweeping in a curve round the edges of the town to a glimpse of the Stockwell and the hills rising behind. Not enticing enough, though, in his opinion, to bring you out of a warm bed on a winter's morning. He lay, lazily content, enjoying watching her without her knowledge, curled up and self-contained in the old rose-patterned chintz armchair. He could see her profile, darker against the still dark sky, her smoothed hair re-forming the memory of it rumpled on his pillow.

She turned slightly when after a while he got out of bed, threw on his bathrobe and padded over to her to put his arms around her, crossing them over her breasts, deciding that now was the time, now, in the aftermath of love, when things could be spoken about.

Alex too was aware that her time of procrastination was over as, stricken with guilt, she listened to his low murmur, but didn't hear, didn't need to hear, knowing what he was saying by heart . . .

'Don't, Gil,' she found courage to interrupt at last, sharper than she meant to, sharp as icicles it came out, so that there was no mistaking either tone or meaning. 'It's no good.'

He was immediately silent, and for so long she thought he wasn't going to reply. 'That's it, then?' he said at last, drawing away. 'No good? And here was I thinking it was. Bloody good. Bloody marvellous, in fact.'

They were facing each other now.

'I didn't mean *that*. You know I didn't. It was lovely, but, oh God – there's no way I can marry you.'

'I see. Good enough in bed, but you can't stand my table manners –'

'Don't blow it up, just listen, won't you? There's a lot I haven't told you.'

'You'd better start then, hadn't you?'

It wasn't going to be easy, but then she'd never thought it would be. He listened, stony-faced, while she told him at last. At last. About her Irish Liam, her dark Celtic charmer with the golden tongue, married to an invalid wife, with no intention of divorcing her. 'Not that I'd want him to, I wouldn't want him under those conditions,' she said – though for years she'd had him under worse conditions than that. Until at last she'd had enough of subterfuge, of not belonging, of feeling herself used, and had made the break and had herself transferred here.

And nothing had changed, because she'd brought herself with her, and she was still the same. Telling yourself you could *make* it be all right didn't work, as last night had proved. Lying awake, it had come to her like a tremendous physical blow that she mustn't go on using Gil Mayo as a substitute. Who wasn't anybody's substitute.

Shared interests, humour, wonderful sex . . . what more did she want? A home, yes. Children – well, maybe, she was still young enough, just – and he was more than willing to give her both. So why couldn't she take a deep breath and plunge?

She was miserably aware that she was demanding something, some perfect combination of attributes that simply didn't exist: Liam, romantic but unstable, shying away from decisions of responsibility; on the other hand Mayo, solid and dependable as the Rock of Gibraltar . . . and ultimately old-fashioned in his views on marriage. She didn't want to be – she *wouldn't* be – taken over, made part of his life, not wholly her own. Because there was

302

ambition too, soaring ambition of a kind she couldn't deny and he might not be able to go along with. She didn't see herself as a substitute, either.

Basically cool and sensible, she was detached enough to realise that this search for unattainable perfection might be an excuse to avoid commitment, to avoid the conflict between marriage and private expectations. But when all was said and done, there was the real, true reason, or rather, two of them: there was Liam still between them – and though Gil hardly realised this himself, Lynne, who wasn't yet forgotten, exorcised. Alex wondered if she ever would be. Her dark, sleek head drooped. She wasn't making sense, and didn't know how to.

He said, 'I won't accept this. What's wrong with me?' The exact words she had used of herself, with a different meaning. Dear God, she couldn't bear it, seeing him humble. Correction, not humble at all, sore and furious. An entirely understandable reaction. At that moment, if he had added only a small endearment, she might even then have succumbed and said it: 'All right, Gil, why not?' But that wasn't his style.

CHAPTER 14

The décor at Charlie Girl, the new unisex hairdressing salon on Peter Street, was painted in hi-tech scarlet, black and grey. The assistants were called stylists, and male and female alike wore freaked-out hairdos in amazing colours, and a weird assortment of baggy white cotton garments that gave them the appearance of refugees from some Indian ashram. Detective-Constable Keith Farrar, who was newly-married, only just out of their generation but worlds apart, could hardly tell one from t'other at first, nor even second, glance. The ear-rings and make-up meant nothing.

There wasn't much going on this Monday morning, he noticed. The framed certificates on the walls, announcing the abilities and prowess of the stylists – Nikki, Vikki, Tamara, Jacqui, Jon and Craig – looked down on empty chairs. A tall thin person with feverish red eye-shadow and hennaed hair cut like a scrubbing brush swanned towards him, a label pinned to a non-existent bosom declaring her to be Sam. It was only the absence of an Adam's apple that decided Farrar on the gender.

'Mrs Who?'

Sam's lack of interest was total. He'd known it was going to be hard going before he began, by the bored, dismissive glance at his regulation haircut and 'straight' clothes, by the hostility aroused when he presented his ID, not by any means the usual reception accorded to Farrar, who was blond, smooth and good-looking. And knew it.

He repeated the name, and after some insistence she was persuaded to look back through the appointments book to December 22nd. 'Oh yeah, she was here. She was Nikki's lady.' A prominent notice declared Nikki to be the leading stylist and colourist. She cost three pounds more.

'Could I see her, please?'

'Nikki!'

She was older, wildly orange-haired, and a little more forthcoming, but not much. She didn't *exactly* recall a Mrs Saville. Well, a lot of people had been coming here just the once, to try the salon out, like, and just before Christmas they'd been specially busy. He couldn't expect her to remember everybody.

He described the dead woman, and showed her photo.

'We-ell, maybe her face is familiar, sort of. What d'you want to know for?'

'She's been murdered, love.'

'You're joking!'

'Afraid not. Haven't you been watching the telly?'

'The stuff they were showing over Christmas? No way! We

stocked up with videos. I never watch the news anyway, it's dead boring.'

Well, at least it wasn't seeing the face on the screen that had rung bells. 'Come on, see if you can't jog your memory somehow.'

Nikki's voice was plaintive. 'I wish I could, but I really can't, I'm sorry.'

'Thanks, love, that's a great help,' Farrar said gloomily.

'No need to be like that, I've done my best. Anyway, I must've done her if she's in the book, mustn't I? There's no cancellation. And like I said, I do faintly remember her, but not exactly.'

A concentrated frown appeared between the plucked arched brows as she pored over the appointments book. She'd never remember. Anyone over twenty-five very likely looked the same to her, Farrar thought, but she said suddenly. 'Hang about, it's coming back to me, I had Mrs Philips in at half past, one of my regulars, and I remember her saying what lovely blonde hair that last lady of yours had, and asking if I couldn't do hers the same. Well, I told her it was natural, and *she's* been every colour under the sun, Mrs Philips, shouldn't think she remembers what her natural colour is –'

'Good girl – you remembered! And you'll be able to tell me what time Mrs Saville would have left?'

'Just before half past, it would've been.'

Farrar smiled and closed his notebook. 'Well done, darling.'

'Be my guest.' Nikki fluttered her eyelashes. Maybe he didn't qualify to join the wrinklies yet. Sort of sexy, really, these older men.

'Tell you what,' she remarked as his hand was pushing open the plate glass door, 'you could do with a cut and blow-dry yourself while you're here, why don't you?'

It was at times like these that Farrar understood the bloke who'd declared himself too old to dance and too young to die.

*

Mayo had walked into the station that morning to find trouble coming at him from all directions, as if Lavenstock's criminal element was suddenly making up for lost time, choosing, right on target, the beginning of what looked like being a 'flu epidemic here at the station, with men and women on the strength going down like flies.

Alex was taking a few days off as part of her entitlement, which precluded the prospect of an immediate meeting. Not that they had parted on bad terms. He thought sourly that he might have felt better if they had. No, they were two mature adults, weren't they, and had ended up rationalising the bloody position so that neither was satisfied. In effect, they were back to square one, with nothing resolved, a situation he'd noticed often happened when you argued with women. But not for long, he told himself. He wasn't a man to live with unresolved situations.

He hadn't been too surprised when Alex had made what for her was evidently a momentous revelation. The possibility that she'd fled to Lavenstock from involvement with some man was one which had occurred to him more than once. What had surprised – and angered – him was her refusal to accept his insistence, his *promise*, that marriage needn't limit her freedom. A career if she wanted it – or a family. But she was like a lot more women in these enlightened days, he reflected bitterly, she wanted to eat her cake and have it. Whereas he only wanted her as a wife, not as a mistress. He was old-fashioned enough to find neither the sentiment nor the phrasing of that amusing.

A murder enquiry naturally took precedence over anything else, but juggling with several other investigations at the same time was a necessity you had to learn to accept. With regard to the Saville case, there wasn't much he need personally occupy himself with at the moment. The results of the forensic tests hadn't yet come in. Nor had the answer to the telephone enquiry he'd made in New York, the outcome of which couldn't reasonably be expected until tomorrow. Routine matters he could leave to others, while he got stuck into the most pressing of the new cases, among which were an overnight break-in at one of the leading jeweller's shops in the town, and a report of cocaine being passed at a teenage party. He plunged into the crisis, and succeeded in taking his mind off his personal problems for a few hours.

But lunch-time arrived with an incipient headache which he hoped to God wasn't heralding 'flu for him as well, and no ease to his soul. He took two aspirin and found himself snapping at Kite for no good reason, demanding to know what the hell Farrar was doing. Why wasn't he back from that hairdresser yet? It was only round the corner, wasn't it, not the bloody North Pole? He heard the injured note in Kite's voice as he answered that Farrar was just typing his report out now, and checked himself sharply. No way to carry on. Whatever private miseries he'd had, he'd never before taken them out on his subordinates. 'Bring him up, Martin,' he said, feeling shabby. 'I'll have it from him in words I can under-stand, not his A-level English.'

'Mind how you go,' Kite warned Farrar, 'His Nibs has been like a bear with a sore backside this morning.'

But the detective-constable's succinct report, confirming that Fleur Saville had indeed kept her hair appointment in Peter Street, earned him an approving word and Farrar, who was out for pro-motion, notched himself up another score .

When he and Kite had gone, Mayo walked to the window, brooding. His office overlooked Milford Road, busy as usual with the one-way traffic speeding through. Another day of raw damp, and though the snow had all but gone in the town centre, pedes-trians were still muffled against the cold. Within his vision was the pet shop on the corner of Peter Street where it curved back on itself to run parallel with the main road, also Woolworth's and the flower-seller who sat under the arched portico of the Victorian Gothic Town Hall, surrounded by a burst of colourful pot plants and baskets of daffodils and tulips from the Scillies. Fleur Saville had loved flowers, had filled her house with them . . . He frowned, dismissing the non-sequitur, trying to connect. Something wasn't right.

She had been alive at two-thirty, and had therefore died some time during the next half-hour – presumably at home. Had she really intended leaving Saville? The removal of her jewellery indicated she had, but if so, the absence of a note worried Mayo. He thought Fleur, a woman to whom words and extravagant gestures were everyday currency, would have left one. Unless she'd been prevented by her murderer, there perhaps by pre-arrangement? During that half-hour the phone had been answered by a man – not Saville, since he was undoubtedly in his shop. And what about the car seen outside? Was it one owned by the murderer – or was it conceivable that he'd had the nerve to use Saville's car to transport his wife to where she'd been found? But remember, she hadn't been dumped until after six o'clock, so if the car had been borrowed from the garage without Saville's knowledge, how had it been returned? He'd been home before five. Or had it been used merely to get the body away, transferring it to some other car which had later been used to dispose of it? And did this indicate collusion?

Mayo rubbed a hand across his face and, turning back to his desk, caught a glimpse from the corner of his eye of a flying figure, a mane of red hair. For an instant he thought the woman from the flower-seller with her arms wrapped around a large azalea in a pot was Zoe Henderson, but no. When she turned, he saw a young girl he didn't recognise, no more than seventeen. He stared after her as she disappeared with springy step around the corner.

He must make time somehow to have another word with Mrs Henderson.

The inquest on Fleur Saville was held on the following day, and adjourned for further police enquiries. By that time, the door-to-door enquiries had been completed. They were predictably unhelpful. No one, it seemed, had noticed anything out of the ordinary on the day in question; and it was certainly too long ago for anyone to remember whether they'd happened to see Saville's own car standing outside his own house. Confronted with questions about his car, Saville had steadfastly refuted all knowledge of its being taken out of the garage that day.

After the inquest was over, Mayo decided to pick up the clock he'd spoken to Zoe Henderson about. If he was going to see her, he would get her to look at the damaged case with a view to having it repaired, which would be an incentive to him to get it working again. He drove home straight from the court.

The owners of the large house in which Mayo's flat was situated were an elderly couple called Vickers, a brother and sister whose family home the entire house had once been. David Vickers, retired from his job as a tax inspector, his children dispersed to various parts of the globe, had lived alone in the house, uneasily and in some disarray, for a considerable time after the death of his wife until his sister Freda, headmistress of the local girls' school, had also retired and consented to come back to share their childhood home. Of an eminently pragmatic and energetic turn of mind, unlike her brother, she had made conditions before moving in, and then immediately set in motion what she had been trying to persuade him was the sensible thing to do for years. Within a very short time the large house had been split up into three self-contained flats, quiet and respectable tenants found, and their own furniture ruthlessly thinned out to make the ground-floor rooms into a comfortable and easily run establishment for two people getting on in years.

Their original tenants had changed once or twice over the next ten years. At present the first floor was occupied by a married couple called Brownlow, with Mayo occupying the top floor, having successfully passed Miss Vickers's stringent tests as to what constituted a good tenant. The arrangement suited them all very well. The elderly brother and sister derived a certain amount of assurance from having a policeman in the house, and Miss Vickers enjoyed entertaining Mayo to the occasional meal. She was sure he must miss his daughter, as she did herself. She'd taken pleasure in their little chats, which she said helped to keep her in touch with the younger generation. Mayo in turn liked the couple's unintrusive friendliness, the fact that his sitting-room overlooked a pleasant garden which he had no need to tend, and the freedom of his own private entrance.

He was just putting his key in the door of his own apartment when Freda Vickers, hearing him, came out with a parcel she'd taken in with her own mail. From the handwriting, and its battered state, he deduced it was the Christmas present from his sister he'd never received, and from the powerful perfume issuing from it, that it was a broken bottle of the kind of after-shave he couldn't be sorry had broken.

Miss Vickers was deploring the carelessness that had caused this. 'Posted well before the last Christmas posting date, too.'

They exchanged opinions on the general fallibility of the Post Office system, and then she said, 'I heard about the murder this weekend, Mr Mayo. Has the culprit been found yet?'

Mayo replied that he hadn't, surprised at her question. She had always shown tact about his work, not expecting him to talk about it, and was certainly not the sort to be avid for lurid detail. Her next words, however, quietly said, explained her interest. 'She was one of my girls at Princess Mary's, you know. I taught her for several years.'

'Did you now?' He looked at Freda Vickers, neat in her check tweed skirt and dark blue cardigan jacket, wearing an impeccable cream silk shirt and gold chain, her becomingly-styled grey hair, her soft elderly skin enhanced by discreet make-up, encountered a shrewd look from her bright blue eyes, and made a decision.

'May I talk to you about her?'

She wasn't a woman for prevarication, and he had a feeling she'd anticipated, even led the way to his question. 'Certainly. Can you spare the time now? My brother's gone down to the bank, and I've just made a pot of coffee.'

He followed her into her tranquil room overlooking the back garden, carpeted in gold Wilton, with long powder blue velvet curtains at the windows, and some excellent gold-framed water-colours on the walls. Little shining polished tables stood about, covered with knick-knacks, except for one which held a coffee tray laid with silver, delicate china and two chocolate digestive biscuits. She fetched another matching cup, saucer and plate, and another two biscuits. The coffee was pale and ladylike, but the biscuits were good, dark, plain chocolate.

'What can I tell you about Fleur, Mr Mayo?'

They'd known each other for nearly six months, were good neighbours and friends, but he was still Mr Mayo to her, and always would be. It was inconceivable that she should be anything but Miss Vickers to almost anyone.

'Things in general – what she was like – anything you can remember.' He was confident she'd know the sort of thing. She was still remembered and respected in the town as being an excellent headmistress of one of the best and most renowned schools in the county, and from personal acquaintance he knew her to be a woman with an open and active mind.

'Where shall I begin?' She nibbled her biscuit, then put it down as if she'd suddenly lost the taste for it, sighing. 'Well, frankly, I have to say that Fleur was a big disappointment. She came to the school on a scholarship, but then never quite came up to the promise she'd shown. When I first heard of her success as a writer, I was pleased for her, and gratified that her years at Princess Mary's hadn't after all been wasted, though I must confess myself astonished. Until on reflection, I realised there was nothing surprising about it, that telling stories was the one thing she was uniquely fitted for.'

Taking up her rose-patterned cup, she sipped gently and watched him over its rim.

'You mean she was a liar, Miss Vickers?'

'That's a little too strong. It implies deceit – and no, she was never really deceitful, I'll give her that.'

But you didn't like her, thought Mayo.

'Let me explain. Her parents, Mr and Mrs Adams, were a very ordinary working-class couple. Deeply religious people, and very strict, as I recall. Good parents in their own lights, but undemonstrative and rather joyless, and totally lacking in imagination. They could never have understood that a girl like Fleur, an only child, might be very lonely and desperate to have attention and affection lavished on her. The result was that Fleur, when she first came to the school, used to – what's the current jargon for it, fantasise? – about herself to the other girls, make up stories about exciting places she'd been to, well-known people she'd met, even that she was really the daughter of someone famous. It's a situation not as uncommon as you might think, many imaginative children do romance from time to time, and coming from such a drab environment . . . her name was really Frances, you know, Fleur was what she called herself, but I didn't insist.'

'The other girls must have known she wasn't telling the truth? Didn't it make her unpopular?'

'Of course they knew. Even eleven-year-old girls are not fools, nor are their teachers. I made it my business to know everything that went on between my girls, Mr Mayo.' It amused him the way she spoke of 'her girls', in the manner of Miss Jean Brodie. 'But if they took her up on anything, Fleur would just laugh and say, "You didn't believe all that, did you? Surely you knew I'd made it all up, just for fun." And I suppose it was fun in a way, and harmless, if you knew you mustn't ever take anything she said seriously. At any rate, she never seemed to lack friends.'

'I've met one or two of them.'

'Let's see if you can recognise any of them from this.' She rose and crossed the room with neat, decisive steps, returning with a leather-bound album from a drawer. It stayed unopened on her knee, however, when she sat down again and said in a low voice,

'She wasn't perfect . . . but whatever could she have done that caused her to die as she did, Mr Mayo?' and then, almost immediately, 'I'm sorry, that's a very improper question which I hope you won't answer.'

'I won't, because I can't. I only wish I did know.'

She stared at him thoughtfully. 'It was thought to be rather smart to be in Fleur Adams's set, you know. As she grew older, there was a circle of girls who always seemed to gather round her – not only girls who were easily led, either. I suppose she had what's called charisma; I used to think they found her style rather glamorous and wanted to copy her sophistication.'

She found a place in the album on her knee, then handed it to Mayo. A dozen or so seventeen- and eighteen-year-old girls were seated around a Miss Vickers who was perhaps at that time a possible fifty, though not looking noticeably different from the present Miss Vickers.

'My Sixth Form, with my Head Girl sitting next to me.'

'Gillian Challis, of course,' Mayo said, instantly recognising the tilt of the head, the confident smile and the hockey-playing physique of the future magistrate and governor of her old school.

'Gillian Lingard-Smith, as she was then. But no. No, it's the girl on my other side who was Head Girl.'

Mayo transferred his gaze to the girl on the right of Miss Vickers. She must have moved when the camera shot was being taken for the image was very slightly blurred, but he knew who it was. 'Fleur?'

He looked up in surprise and met Miss Vickers's bright, speculative look.

'Yes, Fleur Adams. One of the very few judgemental mistakes I made in my career – at least, one hopes they were few. At the time I felt that her qualities of leadership might be put to better use, that learning to use them for the good of the school might make her a little less – shall we say, self-centred? I'm very much afraid it didn't.'

'Later, though? Of recent years, she'd put a lot into working for good causes.'

'So I'm told, so I'm told.' Her tone was dry, her blue eyes told him she had her reservations. He was reminded of Zoe Henderson's assertion that all Fleur's apparent benevolence was a boost to her own ego.

'Perhaps I didn't consider it carefully enough. At the time, as well as other considerations, it seemed to take me off the horns of a dilemma, from having to choose between Gillian and Nell Radlett.'

Mayo searched the photograph again, and it didn't take him long to pick out a smiling girl with dark curls. 'Nell Fennimore?'

'Yes. One of the cleverest girls of her year, Nell, with a place waiting for her at Oxford, and how does she end up? Wasted, married at eighteen, a mother within a couple of years. If Nell hadn't got herself tied up with Gerald Fennimore, what might she not have become? Ah well. I dare say you're thinking I'm banging my drum, and you'd be right. There's nothing wrong with a home and children, if that's what you want, I used to tell my girls, but for goodness' sake get yourself qualified first. But Nell, though she was a level-headed, sensible and responsible sort of girl, never had quite enough ambition.'

'Why not Gillian?' She had Head Prefect written all over her. 'What was wrong with her?'

'Oh, nothing wrong, goodness no, except that she was *expecting* the honour to fall on her. That's not always very good for the Gillians of this world, things come too easily for them. You understand me?'

'Yes, I think so. I think you must have steered the situation through very tactfully. At any rate, the three of them seem to have remained very good friends.'

'That doesn't surprise me. Gillian was brought up to put a good face on things. People's good opinion was always important to her. She took the disappointment well, got her head down and concentrated on her A-levels. Not much sense of humour, Gillian, but uncomplicated. Clever and competent. She got a good degree at Durham. And Nell had a very sweet nature.'

Mayo drained his insipid coffee, and stood up. His thanks to Miss Vickers were sincere, though she herself seemed to feel she hadn't been much help.

'I've said a lot about Fleur's drawbacks, haven't I? Perhaps not enough about her good points – and she had many. I must confess I was hurt at the time by her failure to respond to the faith I put in her – but I came to realise afterwards it was just as much a failure on my part to understand. I could never really *like* her, you see, however I tried, and when one comes down to it, everything she did was due to a need to be loved. Poor Fleur. I wonder if anyone ever understood this?'

Chapter 15

The telephone was ringing as he reached his flat. Kite was on the other end. 'Glad I've caught you. We've somebody here at the station you might want to listen to before you see Mrs Henderson. I think we may have a lead.'

Kite went on to tell him what it was all about, and Mayo said, 'Hold it, I'll be right there.'

The landlord of the Jolly Farmer at Corston Green came into his office wearing a cravat tucked into his open shirt neck, well-polished conker-brown brogues, and a navy blue blazer with brass buttons. He was of middle height, with a luxuriant moustache, receding hairline, handsome in a 1940's RAF way, a man by the name of John Drury, who had come forward to report having seen Fleur Saville and a man together.

'At least I think it was her. Don't get much time for watching television, but there's always a bit of a lull in trade after Christmas, so we had it switched on in the bar last night, and I saw the photograph you've issued. I'm pretty certain she was the same woman who was in my place one night before Christmas with a man. She was wearing a red coat then, as well.'

'Before Christmas? How much before?'

'As a matter of fact, it was the fourteenth of December, the Friday. The reason I can pinpoint it is we had a private party in for a meal that night, get a lot of them around Christmas. About a dozen women who work together in the same office had booked, and when she came in at first I thought she was one of them. I directed her into the corner where they were having a drink before their meal, but she got a bit uptight and said no, she certainly wasn't with them, she was waiting for a friend. Well, I could see she wasn't their sort when I looked – she had real class, and very noisy they were, but you can't throw business away these days, can you?'

Mayo agreed that you couldn't. 'Can you describe the man?'

'Hard to say. We were pretty busy at the time, and anyway he had his back to me most of the time. Big chap though, I can say that – your type, come to think, yes, very much like you, black hair and heavily built. You to a T. Not somebody you'd like to meet in a dark alley on a dark night.' Drury sniggered a little.

'Hm.' Mayo's face showed he didn't share the joke.

'Anything else you remember about him?' Kite asked. 'Specs, for instance? Heavy, dark-rimmed ones?' Mayo threw his sergeant a sharp look.

'He wasn't wearing glasses at all, that I remember.'

'What time was it, and how long did they stay?'

'Oh, not long. Only had the one drink. Maybe about half an hour, round about the eight o'clock mark's the nearest I can say to when they came in. She'd be about five minutes earlier than him. One other thing that might help, though – my barman was out at the back when this chappie drew up into the car park. I didn't see him arrive, myself, but Len swears he was driving a Jag. Pale grey or silver. They didn't leave together. I don't know how she came, but she telephoned for a taxi to take her home.'

'Challis,' said Kite, when Drury had gone.

'Drury said the man wasn't wearing glasses.' But Challis, of course. Mayo's objections were token.

'We don't know that Challis wears them all the time.'

'And he was in Zürich on the twenty-second.'

'We don't know that for certain, either. We've only his word for it. And he drives a silver XJ6.'

He did, he did. Mayo had detested Challis from the moment he set eyes on him, but up to now he'd scarcely been in the picture. There'd been nothing to connect him with the dead woman. He'd said he hardly knew her. Mayo considered that gratuitous piece of information, annoyed with himself on two counts. First, that he hadn't picked up the bloody silly remark on Sunday, recognising it as a lie; and secondly, that he'd misinterpreted Gillian Challis's reaction to it. At the time, he'd thought the agonized glance she'd cast her husband had been a plea for him to stay and give her moral support, whereas she must have been wondering what the hell had made him come out with such an obvious lie. Of course Challis must have known Fleur, and pretty well, if she'd been such a close friend of his wife's all those years.

The idea that had been forming in his mind began to take substance, and as other facts began to click into place, his thoughts went racing ahead. He knew that the case had shifted into the right gear at last. He was as sure in his own mind as he could be that Challis was the man seen in the Jolly Farmer. And therefore the man who'd been at Kelsey Road on the twenty-second? Steady, not so fast, he told himself, but he was tense with excitement. It began to look as though this was the break they'd been looking for.

'I want to talk to him,' he told Kite, 'and have that taxi-driver traced who picked Mrs Saville up – if it was her.' Then, as Kite had his hand on the doorknob, 'Do I really look like that arrogant bastard?'

'We-ell.' Kite stood in the doorway considering his glowering superior. 'Not really. It's the sweetness of the expression that makes the difference.'

Later, Mayo asked for a call to Browne Moulton, the City firm of merchant bankers where he assumed Challis to be this Tuesday morning, and was channelled through a series of secretaries with upmarket voices before being told Mr Challis was in conference, but would ring him back if it was important.

'It's important,' Mayo said. It was a couple of hours later that Challis came on the line.

'What can I do for you, Inspector?'

'Chief Inspector,' corrected Mayo, who scarcely ever bothered about rank, cutting short the apology with a brief request for an interview with Challis. 'As soon as you can make it,' he said. 'Perhaps this evening, at your house?'

Challis put in quickly, 'Oh, no need to go to that trouble. I'll call in and see you on my way home, if that suits you?'

Mayo smiled, grimly satisfied. He'd got precisely the reaction he'd anticipated. He'd have been much less happy if Challis had agreed to see him in the presence of his wife. He arranged to see him about 5.30, which meant Challis, he calculated, having to start out from the City at not less than half past three. Either Challis's working day wasn't as long as Mayo's, or he was suddenly anxious to appear cooperative.

'Please sit down, sir.' Kite indicated a chair in front of the desk behind which the Chief Inspector sat.

'Thank you. Mind if I smoke?'

Mayo, a reformed smoker himself, did, but had resigned himself to the fact that it was necessary to allow others to smoke at times. He didn't keep an ashtray in the room, however, a small disapproval which was made manifest by his pointedly asking Kite to produce one. It took Kite some minutes, and by the time this performance was over, Challis looked in two minds whether to light up or not, as was intended, but his need evidently triumphed. He made a flamboyant performance of it, with a cigarette drawn from a gold, monogrammed case – Mayo couldn't remember when he had last seen anyone using such a thing – and a lighter to match. He was wearing with his formal business suit a very dark blue shirt with white stripes and a white collar and cuffs, accentuating his dark two-shaves-a-day complexion.

'Well,' he began eventually, with a self-conscious half-laugh, 'I know why you want to see me – can't pretend otherwise.'

This man made too many bloody assumptions, Mayo was thinking, when Challis astonished him by adding, 'It wasn't very wise of me to lie to you, but I didn't really see that it mattered one way or the other that I wasn't actually in Switzerland on that Saturday, well, not the whole day, that is.'

'I see.' Mayo's face was expressionless. From the corner of his eye he saw Kite's ballpoint arrested in mid-air.

'The thing is – well, I flew back to London early on Saturday morning. My wife was meeting me with the car at Elmdon Airport, so later in the day I took a train up from London to Birmingham International station, then got myself across to the airport to coincide with the arrival of the seven o'clock flight from Zürich.'

'Very neat,' commented Mayo. And crazy to have admitted such a thing before he was asked. Never explain, never apologise, hadn't he ever heard the dictum? Shrewd, but not clever, Challis, and soft at the centre. Too anxious to save his own skin to be thinking clearly about the situation. 'And what had you been doing with the rest of the day?'

Challis dragged at his cigarette. 'This is all very embarrassing. Do I have to say?'

'Yes.'

'Well then, if you must. The truth is, I spent the day in London.'

'So you said. Doing what?'

Challis looked rueful. 'With my secretary, as a matter of fact . . . you know how it is. I'm sure she – er – won't have any objections – not in the circumstances, you know, to confirming it.'

I'll bet she won't. I'll bet she's the sort of secretary who'll agree to anything, probably thinks it rather a lark to get one over on the fuzz, thought Mayo, who remembered the Roedean voice and recognised a lie even when it wasn't jumping up and hitting him in the face.

'You can check, if you like.'

'Oh, we shall, sir, we shall. What's her name, where does she live?'

'Her name's Carrington, Jane Carrington, she lives in Notting Hill, I think, but that doesn't matter, we weren't at her place. I have a small penthouse flat over the offices which I use if I have to stay in London overnight.'

Did he, oh did he? Mayo wanted the address all the same, but Challis apparently couldn't remember it. He promised it the following day, after which he said, 'Right, then,' stubbing out his half-smoked cigarette and if Mayo wasn't mistaken, looking mighty relieved.

His hands were on the chair arms to lever himself up ready to go when Mayo said smoothly, 'I'd like you to clarify one or two other points for me, if you would, Mr Challis, while you're here.'

Challis looked suddenly wary, raised his eyebrows. 'Such as?'

'Such as where you were on the fourteenth of December, in the evening, that is.'

The only indication of surprise was the slightest flicker of a nerve at the corner of his mouth. 'The fourteenth of December?' Challis puffed out his lips. 'That wouldn't present too many difficulties, if I had my last year's diary with me.'

'Try to remember, sir. It was a Friday.'

'Oh, then I can tell you. I was almost certainly playing squash at the club round the corner from my offices. I stay on late to play most Friday nights, unless I have another engagement.'

'What time did you get there?'

'It's usually around seven. I have a game and then a shower, possibly a drink afterwards. Yes, I'm almost certain I played that night.'

'Who with? Who was your partner?'

'Ah, there you have me. I'll need my diary for that.'

'Did you win?' asked Kite.

'I don't remember that either, but I usually do.' Challis smiled, completely at ease. 'Now, if you don't mind –' His hands, with the black onyx ring on his wedding finger, were again on the arms of his chair. 'I don't know what all this has been about, but I hope I've been able to satisfy you.'

'Not altogether. Because you were seen, at around the time you claim you were playing squash in London, in the Jolly Farmer at Corston Green with a lady we believe to be Mrs Fleur Saville.'

Mayo was taking a chance, speaking as if this were, in fact, established, though the taxi-driver hadn't yet been traced, but Challis, after a longish silence during which he first adjusted his glasses, then his tie, didn't even attempt to deny it.

'All right,' he admitted at last, smiling ruefully. 'It's a fair cop. I was with her, yes. We just went out together a few times, had a bit of fun, nobody was hurt. You know how it is,' he added, using what seemed to be a favourite expression of his, but no, Mayo didn't know how it was. He wasn't one of those who winked at this sort of shabbiness.

'Quite the ladies' man, Mr Challis. First your secretary, and now Mrs Saville.' He ignored the man-to-man smile. 'Well, here's another question I'd like you to answer.'

'Another?' Challis shot his wrist, revealing an inch of pristinely-laundered cuff. His watch, too, was heavy, chunky gold. 'Oh dear. Well, fire away.'

'What can you tell me about Candace Neale?'

This time the silence lasted for perhaps fifteen seconds. A space of time out of all proportion to its quality, that was compounded of electric tension, fear, a suspension of being, as if a clock, or a heart, or the world had stopped.

Then Challis ran a hand through his hair, reached for his cigarettes again, withdrew his hand. 'Candace, did you say?' His voice was without a tremor. 'Candy Neale? That's a name from a long way back. From Oxford, as a matter of fact. I met her when I was up there. She's an American.'

'Is? You've renewed your acquaintance recently?'

'Not to say renewed it, no. But as a matter of fact she's in publishing now, back in the States, an editor in the house that published Fleur. They met not too long ago, and when she knew where Fleur lived, she asked her if she knew me – and sent her regards.'

'How good a friend was she?'

'Very good. But not in the way you mean.' Mayo said nothing, merely looked, and waited. 'Christ, she was just one of the set I went around with, there was nothing more to it than that!'

Mayo smiled. At last he'd got Challis rattled. 'Let's just go over your movements on the weekend of the twenty-second again. Correct me if I'm wrong on any point. You came home from Zürich early Saturday morning, right? Stayed in London until late Saturday afternoon, then took a train from Euston to the Birmingham International station, arriving what time?'

'Six-fifteen. It was late.'

'Then you went to the airport. How d'you get there?'

'By that new Maglev – that new hover thing.'

'Where you were met by your wife – why not your chauffeur?'

'Because he's only expected to drive me during the week – look, what the hell is all this? If you're trying to lay this murder on me, you're bloody –'

'Well, Mr Challis?'

'Oh, go to hell!'

Mayo said blandly, 'We shall need to see you again, sir, I'm sure, and there'll be certain formalities, such as signing your statement and letting us have your fingerprints before you go, but that'll do for now. They'll be destroyed afterwards,' he added, 'if necessary,' and had the dubious satisfaction of seeing Challis open his mouth as if to protest, and then thinking better of it.

Kite returned from escorting Challis out and walked over to the window, where he stood staring at his own reflection in the darkened glass, superimposed upon the spectacle of the neo-Gothic Town Hall and its turreted clock tower, its floodlighting each night giving it a romantic appeal, like soft evening lights of an ageing woman's face, quickly dispersed by the light of day.

'What's on your mind, Martin?'

Kite turned round. 'I'm not sure. Except that it seems all wrong to me. Mainly because Challis doesn't strike me as being one for the women. Rugby, squash – that macho type's more at home with his own sex. And I don't mean . . .'

'I know. And if it's any consolation, I've the same doubts about him myself. Sutcliffe said she wasn't one for the men, either – but that apart, I'm sure there wasn't anything of that sort between the two of them. He was far and away too glib about it – and I'm just as sure he was lying when he implied he was having it off with his secretary as well. I've no doubt she'll give him an alibi, though – jobs with Browne Moulton are probably worth a fib or two.'

'And for another thing, what's with all this confession about not being in Zürich? Jumped the gun a bit there, didn't he? Which you don't do unless you've plenty to hide.'

'He's impulsive, friend Challis. Speaks without thinking, maybe acts that way, too.'

'You mean he panicked? Yes, I suppose he guessed he'd been seen with Fleur in the Jolly Farmer, and that's why we wanted to see him. And of course he'd know we'd be able to check his arrival from Zürich easily enough, so he thought he'd better establish an alibi first off, for the twenty-second. Because he was actually up here in Lavenstock, committing murder?'

'So you do see him as a murderer?'

Kite dug his hands in his pockets. 'Given the right circumstances . . .'

Emptying the ashtray on to scrap paper, Mayo screwed it up and threw it in the waste basket and went to open the window. A blast of icy cold air lifted the papers on the desk, better than getting cancer from inhaling Challis's second-hand cigarette smoke. After a minute he closed the window and went back to sit at his desk.

'Who's Candace Neale, by the way? You scored a bull's eye there.'

'Just an idea I had, may come to nothing, but Challis's reaction was interesting. Bear with me, Martin, I've put some enquiries out in New York and when I get an answer I may be able to put you in the picture.' As if on cue, the telephone rang. Mayo looked at his watch. 'Maybe this is it – I'm expecting it about now.' He stretched out a hand, and after a moment, he nodded at Kite in affirmation.

Kite went out, and when he eventually returned, he was triumphantly waving a sheaf of papers, but he was given no chance to speak. Mayo was leaning forward tensely over his desk. 'Martin, we may have him, motive and all.'

'Motive?'

'Fleur Saville had something on Challis. I think she was blackmailing him – though nothing so crude as money for her own needs. Remember those thumping great donations the Challises made to the Buttercup Club fund? OK, other people have been generous, too, but not to that extent. I'm willing to bet Challis was paying that money to buy her silence.'

'About what? Had they been having an affair, after all?'

'It goes much farther back than that. I'd rather not say any more because until I've seen Candace Neale, it's still largely speculation,' Mayo admitted. 'Apparently she's in London at the moment, and I'm hoping to fix up an interview with her tomorrow.'

Kite said, 'I've got these reports –'

'Just a minute, Martin, hear me out. You come in later if I'm wrong – but how's this for a scenario?' Mayo tipped his swivel chair back, sank his chin on his chest and squinted down at the toes of his brown leather lace-ups, polished like conkers. He wasn't fussy about his clothes, but he was about his shoes. A psychiatrist might have made something out of that. 'Supposing Challis set up the situation, coming home a day early from Zürich, providing a fictitious alibi with his secretary and making elaborate arrangements so his wife wouldn't know, then his being the murderer is a distinct possibility – and logistically speaking, no real problem. If this was what happened, the murder must have been premeditated but how did he hope to get the opportunity? Presumably he knew Fleur would be fully occupied all day, since his wife's day was similarly planned. But what if they'd *agreed* to meet, for the same reason they'd met at other times? Maybe she stipulated Kelsey Road, and at that particular time, because she knew Edwin would be at the shop, Gillian out of the way at the church hall. It wouldn't have mattered after all if she'd been late back after the lunch-break, she could always have found some excuse for it. And he agreed to meeting her there as being the best time to murder her? All he had to do was to hire a car at the airport to get there and back – if it happened to be one of similar colour and shape to Saville's, that would be enough to account for Mrs Tennyson mistaking it for his – she's no expert.'

'I think,' Kite said, 'you'd better see what I've got here, before you go on.'

'What is it?'

'The lab reports on the prints found on the desk at Kelsey Road, also the report on Saville's car. The car's clean ... in a manner of speaking. That's to say, it probably hasn't been cleaned for weeks, but there's no trace of his wife having been transported in the boot, no blood, fibres, nothing. They found one or two of her hairs and some fibres, not from the clothing she was wearing that day, on the upholstery of the front seat, but they would, wouldn't they, if she was used to being a passenger? There were her prints, of course, and his, all over the place – and more besides, the same ones that were on the desk.'

'Identified?

'Michael Saville's. The missing son.'

Not Challis. *Michael Saville*.

The results of the enquiries Kite had put out about him had come in together. 'After he left home, he seems to have followed the fag end of the hippie trail for a while, in various parts of the world, and maybe that was what made him think this country wasn't so bad, after all. At any rate, he came back and bummed around for a while doing whatever job he could find. Ended up working as a baggage handler at Heathrow, only he handled the baggage a bit too personally, see? He was sent down for twelve months.'

That was why his name was in a police dossier; that was how his fingerprints had been traced. It also accounted for Mrs Tennyson's mistaking his voice on the telephone for that of Edwin Saville: fathers and sons often have similar voices. That was what Saville had been hiding, Mayo was sure. He must have suspected that Michael had been at the house that day and kept quiet about it, even to the extent of falling under suspicion himself.

So how did all this fit in with the case he was all set to make out against Challis? Depending, of course, on what he might learn tomorrow. For to London he would still find it necessary to go; he felt it in his bones. But his certainties had been shaken. He just hoped he hadn't been guilty of jumping to conclusions, making the theory fit the facts, something he was forever warning Kite against. He didn't like Challis – it was a personal antipathy from which he couldn't escape – but God forbid he should let that cloud his judgement.

On the other hand, he hoped his judgement hadn't been faulty.

'Where's Michael Saville now?'

'Apparently he's going straight, has a job with a software firm in Leamington.'

'Got his address?'

Kite nodded, and Mayo reached for his jacket. 'Let's go, we might just catch him in, then.'

CHAPTER 16

Leamington Spa. A Regency town, pleasant, bland, with wide streets and public gardens, white classical façades, at its best in the sun. At seven o'clock on a dark January evening, however, with the broad, well-lit main shopping parade left behind, the quiet terraces and crescents had a cold and deserted air about them, though the houses themselves, enviable, owner-occupied and well-groomed, offered glimpses of tastefully lamplit interiors, or spoke of quiet comfort behind their drawn curtains. Along the road into which Kite turned the car, on the other hand, the street lamps served only to emphasise the peeling stucco and general shabbiness of its large flat-fronted houses, mostly converted into flats inhabited by the very young or the very old, the disadvantaged or members of ethnic minorities.

The young woman who answered their ring at the door of a top-floor flat in a run-down terrace house midway along one of these streets spoke abruptly, in an uncompromising manner that went with the straight brows and the dark hair cropped close to her head, and the way the door was opened but left on the chain. 'He's not in,' she told them.

'Then perhaps we could wait.'

'He might be some time.'

'We're in no particular hurry,' Mayo answered pleasantly. 'And anyway, we'd like to talk to you as well.' She gave him a quick, vivid look through the aperture. Mayo didn't think she was surprised to see them, but she made them wait, accepting their IDs with the chain still on the door and then ringing Lavenstock police station to confirm they were who they said they were.

'You can't be too careful,' she said as she finally admitted them to the flat. Mayo agreed that she had done the right and proper thing, though privately he didn't think it was caution that had led her to act as she had done, rather a desire to set the tone of the interview, to show them she knew the score.

A savoury smell of something cooking issued from behind a door in the corner, the table was laid with a lace cloth, cutlery and glasses for two. The young woman herself wore no make-up, a black jersey and a dark, flowered woollen skirt. He judged her age at about twenty-eight, and her attitude towards the police as touchy.

In the event, they had no sooner entered than footsteps were heard running up the stairs, a key was inserted in the lock, and a young man of about the girl's own age came in, a bottle of wine in his hand. Scarcely pausing when he saw the two policemen, he put the bottle on the table, crossed the room and drew the girl towards him with an arm around her shoulders.

'Mr Michael Saville?' Mayo asked. The other acknowledged the question with a barely civil nod.

'It's the police, Mick,' the young woman said.

'I'd noticed. What do you want?' He had his father's tall, lanky frame, light brown hair that fell forward over his brow, a handsome, sulky face and an insolent manner. 'I hope you haven't been giving my wife any hassle.'

Kite stiffened, but had the sense to keep quiet.

Mayo hadn't previously noticed the wedding ring on the young woman's small brown hand, but when he looked now he saw that it was new. He said stolidly, 'Are you aware, sir, that your stepmother, Mrs Fleur Saville, has been found dead in so far unexplained circumstances?'

'That's the good news. So what's the bad?'

'That why you're celebrating?' Kite asked, waving his hand towards the wine bottle on the table.

Saville laughed. 'Celebrating? No – but we might well be. I hated her guts.'

'Mick!'

'It's true, Jane, you know it and I don't suppose it comes as any surprise to these – gentlemen – here.'

'Cut it out, Saville,' Mayo said quietly. 'We've a murder on our hands, and we're not here to waste time, ours or yours. Just you answer my questions. Shall we sit down?'

Saville shrugged, threw himself on to the sofa, tugging his wife's hand to sit beside him, and left the two officers to find seats for themselves. 'For starters,' Mayo said, settling himself composedly, 'we know that you left home several years ago after a quarrel with your stepmother. And you've never been back since?'

'Damn right I haven't.'

'Except, of course, on Saturday, the twenty-second of December last, the day Mrs Saville was murdered? What were you doing there?'

'Interesting question,' Saville drawled, cool as you like. 'But if you think, in view of my past record, which is no doubt why you're here, that I was there on felonious or murderous intent, you're mistaken. I was there legally, availing myself of what was mine by rights.'

'Explain that, please.'

'Mick means –' began his wife. 'No, Mick, let me tell it.' There was a plea in her voice that Mayo guessed was far from habitual with her, and perhaps that was why Michael Saville shrugged and let her go on. 'It was because I persuaded him to go and see his father. It *was* Christmas, after all, and I thought it was an appropriate time to tell his father we were married, and to arrange for us to meet.'

'For Jane and my father to meet, not *her*,' Saville said. 'All right, I'll take it from there, Jane.' His arrogance seemed suddenly to drop from him, and with it something of his good looks, revealing a weak mouth and a slackness of feature that would become more evident with the years. The strong one in this couple was the girl; he was lucky, thought Mayo, to have found her. 'I've never had any real quarrel with my father, and although we were never all that close we've kept in touch, on and off, since I left home. I wanted him to get to know Jane, to know that since I met her, things are beginning to go right for me at last. We've both got good jobs, Jane's teaching A-level science, and I'm not doing badly in computers. Anyway, I drove over the Saturday before Christmas and went to see him at the shop.'

'What time?' Kite asked.

Saville smiled faintly. 'I know he never changes his habits, so I timed it to arrive at one, when he'd be shutting the shop up. I was glad I'd gone, he was like a dog with two tails when he saw me, but all the same he looked ghastly – in a terrible state, he was.'

'Sick, you mean?'

'That's what I thought at first, but it came out gradually that it was because of her. She'd come up with some crazy idea that morning about him selling his business and going to live abroad, and they'd had a row about it. Can you imagine it, my father retiring, giving up, leaving the only things that have ever mattered to him? It would've killed him inside a month – though come to think of it, maybe that would have suited her. But he was worried sick, and I could see why. If she wanted something, she got it in the end, no sweat.' He stopped and said, 'Look, I'm having a drink. Want one?'

'No, thank you.'

Jane Saville walked across to a cupboard, poured a small tot of whisky and brought it back to her husband. 'Go on, please,' Mayo said. 'What happened then?'

'Nothing. We just sat in the back and drank some coffee. It was a long time since we'd seen each other and we'd a lot to talk about. We sat there discussing various things until it was time for him to re-open.'

'Neither of you went out?'

'No. He didn't even answer the door. Somebody knocked about ten minutes before he was due to open, but he ignored it.'

'And at half past two?'

'He opened the shop, and I went to Kelsey Road to pick up several things. That's what we'd been talking about, in and among. When she started throwing out all my mother's belongings, Dad had salvaged one or two small bits and pieces –' he gestured vaguely round the room – 'things she didn't think worth selling even, and put them up in the loft in case I ever wanted them. I said I'd take them back with me that day. I left it till half past two because I'd no desire to bump into her, and he'd told me she'd be at the church hall by then, playing at being Lady Bountiful, organising some sort of charity do for kids.'

Bitter lines pulled down the corners of his mouth into an ugly expression whenever he spoke of his stepmother. Mayo noticed that never once had he referred to Fleur as anything but 'her'.

'So you drove down to Kelsey Road at two-thirty –'

'No, I walked. I drive a Cavalier, and I couldn't have got all the stuff in that. We arranged that I'd leave the Cavalier in the public car park in the centre, so that if my father wanted it he could use it, I'd use the Granada to take the furniture home and bring it back the next day, leaving it in the yard behind the shop. Which is what I did, dropping the house keys back at the shop on my way home.'

'What time would that be?'

'Half past three, something like that? I don't really know.'

'And your father was there, in the shop?'

'Sure.'

'Why did you answer the telephone when you were at Kelsey Road?'

'The telephone?' He hadn't expected that one, a flash of

surprise, even fear in his eyes. 'Oh yeah, I remember,' he said, too late. 'Reflex action, I guess. I was thinking about – about something else entirely, but it didn't matter, did it? I was there quite legally.'

'In Mrs Saville's study? What were you doing in there? It contained nothing you were "entitled" to, legally or otherwise, did it?'

'No?' The immature petulance of Saville's face had set into savage lines. 'Only the one thing I wanted most, the French secretaire – the one possession of my mother's that even she couldn't bring herself to get rid of. But there was no way I could have taken it with me, it wouldn't have gone in the Granada with all the other things, for a start.'

'And?'

'That's all. I locked up, left the keys with Dad and drove home.'

'Are you sure that's all? Your stepmother died approximately between two-thirty and three. When you were in the house, are you sure she didn't come in unexpectedly, that you didn't meet and quarrel, that you didn't kill her?'

'Of course I'm bloody sure!' Saville wheeled round to his wife. 'You see – what did I tell you? If you don't believe me,' he shouted to Mayo, 'you ask that woman from across the road – that Mrs Henderson. She was in the house when I got there, gave me the fright of my life. She'll tell you.'

Zoe Henderson! 'What was she doing there?'

'She said her telephone was out of order, she'd come across to use theirs.'

'She had a key?'

'She didn't fly through the window.' He saw Mayo's face and added sulkily, 'She told me she keeps a spare, because my father's wife had been known to lock herself out on occasions.'

'Which rooms did you go into?'

'All of them, if you must know. I used to live there – remember? It used to be my home, my mother's, I wanted to see it again . . . but I took nothing, nothing except these things from the loft.' He sprang up and went round the room, touching each article as he went. 'This, and this, and this!'

Mayo took no notice of the histrionics. 'When you were in the main bedroom, did you notice any jewellery on the dressing-table?'

'Yes, I bloody did. And fifteen pounds on the kitchen table. And I didn't sodding well take either!'

'Watch your language, Saville,' Kite warned.

'I didn't ask you if you took it,' Mayo said, 'I asked if you'd seen it.'

'I've said I did.'

'Describe it, please.'

Saville looked sullen. 'A couple of rings, I think, and something else – oh, a necklace or a bracelet of some sort, some kind of red stones.'

'Neither your father nor Mrs Henderson have mentioned anything about you being there, Mr Saville. How d'you account for that?'

'Because *they're* part of the human race,' burst out Jane Saville. 'They probably anticipated how you'd react, and they were right, weren't they?'

The silence in the car lasted until they were through Warwick. 'I wouldn't put it past him,' Kite said eventually. 'That he did it, I mean, and his father and Mrs Henderson were shielding him.'

'I think his father may believe he did. That would account for his lies about his car. But my money's still on Challis.' The excitement had returned. Mayo was feeling much more confident than he had before he saw Michael Saville. The visit had cleared away some of the debris that had been hampering their progress. He couldn't see yet exactly how things were likely to go, but one thing he was certain of – Challis's past was about to catch up with him. After that, they'd have to take it from there.

'I'll tell you what else I think, Martin. I think the excuse about

Mrs Henderson's telephone being out of order is a lot of poppy-cock. She was in that house for another reason. Not necessarily to murder Fleur Saville – she'd have had to be pretty nippy to have done so and got her out of sight, maybe into that van of hers, within the time limits – but I reckon she'd seen something which had aroused her curiosity. Whichever, we're about to find out.'

They were doomed to disappointment. When they got back into Lavenstock, both Mrs Henderson's house and the other one down Kelsey Road were locked up and in darkness.

CHAPTER 17

American executives in large publishing houses came less thrust-ing, perhaps younger at first glance than Mayo had expected, until he remembered that he was privy to knowing how old she actually was. Slender and elegant, an ash-blonde with brown eyes, Candace Neale had a sideways smile that was charming and a firm handshake. Her voice, when she spoke, had warm overtones, yet he sensed tension in her. 'What can I do for you, Chief Inspector Mayo, Sergeant Kite?'

She'd taken the trouble to get the names and ranks exactly right. Mayo was impressed. 'Good of you to see us, Miss Neale. I realise you haven't much time, so I'll get straight to the point.'

'Oh, I've fifty minutes before take-off, and I'll be happy to fill in the time. I do a lot of flying, but I'm still not overjoyed about it. Sitting around thinking about it beforehand makes it worse. And of course, in a situation of this sort –'

They had met, with official permission, in one of the empty departure lounges at Heathrow, with time to go before her flight left for New York. Outside, aircraft took off and landed, one a minute. Rain belted down on to the tarmac from a uniformly leaden sky. Foreign tourists walked by to other departure gates, not looking sorry to be leaving behind what England had recently been throwing at them in the way of weather.

'Thank you, I appreciate your cooperation. Shall we sit down?'

When they were seated, it was she who began the conversation, albeit hesitantly, by asking just what she could do to help. 'Because you do realise I hardly knew Miss Lamont – Mrs Saville, that is? I only met her once.'

'And that was here in London on the third of July last year, I understand?'

She nodded, passing her tongue round her lips. 'That's right, I believe that was the date.'

'It's that meeting I wanted to ask you about, first of all.' Mayo was watching her carefully. 'Something you discussed there interested her very much, and I'd like you to try and remember, if you can, what you talked about.'

He wondered if the palpable nervousness she was showing was really due to her phobia about flying, or to something else. Her fingers kept on twisting the narrow strap of her black leather shoulder-bag into a slip-knot, then pulling it out. 'I'll help in any way I can, but you must realise I can't break a confidence.'

'There can't be any question of keeping confidences when it comes to murder. And Mrs Saville is dead.'

The slip-knot came free again as the strap was pulled tight. 'I wasn't actually meaning her . . .' She stopped and plunged into her bag for cigarettes.

'Let me make it easier for you. On Saturday, the twenty-second of December, you met Bryan Challis, here in London.'

He'd counted on the bluff, educated guess, call it what you will, coming off, and it did. 'Did he tell you that?' The cigarette lighter was staying in mid-air.

'We've spoken to him, and we know you met,' he answered ambiguously.

'I see.' She paused, smiling faintly, and some of the tension

335

went from her face. 'It seems to be my fate to meet people at airports. Yes, sure, there was a couple of hours between his flight arriving from Zürich and mine leaving for New York, so it seemed logical to meet here, have a drink together, and talk about old times. Salad days, and all that.'

'Old times in Oxford, when you were students together?'

'What else?'

'About Fleur Saville, perhaps. And the fact that she was, to put it bluntly, blackmailing him?'

For a moment he thought she was going to refuse to answer, or at any rate evade his question, but she said cautiously, after giving him a swift, uncertain look, 'That was what he implied, yes.'

'How long have you known Bryan Challis?'

'I hadn't seen him for nearly twenty-five years. I knew him at Oxford, we went around in the same set for the two years I was there, but we've never met since, not until he contacted me.'

He had to ask her a question that might be an impertinence, but he thought she would answer it truthfully. She had clear eyes that reminded him of Alex's. Candace. The name suited her. 'Were you lovers, Miss Neale?'

She regarded him gravely. 'We had – a relationship, yes.'

'And as a result of that, you had a child.'

'You *have* been doing your homework!'

'We have a copy of Mrs Saville's letter to you, after you'd met. She mentioned your proposed visit to Lavenstock. I made enquiries and found you'd left Oxford sooner than you'd intended, that a daughter was born to you shortly afterwards.'

From below, Concorde lifted off into the air, a big predatory-beaked bird with backswept wings. 'I don't really see what relevance all this has . . .'

'Miss Neale, it isn't likely we should have troubled you, caught you in mid-flight as it were, if it wasn't important.'

She lit the cigarette she'd forgotten until now, drawing on it with small impatient puffs. 'OK, I'm sorry. Yes, I do have a daughter. But Bryan Challis isn't her father. Anything between us was over long before I got pregnant, from the moment he met his wife, in fact.'

He couldn't believe it. He strove to keep the shock and chagrin from showing on his face. He'd been wrong – and what was infinitely worse, so sure he'd been right. If this woman was telling the truth – and he'd swear she was – and Bryan Challis wasn't the father of her child, then his motive for murdering Fleur Saville had vanished. Everything had seemed to fit – the dates, the coincidence of the two women meeting, the unlikely sums of money paid into the Buttercup Club fund – Mayo had never for a moment doubted that Bryan Challis would have done more than murder to prevent this sticky little bit of his past coming to his wife's ears. With any other wife, he might have ridden out the storm, but with Gillian . . . Mayo thought that in Bryan Challis's shoes he too might have trembled.

'Are you sure?' he asked, trying to swallow his disappointment.

'Sure?'

'I'm sorry.' He rubbed a hand across his face. 'I'm not in any way doubting your word. You've surprised me, that's all. Please go on.'

'My child's father was a fellow American. But you know, the idea of being a father appalled him, and he'd absolutely no intentions of marrying me – which was the luckiest break I ever did have, though I sure didn't think so at the time.' For the first time, he noticed grey in the ash-blonde of her hair, faint lines at the corner of her eyes that weren't all laughter lines. It was absurd, the comparison, but into his mind floated the image of Lola Tennyson, shoulder to shoulder with this woman from another kind of life, another continent. Life was rotten, sometimes, but it would never beat either, they'd always fight back. Like Lola Tennyson, Candace Neale too had courage. Her mouth lifted again in her attractive, crooked smile as she leaned forward to stub out her unfinished cigarette and continue her story. 'I went home, and it was tough for a while, but I don't regret it. My daughter Karen's the best thing that ever happened to me.'

Mayo thought about his Julie. He smiled at her. 'That's nice.' He went back to what she'd said, about the end of her affair with Challis. 'So you know Challis's wife as well?'

'Knew. We were very good friends. Oh, I'll admit it, I was so jealous when they first met – he obviously had no eyes for anybody else, and who could blame him, she was so stunning? But I got over it, one way and another. And later, when the baby was on the way, that's when I really got to know her . . .'

Gillian Challis was still a very good-looking woman, with her dusky-peach complexion, her blonde hair. And clever too. She must have been, to get to Durham and take the good degree Miss Vickers had spoken about.

'She was pretty wonderful to me at that time,' Candace Neale was saying. 'I guess I wouldn't have gone through with it, having the baby and all, if she hadn't persuaded me how wrong it would be to have an abortion. She was a lovely person, but very intense, with strong moral principles – and of course that's why they married. Sex without marriage would have been out of the question, at least as far as she was concerned . . . it actually bothered her that most people thought they were "living in sin", as she put it. God, nobody would have cared either way! We all slept around in those days, didn't we? In a way that really shocks my daughter's generation.'

Mayo inclined his head in a non-committal way. Not all, he thought. Some had a bit of self-control, a touch of the Puritans if you like, or maybe were just more particular. Especially people like Gillian Challis. He said, 'Then why didn't they say they were married? Why the secrecy?'

'Oh, he couldn't let it be known, in case it got back to his father.'

'He needed his father's permission to marry?'

'Well, not that, but his approval, I guess, and in the circumstances he didn't want to hurt him.'

'What circumstances?'

'His father was dying, Mr Mayo. There'd apparently been somebody else lined up for Bryan to marry, before he went up to Oxford, somebody with a bit of money and a good Catholic. The way Bryan put it to me was that he couldn't do that to his father on his deathbed, tell him he'd married someone else, I mean. Bad news whichever way, especially her not being a Catholic and all –'

'Not a Catholic?' intervened Kite. 'But –'

'Oh.' She looked unhappily at the two men. 'Oh, I guess you didn't know about Ruth, either.'

Mayo felt as though his brains had been scrambled. Ruth? he thought. *Ruth?*

A Jumbo Jet roared off the tarmac. Candace Neal watched their expressions while the sound died. 'I'm sure you understand about these old Catholic families better than I do. Or maybe you think it's impossible, people still having this sort of attitude, this day and age?'

Mayo did not. Looking at the world around him, he couldn't believe bigotry and religious prejudice had died with Oliver Cromwell. But that wasn't what was concerning him at the moment. 'Let's get this straight. Challis has been married twice? Then his first wife died?'

'Not that I know of.'

'Divorced, then?'

She gave him a level look. 'They must have been, mustn't they?'

With his Catholic principles? Unlikely – unless they weren't so strong that expediency hadn't got the better of them.

'At any rate, he and Ruth pretty soon split. I don't know exactly why, she was very upset and wouldn't talk about it, but anybody could see even by then that their marriage was a fairly total disaster. They'd basically nothing in common, and with hindsight, I can see it just couldn't have lasted. He went overboard for her, I guess, because of her looks, and he's hard to resist when there's something he really wants. She looked real sexy, you know, but she was about as . . . well, anyway, there are some women who should never marry at all, and I think Ruth Whittaker was one of them. She told me once she couldn't understand all the fuss people made about sex, and if she'd listened to herself, she wouldn't have married. Does this make sense?'

He nodded. It was becoming clearer every minute. 'What happened to her, then? What happened to Ruth Whittaker?'

'I don't know, we lost touch. When I asked Bryan the other day, he said she'd gone out to the Far East to work with homeless children, and that figured, it was fairly typical of the sort of thing she'd do. I'd written her several times, to let her know about the baby and so forth, but I never did have an answer.'

'Let's go back to my original question – how much of all this did you tell Fleur Saville when you first met her?'

'When I found out she came from Lavenstock, I mentioned I had friends who came from there and it turned out she knew Bryan Challis well. I was really pleased because with this merger in my company, it was on the cards I'd be over here a lot and I thought it would be kind of fun to look them up again. I even mentioned that I'd probably bring Karen over with me and we'd visit. I asked about Ruth. She looked amazed. "Ruth? –" I remember exactly the way she said it – "But Bryan's wife is called Gillian," she said. By this time I realised I'd put my foot right in it – I figured there must have been a divorce, but maybe he'd kept it quiet, perhaps even from this Gillian. Later, I recalled that was the name of the girl he'd been going to marry before he met Ruth. I was surprised about the divorce, though, because at the time I knew her, Ruth didn't approve of it either. She was very strait-laced, and well, you don't have to be a Catholic, or even very religious I guess, to believe marriage is forever. But people change, they meet someone else, they lose their faith . . . for all sorts of reasons they might have agreed to it later. Anyhow, I began to backtrack fast but I guess she realised there was something fishy, and she must have ferreted it out. After all, she was a journalist one time, wasn't she?'

'Yes,' Mayo said. His thoughts had taken an entirely new turn. He had his motive now. A different one, and possibly more powerful.

Gillian Challis might have been able to swallow, with a struggle, the fact of an illegitimate child of her husband – but a previous marriage was a different kettle of fish. She would never knowingly have married Bryan, otherwise. To a woman such as she was, with a strong Catholic conscience, marriage would be indissoluble, except by death. On the other hand, his first marriage was unlikely, in the circumstances, to have been blessed by a Catholic ceremony and therefore wouldn't have been recognised as a marriage at all by her church, so the question of whether he was divorced or not would have been largely irrelevant. As far as the church was concerned, that was. As for the law, Bryan Challis might be in very hot water indeed.

'So when you met Challis, what did he say about his divorce?' Kite pressed, taking up Mayo's thoughts with the kind of telepathy that their working well together was sometimes apt to induce.

She avoided looking at either of them. 'That's something we never got around to discussing. All he wanted to talk about was exactly what I'd told Fleur.'

Mayo didn't doubt her word that it hadn't been mentioned, but if not, he didn't think it likely to have been an oversight. Candace Neale was no fool, it was very probably something she'd rather not know – and something Challis certainly wouldn't have volunteered.

'I'm sorry, that's my flight call,' she said, as a voice came over the loudspeaker. She was beginning to gather her things together, but slowly, as though there were still things she wanted to say. They stood and shook hands, Mayo thanked her again.

'I don't know about that, Mr Mayo. Right now, I feel a heel. Maybe I'll see it differently when I've had time to think it over . . .

but look, there's something I have to know. You're working on Bryan having killed Fleur, aren't you?'

'It's a possibility we can't rule out,' Mayo replied cautiously.

'Oh God. If I hadn't spoken to her about him, she'd still be alive.'

'No. If she hadn't *used* it, she might be. There's a difference.'

He hoped he'd succeeded in convincing her.

CHAPTER 18

The rain streamed down the windows in torrents, hammering on the roof-tiles of the old stable that was now the garage. It was so dark she'd had to switch the lights on already. She pressed her hand to her aching head and wished Rollo would stop that eternal barking. He hated to be shut up in the garage but she wouldn't have him in the house when she was preparing meals, when his nose was level with the kitchen counter and everything in the way of food was grist to his mill.

Despite her aching head, she moved efficiently about her well-equipped kitchen, preparing for the dinner-party that evening. She'd never felt less like entertaining, but Gillian's feelings always came second to her sense of duty, and the Hammonds had been booked for tonight for weeks. Even if Fleur was dead, appearances had to be kept up, life had to go on.

So, like that other well-conducted person, she went on cutting not bread and butter but cucumber, slicing it rapidly, in the correct, professional manner, the razor-sharp Sabatier knife following her doubled-up fingers with speed and assurance. She arranged salad attractively round the cold salmon trout on the large flat silver dish, decorated it with aspic jelly and expertly piped mayonnaise. She always took the trouble to learn how to do things the correct way, it was so much easier in the end, she told Penny. And Bryan liked things to be done, and people to behave, properly. He wouldn't like the Hammonds to think his wife was going to pieces just because her best friend had died. He would have preferred to keep from them altogether that she had died in such sordid circumstances.

The salmon trout went into the fridge, covered with clingfilm, she turned round and without warning, there in the middle of the kitchen, the tears began to pour down her cheeks. There was no way she could stop, the enormous painful growth that had been swelling up inside her for weeks had finally burst. She sat down at the table, her head in her hands, and with dry racking sobs let her grief have its way, but when the tears eventually stopped she felt no better. She got up and poured cooking brandy into a tumbler, hiccupping as half of it went down in one gulp.

She'd known there was something wrong with her marriage from the first. If she were being honest – and now, if ever, was the time for honesty – even before she walked to the altar with him. But his charm – such a false charm it had turned out to be – had blinded her. She'd even become a Roman Catholic for him when they got engaged – and like most converts, had become more devout than the devout, embracing a faith that had in the end been the truest and most abiding source of comfort in her life.

But she should never have done it, never have held Bryan to the promises made before he'd gone to Oxford, and she to Durham. They'd met at her cousin Elizabeth's twenty-first birthday party, and it had been love at first sight, or at least that was what she'd thought. But by the end of the first year it was evident, to her at least, that their engagement had gone sour on him. He *could* have backed out, of course, there was essentially nothing to stop him, except that it would have needed some courage and Bryan always took the easy way out. And also, his father had died by then, leaving unexpected debts, and the business in a bad way. Bryan had needed her money, the money her parents had settled on her. Not a large sum, but enough to cancel the debts and put him back on his feet. She'd had no illusions, she'd known this, and had traded it for marriage, shutting her eyes to the consequences. She'd believed that because she loved him that didn't matter, and had had to live with the fact that it did for a long time. Because once done, it was too late. Marriage in the sight of God was once and forever.

She drained the rest of her brandy, stood up and, leaning against the sink, stared out of her kitchen window, across the saturated lawn, towards the great stand of yews that she'd always hated, they and their implacable circle of darkness. Why hadn't she asked Bryan to have them cut down? He would have ordered it to be done straight away if she'd ever told him how much she disliked them. She had only to beckon, lately, and he'd do as she asked. It was one of the things which had first made her suspicious. He wasn't naturally a conciliatory person. Another thing was the ostentatious presents he gave her and Penny. That, and the over-generous donations to the Buttercup Club, when money, as she knew, was tight.

Why, she had wondered, had he suddenly found such sympathy with a cause he'd hitherto shown minimal interest in? One *she* hadn't been able to interest him in, but Fleur had, she now realised. Did he think she was such a fool that she'd accept this apparent change of heart without wondering why?

There were so many trees, here at the back of the house. Beech and the yews and some tall elms that had escaped Dutch Elm disease. Dejected rooks cawed and sat in melancholy huddles, high on their bare, dripping branches. The rooks avoided the yews, as did plants, which refused to grow in their shade. As Gillian did, who hated darkness.

She was afraid of the dark. Not afraid of the night, which until recently she had welcomed as a friend who brought sleep, and forgetfulness – but afraid of the darkness of beyond, of eternity, of damnation, to which the sins of omission and commission would condemn her. She had known; she had condoned Bryan's sin for too long. She had been jealous of Fleur all her life, lovely, traitorous Fleur, who struck the match that had lit the furnace. Though she had truly loved her, too.

How long had she been existing in this limbo? Looking for reality when there was none, no sense in trying to find it. It had been a long and lonely road. She found her hand clenched round the cook's knife, her knuckles white. Slowly she made herself unlock her fingers and the knife dropped with a clatter to the tiled surface. It was denied her, the oblivion she longed for, the great quietus, it was denied her. But she had thought she had reached the limits of her endurance before, and she had gone on.

When Kite rang Challis at his office from Heathrow he was told he was seeing a client in Birmingham, and so wouldn't be in the office until the following day. The trip into the City was therefore unnecessary, thank God. Mayo didn't fancy a noisy and tedious journey, jostling and jockeying for position with bad-tempered drivers and wet, scurrying, risk-taking pedestrians in London's overcrowded city streets. Instead, after leaving Heathrow, the car's nose was headed for home.

Kite drove. It gave Mayo an opportunity for silent thought since Kite, who was a good driver, swift, decisive, and alert, with his mind on what he was doing while he was on the motorway, didn't talk too much. Mayo was glad of it, he was in that keyed-up state of mind when he knew he was at the end of a case, when the quarry was in sight. His adrenalin was running high. He had the motive, and the murderer, though the proof was something else. He thought he might even have the means, and the why and how of the jewellery left on the dressing-table. There were still aspects that were puzzling him, though . . .

The going had been slow out of Heathrow and up the motorway, with the heavy rain and several contraflow systems slowing up traffic, but now they were into the cross-country Warwickshire roads and lanes. The steady downpour had spread north, washing away the last traces of snow. The sodden earth could take no more, and water lay in miniature lakes at the sides of the road. There were sounds like tearing silk as the tyres hit water, and the headlights in an afternoon as dark as night picked out the dark humped shapes of hedges rushing urgently past. Fauré, passionately pure, poured into the interior of the car from Radio Three.

'Very enlightening, all that, wasn't it?' Kite asked presently.

'Puts a different complexion on things, certainly.'

'Only I don't see how . . .?'

'I don't myself yet, not entirely. But pin your ears back and listen, and then let's see what we come up with,' Mayo answered, reaching for the radio off button.

For the rest of the journey home they took the case apart, and by the time they got there, they'd reached what seemed to be an inescapable conclusion.

Gillian heard the Jaguar crunch down the drive and swing round towards the front door where it set Bryan down, before continuing towards the garage. Rollo was going frantic. A moment later, freed by Turner, he was hurling himself back and forth between the front door and the kitchen door as he always did, past the study window where she sat, tearing himself apart with indecision and his impatience to get indoors at last. She heard Turner lock the garage, then crunch away towards his cottage, Bryan's footsteps in the hall and his shout to Rollo, the slam of the kitchen door. They came into the study together, man and dog, both large, blustering and noisy. There was a remarkable similarity, too, in the pugnaciousness of the big Airedale's square jaw to that of Bryan's, rather more evident at this time of day, when he needed his second shave, and a drink.

'What's that you're doing?' he asked, giving her a duty kiss and then immediately performing his routine of crossing to the drinks tray and pouring himself a substantial scotch. 'Nothing special.

Bench work.' She turned over the sheets of paper on which she'd been writing, knowing he wouldn't be interested enough to comment further.

'God, I'm tired,' he said. 'Good thing I'm home early, maybe I'll have time for a nap before the Hammonds come. It is tonight, isn't it?'

'They're not coming.'

'Oh? Nothing wrong, is there? I thought Rodney looked a bit off-colour last Friday –'

'They're all right, as far as I know. I put them off.'

She had imagined she had herself under control, that he wouldn't notice anything untoward, but the look he gave her quickly disabused her of this. 'Put them off? Something *is* wrong. You don't look well yourself. Is that what it is?'

She'd managed to erase all signs of tears, but there was nothing she could do about the pallor that lay under her fading tan, giving her a sickly, sallow appearance. She'd rubbed off the blusher she'd never before needed on her cheeks after putting it on; however she applied it, it stood out, making her look like a clown.

'I didn't think you'd want them around with the police here,' she answered his question. 'And I hardly imagined they'd have been and gone before the Hammonds arrived.'

'Police? Here? What are you talking about?'

'Oh, Bryan. What do you *think* I'm talking about? Fleur's murder, of course. What else?'

Silence hung between them. Then, incredibly – or perhaps not so incredibly, because Bryan always got what he regarded as his priorities right – his first question was, 'What did you tell the Hammonds?'

'You don't need to worry about that,' she said drily, in spite of her hurt, 'I didn't tell them the *real* reason – and anyway, here *are* the police.'

CHAPTER 19

The rain had stopped. The winter pansies outside the front door at Boxwinder House had survived the frost and were lifting drenched heads in small glowing pools of yellow and lavender and purple. After the temperatures to which they'd all lately grown accustomed, the early evening seemed to Mayo to hold an almost springlike softness.

On this their second visit, they were shown into an oak-panelled, lamplit study, a small room with each panel carved in pointed arches to the ceiling, just off the vast hall. Like a Lady chapel, thought Mayo, an impression strengthened by the monk's bench drawn up at right-angles to the fire, and the silver vase of spring flowers set on a plain oak credence table. But the analogy fell short at the gas-coal fire flickering in the grate and the television set in the corner, the soft velvet furnishings.

Challis was drinking whisky, not his first if Mayo was any judge. He finished the glass off with a gulp and immediately poured another, affecting unconcern when Mayo declined the offer to speak to him in private.

'I'd like you both to be present, you and Mrs Challis.'

Mayo was watching, not Challis, but his wife, as he spoke, but there was no reaction from her, but for a small, stiff nod of acquiescence. She was sitting in a swivel chair turned round from a small desk in the corner. She looked ill. Perhaps she knew what was coming, too. He suddenly experienced a feeling of revulsion for the whole rotten business, and the part he had to play in it, a momentary feeling, however, which he rigorously suppressed. He was doing what he was paid to do, and what he believed in; if he entertained that kind of doubt for long, he was in the wrong job. He was soberly aware that a family was about to be destroyed, but he had an ultimately simple view of right and wrong: he didn't believe criminals should be allowed to get away with anything.

'There are questions which concern you both. If you don't mind.'

Challis shrugged. 'As you wish.'

Even with his capacity for self-delusion, he must have realised what the presence of police officers here signalled, but he was going to bluff it out to the end, which Mayo could have predicted. What he didn't try to predict was how soon Challis would collapse. That he would collapse was certain. It was written in the character of the man, in the way he'd let himself be carried along with the flow of events, regardless of the rocks that lay submerged under the water and might sink him at any time, until it was too late.

Mayo began as he and his sergeant lowered themselves into the armchairs indicated. 'I want you to go back to our last meeting, Mr Challis. We established then that you came from Zürich, not on the Saturday evening of the twenty-second of December as you'd led your wife to believe, but on the Saturday morning. Why did you do this?'

'I've already told you why.' He slid his wife a quick, cautious glance. The look she gave him was blank and uncomprehending, but he turned away, refusing to meet her eyes. No surprises here, either, that he'd neither told his wife that he'd been questioned nor prepared her for what was to come.

'I – I'd arranged to spend the day otherwise.'

'With your secretary's what in fact you said.' Mayo had no intention of letting him off the hook. 'But we've reason to think there was a different explanation for you returning early.' Despite his effort at seeming indifferent, Mayo could see the man was beginning to sweat. Moisture lay on his skin, which looked grey and, with the dark shadow on his chin, gave him a villainous look. 'Truer to say the reason was because that day you intended to murder Fleur Saville, isn't it?'

'Murder her? No, it bloody wasn't!'

'Wasn't it? How was it, then?'

349

'I told you why I came home.'

'I don't believe you.'

'That's your privilege. But how d'you think I managed to commit murder up here when I was in London?'

'Tell him, Sergeant Kite.'

Kite cleared his throat. 'Possibly because you weren't in London all the time. Let's say you'd previously arranged to meet Mrs Saville at her home after lunch, just before she went back to the church hall. Say you hired a car in London and, having previously set up an alibi with your secretary, drove up here, murdered Fleur Saville and dumped her in the lane near Seddon End. Say you returned the car to the airport branch of the hire car offfices, waited until the Zürich flight came in, then simply walked out to where you'd arranged to be met by your wife, as if you'd just got off it.'

'Say what you damn well like, that's a load of old rubbish, and you know it! What reason had I? Why should I want to murder Fleur Saville anyway?'

'Do you deny you were having an affair with her?'

'Yes – no, I –'

'Well, which is it? It was yes in your previous statement.'

Quite suddenly, all the fight went out of Challis. He looked as though he were deflating slowly, like a limp balloon. 'I wasn't having an affair with her. Christ, that's the last thing I would have done.'

This time Mayo heard the catch of Gillian Challis's breath, almost a slight moan; her hand went to her throat. She averted her face sharply.

'Then why'd you meet her on December fourteenth, to name but one time?'

Challis wouldn't answer. Mayo let the silence build up. The Airedale, sensing the tension of the humans in the room, got up and mooched restlessly round. It had mean eyes and a black and tan coat, curly as astrakhan. It walked across to Kite and began to nudge his notebook with its big, square nose. Gingerly, Kite moved the book away. The dog lifted its lip warningly. Its teeth were yellow, its breath was bad. Challis snapped his fingers and it went reluctantly back to his side, where it sat with ears pricked while Challis nervously scratched its boxy head.

'She wanted to persuade me into giving money to that club of hers,' he came out with at last. 'She'd found out – something – that happened years ago.'

'Not to beat about the bush, she was blackmailing you.'

'She didn't put it like that, not Fleur. She never threatened me, or *asked* for money, just hinted. The first time all she said was she'd met someone who was up with me at Oxford. She understood, only wanted to offer her sympathy, blah blah, blah. She realised I was young at the time, what it must have been like for me all these years – God, as if anyone could know! It was Fleur at her most sickening. Then she changed the subject to that bloody club of hers and how much it needed funds, she was sure I'd understand. I understood all right. I sent her a couple of substantial cheques. But I might have known – she asked to meet me again. and this time she was on about the new wing needed up at the hospital . . . I could see it going on for the rest of my life.'

'And that was when you decided to murder her.' Like many basically weak men, Challis would not act until cornered, when he would be at his most dangerous, lashing out impulsively, without thought or calculation.

'No! I didn't come home from Zürich to murder her, that's crazy. I had to meet someone on their way back to the States, and the only way was to come back early from Zürich. I spent the rest of the day at the penthouse flat – alone – until it was time to get the train home. And that was *all* that happened.'

'Except that the "someone" you were meeting was Candace Neale, wasn't it?'

After a brief struggle with himself, Challis admitted it. 'Well, all right, yes. What about it?' he added, managing to summon up a touch of bravado, but he'd guessed what was coming. You could smell fear on him.

'Why did you lie about this the first time we spoke?'

Challis shrugged.

'Hoped we wouldn't find out that Fleur Saville had threatened to make your wife aware of the situation, didn't you? And had therefore given you a strong motive for murdering her?'

'Gillian's name was never brought into it! I wanted to find out just what Candace had told Fleur, and how much Fleur was making up. She told so many lies, you could never be sure with her. She'd said something the last time I saw her about Candace's daughter, which made me think she might possibly be on the wrong tack – maybe she didn't know, after all.'

'Didn't know what?' Mayo pressed.

Challis cast another agonised glance at his wife. 'Can't we for God's sake go somewhere private?'

'Your wife's going to have to know sometime.'

'I – I can't.'

'This is one you can't dodge, Bryan,' Gillian said suddenly. '*Who* is Candace Neale – and what was it I shouldn't find out?' Since that first involuntary movement, she had sat rigid and almost unmoving, looking like a marble statue, her face colourless, her patrician profile a classical cameo against the rich folds of the dark velvet curtains, with the light making an aureole around her blonde head. Now there was a peculiarly charged concentration in the way she waited for him to answer.

He said nothing.

'It'll come better from you,' Mayo advised, giving him the opportunity to put it to his wife in the way he would know best, but Challis, who was beginning to look as though he was being hammered into the ground, only responded with a groan, sinking his head in his hands.

All right, he'd had his chance. 'Mrs Challis, your husband was allowing Fleur Saville to blackmail him because she had found out from Candace Neale that twenty-five years ago, in Oxford, he married a young woman called Ruth Whittaker.'

Seconds passed.

'Is that true?' Gillian's voice sounded peculiar, quite unrecognisable from her normally confident, magisterial tones. '*Is it true?*'

His bowed shoulders and the refusal to meet her eyes gave her the answer.

'Is she still alive?'

'I don't know, how should I? I've had no contact with her for years.'

'How *could* you?' She was staring at him in a confusion of anger and grief and misery. And yet – surprise? Shock, yes, but disbelief? Mayo couldn't be sure. 'How *could* you have married me when you already had a wife?'

'You mustn't take it so badly – it was all over before you and I were married. It was crazy, a big mistake . . . but these things happen all the time. You know what people are like at that age, you don't know what hell I've gone through . . . I soon knew it wasn't going to work, that's why I left her –'

He was recovering, Mayo saw.

'Who was she?'

'Just someone I met –'

'And married.'

'Not in church. She wasn't my wife, not in the true sense, I mean, that is –'

'You didn't even bother to get a divorce, I take it?'

'She wouldn't entertain the idea. Till death do us part, she said, and meant it. I think she'd some futile idea we might get together again.'

'She wouldn't know you were keeping me as your second string, of course. That you'd let me go on waiting for you all the time you were at Oxford. You've lived a lie and forced me to live one, too. Did you give no thought to what would happen to me if this got out?'

Self-absorbed, neither of them seemed to have given a thought as to what would happen to their daughter either, Mayo thought grimly, and then was confounded when she added, 'What about the child, what about Penny?'

Penny would be all right; she was young, with a strongly independent character, and a survivor, if Mayo was any judge from the brief but definite impression he'd gained of her.

'I – I'm sorry,' Challis muttered, and the huge inadequacy of the apology seemed to sum up the failure of the whole of their lives together.

'Sorry! What does that matter? Shouldn't you have thought of that before?' Mrs Challis had a bitter tongue and a look to match when the need arose. Yet her tone had changed, she sounded oddly apprehensive as she asked, 'Are you going to charge him with murder, as well as – bigamy?'

Mayo stood up and walked past Challis to stand with his back to the fire, where he could better see the reactions of both of them. He said, 'How much of all this did you know, Mrs Challis? How much did Fleur Saville tell you?'

'Know?' In the face she raised to him he caught a glimpse of a secret, inner self, a naked look, gone in a second. She looked him straight in the eye. 'Nothing,' she said.

'Then what *was* the reason? Why did you kill her?'

The silence in the room hung thick as a blanket. Outside the rain overflowed from a blocked spout. The dog gave a low growl. Challis lifted his head, an expression of total disbelief on his face.

Gillian Challis swung round in the swivel chair towards the desk.

She was quick, but Mayo was quicker. The knife glinted in the flames from the artificial coal, but almost on the instant she drew it from under the papers on the desktop, he was across the room, and had her wrist in his grip. A split second later the dog launched itself after him and with an almighty crash they were all on the floor. The dog recovered first. Its jaws were within an inch of his throat when Kite got a stranglehold on its collar, twisting it from behind. At that moment, Challis came to life, taking charge of the animal and getting it out of the door.

When he came back, the two policemen were standing in the middle of the room, Gillian was sitting on the sofa, looking dazed, but without that frozen look she'd had ever since he came home He sat down opposite her in silence, trying not to think about the moments before she'd made that lunge for the knife.

His glance ranged round the room from the desk to the policemen, but the knife was nowhere to be seen. Had he imagined it? Gillian, with a *knife*, for God's sake! Gillian, *killing Fleur*? He told himself, as he had done a thousand times, panicking now as he had done then, that she couldn't have known, how could she? And then remembered that she did now. Mayo had told her, and all pretence between them was over.

She began to speak, addressing herself to Mayo. 'I was trying to write it all down for you – but I haven't got very far. There, on the desk. I knew you'd find out, sooner or later, and I wanted to get it clear, in case – in case – that day, you see, that awful day . . .' She closed her eyes, and it seemed as though she might not, after all, be able to summon up the strength to continue.

Kite shifted his weight. Mayo signalled caution. He recognised the guilty person's need to talk, and knew its usefulness. The police station, the bare facts and stilted sentences of a written confession could come later. He sat down again, and Kite did likewise, opening his notebook.

'All right, Mrs Challis. Let's have it. Everything. Take your time.'

She opened her eyes. 'Yes.' Her voice was so low they could follow her only with difficulty. 'We'd plenty of time, so we drove back to Lavenstock slowly, by way of Kennet Edge. When we got to the Edge, it hadn't yet started sleeting, and I – I didn't tell you the truth, we did get out for some air. There was nobody else about. She began to tell me about the quarrel with Edwin as we got back to the car, about some brilliant idea she'd had of selling up and going to live on one of the Greek islands, but that Edwin had dug his heels in and refused to discuss it sensibly. She said the row had gone off in other directions, and ended with him accusing her of having an affair with another man. She looked sideways at me when she said that, smiling in that way she had, as if she knew something you didn't. Well, it was true, she said, there was a man who was madly attracted to her. I said, "Don't do this to me, Fleur," and I told her I knew about her and Bryan, how I'd known it ever since he began to make those huge gifts to the Buttercup Club. I always read the accounts meticulously, and it came as a shock – he'd never shown any interest before, and why hadn't he discussed it with me, when he knew I was so closely involved? I realised it was conscience money, and I began to put two and two together.'

She paused, clenching her handkerchief tightly in her fist.

'She wouldn't have it arranged any other way,' Challis put in bitterly, 'wanted it all above board, she said. Anyway, you were always on at me to give more – at the time it seemed, well, at least you might think I'd at last done something that met with your approval.'

Gillian glanced at him, then went on again as if he'd never spoken, as if he weren't there. The blood rushed to his face. 'She just stood there by the car, putting a tragic expression on, and she said, "Darling, I'm so sorry, you had to know sooner or later. But it's not how you think." I could see – at least I thought I could see – that she was cooking up one of her wild stories and I – I just felt that everything was falling apart, my marriage, our friendship, and well, that was when . . . oh God, this time she was telling the truth and I didn't believe her! I didn't even mean to kill her.'

A rising note of desperation had crept into her voice towards the end of the flat recital of events. As if of its own accord, her glance travelled to the desk and fixed on what was there with something approaching panic. Mayo said, 'Better if you let us take charge of that, I reckon.'

He picked up her handbag carefully and passed it over to Kite. Square, chunky, with a heavy gold frame that formed a sharp right-angle. She repeated, 'It was an accident. I never meant to kill her.' Her eyes, suddenly wide and horror-struck, beseeched him to believe her.

Perhaps not. Or perhaps not now, when remorse had had time to set in. Mayo watched her, half-convinced. But as he looked at the bag and imagined the fury that had swung it by its straps, giving so much weight to the blow that the edge of the frame had bitten deep into the temple and killed Fleur Saville, he wasn't sure. At that moment – and for how long before that? – Gillian Challis had certainly wanted her friend dead.

'You were always jealous of her.' Challis seemed to have forgotten they weren't alone – or else he was hitting back. She hadn't moved an inch towards him in understanding or forgiveness, and maybe he was beginning to be ready to wash his hands of her.

'Don't be ridiculous.' But it was a truth that had evidently gone home, and this time she didn't make the mistake of ignoring him. 'What reason had I to be jealous?'

'Because she always went one better than you, didn't she? She was famous, she'd more friends. You couldn't bear it that you weren't always top dog, that she got all the kudos. You've been jealous of her all your life. And then you thought she'd taken me.'

Mayo, watching the hostility between them that was at last out in the open, thought this was probably the most acute observation Bryan Challis had ever made. Even Miss Vickers, wise in the ways of her girls, hadn't seen this. She had known that to Gillian Challis appearances were paramount, though. However unsuccessful her marriage had been, Gillian was committed to it through her religious beliefs, and she had made the best of it, in the same way as she had, years ago, made the best of her disappointment at not getting the coveted position of Head Girl. So Miss Vickers had said, who had thought her uncomplicated – because she had been adept at putting on a good face – or at hiding her feelings, depending on how you chose to look at it. Gillian Challis had her complications. If it was possible to love someone and hate them at the same time, he thought that she could. Hers had been a love-hate relationship with Fleur Saville. To the extent that when she killed her, she had possibly hardly realised why – or even whether it was Fleur or her husband she was subconsciously hitting out at when she swung that bag.

When, earlier that morning at the airport, Candace Neale had revealed to them Bryan Challis's long-guarded secret, two bare wire ends of thought had come together and flashed: how far would Bryan Challis go to prevent his wife learning of the one thing which without doubt would have destroyed his marriage?

Or – how far would *Gillian* have gone if she had known of it – if, for instance, that day, Fleur had told her the truth? To stop Fleur from using it, from making it public knowledge – as she, Gillian, must have known she was entirely capable of doing?

Suddenly that remark of hers had been understandable. 'A soul in torment,' she'd said. Applied to herself, Mayo guessed it wasn't far from the truth. Gillian, with her Catholic certainties, must have been shattered to learn of the continued deception which had struck at the very roots of her faith. And desolated by her unchar-acteristic, uncontrollable response to it. A mortal sin, the penalty for which was spiritual death.

From there it had been a short step towards taking a succession of facts, unremarkable in themselves, but which, put together, had in the end assumed a significance that had made him certain it was Gillian Challis, and not her husband, who was the killer.

To what extent even now could they believe her story? She'd been suspicious for weeks that her husband had been having an affair with Fleur, so it wouldn't have come as any great shock to her to have it apparently confirmed. She claimed that she'd misunderstood Fleur over that, and maybe she had. She denied Fleur had told her of her husband's previous marriage, and maybe that was true. They would never know for certain, unless she chose to admit it, whether she had.

Nevertheless, driving back to Lavenstock by way of Kennet Edge – a bracing spot, certainly, but with nothing to recommend it on a morning as bitterly cold as that Saturday, other than the fact that it would have been deserted – that indicated a degree of premeditation. Which one of them, in fact, had suggested getting out of the car, Fleur or Gillian? Certainly, after Fleur was dead she hadn't acted as an innocent woman, driven beyond reason to commit an act of folly, would have done. Wouldn't she have gone to the police, admitted what had happened? Gillian Challis wasn't a woman who would shrink from the consequences of a moment's loss of control. Instead, she had coolly bundled her friend into the boot of her car and immediately gone about setting up an alibi for herself.

'How did she manage it?' Kite had asked. 'If they left the White Boar at ten past one, Fleur must have died around half past, so how did she keep her hair appointment?'

'She didn't. It was Gillian Challis herself who kept the appointment, of course. And that was cool, if you like, but simple. Neither woman was known there, it was Fleur Saville's first appointment, so all Gillian Challis had to do was give the name of Saville when she walked in. She probably counted on the fact that if any checking up was done, to most of these girls all middle-aged women look pretty much the same, it's the hair they look at, and there at least they were superficially alike, both with very fair hair, cut in a similar way.'

'And that's pretty much what did happen, according to what the girl told Farrar,' Kite said. 'She was taking a risk, though. What if someone she knew had come in?'

'I don't think that would have deterred Mrs Challis. It was an unlikely chance. I dare say she was probably prepared to explain that Fleur hadn't been able to keep the appointment and she'd taken it up instead. Then of course she would have had to rethink her alibi. But as it happened, she didn't need to.'

He himself had noticed, when he saw them seated together in that school photograph, how similar they looked, two blonde girls together. That had been just after he had stood at his window and watched the one-way traffic flowing past, and at the back of his mind had been Gillian's assertion that she had last seen Fleur's red coat disappearing into the hairdresser's – when in fact, driving along Milford Road from the right, sitting in her car, she couldn't possibly have seen the entrance to the shop, with Peter Street almost doubling back on itself from the corner.

'And when she left the hairdresser's, all she had to do was drive down to Kelsey Road, let herself in with Fleur's keys and leave the jewellery. It couldn't have taken her more than a minute or two to slip into the house, but that, if I'm not very much mistaken,' Mayo said grimly, 'was what Mrs Henderson saw – Gillian's distinctive white car. She was very likely on her way to the shop at the time and being naturally inquisitive, and taking an interest in Edwin Saville as she does, she used the excuse of her out-of-order telephone to go across and see what was happening. That would be when Michael Saville came in and found her.'

'If she'd told us she'd seen the car there, she could have saved us a lot of trouble. Why the devil didn't she?'

'Who can tell what motivates a woman like Zoe Henderson? She detested Fleur Saville – probably thinks whoever killed her deserves to get away with it. She's devious, as well as a lot more things – Saville's welcome to her. Maybe she doesn't know about the penalties for hindering the police, but she's going to find out in the very near future – both she and Edwin Saville, though the reason he kept quiet is more understandable.'

'It's like most problems, simple when you know the answer,' Kite said. 'If Fleur hadn't put her rings and her bracelet on the dressing-table herself, it must have been somebody else who knew of the quarrel. Somebody who saw the value of using them to indicate she had decided to leave Edwin because of it. The only other person who knew – apart from Mrs Tennyson, and of course Saville himself – was Gillian Challis. The thing that amazes me is that she was able to go back to the church hall, with the body in the boot, and carry on as though nothing had happened.'

'Not only that – but drive home that evening with it still there, until she could dump it in the lane at Seddon End on the way to pick Challis up at the airport. Maybe it was simply a convenient spot en route, but more likely she intended to leave her in the gravel pits and found the lane blocked. Remember telling me about a case last year, an uproar over a possible prosecution? Who better than Mrs Challis, JP to have remembered that?'

'She'll get away with manslaughter,' Kite said, 'if they can prove provocation.'

Provocation or not, she had killed. When she made that lunge for the knife, she intended to kill again – either herself or Challis. Mayo somehow didn't think that the length of her sentence was going to be the cross Gillian Challis would have to bear.

CHAPTER 20

A few days later Edwin Saville sat in the back room at his shop, hunched over a pile of books in which he could summon no interest.

The bell rang as the shop door opened. Edwin sighed and didn't immediately stir. He was just rousing himself to answer it when Zoe came through. She'd brought teacakes again from the shop next door, the spicy ones he liked, crammed with currants and sultanas, to be served split and toasted and dripping with butter. It was becoming a daily routine with them.

There was a lot of confidence about her these days. Everything about her seemed more clearly defined – her hair redder, her skin whiter, her eyes more green than blue. He knew, sadly, that she was glad Fleur was dead.

She thought, like everyone else, that he had been deceived by Fleur, taken in and touched by her glamour, as the rest of them were. She was wrong. His marriage to Fleur hadn't been perfect, but he had known her through and through, and he'd loved her in spite of it . . . though he'd never been able to manage her. If he had, he'd never have allowed the quarrel that day to escalate, he'd have coped with things better, smoothed it over until she'd come to see the impossibilities of the situation, or until they could reach some compromise. But he'd never been very good at that sort of thing, it had always been easier, even with Margaret, his first wife, to give in. As he had when she'd insisted on going out in the boat that day, in rough weather with which he'd known he couldn't really cope. As he had with Zoe, too, agreeing to saying nothing to the police about Michael's visit to the house on the day Fleur disappeared . . .

It was a hard thing for a father to have to admit he had believed his son capable of murder. It was part of the guilt he was going to have to live with. The other part lay in believing that Fleur would ever have left him for that Waterton chap. She would never have done it, he knew that now. She had needed him as much as he had needed her, perhaps more.

His shoulders sagged, his hand rested slackly on the table. Zoe brought her own hand to lie next to it, the tips of her strong, thin fingers brushing his. There was suddenly uncertainty in the faint closed smile on her lips, a question in her eyes. He stayed where he was, unmoving, and presently, when the silence became unbearable, she took her hand away.

REQUIEM FOR
A DOVE

CHAPTER 1

Was it the woman herself, living self-contained and solitary, who had intrigued him so much, maybe because some awareness of the inescapable link between them, yet to be forged, was already with him? But he had no sense of that, then. It was only later that he came to feel that way. Perhaps it was simply the place.

A deep, narrow cutting through red rock, thickly wooded. Coins of light dancing on khaki-green water, still and sluggish between banks high with cow parsley and willow herb, and orange balsam bending to its own reflection. The tow-path overgrown with elder and hawthorn and willow, dangerously undercut in places, bounded by the dark mouth of the tunnel entrance at one end and the first of the flight of three locks at the other.

Beyond the tunnel was the canal basin by the old gasworks and a flat grey wasteland of abandoned factories and warehouses; above the locks the industrial suburb of Holden Hill began. But here in this hidden valley, between a B road and the railway, the traffic noise baffled by trees, lay this place of silence and secrets.

The waterway, he'd learned, had been a branch constructed originally in Lavenstock's industrial heyday to bring sand up to the local glass factory, as well as iron ore for the foundries and coal for the gasworks, but no barge or narrowboat had passed along it within years. At this point the canal was choked with weeds and silted with mud; green slime covered the lock gates, though its upper reaches had been cleared by bands of volunteers and it was now navigable as far as the locks. There were plans to repair the flight and develop the section beyond the tunnel as a leisure area. Landscaping for that had already begun. Factories were being pulled down, warehouses had been converted into luxury flats and the basin into a marina connecting the canal with the Stockwell, which ran parallel with it for several miles in the valley.

It was this last which had led to Mayo's discovery of the place on a day when he'd been inspecting one of the warehouse flats with a vague idea of buying, believing over-optimistically that he might not always be living alone and that one of the flats might not be beyond the means of a detective chief inspector. But although both hopes had been summarily dashed, his irredeemably inquisitive nature – and even, he admitted with a grim wryness, a certain masochism – had led him on to explore the whole area further, pushing through the dank, echoing, bat-hung tunnel to emerge with surprised delight into a golden evening silence, tree-dappled and shot through with the iridescence of dragonflies.

He suspected few people used the canal at this particular spot. The absence of the usual detritus of rusty bicycle wheels and abandoned fridges, floating islands of indestructible polystyrene foam and old mattresses disfiguring the stretch beyond the tunnel, was enough indication of this. The odd fisherman might occasionally manage to find somewhere to set up a stool and an umbrella, and an old rope dangling from a leaning sycamore led him to suppose unsupervised kids might lark about here from time to time. But he imagined the woman living in the old lock-keeper's house, at the point where the ground widened in front of the first lock, would be virtually undisturbed, left to the peace and the humming silence and the green water sliding soundlessly through the wooded clearing.

He realised he was seeing with temporarily enchanted eyes. In the dark winter days when there was no sun, or when mist rose from the canal like a miasma, it would be dismal. The dark little lockhouse wasn't convenient, being approached via a rutted lane with no easy access for vehicles. And yet – preoccupied with personal problems, walking along here several times lately in the hot dry spell that had come like a late redemption for a poor spring and summer – when he'd seen her sitting reading under the trees, or gardening, sometimes feeding her ducks, she had seemed apparently entirely contented and self-sufficient. She appeared so calm, so much a part of the place, shadowed and secret. A mythical figure almost, timeless, fixed in storyland . . . *Once upon a time, there was an old woman who lived alone in her cottage with her six white ducks . . .*

Only she wasn't old, not what you'd call old nowadays. A slim, nice-looking woman in her late fifties or early sixties, she'd raised her head when he passed, regarded him calmly with large grey eyes and then returned to whatever was occupying her. Apart from passing the time of day they'd never spoken.

CHAPTER 2

Poised symbolically over the huge metal entrance arch into which DOVE'S GLASS was writ large were a pair of white marble doves, as artistically intertwined as if on some tomb of the Victorian era in which they had originated. More doves were engraved on the glass panels of the mahogany entrance doors to the offices, in case you might have missed the significance of the others. The carpet in Kenneth Dainty's large, old-fashioned but airy office was dove grey, though this may not have been intentional. Ken was not given to flights of fancy.

'Oh dear me, not at our best today, are we?' Mr Bainbridge's ironic glance had followed Ken as he stalked through the outer office that morning with barely a nod to those present.

'Poor man, it's most likely Mrs Ken on at him again over something.'

'None of your business, Valerie!' Eyebrows lifted reprovingly over half-moon spectacles, his voice called her sharply to order. He was Ken's uncle by marriage, and the office manager, and thereafter entitled to take occasional liberties, but she as Ken's secretary – and office typist and tea-maker when the occasion demanded it – wasn't so privileged. In an office where everyone was known by their Christian names, he was never anything else but Mr Bainbridge. He was painfully arthritic and walked with a stick. He was due to retire shortly and should have gone years ago, but nobody had dared suggest it. In any case, no one, including Ken, could imagine how the office would run without him.

'I'll bet it's true, though,' Val had retorted, unrepentant.

Ken was at that moment making a half-hearted attempt at dictating to her, with many ums and ers and constant second thoughts to interrupt the flow of her neat shorthand. She was a plump, cheerful girl who liked working for him because he overlooked her tendency to misspell occasionally, largely because his own spelling was worse than hers, let her go promptly at five-fifteen and gave her generous bonuses at Christmas. She sighed now as ostentatiously as she dared and the unlikely object of her sympathy, taking the hint, pulled himself together and began to concentrate.

When he was finally through with his correspondence and she'd gone away to deal with it, Ken left his desk and walked heavily to the window where he stood, one hand braced against the frame, the other thrust deep into the trouser pocket of his well-tailored grey suit, staring without pleasure over a familiar view that normally gave him a good deal of satisfaction. He was a powerful man with muscular shoulders and a short neck, with fresh-coloured smoothly-tanned skin and the curly forelock, rounded forehead and wide nostrils of a handsome pedigree bull. It was a not unattractive face, especially when people were doing what he wanted, but just now set in a deep frown. What was he going to do about Shirley's mother? What, for Christ's sake, *could* he do? He'd spent most of last night lying awake worrying and was no nearer a solution.

There must be one, somewhere. After nearly twenty-five years with the firm, fifteen of them as an honorary member of the Dove family through his marriage to Shirley and the last ten as MD, virtually running the whole show – with Marion content to let him do so – he wasn't going to allow her to ruin everything he'd built up, have it come crashing round his ears. What daft whim had got into her, what in God's name did she think she was playing at? He'd always considered her too deep for her own good, too deep for him at any rate, though they usually got on well enough, considering. But this latest thing, he raged, staring moodily out, was beyond belief. It just wasn't on.

From this favourite vantage-point at the window, with the Stockwell valley spread out in front and descending gently towards Lavenstock, it was nearly possible to believe the sprawl and workaday clatter of industrial Holden Hill, stretching down and behind the factory, didn't exist. On this side of the slope, where he could remember the last of the old nailers and chain-makers and foundries standing cheek by jowl with corner shops and the unlamented back-to-back houses of the sort in which he'd been born, a private estate now stood, thrusting up red gabled roofs through trees that had been planted and had matured over the thirty-odd years of its existence. Gone were the other factories. Only Dove's remained, foursquare on the broad brow where it had been built 150 years ago, when old Enoch Dove had first trekked over here with his glassmaker's tools to set up on cheap land after a disastrous fire at his glasshouse in Stourbridge had almost ruined him. Here sons and grandsons and great-great-grandsons had continued in a small way their proud inherited Huguenot tradition of working glass until Wesley, the last and most ambitious of them, had died. After striving all his life to make the name of Dove synonymous throughout the world with elegant cut crystal and only partially succeeding, he had died a bitterly disappointed man, leaving only daughters, with no sons to carry on his name.

Shortly before Ken's marriage to Shirley, it had seemed to him that as a future son-in-law it couldn't do his prospects any harm at all to let it be known to Wesley that he was willing to change his own name to Dove, in the same spirit as the original Huguenots, founders of the family, had anglicised the French name of Douvre four hundred years ago. It was one of his few tactical mistakes. The old devil had soon silenced him with one of his sardonic looks and told him not to push his luck, and he hadn't made the suggestion again.

The canal flowed along behind the works before descending into the valley and where it curved gently in the distance some of the now converted warehouses by the old gasworks basin could be seen on their newly landscaped site. Because of the trees the flight of locks known as the Jubilee wasn't visible from here, but Ken could unerringly pinpoint the exact spot where his mother-in-law now lived. He would never understand why anyone with the money she had could actually choose to live in a hovel like that. And *ducks*, for God's sake! She could have had a nice little bungalow with every mod. con. plus her own car – even someone to drive it if she'd wanted – but no. Not Marion.

Her obstinacy had been a source of mild irritation to him for years but Shirley, from whom in this at the very least he might have expected a bit of support, chose to defend her mother. 'Oh, leave her alone, I've wasted enough breath trying to persuade her to get something better and it never does any good. Whatever people must think of me, I dread to imagine, but she never listens to my advice, so she certainly won't listen to yours. All she'll say is it suits her to live there better than living at The Mount.'

'Anything'd be better than rattling round in that damn great mausoleum!' It stood there alongside the factory, unlived in but still fully furnished, the original inimical Victorian red-brick monstrosity built by the second Dove, shrouded in banks of rusty laurel and overgrown rhododendron. When old Wesley had died Marion had simply walked out and refused to go back, and for ten years she'd categorically refused to do anything about it. The doors would never since have been opened had Shirley not felt obliged to check things over occasionally, ensure the house was aired and arrange to have someone see to the garden every so often to keep the grass down. 'I can understand her wanting to get out of there,' Ken continued, 'but there's no need to jump off the other end of the bloody plank!'

'Must you be so coarse about everything?'

'I could be a lot coarser if I set my mind to it!'

She didn't laugh, as she would have done once. She hadn't turned her nose up at a bit of rough in those days. But now, the local accent he'd never managed to get rid of, his mannerisms, his working-class relatives still living in the humbler parts of Lavenstock, she regularly had a go at them all. It was his good luck, he reckoned sardonically, that they'd met when she was so young, before she'd learned to be a snob, otherwise she'd never have looked at him and he'd still be where he'd started, on the shop floor.

What was it that had turned her eagerness into restlessness and discontent? What – apart from that bit of bother she'd had nine years ago – had happened to the lovely, impulsive girl who couldn't wait for them to marry, he occasionally asked himself, though not consciously. He shied away from thinking about things like that, and not only because he wouldn't have wanted to face the answer. Leave such fancy thinking to people with more brains than he had, he told himself, people like Rachel. But sometimes, he couldn't help wondering.

At nineteen she'd been eager for life and experience, too impatient to get on with it to waste, as she put it, three or four years at university, as her sister was all set to do. OK, she'd done what she wanted, even to the extent of overriding the objections to Ken's own lowly status by the father she'd feared . . . she could find courage enough when she really must . . . but it hadn't stopped her from being bitterly envious of what she constantly and acidly referred to as Rachel's liberated lifestyle.

371

What did she want, for crying out loud? He spent his life trying to find ways of coping with Shirley, but he hadn't yet found the answer. In her own way she was as impossible as her mother was being over this latest thing.

Five to ten. His unproductive thoughts coming full circle were interrupted by Val buzzing to ask if he'd forgotten he was due to meet Jim Thorburn in the cutting shop at ten. 'OK, Val, I'm on my way.'

He took the back steps, pausing on his way across the yard to glance in at the furnace hall and reassure himself that all was well, though he'd have been both surprised and annoyed if it hadn't been. He never could resist the pull that drew him there, however. Here was the heart and centre of the factory that was so intimate a part of him, where the raw, unpromising materials of sand and red lead and the broken and waste glass known as cullett were melted in the great domed furnace and the resulting glass metal spun into objects of astonishing and fragile beauty.

He stood inside the door, watching, his eyes growing accustomed to the darkness, the quiet broken only by a snatch of pop song from one of the youngsters, the tinkle of broken glass as a wineglass foot was cracked off a punty, the purring roar of the furnace. Traditionally it had been fired by cleft beechwood billets, later by coal, but now it was gas-fired, no longer dependent on the fickle direction of the wind or the reliability or otherwise of a stoker. From the rotunda of the furnace, the red eyes of the glory-holes glared out. Inside, the glass metal pulsated in the pots. The teams of men working it were stripped to the waist, sweat pouring as they dipped the long iron, spun and swung the fiery gather of glass and threw the iron with split-second timing from one to the other, with disciplined, organised, balletic movements. He remembered almost jealously how it was, he felt the old upsurge of pride, the sense of continuity, of belonging to a centuries-old tradition. He'd worked at the furnace himself, man and boy, rising to gaffer of one of the 'chairs' working the glass, making objects shaped by his own will and sleight of hand, by the quick precision of his movements. He still got the itch to seize the blower's iron with its potentially dangerous orange-gold gather of molten glass, swing it, shape it with his breath, manipulate it and demonstrate his power to subdue the forces of gravity.

But he'd come a long way since his gaffer's days and his power was of a different kind now. He knew the business inside out, having started at fifteen as an apprentice glass-blower, with marriage to the boss's daughter ten years later advancing him to managerial level. Some of his mates had looked askance at that but Wesley Dove had known what he was doing. He'd been a right old bastard but he didn't make mistakes about the men who worked for him. Ken had justified the faith put in him by revealing a flair for administration and a head for figures, and with his practical experience and capacity for hard, untiring work, plus a certain ruthlessness, was soon master of every facet of the business. In the years since Wesley had died he'd increased the viability of Dove's Glass beyond all expectations.

And standing here at the hub of his universe, with all the world he knew and wanted around him, he felt a sudden access of resolution: he'd faced trickier situations than this one by far and got out of them. All it needed was a measure of concentrated thought until at last a plan of action would appear, plus a nimbleness of wit to foresee any difficulties that might arise, and the nerve to carry it through. His Taurean head lifted and he smiled. He was confident he had a good measure of all three.

CHAPTER 3

Mayo would have had difficulty in believing the body was hers if it hadn't been for the spot where she was found. She'd been in the water too long and wasn't a pretty sight. Fish had already begun their nibbling at her water-sodden skin. Her tongue protruded horribly. She was wearing what had once been a navy and white silk shirtwaister and one smart white shoe, and her dark hair had come loose from its French pleat and streamed like Ophelia's. Her elegant pearl earbobs were still in place.

He looked down at what might once have been the woman who lived in the lockhouse and then put the polythene carefully back over the sodden body lying on the ground, breathing deeply. His stomach heaved as if this were his first corpse. God!

After all these years he thought he'd learned to control his physical reaction to the sight of a gruesomely dead body, though he was still moved every time to something like despair by the waste and futility of it. In this case it also affected him irrationally with a sense of personal affront, a shock of disbelief: this woman's life and his own had touched, however glancingly. What usually saved him from total despondency – and did so now – was the small, half-shamed yet undeniable frisson of professional excitement and yes, pleasure; such an end was after all a beginning for him, the unravelling of the threads to get at the centre of the knot. Or the start of the chase and the hunting down of the killer, depending on your terminology.

It was five to eight on a Tuesday morning early in September and although there had been a heavy dew it was already humming with heat, promising another scorcher. Mayo had only just arrived at the scene, thrown straight back into the thick of it the very day of his return from a fortnight's leave. He'd arrived at the station half an hour after the call had been received in the control room and when they'd told him a dead body had been found at the Jubilee Locks he'd driven over immediately, to find routine procedures already in motion.

'Everything under control, sir,' DC Keith Farrar assured him officiously, as if he, and not Inspector George Atkins, tirelessly plodding his conscientious unimaginative way towards retirement, was responsible.

Nevertheless, Mayo did a quick check round. A mortuary van was standing by with the other police cars, lights flashing, on the road above the rough track which led down to the canal, ready to take away the body after the police surgeon and the pathologist had examined it. The track itself had been sealed off by barriers. Two constables were marking off the area around her with yards of white tape, and Napier was busying himself with preliminary camera shots. Plain clothes men and uniformed constables in shirtsleeves and helmets were grouping, ready to move in when instructed.

'Have we identified her yet?'

Mayo had swiftly regained command of himself and now asked the question routinely of Farrar, who despite the heat was looking his usual cool and uncreased self. He was an excellent young man of whom Mayo had high hopes, but who sometimes annoyed him with his too-obvious ambition, his determined keenness, his fancy dressing. Today he wore a crisp white shirt and light cotton trousers, his blond hair was smooth and unrufffled. One day, thought Mayo sardonically, he'd forget and bring his tennis racquet with him as well.

The good-looking young detective-constable hadn't failed to observe Mayo's pallor on seeing the body but was careful to keep his interest to himself. While acknowledging his superior's reputation, and conceding admiration, Farrar fully intended in time to surpass him and was therefore circumspect in his speech and actions. 'The man who found her says she's the woman who lives here in the lockhouse, sir, name of Dove, Mrs Marion Dove. Sergeant Kite's taking a statement from him now.'

Mayo nodded at this confirmation of what he'd already guessed.

'She was found in the pound, sir.'

'The what?'

'The pound, that's what they call the bit below the locks, sir.'

'Do they? Thank you, Farrar, for that information.'

Mayo walked across to where Kite was sitting with an old man on a bench set underneath the window of the lockhouse, notepad on his knee, ballpoint in one hand and what looked suspiciously like the screwed up wrapper of a Mars bar in the other. The lanky, perpetually hungry sergeant, like the rest, was in his shirtsleeves and sweating profusely. He stood up and greeted Mayo with his likeable, cheerful grin.

The old man's name, Mayo learned as he was introduced, was Percy Collis, a nimble old pensioner with a bright eye who had on a light blue buttoned cardigan and a peaked cotton cap that gave him the appearance of an elderly budgie.

'Terrible shock, summat like this, for an owd 'un like me,' he greeted Mayo. 'I'm eighty-six come next Thursday, yo' know.'

Mayo dutifully expressed his surprise, put a few questions which launched the old man, who was nothing loath, into a repetition of what he'd already told Kite, of how he'd come across the body suspended in the reeds not far from the lock gates. He'd got over his initial shock, being too old for death to hold permanent terror for him, too experienced in human tragedy to be appalled for long and by now he'd reached the point where he was beginning to enjoy his moment in the spotlight. Play his cards right and he might even get his name in the papers, you could see him thinking it.

'I come down the cut most days when the weather holds, see, for a bit o' fishing, like. There's a cunning old devil of a pike I've been after for weeks down yonder. Yo' hadn't used to be able to cotch a lot but it's better nowadays, they stop 'em turning out so much muck into the water.' He paused, his glance travelling thoughtfully towards the sheeted bundle on the bank. He took another gulp from the beer bottle in his hand. 'Reckon I might give it a miss for a bit, eh?'

Beside him on the ground by the seat lay his gear for the day, his picnic bag piled on top of his rods and lines, keep nets, collapsible stool and umbrella, his can of maggots. 'Want a wet?

There's another bottle,' he offered Mayo generously. And with a nod towards Kite, 'I've asked him but he don't want one.'

'Keep it for yourself, dad, bit early in the day for me,' Kite said, and Mayo also shook his head.

'Suit yersels.' Unoffended, the old man belched and eyed Mayo. 'Reckon her fell, then? Them steps is slippy sometimes. Only last week her sang out to me to watch how I come down.'

Mayo had already made sure there were no obvious signs of anyone having slipped from the steep stairs at the side of the lock, though at the point where she'd been found the bank had broken away where someone might easily have accidentally missed their footing. Someone as familiar with those few yards of bank as the dead woman? In any case, he didn't think so.

The mud and debris of years had silted the canal up at the edges. Reeds and waterweeds with tough stems and flat, cabbage-like leaves had grown into it, making a thick, impenetrable mat, supporting the body just under the surface of the water.

'What made you so sure it was Mrs Dove you found, Mr Collis?'

'Who else could it ha' been? But it wor them ducks as made me wonder in the fust place. Gooing mad, poor little buggers, no food nor water in this heat and one of 'em already dead. Her wouldn't never've left 'em like that. When I rattled the door and give her a shout, no answer, so I knew summat was up and I started to have a good look round. I loosed the pen for a start – yo' should ha' seen 'em goo!' Mayo glanced towards the canal and the five remaining ducks. Survivors, unconcernedly upending themselves into the water. 'And then – then I come across her, poor wench.'

'Known her a long time, have you?'

'Oh ar, ever since her wor a nipper. Come from Chapel Street her did, Bert and Flo Waldron's youngest. Her wed Wesley Dove, him what owned the glassworks, though he could've give her twenty year easy. Rolling in it, the miserable owd sod, and he couldn't even see her orright when he died! Her shouldn't've had no need to live poor like this.'

The tone of voice wasn't unfamiliar to Mayo, evoking echoes of his own northern childhood, an environment with this same sense of tight community, where everybody knew everybody else and some did better than others, but good luck to them all the same. A good feeling of belonging, except that you couldn't blow your nose without everybody knowing. He asked Percy Collis how long Mrs Dove had lived here.

'I'd be guessing if I said. Ten year? Dunno, rightly. Her used to mek me a cuppa tea now and again and I once asked her why her come here but her told me: "I just like it quiet, Perce." Well, it's all according, ain't it?'

'No accounting for tastes,' Kite agreed. 'What is it, Farrar?'

'Doc Ison's car's here, Sarge.'

Mayo stood up. 'Carry on with your statement to Sergeant Kite, Mr Collis, if you don't mind, then we'll get a car to take you down to the station so it can be typed and you can sign it.'

Percy Collis made no objections, signifying his willingness with a nod and another swig at the bottle, and Mayo followed Farrar down the path where he met the police doctor and Atkins at the foot of the steep stairs which descended from the first lock. ''Morning, Doc.'

The doctor acknowledged the greeting, his face grave. 'This isn't what I expected, I must say.'

'Expected?' Mayo looked sharply at the doctor.

'It's Marion Dove, isn't it?'

'You know her?'

Ison nodded briefly and knelt down on the grass beside the body. For what seemed like several minutes he stayed motionless, an unreadable expression on his face, then he said quietly, 'Yes, it's Marion Dove, God rest her.' He lifted the sodden left hand with its bleached and wrinkled skin, indicating where, across the back, ran a thick, ridgy scar, white as a worm. 'Cut herself badly with a bread knife, years ago.'

'Tell me about her, will you?' Mayo asked abruptly.

'I don't think I can tell you much. I've known her – and all the rest of her family – a long time, but only as patients. She's the widow of Wesley Dove – you know, Dove's Glass. There's a couple of daughters. The eldest's married to Ken Dainty, the chap who runs the works now.'

'She'll have to be told. Where can we get hold of her?'

'They live out at Henchard, on The Ridgeway,' volunteered Atkins, the fount of all local knowledge, naming the most prestigious road in Lavenstock's most affluent suburb.

Ison said, 'Go carefully, she's inclined to be neurotic. I should try the works first, get hold of the husband and let him break it to her.' He had shed his jacket and now began rolling up his sleeves preparatory to starting his examination. 'All right, I'd better see what's what.'

Mayo said, 'You won't want me getting in the way. Tell them to give me a shout when you've finished, will you? George, you come and give me a rundown on what's happened so far.' He walked away, Atkins following like a faithful St Bernard. Mayo was a big man who carried himself well, but Atkins overtopped him. 'Anybody been inside the house yet?'

'Had a quick look round myself. Nothing obvious. It wasn't locked, and the kitchen window'd been left open. Won't be told, will they?' The inspector shook his head sorrowfully. 'A lot of money left in a drawer in the bedroom besides, but not touched seemingly. Her handbag's missing, though.'

'How much? In the drawer?'

'Five hundred, at a guess. In tens and fives.'

Mayo's eyebrows shot up. He told Atkins he would have a look round the cottage himself before Forensics arrived. 'I'll come back to you.'

'Right you are.'

His long strides covered the distance back to the house and through the gate set in the low, dark-green painted fence which surrounded the garden. Kite and the old man had moved away. A

379

short flagged path led from the gate to the front door, through a small plot bright with asters, pot marigold and nasturtium and fragrant with lad's love, with a Dorothy Perkins rambler and a honeysuckle either side of the door.

At the door the path divided and circled the lockhouse. Before going inside Mayo followed it round, shielding his eyes with his hands to peer through the windows. He got the general layout but could see little except that everything appeared to be in order, the kitchen tidy, the bed made. The building was one storey, rectangular, built of dark red Victorian brick. Its plan was simple. Just a front room with a kitchen behind it to one side of the central front door, with one bedroom and a bathroom made from what had probably once been a second bedroom on the opposite side. The cutting rose almost vertically behind the house and windows to the back had evidently been deemed unnecessary, those of the kitchen and bathroom being set in the side walls, the one overlooking a small vegetable garden with an abundant Cox's apple and a purple damson tree, the other the duckpen.

Among the vegetables a row of lettuces and a tomato plant in a growing bag, heavy with fruit, were flagging from lack of water. In the duckpen the dead duck lay with its head tucked under its wing, the water-trough was bone dry. How long could a duck survive without food or water? It sounded like a facetious riddle inside a Christmas cracker, but the answer might help to establish the time when their owner had died.

Pulling on protective gloves, he opened the front door. His first impression was of darkness, though all the walls had been emulsioned in pastel colours to maximise the light. An open door showed him the bedroom, easily examined since it contained nothing except a single bed covered with a white hand-crocheted cotton spread, a chest of drawers with one top drawer locked and the money Atkins had mentioned in the other – all of five hundred pounds, yes – and why wasn't that in the locked drawer? He'd have that one opened as soon as Scenes of Crime had finished with it.

The wardrobe he found as he opened it housed a modest collection of unremarkable clothes. It looked as though she had been wearing her best when she died . . . The rest comprised the sort of garments he'd always seen her in: simple cotton dresses, blouses and skirts, a few sweaters and a mac with a detachable fur-fabric lining that would have doubled as a winter coat. The chest of drawers served as a bedside table and on it was a lamp, two half-full bottles of prescription pills and a thick volume of the *Complete Poems and Illustrations of William Blake*, inscribed in confident handwriting on the flyleaf, 'To Mother, with love from Rachel'. A Tesco checkout receipt for a modest £7.39 marked the place where a couple of lines were underscored in pencil: 'He who kisses the joy as it flies, lives in Eternity's sunrise.'

An unusual choice, Blake, not to everyone's taste by a long chalk. And whose choice, in this case? The mother's or the daughter's? He flicked through it. Difficult poems, some of them, well-nigh incomprehensible to him, the weird drawings and colour prints equally so. Visionary, said the accompanying text. Surrealist, he would have described them himself. The subject of one entitled 'Pity' had a particularly unnerving effect on him. He *thought* it was a dead or dying young woman with a newborn child being taken up into heaven by a messenger on a winged horse, but whatever it was supposed to be the prone figure with streaming hair and hands clasped across her breast bore a shocking resemblance to the shrouded figure lying on the canal bank.

He closed the book abruptly and as he did so the supermarket receipt slipped out and fluttered to the floor. Bending to retrieve it, he saw there was something written on the back. In a very different handwriting from that inside the book's cover, small and slightly backward-sloping, someone had written: 'Steven, 10.30 Sunday.' Before putting it in his wallet, he noted that the date was last Friday's, and slid it carefully into a small plastic envelope so that it could be tested later for traces.

The kitchen and bathroom were neat and orderly with nothing

special to interest him. And very little in the tiny sitting-room, except for a plain oak sideboard, the contents of which mildly surprised him. An Indian-style rug in front of the hearth stood on a floor of polished red brick, there were almond green slubbed linen curtains and two armchairs slip-covered in flowered cretonne, and a low table upon which was set a chessboard with a game in progress. There was also a small bookcase which on inspection contained predominantly travel books and more volumes of poetry, mostly modern, with several library books on the top shelf of the same persuasion.

A simple home. Simple but not, as the old man had implied, poor. And through choice rather than necessity, Mayo was sure. Deliberate simplicity, almost to the point of anonymity. Marion Dove seemed to him to have pared down her life to all but essentials. No music, even. He, who found poetry difficult to understand and appreciate but to whom life without music was unthinkable, had of course noticed at once that this hadn't been an obvious way in which her life was enriched.

Yet it was extraordinary what a peaceful atmosphere there was in this room. So strong as to be almost a force, as if the woman who had lived there had left her own attainment of it as an impression on the very air, so that he might pick it up. How much of this was due to the curious effect his own obsession with the place had on him? Mayo stood for a moment in the centre of the room, being very still, then went out of the house, closing the door behind him.

CHAPTER 4

Ison was standing up, brushing the red sandy soil off the knees of his trousers. 'That's it, then,' he announced in typically brusque manner. 'She didn't drown, she was strangled. Dead before she went into the water – though don't quote me. You'll have to wait for the PM to be certain.'

The doctor's natural caution was always added to by his professional reluctance to commit himself, but Mayo knew him well enough by now to realise this practically amounted to a direct statement, and in any case the information came as little surprise to him. He'd seen enough bodies to have recognised the signs on this one and to have made a fairly accurate guess, even from his brief look at her, that someone had choked the life out of Marion Dove.

'Strangled, how?'

'Manually, by the look of the bruises on her neck . . . if she fought back, there's no other bruises to say so. They may of course find skin and tissue under her nails.'

At least there'd be no dragging the canal, no rubbish tips to sift through, no waste ground to search for the murder weapon.

'Anything more?'

'I take it you mean when did she die? A couple of days, I'd say, three at the outside. Sorry, Gil, I know it's important to you to know, but it's not something I'm prepared to stick my neck out on at this point. Maybe Timpson-Ludgate will be able to be more precise at the autopsy, but I wouldn't count on it. You know as well as I do how difficult it is to tell. Find out when she had her last meal and we might be in a better position to say.'

'Two to three days? That takes us back roughly to – Saturday, Sunday.' Mayo thought for a while, then remembering what the doctor had said when he arrived, he asked, 'What did you mean by saying this wasn't what you'd expected to find?'

Ison brought out a handkerchief to mop the perspiration from his brow and stared across the water, not answering immediately. A dabchick dived underwater with a plop, and a shaft of sunlight penetrating the canopy of leaves shone on a cluster of half-ripe elderberries, emerald bloomed with dusky purple. The scent of meadowsweet was strong, mingling with the dank, faintly rotten smell of the canal and the taint of corruption on the air.

'No,' he said at last, 'it wasn't what I anticipated. When I heard a woman had been fished out of the canal just here I automatically thought of Marion Dove, knowing she lived here. I expected to find she'd taken her own life.'

'*Suicide?* Was she suffering from depression? Had she attempted it before?'

Ison said, 'No, not clinical depression, that is. But she'd been having treatment for some time. She was suffering from inoperable cancer. She'd left it too late and I had to tell her a few weeks ago that her chances of surviving more than another month or so were so slim as to be non-existent.'

'He who kisses the joy as it flies.' Those underscored lines of poetry suddenly seemed unbearably poignant. A sense of fleeting melancholy assailed Mayo as he looked at Ison, shortish, bespectacled, middle-aged, tired. Of such stuff are heroes made. 'It's a devil of a way to earn a living, Henry, yours.'

Ison grunted, briskly rolling down his sleeves. 'Yes, well, nobody ever made you become a policeman, either.' Picking up his bag, he hesitated.

'Something bothering you?'

'No. No, not really.' Ison frowned and ran a hand through what was left of his hair. 'Just something niggling, but damned if I know what. Probably left the garage door unlocked or some such. Forget it.'

He wasn't a man to be pressed and when he'd left, Mayo rejoined Atkins, who was standing with DC Deeley looking at the taped-off section at the edge of the canal where the bank had broken away. He looked around for Kite, found he had just sent old man Collis off to the station with Farrar, and beckoned him over. He then repeated what Ison had said for the benefit of the others.

'That's bad,' Kite said.

'That's life, son,' replied Atkins, but the irony of it subdued them all for a moment.

'Her handbag turned up yet?' Mayo asked Atkins.

'Not so far. After her attacker had got what he wanted, he probably chucked it in the bushes, or the canal. We'll drag for it, if necessary.'

'She was mugged then, sir?' Deeley surprised them with the doubt evident in his voice.

'She was strangled, Pete, throttled,' Kite pointed out patiently to the young DC. Deeley sometimes exasperated them all with his slowness, but he was showing promise and any initiative was to be encouraged. 'Not knifed, or knocked to the ground, or clouted over the head. Deliberately strangled.'

Deeley looked abashed, but unoffended. He was used to being put down. He accepted the fact that they couldn't all be smart alecks, like Farrar, but he knew he had his uses. He had hands like York hams, weighed fourteen stone. Put him in a punch-up and nobody had the edge on him, and though he was slow-thinking, he got there, in time. 'She must have been going out, or coming back in, then,' he said.

'Her door wasn't locked, nor the windows, and there was money in the house, so that seems unlikely.'

'Then why did she have her handbag with her? She wouldn't take a handbag with her for a walk outside her own front door, sir, would she?'

He had a point, Mayo thought. Perhaps she had for some reason rushed out, handbag in hand, forgetting to lock up, and had been attacked. Why? Why had she rushed out, why had she been attacked? This didn't, he was thinking, have the appearance of an opportunist crime, a chance encounter on a dark night, a handbag snatch gone wrong, with death an unforeseen result of the attack. Yet if it had been a deliberately planned robbery, that implied someone with prior knowledge of something worth stealing, either in the house or on her person. Curious, then, considering the money in the drawer, and the unlocked house. 'It doesn't make much sense. Anyone attacking with robbery in mind would have taken the opportunity of seeing what he could find in the house.'

'Not if he panicked when he saw she was dead,' Kite said.

'Fair enough. But don't let's get sold on the idea of this as a casual, unpremeditated attack.'

'So if robbery wasn't the motive . . .' Kite let the rest of his sentence hang.

But Mayo was not, at this point, overly-concerned with speculation about motives. 'Then we're looking for something else, aren't we?' he said.

The pathologist, Timpson-Ludgate, in a great hurry and not as exuberantly cheerful as usual, thank God, had been and gone, promising to carry out the autopsy as quickly as possible, not adding anything material to Ison's findings. The body, sheeted in polythene, had been carried up the steep path to the mortuary van. Leaving Atkins to take care of what still had to be done at the scene, Mayo left with Kite to go back to Milford Road to put his superintendent, Howard Cherry, in the picture. Fortunately, on this occasion the station was within striking distance, near enough to make the setting up of a separate incident room unnecessary, a situation Mayo always avoided if possible. He always preferred to work from base, where all the investigating machinery – telephones, computers, transport, the rest – was already to hand.

'When I've seen Cherry I want you to come with me to see the daughter's husband – what's his name – Dainty, Kenneth Dainty,' he told Kite as they followed the same path as the victim.

He wanted somebody with him at the first, all-important interviews with the next of kin, another pair of perceptive ears and eyes, and there was nobody he'd rather have than Kite. Competent, tenacious and energetic under a sometimes regrettably flip exterior, despite his youthful, ingenuous appearance, he was an experienced detective and there wasn't much he missed. He had plenty of the same sort of drive that Mayo had, and they'd worked together long enough now to be on the same wavelength, so that there was the minimum of time wasted. Time which was a crucial factor in every murder investigation, before the trail went cold.

As they left the canal bank and began to walk up to the road, Kite said, 'I'd nearly forgotten . . . have a good holiday, sir?'

His own, taken at the beginning of the school holidays with his wife Sheila and their two young sons, seemed a long way behind, and his tone was a bit wistful.

'Fair to middlin', thanks. Restful.'

'Glad to hear it.' Kite took the answer for what it was, true Yorkshire understatement. Circumspect as ever about his personal life, the DCI, but his holiday had evidently done him good. He looked fit and tanned, a lot more relaxed than he had for some time.

Kite's surmise was correct, as it happened. Holidays weren't something Mayo relished these days. They never had been, truth to tell, even when Julie had been a little girl and Lynne was still alive and seaside or country holidays had been one of the great occasions of the year, like Christmas, planned months ahead. Now that he was alone and could please himself he generally managed to avoid taking the whole of his annual allotted leave. This time, however, he had felt the need for a break and had just spent ten days walking alone in the Western Highlands, staying at a small hotel which provided ample, wholesome food, plentiful hot water for luxurious baths when he returned tired out at the end of each day, and excellent malt whisky. It had only rained three or four times, he'd seen a golden eagle on the Isle of Eigg and he'd returned sunburned, full of well-being and rarin' to go.

During the long days tramping the hills alone, when he had met nothing that lived except for sheep and the occasional magnificent stag glimpsed dramatically on the skyline, he'd done a lot of thinking. Mainly about Alex and himself. He wasn't a man to go on bashing his head against a brick wall, he decided at last. What he needed was a strategy, and the strategy called for at the moment was to play a waiting game, to go along with the uncommitted relationship Alex wanted. Looking down from the height of a barren moor, ravished by the unexpected sight of a hidden loch between the hills mirroring the racing clouds of a blue sky, his mind blown clear and exhilarated with wind and sun and pure air, he'd suddenly been able to put things in perspective.

Alex was ambitious, sooner or later she would be off. She wouldn't stay a police sergeant for much longer. Whereas he, perhaps, had reached the desired limits of his own ambition – for further promotion would mean a more and more deskbound future, which was not where he was at. Maybe also she was wiser than he. Maybe it was only propinquity after his wife's death and his daughter's leaving home to train for a career which had brought them together, and anything long term was not on. But this was travelling further than he was prepared to go at the moment.

'Kiss the joy as it flies.' The words of the quotation came back to him. It was as good a philosophy as any.

There was a shout from one of the constables up by the lock gates. 'Looks as though they've found it, the handbag,' Kite said. But the constable was holding aloft the other white shoe.

They walked up the lane, small round stones slithering under their feet, and emerged on to the Compsall road, where Kite stood looking round, his face registering utter incomprehension. 'Why in God's name would *anyone* want to live here?'

The road bridged the canal at the top of the first lock and crossed a further stretch of industrial spoliation, long awaiting redevelopment. As so often hereabouts, topographical contrasts were marked. These desolate acres which signified the limits of Lavenstock's industrial area came to an end half a mile away at the Evening Lock, whereafter, like going through the gateway to another world, the canal wound lazily through a landscape in which cattle grazed in lush meadows, crops flourished and woods rose gently to the hills. But here was scrubby emergent grassland where the only signs of life were a few aged, motheaten donkeys and ponies looked after by some cranky woman. Almost treeless, bisected by the canal, bounded by Compsall Road. Along the roadside survived two or three scattered, tiny dark brick cottages of the sort that had been shoved up in a day and a night to establish squatters' rights during the last century, it was said. Holden Hill and its crowded factories and engineering shops veered off upwards to the right. Far to the left lay the remains of a forsaken brickworks, merely a blunt chimney now and some tumbledown walls. Further along was the Dog and Fox, a pub of unsavoury reputation.

Why live here? Looking round, Mayo couldn't argue with Kite's point of view; but below he had been vouchsafed a glimpse of Marion Dove's small secret world, and he thought he could understand.

He got into his car, then leaned out to speak to Kite. 'By the way – those ducks. Get somebody to do something about them, see they're taken care of.'

Kite looked blank. He knew nothing about ducks except that they tasted good with orange sauce. 'Couldn't they be left to – er – take care of themselves? I mean, other ducks manage all right, don't they? Worms and things. Or have these forgotten how to forage for their own food?'

Mayo looked equally blank. 'I haven't a clue. But see to it anyway.' He grinned. 'Or ask Farrar, he's sure to know.'

CHAPTER 5

Rachel was packing when Ken telephoned with the news.

'I can't believe it,' she heard him say, from a long way off, it seemed. 'The last time I saw her, on Saturday night . . . I can't believe it!'

What did he mean? She was too shaken for it to matter.

She was a sturdy, positive young woman with straight fair hair which she wore pushed behind her ears and clear hazel-green eyes under strongly marked brows. Decisions didn't normally present her with difficulties. Yet when Ken had at last rung off she sat where she was, unable to move, in a patch of sunlight that filtered through the Edwardian stained glass in the front door panels and dabbled her white cotton skirt with rich lozenges of colour. Gold, sapphire, blood red. Blood. But there would have been no blood, would there? Oh God.

She was quite steady. She wasn't shaking, there were no tears, just a hollow feeling of complete unreality. And coldness. How could she be cold in this stifling heat? Half an hour ago just the effort of putting her things into her case had been making the sweat run down her back.

Theory, she discovered, was of no use at all. In theory she was fully aware that she was in shock and knew what she ought to do about it. In reality she seemed to be totally incapable of even moving, simply overwhelmed by things which seemed complex beyond her power to do anything about .

Josh. Josh, she thought with release. Thank God, he would know exactly what to do. With stiff fingers she dialled. But when he answered she didn't know where to start. There seemed nothing to say except, baldly, 'I can't go to Florence. My mother's dead.' Somehow she managed to tell him how.

There followed the briefest of pauses. 'I'll come over right away. Ten minutes.'

And in fifteen, after a hard and steadying embrace and a foray into the kitchen to make a cup of strong, sweet tea, he was leaning his shoulders against the mantelpiece, a slight man with a clever, mobile face and horn-rimmed spectacles, watching her while she sipped.

'You go,' she said, 'there's no need to spoil the holiday for both of us.'

'Go? Without you? The whole point of Florence was to show it to you, my darling. It'll wait until we can go together.'

The endearment, which came as a slight shock, she recognised with mute gratefulness as a measure of his concern. Endearments weren't his usual style. That was more a matter of laconic, amused tolerance which she at least knew masked a deeper sensitivity, plus a lack of pomposity and the sort of irreverent, ironic wit that made him popular with his students.

An art historian of some seriousness and distinction, with several well-received publications to his name, Josh Amory had so far managed to survive critical acclaim with modesty and humour. They'd met when she'd taken up her own appointment here as lecturer in the history department at the university three years ago and had been lovers for the last two. He'd never asked her directly to marry him, nor had they ever discussed the possibility in theory. She'd sometimes wondered whether this was from some reluctance of his own or whether it sprang from an innate delicacy which sensed without being told that she didn't want to share the life she'd made for herself, even with him. Their relationship was deep and tender, emotionally satisfying, but marriage was the final commitment and as far as she was concerned, one demanding total honesty. There were still areas of her life closed from him.

'You'll have to go to Lavenstock,' he said.

'I suppose I shall.'

'I'll drive you there.'

'No!'

She was appalled at the strength and crudity of her denial and laid her hand on his to lessen the impact but if he was offended he gave no sign. 'If that's what you want,' was all he said, adding after a moment, 'You're still cold, is there any brandy?'

'I think so.

Unruffled, as familiar with her flat as with his own, he went to the cupboard where she kept her drink, poured cognac and brought it back to her, moulding her fingers around the glass until he was sure she held it steady. His touch was firm and comforting.

Like her, Josh had been brought up to control his emotions, though for different reasons. His family, unlike hers, was impeccable upper-class, a long line of distinguished soldiers with several brigadiers and a famous general adding lustre to his ancestry; public school and Cambridge had followed a sheltered childhood. Her own circumstances were undeniably more proletarian, grammar school and a redbrick university, because such wealth as her father had possessed hadn't persuaded him to expend it in the buying of privilege, either for himself or his daughters.

Diverse as their backgrounds were, however, it had never seemed to matter. What was important was their common ground here in the civilised and perhaps remote tranquillity of this quiet, academic city. It wasn't any sort of inverted snobbery which made her want to keep the two strands of her life apart but simply that they were like two parallel lines, never converging, or only at some distant, illusory point. Here at Northumbria was fulfilment, shared assumptions and an intellectually stimulating, well-ordered life. And there in Lavenstock were ghosts. Ghosts from the old house in Holden Hill – private ghosts, never far behind.

Something inside her shivered uncontrollably. She knew she had something of her father's darkness in her, something of her mother's hidden waywardness. It had always frightened her, now it threatened. There was always guilt somewhere when someone died, which had to be accepted and sooner or later be forgiven in oneself – she didn't fool herself that she was unique in that. If her mother had died from natural causes the remorse would still have been there – but now it had added to it the burden of anger. It was an obscenity that after all she had been through, and endured, Marion's life should have ended like this.

The anger was not new. Rachel had rarely, if ever, asked her mother for advice but had rather been prone to give it even from a very early age, and been annoyed and impatient when it was rejected. She'd always been so sure of herself, so certain that her rational way of thinking was right not only for her but for her mother. That last meeting, for instance . . .

She told herself that she'd tried. But Marion had been adamant, gently stubborn and unyielding in the way only she knew how to be. It had driven her mad, she knew her mother's decision had been the wrong one, but how could you argue with someone in her position? She had by then had the answers to much of what had puzzled her in her mother's life, that she might have known before had she asked in the right way. She had spent the journey home bitterly regretting that she had never before paused long enough in her headlong pursuit of career and self-fulfilment to think it through.

She tried to remember what Ken had said, what he'd meant, but somehow it didn't seem to have registered. It was irrelevant anyway, what did it matter now? He ought to be concerning himself with how Shirley was going to take the news. Poor Shirley, in her expensive new house, so careful of her vowels and the friends she kept, with her own personal hang-ups. How much had she known about what had gone on in those dark years? Rachel imagined herself asking her sister but knew she'd never do so. Shirley would grow scarlet and uptight, and even if she'd known, she would never admit it. Not she, not Shirley. She would much prefer to pretend it had never happened.

But as the elder child, she must have known, thought Rachel. What else had contributed to that horrifying business nine, ten years – Michael was how old? – nine years ago. As it had contributed to Rachel's own attitude to marriage. They'd neither of them ever be free. It was a cycle, a vicious circle, spiralling from one generation to another.

CHAPTER 6

Mayo kept his eyes on the back of Ken Dainty's dark red Volvo as the CID car followed it, weaving expertly through Lavenstock's twisting, busy streets, noisy with market-day traffic. Kite drove. In the back sat WDC Rhoda Piper, a silent, stolid woman with red hair and a broad freckled face, who had remained in the car reading the *Guardian* while Kenneth Dainty was informed of the death of his mother-in-law, his brief telephone call to break the news to his wife's sister, and his later formal identification of Mrs Dove's body at the mortuary.

Out towards Henchard, where the soil was red and the hills crowned with trees heavy with the heat of late summer, the harvest was in and the stubble fields, pale and golden, stretched either side of lanes becoming increasingly steep and narrow. Presently they were running along the elevated country road known as The Ridgeway bordering which, for about a mile, were architect-designed houses with landscaped gardens and sweeping panoramic views either side.

'Millionaire's Row,' Kite commented laconically. Mayo grunted. There were some very showy houses along here, one of them occupied by a pop singer who had enjoyed a moment of fame, but in Mayo's opinion their reputation was exaggerated by the inflated prices they commanded when they were sold.

Dainty, driving his Volvo fast and surely, eventually made a stylish turn into a red tarmac drive which led up to a split-level house with low sloping roofs and picture windows. Though not as large as some of its neighbours, it was still a house making a statement about the prosperity of its owners. Either side of the drive shaven lawns swept down, with specimen trees strategically placed. Flowerbeds surrounded it in which were lavish displays of roses of every hue in their second flowering, unsullied by black spot or aphid. Even Rhoda Piper was moved to comment on the perfume which almost overwhelmed them as they alighted from the car and went to the door, where Dainty waited for them .

'Oh, the roses!' He shrugged. 'Yes, they do well round here. Come in, will you?'

A short while before, Shirley Dainty had been staring round her expensively furnished home, impatient and dissatisfied with it.

The room itself in which she was standing was attractive, long and low, with pine-clad walls and a ceiling-high fireplace in natural stone and a big picture window, but it somehow didn't look as it ought, the overall effect jangled and she didn't know why. It should have been perfect, everything in the room was new, and colour-coordinated, and the draped silks and velvets of the soft furnishings had looked so lovely in the department store room display. Perhaps velvet and silk were wrong, maybe she ought to have kept to the plain carpet, and not substituted the brighter, patterned one. A shaft of sunlight caught the prisms of the cut-glass chandelier and made her blink. The shiny new brocade cushions she'd bought yesterday, punished into stiff diamond shapes, marched along the length of the velvet settee and suddenly furious, she punched them into softer shapes, flung herself down and lit another cigarette.

Why was nothing ever perfect? Why did everything, once so earnestly desired, turn to dust and ashes once you'd got it?

Ten minutes later she was still sitting there, looking at the two men and the woman who'd accompanied Ken into the room. Detectives! She told herself she wasn't impressed with the Chief Inspector, despite his size and those grey eyes that were watchful and missed nothing. She reached out and lit another cigarette and his eyes flickered. He didn't like to see a woman smoking; she could always tell, but what was it to him? She tapped the ash off impatiently. Ken began to speak.

She heard what he said and didn't believe it. Then she looked at his face and saw that it was true. She felt her face crumple. She put her cigarette in the ashtray and Ken put his arms round her and for the first time in a long while there was, for a moment or two, that old feeling of closeness and warmth.

Was there an easy way to communicate the appalling fact of murder? If so, Mayo wished he knew. They let her husband tell her and sat awkwardly by while he comforted her with a tenderness that sat oddly with his bullish appearance, his large hands gentle and a curious expression on his face as she allowed him to hold her head against his shoulder for a few minutes. Then her body gradually became more rigidly held away from him and presently she raised herself from his arms altogether and moved slightly along the sofa. Dainty sat up more slowly and stared fixedly through the window, his jaw set.

'It's not fair,' his wife was moaning, echoing the uncomprehending and unanswerable lament of the bereaved everywhere. 'She wasn't old, or helpless. She could have had a good twenty years in front of her.'

So Shirley Dainty hadn't known about her mother's medical condition. For reasons of her own, Marion Dove had kept that to herself, and Mayo didn't feel it was up to him to add to her daughter's misery at the moment by informing her. She had cared for her mother, that was evident – unless she was a damned good actress. Her eyes were reddened with weeping, her mouth swollen, though the first genuine outburst of grief over, she was beginning to react with hostility and accusation, her tone if not her words suggesting she was almost as much outraged by the fact of her mother being murdered as saddened because she was dead. It was becoming ever more apparent that she was also deeply affronted by the manner of her dying, and alarmed at the thought of the unwelcome notoriety it would inevitably bring.

'It's disgraceful, this sort of thing – isn't it about time your people did something to stop it? Just what has to happen before one can be allowed to walk outside one's own home in peace without being mugged?'

'Forgive me, Mrs Dainty, but it's by no means established your mother *was* mugged yet,' he said gently.

'She was attacked, wasn't she? Her handbag's missing. What more do you want?'

'More facts at this juncture. But this has been a shock, very upsetting for you. We can come back later if you don't feel up to it, though naturally we don't want to lose any more time than we have to.'

Dainty said quickly, 'Would you rather they did, Shirley?' He for one looked as though he'd be glad of a reprieve.

She shook her head and said she was all right. And despite her nerviness, Mayo was sure she would be. There was no sign that she was about to collapse or go into hysterics. Rhoda Piper wasn't going to be needed for tea and sympathy. 'What do you want to know?'

Anything you can tell me about your mother, Mayo thought, what sort of woman she was, what her relationships with other people were . . . but knew instinctively she wasn't the person to ask, even if the circumstances had been propitious. Everything would be subjective with her, everything judged by how it affected her personally.

She was a good-looking woman, her bone structure excellent, she had large hazel eyes and fine light brown hair that she constantly brushed back from her face, but she was too thin, at thirty-five or so already on the way to becoming scrawny. Lines of discontent pulled down the corners of her mouth and her constant fidgeting – with her hair, her cigarettes, the fringe on the armchair, her red-nailed fingers twisting together – were beginning to get on his nerves. But there was a dazed look behind her eyes that prompted him to be patient.

'Thank you. It would help us if you could answer a few questions,' he said, keeping to practicalities. 'For instance, whether your mother was in the habit of keeping large sums of money about her?'

397

She stared blankly at him. 'Cash? Good heavens, no! Who does nowadays – it's all plastic money, isn't it? Not that my mother bothered with credit cards. She paid what bills she had by cheque and I know for a fact she never kept more than a few pounds by her. But what difference would it have made if she had? People are mugged for whatever can be got, aren't they?'

'We found five hundred pounds in a drawer in her bedroom.'

'Five hundred pounds!' Her voice rose several tones. 'But that's not possible!' Astonishment silenced her, but only momentarily. 'In the bedroom? Well, she was mugged outside, and whoever did it wasn't to know that, was he?'

He could appreciate her insistence on the mugging theory. It would be easier for everyone if that's how it turned out to be. The alternatives were undeniably more horrible. He wondered if they'd occurred to her.

He asked the question that always made him feel like a Roundhead inquisitor – when had she last seen her mother? She blinked. Dainty said, 'Saturday evening, wasn't it, when she had supper with us.'

'Oh, yes. Yes, Saturday.'

At that moment the telephone rang in the hall. Mayo made a signal for WDC Piper to answer it and waited. He eased the hard cushion at his back. The room smelled aggressively of furniture polish and was an uneasy mixture of studied, conventional good taste and expensive, glitzy ostentation. That chandelier must have cost a couple of weeks' wages. It was as unlike her mother's home as it was possible to be. I know which I'd rather have, thought Mayo.

Rhoda came back. 'Mrs Dainty, it's your sister.'

Shirley rose and walked quickly through the door Rhoda held open for her and left open after she'd gone through. 'Rachel? Oh, Rachel! Isn't it *awful*?'

Her voice was clearly audible to anyone at the other end of the room and since Rhoda was evidently obeying her instructions to keep her ears and eyes open and making a mental note of what she could hear, Mayo turned his attention to Dainty.

'Yes, as we've told you, she came over and had a meal with us on Saturday and spent the evening here. Most weeks she'd come over one of the days. Not Sundays, though. She nearly always spent Sunday with her sister.'

'This week as well?'

'Presumably. She didn't specifically say so, but it was a fairly routine thing.'

Kite made a note of the sister's name, and an address in Holden Hill.

'What time did she leave?'

'I drove her home at about twenty to eleven . . . later than usual, but we'd been watching an old Western and she wanted to see the end.' He smiled faintly. 'She dearly loved a Western.'

'When you say "home" I take it you mean right down to her door?'

'Have a heart, I've more respect for my suspension than that! I stopped at the top of the lane.'

'And presumably walked with her down to the house?'

There was a small silence. 'Well, no.'

'No? There was no moon on Saturday night. It must have been very dark down by the canal.'

'Look, I did try. We had the same argument every time I took her home. I always offered to go down to the door with her, but she'd never let me.' The truculence in his tone, his bull-like appearance and the held-down energy that radiated from him didn't suggest a man so easily deflected. 'She always said she knew the lane like the back of her hand and there was no need. She was a very independent lady, my mother-in-law.'

All the same, thought Mayo, all the same. Who would let a woman go unescorted down a lonely lane late on a moonless night? Into the dark shadows, where on that particular night, a silent watcher might have been waiting? Perhaps Dainty hadn't. Perhaps he was lying and had in fact gone down with her, down that dark track. He was jumpy and anxious, not, Mayo suspected, telling the whole truth. He was big and forceful, though not especially tall, with powerful shoulders and broad hands, capable of great strength. Workman's hands, still scarred with old burn tissue from his trade but, Mayo had already noticed, with no recent, visible scratches. Dainty was an unfortunate name for one with his appearance to be saddled with, though Mayo guessed he'd probably long since ceased to be either amused or annoyed by jokes about it.

He tried a different tack. 'Would you say you got on well with her?'

Dainty stood up and went across to a section of the wall unit that held drinks and held up a bottle, but when Mayo waved away the offer, he poured himself a stiff gin, barely diluted with tonic, drank it straight down and poured another. No doubt the horror of that mutilated body on the mortuary slab he had formally identified was still with him. No doubt he needed time to get his act together. Whatever the reason he was, under that brusque exterior, almost as tense as his wife. 'She wasn't a person you could ever get close to,' he said, coming back to his place on the settee, glass in hand. 'But I think we understood one another.'

Not a very satisfactory reply. The reply of a man who, despite the assurance and authority he'd shown at his office, seemed to need to tread warily in his own home.

His wife came back into the room. She'd been crying again, her handkerchief was a crumpled ball in her hand. She stood in the centre of the room and said, 'She's coming down – she wanted to stay at the King's Arms to save bother but I said that was ridiculous, of course she couldn't.' She looked hurriedly at her watch. 'I shall have to make the spare bed up, get a meal –'

'Shirley, sit down. Rachel will have to take pot luck, she won't mind anyway.'

'That's what she said, but that's not the way I look at it,' she answered petulantly; nevertheless, she resumed her seat, perching

400

on the edge of the settee, obedient to an authority in him hitherto not apparent, and surprised by it, perhaps.

Mayo cleared his throat. 'Had there been anything untoward, any trouble of any sort between Mrs Dove and anyone lately? If there was anyone who didn't wish her well, we should know about it.'

'If you'd known her, you wouldn't need to ask that,' Dainty said. 'She wasn't the sort to get involved in trouble, not Marion.'

'Didn't wish her well?' Mrs Dainty echoed, slightly contemptuous in a way Mayo didn't much like. 'I suppose by that you mean did she have any enemies. Well, of course not – she didn't have many friends, let alone enemies.' She bit her lip. 'What I mean is, she didn't socialise. She led a quiet life, she was a very private person, you might say a bit strait-laced. She didn't even smoke or drink.'

After that put-down of hers, he couldn't help but take pleasure in one of his own. 'There was drink in her sideboard, half-full bottles of sherry, whisky, gin.'

'Oh!' There was a split-second hesitation. 'Oh well, of course that doesn't mean she didn't keep some to offer her guests.'

And yet she had just said she didn't have many. There'd also been an empty gin bottle in the dustbin. Maybe Shirley Dainty didn't know her mother as well as she thought. He said, 'A game of chess was set up inside the cottage. Who d'you think her partner might have been?'

She took her time before answering. 'I suppose that must have been Paul.'

'Who's Paul, then?'

'Paul Fish.' The very faintest head toss was discernible as she told him that he was the grandson of her mother's eldest sister, now dead.

'How old is he?'

She shrugged. 'Sixteen, seventeen? One loses track.'

'And they played regularly?'

401

'Not regularly, but fairly often, I suppose. He was always down there, doing jobs for her, or that's what he used to claim. We all know why, of course. Why else would a young boy spend so much time with a woman her age? Out for what he could get, that's obvious, after she'd told him she'd see him all right in her will, wasn't he? Don't think, Inspector,' she added sharply, her colour heightened, 'that my mother lived down there in Jubilee Cottage because she couldn't *afford* anything else. She wasn't a pauper, far from it! Besides which, she had The Mount, the family house on Holden Hill to live in if she'd chosen to.'

'I think I know it – a big house for one person living alone, if it's the one I'm thinking of. Next door to the glassworks, isn't it?' Mayo asked, interested in her terminology. How much more upmarket 'Jubilee Cottage' sounded than 'the lockhouse'! 'Who lives there now?'

'Nobody.' It was Dainty who answered. 'She refused to sell it or even to get rid of the furniture, though we're chronically short of space at the works, and we could at least have used it for offices.' His tone was resentful, but the thought occurred to Mayo, and must at the same time have occurred to Dainty, because he attempted to shrug off what he'd said with a rueful gesture, that now there was nothing preventing it.

Mayo had come across many motives for murder and learned to discount nothing, though he thought it rather fanciful to imagine Dainty might have killed his mother-in-law for more office space. And yet – a quarrel on the subject, tempers raised . . . But he thought Dainty a very self-controlled man, and by no means a fool, who didn't easily lose his temper. He might, on the other hand, very well be the sort to nurse a grudge.

'I'd like to have a look around The Mount, if I may.'

Shirley Dainty threw him the incredulous sort of look he might have received if he'd asked permission to wander around Buckingham Palace, but Dainty seemed unconcerned. 'If you wish. One of us will go with you.'

'That won't be necessary. If you could just let me have a key. I'll give you a receipt for it, of course.'

He could see Mrs Dainty welcomed this request even less, but he held out his hand and while she unwillingly fished a key ring from her handbag and began to work a large mortice lock key from it, he took the supermarket receipt from his wallet and asked if she recognised the handwriting on it.

She handed over the key and looked at the back of the receipt, still in its plastic envelope and confirmed that it was her mother's. A tiny pause. 'Steven? Who's that?'

'I was hoping you might know.'

He kept his eyes on the two of them and there was no response. But as sure as God made little apples, one of them knew. Which one, he couldn't tell, maybe both, but the enquiry had prompted a frisson of recognition – alarm – fear – emanating from someone in that room.

'What time did you go to bed on Saturday night, Mrs Dainty?' he asked.

'About ten minutes after I'd said good night to my mother, it would be. I emptied the dishwasher and set the breakfast things out because we were playing golf the next morning and had an early start. Then I went to bed. Oh yes, I also stacked some left-overs in the fridge, so it might have been a few minutes more.'

'What did you have for dinner?' he asked, apparently idly.

'A *ragoût* of beef with courgettes and potatoes *Lyonnaise*, *tarte aux pommes Normandie*, coffee and biscuits to follow,' she pronounced immediately, without batting an eyelid.

'And garlic,' said Dainty.

His wife ignored this. 'Why?' she asked Mayo. 'Why do you want to know that?'

He thought it best not to enlighten her. Relatives were apt to get upset at the thought of what went on at post-mortems. Instead, he said, 'A heavy meal like that, you must have slept well.'

'Yes, but then I always do because I take a sleeping tablet, otherwise I'd never sleep at all.'

'So you wouldn't hear what time your husband came in?'

'As a matter of fact, I did. I hadn't quite dropped off, and I looked at the clock when I heard the door. It had just gone eleven. Now look, if you've finished, I have to get ready for my sister coming –'

'We'll just go through Sunday, if you don't mind,' he said, unmoved. She made an irritable gesture and sat impatiently while he found out how they'd spent the day . . . golf in the morning, drinks and a snack at the clubhouse, home and a snooze with the Sunday papers, then out to dinner with friends.

'Well, that's it for now,' he said at last, standing. 'Unless my sergeant has anything to ask.'

Kite looked over the notes he'd taken and shook his head. Rhoda coughed, and looked at Mayo. He nodded. She asked, 'Do you remember what your mother was wearing on Saturday night, Mrs Dainty?'

'Of course.' There was a split-second hesitation. 'She had her Liberty print skirt on, with a cream silk shirt and a caramel-coloured cardigan.'

'Thank you.'

'He'll have to come up with a better story than that, otherwise he won't be getting *ragoût* of beef and *tarte aux pommes* where he's going,' Kite said.

'Oh, I don't know,' Rhoda offered, with unexpected humour. 'Except they call it beef stew and apple pie in there.'

Mayo grinned, then complimented her on the question about Mrs Dove's clothes, causing her to flush, though not very becomingly, with her red hair. 'And since she wasn't wearing what Mrs Dainty described when she was found –'

'Maybe we're meant to assume she wasn't murdered until Sunday? You think she's covering up for Dainty, then, sir?' Kite asked. 'Though they weren't exactly lovey-dovey, were they?'

'That doesn't mean a thing,' Rhoda answered, encouraged out of her usual taciturnity.

'We're jumping the gun a bit, anyway, aren't we, assuming that he did it?' Mayo said, but he said it absently. He was half thinking on the same lines as Kite, that at the moment it did seem that Dainty was the most likely suspect, and that the obvious one was usually the right one. It looked as though he'd had the opportunity, he was certainly physically capable of it, and probably, if Mrs Dove had been as wealthy as her daughter implied, he might well have had a strong motive.

But the other half of his mind had been thinking that there had been something odd about Mrs Dainty's reception of the news. She might well indeed, despite appearances to the contrary, be worried for her husband, or trying to cover up for him, but he'd be very interested to know why also, deep under the layers of shock or grief or affront, or whatever other emotion she'd shown, she was also personally very much afraid.

CHAPTER 7

It had turned up in the water at the very edge of the canal, down in the reeds where the body had been found and that, unless it had indeed been a mugging gone wrong, disposed of Mrs Dainty's favourite theory, because the contents of the handbag were apparently intact. It seemed probable that it had fallen in while she was being attacked, rather than having been tossed away. It was a shoulder-type, of soft navy-blue leather and now that the canal mud and slime had been cleared off, was seen to be of excellent quality, though well worn. In it were: a purse containing just over twenty-four pounds in notes and coins, a cheque-book and an appointments diary in a leather wallet, a comb and a compact, one crumpled lace-edged handkerchief and one folded one, a pair of spectacles in a case and a small bunch of keys, one of them presumably the key to the locked drawer. But that had already been opened, and found to contain, apart from predictable personal papers such as insurances, bank statements and bank books showing appreciable balances, only some old photographs of her children, a lock of baby hair curled into a piece of tissue paper, and two pairs of baby shoes.

Kite regarded with an appraising eye the contents of the bag spread out on a table in the corner of Mayo's office. 'A lot less than most women cart around with them,' he remarked. 'You need a forklift truck to pick Sheila's bag up.'

But it was what Mayo was coming to expect of Marion Dove. Neat, sparing, nothing unnecessary. Even the things found in the drawer, a mother's usual sentimental trivia, had been few. He picked up the cheque-book, which had been inside the leather wallet and now that it had been dried out was reasonably legible. There were only two blank cheques left of the original thirty. Mayo examined the counterfoils at the front of the book and after studying it for a while handed it to Kite.

'Take a look at this. What does it say to you?'

Kite said presently, 'Fairly obvious, isn't it, if you look at those bank statements as well. Why else would she draw all these large amounts out? It's a fair bet she was being blackmailed. Very interesting.'

'Interesting, but not conclusive. It's more often the blackmailer who gets the chop, rather than the victim.'

'Unless she refused to pay.'

'The last withdrawal was on Friday. A thousand pounds drawn out in cash – and only five hundred of it's missing,' Mayo pointed out.

'Perhaps she was paying in five hundred pound instalments.'

'Not as a regular thing. Not according to the statements. She's been drawing a lot of money out, but not regular amounts, or at regular intervals. But if it wasn't blackmail money, I'd very much like to know what she was doing with it.'

The sister's house turned out to be small and brick-built in a long terrace of similar houses whose front doors opened straight off one of the sloping back streets of Holden Hill. She was smartly got up in a silk blouse and tailored skirt, a plump and robust woman with careful make-up whose hair had been streaked and touched up back to the warm blonde it must once have been. Looking a sprightly fifty-four rather than the sixty-four he knew she was. Not much like her sister, Mayo guessed, and rough-edged but good as gold. A mouth that looked as though in normal circumstances it would smile easily.

'Cuppa?' The invitation was issued as soon as they stepped into a tiny hallway at the foot of a steep flight of stairs. Thanking Kite for the post he'd picked up off the mat, remarking that it seemed to arrive at any time these days, Mrs Bainbridge manoeuvred them from the hallway into a small, cheerful front room where a tray was set out on the coffee table.

'Please don't go to any bother.'

'A cup of tea's no bother to me. Don't know what I'd do without it.'

'In that case, thank you, it would be very welcome.'

The kettle, she assured them, was already on the boil. With instructions to make themselves comfortable, she left them while she went out to the kitchen.

Mayo used the opportunity to take in the sort of details his policeman's training had taught him to observe: the shining bay window, curtained in crisp, spotless net shaped to rise above the sill at the centre though not, it seemed, to let in more light, for in the space thus provided stood a large and healthy sansevieria, its leaves as glossy and polished as everything else in the room. The three-piece suite, one with the exaggerated wings and splayed legs of the 1950s, worn and shabby on the arms, standing on a carpet with a pattern of the same vintage that was wearing threadbare. A gas fire fixed into a tiled surround, with framed photographs set out on the mantel.

Mayo bent to study them. At one end was a pretty, laughing girl with a firm rounded chin, wearing the WAAF uniform of the last war, recognisably Gwen Bainbridge. At the other a distinctively good-looking young flight-sergeant sporting the one white flash of an airgunner above the breast pocket and grinning at the camera with the youthful certainty of immortality. In the middle, in the place of honour, was their wedding photograph. He in uniform, she in white with a veil, the bridesmaids flower-wreathed and long-skirted . . . even in wartime it had been managed somehow, dried fruit for the wedding cake and clothing coupons garnered from far and near. There were two bridesmaids, neither of whom Mayo could identify as her sister Marion.

'I see you're looking at my photos, Robert and me,' remarked Mrs Bainbridge, returning with the teapot under a cosy in one hand and a plate of biscuits in the other.

Mayo suddenly made the connection. Robert Bainbridge? Wasn't that the name of the office manager who'd received them at Dainty's office that morning? It took an act of will to relate that precisely spoken, painfully moving, bloodless little man with this dashing rear-gunner, but substitute a bald dome for that abundant dark hair, add a pair of gold rimmed specs and forty-odd years and it could be done. Even possible, then, to partner him with this woman. Gwen Bainbridge in her prime must have been quite a girl. She wasn't bad now. Nice-looking legs, her feet shapely in high-heeled shoes. Good skin still, carefully made up. He liked the courage of that. She was putting a brave face on it and what it was costing her was showing only in the misery in her eyes and the exaggerated steadiness with which she poured tea into generous-sized mugs. 'You won't want teacups, that right?' she announced, rather than asked, in a matter-of-fact way.

'Right, missis,' Kite assured her colloquially, as comfortably at home with her as with his Auntie May up Mapleton Street and striking exactly the right note, Mayo was pleased to see, as Mrs Bainbridge's rigid grip on the teapot handle relaxed and she gave him a glance that was very nearly a smile. 'Three sugars, please.'

The offer of a little drop of something in the tea having been refused, she shrugged and sloshed a generous amount into her own before handing out the biscuits. 'Go on, they're ginger, fresh-baked . . . gave me something to do, it did. They insisted at the shop I have the rest of the week off, but I wish they hadn't. I'm that lost already . . .'

She was suddenly too choked with emotion to go on. 'Oh God, I'm sorry,' she managed after a moment, blinking and pulling out her handkerchief. 'I can't hardly get used to it, yet.'

'Don't apologise, Mrs Bainbridge – I'm only sorry to have to face you with questioning at a time like this –' Mayo began.

She tucked the handkerchief away, reached out for her mug and took a big gulp of tea. 'That's all right, m'duck, you have your job to do. Don't take no notice of me, I'm all right, now. It just keeps coming over me, that's all. Ask me anything you want – anything that'll help catch him that did it.'

As she gradually relaxed with the help of the whisky-laced tea, she became talkative. Talking was a natural state with her, Mayo guessed. Bit of a rattle-pate probably, but all the better from his point of view, the more garrulous the better. They quickly learned that she was employed part-time at Betty's, the small dress shop down Holden Hill Road where she'd worked for over twenty years. It was a nice little job, she got her clothes at discount (which explained her smart and up-to-date appearance, Mayo thought) and she wouldn't deny that every little helped. Maybe she'd give it up when her husband retired next year, but she'd miss it, though not as much as Robert would miss working for Dove's. They thought a lot about him up there, Ken Dainty was always saying he'd be hard put to it to find anybody else who could run the office like he did. She fetched up a deep sigh. 'He should have finished long since, but he can't abide not being occupied. Which is all very well, but look where it gets him – laid up in bed half the weekend! But he won't be said, nothing'll stop him if he's determined. He makes me that mad sometimes.' She said it as though she loved him. Her face shone as she spoke of him.

So it was as Mayo had thought – he *was* the same Bainbridge. Well, we all have our moments of glory, all are golden lads and lasses come to dust.

'It's in his spine, you know, trouble from his old war wounds, or so they say. He was shot down just after we were married and never been right since. It's hard, though, watching him go downhill. They gave him a DFC for bravery, but that's not a lot of compensation, is it?'

It was obvious that, like many childless women, she lavished all the warmth and love of which she was capable on her husband. Mayo guessed she would face the prospect, bleak enough for both of them, with as much fortitude as she attributed to her husband.

She said abruptly, 'Who could have hated her enough to kill her like that? She wouldn't have hurt a fly, our Marion.' It was a universal comment Mayo had learned as a rule to take with a pinch of salt, though it was always possible this might be one of the exceptions. He asked Mrs Bainbridge when she'd last seen her sister.

'Friday afternoon. She stepped into the shop for a few minutes.'

'Not later than that? Didn't she come to you as a regular arrangement on Sundays for lunch?'

'Not this Sunday she didn't. She usually came about half past twelve, left home at quarter past. We waited for her till half past one, then I gave her a ring but there was no reply so we gave it up as a bad job and carried on without her. I had a nice shoulder of pork and there wasn't no point in letting good food spoil and dry up.'

Kite's pen was busy noting the times. If she had been dead by then, and assuming all parties were telling the truth, if Ken Dainty had last seen her about 10.40 the previous evening, this narrowed the length of time during which she could have been killed to about twelve hours. 'Weren't you worried when she didn't turn up?' he asked.

'Not specially. Mad, more like, that she hadn't bothered to let me know.' She hesitated. 'To tell you the truth . . . we'd had a few words.'

Another revivifying gulp of tea helped her to go on. Mayo picked up his own mug and took a scalding sip. It was strong enough to strip paint.

'Look, she was my *sister*, we could have a difference of opinion and not let it rankle after. I just expected she'd turn up as usual for her dinner, we'd both say we were sorry and that'd be the end of it. When she didn't I thought she'd taken the huff, though that wasn't like our Marion at all. I reckoned I'd give it a couple of days and then go down and see her and smooth things over. And now it's too late.' She pushed biscuit crumbs around her plate with her forefinger. 'Our mum used to say, "Never let the sun go down on your disagreements." She was right, wasn't she?'

The terrible thing about death was that it brought out all the old hackneyed sentiments, and it wasn't any less irritating when many of them turned out to be truisms, Mayo reflected, but she was welcome to them. Comfort came in all guises.

He said gently, 'Could I ask you what it was you'd disagreed about?'

'You could, but I'm not going to tell you,' she answered decisively, rallying with some spirit. 'It's got nothing to do with what's happened.'

When it came to murder, in fact, Mayo regarded nothing as too irrelevant to consider, but she'd closed her lips firmly and he had to accept he would get nothing by pressing her. He took another cautious sip of the tea which seemed to have acted on her like a shot in the arm, then put the mug firmly back on the tray, declining to have it topped up. If Mrs Bainbridge could drink that, especially laced with whisky, she was a braver man than he. He made a better bargain by taking one of the only two biscuits Kite had left.

'I'll tell you something, though,' she said abruptly. 'I don't know what it was, but she was different lately. It wasn't anything I could put my finger on, know what I mean? But she'd lost a lot of weight and if it hadn't been that in a funny sort of way she somehow seemed happier than she had for years, I'd have thought she had something the matter with her – you know, that she was poorly. She'd had a few days in hospital for observation a couple of months since and I did ask her, but she said everything was all right . . .' Her voice trailed off as she felt the silence. 'Oh God, there *was* something, wasn't there?'

Her glance travelled from one face to the other. She needed no answer. 'Cancer, was it? Was that it?'

'I believe so. But according to Dr Ison, if that's any consolation, she couldn't have lived long in any case, Mrs Bainbridge.'

At that she turned on him with unexpected fury. 'Oh, so that makes it all right, does it? She'd outlived her usefulness anyway so it doesn't matter she was got rid of and thrown into the cut like a piece of old rubbish?'

'Now, Mrs Bainbridge –' Kite began.

'All right, I shouldn't have said that, it wasn't called for – but she'd a right to what was left of her life, hadn't she? I just wish I'd known, that's all. I wish I'd known.'

There were no tears now, but the silence was heavy. Mayo gave her time to collect herself. She struggled for composure and presently she was able to speak. 'I shouldn't really be surprised she didn't tell me, she was always a bit secretive, you never knew what she was thinking. She was the clever one, got a scholarship to the High School, and all. Not like me, I never could add two and two together. Her teachers wanted her to go on to university, but . . . well, anyway. "What's it matter, where's it going to get you, all that reading and swotting?" I used to say to her. "Take life as it comes . . . have a good time while you can." No use talking to her, though. She could be stubborn, and she'd just go on in her own quiet way, doing what she wanted.'

She underestimated herself, Gwen Bainbridge. Not a clever woman maybe, not in the same way she said her sister had been, but not lacking in common sense and shrewdness.

'It paid off though, didn't it?' he suggested. 'Mr Dainty has told us she ended up owning Dove's glassworks.'

'Well, if you mean it paid off for her to marry her boss, then it did. She was Wesley Dove's secretary before she married him, that's how she came by all that. Twenty-five she was to his fifty-one, and that never seems right to me, big difference like that. Everybody thought she'd done it for his money, but it wasn't that, she was never interested in money. Though of course,' she added wryly, 'that's easy when you have plenty, isn't it?'

Did he detect the shade of an old envy, perhaps unrecognised, almost certainly never admitted, but never quite exorcised? It would be understandable. It seemed self-evident that there was little spare money to throw around in the Bainbridge household.

'God knows why she did marry him, but she was a good wife to him, and she was entitled to a bit more than she got. He was, excuse me, a bastard, and living with him was no bed of roses, to put it mildly.'

'They weren't happy?'

'Happy?' Her laugh wasn't amused. 'God, that house – The Mount – used to give me the creeps every time I went in. It takes some crediting, but it's gospel truth – he wouldn't have a stick nor a stone changed, every blessed thing was just as his mother had left it – and his grandmother and all, I shouldn't wonder. You should have seen that cooker – and as for the bathroom, well! How she stuck it, I'll never know. No wonder she got out as fast as she could when he died.'

'Is that when she went to live down in the lockhouse?'

'That's right. They didn't want her to live there – Shirley didn't, anyway, not good enough in her opinion – but it wasn't a bad little place. Better than the one in Chapel Street where we lived when we were kids, I can tell you. That got a bomb on it during the war and good riddance. It was what she chose, the lockhouse, it was quiet, but she wasn't lonely. She wasn't a what-you-call-it, a recluse, you know, she was always happy with her own company, just dreamy, romantic like. Anyway, I used to pop down to see her a fair bit, she came up here every Sunday and Shirley would ask her up to that posh house at Henchard for a meal – when they didn't have company, that is.' She added drily, and with a sharp look that said a lot, 'They'll come in for a fair bit, you know, her two girls. She's left The Mount to the pair of them, and money besides. I expect they'll be selling up – there's stuff in there worth a mint, whatever my opinion of it. It's thought a lot of nowadays, they tell me. Shirley won't be able to get her hands on it fast enough – she's greedy, that one, always was. Grab, grab. Hopeless, she is. Lives on her nerves.' She checked herself sharply, whatever she'd been going to say – and there had been something – was left unsaid.

Mayo saw wisdom in not replying to derogatory remarks about one of the family. He was beginning to have a hunch that there was no need to look for an alien element in this murder, that whatever had occurred to cause the death of Marion Dove had its roots within the intricate web of family relationships. And such close-knit entities might be at daggers drawn among themselves but let any interloper or outsider, any comer-in as he was known hereabouts, dare to interfere or criticise or want to know why and they would rise as one against him. He'd had to conduct other similar enquiries on countless other occasions and the prospect of doing so again didn't fill him with unalloyed pleasure.

'You understand in a case like this it's necessary to check on the movements of everyone close to Mrs Dove,' he said. 'So what about Saturday evening, what did you do then – and what about Sunday?'

'It wasn't what you'd call a cheerful weekend, what with Robert being so bad and all. I stayed in Sunday afternoon watching telly while he went up to rest, but I popped out both Saturday and Sunday night to help out in the bar at the Fighting Cocks – I do occasionally when they're short-handed, it's a bit extra. I wasn't keen on leaving Robert, him feeling so poorly, but I'd promised and I didn't like to let them down, and there wasn't anything I could do for him after I'd given him his pills. I left as soon as they closed, and I was home both nights before quarter to eleven.'

Kite looked up from his notes. 'That was good going, from the Fighting Cocks.'

'I didn't walk – least, I walked there but I was driven home. We don't use the car a lot. It's on its last legs, I'm no driver and Robert can't manage it now. That nice Valerie from the office gives Robert a lift to and from work, so we let a young relative of ours use the car on condition he pays for his own petrol and runs me about now and again when I need it.'

'What's his name?'

'Paul Fish. He's the grandson of my sister Beattie that died, her daughter Norma's son.'

A shade of reserve had crept into her voice as she gave the information. Kite wrote the address down. Wasn't that the young man who used to play chess with her sister? he asked.

'How d'you know that?'

Mayo told her about the chessboard which had been set up, and what the Daintys had told him about Paul playing with Marion. 'Nice of him to bother. Not every lad his age would.'

'That's right.' Her face softened. 'But Paul's like that. Marion thought the world of him. He'd run errands for her and keep things fixed up for her, he's handy that way. He does the same for us, we've always made him welcome here, and so did she. Here, you're not thinking he had anything to do with it, for heaven's sake? Not Paul, never! He's still at school, he's only just gone seventeen!'

415

Since when had being seventeen been a bar to violence, theft, rape, murder, or any other crime that could be thought of? But no, he told her, they'd no reason at all to suppose Paul was involved in the murder at the moment, but as they weren't in a position to know yet who might have information that would help, they needed to talk to everybody who'd seen her recently, and that included Paul.

'Well, God help you if Charlie Fish's around when you do.'

'His father? Likely to cause bother, is he?'

She hesitated, then closed her lips firmly. 'Better not say, I've been in too much hot water as it is for interfering in that direction. You'll find out for yourself. But go easy. There's been enough trouble down there.'

They drove off, Mayo thinking about the worn carpet, the shabby, dated furniture, the references to needing money. 'Wonder why they're so hard up?' he remarked.

'I was thinking that, too, but did you see that big envelope in the post?' Kite asked. 'It was from Tixall's, in Sheep Street.'

'The estate agents?'

'Right. Think how much more convenient a bungalow would be than that house. Not one for anybody who finds it hard to get about, is it? Those stairs, for one thing! What I thought was, if he's due to retire, they've likely been thinking of moving and they've been pulling in their horns a bit – you need all your resources these days, property the price it is . . .'

'You're probably right, Martin. So a nice little nest-egg from her sister isn't going to come amiss. They seemed close, it'd be funny if she hadn't left her anything.'

From the size of those bank balances alone, never mind what else Mrs Dove had owned, somebody was going to be appreciably better off, unless she'd left it to the cat's home or something. Money was always high up on the list of motives for murder. It was time he made contact with Mrs Dove's solicitor.

CHAPTER 8

In the event, he was saved from the trouble of finding out by a telephone call immediately following on Kite's departure from the station to catch Paul Fish on his arrival home from the comprehensive school. It was from Deeley, who had been left on duty down at the Jubilee Locks, a stolid and immovable presence to repel the inevitable ghoulish onlookers drawn to the scene like iron filings to a magnet whenever word got around that a murder might have taken place.

'The phone in the house here rang a few minutes ago, sir – Mr Crytch, the solicitor it was, ringing Mrs Dove. He hadn't heard the news about her and he's on his way to see you, sir, says he'll be with you in a few minutes. He seemed to think he ought to see you straight away.'

'Thanks for letting me know, Deeley.' Mayo broke the connection and then rang down to the front desk, instructing them to send the solicitor up to his office immediately he arrived. If Geoffrey Crytch – of Crytch, Masterson and Crytch, a pleasant, elderly man with whom he'd had one or two dealings – thought it was important, that was enough for Mayo.

'An appalling thing to have happened, appalling,' were Crytch's first conventionally expressed words on entering Mayo's room. He had come straight round from his office, which was just along the road from the police station, and though he must have hurried, he was puffing only slightly. A plump man with a deep double chin, well past sixty, silver-haired and well-preserved, he had the milky, replete look of a well-fed baby and a look of mild surprise, maybe at having married a woman much younger than he was, a doctor in professional practice, and having produced, so late in life, a family now just out of their teens. These ingenuous externals were at variance with the sharp mind Mayo knew him to have and a

417

propensity, not usually attributable to solicitors, for getting things done.

They shook hands and Crytch came straight to the point without waste of time, explaining, in the fruity voice that served him so well in court, that Mrs Dove had made an appointment to see him at two that afternoon. 'When she hadn't turned up by four, my secretary decided she'd better speak to her and find out whether we'd got our dates crossed. Your policeman who answered the phone told her the dreadful news but quite rightly wouldn't give any detail. Are you at liberty to do so?'

'There's no reason why you shouldn't know – I'm sorry to have to tell you Mrs Dove's been murdered.'

'Murdered? Surely not!' Crytch looked shaken to the core, and his complexion abruptly lost some of its rosiness. The presence of the police at the lockhouse must have prepared him and alerted him to the fact that more than a simple death had occurred, however. He sat deep in thought for a while, before suggesting tentatively, 'It couldn't have been an accident?'

'It was no accident, she was strangled.'

'Good God!'

'You knew her well, I take it?'

'Yes, indeed. Very well. The firm have looked after the Dove family since before I was born. My grandfather first acted for them, if I remember rightly.' He hesitated. Presumably, being a solicitor, caution was second nature to him. Presumably he also believed it was good tactics to be completely honest with the police. 'Actually, I knew Marion better than that. We were going out together at one time – only a boy and girl romance, but I always hoped when I came back home after the war she'd become my wife. Unfortunately, it didn't quite work out that way.'

'Changed her mind, did she?'

Crytch spread plump white hands. 'She seemed to lose interest. People change . . . at any rate, she did. In fact, it surprised me she married at all. I'd have laid bets on it she'd have stayed single.' He smiled wryly. 'Well, she didn't – and in the end she did better for herself by marrying Wesley Dove rather than me.'

It sounded as if the memory might have been painful, all the same. No man likes to admit rejection, even after forty years. They'd all been young once, these elderly people, Geoffrey Crytch, Marion Dove, Gwen Bainbridge, their blood had run hot. You had to remember that.

Giving Mayo an assessing look, Crytch said carefully, 'In view of what you've just told me, I don't think I should be stepping out of line if I told you why she wanted to see me today. She was a woman of some substance, I expect you know that by now . . . well, she'd suddenly taken it into her head she ought to give some of it away to charity and wanted to discuss ways and means with me. I suggested the best way was probably by deed of covenant, and she said, rather curiously I thought, that she was thinking of more immediate arrangements.' He paused, thoughtfully. 'Strangled? There's no question about that?'

'No question at all. It certainly wasn't suicide, Mr Crytch.'

Mayo was beginning to wonder if he'd found the explanation for the sums Mrs Dove had recently drawn from her bank account, but on reflection that struck him as fairly unlikely. Surely she would have made out cheques, not donated such large amounts in cash. 'So that was what your appointment today was about?'

'Not entirely. As a matter of fact,' Crytch said, 'she told me she also wanted to make some changes to her will.'

At that moment the tea Mayo had requested came in, brought by a shirt-sleeved constable. Mayo poured two cups and handed one to Crytch, who sipped it thirstily. The cup rattled slightly as he put it back on the saucer.

'Now that's a very interesting fact, Mr Crytch. Did she give any indication of how she was going to change it?'

'No. No, she said she'd explain when she saw me. No great changes, and she'd already worked out a rough draft on paper . . .

you may possibly,' he suggested carefully, 'have come across it?' It was a question which Mayo chose to evade by regarding it as a statement.

'I wonder who else she told?' he said.

'That's something I'm hardly in a position to know.' But would dearly like to, Mayo thought, and wondered why. His mind began again to run on those sums the dead woman had drawn out – and also to play around lightly with notions of the opportunities solicitors had to fiddle.

'You realise that if this change in her will was to someone's disadvantage, and he learned about it, that could be a strong motive for murder?'

'I do realise that,' Crytch answered stiffly.

'What are the terms of her will as it stands?'

Crytch ummed and aahed at that. Having gone further than perhaps he thought cautious, he now began to stand on his professional dignity, saying he couldn't possibly breach his client's confidentiality, but in the end he compromised, agreeing to produce the will on the following day, as if it would need to be laboriously retrieved from the back of some dusty filing cabinet. In view of the sharpness of lawyers in general, and Mr Crytch in particular, it was more likely to be lodged firmly in the forefront of his mind. However . . .

'All right. But I need to have it. It may contain information material to the case.'

Not principally who stood to gain, but who might have been disadvantaged by any alterations, and therefore have had reason to do away with Mrs Dove before these could have been implemented.

Not long after Crytch had left, Kite came on the line.

'I've been hanging about here waiting for Paul Fish to come home from school. Then his dad arrives and says he's gone, scarpered. He went off this Monday morning, told him he doesn't know when he'll be back.'

'Where are you? Still at Stubbs Road? Stay where you are,' Mayo told him, 'I'll join you as soon as I can.'

Stubbs Road clung tenaciously to the side of a hill, a road in a pre-war housing estate which the council, against much opposition, had sold off at favourable prices to sitting tenants. Most of the houses, small and semi-detached, with a forest of TV aerials sprouting from the chimneys, had had a miscellany of improvements added by way of garages or car-ports, bay windows and porches. Bull's-eye glass and stone facings put on to what had been grey pebble-dash were much in evidence, and most were smartly painted.

No. 47 had once upon a time had its pebble-dash painted in beige and its paintwork done blue, but by now most of that was a memory. Dandelion and twitch were breaking up the short concrete front path and the front gate was hardly visible under a tangle of quickthorn, indicating its long disuse, so Mayo pushed open the side gate that warned *Beware of the Dog*. The warning was superfluous. As soon as his hand had touched the latch a Staffordshire bull terrier, a caricature of rage and ferocity, began to raise hell from a barred kennel strong enough to cage a tiger, with 'Caesar' painted crudely in white over its opening.

Mayo trusted the neighbours were deaf. He knocked loudly enough to hope he'd be heard above the din, with the dog choking on the chain behind him. It was Kite who opened the door. As he stepped inside, a powerful combination of old frying fat and stale cigarette smoke solid enough to cut with a knife almost made him reel. Charlie Fish was sitting at the kitchen table with his head in his hands, in a welter of dirty coffee mugs and cold greasy plates bearing the remains of old junk-food meals, the one on the table containing some congealed chips and the remains of a piece of battered fish. A pile of used crockery was jumbled into the sink, along with old tea-bags and a grey dishcloth of uncertain provenance. On the drainer was about two pounds of good quality beef, some of it already cut up and put into the dog's dish. What kind of a man would buy rump steak for his dog and live off fish and chips himself?

Kite leaned against the wall. 'Isn't there anywhere else we can talk?' Mayo asked, revolted.

'What for?' Fish raised a bleary unshaven face and breathed out beer fumes strong enough to indicate that his posture was more likely to be due to a thick head than despair. He blinked, his eyes focused on Mayo's cold grey gaze, and shrugged. 'Oh, orright. Come on into the lounge.'

'I'd get some black coffee down you first to pull yourself together, if I were you.'

'I don't need no coffee.' Fish shambled gracelessly out of the kitchen, through the passageway and into the room he euphemistically called the lounge. It was only slightly less squalid than the kitchen. Flinging himself on to a sofa transmogrified to mud-colour and scarred on the arms with old cigarette burns, he lit up again, while the two policemen gingerly found places on the least encumbered of the grease-spotted armchairs.

'Well, what you wanting?'

Mayo regarded the unprepossessing specimen of humanity before him without charity. Charlie Fish, properly dressed and reasonably sober, could still have been handsome in a dark, gipsy sort of way. He had a head of curly black hair, at present overlong and unkempt, and a raffish, foxy look that might once have been attractive to a certain type of woman, but the years had coarsened his features, a beer belly rolled over the belt that held his trousers up.

'Where's your wife?' Mayo asked.

'My wife? Norma?' Fish laughed unpleasantly. 'How the hell should I know? Buggered off with the TV man seven or eight years ago her did, and nobody's seen hide nor hair of her since. Story of my life, that is. They all leave me. First her. Then my eldest lad, every encouragement to get to bloody university, then

422

too bloody stuck up to come back home once he's there. Now Paul.'

'I'm crying my eyes out,' Kite said. 'What's your other son's name? Steven?'

'No, it's not. It's Graham. Why?'

'Never mind. Is Paul in touch with his mother?' Mayo asked.

'You must be joking! Her left him when he was eight years old – wouldn't know one another from Adam now. Anyway, what's it to you? What is all this?'

'You've no idea at all where he could have gone?'

'He don't tell me nothink – I'm only his father.'

'Didn't you ask him why he was going – or try and stop him?'

Fish shrugged. 'He's old enough to please hisself. He's seven-teen.'

Mayo held on to his disgust and asked shortly whether it was likely that Paul could be with his brother, but clearly Charlie Fish had no notion. He evidently had little idea how his son had spent his time, nor, it seemed, did he care. They were nominally father and son, they occupied the same house but might have existed on different planets. Poor little devil, Mayo thought. What sort of chances could they ever have, kids like this, what values were they expected to learn? He gave up the idea of questioning Fish as a bad job and asked if they could see Paul's room.

'Not unless you tell me what all this is about. You can't come in here, just like that, without no search warrant, I know me rights.'

'Cut it out, Fish. We're on a murder enquiry.'

'What's that got to do with our Paul? Here, hold on –'

'Last night Marion Dove was murdered. That's your wife's aunt, in case you'd forgotten.'

'Forgotten that bloody lot?. Not likely! It's her and them Bainbridges between 'em as have put all these fancy ideas into my lads' heads. Interfering old buggers.'

'You just watch your language, or we might just decide to have you in for insulting behaviour – or even on suspicion.' The craven

423

fear that sprang into Fish's face as Mayo said this made him pause. 'You didn't do it, did you, Fish?' he asked softly. 'You knew she was well off, you didn't go there on Sunday morning demanding money and then kill her when she refused?'

'No! No, I never did! I was up the Dog, Sunday morning!'

'The Dog and Fox, eh? Not a million miles from the Jubilee! In fact, less than half a mile on the Compsall road.'

'I was in the pub, I tell you, till they closed. Anybody'll tell you.'

'And after they closed?'

'I was here, having a kip, wasn't I? Then back to the Dog, Sunday night.'

'And after *that*?'

'It's got sod all to do with you, but I was with – somebody else.'

'Oh yes, who?' Fish said nothing. 'Who?' repeated Mayo. 'Who were you with?'

'Right, then, I was with Ruby Deacon. Orright?'

'Ruby Deacon! Dear oh dear!' What sort of alibi was that? She'd say anything for tuppence, that one, do anything, some said. A hard case. 'Come off it, Fish, don't make me laugh. You'll have to do better than that. And while you have another think, we'll go and have a look at Paul's room.'

They'd hit on something, Mayo felt sure, though whether it had anything to do with Marion Dove's murder he was less sure. At any rate, Fish became suddenly, if not more cooperative, at least less obstructive. Reduced to silence, he stood sullenly aside and let them pass up the narrow staircase. By chance the first door they opened turned out to be Paul's bedroom. Sparsely furnished, a single bed covered by a red blanket tidily tucked in, and a small dressing-table that evidently served as a desk, with a chair in front and on it a pile of exercise books with 'Paul Fish' printed on the cover. Its neatness, in contrast with the rooms downstairs, made it seem almost monastic, but any bareness was dissipated by the squadron of model aircraft dancing from the ceiling on cotton threads, and the photographs and drawings, all of them representing aircraft of some description, which nearly covered the shabby old Snoopy wallpaper. A homemade bookshelf held a row of library books and paperbacks. Mayo recalled with what passionate intensity as a schoolboy he'd pursued the hobby of the moment, to the exclusion of everything else: model railways, stamp collecting, all the usual things. Though by seventeen, he reckoned, he'd outgrown most of them. He reached up and touched one of the models. It was clean enough, with only a light film of dust, and so were the others. Some of the library books had current date stamps. *Aircraft of the World*; *Learning to Fly*; *Enemy Coast Ahead*. Farnborough, Sheila Scott, Neville Duke.

Kite said, opening the cupboard in one corner, 'If he's gone for good, he hasn't taken all his clothes.' Sportsgear piled up in one corner and a school blazer hanging up beside a pair of dark grey school trousers were understandably left behind, but there were also jeans and T-shirts, underclothes, a pair of nearly new shoes and some trainers.

Mayo replaced *Flight Briefing for Pilots* and looked out of the window. The streets of the estate were in tiers; the downstairs windows of the street above looked directly into the bedroom windows of the one below. Between were tiny gardens crammed with sheds and greenhouses, rabbit hutches, swings and dustbins. The only space and freedom was in the empty skies above. He said, 'I'm going over to see Mrs Bainbridge. You can come with me. She saw Paul on Sunday night when he took her home, didn't she? And I shall want Forensics up here to take some of Paul's prints.'

The same unspoken thought, of the five hundred pounds as yet unaccounted for, passed between them. Kite said, 'What you just said to Fish downstairs went home. Think he knows something?'

'I wouldn't bank on it – but he's up to something diabolical, you can bet your boot soles. One of our customers, is he?'

'Not to my knowledge.'

'Well, whichever way up, he's a nasty piece of work. So watch him. Don't let him slip.'

'No way,' Kite said, grinning, 'it'll be a pleasure.'

Yes, they kept the car in one of the lock-up garages round the corner. Paul had keys, both for the garage and the car – but he always came and asked permission before he took it out, always. As Mrs Bainbridge gave Kite her key, her hand trembled.

But of course the fifteen-year-old Mini had gone.

'Now think back to when you saw him Sunday night, Mrs Bainbridge,' Mayo said. 'That was just after half past ten, right?' She nodded miserably. 'How did he seem – different, or just as usual?'

'He was in a state,' she admitted at last. 'I could tell there was something the matter. He hadn't long passed his test, but he usually drove very careful, at least when I was with him, but Sunday night he was, you know, erratic, grinding the gears and jamming the brakes on. I told him to go steady and he did, I don't think he realised how badly he'd been driving.'

'And?'

'That's all. I asked him what was wrong, but he said there was nothing the matter. I didn't push it, I thought it was likely another row with that Charlie Fish and least said about it the better.'

'You were right about that anyway, they had had an argument, his father admits it.' Fish had insisted it was nothing more than the usual row. Paul had asked for some spending money, his father had refused. It was the same old set-to they had every week. He'd get over it, he always did. Did Paul think he was made of lousy money? He was unemployed and had been living on social security for years. Anyhow, he knew for a fact that Marion Dove was in the habit of slipping Paul the odd fiver or so for the jobs he did for her, so why should he subsidise him as well?

'Was the tank full?' Kite asked. 'He might not have had much money, in which case he can't have got far . . . What's the matter, Mrs Bainbridge?'

Her hand had gone to her mouth. 'It's just – I've remembered – my Visa card's missing. I thought I'd lost it – the clasp on my bag's not very clever – and I was going to report it, but with all that's happened today that was the last thing I was thinking about . . . oh, my God.'

'Could Paul have taken it?'

'He'd never do a thing like that!'

'Did he have the opportunity?'

After a moment she reluctantly admitted it was possible. 'He came in with me for a coffee when we got home. I went straight upstairs to see that Robert was all right, but he was still asleep. I left my bag on the kitchen table while I went upstairs . . .'

Mayo said, 'We'll have a stop put on your card, and if Paul does try to use it, that'll help us to find him.'

In a moment of unprofessional but spontaneous sympathy, Kite put his arm round her shoulder as they were leaving. 'Don't worry, m'duck, he might have run away for all sorts of reasons.' It wasn't what he thought himself, but he didn't see any point in increasing her alarm and anxiety.

CHAPTER 9

The cheese rolls from the canteen were more than usually uninspired, and the coffee was anaemic. A pile of work, not all of it connected with the present case, was waiting on Mayo's desk. The air-conditioning seemed to be going berserk. His office was like an oven.

'What are they trying to do, suffocate us?' Mayo flung open the window and the door, and slung his jacket over the back of a chair. It was only seven o'clock and it was already beginning to feel like the end of a very long day.

427

On the same principle as he'd used as a child when eating his greens or liver first and saving the chips until last, he put the day's reports on one side and looked through the other documents, unmistakably the work of Atkins, without doubt the most economical user of typewriter ribbons and punctuation in the whole of the Lavenstock police force. Deciphering them as he masticated his way through the cheese rolls, he saw that two of them concerned missing young people. One girl disappearing – nasty, that always gave him a sinking feeling – and one boy turning up. Another latter-day Dick Whittington, this one, looking not for fame and fortune, but freedom and excitement in the big city. One of the thousands, heartbreak left in his wake, and appeals on the London Underground to ring home with no strings attached. Was this in fact all that had happened to Paul Fish? Well, this particular Whittington had had enough of sleeping rough, running out of money, not enough to eat. He'd turned and come home, disillusioned. Maybe Paul would, too.

They'd barely finished eating when Cherry rang down and spoke to Mayo. Before he went home to his supper, the Superintendent wanted updating on the present case, and also a word about his own attendance together with Mayo in court the next morning, where they were required to give evidence in a case concerning a series of organised shoplifting from local supermarkets. He wanted to get home himself, he said, so he'd not take up more than ten minutes of Mayo's time. Which meant half an hour, Mayo reckoned, if Cherry was hungry, three-quarters if not.

'Home!' Mayo grunted as he put the receiver back, annoyed at being reminded of the time he was going to have to waste in court tomorrow, something he'd been trying hard not to remember all day. 'We'll be lucky if we get there before midnight.'

For a while after he'd left the office, Kite sat mulling over what they'd discussed. Then he picked up the telephone and dialled. He announced himself to the woman at the other end and after her surprised reaction asked, 'Fiona, is Colin there?'

He was told that he was not.

'What, still down at school at this time? Them's policeman's hours!' he joked.

'I know,' Fiona Massey answered rather crisply.

Kite knew all about that tone of voice. Not that he heard it too often nowadays, now that Sheila had her own career to occupy her and little time to dwell on the injustices of being a policeman's wife, but when he did, he knew it was time to wave the white flag.

Fiona went on to explain that some new schedule or other that Colin worked on during the holidays wasn't going according to plan and needed adjustments. He'd tried bringing the work home, but what with three kids under his feet, he'd packed in the idea and decided staying on at school was a better bet after all. It was all right for some, wasn't it?

'Well, thanks, I'll go down and see him there,' Kite rejoined hastily. 'Promise I won't keep him too long! Take care, love. 'Bye.'

'If the gaffer wants me,' he said to the sergeant on the front desk as he went out, 'tell him I'll be back within the hour.'

Colin Massey was sandy-haired and bearded, a big raw-boned man of Scottish descent whose appearance brought Porage Oat packets and the skirl of the bagpipes irresistibly to mind. He and Kite had been at school together. The friendship had continued after they left and been strong enough to survive the separation of Colin's university years but had lapsed somewhat, like so many other things, since Kite had joined the police force and even more since he joined the CID. He was now deputy headmaster at the comprehensive, and although the occasions when they now saw each other were fairly infrequent, the two men never found any difficulty in picking up where they had left off. He was delighted to see Kite again and said he was quite prepared to help; nevertheless his response became guarded when he learned who it was Kite was enquiring about.

'Paul Fish? A quiet lad, a bit of a dreamer. Likeable enough, though.' He leaned back in his chair at full stretch, his hands in the pockets of his corduroys and heels dug into the hairy tiles that carpeted his room. 'Well, you could say *very* likeable, considering his background.'

'I've seen something of that.'

'Then you'll know what I mean. Why do you want to know? Not in trouble, is he, Martin?'

'I hope not. Didn't you know he hasn't been at school these last two days?'

'No, but I wouldn't. He's only with me on Thursdays this term.'

'It looks very much as though he may have done a bunk.'

'Oh. Oh Lord, has he?'

Kite looked at him sharply. 'You don't sound surprised.'

'Should I be? With a father like that.'

Kite soon found out that Massey was familiar not only with Paul's immediate family circumstances but also knew of his connection with Mrs Dove and the Bainbridges. He watched his friend's face lengthen as he told him what he knew of the situation. 'So tell me anything you can about Paul, will you, Colin? Anything you think might help.'

'Well . . .' The schoolmaster tugged at his beard and thought. 'Scholastically he's only average, in fact he came a cropper in his O-levels. He re-sat a couple and did better, and now he's determined to get good A grades. He won't manage it, I'm bound to say, never mind beat Graham . . . that's his brother. Very bright indeed, Graham, but a hard act to follow. He could've made it to Oxbridge, but he couldn't be dissuaded from Northumbria – not entirely uninfluenced by the fact that his girlfriend was going there, I imagine, but mainly because they've a particularly good fine arts course up there.'

That was where Rachel Dove lectured, Kite recalled. University of Northumbria, situated midway between York and Durham. 'Are they close, the brothers? I'm wondering if Paul might have gone up there.'

'The university term doesn't start until mid-October, remember, and anyway, I happen to know Graham's in China.'

'*China?*'

'It's the latest student thing. Getting there's the main problem, but once there, food and transport costs are dirt cheap by our standards, they sleep travelling on the trains . . . yes, I suppose the two boys are close in a way. Paul's crazy about flying, did you know?' he added, with seeming inconsequence. Kite said he'd guessed. 'I've sometimes wondered if that's what it's all about – sibling rivalry and all that sort of thing – if he can't beat Graham one way, he'll do it another. He hasn't really a hope of getting a university place anywhere, if we're being honest. Actually, I think he's admitted it to himself deep down.'

The room faced over the playing fields and a netball court where a group of teenage girls were playing an energetic and noisy after-school game. Echoes of their shouts floated through the open window, the sun, low in the sky, flashed on heated faces and young limbs.

'This flying's a bit more than a hobby with him, isn't it?' Kite asked.

'It's an obsession. I didn't know about it until I had him in for a heart to heart when he flunked his O-levels. I got him talking about himself, the usual thing, what he wanted to do with his life, what his interests were and so on. I'd never got near him before, but suddenly, wham, there it was – the only thing he cared a jot about. Flying. Apparently this Bainbridge uncle was a rear-gunner in the war and it seems they talk about nothing else. He's encouraged Paul to the extent where he's even fantasising about having flying lessons. I told him not to get his feet off the ground, if you'll pardon the pun, reminded him the lessons cost a fortune, but he said no, Mrs Dove had promised to pay for them when he was eighteen.'

'She had?'

'That's what he said . . . the only snag was there were conditions attached, and they went very much against the grain.'

'What conditions?'

'She wanted him to join the family firm when he left school. Definitely not what Paul has in mind. He's got one idea in his head when it comes to thinking of a career – and that's not concerned with making glass. I could see it wasn't a lot of use reminding him that in the present climate plenty of kids would give their eye teeth to have a job like that waiting for them when they left school, not to mention one with such prospects – which I imagine would mean he'd eventually have enough cash to fly all he wanted – but when I pointed this out, it cut no ice, I doubt he was even listening.'

Perhaps, thought Kite, he was thinking of that promised legacy of his great-aunt's. If Shirley Dainty had told the truth about it, perhaps that and the flying lessons – without conditions attached – had suddenly seemed accessible. Or what if she'd told him she'd decided *not* to leave him anything in her new will if he wouldn't promise to go into the firm? Fed up with his father, he might have felt that the last straw. He asked abruptly, 'Would you say he could be a violent lad?'

Massey replied with careful qualification. 'Not under normal circumstances, but you can never really tell with adolescents. They can become emotionally disturbed over what might appear to be trifles. It's a hell of a time for them, particularly with today's pressures. They're not kids any longer, but they're expected to be adults before they've the maturity to cope with it.'

'Yes.' Kite watched a young Amazon raising the ball high in front of her to shoot into the net. When he was fifteen he'd been desperately in love with a girl like that, a blonde with long legs and big, bouncing breasts. 'Remember Maxine Thompson, Colin?'

Massey followed his glance and grinned. 'She's a physiotherapist up at the hospital now.'

'Wouldn't you know.'

He'd privately thought himself no end of a lad at that age. But in public, that was different. Desperately unsure of himself, abashed at the size of his hands and feet, his clumsiness and his sprouting moustache . . . it hadn't helped when the lovely Maxine had rejected him for a wimp named Julian Something-or-other, a pimply undersized youth with greasy locks, and he could remember even now the burning humiliation, the painful sense of rejection, the strong desire to grind Julian Something-or-other between his back teeth and spit him out in little bits. Adolescence was one hell of a time.

Kite drove back to Milford Road and told Mayo what he had learned. 'He's evidently been under a lot of pressure lately, from one direction or another. It's conceivable he may have found it all too much.'

'All right, Mrs Dove was putting pressure on him to join the firm, but it wasn't imminent, he still has another year at school. And we've no evidence at all that he was anywhere near the lockhouse that weekend. We can't go round suspecting him until we have.'

It also seemed to Mayo that it was a point in Paul's favour that if Mrs Dove had been dead by the time her sister rang her at one-thirty, and Paul *had* been responsible and had subsequently made off with the missing five hundred pounds, then he would hardly have pestered his father afterwards for the few pounds he might or might not have got from him.

Kite said, 'I've got a list of some of his friends from Colin Massey. I'll get somebody on to it tomorrow, see if we can get a lead on what he was doing.'

He could leave it to Kite. For himself, Mayo couldn't summon up much interest for pursuing something he didn't really want to pursue. Not because Paul's youth made the possibility unlikely – doubts about that kind of objection had taken a nose dive long ago in the teeth of evidence to the contrary – and he'd do it if he had to, but he'd need to be more convinced than he was at present.

All the same, there *were* disturbing lines of connection between Paul and Marion Dove.

It was indeed after midnight when they finally called it a day.

Kite drove home to his semi-detached house on a private estate at the edge of the town, left the car in the drive and let himself into the bright kitchen he'd recently redecorated. As a finishing touch, Sheila had persuaded him to invest in a microwave oven, a boon, she'd argued, for getting the children a quick meal when she came in late, and with Kite working the odd hours he did. So far he'd steered clear of it, but the effect of the cheese rolls had long since worn off and he was starving, and Sheila had left a note to say there was a chicken casserole in the fridge which just needed heating up if he fancied it. It really did heat up in the incredibly short space of time the instructions said it would, and with no kids around to set a bad example to he polished it off straight from the dish.

On his way upstairs he looked into his sons' room, as he always did. Daniel, on the top bunk, was flat on his stomach as usual and Davy, also as usual, was invisible in a mighty tangle of bedclothes. How could a duvet get tied into a knot? He didn't attempt to untangle his son; in a few minutes he'd be in the same state again.

'What time is it?' Sheila murmured sleepily as he crept into bed, her curly brown head just visible above the sheets. 'Ouch, your feet are freezing, you've been walking about without shoes again.'

'I didn't want to disturb you.'

'Why not?' she asked. Warming his feet with her own, she turned towards him and lifted her face and curled her small warm body into his arms.

Mayo couldn't sleep. He had, over the years, taught himself to relax at will, snatching sleep and rest when he could, but tonight his technique wasn't working. He'd done himself some half-hearted beans on toast and then been too tired to taste them and now he lay unsleeping, the events of the case turning over and over in his mind no matter how he tried to blank them out. He tried thinking of other things, but that was worse. The cheerful optimism with which he'd returned from holiday now seemed quite unjustified. He'd only had the chance of a few unsatisfactory words with Alex during the day, but looking back on them, he couldn't recall that she had appeared to have missed him unduly while he'd been away.

Damn these self-sufficient, career-minded women. And yet, wasn't that what he wanted? Lynne had been content to be a housewife and mother, without outside interests of her own, dependent on him for companionship and resentful of a job that wasn't nine to five, and the tensions had become unbearable. Poor Lynne. If she hadn't died, the marriage would inevitably sooner or later have ended in divorce, he knew it. Paradoxically, that would perhaps have left him less guilt-ridden. As it was, her pert little face that had turned sharp and discontented with the years, the soft voice that had too often become a whingeing monotone, haunted him yet.

He finally gave up the attempt to sleep altogether, turned on the light and picked up his current book. In a few minutes, he was fast asleep.

CHAPTER 10

'The PM report's in, sir,' Kite announced, looking up from his first half-pint of coffee of the morning. 'It's on your desk.'

Timpson-Ludgate had come up with no surprises. The substance of the report was that Marion Elizabeth Dove, sixty-two years of age and suffering from advanced carcinoma of the liver, had died by manual strangulation, prior to the body being immersed in the canal for some thirty-six to forty-eight hours before it had been taken out on Tuesday morning. Examination of the stomach contents showed that a small quantity of toast and some tea had been consumed a few hours before death. Reasonable then to work on the assumption it had been breakfast, and that death had occurred on Sunday morning, some time between then and one-thirty, when her sister had rung. No traces of skin or fibre had been found under her nails to indicate she had fought her attacker . . . no bruises were reported, other than where heavy hands had gripped her upper arms, before moving on to her throat. There was considerable bruising there, and enough force had been used to break the hyoid bone; her age, however, made it probable that this, situated just above the Adam's apple, was brittle and therefore easily broken.

There'd been no indication of any great struggle on the canal bank, either, Mayo recalled. It was almost as though she hadn't *tried* to defend herself.

Later, Mayo dutifully presented himself at court along with Cherry, prepared for a long and tedious morning. He wasn't in for any surprises there, either, and it wasn't until after lunch that he was free to make his way to the glassworks. He'd learned that Ken Dainty would be closeted with important customers that afternoon and was not to be disturbed unless it was absolutely necessary. So it was business as usual, was it, the small matter of his wife's mother being killed wasn't going to change anything. To be fair, though, Dainty wasn't going to achieve anything by letting his affairs go to pot – and his wife would have her sister with her now. While Mayo wouldn't have had any compunction in bringing Dainty from his meeting had it suited him, he'd decided to leave him for the time being and instead made arrangements to see Mr Bainbridge. He suspected that in any case at this point he'd probably get more of what he wanted from him than from Dainty.

The factory, just off the main road, with a glimpse of water, the now disused arm of the canal, running behind it, could best have been described as a fine example of Victorian sham. Behind the elegant and impressive wrought-iron gates with their intertwined doves, a shabby, haphazard collection of old buildings was roughly grouped together, in dire need of smartening up. The office block was about on a par, the reception area reminiscent of dentists' waiting-rooms, with a glassed-in switchboard cubicle in the corner and a concession to the nature of their business in the form of a showcase where various pieces of crystal were displayed against dark blue velvet.

Business, however, was brisk. He had to wait several minutes before the telephonist was free, a girl with the face of a Botticelli angel, blonde curls, and a skin like painted porcelain, chiming 'Dove's-Glass-can-I-help-yew?' as if she were wound up by a little key in her back. At last another girl appeared to lead him to Mr Bainbridge. She was plump and rather plain, but the intelligence in her face, and her silence, were a change after the Botticelli angel. Twice as they progressed upstairs he thought she was going to speak, but she was young and he guessed she found the situation embarrassing and didn't quite know what to say to him in the circumstances. She showed him into an office next door to where he'd been received yesterday and had imparted the news of Mrs Dove's death. Not anywhere near as spacious, but light and pleasant, with a high ceiling and the desk placed so that Bainbridge had the same, though narrower, view that Ken had.

Mayo suspected this was not a good day for the old man. He had almost asked him not to bother getting up as he was shown into the room, but saw in time that his consideration would not have been appreciated. Robert Bainbridge evidently chose not to spare himself. An authoritative figure behind his desk or when moving by the aid of strategically-placed pieces of furniture, his lameness was not as apparent as it had been when he had met them yesterday in the outer office, leaning on his stick. What it cost him to keep up his self-imposed discipline was anybody's guess – to reach this office, there were had been two flights of steep stairs and no lifts. Negotiating them must be a twice-daily feat of heroism, but work, a view of himself as a still-useful member of society, being a lynchpin here in the office, Mayo could see would be more important to a man like Bainbridge. It was something he understood. He worked better under tension himself, it kept the adrenalin going and pushed you further than you knew you could go.

'Is there any news of the boy?' were Bainbridge's first words.

Mayo told him they were doing their best, but nothing had transpired so far. 'But I'd like to take this opportunity of having a few words with you about him. As I understand it, you probably know him better than anyone else.' He studied the man's face as he spoke, with its deeply moulded contours, spare and bleached as a bone, its deep-set eyes regarding him shrewdly. The face was severe with pain but Mayo saw evidence of an ironic humour and perhaps a wry kindliness there.

'Do I? Yes. Yes, I suppose I do. We talk – or rather he lets me talk, about my flying days, you know. There are few people who are interested in one's wartime exploits, but Paul's an appreciative audience. I can understand that – aeroplanes have always had a fascination for me, too.' He had a precise, pedantic way of speaking, either natural or more likely something he'd acquired as part of his persona as office patriarch.

'You didn't feel that you were perhaps over-encouraging him?'

'I don't think that's possible. "A man's reach should exceed his grasp – or what's a Heaven for?" Isn't that what the poet said?'

Mayo wasn't sure that the analogy would stand up. It was one thing to encourage the young to aim high, but not so high that, like the young Icarus, they burned their wings on the sun. He said, 'Why do you think he's disappeared?'

'Not because he's killed Marion. That's not possible,' Bainbridge said flatly. 'He was extremely fond of her, and anyway, he's not that sort of boy. His home life isn't very satisfactory, as you're no doubt aware, but he doesn't make that an excuse to act the young tearaway. He's a decent boy and I gather he's had another row with his father, which always upsets him. He'll come back when he's got it out of his system.'

He spoke with such calm assurance, his intense dark eyes, deeply contrasting with his pale polished face, looking over the halfmoon glasses, intelligent and alert, that it was difficult not to be carried along by his positiveness.

Mayo said, 'He's disappeared though, hasn't he? Apparently with your car and your wife's Visa card. We also have reason to believe there's a large amount of money missing from Mrs Dove's possession.'

Bainbridge regarded him steadily. 'I stand by what I said. Paul could never have murdered Marion.'

At that point, the tea Mr Bainbridge had asked for was brought in by the girl who'd shown him up. 'Thank you, Valerie, perhaps you wouldn't mind . . .'

Conversation lapsed during the business of pouring the tea, settling whether milk and sugar was required. When the girl had gone, casting him another of those slightly agonised looks, Mayo began again by asking Bainbridge how long he'd worked at Dove's.

The answer came promptly. 'Forty-four years to be exact.' Stirring sugar into his tea he leaned back, seeming glad that Mayo was not pursuing the question of Paul and the missing money. 'I'd always intended to go in for accountancy but the war put a stop to that. It needn't have done, there was no lack of schemes for training ex-servicemen, but I'd spent the last eighteen months of the war getting myself patched up and there wasn't much energy left for raising new initiatives. When Wesley Dove offered me a job in his office, I thought why not?' He smiled faintly. 'I took it as a stopgap, later I turned it to my advantage and learned to enjoy it for its own sake.'

Yes, he'd know all about the company, everything that went on, which Mayo had counted on. But . . . he might not tell. He looked like a man who could keep secrets.

'Funny how things happen,' Bainbridge mused, encouraged to continue by the apparently unhurried attitude Mayo was prepared to assume to hide his contained impatience. 'I never intended coming back to Lavenstock after the war. At nineteen, it seemed a dump to me and I couldn't wait to shake the dust off my feet. Then when I saw it the morning after that bad raid, that was it. I suddenly realised how much the place meant to me – it was my town and I knew I'd come back despite everything and settle down. Gwennie and I were going to be married and I decided then and there we weren't going to wait. We were only nineteen. Too young? In wartime it didn't seem so. Nor has it ever.' A smile, fleeting and brilliant as a shooting star, lit his eyes. 'I've been a very fortunate man, Mr Mayo.'

Mayo was reminded of his wife's face when she had spoken of him. They'd been married – how long? – forty-odd years? And still considered themselves lucky. Unaccountably, Mayo felt left out in the cold.

'You didn't meet your wife in the forces, then?'

'We'd known each other by sight all our lives but it wasn't until we found ourselves on the same RAF station that we got to know each other – and fell in love. Things being what they were, of course we were immediately posted to different parts of the country! Our leaves never seemed to coincide – but that's the fortunes of war. Good fortune sometimes – she'd just been posted and her leave cancelled, otherwise she'd have been home too when the bomb fell.'

'I hadn't realised there was enemy action in Lavenstock.'

'Not if you're comparing it with Coventry, but enough for a small town. It wasn't good that night. The house in Chapel Street was hit, her parents taken to hospital with minor injuries. When Gwennie heard, she applied for compassionate leave but she was stationed in the north of Scotland and didn't get home straight away, so young Marion had to cope alone. You could tell she was very shocked, but she was exceedingly brave. But then, she always was. She had her own inner resources, even then. She never deserved what she got.'

A small silence fell. The tea was drunk, it seemed appropriate to begin more immediate questions. He felt Bainbridge was a shrewd observer and would be an impartial witness. 'Do you have any suspicions at all as to who might have killed her?' he asked. When asked that particular question direct, it was surprising how many people responded with answers which often led to the truth.

Bainbridge picked up his pen and rolled it between his steepled fingers, considering. 'I've thought it over, naturally, but I've come to the conclusion that it would be invidious to suppose anyone close would be capable of such malice towards her.'

'What about others? Had there been trouble with anyone here, for instance?'

'Not to my knowledge – and I'm sure I would have known if there was.'

'Well then, let's talk about Mrs Dove herself, if you don't mind, sir.'

'Not at all. I'll say straight away it's been a great shock, not only to my wife and myself, but to everyone here, too. Dove's is above all a family concern and we were all of us deeply fond of Marion.'

'I believe she took an active part in the business until recently?'

Bainbridge inclined his head and said she had, until two years ago. When she reached sixty, she had thought it time to retire, though for a some time before that, she'd been leaving things more and more to Mr Dainty. 'Quite rightly. He's very capable, very sound.'

'She'd some idea of young Paul coming into the company when he left school, I believe?'

'So you've heard about that?' Bainbridge smiled, rather coolly, but didn't ask how Mayo knew. 'Well, yes, that was so – but I'm not sure she was right in this instance. Paul isn't very interested and you really can't impose conditions of that sort. It was understandable, though; she was very concerned, as we all are, with family continuity in the firm. The name of Dove in one form or another has been connected with glassmaking for at least five centuries, did you know that?'

'That's a long time. And now?'

'The name may not be the same, but the tradition will still be there, Mr Mayo. I know of no other industry with such a proud and continuous history as glassmaking. Nor one so family-orientated, come to that. I suppose it's unique. It's always been the custom for members of one family to work together in teams – "chairs" as they're called. At one time here at Dove's, we'd no less than twenty members of the same family working for us in one capacity or another! Mr Dainty was part of that particular clan, his father, uncles, grandfather were all blowers here. And in fact, a long way back, they were connected with the Doves through marriage. His two sons are very young yet, but I know he's extremely keen that they'll carry on the tradition.'

'Perhaps they'll be like Paul, and won't want to.'

'Then he'll be bitterly disappointed. Glassmaking's his whole life, and there's nothing he doesn't know about the business. The firm had unfortunately rather dwindled during Mr Wesley Dove's last years, but Ken's getting it back on its feet. There's much to be done, but he understands that change for its own sake isn't necessarily a good thing, it's better to make haste slowly, to consolidate and build on what you have. He's doing a splendid job. It would be a great pity if anything were allowed to spoil what he's worked for, but of course that won't happen now that he'll be totally in control.'

Mayo caught some nuance of something there, but the significance escaped him. Eventually he said, 'How can you be certain he will be?'

'It's never been any secret in the family,' Bainbridge answered calmly, 'that he was the heir apparent. Old Mr Wesley, now – he

442

thought he was immortal and would live forever, but in the end he died suddenly and without warning, without making any real provision for who was to follow him. Marion had no intention of allowing that to happen again.'

Mayo wondered if Bainbridge realised how he was implicating Dainty by what he'd revealed. He said, his eyes resting on the other man's face assessingly, 'Would it surprise you to know that she intended changing her will?'

'Did she? No, it wouldn't surprise me. I believe the will was made out a long time ago, and as one gets older, circumstances change, time no longer seems infinite. I've felt myself from the age of sixty that every day is a bonus.'

'I take it you didn't know Mrs Dove was seriously ill?'

The other man looked suddenly a little greyer, a little more stooped. 'Not until my wife told me. That makes it even more understandable that she should want to put her affairs in order.'

A reminder of mortality briefly silenced both men. 'You don't think the new will might have concerned Mr Dainty's succession? Could they have disagreed in some way about it?'

'I think it highly unlikely.' A faint smile lifted the corners of his mouth. 'First because I don't believe, even if she'd told him about any changes she was going to make, that they'd have been substantial enough to affect him. Secondly, because neither has ever been the quarrelling type. Ken would simply bide his time, then try another tack, and Marion could be stubborn on occasions but she'd usually give in rather than have any trouble, which she couldn't bear. She'd had a few words with Gwennie, for instance, last Friday and it had upset her terribly.'

'Your wife mentioned there'd been an argument.'

'Oh, I'd hardly call it an argument, just a difference of opinion. Marion admitted to me she'd been rather tactless. It was nothing, just a few words over a bungalow we'd put in an offer for. I'd had a rather more substantial win than usual last week – I like a harmless little flutter occasionally – and we thought we could manage it, but the price turned out to be way above our heads. Gwennie was rather down in the mouth about it when Marion popped in to see her at the shop and offered to make up the difference, but I'm afraid Gwennie's always been inclined to be touchy about what she sees as charity and took exception to that.'

So this was where the money went in the Bainbridge household – the 'occasional little flutters' which weren't perhaps quite so harmless when they meant his wife going out at nights pulling pints for the locals at a time of life when she might have expected to stay at home with her knitting. Or when it meant they couldn't afford the bungalow that could mean so much in terms of ease and comfort for them both. He was sure neither of them looked at it in this light, and on the whole this surprising streak of rashness in the pedantic Mr Bainbridge seemed endearing rather than otherwise, a peccadillo bringing him down to the level of other mortals.

He stood up. 'I won't keep you any longer, Mr Bainbridge. Thank you for being so helpful.'

The girl called Valerie was hanging about in the corridor when he came out. 'I'll show you out.'

He smiled at her. 'Don't bother. I can find my own way.'

'Oh, it's no bother.'

An uneasy silence hung between them as he followed her down the narrow stairs again. At the foot, she stood hesitating with her hand on the knob of the door into the reception area.

'Was there something you wanted to say to me?'

She gave a sort of gasp and went very pink. 'Oh no, only that we're all terribly upset,' she said in a rush, tears springing to her eyes, 'about Mrs Dove.'

A man in a brown smock came through the door from the other side. 'Orright, Val?' he asked, looking curiously at her.

'Yes, thanks, Jim. I – I'm sorry, I have to go now,' she said breathlessly to Mayo and, turning, followed the man quickly up the stairs.

*

It was after four when he came out into the yard and made his way across to his car. Inserting his key into the lock, he chanced to look up, his eye caught by a flight of pigeons swooping round the tall red brick house in the garden beyond the wall, the house that was called The Mount.

It was a house that had always interested him as he passed in his car, and since Shirley Dainty had mentioned it, he had had a feeling at the back of his mind that in it lay some connection with the case, that there at least he might find some of the answers to the questions which had started up in his mind when Gwen Bainbridge had spoken about her sister's marriage. He decided now was as good an opportunity as any of looking it over. He left the car in the car park and walked across.

CHAPTER 11

If it were possible to concentrate all your efforts on one particular case to the exclusion of all the rest, mused George Atkins, running his hand through his grizzled hair and ensuring himself a period of undisturbed privacy by lighting up his noxious pipe, life would be a darned sight easier – but when had it ever been? Just now the DCI needed all the men he could get on the Marion Dove case, but everything else couldn't be ignored. He pondered in particular the problem of this girl, this fifteen-year-old who'd gone missing while her parents had been on holiday abroad. He sat down, shuffled a few names and allocated jobs and in the end, not without some trepidation, he sent Deeley to see what he could get out of the friend who'd supposedly been staying with her during the absence of the parents, whom Atkins had already interviewed himself, and of whom he hadn't formed a very high opinion.

★

Nicola Parkin was, fortunately for Deeley, away from school with a cold, though when he was confronted with her he could see no signs of it.

She was a tall, etiolated fifteen-year-old, blonde, and so thin as to be almost anorexic, and her voice was scarcely more than a whisper, so that Deeley had to strain to hear what she was saying. Her mother, on the other hand, had a loud and hectoring voice to match her presence. So far she'd done most of the talking. Deeley let her run on, waiting patiently for the time when in the nature of things she must pause for breath. Nicola, it seemed, was in disgrace, but it was 'that Katie Lazenby' who was bearing the brunt of Mrs Parkin's wrath.

'I never did trust her, really. Sly, she is, I always said so –'

'Oh, Mum!' breathed Nicola.

'Oh yes I did, always. Involving my daughter in her lying and scheming, how dare she! And you –' turning to her daughter – 'I shall have something to say to you, my girl, about all that just now, don't think you'll get away with it, telling lies just so *she* could carry on and get up to God knows what while her parents were out of the way! And what about her mother?' she demanded of Deeley. 'Disgusting, I call it, willing to leave two young girls on their own while they gad off abroad – Acapulco, wasn't it?'

'The Algarve, Mum.'

'Well, wherever. And not even taking the trouble to check with me that I was agreeable. As if I would've been! Her dad'll have something to say about that, I can tell you. My Nicola, and all my children, have been brought up right!'

'Mrs Parkin, do you think I could trouble you for a drink?' Deeley asked at last in desperation. 'I've got a real thirst on.' The three of them in that little sitting-room, with the large three-piece suite and the enormous TV set and music centre dominating one side of it, seemed to take up a lot of air.

She looked at him sharply, but he was indeed looking warm. 'Go get the policeman a glass of water, Nicola,' she ordered and

Deeley, mortified, saw that his ploy hadn't succeeded. He wasn't going to get a cup of tea, as he'd hoped, and he wasn't going to get Mrs Parkin out of the room, either. She talked all the time her daughter was absent, which seemed an inordinately long time. Eventually Nicola came back and handed him the glass of water, then folded herself like an Anglepoise lamp and sat down. Deeley took a long swig and said firmly, 'Mrs Parkin, I'd like to hear Nicola's own account of what's happened, now, if you don't mind.'

Nicola shrank further into the corner of the settee, her mother crossed her arms over her militant bosom and tightened her lips, looking offended. 'Well, I don't know what more she can tell you than I've done, I'm sure.'

It took more patience than Deeley knew he possessed to get a coherent story out of Nicola, who was terrified at what she'd done, and even more to prevent her formidable mother from interfering, but eventually Deeley's notes were complete and, as it turned out, a good deal more relevant than anyone might have thought.

He was chuffed. This'd bring a bit of colour to the DCI's cheeks.

After he left the glassworks, not quite knowing what to expect at The Mount, Mayo made his way up the drive between craggy stone rockeries dankly overhung with evergreens.

It was as Gwen Bainbridge had suggested, fixed in a time-warp, an old dinosaur of a house. He wasn't averse to Victorian architecture; at its best he admitted it could be magnificent, but this was a different matter. Over-ornate for its size and propor-tions, The Mount was ugly by any standards. Constructed of dull red brick with string courses of yellow stone like marzipan in a Simnel cake, with its steeply-sloping grey slate roofs and tall chimneys and unnecessary turrets, it had a slightly top-heavy look, as though too high for its base, as though a good push from behind would send it toppling into the neglected garden.

Before going into the house, he took stock of the surroundings, walking round the trodden and moss-grown red gravel path that circled the lawn, gingerly pushing aside the long, rampant tentacles of climbing roses which had long since blown away from the supports of their metal arches.

This had once been a fine garden but now the earth was sad and heavy, uncultivated beneath the unpruned shrubs. A lovely Victorian oval lead pond was choked with weeds and almost obscured by a small thicket of seedlings from the weeping ash at the corner of the path. Someone had carelessly rough-cut the lawn fairly recently, leaving long grass high between the swathes of the mower and at the lawn edges where old blue bricks set diagonally upright made a broken picot edge. Pigeons had roosted in the crannies and gullies of the angled roofs and behind the chimney stacks, and evidence of their presence was all around. Stepping carefully towards the massive front door, he put the key into the lock with some feeling of anticipation, instinctively ducking as an alarmed clatter of wings sounded and two pigeons swooped down and away.

Inside was a museum, furniture and fittings circa 1880. Ornate dark marble fireplaces with heavy overmantels, elaborate plaster ceilings and tall windows, leather and plush-covered armchairs and sofas, a smell of dust. Mrs Bainbridge had exaggerated, but not much, in saying nothing had been allowed to change. There were a few later, obviously replacement furnishings here and there, anachronisms which did nothing to relieve the prevailing ambience of overall gloom. He walked in growing wonder from room to room – seven bedrooms, attics, one amazing, unbelievable bathroom. A huge drawing-room, a sombre dining-room off which led a sunless conservatory, a study, a depressing kitchen and sculleries and – the only pleasant room in the house – what he took to be a breakfast-room of sorts. He was upstairs in one of the main bedrooms when he heard the sound of wheels on the gravel.

Walking swiftly to the window, he stood to one side, screened by dark green chenille curtains and a layer of yellowed lace, watching the small silver Peugeot climb the drive. The car drew to a halt beside the front door but no one alighted for some time. He waited patiently and presently a young woman got out, slamming the door behind her.

She stood for a moment facing the garden and then turned abruptly to the house and stopped, her figure foreshortened from his angle of perception, her hands thrust into the pockets of her denim skirt. Slowly then she walked towards the door and let herself in.

She'd been fooling herself to think it would be any different, that there would be no stifling sense of suffocation, that the grim, dimly-lit hall where ghosts and witches had lurked in the shadows when she was a child on her way to bed would have been mysteriously lightened, that the pounding of her heart would be any less painful now than it had been then. Only now she couldn't, once the drawing-room door had closed behind them, grasp Shirley's hand tight as they raced up the stairs together. Even Shirley must have felt fear at times, pretend as she might.

She forced herself to walk through rooms she hadn't entered for ten years and more, while memory rushed back. The vast Victorian Gothic furniture in carved black oak, the oppressive wallpapers, Turkey carpets and heavy dark velvet hangings, the thick lace curtains – some of her friends would have drooled over its authenticity, the furnishings alone were going to be worth a fortune, but Rachel could only regard it with loathing. For a long time she stood looking at the leather wing chair that only her father had been allowed to occupy, still standing in front of the big mahogany desk in his study. Without looking at the portrait of him that hung over the mantel, she walked quickly out to the hall.

Her footsteps rang on the cold Minton-tiled floor and so familiar was its pattern of tans, blues and reds, with a black and white chequerboard edging, that she could have drawn it with her eyes shut. She halted at the foot of the oak staircase, the murky colours of the big mournful stained glass window on the half-landing obscuring what light there was, feeling again the deep chill that the vast old-fashioned radiators could never dispel seeping into her bones, seeing the iron grating on the floor where the wavering heat from the hot pipes came through and the fluff and grit went in . . . how could her mother have *endured* it?

Utter dejection swept her, she stood there without moving, consumed by it, weeping inwardly for Marion. Had there ever been happiness in this house, or laughter? There must have been, once. Children had lived here – and children and unrelieved gloom and misery were a contradiction in terms.

She lifted her head and her eyes lit on the mounted antlers half way up the staircase upon which, on the day she left school, Shirley had irreverently and joyously thrown and impaled her school hat. For the first time since entering the house, her misery lifted a little.

Mayo heard her moving from room to room downstairs and then into the hall. As he came out of the bedroom and on to the galleried landing, his footsteps muffled by thick carpets, he could see her at the foot of the stairs, her head bowed, clasping the newel-post with her forehead against the cold marble of the ball that surmounted it. Her unhappiness was so evident that to disturb her now would be an unpardonable intrusion and he moved swiftly and silently back into the bedroom, gave it a few minutes and then walked out again, this time making enough noise to warn her of his presence.

'Miss Dove?' he said, coming down the stairs. 'Detective Chief Inspector Mayo, Lavenstock CID.'

She waited for him, showing no surprise. 'My sister told me she'd given you a key.'

She accepted his condolences gravely, but with no trace of the grieving young woman he had glimpsed from upstairs. Her voice was quick and decisive and her handshake firm, though her fingers were icy cold and she was exceedingly pale. There was a strong resemblance between the two sisters but she was fairer and more sturdily built than Shirley Dainty and had that calm direct gaze of her mother's that had been his most lasting impression of her.

'I suppose you want to talk to me? Then if you've seen all you want, I'd prefer to go outside. This place hasn't changed. It still has all the welcome of a morgue.' She caught her breath slightly, and as if her unfortunate choice of words could be exorcised by movement, walked rapidly out of the door, slamming it when he had followed her outside. 'I can understand my mother walking out after my father died, not wanting to have anything to do with it ever again, even the business of selling it.'

He'd have preferred to be able to watch the expressions on her face, to see if they echoed the uncompromising tones; it was difficult, pacing awkwardly side by side on the gravel and he was looking around for a seat of some kind when she said suddenly, 'I don't know about you, but I could do with a cup of tea. I wonder if Hawley's are still in business? Shall we walk down and see?'

'That sounds like a good idea.' He was awash with tea at the moment but willing to suffer if it would help to elicit information.

The steeply descending road that led past the glassworks at the side of the house and thence to the Lavenstock bypass had never been designed for the heavy traffic it now took. They had to wait several minutes, nearly asphyxiated by the hot smell of tarmac, dust and petrol, while a stream of container lorries and tankers thundered past and a space finally occurred which allowed them to cross. When they got there they discovered to her obvious satisfaction that the small baker's with its half-dozen little chequered-cloth tables set out towards the back of the shop was still in the business of serving teas and homemade cakes. He ordered tea for two and it was brought almost immediately with scones and a selection of cakes.

She filled their cups from a large brown teapot and selected a slice of chocolate cake from the plate he offered. 'I shall no doubt regret this later,' she remarked as she proceeded to eat it slowly and with serious concentration. 'Shirley will have cooked an elaborate meal and if I don't do it justice she'll get all uptight and think it's not good enough, but there are times when something sweet is necessary, don't you agree? Echoes of the nursery?'

'Or something to do with the blood sugar, I suppose.'

They sat in a small oasis of privacy among the other unoccupied tables, the only seated customers at that moment. It was nearly five o'clock and the women of Holden Hill who weren't still at work would be at home giving children their tea, preparing an evening meal. Mayo ate his scone and drank his tea while customers came in and bought from the counter sweet-smelling brown loaves and the meat pasties for which Rachel told him the shop was famed. Outside the heavy traffic continued to roar by.

'Thank you for being patient,' she said presently. 'I feel better now.' But she'd pushed away her plate and he noticed she'd eaten barely a third of the cake. A little colour had come into her cheeks. Her hair had fallen forward, making her seem less strained.

'I'd like to talk to you about your mother, though it's more a matter of background than anything, since you weren't here at the weekend.'

'Wasn't I? Who told you that?' The glance she gave him was sharp and speculative, and somewhat impatiently she told him she'd driven down on Sunday morning because her mother had rung and said she'd like to see her rather urgently before she went on holiday. 'She wouldn't say what it was over the telephone, but she sounded concerned, and as I was due to leave tomorrow to spend three weeks in Florence I came down straight away.'

'What was it she wanted to see you about?'

The impatience drained away and a sadness settled on her face. 'This is going to be difficult.' She stared down at the chequered pattern of the tablecloth. When she eventually spoke her voice was

452

husky, yet controlled. 'She'd recently been told she didn't have long to live, and she wanted to talk to me. She – she thought I ought to know, in case anything happened while I was away . . .' She broke off. 'Stupid of me, the post-mortem. I see you know that already?'

'I'm sorry.' It was lame, inadequate, but what else was there to say? 'That was all your mother wanted to see you about?'

'What else?' She shrugged, but suddenly wary it seemed to him. He thought she might have been going to elaborate, but though he waited, she said nothing more.

'What time did you leave her?'

'I started out early and arrived somewhere around half past nine, and left about – oh, about half past eleven, because I knew she usually had lunch with my Aunt Gwen on Sundays. I'd have driven her up there but I had to get back.'

So – if Rachel Dove had left her mother at eleven-thirty, and she had been dead by the time Gwen Bainbridge rang at one-thirty, this further reduced the time during which she might have met her death. In broad daylight? With someone coming to walk their dog, say, liable to pass by at any moment? Quite possible. A spur of the moment killing which could have taken less than a minute, another minute to pitch her into the canal. But equally, there might have been another reason why she hadn't answered the telephone. He thought of the supermarket receipt, and the name Steven. And the time, 10.30, which wouldn't fit.

'Did she ever mention anyone called Steven?'

'Steven? Not that I remember. Someone up at the works, perhaps?' she said vaguely. 'She promised she'd rest after I'd gone. She looked exhausted, and I felt guilty that I'd kept her talking so long. We'd talked, perhaps too much, about things that ought to have been said years ago . . .' She pushed her hair back behind her ears. Her face had become pinched and plain again. 'We were at cross-purposes, as usual.'

'Cross-purposes?'

'What I mean is, I was frantically upset at the news and I wanted her to let me arrange for her to have some sort of care. At the same time she was trying to persuade me not to cancel my holiday. She pointed out I couldn't do anything if I stayed and that she'd no intention of leaving the lockhouse until she had to.'

He wondered why Marion Dove had chosen this particular moment to tell her daughter such a thing, if she hadn't wanted her to cancel her holiday. Telling her could have served no useful purpose, surely, other than ruining the holiday for her. The sudden shock of hearing of her mother's death would have been no worse than worrying that it might happen while she was away. There was more to it.

'Did you know she intended changing her will?'

It took her some time to consider her answer, but in the end she said yes, her mother had told her that.

'Did she tell you how?'

With slight irony, she answered, 'No. Except that it wasn't going to affect me.'

Mayo didn't believe her. He was sure her mother *had* told her, and that for reasons of her own Rachel was being less than frank about revealing what it was. He decided, because he believed she was on the point of telling him other things and he didn't want to lose her, to let the lie pass for the moment .

'I gave up arguing in the end, about her leaving. You couldn't ever persuade my mother into something she didn't want to do, and anyway, I believe she was happier down there at the Jubilee than she'd ever been. It seemed to me that if that was her wish, if she wanted to stay there right up to the end, then no one else had the right to make her choice for her – though my sister didn't entirely agree with me over this.'

He could imagine that.

She said suddenly, almost as if she couldn't help herself, 'My mother had a rotten life, you know, with my father. He was a violent man and I hated him. Not that it matters now, I don't suppose. It was all pretty sordid, but he's dead, she's dead, it's all done with.' After a bleak pause, she added, 'No, that's never true, is it? The past always has a bearing on the present . . . I for one can never forget it, as for Shirley . . . Well, anyway.'

With a deliberate effort of will, she seemed to shift her mind back from some disturbing thought about her sister. 'The truth is, they had rows, he and my mother, when he'd beat her up. He was careful never to give her a black eye or anything that could be seen, except he once attacked her with a knife. She had a huge gash across the back of her hand – she said she'd done it herself, cutting bread, but I never believed it. It's a fallacy to think it's only drunken labourers who beat up their wives, isn't it? I simply could not understand why she wouldn't leave him. No one *has* to endure *that*!'

Indeed they did not. But the reasons why so many women did, and allowed themselves to be battered again and again by their men were complex and often defied understanding.

Financial dependency, he suggested, especially when there were children.

'She could have got a job. She was more than competent.' Her lips tightened. Remembered anger was competing with distress and anger won. 'I've tried to understand why he needed to be like that, and believe me, I know all the fashionable excuses . . . frustration, low self-esteem, insecurity about his masculinity. Or just that maybe *his* father beat his mother. Violence creates violence, that's the current thinking, isn't it, that brutality is inherited? Do you think that's true? Do you think it's in the blood?' She shot the question at him as if he were one of her students.

'No,' he said, though his views were not as rigid as that. But it was what she needed to hear, and it saved him from the sort of digressive discussion he'd no desire to get involved in at the moment. 'What did they quarrel about?'

'About? I think it was mostly about us, Shirley and me. He was disappointed in having daughters instead of sons for his precious business. If he'd had more wit to see it, he could have trained us to carry it on, but I don't suppose that ever occurred to him – that a woman could ever do a thing like that – he'd have been amazed to see how my mother ran the business after he died, much better than he ever did.'

'Did he ever use violence against you and your sister?'

A lorry, crashing its gears on the hill outside, provided time for her to frame a cautious answer. 'Occasionally, when we were children, though never if my mother was there, and only once later, in my case. I see – I believe now, because of what she told me – that he was afraid of us.'

She was watching him, waiting for him to ask what she meant, but he had no need; he knew, immediately. 'Afraid of you?' he asked nevertheless, more gently than he'd replied to her other question.

'He had a fancy, my father, for young girls. Under age, to be precise, fourteen or fifteen.'

He understood now, only too well. He appreciated, too, that moment of despair at the bottom of the staircase, but softly she added, so softly he had to strain to hear, 'No, he never touched us, he wouldn't have dared. My mother knew too much about him, you see.' She looked at him with that clear, direct gaze of her mother's, but tinged with defiance. 'You're shocked, aren't you?'

'I've been a policeman too long for that, Miss Dove.'

Not shocked – but some things could still sicken him.

'She tried to make me see on Sunday that he wasn't really evil, just weak and insecure. Oh, I dare say he *had* a pretty low self-esteem, which isn't surprising, considering everything. But it didn't make me feel one jot differently about him. I still feel he was a bastard, hard as nails, but soft and rotten at the core.'

Despite the harshness of her judgement, some of the bitterness seemed to have drained out of her. She sounded suddenly very tired. 'I think she was sorry for him in a way, but that wasn't the real reason why she'd stayed with him. She didn't care about money, not for its own sake, not for herself . . . that was something

456

we *were* agreed on. Money doesn't matter greatly to me, either. But her attitude was she'd brought us into the world and it was up to her to provide for us as best she could. What an inheritance!'

'Thank you for telling me.' He realised the effort it had cost her. Even Gwen Bainbridge, who had very nearly told him yesterday, hadn't quite been able to bring herself to do so .

'Thank *you* for the tea, I must be going now.' She pushed her chair back and said with a difficult smile, 'It's the only thing in my life I've ever found it impossible to discuss, until now. You're very easy to confide in.'

He grinned to himself, thinking what Kite and a few others would have said if they'd heard that. He didn't actually believe it himself in any case. It was simply that he'd been there, available, at a vulnerable and unguarded moment when she had felt it possible to unburden herself of years of inhibition. If she'd thought about it, she wouldn't have done it, she was too sharp and self-aware for that. He had the impression she was glad that she had spoken, however. He sat for several minutes more after she had left him, thinking over what she'd said. It might well turn out to have a bearing on the case. He would need to see her again, when the pattern had emerged more clearly. And the next time, he wouldn't let her get away with less than the truth.

CHAPTER 12

When he heard what Atkins and Deeley wanted to see him about, Mayo sent for Kite and had them all three come up to his office. Kite, who had spent all afternoon checking through the interviews with the various people Ken Dainty had produced to support his alibi, and felt he could do with a change of direction, came in with alacrity, just behind the other two.

Mayo waved them all to sit down and perched himself on the edge of the desk. 'All right, let's have it right from the beginning.'

Atkins began with his own account of seeing the parents of Katie Lazenby after they'd discovered their daughter missing on their arrival home from holiday, three days earlier than expected. 'Didn't come up to scratch, I gather, the Algarve, so they packed-it in.'

It appeared that the only time they'd been able to get a suitable booking was when Katie was back at school after the holidays, and so they'd arranged for the grandmother to stay with her. However, just before they were due to go, the old lady had broken her hip in a fall and had been in hospital ever since. Young Katie had pestered her parents not to cancel their holiday and to be allowed to stay on her own. Eventually they'd agreed, on condition that she had her friend, Nicola Parkin, to stay with her.

Deeley, who had taken his notebook out to make sure of getting his facts straight, took up his part of the story eagerly. 'Nicola told Mrs Lazenby she'd asked her mother's permission, and got it – which wasn't true of course, sir.'

'Didn't Mrs Lazenby check?'

'Apparently not, she just took Nicola's word.'

'Shouldn't think, from what I saw of her,' Atkins intervened, 'she'd bother much with that sort of thing, in case it interfered with her own plans. And of course Nicola had no need to mention it to her mother, because there was never any intention of her going to stay with Katie – that was all malarkey, just a blind. She'd other fish to fry, young Katie. Sounds a right little madam, if you ask me.'

'She was making use of Nicola, sir,' Deeley said. 'The poor kid's frightened to death at what she's done, incidentally.'

'And so she should be. What made her agree to it?'

'Seems this Katie's one of the clever ones at school, shines at everything, and she agreed to help Nicola, who's always in trouble with her maths, if she'd do as she asked.'

'And why was she so anxious to be alone?' Mayo asked wearily, because he knew the answer that was coming and didn't want to hear it. Another precocious child, prepared to jeopardize her future, mess up her life – there'd be a boy in it somewhere, no doubt . . . and then knew where it was all leading, and why Deeley was so excited. 'Paul Fish?' he asked softly.

'That's right, sir. Seems he's been soft on her for months, but she's kept him on a string, made him pretty miserable with it, and then suddenly she gives in and they start going out with one another . . .'

So there could now be an entirely different reason for Paul's abrupt departure from the scene, a much more acceptable one. What, after all, was the hard evidence against him regarding Marion Dove? Nothing but speculation. On the other hand, it seemed fairly conclusive that Paul *had* taken Gwen Bainbridge's car – not to mention her Visa card – and that was more in line with the sort of thing a boy might do if he was setting out to impress a girl and needed money. Five hundred pounds in cash, of course, the missing five hundred, would have been even more useful.

'What d'you think, Martin?' he asked when the other two had gone.

'I'd put money on it that Paul was just fed up after the row with his father and decided to push off, probably only for a few days until he'd cooled off, taking Katie with him, know what I mean?'

'I do know what you mean. But – robbing his aunt of the five hundred pounds to finance the jaunt? Having first murdered her? If he did, it would have meant him going about his business for the rest of the day as if nothing had happened, even to ferrying Mrs Bainbridge about, only deciding to decamp either very late that night or early the next morning. Which seems pretty cool – and indicates a certain complicity on the part of Katie Lazenby.' Mayo shook his head. 'Possible, of course, but probable? I don't know. I just don't know.'

★

He liked Alex in uniform. She was one of the few women who could wear it without looking either lumpy or butch. But he preferred her as she was tonight. She'd been dozing in front of the television when he rang the bell, relaxed in a dark blue shirt in some silky material and a longish sort of skirt that drifted as she walked, and her hair was a little tousled where her head had rested on the cushion, her cheeks flushed with sleep.

After all these months, he still felt it necessary to apologise for arriving without warning but she welcomed him as if his unexpected appearance was the most agreeable thing that had happened to her all week. That was one of the best things about her – her readiness and ability to understand the haphazard irregularity of his life without fuss, to provide a warm and loving atmosphere with no hassle. The other side of the coin was that Mayo wanted to be married and Alex didn't. He told himself in moments of trying to understand her point of view it was simply that he wanted a hand to hold, a presence in the dark, someone in the other chair. Maybe. But whatever it was, he wanted it permanent, and because she was wary of anything less than a perfect relationship and saw that there were reasons on both sides why this might never be possible, she preferred – insisted on – remaining uncommitted.

'You look bushed, Gil. I'm afraid I've already eaten, but I can do you a couple of lamb chops. Will that do?'

'Fine.' They'd be perfect, too. She was incapable of doing anything less than excellently. All very well, but she tended to have the same expectations of others. It was a nagging fact that occasionally disquieted the corners of his mind when he was trying to persuade her that she couldn't eat her cake and have it. Which was how he saw it, but she didn't.

'Get yourself a drink while you're waiting.'

He followed her into the small kitchen, helped himself to a beer and hitched a hip on to the edge of the table, watching her while she moved efficiently around, admiring her back view, the tall slimness of her. 'Any leads yet?' she asked over her shoulder, taking salad from the fridge.

Briefly, he brought her up to date with what had happened, the latest about Paul Fish.

The chops, succulent and pink inside, exactly as he liked them, arrived on the table, magically accompanied by a crisp salad, a couple of warm rolls and butter and a pot of strong dark coffee. She poured herself a cup and sat opposite while he ate.

'What do these wretched parents expect, for heaven's sake? Leaving a girl that age?' she commented. But she seemed to sense that he didn't want to talk about the case, that tonight he wanted to switch off, and while he ate they talked about his holiday, or rather he talked and she listened.

'It sounds marvellous!'

For a moment he regretted not having asked her to accompany him to Scotland, but when he tried to imagine her struggling across the boggy moors in a drenching Scottish mist, he failed. Her dark blue skirt exactly matched the dark blue of her shirt, which exactly matched the blue of her eyes. Her nails were short and very clean, polished to pale, pearly pink ovals. Yet he knew how tough she was, she knew how to take care of herself in a rough-house, she knew what was what, having done her share of the rotten, sometimes unspeakable jobs, like any other police officer, man or woman.

He really enjoyed the food, finding himself more hungry than he'd known he was. 'This is good, love. The two women in my life, both super cooks – what have I done to deserve that?'

He saw immediately that she didn't altogether like that, that for some reason he'd said the wrong thing, but couldn't for the life of him see why. Sometimes he felt that conversation with Alex was like stepping through a minefield. You never knew what you were going to put your foot on next. She could be acid about remarks he considered quite innocent, but this seemed to apply to ninety per cent of women these days.

His meal finished, they went back into her sitting-room. She put on a new record she'd bought, a collection of Scarlatti harpsichord sonatas. He suspected, because their tastes in music rarely coincided, that she'd bought the record especially because she knew he liked it, and was touched.

She'd created a lovely restful room, decorated in the cool, neutral colours she loved, resisting the blandishments of her sister to reconstruct and reproduce a facsimile of the apartment's elegant Edwardian past. Lois, who ran a swish interior decorator's business from a shop in the town and thought nothing of redoing a room entirely, throwing out everything else simply on account of some new chair or cabinet or even a picture she'd bought, thought it a chance wasted, but Alex liked and kept the things she'd collected over the years, and with them had achieved an elegance of her own.

She hadn't drawn the curtains across the open window and framed between their lavender grey velvet folds he could see the three-dimensional tracery of leaves and branches of one of the trees in the park opposite, lit by the street lamp, a blurred, grainy light emphasising the darkness beyond. The jungle outside the territory of the campfire, where in the night lurked lawlessness, the unknown, terror and murder. 'Tyger, tyger, burning bright, in the forests of the night . . .' Blake. Marion Dove.

She had liked poetry. These cool, precise Scarlatti cadences, or Mozart, Bach, Elgar, Prokofiev, none of them had probably meant a thing to her, but words forming patterns on the page had said something to her heart. He still didn't know what sort of woman she really was. She had been quiet and unassuming, leading a quiet, uneventful life. An ordinary woman, with nothing so far revealed in her lifestyle or her make-up to lead anyone to murder her. Except for one thing.

She had had money, and the power that money brings. Had she been the sort to wield that power? To enjoy manipulating people, using her money as a lever? From what he had gathered, that seemed to be the last thing she would do. Her interest in money had seemingly been for her daughters only, but it had been strong enough to induce her to stay married to a man like Wesley Dove for more than twenty-five years.

But there had to be, somewhere, a reason for her having met so horrible, so sad a death. He had a strong ineluctable feeling that he ought to know, that he had already been told the facts that would lead him to his murderer. The facts were there, randomly distributed in his subconscious. It was a matter of looking at what there was to see and seeing its relevance, but gathering them together felt maddeningly beyond him tonight. And also, his eyes kept straying to an opened envelope with a Bradford postmark propped on the mantelpiece, addressed to Alex in stylish handwriting, cursive, thick and black.

Liam. He'd never seen this Liam's handwriting, the man on whose account Alex had left Yorkshire and been transferred down here, but he knew it was his. His handwriting *would* be like that, fancy, the handwriting of an Irish Don Juan; flamboyant, untrustworthy, a man who'd no intention of leaving his wife, or letting Alex alone, either. He'd have smiling Irish eyes, too, and that he had a great line in blarney was implicit in the fact that she evidently couldn't, despite the way he'd treated her, break entirely free.

He made an effort to empty his mind. He'd been at it fourteen hours on the trot . . . he heard the record come to an end . . . The telephone rang, jerking him fully awake. Alex went into the hall to answer it and after a few minutes' conversation, during which he heard laughter, she came back and said, 'It's for you, it's Julie.'

'Here?' He felt ridiculously guilty, and annoyed with himself for being so. Like many men, he was prudish as far as his daughter was concerned; so far, he'd preferred not to think about whether she'd correctly interpreted Alex's place in his life. Whenever they met, Alex and Julie got along fine, they seemed to understand each other very well. Sometimes he had a suspicion they were ganging up on him.

'Julie?' he said, cautiously.

'Hi, Dad! Hope you don't mind my ringing so late,' she said cheerfully. 'I tried the flat and thought maybe Alex could give you a message. I was just wondering, there's a concert in Leeds we could go to after the do on Saturday, shall I book? Everything should be over by six at the latest and you won't want to hang around talking to the relatives, will you?'

God, he thought, the wedding!

He said, 'Julie, I'll do my best, but the chances are I shan't make it – the wedding, I mean. There's something come up – it's a murder case, and I don't think there's a hope we shall be clear by Saturday. I'm sorry.'

She knew he'd forgotten. The slight pause before she answered was fractionally too long, it seemed to him, her voice when she did answer was to his ears just too light and unconcerned. Thus, and thus, and thus, the pattern of his life with Lynne. Or was he being over-sensitive? 'I'm sorry as well, Dad, but never mind – murder, that's important. Anyway, family weddings aren't exactly your scene, are they?'

He wasn't sorry actually to have the best of excuses for getting out of it. He might approve of marriage, but with scornful masculinity he hated weddings, even the wedding of a favourite niece, his sister's daughter. He was sorry, however, to rob Julie of her good intentions. It had been a gentle thought.

His daughter was in the middle of her training in catering and hotel management and had very definite ideas about one day owning her own restaurant. As part of her course she was doing a stint in a hotel in Yorkshire, and had as a consequence been seeing a lot of her northern relatives, and been involved in the preparations for her cousin's wedding.

'Maybe it's not in my line but I'd have been there if I could, you know that. Isn't there a disco thing afterwards for the younger end?'

'Yes, Dad, I'll stay on for that. I expect Aunt Isobel or someone will put me up. I'll make your excuses. And listen, don't *worry* about it, I only thought, if you were going to be at a loose end . . .'

Perhaps she wasn't feeling let down. Perhaps she was feeling quite relieved, really, that she'd be free to enjoy herself with the other young people. Perhaps it was only his own conscience, and the echoes of Lynne, and the times he'd let her down, that was bothering him.

'I'm really sorry, love, but I'll make my own excuses, thanks all the same. Look, the next weekend you're free, come home and we'll fix something up, right?'

'Right, Dad, I will, that'll be great.'

If nothing else crops up, he thought, no more murder, arson, robbery with violence, shoplifting, indecent exposure. He went back to Scarlatti and his – Alex's – armchair, his peace of mind thoroughly shattered.

As he picked up his whisky tumbler, he saw that the envelope from Bradford had gone from the mantelpiece.

CHAPTER 13

It had rained during the night. The morning had a tranquil grey coolness, the hiatus of late summer before the smoky hazes of autumn came. Kite was wearing a jacket for the first time in weeks. Mayo strode into the office, restless, impatient, demanding feedback from Forensics, not yet through.

'I'll chase them up,' Kite told him, 'but you know what they'll say. They're convinced we expect miracles.'

'And why not? A miracle's the only way we're going to get this job started, as I see it. And they've had two days, for God's sake! Never mind their tender feelings, you jump on them. Make 'em earn their keep.'

And *he* was supposed to be the impatient one! Kite deemed it wiser not to say that two days was no time at all, even by Mayo's standards. For now, it was a case of collecting facts, questioning witnesses, checking alibis until sooner or later a clear suspect with a strong enough motive would emerge. Unless this turned out to be a mindless, motiveless killing – a thing far rarer than people imagined, most murders being committed by people who knew their victim.

Kite was for once more tactful than Mayo had suggested, and as a result the forensic people were prepared to be helpful. Prints found in the house had belonged to the victim and to both her daughters; those on the chessmen corresponded with Mrs Dove's and those of Paul Fish, taken from his room. There were none anywhere belonging to Ken Dainty. But – an unidentified set had been found on the gin bottle in the sideboard and the empty one in the dustbin.

And one other fact interested Mayo very much. At the spot where the body had been found it was impossible to detect any footprints. At a little distance under the trees, however, were some deep indentations in the grass, not precise or easily identifiable because of the loose, stony nature of the soil, but consistent with, say, the high heel of a woman's shoe.

Marion Dove's white shoes, though fairly new and quite fashionable, had been low, almost flat-heeled. She had not, apparently, possessed a pair of high-heeled shoes. There were three other women whom they had interviewed, of course – but two of them were her daughters, the other her sister. Nevertheless . . .

'A woman?' Kite made a dubious face. Women were not notably stranglers. 'That's a bizarre thought!' But he knew that the possibility, however unlikely or unwelcome, couldn't be dismissed. Nothing could or indeed should be ruled out. It had been a straightforward strangulation, not, as such cases often were, accompanied by rape or sexual assault. Nor had any considerable strength been needed to kill her. Marion Dove, like Anne Boleyn, had had 'a very little neck'. A woman could easily have done it.

'Though at the moment, it's hard to see how or why.' Mayo began to tick the women off on his fingers. 'Gwen Bainbridge had had words with her. She's no spring chicken, admittedly, but she's far from decrepit. Also, she probably stands to gain from the will. Then there's Shirley Dainty – a neurotic woman with an expensive lifestyle, and hiding something, if I'm not mistaken . . .'

'She has nails an inch long, and there were no nail-marks on the neck,' Kite remarked.

'True,' Mayo agreed. 'And they can both account for the two hours in question – Mrs Bainbridge cooking the roast pork and stuffing, Mrs Dainty knocking back the G & Ts at the golf club. That leaves Rachel Dove. Of the three, she's the most problematic, the one with the best opportunity, and the least motive – if we can believe her claim not to be interested in money.'

'Is anybody?' Kite asked cynically, as Farrar knocked and put his blond head round the door, looking alert and for some reason slightly amused.

'It looks as though things are hotting up, sir. We've got a witness downstairs – the woman who looks after the donkeys on the Compsall road, a Miss Martha Witherspoon. She says she might have seen someone coming out of the lane on Sunday night.'

'Might have seen?' Mayo repeated, following Farrar down the corridor. 'Did she or didn't she?'

'Don't know, sir, she hasn't been properly questioned yet. The inspector thought you'd like to do that.' Farrar was passing the overhead fan as he spoke, and it lifted the clutch of paper in his hand. Not a hair of his blond head moved. Does he use *hair spray*? wondered Mayo, fascinated.

The reason for Farrar's amusement became clear as soon as Mayo entered the room. Miss Witherspoon, Martha, wasn't in the least what he'd expected. Someone with a name like that who cared for superannuated donkeys had prepared him for a kind of dotty Margaret Rutherford look-alike, not this tiny girl of about twenty or so with a slim, boyish figure and shining fair hair clasped at the side with a tortoiseshell slide, a face innocent of make-up. Her jeans were pressed with a crease down the centre of the leg and her spanking white T-shirt showed an almost breastless figure. She was cradling a cup of tea, the thick white china looking too heavy for her too small hands to support as she drank in a series of delicate sips.

'Now, Miss Witherspoon,' he began, feeling faintly foolish at using the inappropriate name.

'Marty,' she said, with a shy smile. 'Please call me Marty.'

'I know you've already told Inspector Atkins why you're here, er, Marty, but perhaps you wouldn't mind repeating it?'

'Oh no, not at all. Daddy warned me I should have to make a statement and I was quite prepared.' Her voice was little-girl to match her appearance. She had the hint of a lisp and her face shone with cleanliness and earnestness. She sat well back in her chair, so that her feet in their red and white trainers scarcely touched the ground. He was already beginning to find her irritating. Mainly because she was much older than he'd first thought, he was almost sure nearer thirty than twenty, and he'd no patience with anyone who refused to keep pace with their age.

'We-ell . . . I go down to the Compsall road twice a day to see to my animals, to give them food and water and things, once in the morning before I go to work –' he glanced at the particulars Farrar had taken down: Marty Witherspoon worked in the Midland Bank and lived in one of the large Victorian houses in Park Road, not far from the house where Alex had her flat – 'and once in the evening. I was quite late finishing on Sunday, I have a newcomer to my little family and he's taking time to settle down, poor thing.' The corners of her mouth turned down censoriously. 'He wasn't well-treated in his previous home and –'

'Sunday *night*, you said. What time was this?' Mayo interrupted, fearing some diatribe on animal rights. 'Do you remember?'

'Oh yes, I do, it was half past nine. It was getting quite dark and I'd promised the parents I wouldn't be late . . . Daddy usually drives me down in the evening, but they had guests on Sunday.'

'I see. So tell me what you saw.'

'I was just padlocking the gate, and I saw this man come staggering out of the entrance to the lane . . . I mean, *reeling*. I shut my flashlight off and kept very quiet and just hoped he wouldn't see me. Daddy's always warning me to be careful when I go down there alone at night. I mean, the Dog and Fox is just along the road and I assumed he'd probably come from there and was drunk.'

'But you said he'd come from the lane.'

'Oh yes, he had. But I expect he'd been – well, you know, if he'd come from the pub . . .' She wriggled in her chair and lowered her eyes modestly.

'You thought he'd been to obey a call of nature, Miss Witherspoon?' Mayo asked, despising the euphemism but resisting the temptation to be plainer.

'Mmm.'

'Which direction did he take?'

'Towards Holden Hill.'

'Would you recognise him again?'

'Oh no, I've told you it was quite dark and he was under the trees and he never turned his face towards me.'

'How was he dressed?' She shook her head helplessly. 'Tall or short, heavily built or slight? Did you get any impression of his age?'

'I really didn't notice. I got into my car rather quickly, you see, and drove off.'

'You'd see him again in your headlights, then?'

'No, because I always go the other way, the way my car's facing, and circle back into the town. It's easier than trying to turn on the Compsall road.'

'Was there a vehicle of any sort parked nearby?'

'I – don't think so.'

'But you can't be sure.'

'There wasn't when I left. There *may* have been one when I got there, there sometimes is, but I wouldn't like to swear to it . . . I'm sorry.'

Her confidence was shaken. She looked so woebegone he told her not to worry, she'd been a great help. He thanked her for her public-spirited action in coming forward, he'd contact her again if necessary. She beamed, wriggled off the chair like a child, and trotted away.

The most likely explanation of what she'd seen was most probably the right one – some drunk staggering along from the Dog and Fox rather than the murderer, unless the murder had taken place some fifteen hours later than had been thought. But by an association of ideas, he decided it wouldn't do any harm to find out where Charlie Fish had been at 9.30 on Sunday evening.

'That's a pleasure in store for you,' he told Kite as they eventually set out to drive up to the glassworks, with Kite at the wheel. 'But for now, get your skates on, Martin, I've got the inquest at half eleven and I don't want to rush this interview with Dainty.'

Ken Dainty had barely had time to open his post that morning before Rachel was shown into his office.

'Come in, sit down.'

He spoke without turning round, carefully closing and locking the two illuminated corner cabinets in the room, where the colours and lustrous textures of a magnificent collection of old glass glowed behind the panels of the doors. 'Rustle up some coffee for us, will you, Val?' he asked, and only then did he give his full attention to his sister-in-law. 'Well, what is it that's so important that you have to come down here for, Rachel? Couldn't you have seen me at home?'

'I've been trying to get you alone, ever since I came down. You were busy all day yesterday and we simply can't talk when

470

Shirley's around, the way she is. I know she's upset, but so are we all, and refusing to discuss it isn't going to make things easier.'

'Discuss what?'

'You know perfectly well what I mean. There isn't any need to pretend obtuseness with me. I've known you long enough to believe better of you than that. What are we going to tell the police about Sunday?'

'I thought we'd agreed on that, right from the first. We say nothing. That way, no one will be wiser, no one will be hurt.'

'Ken, I've been in a state of shock ever since you rang me with the news. I wouldn't otherwise have agreed to anything so morally indefensible and ultimately futile. Legally obstructive too, I shouldn't wonder.'

Ken gave a short bark of derisive laughter at the high-flown words, and she flushed as she realised how ridiculous she'd sounded. 'Wouldn't you?' he said drily. 'You were there as well, remember?'

'I spoke with the Chief Inspector yesterday, as I told you. The only reason I didn't say anything then was because I thought she'd be –'

Oh God, you had to be so careful, not only in *what* you said to Shirley but in what you said *about* her, but it was high time all that pretence was stopped. Yesterday, and her talk with Mayo, had made her see that. She'd spent a sleepless night and felt physically wretched, but had come to the decision that the hoary old skeleton in the cupboard must be brought out into the light of day. Otherwise its grisly unseen presence was going to go on disrupting all their lives, not least her own – and Josh's. It saddened her that it had taken the horror of her mother's death and a talk with Mayo, a stranger, to show her how unfair she'd been in not telling Josh the truth and letting him make his own assessments, in not allowing him to help her. In admitting that she needed help. Was it, she thought with something approaching terror, too late? Too late for her, too late for Shirley? She wondered how much, if at all,

Ken and Shirley had ever discussed the problem. Very little, she suspected, that was why they were in this mess.

At that moment the coffee came in. When it had been served and they were alone once again she determined to grasp the opportunity. 'She isn't very happy, is she, Ken?'

He didn't pretend this time not to understand who she meant. 'Shirley wouldn't be happy if you gave her the moon and wrapped the stars up with it.'

She sipped her coffee and watched him steadily. They'd never had much to say to one another, she and Shirley's husband, they operated on different wavelengths, but up to now she'd always respected him, and liked him well enough to be sorry at the change in him. He never used to be bitter. Poor Ken, who didn't try to be anything other than he was and didn't realise he was all the better for that. Who was, for all that, a dark horse.

He drained his coffee and looked pointedly at the clock on the wall. 'If that's all you've got to say, you'd better go. I've got that detective-inspector coming to see me in a few minutes.'

'In that case *you* can tell him.'

He ignored that, saying in his abrupt way, 'I've had a phone call this morning.'

'From –?'

'Yes.'

'There you are, then. What if he tells them we were there?'

'Not he. He'll be putting himself right in it if he does, don't forget. We can all testify what went on between him and Marion.'

'What did he want?'

'He says he wants what he was promised.'

She said slowly, after a moment, 'Why not? Don't we have a moral obligation? My mother *did* intend him having something, after all. It was only his attitude that made her so reluctant to say so definitely. That – and what you'd told her, I suppose. She was always like that – if you tried to push her, she dug her heels in all the more.'

His head had jerked up and he stared at her in uncomprehending silence as she spoke. He thought how plain she looked this morning, colourless. She'd always been one whose looks depended on her moods and feelings. When she was happy, she was lit up and looked nearly beautiful. Today the lamp burned very low, she was turned right down. He'd heard Shirley say there was a man, up there at Northumbria. Well, good luck to him! Rachel wasn't a gift he'd wish on anybody. 'Like hell we will,' he said. 'And aren't you forgetting something? What if he killed her?'

'Did he, though? Did he, Ken?' Her steady, unwavering gaze fixed itself on his face, his truculent pose across the desk, arms folded, head lowered, like an angry bull looking over a fence.

'I'm not sure I understand what you're getting at,' he said, dangerously quiet. 'What's that supposed to mean?'

'Well, don't let's pretend you wouldn't do just about *anything* for your old glassworks, shall we?' she said, suddenly hostile, moving her arm in a sweeping gesture that encompassed the yard outside and the glowing cabinets in the corner, and five hundred years of family history, pride and arrogance. 'What you did to my mother – that was cruel, and it proves what I mean. It's an obsession with you, just as it became an obsession with her. It seems you get like that when you marry into this family.'

His face was suffused with temper. 'That is so bloody stupid,' he said, enunciating each word carefully, 'it doesn't need an answer.'

Her own anger flared up. 'The whole thing's stupid! We should have told the truth in the first place. I'm supposed to be making a signed statement to the police, and I'm certainly not prepared to put my name to a load of downright lies. I shall tell them he was there.'

'Don't do that,' he said, his voice suddenly cold. 'Not before you think a lot more carefully about it. If we start changing our story now, they'll think we really have got something to hide. We say nothing. You say not one word, is that clear? Right, then – end of story.'

CHAPTER 14

Half-running across the car park towards a silver Peugeot in the far corner when they arrived at Dove's Glass was a woman Mayo instantly recognised as Rachel Dove.

'That's her – the younger daughter I saw yesterday at The Mount!'

They followed her progress with interest, a young woman obviously in a fair old temper. A hundred yards of car park couldn't disguise the fury. It seemed Rachel Dove might have inherited her mother's level gaze but not her calm temperament. The set of her head and shoulders showed it, the swift angry flick of her skirt as she got into the driving seat, the quick reverse and the speed with which she shot out of the car park. Mayo wasn't sure whether she'd noticed their car or not, but it didn't matter. He wasn't yet ready to see her again.

They found Kenneth Dainty dusting the contents of the top shelf of a tall, illuminated glass-fronted cabinet, one of two in the corners of his office. He greeted them with a faintly embarrassed nod and a quick excuse for the duster in his hand. 'Won't be long. Always see to this myself, you have to take it slow, see. Just the job for lowering the blood pressure, they tell me.'

'Please carry on, we're in no particular hurry.' Not true at all, but truth was an expendable commodity in the interests of achieving cooperation, which might not in the circumstances be easy if Rachel Dove had left Dainty in a condition where he needed calming down – which might well be the case. Mayo had an idea that she could be a very unsettling young woman if she chose.

It *was* Dainty she'd been to see. On his desk were two empty coffee cups. The air held a faint evocation of the scent she used, sophisticated yet romantic, sharp, with hints of rose: a surprising choice, though perhaps someone else had chosen it for her, someone who knew her better than she knew herself.

It was hard to tell whether the anger he'd sensed in her was reciprocated in Ken Dainty. His appearance was much as it had been the only other time Mayo had seen him, tough, uncommunicative, facing the world with his own brand of head-down truculence, frowning with concentration as he completed his task.

'You've a pretty good collection of glass there, Mr Dainty.'

'Not bad, I suppose.' But Dainty's expression lightened. 'You interested?'

Mayo nodded. He was moderately interested in the glass but more intrigued by the way the big man's hands caressed each fragile object as he replaced it precisely. 'What are these little things here?'

'You'll very likely have seen them in the local antique shops, sir,' Kite offered.

'And ridiculous prices they ask for them, too!' Dainty intervened.

'I knew an old man used to work here and he'd make them for us when we were kids. Aren't they called friggers, Mr Dainty?'

'That's right, they are.' They were apprentice pieces, he explained, or bits of spare-time nonsense made from waste glass. 'Blown scores myself, in my time,' he said. But he reckoned most of those in the cabinet went back further than that. They were charming little specimens of the glassmaker's art, objects ranging through minute replicas of umbrellas, swans, a pair of tiny bellows and a miniature pump, complete with bucket, to a fully-rigged sailing ship. He didn't trust them into his audience's hands, doubtless believing, quite wrongly, they wouldn't exercise the necessary care, not knowing Mayo's expertise with the tiniest of watch and clock parts.

'If you want to see something really old, though, take a look at these.' He opened the twin cabinet in the opposite corner, and began to explain with mounting enthusiasm the various pieces of glass and their origins – Rhenish and Bohemian glass, English flintglass, beakers and rummers, posset pots and goblets, greenish bottles made iridescent by time and weather, enamelled and cameo glass, soda glass, cranberry and Bristol opaque . . . He brought himself up short. 'Sorry, once you start collecting it gets you, like a virus.'

Mayo waved a deprecatory hand. 'Worth a fair amount, I expect?'

'Can't say I've ever totted it up, but likely it's worth a bob or two. But if you're talking of *value* . . . this is what you should be looking at. Not in money terms maybe, but there's other sorts. It's only a fragment broken off one of the pots used to melt the glass – if you look, you can still see some of the vitrified metal on the side – but it must be about four or five hundred years old. It came from one of the original furnaces in the Darney Forest in Lorraine.'

He picked up, and this time handed to Mayo, what looked like nothing more than a piece of jagged grey rock but was really, he explained, a lump of grainy rock-hard clay to which was bonded an eighth of an inch layer of glass, translucent, bluish-green, the colour of sea water.

'They were making this sort of glass as far back as the fifteenth century and before, our ancestors over there. There was a mystique about making glass in those days – and a lot of superstition. Folks thought it was black magic, but I don't suppose the old lads cared, why should they? They were gentlemen glassmakers, they owned lands and property, they had titles to their name. All had to be left behind, of course.'

'What brought them over here?'

'Oh, religious persecution among other things.' They had been Huguenots, he said, and had come to England at the royal request of Queen Elizabeth, to revive her dying glass industry, first to the Sussex Weald, then later, when they had been forced to start using coal for their furnaces, to Stourbridge. At that time they'd been mainly manufacturers of broadglass, made by blowing a big cylinder of glass metal and then splitting it open to form a square which was afterwards cut into quarries – the little squares seen in old lattice windows. 'I'm a practical glassmaker myself and I can tell you that must have been heavy work, swinging and working a hot bulb of molten glass weighing several pounds –' Dainty stopped abruptly, the animation leaving his face. 'I'm talking too much. Glassmaking's been my life, I get carried away.'

'No, no, please go on.' By this time Mayo's curiosity was aroused. It was a fallacy, he thought, to believe that people were necessarily boring when they talked shop – especially when it was their all-consuming passion. He'd known otherwise dull and tedious people suddenly become fascinating when speaking of what was overridingly important to them. It was enlightening to have seen what motivated this man, what might release that controlled force one could sense just under the surface. He could see Kite also looking at Dainty with speculative interest, and wondered if he too, had noticed how the other man had spoken of 'our' ancestors, quite unself-consciously. Meaning perhaps the whole race of glassmakers, or simply the Dove family, with whom he had apparently so wholeheartedly identified himself? Whichever, passion had been there when he spoke and when he handled the glass, and where there is passion, there is single-mindedness, often a refusal to admit any other point of view, sometimes a ruthlessness in achieving the desired object, Mayo thought.

'On the contrary,' he said, 'you've whetted my appetite. I'd like to see the manufacturing process some time, if that wouldn't be too disruptive.'

'No problem – the men are used to it, they'll take no notice. We don't often take parties round, but there's always some individual or other interested in seeing what goes on. We used to call on Marion regularly whenever necessary, she really enjoyed acting as guide. Just let me know when you're ready,' he finished abruptly. He waved them to a couple of seats. 'I've wasted enough of your time. What did you want to see me about?' Assuming what is

477

generally regarded as the dominant position in the chair behind the desk, his guarded expression as he asked the question nevertheless suggested he felt the desk more of an entrenchment or a barricade put between them.

Mayo had no intention of being rushed. He settled himself comfortably and asked whether they had ever thought of expanding.

'No, not really. There's always a ready market for the traditional ware we make. We don't make anything very fancy nowadays. We have our lines, top-quality lead crystal with mostly traditional patterns, and we stick to them. Run of the mill stuff. We have as much as we can cope with. We're only a small firm, not like the big boys over in Stourbridge.'

It sounded a fairly mechanical answer, and didn't square with what Bainbridge had hinted yesterday. Mayo said, 'When I spoke to your offfice manager yesterday, I rather gathered you had some future plans, though.'

'I'd like to do some reorganisation, yes, starting with the offices. As I told you the other day, we're short of space, and I want to computerise the accounts when Robert Bainbridge goes. He runs the place efficiently enough at the moment, but it's too much in his head. When he goes, we could be in dead trouble if we don't watch it. We need to reorganise the factory, too – not the manufacturing process, that's still basically the same as it always was – but the buildings are a shambles. They've been patched up for so long, there's nothing for it but to start again . . .'

'What did Mrs Dove think of all this?'

'She was coming round.'

'That means she *hadn't* altogether agreed?'

'No, that's right – but my mother-in-law was inclined to put things off. She'd do anything sometimes rather than make her mind up, and you couldn't budge her. But I knew it was just a matter of patience.' Dainty looked pointedly at his watch.

Mayo said, 'I've just one more question, sir.'

478

'Yes?' The curt monosyllable couldn't hide the sudden tension that radiated from him, the wariness that sprang to his eyes.

'I've spoken with Mr Crytch this morning about Mrs Dove's will. I believe he's made it known to you that you were the principal beneficiary in Mrs Dove's will. Were you aware of this?'

'Of course.' Dainty smiled for the first time that morning. His shoulders almost visibly sagged. He'd been expecting a question, but not that. Whatever he'd been afraid of, it wasn't the police knowing that he would now, through the death of his wife's mother, be a considerably richer man.

The will had in fact been brief and unsurprising. There had been several small bequests, and ten thousand pounds for Paul Fish on his eighteenth birthday, without conditions attached. Jubilee Cottage had been left to Mrs Bainbridge, plus a generous annuity. Equal shares in the glassworks were left to her daughters, plus The Mount and the residue of her estate to be shared between them. But the majority holding in Dove's Glass was to go to Kenneth Dainty. Which might well be seen as a will heavily weighted in favour of the Daintys, as husband and wife. But perhaps Rachel had meant it, when she said she didn't care about money.

Mayo stood up. 'We won't keep you any longer, sir. You've got to be at the inquest like me at eleven-thirty, and you'll have things to do.'

'Is that all you want?' Relief mingled with Dainty's evident surprise.

'Yes, sir, that's all,' said Mayo blandly. 'Thank you for your time.'

They left the building and Mayo waited impatiently for Kite, lingering behind, to join him in the car. 'What kept you?' he asked as the sergeant eventually slid in beside him.

'It was that girl, Valerie. She's had something on her mind that she feels she ought to tell us. She nearly told you yesterday but she was too scared.'

'Scared, of me?' Mayo wasn't sure whether or not he entirely welcomed the idea that he was less approachable than Kite.

'She feels as though she's being disloyal, telling tales, but anyway she told me that Mrs Dainty came in on Friday and she overheard some sort of quarrel between her and Dainty – more correctly, it appears it was Dainty who was doing the shouting, and he stopped when she went in, but she's sure they'd been arguing. Mrs Dove looked upset and he was red in the face. And she quite distinctly heard the name of Steven mentioned.'

The inquest went as expected. Dainty was called to give evidence of identification, medical evidence as to the cause of death was produced and the coroner, as was usual in such circumstances, adjourned the inquest for further police enquiries. The Press got a statement from Mayo which amounted to very little, but had to be satisfied with it.

Afterwards, he crossed the Cornmarket and went to the Red Lion where he had arranged to meet Kite for lunch, for no other reason than because it was usually less crowded than the Saracen's. He had barely seated himself before a hand touched his shoulder. Dr Ison said, 'I was told I should find you here.'

'Henry, have you come to join us for lunch?'

'I don't eat lunch,' Ison said virtuously, looking pointedly at the locally made faggots, mushy peas and chips which was the Red Lion's idea of gourmet food. Mayo ignored the look. As an occasional one-off, the meal wasn't going to put him in his box. In fact it was very tasty.

'You'll have a drink, though?' he asked. 'What would you like?'

'I'd like a scotch but I'll have a non-alcoholic lager, please.'

Ison in his most irritating mood, Mayo reflected. When Kite returned with the lager, remarking that he didn't know how the doctor could drink it, he said blandly, pointing his pipe stem at Kite's half of bitter, 'You can get used to it, son. Better than that stuff you're drinking. Thickens your blood and gums up your arteries, that does. Stick to whisky, and your blood'll pour like the best claret through your veins. Cheers!'

'What can we do for you?' Mayo asked. 'You don't usually honour us with your presence at lunch.'

'No, but there's something about Marion Dove I think you might like to know, I remembered it just as I was getting into my car a few minutes ago. There's something been niggling me ever since she was found and then suddenly it came to me, just like that, you know how it does. It may not be of any significance, of course, being so long ago, but on the other hand . . .'

'Anything's welcome at this stage.'

'That's what I thought.' Ison fiddled with the pipe he had substituted for the cigarettes he had renounced on the premise that by the time it was lit the desire had gone.

'Get to the point, Henry.'

'All right, all right, don't rush me, I've had a trying morning. The thing is, Marion Dove's been my patient a long time, but when I first joined the practice, that was in 1953, she was still under old Dr Wade, the senior partner. When he retired I took over his list, and that was when she became my patient. Before that, I only had occasion to see her once, when Doc Wade had 'flu and I was standing in for him.' The pipe well alight, he leaned back. 'She was expecting a child at the time and I was called out because she was haemorrhaging slightly and there were obviously fears of a miscarriage. I did what I could, kept her in bed and so on and all was well as it turned out. I'd forgotten all about it until now.'

'What's the connection?'

'The point is, it was her first child she was supposed to be having. I knew immediately that this was rubbish, of course, as any doctor would. But I also knew she hadn't been married long, and if that was how she wanted it to appear and Doc Wade was going along with it, it wasn't my business to upset the apple-cart. One of the first things a doctor learns is to keep his mouth shut.'

481

'When did she have this baby – the first, I mean?'

'It wasn't noted on her records. I assume that may be because she didn't have the child here, in Lavenstock. Was she away in the forces during the war?'

'Her sister was. I'll have it checked, but I had the impression Marion had stayed at home – she may have been on war work or something.'

'It'll be the usual story, you'll see, father not able to marry her. A lot of that sort of thing happened in the war – but that didn't make it any better for the poor girls, being an unmarried mother was a scandal folks would do anything to hush up, especially if they were strong chapel-goers, as I believe the Waldrons were. Mind you, it doesn't necessarily mean she *was* unmarried. For all I know, she may have been married before, but then why the secrecy? Anyway, that's your problem. I just thought you'd like to know.'

'Yes, indeed. Thank you, Henry. It's very interesting.' The doctor nodded, drank up and knocked out his pipe. Mayo put down his knife and fork and pushed his plate away. 'Before you go.' He hesitated, wondering whether to chance it with Ison, then decided he'd nothing to lose and reminded Ison what he'd said about Shirley Dainty being a neurotic woman. 'Just how neurotic is she?'

'Hm.' Ison looked at him consideringly for a while before answering. 'Let's say I've been treating her for eight or nine years.'

'For what?'

'Come on, Gil, you ought to know better than that! What I told you about Marion can't hurt her, she's dead. Breaching my living patients' confidence is another thing.'

'It may be important, Henry. It won't go any further, you know that.'

'It won't because I won't tell you. She has every right to demand privacy in this respect. Moreover, it's my considered opinion that her condition has nothing whatever to do with the enquiries you're pursuing,' Ison said pompously.

And with that, Mayo had to be content. After Ison had left he sat looking reflectively into his beer, thinking about what he'd just been told. 'What would you do if you found you were terminally ill, Martin?'

'I'd want to see my kids and Sheila provided for, check up on her pension rights, make sure the insurance was up to date and so on,' Kite said with unwonted sobriety. 'Square my conscience, too, I suppose. If we're talking about Marion Dove, it's possible she might have felt she had to do the right thing by this illegitimate child, see him OK in her will . . . but my God, that would really put the cat among the pigeons, wouldn't it?'

'Very probably,' said Mayo slowly. 'In more ways than one.'

Kite didn't have the imagination Mayo had, but he caught on quickly, and the possibility enlarged as he surveyed it. 'We really have to find this Steven, don't we? – incidentally, I rang Dove's and there's no Steven on the payroll – though wouldn't he have more reason for wanting her alive, at least until she'd changed her will, rather than wanting to kill her?'

All the same, they had to find Steven, whoever he was, more especially after what Ison had told them, Mayo knew. He was perhaps making too much out of a name scribbled on the back of a till receipt, but he didn't really believe that. It could have been anybody's name, something totally dissociated with what had happened, someone coming to see her about decorating her bathroom, for instance, or something equally trivial. The note need not even have been referring to that particular Sunday, though there had been no date indicative of which future Sunday it might be. Much more likely in Mayo's mind was the idea that the events that combine to make what is called coincidence were all part of a pattern, one which had on that day led to murder. And that the mysterious Steven was an essential part of this pattern.

CHAPTER 15

Mayo banged loudly for the second time with Mrs Bainbridge's shining brass doorknocker, then stepped back and gazed speculatively at the closed, gleaming sash windows before turning away and getting into his car. He was just about to click in his seat-belt when the door of the next house opened and a young, miniskirted woman emerged, pushing a pram on to the pavement towards him, waving him to stop.

'Hello, I heard you knocking next door. If you want Mrs Bainbridge, she's gone back in to work. Betty's, down Holden Hill Road, d'you know it?'

'Thanks – I do,' Mayo told her, switching on the engine.

'You the police?'

'Now what makes you think that, love?'

'You must be joking! Well, if you do see her, tell her the telephone's been ringing half the day, somebody wants to get hold of her urgent by the sound of it. If she'd left me a key like she usually does, I could've answered it, couldn't I, but I expect she forgot, what with everything. Terrible about her sister, isn't it?'

These little houses, you could hear everything. Television, telephone. Babies crying. Family rows. He thanked the girl again, and drove off down the street and eased into the grinding traffic of Holden Hill Road. 'Betty's' was a small shop with only one front window, not far from the confectioner's shop where he'd had tea with Rachel Dove, and he had to park round the corner in a side street. When he returned Mrs Bainbridge was in the window, pinning a slim, coyly-posed model with a winsome face and outdated bouffant hairstyle into a dress of matronly proportions. The bell clanged as he pushed open the door, and when she looked up and saw him, she backed out immediately, careful not to disturb the other figures modestly draped in cotton sheets.

'Is it Paul, have you found him?'

He had to tell her they were still looking and watch her face settle into disappointment. But when he passed on the message about the ringing telephone, she brightened. 'That'll be him,' she said at once, 'I knew he wouldn't just disappear, like that.'

'Did he ever mention a girl to you, a girl called Katie Lazenby?'

'No, he never talked about girls, not to me.'

'It looks as though they might have gone off together.'

She looked first astonished, then relieved. 'Well, that's more natural – more likely than running away because he killed Marion. I told you there was nothing wrong with Paul. Not that he's done right, mind, if that's what it is.'

'There's still the question of your Visa card.'

'Which he'll have to answer to me for when I see him . . . if he *has* taken it.' She was still unwilling to believe that of him. 'Give him time, he's sure to turn up.'

Not necessarily, Mayo thought, but he didn't feel it incumbent upon himself to disillusion her by saying so. If Paul wanted to disappear, he could. If he were determined enough, strong enough. Afraid enough.

'I've something else I'd like to talk to you about, Mrs Bainbridge, if you could spare me a few minutes.'

'As long as you like,' she said, turning the card on the door from Open to Closed, remarking that nobody else except her employer would expect customers today anyway, when everyone else around kept half day. She showed him into a small windowless room, part store-room, part kitchenette, at the back. Among a stack of cardboard boxes spilling tissue paper two little chairs, relegated to the back premises presumably on account of their chipped gold paint and rubbed silk seats, were squashed into the tiny space, together with a small flap table hinged to the wall, with an electric kettle on it, two mugs and a teapot under a cosy.

'There's some tea brewed.'

Having declined the offer, and congratulating himself on his prudence when he saw the caustic nature of what she poured out for herself, Mayo gingerly lowered his large frame on to one of the fragile chairs before approaching his reason for being there. She sat opposite him, elbows on the table, the uncompromising fluorescent strip light overhead revealing lines on her face that grew visibly more taut as she listened to what he had to say. She heard him out, not interrupting. When he'd finished, however, she took him up with angry impatience.

'Haven't we enough to put up with just now, without you raking all that muck up?'

'Murder's a dirty business. Nobody can have any secrets, not even the dead.'

Especially the dead.

'It's past and gone. It can't have anything to do with what happened to her.'

He said patiently, 'You must know that's not necessarily true. Your sister's been murdered and there's nothing about her life we can leave uninvestigated until we've found out why.'

'What d'you expect me to say? You know all there is to know. She had a baby without being married. She wasn't the first and she won't be the last neither. Except nowadays they get rid and no disgrace if they don't want them.'

'Listen, Mrs Bainbridge. There was a baby, that much we know. What we need now is more detail – and you're the person who can most easily fill us out.'

'And if I don't?'

'You'd be wiser to do so. I can't force you, of course, but we *can* find out from other sources, and they mightn't be so discreet.'

She bit her lip. She was more upset than he'd imagined she would be. She knew about gossip and what it could do, and was dismayed, which surprised him, though perhaps it shouldn't have. Natural enough, he supposed, to want a family scandal hushed up, but who would really care, forty-odd years later? She was more concerned with her position in the community than he'd supposed.

He gave her time to think over what he'd said and in the end she gave in, albeit unwillingly, making him wonder at her sudden antagonism. When he'd questioned her before, she'd been upset, but cooperative, now she seemed actively hostile. 'All right. It doesn't look as though I've much choice, does it? But I don't know much, and that's the truth. I was in the WAAF when all that happened.'

'Let's start with what you do know. To begin with, can you remember the date the baby was born?'

After a moment's thought, she said it would have been early in 1944, probably about March. She had come home on leave herself in late April, and it was all over by then, Marion was back home.

It seemed that Ison had been correct in surmising the child hadn't been born here, and Mrs Bainbridge confirmed this when he spoke the thought aloud. 'Of course it wasn't! They'd concocted a story about her having some sort of nervous breakdown – the after-effects of the bomb on Chapel Street it was supposed to be. They sent her away to our aunt near Wolverhampton to convalesce. Who did they think they were kidding, her not even home for my wedding? But it saved everybody's face. It would have killed our Mum to have it out in the open, not to mention my Dad. Little Marion, good as gold, quiet as a mouse – I reckon if it'd been me nobody would have been all that surprised, just because I liked a good time, though they'd have been wrong, for all that.'

She pushed away her empty mug and scraped her chair back, swinging her legs round, preparing to get up. They were nice legs for her age, as he'd noticed before, and she was evidently not unaware of the fact. Her tights were sheer and her patent court shoes had high heels. 'Well, that's about it, then. That's all you need to know.'

'Not quite. What happened to the baby?'

'Adopted, of course. Abortions weren't ten a penny then!'

'Was it a boy or girl?'

'I have no idea,' she said, looking at her watch, 'and if that's all, I'd better get the shop opened again.'

'Just a minute, I haven't quite finished yet. What about your aunt's name and address –'

'I don't even know if she's still alive! She must be a hundred if she is.'

'All the same . . .'

Reluctantly, she told him. 'It was Copley. Edith Copley. She wasn't really our aunt, only our mother's best friend. She was a district nurse, went to live near Wolverhampton when she got married. I don't remember her address, but Marion used to write to her at one time, I think.'

'That'll be a start, thanks.' The address book that had been in the locked drawer in the bedroom might give them the answer. 'Just one more thing, but the most important.' He paused. 'Are you going to tell me who the father was?'

She eyed him sardonically. 'Am I going to tell you what? Well, maybe I would if I knew – but that's what we all wanted to know, didn't we, and wild horses wouldn't drag it out of her. She wouldn't let on, not even to me, though I could've helped her. I *would* have, poor kid. That's all she was, a kid. Seventeen.' She stared at the chipped varnish on her thumbnail for a while, hesitated then said suddenly, 'It was Wesley Dove, of course.'

'*Wesley Dove?* The man she later married?'

'It stands to reason. She'd started working at Dove's when she left school. Maybe she was flattered he paid her attention, I don't know. He was handsome enough in those days,' she admitted grudgingly, 'but he was married, though his wife was sickly and he always had an eye for – for a pretty face,' she ended lamely.

'Don't you mean for a young girl?'

Her lips tightened. 'How d'you get to know about that?'

'Oh, we hear things. But isn't it unlikely she'd want to marry the man who'd given her such a hard time? Unless you mean there'd been something between them all along?'

'No, I don't! Like I told you before, it's something I've never been able to work out, why she married him, of all people, when she'd plenty other chances – and turned them all down. All I do know is she suddenly realised she wanted another child, she told me she'd never be rid of the ghost of the other until she did. That was the sort of thing she sometimes said, out of the blue, so you didn't know how to answer. By then Wesley's wife was dead and Marion had got to be his secretary, and what I think is she saw her chances and reckoned she'd a right to something from him, after all she'd been through.'

It was possible, he supposed. Marion had been sixteen when she found she was pregnant, the age Wesley apparently preferred a girl to be. And what Gwen Bainbridge saw as her reasons for marrying him later was only confirmation of what Rachel Dove had told him.

'If he *was* the father, then that,' he said gently, 'sounds suspiciously like a form of blackmail.'

'Oh no! You'd have to have known Marion to understand. She wasn't vengeful. Never that. But subtle,' she said, as if surprised that such a word had come to mind.

He put the next question in the expectation of getting a short answer, or none at all, and wasn't therefore surprised at her reaction. When he asked if either of Marion's daughters had known about this other child, her skin flushed a dull, dark red. 'They do not – and I hope you won't go letting on! Especially to Shirley.'

He could make no such promise. 'We may have to,' he had to insist. 'But why especially not Mrs Dainty? What's wrong with her?'

She looked very much as though she regretted her outburst, closing her lips with the stubbornness he was coming to see might well be a family trait. It had more than once been remarked so far during the investigation that Marion Dove had been stubborn, not to be moved, but he too was prepared to sit this one out. There had been too many dark hints about Shirley Dainty and her obviously neurotic condition. He waited, letting the silence lengthen, and finally unable to stand it any longer, she gave in.

'Oh, Shirley's all right. I get impatient with her, that's all. She had a bit of trouble a few years back, after little Michael was born, and I just think it's time she pulled herself together, but I wouldn't want to go upsetting her, for all that. She's had a lot to go through.'

His kept his expression carefully non-committal, and with a sigh she poured herself another cup of tea, and, thus prepared, told him.

'Post-natal depression? Sergeant Thomson's wife had that, but it didn't last for ten years!' Atkins said.

'Nor did Mrs Dainty's,' Ison responded sharply. 'Her case is somewhat different.' He had called in at the station on a small matter of routine connected with the autopsy report and found himself involved, willy-nilly, in the discussion. He looked mightily as though he wished himself elsewhere. His face had deepened with disapproval when Mayo told him what he had learned from Gwen Bainbridge.

'We can take it as fact?' Mayo asked.

'Oh yes, it's true enough. She called me out one night in a terrible state. She was terrified of what she might do – what she might even have already done . . . she was in such a condition of collapse she couldn't even remember. I examined the child but I could find no evidence of any physical abuse. I believe she cried for help just in time . . . she had excellent treatment, she got over it.'

Kite was doodling on the pad in front of him. 'It can be hell, a baby who cries all the time,' he said slowly, looking up. 'Daniel was like that for a while, never seemed to stop, for no reason we could ever find out. They go on and on and there are times when you feel as though you'd do *anything* to stop them and get a good night's sleep.'

'Only most people don't,' Mayo said.

'Most people don't have the background she had,' Ison retorted. 'And anyway, she *didn't* harm the child. The nervous condition she suffers from is something quite different.'

'We all know about her background, we know her father was a violent man – maybe he used violence on her as a child.' Ison didn't reply. 'I don't want to push you further than you feel you've a right to go, Henry, but tell me this: Is she potentially dangerous?'

'I don't know what you mean by that. Things are rarely if ever so clear-cut.'

'It'll make it clearer. Is her mental condition such that she would be capable of murder in certain circumstances?'

'Gil, I'm a GP, not a psychiatrist! Besides, that's a hypothetical question. You're really wanting my personal opinion as to whether she murdered her mother, and – very well, the answer's no. I believe the two incidents are entirely different and quite unrelated – but your own opinion would be just as valid. I'll ask you: Do you think she did?'

'I'm keeping my options open,' Mayo said shortly. He wouldn't, whatever happened, let his compassion blind him.

Marion Dove's address book had been searched through in vain for the name Steven, as Christian or surname, but when Mayo looked through it this time, he met with instant success.

'Here we are, Martin, Mrs Edith Copley!'

The address was an old people's home near Wolverhampton. A telephone call by Kite established that she was still there and an appointment made for him to see her the next day.

CHAPTER 16

Geoffrey Crytch's secretary was a Mrs Lorne, of the breed which always seem to see their mission in life as being one which necessitates at all costs preventing anyone but themselves from having easy access to their employer. She informed Mayo with great pleasure that he'd just missed Mr Crytch, who'd left for home five minutes before. He was lucky to have caught *her*, she was on the points of locking up, and no, she added firmly, she didn't think Mr Crytch would be willing to see Chief Inspector Mayo at home. He'd had a very busy day. Why not make an appointment for tomorrow?

'Because I want to see him tonight!' Mayo had a short, sharp way of dealing with people like her, and Crytch wasn't the only one who'd been pressed that day. Over the indignant bridling that followed, he said, 'Don't bother, Mrs Lorne, I'll make my own arrangements with him.'

Crytch had already arrived home when he telephoned and was about to have his dinner in half an hour, but agreed to see Mayo who promised he wouldn't keep him longer than that.

Kite, meanwhile, was on his way to the Dog and Fox. There were only a couple of cars as yet in the car park when he arrived, neither registration less than ten years old. An elderly bull terrier that might have been the progenitor of Charlie Fish's Caesar and a hundred others like him sat militantly by the door, a watchful, heavyweight Cerberus guarding the gates of Hades. Kite was allowed in and hoped he'd get out without losing a piece of his trousers.

The public bar looked as though it hadn't been redecorated since the Festival of Britain, the coco matting on the floor threatened to trip the unwary, the wallpaper pattern hadn't been visible for decades and the ceiling was pickled a rich brown from tobacco smoke. Two elderly men sat drinking Guinness beside a fireplace that contained nothing but a hopeless arrangement of tired plastic daffodils in a red glass vase. The landlord, Jim Littlebank, was at the bar in a washed-out navy sweatshirt that did nothing for his complexion or his figure. A silence fell as Kite entered. The police were known here and not liked, for manifold reasons. Kite ordered his half-pint (one of the reasons: they rarely drank more than halves), took it over to a corner table and opened his evening paper.

When he'd managed to down half his beer he folded the paper and went to the bar to begin his questions. 'Police,' he said, showing his card. The two customers began a game of dominoes.

'The fuzz, Rita,' the landlord repeated to his wife. She laughed.

Kite gave her a look which suddenly made her busy herself with arranging the bottles behind the bar. She was Ruby Deacon's sister, and neither had much to crow about over the other.

The landlord's memory was short, his willingness to cooperate negligible, this being the second time the police had questioned him, the first time being in the course of their house to house enquiries. No, he disremembered Charlie Fish being in the pub any time on Sunday. On the other hand he might have been. He was so much a part of the furniture it was hard to say, especially when you were crowded. Very crowded they always were, weekends.

'What do they come for?' Kite asked. 'It can't be the beer.'

'What's wrong with the beer?'

'It's flat,' Kite said, and went out.

Cerberus stood up and saw him suspiciously off the premises. It hadn't been the most successful interview he'd ever conducted, Kite reckoned, and the beer was sour on his stomach. He sat in the driving seat and stared round at the desolate landscape spread before him. Even in the golden hanging stillness of the furry-lit September evening it couldn't escape grimness. Even the knackered ponies in the field, cropping desultorily, seemed to have lost

493

heart. He followed their progress, his eye coming to rest on the deserted brickworks three or four fields away, random and forlorn.

For a while, he let his thoughts wander, then suddenly something clicked and he jumped up as if scalded. That was it! He grinned and buckled on his seat-belt and put the key in the ignition. A slight noise made him look round. Long red nails like talons dipped in blood were scratching on the glass. The publican's wife, Rita Littlebank, was peering in at the window, her face distorted in an effort to gain his attention. He wound the window down and her scent invaded the car, not cheap scent either, but too much of it, musky and heavy.

'Here,' she said, with a nervous glance over her shoulder, 'don't you go thinking Charlie Fish did that there murder, 'cause he never did. That's what you was on about, wasn't it?'

'And how would you know he didn't, missis?'

''Cause I know where he was on Sunday night, see.' She added unnecessarily, with a jerk of her head towards the pub, 'He don't like you lot, he wouldn't give you the time of day, but he don't like Charlie Fish, neither, that's why he wouldn't say one way nor another.'

'Who's talking about Sunday night, just?'

'I am, aren't I? Because she was here on Sunday, about six, and Charlie was – well, he was down my sister Ruby's then. I know, I'd just left him there, and he stayed all night.'

Kite said, 'Let's get this straight. *Who* was here?'

'I mean *she* was here, Mrs Dove, in the car park, sitting in a red Sierra. She was with a young feller, good-looking chap, he went inside while she waited for him in the car.'

Kite sat and looked at her, flashily dressed, her face raddled with too much make-up, but good-natured enough. He didn't think she was lying. 'How well did you know her?'

'If you're thinking I could've been mistaken, I wasn't. I knew her right enough, I used to work in the canteen up at Dove's, one time. Nice lady, she was, and anyhow, we spoke to one another. I said good evening and she asked me how I was. I didn't stop, Jim'd already opened and I knew he'd be mad at me for being late. The young feller came out with a bottle of gin in his hands as I went in and they drove off.'

'What time was this?'

'Just after six – about ten past.'

'Why didn't you tell us this when we called round making enquiries?'

'I wasn't here, was I? I'd gone shopping.'

She could have let them know, all the same. But better late than never.

'Well, thanks, m'duck. Pop into the station and make it all official-like tomorrow, will you?'

'All right, but I don't want no thanks. Just, I don't want Charlie Fish blamed for somethink he didn't do. We used to be good mates once. He's a boozy old sod now, but you should've seen him when he was eighteen!'

Kite drove straight down to Milford Road and went immediately up to Mayo's office, but by that time Mayo had already left some time ago to see Geoffrey Crytch. After a moment's thought, he picked up the phone and had an interesting conversation with the person at the other end.

The Crytch home was a spacious and pleasant Edwardian villa in a quiet cul-de-sac within walking distance of the town centre. Mayo had left his car at the station, but was there within five minutes. There was no nameplate on the door, but he recalled that Laura Crytch was in partnership with several other doctors at the medical centre in the town. She answered his ring herself and showed him into a comfortably furnished room at the back of the house, where Crytch was seated at a grand piano playing Chopin and drinking sherry. The wide glazed doors stood open to a long garden with a manicured lawn and glowing three-dimensional flowerbeds throwing long shadows in the golden evening light, framed by conifers of artfully varied form and colour.

Mrs Crytch was a tall woman, many years younger than her husband, with straight brown hair and a wide, lovely smile that beautified otherwise unremarkable features. She herself saw Mayo supplied with sherry and then after a few moments' conversation made excuses with commendable tact about seeing to the dinner and left him alone with her husband. Crytch's eyes followed her as she left the room.

'I won't keep you very long, sir.'

The other man apologised for stipulating only half an hour for the meeting. 'It's Laura's day off, y'see, and we've a free evening for once. She's not on call and all the girls are away so I've none of this confounded ferrying here, there and everywhere to do. Bought Jennifer, our second, a car for her birthday, but the others still have me on a bit of string.' He smiled indulgently. There was a photograph of him, surrounded by a bevy of women, his wife and his four pretty daughters, on the table beside him. They could almost have been daughter and granddaughters. He added more soberly, 'Have you found anything new – about Marion? I take it that's why you want to see me.'

'We've come across something which may possibly have some connection, and yes, I think you might be able to help us .

'Oh?' Mayo felt that a distinct wariness had entered his tone.

'We've found out she had a child, long before she married Wesley Dove, whom we're trying to trace. We think she may have intended changing her will to include him. Is that likely in your view?'

Crytch's response was unexpected. His fair-skinned, already pink complexion became further suffused, and then the flush faded, leaving his skin mottled and unhealthy-looking. He gulped down the rest of his drink. 'I – I don't know whether that was so or not. She didn't say so to me.'

'But you guessed it might be . . . an educated guess? Did you perhaps know about this child?'

'No, I –' Crytch picked up his glass, found it empty, looked round rather desperately for the decanter and poured another. Both his acquired lawyer's caution and his own natural *savoir-faire* seemed to have deserted him. 'Oh God, yes. That is, there were rumours.'

Mayo suddenly understood. 'The child was yours.'

'No! I don't know. It – it could have been.'

Abruptly he jumped up and despite the warmth of the evening, closed the doors to the garden, shutting out the sweet, heavy evening scent of a white-flowered shrub near the door that Mayo couldn't identify, as if afraid his wife might suddenly have taken it into her head to eavesdrop outside. He was evidently terrified of her learning this secret he'd managed to conceal for more than forty years, a trivial one in today's world, but perhaps not to a man of Crytch's generation and temperament, who was also a lay preacher and a prominent member of the local Methodist church. To have it made known now would not only intrude into his tranquil, civilised and self-satisfied mode of living; it would reveal him as a humbug and hypocrite, no longer the upright, respected citizen, or the ideal husband. It would do a lot of harm to his self-regard, Mayo could see; it would be a calamity.

Could such a humiliating prospect have stirred this mild man into violence? Unfortunately for Crytch, Mayo knew this to be entirely possible. He'd lost count of the murderers he'd met who looked as though they couldn't swat a fly. Moreover, he didn't allow himself to forget that Crytch was intelligent and shrewd, quite probably not as mild as he seemed, and was in a position to know more about Marion Dove's affairs than anyone else connected with the case.

'I'm afraid I shall have to ask you to tell me about it, please.'

Crytch stared out of the window, at the picture-book garden, saying nothing. 'Very well,' he said at last. His colour had returned to normal, but a dull, heavy lassitude had replaced his usual smiling vigour. For the first time since Mayo had known him, he looked his age. 'I'd been going out with Marion before I went into the army, as I told you, but you must realise I didn't know anything about any baby until I came out. It was actually my mother who told me. We all went to the same chapel, you see, Marion's family and mine, though my mother didn't like Marion – at least she thought she didn't come of a good enough family, but I was in love with her and I thought she was with me. All right, we were very young, but I swear it was genuine.'

Footsteps approaching the door made him pause, but they went away again. 'When I was called up she said she wouldn't hold me to any promises, we might both feel differently after the war had ended, but when I was demobbed and came home I still felt the same. I asked her to marry me, and she refused. I was pretty fed up about that, impossible to live with at home, I suppose, and that was when my mother told me what folks had been saying.'

It all came out very smoothly, with practised courtroom fluency, but there was little doubt also that this was an oft-remembered tale. Remembered with resentment, the fires stoked up to keep the pot simmering? Mayo wouldn't have been surprised. 'What about Marion herself? Didn't you ask her?'

'Not for a long time. Things had become different between us. She'd changed, there was no question of carrying on as we had before. She was unapproachable, she wouldn't let me touch her – we couldn't even talk. But one day I braced myself and asked her if it was true that she'd had a child, and if it were mine.' He swizzled the remainder of his sherry round in the bottom of his glass, and then drained it in a gulp.

'What did she say?'

'She froze, then said she didn't want to talk about it, clammed up like an oyster and wouldn't say another word. After that we just saw less and less of each other until finally we stopped meeting at all. I could understand it in a way, her not wanting to have anything to do with me after what she'd had to face on her own . . . though she needn't have. If only she'd told me, it would have been all right, I'd have married her, she must have known that.'

There was genuine regret . . . but underlying that, the shadow of an old, deep hurt. He had not, even yet, completely forgiven. It had taken him years to come to terms with his rejection, to reach the stage where he found it possible to marry. Would he have tolerated any possibility of disruption to his present happiness?

It all began to make sense, much more sense at any rate than believing Wesley Dove was the father. It explained Marion's refusal to marry Crytch, if she'd found herself pregnant and then discovered she didn't love him. That stacked with the sort of introverted, romantic young girl he'd come to envisage: a young girl strictly brought up and coming face to face with her own sexuality and its consequences. She'd be determined not to let her emotions run away with her ever again. That could be why she'd eventually married Wesley Dove, an arrangement of convenience, surely, committed solely to providing him with no more than a wife and the sons he hoped for to carry on his name, while she could have the children she longed for, the means of exorcising the ghost of her first child, as she had put it to her sister.

'Did she in fact tell you she was going to make provision for this child in her new will when she made the appointment to see you?' he asked Crytch. There'd be more to it than that, of course. More than a name in a will and a few thousand pounds as a sop to her conscience. Enough to make someone decide to stop her before she could make the change? And who was in a better position than Crytch to know about that?

'Not in so many words. She said, "I'm going to right a few wrongs and tell you the truth. Poor Geoffrey, I ought to have trusted you before." I've been in a panic ever since. If my wife and children got to know . . .' Crytch pulled out a handkerchief and mopped his brow.

Mayo wished he had a fiver for every time he'd heard that fear expressed. Often a quite unjustified fear, if the wife – or the husband – was worth his salt. After all, what did this amount to? A boy and girl love-affair, over forty years ago, with an outcome that wasn't so unusual. And if Mayo was any judge, Laura Crytch, who must have come across many similar happenings in her professional life, would not judge too harshly.

'I didn't kill her,' Crytch said suddenly, desperately. Beads of sweat stood on his forehead.

Was he capable of it? On the face of it, he was woman-dominated, a role he apparently sought and preferred, perhaps patterned by his mother. When she had died, he had chosen another strong, capable woman in his wife Laura. His daughters also had him twisted round their little fingers. Even his secretary fell into the same category. But it would be a mistake to regard him as ineffectual. That he was not. He was a shrewd, clever and at the moment very worried man.

Mayo said, 'I suppose you realise I'm going to have to ask you to account for your movements on Sunday, sir?'

Crytch looked out into the glowing evening garden, the white scented shrub sweeping to the lawn like a cascade of stars. 'I was at home here all day with my wife. We did some gardening, I cut the lawn, trimmed the edges, that sort of thing.'

'And in the evening?'

'We had dinner and read a little, listened to some music. Laura was called out for a while – it was an emergency. Some child who'd swallowed something toxic, I believe, and had to be rushed off to hospital.'

'What time was that?'

'I think about eight' – I don't remember, I dozed a little.'

He went through it all again, questioning Crytch closely about the two hours between 11.30 and 1.30, but he had been with his wife the whole of that time. So Crytch, too, had had an alibi for the crucial hours.

★

500

He went back to the station to pick up his car and walked upstairs to see if anything had come in for him. He found Kite waiting in a state of excitement, and listened carefully to what his sergeant had to tell him. 'You think she's telling the truth, this Mrs Littlebank?' he asked.

'No reason for her not to, that I can see – and yes, I do think so. She's coming down to make a statement tomorrow.'

So the murder must have taken place in the evening, which meant Crytch's alibi wasn't as watertight as he'd thought. Nor, for that matter, was Ken Dainty's. And what about Paul Fish? And the drunken figure Marty Witherspoon had seen? If Rita Littlebank's statement was to be believed, it couldn't have been Charlie Fish. But Charlie Fish, according to Kite, was in dead trouble anyway.

CHAPTER 17

Kite found the Aysgarth Home for the Elderly without difficulty, a big converted Georgian house about five miles out of Wolverhampton town centre, fronted by a long garden and with a large, sunny conservatory at the side where chairs were set out and the old people were taking coffee. The matron, Mrs O'Shea, was a young and cheerful Irishwoman who took him straight into her office, a comfortable chintzy room overlooking the garden.

'I hope what I've got to say won't bother the old lady,' Kite said, after he'd told the matron briefly the reason for wanting to see her. 'I'll do my best not to upset her.'

The matron laughed.

'Don't you worry about that, she's more than able to cope, you'll find out. You'd like to be private, I expect, so I'll bring her in here.' She left him with a copy of *Good Housekeeping* and returned a few minutes later accompanied by a neat little person, well below the level of Kite's shoulder, with carefully permed white hair and small intelligent eyes like blackcurrants, who was wearing a blue woollen dress with a pretty silk scarf tucked into the neck. Kite found his hand gripped with surprising strength.

'You'll have had your coffee,' she announced, seating herself firmly in a high-backed chair, 'so let's get on with it.'

The matron said, 'Now, Edie, it's no trouble at all to get Mr Kite a cup.'

'As a matter of fact I *have* just had one,' Kite lied cravenly, intimidated before he'd started.

'If you're sure, then? All right, I'll leave you to it.'

Kite gathered his forces while Mrs Copley summed him up with her bright little eyes and then spoke to him.

'Well, let's hear what you've got to say for yourself, young man, I haven't all day. I've got me serial at eleven. What do you want to know?' She'd been away from Lavenstock for more than most people's lifespan, but it hadn't altogether robbed her speech of the local rhythms and intonations, and her voice was strong and without a quaver.

'All right, Mrs Copley, I'll be as quick as I can. Do you remember a girl called Marion Waldron, Marion Dove as she later was?'

Mrs Copley gave him a withering look. 'Of course I remember her. I might be ninety-one, but I'm not off me chump, not like some of 'em here. Got herself murdered, hasn't she? I saw it on the telly, and I said to meself when I heard you was coming, "Edie, that's what that bobby's after." It's about that baby she had, I suppose?'

'That's it,' Kite said, leaning back. There were no flies on Mrs Copley. He could see she had it all sussed out and he'd no objection to her making his job easier.

'Don't you go getting the idea she was a bad girl then, for a start. She wasn't, just unlucky that he couldn't marry her – or wouldn't. You lot, you men, you're all the same, you want your fun but you don't want to pay for it.'

'Did she tell you who the father was?'

'She'd more sense! Wasn't much more than a kid herself, but she had her head screwed on the right way. I didn't ask and she didn't tell me. It was better that way. Anyway, she'd had enough of being badgered by the time she came to me. Her dad had shown her the back of his hand more than once, trying to get it out of her who was responsible, but she wouldn't let on. Never had much sense though, Bert Waldron, more concerned with what they thought of him up the chapel than how his daughter felt. Good job they'd me to turn to. Flo and me, that's Marion's mother, we'd always been good friends so it was natural she'd turn to me when she was in trouble, especially me being a district nurse and all. 'Sides, I was glad of the company, my husband and both boys being in the army.'

Her bright eyes studied him. Suddenly she leaned forward. 'You a Lavenstock man?'

'Born and bred there.'

'Thought so, with that name! Any relation to Arthur Kite, worked up the waterworks?'

'He was my uncle, but he's dead now.'

'I'd be surprised if he wasn't,' she retorted, with the satisfaction of having outlived most of her contemporaries. 'Cheeky young devil, he was. I expect you're the same, eh?'

'So they used to tell me,' Kite replied, wondering how to get back to the subject, when she returned abruptly to it herself.

'Given half a chance she'd have kept that child, I'll tell you that, but you have to face facts and she knew it. It was a stigma, then, having a baby out of wedlock, she'd've spent the rest of her life living it down. I've seen enough of that in my time, and the trouble it brings. You made your bed and you had to lie on it in them days and it was best for everybody she let the baby go, but I've had children of me own and I know how she must've felt. Nearly broke her heart to let it go, it did.'

'Where *did* the baby go?'

503

'That I can't tell you, 'cause I don't know. The vicar, the Reverend Archibald, he took care of all that. He knew somebody who was desperate for a baby and he fixed it up, all legal. It'd be a good home, mind, he wouldn't've let the baby go to just anybody. Nice chap he was, he had ginger hair, looked like Mickey Rooney.'

'Who?'

She leaned forward and slapped his hand. 'I might as well've been talking to meself – haven't you been listening? The vicar, of course!'

'I meant who's Mickey Rooney?'

She looked at him as though there was no hope for the younger generation, in particular those in the police force. 'He was a film star, wasn't he? Used to sing and dance and that with Judy Garland. You've heard of Judy Garland, I suppose?'

'The baby, what happened to him?' Kite asked, holding on.

'Oh, it wasn't a him.' Mrs Copley's indomitable old face softened. 'It was a little girl she had, a beautiful little girl. Born into my own hands. She called her Rose.' She fell silent for a while and then said suddenly, 'You get used to the idea of death by the time you get to my age. It don't bother you so much. But strangled, eh? That's a terrible way to die. I was that upset when I heard. You hear about these things and you think, well, likely they asked for it, but Marion wasn't that sort. She was a nice girl, and don't you listen to nobody that tells you different. Thoughtful, never forget me, never failed to send me a Christmas card, she didn't – and this scarf last birthday. She had a bad start, poor wench – some folk seem to be born under an unlucky star and I used to think she was one of them, but it turned out all right in the end, didn't it? She married well, she had two more little girls. I was glad to know she was happy at last.'

Kite saw no point in enlightening Mrs Copley about the true state of Marion Dove's marriage. She seemed to have a low enough opinion of men already.

'Don't suppose you know where that vicar is now?' he asked without much hope.

'Oh yes, I can tell you that. He comes to see me now and again, though he's retired now. He's not as old as me, mind! He has a little cottage in a village called Shenningstone, know where that is?'

It was the other side of Lavenstock, but with luck, he might make it before lunch. He'd a hunch Mayo would want to go along, too.

'Is that all, then?' Mrs Copley asked, standing up in one brisk movement.

'That's about it.' Kite rose too and thanked her for being so frank with him. 'I'll get over to Shenningstone as soon as I can.'

'I hope you catch him,' she said, as he opened the door for her. Kite didn't ask who, this time. He knew she didn't mean the vicar.

A steady stream of elderly people met him in the corridor, making for an open door from whence issued the sound of a TV set advertising the newest, cleanest, whitest, improved, environmental-friendly washing liquid. It was 11.26. He'd timed that very nicely. Mrs Copley would get to watch her serial after all.

The Reverend James Archibald was picking up windfalls in his garden, a back-breaking job for one of his age, and he was glad of the diversion when the telephone, connected to an outside bell, rang. After he'd answered it, he abandoned the apples altogether and allowed himself a few minutes' reflection, sitting on the wooden seat that encircled the apple tree, with the winey smell of the fruit all around him and the sun on his face.

It had all been so long ago, that impulsive act, the consequences of which continued to haunt him still. Marion Waldron. That young girl whose image wouldn't be dismissed whenever he had cause to examine his conscience. He wished Cecily were here to reassure him that it wasn't his fault, that he'd acted in good faith and with the best of intentions. He might then be comforted for a while and believe the intention was what mattered. But Cecily had been dead these seven years, and now he had to wrestle with his conscience alone, or with God.

He was a simple man, a practical Christian who had always taken each day as it came and each person for what they were when they came under his pastoral care, and had left the probing of minds and motivations to others, and he only knew he'd been desperately sorry for the woman and her husband.

She'd been such an *intense* woman, Angela Feldon. She'd got into the habit of catching him at the church at every conceivable moment, she telephoned him at inconvenient times, she called at the vicarage and insisted on unburdening herself, she had declared that life meant nothing to her if she had no child to love, she needed fulfilment; it became an obsession and he'd feared that she really was in danger of taking her own life, as she threatened. How terrible it must be, he'd thought with compassion, to long for a child with such intensity, to know that it would always be denied. He and Cecily had been blessed with five children of their own, a source of love and delight that had withstood every trauma of adolescence and young adulthood.

So he'd done what he thought was best for everyone in the circumstances. It was only in the light of what happened later that he wondered guiltily if he hadn't acted as he did simply to get rid of her. Only very gradually and painfully did he later come to realise that there were women, hysterical women, to whom anything unattainable immediately became a necessity, a terrible truth that he found very hard to accept: that it was possible for children, to some women, to be just another consumer product, that they had to have a child as they had to have a second freezer, or the latest food mixer.

A wasp, drunk on apple juice, buzzed round his ear. He wafted it away and after a while decided that self-pity was a greater indulgence than remorse and he'd better go and get himself cleaned up before the policemen arrived.

*

When Mayo pushed open the gate of the cottage just off the village street at Shenningstone just before lunch and walked up the path with Kite behind him, he saw an old man in a linen jacket sitting at a table on the small sunny terrace, a man spherical in shape, whose receding hair, eyebrows and eyelashes had all taken on that indeterminate dusty sand-colour between auburn and white. His pale blue eyes were a little rheumy, but his smile was kindly and benevolent, like a jolly old monk.

'Please sit down, Chief Inspector, Sergeant. You'll join me in a glass of sherry? It's a luxury I allow myself, a glass half an hour before luncheon, another before supper. Thereby I measure out my life like J. Alfred Prufrock.' His smiling gaze travelled benignly from one to the other. 'You don't know your Eliot? Ah well.'

You'd imagine, Kite thought, that with all the time they have, these old folks, they'd be glad of something to fill it up. Measuring out his days! A poetry-spouting vicar's all we need. He felt relieved Mayo had thought it necessary to come along, watching the old man as he poured three careful glasses of the pale, dry liquid. He'd rather have had a glass of cold beer, himself, but he didn't like to ask.

'How can I help you?' He seemed a nice old boy. The tone was gentle, the voice cultured, an Eton and Oxford sort of voice.

Mayo said, 'I believe I mentioned on the phone that it was about the girl you knew as Marion Waldron that I wanted to talk to you.'

Archibald nodded, a crease of worry appearing between the sandy brows.

'Specifically, it's her child we're trying to trace.'

'She hasn't been successful, then? I feared as much. She's making a mistake, after all these years, and so I told her.'

'You told her? When was this?'

'Two or three weeks ago, maybe a month, when she came to see me. May I ask what your interest is in this?'

Mayo stared across the sunny terrace to the small orchard. The wind moved through the branches and lifted the leaves, and the apples still on the trees, almost at the peak of perfection, glowed like Chinese lanterns. 'I don't believe you know what's happened, sir.'

'Happened? What has happened?'

As gently as he could, Mayo told him. He could see it was a shock to the old man. He closed his eyes for a moment or two and Mayo wondered if he could be praying. Then he said, a little shakily, 'That woman who was murdered was Marion Waldron? I read about it in the papers, but I never dreamed . . . You see, she didn't give me her married name. You know why I was the one, particularly, she came to see?'

'Presumably because you arranged the adoption.'

The old man nodded, slowly. 'She was adamant about finding her daughter. I thought she was making a mistake, as I told you. These things are possibly better left, after so many years, but she was very . . . well, she had her reasons.' He didn't say what they were but Mayo guessed she had used her illness to persuade him into giving the information. Doubtless she could have found out herself, given time, but no one knew better than she that this was something of which she had only a limited amount. 'I see I shall have to tell you about it. It's not a pretty story, and I'm not particularly proud of the part I played in it, with hindsight, but I ask you to be patient while I tell you. May I give you another glass of sherry? No? Perhaps you'll take pot luck and have luncheon with me? Mrs Wilson leaves me casseroles, always far too much . . .'

'Thank you kindly, but we really must get on,' Mayo said. The old gentleman looked disappointed, but began his story.

And it didn't, after all, take long to hear how James Archibald, then rector of the parish where Edith Copley had lived, had helped to arrange for the legal adoption of Marion's child by a comfortably-off, childless couple who were desperate for a child of their own. How the husband had then been killed in the latter stages of the war, and the wife, a neurotic woman called Angela

Feldon, left alone and with no one to lean on, had been unable to cope. The child, the little girl Rose, had grown up self-willed and uncontrollable. The wilder she became as she grew up, the more her adoptive mother retreated and washed her hands of her. Finally, the girl ran away from home at sixteen to marry a disreputable young local tearaway called Steven Cordingley.

So 'Steven' now had a surname. 'Where is he now – this Steven Cordingley?' Kite asked.

'He was killed, driving a car while he was drunk.'

Mayo would have gnashed his teeth like Charlie Fish's bull terrier, if it would have done any good. But there was a Steven, and maybe . . . 'Do you know if there were children of the marriage, Mr Archibald?'

'I believe there was at least one, a son.'

'What happened to Rose?'

'I can't tell you that. I'd moved from the parish by then and it was only through reading about the crash in the papers that I knew of it at all.'

'The Cordingleys . . . Steven's parents? Would they know? Were you able to tell Marion – Mrs Dove – where she could get in touch with them?'

'I wasn't sure I could help her – that I ought . . .'

'But you did.'

'Only as far as finding out where the Cordingley parents live now. I made some telephone calls while she was here, to people I still know in the parish. After that, I felt it was up to her.'

'In the circumstances, sir, it would be helpful if you could pass on the address.'

They left, ten minutes later, furnished with the address and each weighed down with a plastic carrier bag full of windfall apples which had been pressed on to them by Mr Archibald, who wouldn't take no for an answer. Kite didn't want Mayo's share, and Mayo had no use for them, which meant, when they got back to the station, looking around for someone with a wife who'd be willing to make apple pies from his kindly-meant but unwanted gift. To his mild surprise, it was Rhoda Piper who said she'd have them, in order to make apple chutney.

'It'll help start off my store cupboard when the house is ready. I'll let you have a jar when I've made it, sir.'

Mystified, Mayo handed them over and she walked away before he could ask her what she meant. He asked Kite instead, as they walked upstairs. 'She's getting married next month, they're buying one of those new houses by the river,' Kite answered.

Mayo was astounded. Rhoda, getting married? She was all of forty, plain and worthy and somehow, if he'd thought of her private life at all, he would have imagined her as the sort of willing-horse daughter who'd been left by the rest of the family to take care of an elderly mother, the sort who'd never had the opportunity to get married, but who probably wouldn't want to, now.

'Her father's just died,' Kite said, 'been a semi-invalid for years, and now she's marrying this widower, not without a bit of money, either.'

Mayo just stopped himself from grinning. 'You do surprise me,' he said.

It wasn't the only surprise of the afternoon. He'd been back in his office barely five minutes before the news came to him that Paul Fish and Katie Lazenby had turned up.

CHAPTER 18

He sat hunched on the hard, upright chair in the interview room with his head in his hands and wished he were dead.

He might as well be. His life was a total mess, he loathed himself nearly as much as he hated his father. He was useless at everything, he'd never be brainy like Gray, and what was worse, no way was he ever going to be able to pay for flying lessons. He couldn't seem to get one single thing right, not even with Katie Lazenby, and that was a laugh, when half the guys at school claimed they'd made it with her. (Though after the last few days he reckoned most of that was a load of bull.) And now his Aunt Marion was dead. Murdered. And the fuzz here were so thick they thought he'd done it.

He felt sick. It was like an oven in the room. They'd obviously just redecorated it and the hot sun on the window-frames brought out the pungent smell of new paint. And if Katie's father, the stupid old git, told him just once more that if he got his hands on him he'd have his guts for garters, he'd – he'd smash his face in! It was Katie's fault just as much as his, she'd been the one who'd needled him into taking Aunt Gwen's car in the first place, though nobody was ever going to believe that. The one who'd jeered when he'd lost his nerve and wouldn't use the credit card. He wondered what he'd ever seen in her.

She sat as if butter wouldn't melt in her mouth, next to her mother, who was wearing jeans and a T-shirt just like Katie, trying to look young, only she didn't. They were quite alike and Katie said they often passed for sisters. That was how Katie would look when she was old, it was weird.

He couldn't bear the thought of Aunt Marion being dead, he didn't want to think of it, because if he did he might blub, and they were already treating him like he was about twelve years old. He couldn't stop thinking about her, though. How they'd played chess, sometimes sitting for an hour without saying a word, that was brilliant. How he'd put up the fence round the duckpen for her and how she used to read poetry out to him. Not that he was into poetry – he hadn't understood most of it, but he'd liked the sound of her quiet voice . . .

He wished now he'd stayed away and never come back, let Katie come home on her own. Or that he'd agreed to do what

511

Marion wanted and settle for that boring job at the glassworks. Maybe he might as well end up doing that, after all, if the offer was still open, it was what she'd wanted him to do . . . or he might even join the RAF, like old Mass had suggested. Probably he'd do neither, if he was going to make such a pig's ear of everything he might just as well kill himself and be done with it.

'Let me just get my hands on him, the young devil!' Lazenby said again.

Paul didn't even raise his head.

'All right, all right, cut it out, Mr Lazenby, please!'

Mayo had neither time nor inclination to listen while Rick Lazenby, the skin peeling off his nose from sitting too long in the unaccustomed sun, vented his feelings. He should have thought of that before he went off to the Algarve, and serve them right the holiday hadn't turned out as they hoped . . . the hotel hadn't come up to expectations, there was nothing to do all day except sit in the sun, the food wasn't up to much, either. Denise had caught a bug, she'd started worrying belatedly over leaving Katie, wondering if they'd done the right thing . . . and altogether, Mayo gathered, the holiday hadn't exactly cemented marital relations.

'We wouldn't have gone without her,' the mother was saying now, defensively, 'only the travel agents couldn't give me any other dates, and she had to be back at school, and we really *needed* this holiday, her dad and me. I've got a job in Catesby's office and I work hard – we both work hard – we like things nice at home, we're entitled to a nice lifestyle, we've done it all for her, anyway!' Denise Lazenby cast a look of venom at her daughter, who remained quite unaffected by it. 'She's never gone short of a thing. I thought I could trust her!'

They were running predictably true to type, Denise Lazenby and her husband. She was the dominant partner, while Lazenby just went along with her, both of them paying lip-service to his macho image. She'd be the one who paid the bills and decided on the holidays and had their social life planned to a T. Mayo was certain that her cool, clever daughter, with her inscrutable eyes, was beyond her. She'd run rings round the pair of them, in fact. A right little madam, Atkins had said. Mayo, sitting opposite her in the interview room, wasn't prepared to argue.

She was a dark beauty, young Katie, with high cheekbones and vivid green eyes, slanting and thickly lashed. White-skinned and with her black hair bobbed and cut in a straight fringe, she looked like a pert, sexy maid in a French farce. Unlike Paul, she was old for her age and self-confident, but underneath it still young enough to be very frightened at the moment, answering his questions meekly and with downcast eyes. Yes, Paul had rung her very late on Sunday night and begged her to go away with him first thing the next morning. She'd agreed in the end – just until her parents came home, she said, ignoring both her mother's indrawn breath and Paul's. He'd told her he could borrow his aunt's car, and said he'd plenty of money. She raised her eyes and Mayo saw a flash in them like the sun on a kingfisher's wings. 'It wasn't true,' she said, with soft scorn. 'He hadn't any money, all we had was what I had with me and when that was gone we had to come home.'

'What about that credit card of your aunt's, Paul?' Kite asked.

The boy made an attempt at evasion. 'What credit card?'

'The one you pinched, right?'

'No, I never! I found it on the floor of the car and OK, that was what gave me the idea. But I put it in the dash and it's still there.'

'That's true enough,' Katie said, but the way she said it, it was as though she might have admired him more if he'd been prepared to forge the signature, to squander recklessly, to buy them the romantic, exciting time she'd envisaged when she'd agreed to go away with him. She was only fifteen, and for all her acquired sophistication, imagined that was what escapades like that ought to be. 'We had to sleep in the car!'

Her father began, 'By God –!' but Mayo interrupted him and spoke to the two youngsters.

'I'll be frank with you both. I don't much care what you've been doing this last week, as long as you've been within the law. You've caused us a lot of bother one way and another, but what I'm interested in now is what happened last Sunday.'

'Nothing happened.' The boy's tone was muffled. He was doing his best not to break down in front of the adults, and especially not in front of Katie.

Mayo decided to take pity on him, not for altogether altruistic reasons. He was certain to get more out of him alone, without all this flak from the opposition. He turned to Katie and her parents and told them they could go home.

'Is that all, then?' Lazenby asked, the wind taken out of his sails. Yet he was relieved, both parents jumped up immediately, anxious to shake the dust of the police station off their feet as soon as possible. Katie seemed hardly to believe her good fortune, but to do her credit, she did appear slightly shamefaced at being freed and leaving Paul there. She refused to look in his direction, keeping her green eyes veiled.

'Inspector Atkins will do the necessary before you go – oh, and Mr Lazenby, don't let's have any more threats against Paul here, eh?'

Rick Lazenby answered with a ferocious scowl at Paul that didn't impress Mayo. There'd be no more trouble from him. He'd got his daughter back, he'd gone through the necessary motions and wouldn't want any more bother. He must have known his own part in the affair wouldn't stand up to much scrutiny.

When Rhoda Piper had led them out, Mayo flung open the window and then resumed his seat. With more air circulating, and fewer people in it, the small room was cooler and reeked less of new paint. 'Now,' he began, turning to Paul, 'let's have a talk about Sunday. Did you go down to the Jubilee to see Mrs Dove at any time that day?'

'On Sunday? Yes. Well, no, not properly.'

'What do you mean, not properly, Paul? Make your mind up.'

'Well, I went, but when I got there she'd got somebody with her, there was a car parked in the entrance to the lane, so I went away again.' The lad seemed at last to be coming out of the stricken silence that had overtaken him ever since he'd walked into the room. He was a compactly built youth with a tanned skin and short-cut brown hair whose regular features hadn't yet hardened into those of the man he would become. He wore old jeans and a red T-shirt with 'University of the World' printed on it. If Katie seemed older than her years, Paul was very young for seventeen. Immaturity still clung to him like the half-shed pupa case of a chrysalis moth.

'What time would that have been?'

'I don't know – round about seven I should think, but I don't remember for sure.'

Mayo noticed he didn't wear a watch, so this was possibly true. 'What was your reason for going to see Mrs Dove?'

A spasm of misery crossed the boy's face. 'I wanted to talk to her about something. I wanted her advice. She'd have understood, but I couldn't talk to her with somebody else already there, could I, so I went away.'

'You'd had a row with your dad and you were upset, was that it?'

'Yes.' Paul didn't ask how Mayo knew about it, he seemed to take it for granted that he would.

'Was it about money?'

'No!' The boy's fists inside the pockets of his tight jeans bunched with anger.

'It usually was, wasn't it?'

'Well, it wasn't this time! If you must know – it was something to do with Caesar.'

'Your dog?'

'He's not mine! I wouldn't treat him like that if he was! It's sick, and I told him I was going to –' He stopped, flushing a dull red, aware that he'd gone beyond limits. 'Oh never mind, I wouldn't expect you lot to understand.'

515

'You were going to report him? Isn't that what you were going to say? Come on, what d'you take us for? We don't approve of dog-fighting either, lad. And not just because it's against the law.'

Kite had been the one who'd spotted it, made the connection between the splendid dog, kept in fighting trim, with the sort of man Charlie Fish was, and put two and two together. Breeding fighting dogs for the ring was nothing new in this part of the world. It was a barbarous custom going back centuries, which hadn't yet been entirely stamped out. It still cropped up sporadically, despite the risks and penalties. It had its appeal among those who got their kicks from blood sports and illegal gambling. Typical of Charlie Fish, this particular set-up was haphazard, illorganised and amateur, the abandoned brickworks serving as a venue, with the Dog and Fox being the only habitation in the vicinity, where the landlord, whose suspected involvement with the dirty business of his customers had yet to be proved, had almost certainly turned a blind eye.

Before the look of stunned surprise had faded from the boy's face, Mayo said, 'Don't worry about it, everything's been taken care of, including Caesar, but things might not be very easy for a while . . . I'm afraid your father's going to have to face charges . . .'

'Tough,' said Paul, but not with total conviction. Trying to look as if he didn't care, he began to stand up, seeming uncertain whether anything else was required of him or not.

'Don't go yet, Paul, we haven't quite finished, but I'll not keep you any longer than I have to. You'll want to be off home, I expect.'

The uncertainty was replaced by a sullen defiance as he slumped back on to the chair. 'I'm not going home, not back there, I won't, not ever. My Aunt Gwen says I can stay with them.'

Mayo thought he might have expected that of Mrs Bainbridge, but if Paul expected roses all the way, he was in for a shock. There was trouble ahead there for him, too. But he thought it would – in the end – be the best thing for all concerned in the circumstances.

Kite took up the questioning. 'Let's get back to what we were talking about. How did you get down to the Jubilee?'

'In the Mini. They let me use it, you know.'

'OK, I know. Presumably you recognised the car that was parked in the lane on Sunday as belonging to someone who was likely to be visiting Mrs Dove? Not just anyone leaving it there while they went for a walk on the canal bank, for instance – otherwise you'd have gone down to the lockhouse?'

'Sure I recognised it. It was that silver D reg Peugeot of Rachel's – Mrs Dove's daughter.'

There was no need to ask him whether he was certain. Any boy of Paul's type and age could probably tell him not only the registration number and colour but also the condition of the tyres and the miles it had done, together with any optional extras it might have into the bargain.

'Was there any other car there?' he asked, thinking of the red Sierra in the Dog and Fox car park in which Mrs Dove had waited.

'Not unless it was right down by the lockhouse, I'd've noticed else. There's not much room for more than one at the top of the lane, and it's dodgy parking on the road, with the bridge and that bend there. But it's not a lane I'd take my car down, if I had one.'

Perhaps it had been down by the lockhouse, all the same. Or perhaps Marion had simply been brought home, and the driver hadn't stayed. Perhaps he *had* stayed, long enough to murder her and leave her body behind him in the canal. Perhaps that was why he hadn't come forward. Perhaps . . . Mayo could think of at least half a dozen more variations of that little scenario.

There seemed little point in keeping Paul any longer. He was telling the truth. It didn't take two experienced detectives to realise that he was almost certainly innocent of any involvement in his aunt's death. They let him go.

'Where does that leave us?' Kite asked.

On one thing both men were agreed – the elusive Steven with

whom Marion Dove had had an appointment had to be her daughter Rose's son, with the same name, Steven, as his father. And almost certainly, he was the man in the red Sierra. 'He could easily have killed his grandmother after Rita Littlebank saw them in the car park and got away before Paul arrived,' Kite said.

'Then what about Rachel Dove?'

She'd lied about driving straight back to Northumbria, if only by implication, when she'd spoken to him. She had returned to the lockhouse that evening. He imagined her going into the house, finding it empty, searching around for her mother, as Percy Collis had done, and then finally discovering her. Easy enough to imagine. What he did find impossible to swallow was the idea of her simply leaving her mother's body, going back up north and carrying on with her normal life, packing for her holiday in Florence. Unless, of course, Marion Dove had still been alive when she left her car and went down that steep path . . .

It was time to see her again. He was a fool to have allowed himself to pity her evident distress over her mother. That was when he ought, professionally speaking, to have pressed her more, but he had never been one to take advantage of another's grief, unless he absolutely had to. If it had been necessary, he would have done it, but he hadn't deemed it so at the time and it was no use now wishing he had.

He decided on reflection, however, his annoyance with himself having cooled somewhat, that it would wait a little longer. Kite deserved an evening with his family, for once. For himself, he was going to go home, cook a decent meal, listen to some music with a glass of scotch at his elbow and for the twentieth time go through the files, slowly and without interruption. He needed an overview, to see if, somewhere, he could find any connections or discrepancies in all the various reports and statements which had been made. He had this tantalising sense of pressure building up which told him they were very nearly there, but not quite. On the edge of discovering the key to the solution. Not by blinding intuition –

experience had taught him this rarely if ever happened – but through methodically gathering the facts together and perhaps drawing a conclusion from them. He thought he might be in for a long evening.

CHAPTER 19

They were going to seek out Mrs Cordingley this morning, at the address Mr Archibald had given them. Mayo was up betimes, impatient to follow up the information. It was a Saturday morning, crisp and sweet and mellow as a September apple. A perfect day for the wedding Mayo wasn't going to. At least he'd remembered to make his apologies earlier in the week, and he'd found time to arrange for a greetings telegram to be sent to the happy pair. It wasn't very satisfactory, but it was the best he could do in the circumstances.

He'd asked Kite to meet him at Milford Road, but first he drove his car down to the canal-side flats and parked it there, having decided to walk through the tunnel towards the Jubilee Locks. He wanted to have another look at the murder scene, he didn't know that it could tell him anything, but he wanted to have another look all the same. It was necessary to test certain theories, to see whether they were as feasible as they'd seemed in the small hours, or whether they were merely the product of euphoria induced by a good malt and the glories of Elgar.

As he walked, he noticed *en passant* that yet another of the old factories had disappeared under the demolition hammer, revealing open spaces and an ancestral view of distant hills out beyond Henchard, hills once thickly forested where deer had roamed and kings had hunted, but not for hundreds of years. Hills never before seen within living memory from this point because of the solid mass of tall brick factories, chimneys and warehouses that had obscured them. Soon they'll all be gone, these old relics of the Industrial Revolution, another new instant landscape would be created around the still raw-looking blocks of flats, bewildering the older generation, still accustomed here in Lavenstock to the slow, imperceptible changes of time.

The new marina, where once a gasholder had stood, wasn't waiting for this, it was already briskly in business. A few brightly-painted narrowboats and several motor-launches were moored in the basin, and outside the shop which catered for the boaters roses and castles bloomed on a new delivery of repro bargeware intended for the influx of visitors expected over the weekend. This was at present as far upstream as they could come, until the uncleared stretch beyond the tunnel and up to the Jubilee was tackled.

He came out of the darkness of the tunnel and into the bright morning and was struck by the notion of trying his hand some-time at painting the scene. He grinned to himself and the idea passed. He knew he'd never have the ability to depict the scene on canvas, to capture it as it was, tranquil and undisturbed as it might not be for long, the trees dappling the green water with sunlight, the old man fishing quietly on the bank. As he approached, Percy Collis caught a fish, removed it from the hook and threw it back. Perhaps it was too small, maybe the memory of what he'd found further down was still with him. They exchanged greetings and Mayo found a place beside him on the bank while the old man rebaited his hook and cast again into the water.

'Making much progress?' Collis asked when this had been accomplished.

'These things take time, Mr Collis.'

This attitude seemed to meet with Collis's approval. He was of that lost age to whom it seemed right and natural to take your time over everything. They sat in companionable silence for a while. The old man remarked, 'Days like this, I can see why her wanted to live here. Not much of a place, but better'n rattling round in that bloomin' old mansion next the glassworks.'

'Or Chapel Street, so I've heard. Folks I've talked to seem to think that bomb on it was a blessing in disguise.'

'It wor that orright – though we didn't think so at the time.'

'You'd never forget a night like that,' Mayo agreed.

'Suppose not. Surprising, though, how much yo' do forget, good thing too, I reckon.' What he was saying, of course, was that memory had of necessity to be selective. No one person could bear the weight of every single remembered misery, such as were witnessed in wartime. Mayo could wish his own memory was, at that point, slightly less selective; he could do with remembering everything that had been said to him during the last week.

The old man suddenly gave a reminiscent chuckle. 'Funny thing, what I've never forgot about that night is how it spoilt my Whit Sunday dinner! My missis'd been lucky and she'd got a chicken for us, see – a real luxury in the war. Being in the ARP, I'd spent all Saturday night getting injured folks out and somehow it didn't seem right, tucking into chicken and that next day, Whitsun or no.'

There was a tug on his line. For several minutes he was occupied with more immediate matters. Again the fish was landed, then thrown back into the khaki-coloured water, the hook rebaited, the line cast. 'And that soldier. I do remember him. And I can still see Marion, only a bit of a kid as she wor then, but more guts than some o' the lads, that night.'

'What soldier was that, then?'

'Dunno who he could've been, never saw him after that, not that I know to. We was all black as the ace o' spades with all the smoke, yo' wouldn't've knowed your own brother that night. But a real hero he turned out to be. Funny what yo' remember, ain't it?'

Mayo left old man Collis and walked along the overgrown tow-path to the lockhouse. He walked around, he looked at the crumbled bank and the slimy lock gates, he assessed the steep, stony lane and the slippery stairs by the side of the lock. And as he stood by the green-painted fence and looked up at the red rocks and the loose, unpromising shaly soil from which the tall, graceful trees had sprung and flourished until they now formed a deep and bosky green glade, he wondered, with a sense of loss, what would happen to the lockhouse now. Gwen Bainbridge would try to sell it to help finance her bungalow . . . if they could find anyone prepared to live in such a place, knowing a murder had been committed here. But of course someone would be found, despite that, despite the desolation that now seemed, even on a morning like this, to hang over the cutting; perhaps people who'd turn it into another weekend cottage, whitewash the outside and prettify the inside, build a garage where the kitchen garden and the duck-pen had been and lay down a proper drive from the road. He noticed the ducks had gone, and wondered whether Kite had got someone to take care of them, or if a fox had had them. He must remember to ask. It seemed important to him to know that her ducks would be looked after.

Kite was ready for him at the station, but Mayo asked him to wait and went upstairs to his office. He wanted to make arrangements to see Rachel Dove immediately when he got back. But first, what had she said on her official statement?

Nothing, he found when he looked for it, because the statement wasn't there.

'She was supposed to have come in yesterday to make it,' he told Atkins.

It appeared that she had not. Further enquiries elicited the fact that not only had she not been in to the Milford Road station, but that she had in fact left Lavenstock.

She'd been asked to come in and make her official statement, she'd been asked not to leave Lavenstock without informing the police. She'd done neither. Nor did her sister know where she had gone, when Mayo, tight-lipped, had Kite make a detour round by Henchard because he wanted to speak to Mrs Dainty himself.

Ken Dainty wasn't at home, and a cleaning woman was busy in the sitting-room, so she took them into the kitchen, a miracle of modern technology allied to olde worlde nostalgia. They were offered chairs that matched the stripped pine table in an alcove papered with Victorian rosebuds, while the washing-machine and the dishwasher clicked and sloshed through their various programmes and the fridge and the king-size freezer hummed in concert.

'You've no idea where she's gone?'

'No,' she said, pouring coffee from a fancy glass jug with a plunger device.

'Has she gone for good? I mean, is she coming back tonight?'

'How should I know?' she answered tightly. 'I'm not her keeper!'

So they'd quarrelled. About the will? Had death, instead of bringing them closer, caused a rift, as it so often unhappily did?

She was getting worked up. She'd drunk her coffee, hot, black and strong, before Mayo had started his, and nearly smoked through a cigarette. After what he'd learned yesterday, he was disposed to try and be more gentle with her than her attitude to him warranted, but he was decidedly fed up with chasing after the various members of this family. 'Didn't your sister leave an address?'

She was twisting a dull, inexpensive-looking little gold signet ring round and round on her finger. She saw him looking. 'My mother's,' she said, and her eyes filled with tears. It was at this point, Mayo realised later, that he'd began to feel sorry for Shirley Dainty. Up to then, she had merely irritated him, and there was really no reason for him to feel otherwise now, but he did.

No, she'd left no address, but there was someone, Mrs Dainty said, either relenting or sensing the change in his attitude, who might just know where she was. His name was Josh Amory, Dr Amory, and Mayo could get him at this number at Northumbria.

Josh Amory. He knew the name, he'd seen the man presenting a very enjoyable television series of programmes on Renaissance art. He rang the number he'd been given from his car, expecting to hear the pleasant voice with the amused, ironic note he remembered. He let it ring twenty times, but there was no reply.

It was clear from the start that Mrs Alma Cordingley was not one of the world's fighters. She had lost the battle with the hem of her skirt, her wispy grey hair and her ill-fitting false teeth, through which she spoke with almost closed lips, as if afraid they might otherwise snap out and savage her unawares. Her thin figure drooped hopelessly, her face was anxious. In the struggle for respectability, however, hers was the victory. Alone in a neighbourhood not renowned for its salubriousness, her house shone with conspicuous cleanliness, the tiles in the tiny porch were a gleaming cardinal red, the white lace curtains stiffly crisp and spotless. A washing-machine whirred in the background as she let them in. A Hoover stood at the foot of the stairs.

She perched on the edge of a straight chair in the evidently little-used front room, where the three-piece suite was protected with antimacassars embroidered with lazy daisies and the only picture in the room, a print of a malevolent-looking Persian cat, hung two feet above eye level. Yes, she confirmed, Steven Cordingley was her grandson. Yes, he was over here from Canada. No, no, not *staying* with her, she couldn't do with him here! she exclaimed in fright, as if looking after her grown-up grandson would be a task as totally beyond the scope of her abilities as sailing single-handed round the world. It probably was, poor woman, Mayo thought; thirty years younger than she was now, she hadn't seemingly had much success in handling her son.

'Presumably you know where he's staying?'

'He's taken a furnished flat somewhere over the other side of the town. I have the address if you want it, and the telephone number.'

'Thank you, Mrs Cordingley, that would be most helpful.'

She gave them the details, taken from a postcard kept in her handbag. 'He – he hasn't got himself into trouble, has he?'

'Not that we know of.'

'Only – I hope I've done right. When that woman came – the one said she was Rose's mother – I didn't know what to do. I had to tell her Rose – my son's wife – was dead, see, and I could see it upset her, but she still wanted to know all I could tell her.' She hesitated, fiddling with a button on her cardigan. 'You know Rose was adopted as a baby?'

'Yes.' So Rose, too, was dead. Somehow, Mayo had half-expected it.

'She was upset about that, but so was I when she died, you know.' Momentary rebellion lifted Mrs Cordingley's defeated shoulders. 'She'd never known Rose, but I'd grown fond of her, in spite of everything.' Her mode of expression was limited, she wasn't given to extravagant phrases, but Mayo knew immediately that she had loved the girl and resented the real mother who had, as she saw it, deserted her baby. 'She'd made such a big effort to put herself to rights after Steven was killed. It was that car crash did it, made her realise what sort of life they'd both been leading, though the crash was his fault, he was drunk when it happened. He was always wild, Steven, I always knew he'd come to a bad end one way or another.' Her lips tightened against emotion. 'But Rose knew she had to pull herself together for the sake of the child, and when she said she was going to try to make a new start in Canada, I encouraged her. I didn't want to lose them, but it was best that way.'

She shivered and pulled the cardigan closer round her thin shoulders. It had evidently been a long speech for Mrs Cordingley. She looked exhausted. Mayo said gently, 'What happened to her over there?'

'Oh, she knocked around a bit. I don't think everything came all right straight away, but she got married again after a while, chap called Jack McKinley. Well, she would, she was a lovely girl, you know, always laughing, full of joy. This is her and Steven, and the baby, taken on her birthday. "I only have a birthday once every four years," she said, "so I'm going to have a real celebration." A leap year baby she was, see.'

Mayo looked at the photograph she took from the place of honour in the centre of the sideboard. Even by flash, you could see that Rose was smiling and dark and vividly beautiful, and not in the least like Marion Dove's other daughters.

'See what I mean?' Mrs Cordingley, who could never have been beautiful, and couldn't have had much joy in her life, gave the photograph a rub with the corner of her apron and put it tenderly back.

'So what happened after she married McKinley?'

'She seemed very happy, and after a bit she wrote to tell me she was having a baby. She died having it, and the baby as well, you don't hear of that so much nowadays, do you? Maybe she was a bit too old, she was getting on for forty. They said there were complications.'

'And young Steven, what happened to him?'

'Well, he didn't keep in touch with me like his mother had, but then he'd never known me, really. He was only a baby when they left. I was just a name to him. He stayed with his stepfather for a while after his mother died, but I don't think it worked out. He seems to have done all sorts of things since. I gave Rose's mother Jack McKinley's address and that's how she got in touch. Steven called to see me when he came over from Canada about six or seven weeks ago.' She didn't sound as though she expected him to call again.

Mayo stood up. 'Thank you, Mrs Cordingley, I don't think we shall need to trouble you any more.'

Relief was evident as she smiled her closed-lip smile and showed them to the door. However curious she was, she hadn't asked them why they wanted to know about Rose, nor even much about Steven. She'd had her troubles and wanted no more. She closed the door firmly behind them and the Hoover started up before they reached the gate.

'There's another one who didn't seem to know about the murder,' remarked Kite when they were in the car.

'There's no reason why she should have made the connection, any more than Mr Archibald did, if Marion didn't give her name. I saw no need to tell her, not at the moment at any rate, no point in it.'

Mayo spoke absently. He agreed with Kite that Steven Cordinglev would have to be picked up and brought into the station, and then fell silent, staring unseeingly through the windscreen as the car sped towards Lavenstock. After a while, he asked Kite to get someone to find out details of Geoffrey Crytch's army war service and his leaves. 'It's possible he could be this soldier that Collis remembers.'

'Crytch?' Kite whistled softly. 'I'll put Farrar on to it, it's just the sort of job he enjoys – but he won't be able to get much over the weekend.' He made a swift calculation. 'That would be May 1943, I take it? Nine months before the twenty-ninth of February, 1944?'

'Whitsuntide.' Mayo tried the call to Northumbria once more. There was still no reply. After which, Mayo relapsed back into a deep silence, breaking it only to ask, 'What happened to those ducks?'

'Which ducks? Oh, they've gone to a farmer the other side of Brome who has a flock. By the way, he says they can't exist long without water. They ought to have it for swimming in, but it's not essential. They must have plenty of drinking water, though, and deep enough to immerse their heads when they drink.'

'Interesting.' But it didn't really matter now. The limits within which Marion Dove had died had been established as no more than thirty-six hours, but Mayo thought he could pinpoint the time now more exactly than that. He was almost certain now he knew when she'd been killed, and why and who the killer was.

Another call to Northumbria when they got back produced the same negative results. Mayo decided to give it another day – Amory might be away for the weekend – and then enlist the help of a friend and colleague who lived in the area.

CHAPTER 20

So here he was at last, Steven.

Steven Cordingley, twenty-six years old, tall and narrowly built, with dark straight hair, good teeth and the sort of mid-Atlantic accent that said he was not anxious to be classified as belonging to one side or the other. A young man whose life had been such that he found it hard to settle anywhere, who made no allegiances as a matter of principle, perhaps never would. He smiled often, but fleetingly, and never with warmth. His eyes considered, explored, rejected. He held a kind of violence contained within his thin, taut body.

He refused tea or coffee and sat silently opposite Mayo in his upstairs office, chosen because the decorators hadn't yet reached here and there was no paint smell. Two of the DCs, Pete Deeley and Nick Spalding, had been sent out this morning to fetch Cordingley and they'd only just returned. He had, he explained, been busy trying to book himself a seat back to Toronto.

'Not even staying for your grandmother's funeral?' Mayo asked.

He shrugged. 'I don't go for that kind of thing.' He had the kind of eyes that reminded Mayo of Katie Lazenby's, though his were very blue. He found it very hard to trust anyone with eyes like that.

It was less odoriferous than downstairs, but the room was still very hot. The air-conditioning seemed to be having another of its go-slow periods. Kite opened a window experimentally, but closed it immediately. It was marginally better without the traffic noise from Milford Road.

'Well, Mr Cordingley, I'm waiting.'

'I don't know what you want to know, for God's sake.'

'Don't play games with me, I've other things to do with my time. I've told you once and I'll tell you again – I want to know exactly what happened from the time your grandmother first contacted you, right up until last Sunday, the day she was killed. Exactly one week ago today, when you were the last person known to have seen her.'

'I take it this means you think I killed her, but you'd be wrong. I wouldn't do that, I liked her, I really liked her. We'd got to be friends . . . it didn't seem like she was my grandmother at all –'

Mayo took all this with a pinch of salt. 'Stick to the facts for now, Mr Cordingley, if you please.'

'If it makes you any happier.' Cordingley stuck his hands in his pockets and leaned back, digging his heels into the carpet. 'She wrote me about eight weeks ago and told me who she was. She asked me to come over as soon as I could and sent me the money for my fare. I was knocked over . . . I'd no idea there was anything like that in the family background and I was intrigued. I'd always intended to trace my family if ever I got the opportunity, find out what kind of genes I'd inherited, that sort of thing. Well, I came over immediately, there wasn't anything particular to keep me in Canada.'

'Isn't that a long time to take leave from your job? Two months?'

'Luckily, I'd quit the job I was in a couple of weeks before I heard from her.' He offered no further explanation for what seemed a fortuitous occurrence. A timely leavetaking, Mayo suspected, capable of varied interpretation as to the exact date. He'd be willing to bet Cordingley had packed his job in as soon as he heard from Marion, he wouldn't have been able to wait to see what was in it for him. It was unlikely that Mrs Dove would have told him what her intentions were before seeing him.

'Carry on, please.'

'I contacted her as soon as I arrived over here, we struck up a rapport, and that's all there is to it.'

'A little more than that, I fancy.'

'What's that supposed to mean?'

'I believe Mrs Dove has been very generous to you, financially, over the last few weeks.'

'She helped me out a little, yes. I had to have somewhere to live –'

'And a car?'

'It's on hire.'

'Still costs money. But I think there was more, wasn't there, Mr Cordingley? I think she indicated that she was prepared to provide for you in her will and that's why you hung around.'

The young man threw him a narrow look, leaned back and folded his arms. He wasn't smiling any more. 'You think so?' he said. 'Then you're way out. I wasn't interested in any long-term projects.'

'Perhaps you'll be good enough to tell me what you were interested in.'

'Why not? She offered me a stake in the company – a marvellous chance, something right up my street, that would really give me scope. I could hardly believe it! She took me round the works and I could see the potential right away. They're dead from the neck upwards there, you know? So laid back they're damn nearly asleep. There's Ken Dainty, a wonderful craftsman but steeped in that damned family tradition, no ideas about branching out. Why do they need to keep to crystal ware, when the world's crying out for industrial glass, for instance? Money, he says, that needs money, to launch into something like that. My God, go in with one of the big conglomerates and their troubles are over! But he would never agree to that, he's still got the last five hundred years round his neck. And that old guy Bainbridge in charge of the offices! I tell you, they haven't seen anything like him in Canada in a hundred years. What it needs at Dove's is a clean sweep, something to take them into the twenty-first century, and forget the last five hundred years, for once. And she was going to give me the chance to do it!' His face had set with fury. 'So why, may I ask, should you think I killed her? I'd every reason for keeping her *alive*! What do I get now? Damn-all.'

'What did Mrs Dove say to these ideas of yours?'

'We didn't discuss that side of things.'

No, they wouldn't have done. He would have been careful not to. He knew just which side his bread was buttered on, this young man, and he wanted the jam as well. He'd have been careful to have his foot in the door before doing anything that might prevent his getting it.

'Tell me what happened on Sunday. Exactly.'

Cordingley had swiftly regained control. His white teeth flashed in one of those smiles of his as he said, 'I'd told her how I liked Lavenstock, that I was growing fond of it, and she said it was high time I saw some of the real English countryside, so we arranged to go out for a drive at about two o'clock.'

'Two? Not earlier?'

'No, it was two, though originally we'd arranged to start out mid-morning. She usually went to her sister's for Sunday lunch, but she'd cancelled that.'

'Is that what she told you? That she'd cancelled it?'

'That's right.'

This was a point that had troubled Mayo from the first. Marion Dove hadn't seemed to be the sort of person who would not turn up for a lunch without apology when she was expected. At first it had been assumed this was because she was dead by then, but now they knew she was alive until six at the least. And if

531

Cordingley – who appeared to have no reason to lie about it – was correct, then why had Gwen Bainbridge kept the meal waiting? Or *said* she had?

'But she rang me and said someone – her daughter, to be exact – was driving down to see her from that place in Northumbria where she teaches, and would I mind if we started out later, in the afternoon. It was a little early when I got there, about one-thirty. I fed the ducks for her while she changed, and then we went out.'

'Where did you go for your drive?'

'Oh, we just drove around through the country lanes, had a pot of tea and a toasted teacake at a little place in the Cotswolds, and then came back. It was a lovely day and we didn't hurry. We got back later than we intended.'

'When, exactly?'

'I don't know, exactly. Just after six, I guess.'

'Where did you park your car?'

'Right down by the house. Not where I normally left it, but I had to leave room at the top for the others.'

'Others? What others?'

'Oh my, haven't they told you? Ken Dainty – and Marion's daughters. I hadn't met the daughters. They were all supposed to be down at the lockhouse for seven-fifteen, so there could be a grand introduction. She was going to tell them formally what she intended to do.'

'I see. Did you call anywhere on your way back?'

'No. Apart from that ratty old place up the road, the Dog and Fox, to pick up some gin. I'd noticed before we left she only had a couple of shots left in the bottle and Ken's capacity alone is more than that. I'd an idea I was going to need more than that myself. It didn't seem to me the meeting was likely to go very smoothly.'

'You mean because Mr Dainty was likely to oppose your introduction into the firm?'

'Well, I knew that already! But I suspected there was something

532

else. Marion hadn't been herself all day. She seemed moody and she'd been probing into my past, wanting to know why I'd had so many jobs and all that. I told her, nobody nowadays stays with the same firm half a century like old Bainbridge. And of course it all came out when the others arrived. Dainty, the slimy bastard, had had enquiries made about what he called my track record. Well, you can cook up anything to look bad if you want to! The upshot of it was that Marion couldn't bring herself to tell them what she'd promised me she would. I tried all ways to get her to say but she refused to discuss it. In the end I lost my temper a little.'

His frankness, maybe because of the way he projected himself, was suspect, posing the question of why he should want to lie. Again he smiled. 'I could see *that* wasn't going to do my prospects any good, so I decided I'd better leave and go and think it all over. Dainty said not to bother, they were going anyway, he and Shirley had this dinner-party and were already late. Rachel went too, she'd driven them all down to her mother's and she had to get back up north.'

'So you were left alone with Mrs Dove?'

'I was, but I'd calmed down by then. I tried to get her to see reason, but she wouldn't promise me anything. She said she needed time to think, and in the end I had to be content with that. I helped her to clear up before I went. I was just getting into the car when she came running after me, waving her bag. She had five hundred pounds in it that she'd promised me and forgotten to hand over. I almost told her to take it back, but I didn't want to start anything up again, and there was the rent for my apartment, Lord knows what else . . .'

He'd known how to get round her. Feeding the ducks. Helping to clear up. And had been well rewarded. 'And that's all that happened? Are you sure your quarrel with your grandmother didn't escalate and end with your strangling her?'

Mayo waited for the outburst, which surprisingly wasn't immediate, though it would come, soon enough. Cordingley was fluent and plausible, he wouldn't waste time that he could otherwise use to justify himself. But he didn't hurry, and when he did speak, his natural arrogance seemed to have drained away. 'I just can't believe this! Two months ago I was in Toronto, not exactly living it up, but at least I was free. And now I'm in this mess, suspected of murder!'

'If you're innocent, you've nothing to worry about,' Mayo assured him, a statement he'd always considered particularly inane but which in the circumstances he considered was fair enough.

'You really believe that, do you? I've heard of British justice. I guess I'm not seeing much evidence of it. No, I didn't kill her! I did not!' Sweat stood on his forehead.

Mayo asked suddenly, 'You seem to have become very close to your grandmother . . . did she ever tell you who your grandfather was?'

It was the sort of random question that was apt to rattle witnesses and for a moment Cordingley seemed disorientated by it. 'No,' he answered, recovering quickly. 'I wasn't interested.'

Mayo had to listen to a lot of lies in his job. He would have imagined Cordingley would have made a better shot at this one, would have remembered sooner that he'd just said it was something he'd always intended to do as soon as he got the chance. He was remembering it now, too late.

Mayo had heard enough. This was as far as he was prepared to go at this point. 'All right, Mr Cordingley. Sergeant Kite here will get your statement typed and when you've signed it you can go.'

'Go?'

'What d'you expect, bed and breakfast as well as a ride back? But if I were you, I'd cancel that ticket back to Canada. You're not about to cross the Atlantic yet awhile.'

When Kite returned from following out his instructions an hour later, he found a message from Mayo, who had for some reason best known to himself decided to have another look at The Mount on his way home.

★

He had opened his desk drawer and found the big, old-fashioned key to the house staring up at him. It had been there since his first visit, waiting to be returned, and he must have opened the drawer dozens of times since without actually being aware of it, but now he picked it up, weighed it on his palm for a minute, then pocketed it and went down the stairs to his car.

He didn't need the key, after all. There was a car parked in the drive; a big, ten-year-old Vauxhall with a Leeds number-plate, and the front door of the house stood wide open. Some of the windows were open, too, letting in the evening sun that was shedding a misted radiance over the garden. The acrid smell of a bonfire was strong on the air. Smoke blew over the gate that led to the back of the house. He raised his hand to bang the knocker, but before he could do so, a man in shirtsleeves and corduroys came out through the gate.

This was no jobbing gardener. Mayo knew him at once, though he was taller and much thinner and altogether more ordinary than he'd appeared on the television screen. That phone call to his colleague wouldn't be necessary now.

'Dr Amory?' Mayo introduced himself and the man smiled and apologised for not shaking hands, spreading his own, begrimed from the bonfire, in explanation.

'I suppose you want to see Miss Dove?'

'If she's here, yes I do. I've needed to see her for the last couple of days.'

Mayo felt himself being assessed with a sharpness that wasn't disguised by a pair of horn-rimmed spectacles and a mild manner. You could wilt under a scrutiny like that, if you were maybe a young student, unsure of yourself and how your opinions were being received, but Mayo was made of sterner stuff and said, 'And I'd rather not waste any more time, if you don't mind.'

'I'm sorry. I was just wondering how I could ask you to go easy on her. She's had a pretty bad time, one way and another.'

'You can stay with her if you like and see I don't try any rough stuff. All I want is a few facts.'

'I've been telling her that since Friday,' Amory said mildly.

'She's been with you? Where?'

'We have a cottage on the Yorkshire coast. It's very quiet. She came to me on Friday and we went down the next day. I believe over the weekend she's been able to sort a few things out in her mind. Come inside.' In a relaxed and easy manner he led the way into the room off the hall which Mayo had on his previous visit assumed to be the study.

'Rachel,' Amory said as he went in, 'there's someone to see you. It's –'

'I heard, Josh. Hello, Mr Mayo.'

'Miss Dove.'

Now that she was here in front of him he found it curiously difficult to begin. She had resumed her seat at the large mahogany desk, which was piled with papers she was stuffing into cardboard boxes, presumably for the fire. Amory perched on the corner, swinging a negligent foot, while he himself occupied the chair opposite. He had the feeling they were ranged together, maybe against him. But she smiled suddenly and said, 'I owe you an apology. I shouldn't have gone away like that, but I needed time to think.'

'Next time you need to,' he answered austerely, not willing to forgive quite so easily, 'just let me know first. In fact, while you were away thinking, we've learned quite a bit about what happened last Sunday. So now I'd like to hear the truth from you, if you please.'

'Yes, of course. It wasn't very sensible not to have told you in the first place.'

He didn't feel an answer to this was called for. It confirmed a long-held belief of his, that a high IQ had very little to do with natural common sense. Those who claimed to be intellectuals were often quite spectacularly lacking in that commodity and the ability to manage the everyday affairs of life. Amory didn't on first acquaintance seem to fall into this category. He appeared pretty down to earth, and with a leavening of humour which he didn't think Rachel possessed. She looked happier, however, and more relaxed than when he'd seen her before. He suddenly noticed that the portrait over the desk, presumably of her father, had been taken down. He wasn't surprised. He imagined it had been the first thing she'd done before sitting at the desk. How her father had managed to sit under the cold regard of his own flat brown eyes, the mouth closed like a trap, perhaps to disguise its weakness, was unanswerable. His daughter didn't have to.

He collected himself and began to take her through the events of Sunday, starting with her arrival at the lockhouse and her departure back to her university. Amory was able to confirm the time of her arrival. He lived in college and it appeared she had gone straight to his rooms. Her account of what had happened at the lockhouse tallied in every respect with what Steven Cordingley had said.

'You saw them quarrelling and yet you were quite happy to leave her alone with him?'

'It had blown over by the time we left. I think he was genuinely sorry that he'd upset her and he was being especially nice to her. He's really quite charming when he wants to be.'

Mayo hadn't found him charming at all, but he allowed that women looked at things in a different way. 'And after you left the Jubilee?'

'I drove straight back up north, dropping Ken and Shirley at the Wainwrights' on the way. That was the reason we'd gone in my car, Ken's very sensible about not driving after he's been drinking, and someone else at the dinner-party had previously agreed to give them a lift home.'

One more thing he wanted to know. 'When we spoke before, you told me the reason your mother asked to see you was to tell you about her illness.'

'That's right, it was.'

'And that was all?' She didn't answer. 'Wasn't it about Steven she wanted to talk as well? Or did you know about him before then?'

She flushed and looked unhappily at Amory for support. What she saw there Mayo couldn't tell, but she said, 'No. Actually, neither Shirley nor I had ever heard of him until then. We'd neither of us any idea. It was something of a shock when she asked us to meet him that evening.'

He thought that quite an understatement, too. It must have been traumatic to say the least, even for Rachel, but in particular for Shirley Dainty.

'So she told you Steven Cordingley was her illegitimate grandson. I imagine she also told you who his grandfather had been?'

'Why should you imagine that? Why should she give away a secret she'd kept all her life?'

She knew, and she was lying because she also knew the father was still alive.

'It's Crytch,' said Kite when Mayo told him next morning what had happened. 'It has to be. Farrar's already found out he was stationed in North Wales at the time, so he could easily have been our unknown soldier, home on leave. We haven't got that far yet, but it'll be him.'

Mayo nodded approval of Farrar's efforts. He was damned annoying sometimes, with his know-all airs, but give him a job like this and he'd keep his nose to the ground like a bloodhound.

'I don't want to steal his thunder, let him carry on because we shall need confirmation, but it'll cut a corner if you and I go and see Crytch personally at his office. And I want you to tell me again exactly what young Valerie said to you when she ran after you in the car park at Dove's.' Kite had an excellent memory and was able to repeat the conversation word for word. 'We've got our man, Martin! But before we go and get him, get yourself a coffee.

You might need fortifying while you listen to me and see if you can pick holes in what I say. I don't want there to be any cock-up at this juncture.'

CHAPTER 21

Dull heavy weather had replaced the crisp sunny days, seeming to drain even the bright colour of the dahlias and gladioli crammed into the buckets of the flower-seller outside the Town Hall, and the last of the gaudy bedding-out schemes in the square of the new shopping precinct. The unstirring leaves on the trees in the park were now the heavy, dark green which says they've been there too long, it's time for a change. Some of them had already made the transmutation to pale gold. Today, the sky was that colour which is the absence of colour, all cloud. A flat, muted, nothing sort of a day. It might rain. A wind might get up and blow the cloud layer away. It might stay like this for days.

The Botticelli angel in the telephonist's cubicle at Dove's Glass had painted her porcelain features with a different palette. Her eyelids, lips and cheeks were a curious shade of tan and her hair, newly arranged in a stiff coxcomb, stood up straight from her head in no way nature ever intended, as though in fright at what had gone on underneath it.

'We'd like to see Mr Dainty, please.'

'Have you an appointment?' She didn't recognise Mayo. Callers were all one to her. He shook his head. 'I'm sorry, then,' she said, 'but he isn't seeing anyone.'

'He'll see us.' Mayo produced his warrant card and after a scared glance at their grim faces and a quick word on the internal telephone she told them that Mr Bainbridge said he was in the furnace hall but someone had been sent along to fetch him.

'Where is this furnace hall?' Mayo asked.

'Oh, but you can't –' She hastily changed her mind and directed them along a route which involved going out again into the car park and turning right into the yard, where they found the place easily enough. They went into the long, low, seemingly ramshackle building, and as soon as their eyes had become accustomed to the darkness saw Dainty standing in conversation with someone over by one of the glory-holes that was set into the huge domed furnace. The scene was like something out of hell, Mayo thought, the heat, the dark, the half-naked men, the swinging irons to which orange-hot gathers of molten glass were attached swishing through the air with little apparent respect for anyone in the way. Dainty stood waiting for them to approach, his face expressionless, his hand on the back of a bench with long wooden arms where the sitter rolled a bulb of fiery glass metal on the end of a pipe. This man would be the blower, the head of the team, the gaffer, supreme in the glassworks succession, Dainty as he had once been.

It was easy to imagine Dainty at home and content here before the furnace, stripped to the waist, his torso gleaming with sweat, ox-like shoulders lifting and swinging and wielding the heavy weight of glass. Now he looked haggard, Mayo saw as they came nearer, his forehead was dewed with sweat, but that might have been merely due to the dimness of the interior and the searing heat.

'Come to look round then, have you?'

No one could seriously believe they would take time off in the middle of a murder enquiry to be taken round the works like a Women's Institute outing, no one could be that naive. It showed his mind had been elsewhere. It had been something said without thought, a banality uttered to cover up the awkwardness, the embarrassment of their arrival. Men were looking speculatively at them, putting two and two together.

'We'd like a word in private, Mr Dainty, if you please.'

He turned and spoke briefly to the man beside him and then motioned them to follow him. They walked in silence out through the back door of the hall, then in single file up some steep, narrow back stairs and finally into his office. The light was poor on this dull day. Automatically, Dainty crossed the dove grey carpet and pressed the switch that illuminated the corner cabinets, another that lit a single green lamp on his desk. He lowered himself into his chair like an old man, all his vitality and energy gone, a defeated Minotaur. The effect of that vibrant colour and lighting in the dim room, and the solitary man sitting with his head supported by his hand was that of an actor sitting on a stage, waiting for the curtain to go up and the play to begin.

Mayo waited for Dainty to speak first. At last he said, 'What is it you want of me?'

'The truth about what happened last Sunday.'

'The truth?' He looked round the room in a vague distracted way, as if that were something he'd lost and might never find again. 'Well I – well.' On his desk was a carafe of water with a tumbler over its neck. He poured a glassful and drank it thirstily. 'Where do you want me to start?'

'After you got back from the golf club in the afternoon will do for the moment.'

'We came home and read the Sunday papers, dozed in front of the telly, went out to dinner with the Wainwrights . . . you know all this, I've already told you.'

'What you haven't told us is where you went after you had your snooze and before you had dinner.'

'Ah,' he said, then looked up with a show of his old belligerence. 'If you're asking that then you must know the answer.'

'You tell me, all the same – and no more funny tricks. You're already in serious trouble for wasting police time . . . you, and your wife, and your sister-in-law.'

'I don't know what you mean,' Dainty said, but he did. And he knew that Mayo already knew the answer. The bluster went out of him. 'All right, we called in to see Marion. Who's told you, Rachel?'

Mayo shook his head, and the blood rushed to Dainty's face as further realisation struck. 'All right,' he said again after a minute. 'Since he's obviously told you his version, I'll just put the record straight.'

'We're listening.'

But his account of what had happened at the lockhouse turned out not to differ substantially from that of Rachel or Cordingley. The disparity with the latter was only in the interpretation. Where Cordingley had implied treachery in Dainty's having him investigated, Dainty insisted that this had been the right and proper and only thing to do to avert total disaster within the firm. The slight disagreement Steven said he'd had with his grandmother over her refusal to come out with her plans for him Dainty implied had been a major row.

'Yet you left her alone with him?'

'By that time things had simmered down,' Dainty admitted. 'He'd apologised to her, and we had to go, we had a dinner date, remember? But if you think I came back and murdered her, you're mistaken. I wasn't going to have that young puppy putting his penn'orth in here at Dove's, mucking up everything I've been trying to do, I'd have fought like hell to stop it, but I didn't kill her!'

'Let me ask you something, Mr Dainty. You obviously knew Steven Cordingley was a protégé of Mrs Dove's, but do you know who he really is?'

'I don't give a toss who he is, he could be the Prince of Wales for all I care, it won't alter my attitude! She said he was her grandson, but who the father was is anybody's guess. Somebody she had an affair with during the war, I reckon. Ships that pass in the night.'

Did he really believe Marion Dove had been like that?

The thought communicated itself to Dainty. He had the grace to look ashamed, but it was himself he was really thinking of. 'You

542

have to believe me, you know! I didn't kill her – why should I be such a fool as to risk everything I've ever worked for? What I mean is, I wouldn't have killed her anyway –'

'As you say,' Mayo answered. 'It's good to know your heart's in the right place, Mr Dainty. But just now I'd like to have a talk with Mr Bainbridge, if it's all the same to you.'

He came into the otfice, leaning heavily on his stick but looking rather better, presumably after a weekend of rest, than Mayo would have expected. There was some slight colour in the marble face, less rigidity in the way he moved, the way he lowered himself in silence on to the upright chair by the window and waited for what they had to say.

Mayo began, 'The last time I saw you, you told me you weren't able to help us in the matter of Mrs Dove's murder. That was nearly a week ago. We've reason to think you might want to change your mind.'

Bainbridge's eyes, over his half-moon spectacles, regarded him steadily. 'Now why should you think that?'

'We've traced Steven Cordingley.'

'Ah.'

'We're aware of the circumstances surrounding his proposed introduction into the firm here, and the objections to it. I think you know all about that – and precisely what happened last Sunday evening. Whoever you think you're protecting, I'd advise you to think again and tell us what you know. I presume you know why we're here and you're now prepared to tell us?'

A slight, bitter smile twisted Bainbridge's pale features. His answer was bleak. 'There's really no need to presume at all. I'm quite ready to tell you what happened.'

It had been very dark, under the trees up by the old lock gates. He was grateful for that, and the respite. He could rest on the lock stairs, swallow one of his pills and wait stoically for the pain to assume more manageable proportions. He sat there in the shadows, the Malacca cane with the silver handle that had been his father's a support to lean against, and waited for the car parked beside the house to leave. That boy should have been gone long before now, it was getting late, time was pressing. It had taken him an hour, possibly more, he couldn't remember, to drag himself here, yard by painful yard, sliding each foot forward, hesitantly, so that if anyone had seen him, they'd have thought him a drunken man. He'd pretended to Gwennie over the weekend to be worse than he was, but now he had no need for pretence, he'd scarcely ever felt worse. But he would spoil nothing by giving in, at this stage. He was a patient man, prepared to go on waiting, and it was essential that he should remain calm for what he had to face.

The sweet, heavy scent of the honeysuckle climbing round her door pervaded the night. While phlox, starring the darkness, added its own layer of fragrance. A car's headlights scimitared the darkening road above, the noise of its engine increased as it crossed the bridge that spanned the canal, stopped and then after a while started up again. The door slammed, and then silence again, but for the gentle papery sound of the breeze ruffling the reeds.

He lost track of how long he had waited, occasionally getting up heavily and moving around with the aid of his stick so that he wouldn't stiffen up, but the dusk had deepened into dark when presently a rectangle of light showed in the lockhouse doorway, framing the figure of a man he knew to be Steven Cordingley. The door slammed behind him and he began walking with rapid strides towards his car. He'd barely reached it when the door opened again and Marion came out, calling to him. He stopped, and after a moment, turned.

Robert could hear their voices but not what they were saying. It was like a pantomime in dumb show. Her hand was on his arm, her face lifted to him, as if pleading. He saw her open her bag and press something on to him. Bile rose in his throat as Cordingley, after a show of reluctance, pocketed what Robert knew must be money. Finally he bent his head and kissed her on the forehead. A Judas kiss! She stood and watched him until he'd disappeared up the lane, and even after he'd gone and the noise of his car engine had faded, she stayed outside in the warm dark, unafraid and unaware that anyone might be watching, walking slowly back and forth along the towpath, her head bent.

He rose and stepped out of the shadows long before she reached him, so that she might see him. He didn't want to terrify her, to make her turn and run and start their meeting off at a disadvantage. But when she first saw him, he thought that was what she was going to do. She drew in her breath, and though she stood stock still, he could sense her gathering herself to turn and flee. He spoke her name, gently.

'Robert!' Her voice was constricted with shock. 'What *are* you doing here, this time of night? Where's Gwennie?'

'I'm on my own.'

'Gracious, how ever did you get here?'

'I walked.

'*Walked?* My dear Robert, you must be exhausted! Come inside and sit down, I'll make you a cup of tea.'

'I'd rather stay out here. I want to talk to you. It may be easier in the dark.'

She was immediately on the defensive. He could barely see her face, but her voice was low and urgent and he sensed the tension emanating from her. 'If it's about that business, I've already told you I don't want to talk about it. I'll make my own mind up when the time is right. I'll not be pushed into any decisions. Come on now, do let's go into the house and have that tea. I need a cup myself. Today's been absolutely exhausting.'

His own tiredness had gone beyond the point of exhaustion. He had made a superhuman effort and the small strength he'd regained from his rest had drained away, but he no longer felt tired or otherwise, rather a lack of sensation, a feeling of being weightless, in limbo.

'I want to ask you to think again,' he said.

In the silence a far-off dog barked, the reeds at the foot of the lock gates stirred with the presence of some unseen animal and the leaves overhead rustled in some faint atavistic empathy. She turned and took a few slow paces along the towpath towards him, as if each one were an effort. It occurred to him that Marion – Marion, strong and indestructible and ageless – had begun to seem older recently.

'I have thought, Robert.'

'And?'

'I can't do what you want.'

'But you must not do the other.'

There was a familiar, stubborn quality about her silence. Finally she said, 'I thought you, of all of them, would understand. I thought you'd be *glad* to welcome your own flesh and blood. Don't you see, I have to do this last thing for him – he's never had the chances that Shirley and Rachel have had.'

'Then give him money, for God's sake! There's no need for you to do more. It isn't you he cares for, all he wants is money.'

'That's cruel! I never thought I'd hear you being cruel!'

'I'm being realistic. Face it, Marion. He'll destroy Dove's for what he can get out of it, and others into the bargain. Look at him and see him as he is. Are you proud of what we created between us? I'm not.'

She raised her right hand and struck him, right across the face, and almost lost her balance. She closed her eyes and gave a little whimper, of pain, of surprise and shame at her own action. He dropped his stick and took her by the upper arms and her eyes flew open. 'Come to your senses, don't be such *a fool*! Can't you see what you're going to do to everyone, to Rachel and Shirley – most of all, to Gwennie? My God, have you even *thought* what it will do to Gwennie?'

He shook her violently and for a moment they teetered together on the edge of the canal. Part of it fell away and his grip tightened, pulling her away from the edge, afraid she might go into the water. She moaned again, and as he looked at her, he could see death in her face, the stark shape of the skull beneath the tight-drawn skin. She was a gargoyle, her lips drawn back in fear, her eyes wild. But still she shook her head. He lost all sense of time, or reason, he could see nothing but a red mist in front of his eyes. His hands round her neck felt preternaturally strong, as they hadn't felt for years.

It didn't take much effort. She hardly struggled at all. She went limp and quite soon he knew she was dead.

He released his hands and she fell away from him backwards into the water. He stayed where he was, petrified as sense returned, unable to move for several minutes. Then he looked down, and saw with horror that her body hadn't sunk much below the surface, it was supported by the mud and reeds that had silted up the canal. He had no strength left to move her, to push her out into the deeper water at the centre where she would sink. With an anguished cry, he groped for his stick, then staggered, almost crawled, up the lane.

At the top, where it emerged on to the road, a girl was manoeuvring a car out through the gate of a field where it had been parked, the car he'd heard draw up earlier. She got out to lock and close the gate behind her and for a crazy moment he was tempted, almost beyond resistance, to beg a lift of her, but sanity, or self-preservation, triumphed over his weakness. He thought he might well die before he reached the sanctuary of home again, and at that moment would have welcomed it. It didn't matter what happened to him now. He had done what was necessary, now Gwennie would never, ever know how he'd betrayed her.

After Bainbridge had finished speaking, no one seemed inclined to say anything. Dainty looked like a man in shock. In the dim light, with his pale polished face, Robert Bainbridge bore an uncanny resemblance to that black and white photograph of his daughter, to Rose.

Dainty poured another tumbler of water and drank. '*You* were the father of Marion's child?' He sounded stupefied. 'I don't believe it!'

'I don't suppose you do, but I wasn't always old, and a cripple.' Exhaustion was evident now in the dragging way he spoke, the faint flush had intensified to two bright spots on either cheek, and his eyes were very bright. His speech had lost its pedantry, and seemed to have regained some of its former local intonation.

'I came home on leave the day after their house in Chapel Street was bombed. The place was in ruins, her mother and father had both been taken to hospital. Marion was staying with relatives.' He paused but went on almost immediately, and there seemed little point in trying to stop him, since he evidently had the guilty person's intention of making a clean breast, and enough of his own brand of determination to carry it through. 'She used to cycle up to the hospital every evening to see her parents. I was at a loose end, so I took to going with her, for company. One time, after the visiting, we rode round the countryside a bit . . . it was a beautiful evening, it was May, the May blossom was out on the trees. Well, she'd been very brave about it all but that evening for some reason she broke down. I tried to comfort her, one thing led to another . . .'

He'd forgotten the others by now, he was speaking to himself, looking inside himself. 'God alone knows what got into me – except that she was there and Gwennie wasn't – when all I wanted, all I've ever wanted, was Gwennie. Nobody could have been more shamed than I was, than I've always been.' He closed his eyes and then said tonelessly, 'I didn't rape her, you know. She wasn't unwilling. And I – I wasn't the first, either.'

No. There had been Geoffrey Crytch. But Crytch's unit had left Wales and had been fighting in North Africa in May 1943. That was what he'd told them an hour ago. It had been necessary to check that he couldn't have been the soldier Collis had remembered, although Mayo had been as nearly positive as ever he could be, after Mrs Cordingley's mention of Rose's birthday, that Robert Bainbridge, on leave at the time of the bombing, the relevant time, was the father. And that, as far as Robert Bainbridge was concerned, had constituted motive enough.

'That's why, when I eventually learned about the baby,' Bainbridge was doggedly going on, 'I never thought it could have been mine. But I *didn't* know about it, not until long after we'd been married, Gwennie and me. I'd no reason not to believe the story about Marion having some sort of nervous trouble and going away to stay with that aunt – I'd seen how upset she'd been that night, so it didn't surprise me. It was years later Gwennie told me the truth. Neither the parents nor Marion ever mentioned it, there was this conspiracy of silence, pretending nothing had happened, nobody was supposed to breathe a word about it. So I couldn't have asked Marion herself without letting her think Gwennie had broken her promise never to speak of it. And anyway, I reckoned if she'd thought the baby was mine, she'd have told me, wouldn't she?'

It was what he wanted to believe, he had convinced himself that it was so. 'Besides, we've never had children of our own, we've never been lucky that way. What a terrible thing it would have been for Gwennie to know . . .'

He leaned back in the chair and ran a finger round the inside of his collar. His knuckles were white as he leaned forward on his stick. As he must have leaned on the fateful night, waiting for Steven Cordingley to go, making indentations in the ground which might have been, but were not, the marks of high heels.

'When did you realise the child was yours?' Mayo asked.

'Not until a few weeks ago. She came to me and told me she'd always bitterly regretted having the baby adopted and finally she'd decided to do something about it and have it – the little girl she'd called Rose – traced. I begged her not to do it, to let sleeping dogs lie, but she'd made her mind up and she wouldn't listen. She said nobody need ever know that Rose had anything to do with me,

549

she'd kept her silence all these years and she was wasn't about to break it now. Well, as you know, the trail ended in Steven Cordingley.'

He broke off once more to mop his forehead. He'd been talking practically non-stop, feverishly, as if he had to get everything out as quickly as possible. 'Take your time, Mr Bainbridge,' Mayo said. Bainbridge merely waved his hand impatiently and went on. Mayo didn't try to stop him. They were getting the confession they needed, which was just as well, since without it, there was precious little to prove him guilty of the crime he'd committed.

'I knew as soon as I saw him that he was trouble, in every way. Bad for the firm, but even worse for me – and Gwennie. You've seen that young man. Does he strike you as the sort to pass by the chance of finding out who his grandfather was? The first time he met me, he began asking questions. He's the sort who'd not stop until he'd ferreted the truth out. And he'd have used it, believe me!'

Mayo didn't doubt this for a minute.

'She went a little mad, I think. Now that she'd found him, there wasn't enough she could do for him, even to standing by and seeing him ruining the firm she'd given most of her life to.'

'And that was important to you?'

'Yes, of course it was, in a way. But there's only one thing – one person – really important to me, who's ever mattered, and that's Gwennie. She's stood by me through thick and thin, even when I came out of the forces a crock. I couldn't – I *wouldn't* – let her know, that I'd been disloyal to her, and with her sister, her sixteen-year-old sister. How could I? What has she done that she should be made to suffer? To share my guilt? There was *nothing* I wouldn't have done to protect her from that kind of hurt.'

It occurred to Mayo as he looked at the man that here was the face of a fanatic. Men with eyes like this, burning in their sockets, the skin of the face stretched taut over the bones, had roasted at the stake for their beliefs. Men who'd achieved unbelievable feats of heroism, near-miracles, by the sheer strength of their willpower, by an unswerving single-mindedness. It no longer seemed impossible, or even unlikely to believe, that Bainbridge, lame and in constant pain, had dragged himself from Holden Hill to the Jubilee Locks and then strangled a woman with his bare hands.

'But, good God, to kill her!' Dainty exclaimed, appalled.

'I didn't mean to,' he said, as they so often did, afterwards. 'I loved her, as we all did. If she'd listened to reason, it wouldn't have happened. And I – I didn't know she was ill, dying.'

'If you had, would it have made any difference?'

Bainbridge said nothing. His face was livid, he looked very ill. Then he said, bleakly, 'No, very probably not.'

He might not have planned to murder her, but had it been entirely an accident? He must have made his schemes for that day, a last bid to make her see sense. He had let slip that he had seen Marion the previous Friday, *after* her quarrel with her sister, he'd told Mayo how upset she was about it. She had been in the office at Dove's on the Friday afternoon and according to Valerie had seen Bainbridge as well as Dainty. Steven Cordingley was certain she had cancelled her usual Sunday lunch arrangement. Not with her sister, however, but obviously through Bainbridge. He hadn't told Gwen, because that would have involved explaining about Steven. Presumably, he had hoped to persuade Marion to think again and they could have found some way of accounting for her absence.

That was how Mayo and Kite had thought it must have happened. Mayo turned to ask Bainbridge, but he was speaking again, his voice sounding strange and slurred. 'It's very warm in here, a glass of water –'

Dainty blinked like a man coming out of hypnosis and picked up the half-empty carafe on his desk. 'I'll get a clean glass.'

'Never mind that, use the one that's there,' Mayo ordered, springing to the old man's side. With equal alacrity, Kite leapt to fill the tumbler and Mayo said to Bainbridge, loosening his collar, 'Have you any pills?'

A faint shake of the head. The flush had gone, the face was a pallid grey, like cold porridge, but his mouth twisted into a parody of his old, ironic smile.

'None left,' he said.

He wasn't going to need them, anyway. Not now.

CHAPTER 22

He'd rarely felt less inclined to meet and talk over the events of a case with anyone. At the lockhouse, what was more, a rendezvous he liked no better. But Mrs Bainbridge had asked to meet him there and he felt he owed her that, at least, so he took himself off with as good grace as he could muster.

The leaves were falling from the trees in great autumn drifts, but the little house didn't have the forlorn, deserted air he'd expected. It was still furnished as it had been when Marion Dove lived there, Mrs Bainbridge had lit a fire against the chill and there was the everlasting pot of tea ready, and a plate of warm, lavishly buttered scones. Then he noticed the net curtains at the windows, the brass ornaments . . .

'You're living here,' he said, taken aback and trying not to show it.

'I couldn't stand it, up there in Harmer Street, not without – not on my own, but I'd nowhere else to go until I thought of this. I like it here anyway, and I've got Paul living with me. He has a makeshift bed on the sofa for now, but we've got other plans. I'm going to have an extension built on with a room behind he can have for his own. It won't be very big, but I don't suppose he'll be with me for long, they want to be off and on their own these days. I shall miss him, he's been such a comfort. But by the time I get the extension finished they'll have opened up the canal and what

I thought was, I'd start up a little tea-room, for people on the boats. What d'you think of that?'

At first thought the whole idea seemed macabre and ghoulish in the extreme, planning to live here where such a horrific tragedy had occurred, involving the two people she had loved best. But perhaps it wasn't. Maybe, by not shutting it out of her mind, she'd more easily be able to come to terms with what had happened, find the same sort of peace her sister had found, be able to 'kiss the joy as it flies'.

In the last weeks she'd put on weight. She was evidently one of those who ate for comfort, not one who dwindled away to nothing through grief. Her hair was white at the roots where the tint was growing out, and if she was pale, her make-up concealed it. She was as smartly dressed as ever, and the black suited her. He felt like clapping, or perhaps weeping.

When he'd eaten as many scones as he could manage – he was taking Alex out to supper tonight – and manfully drunk two cups of tea, she poured herself a third cup with plenty of sugar, then settled back in her chair and fell silent. The logs on the fire threw sparks up the chimney. Suddenly she said, her voice not quite steady, 'He did it for me, you know. He did it all for me, and there was no need. That's what upsets me. No need for any of it, because I knew.'

Once more she'd succeeded in astonishing him. 'You knew?'

For a moment the lines of communication were crossed. Then she saw what he meant. 'I'm not talking about Marion dying, though that's all part of it, of course. I meant I'm the one who's to blame for all this. I ought to have told him, but I didn't have the courage.'

'What did you ought to have told him, Mrs Bainbridge?'

'That I knew about the baby. I've always known it was his, see. Well, not always, but soon enough. The more she refused to talk about it, the more it made me think. I started putting two and two together and well . . . once I'd faced the possibility, everything else

553

fell into place. I'd nothing to prove I was right, but there's times when you don't need proof, when you just know. I wasn't jealous or anything, I knew there couldn't ever have been anything serious – and anyway, he was married to *me*, it was *me* he loved. Always.'

'You can't blame yourself,' he told her, but couldn't quite bring himself to add what he also felt, that Bainbridge should have been the one to tell her the truth. Of all people, surely he could have trusted Gwen to understand. Not allowing her to forgive indicated a kind of arrogance.

'As to the other – I didn't know he was responsible for – for her dying, not at first, how could I? It was only when you started asking questions about the baby that I began to be frightened it might be that. But I put it to the back of my mind, I refused to admit it could be possible. I wouldn't think about it. The other felt worse, somehow, him finding out that I knew about the baby. It was something I'd dreaded happening for years. He'd never have been able to bear it, you know.'

Their eyes met. She knew why her husband had done what he had done. It was probable, if hard to credit, that Bainbridge had acted as he did simply to protect his wife. So hard that Mayo would never wholly countenance it. In part, it must have been true, and Bainbridge himself had undoubtedly believed it, but motives are seldom so selfless, or unmixed. Gwen Bainbridge too, he saw now, had her doubts. She and Bainbridge between them had created this image of the perfect marriage, the perfect husband, and she alone knew that it had not been in his nature to admit to her he had, even once, had feet of clay.

So this was why she had asked him to come here. She'd realised too late that if the subject had been broached early in their marriage, such a situation would never have arisen, her sister's death would never have happened, but this was looking at events with tragic hindsight. It wasn't his job to reassure her, to tell her what she needed to be told, that she had done the only thing possible in the circumstances. Probably there was no one else she could talk to, no one who knew all the facts. He did his best. They talked for a long time. But he didn't think she'd ever be totally convinced.

He came out of the overheated cottage and stood at the foot of the first lock for a moment or two before walking up the lane to his car. The tall plants by the water's edge had a black, shrivelled look, the water was no longer green but dark and oily, brambles that the Devil had spit on caught at his trouser legs as he turned to leave. He wouldn't come here again. He walked up the rutted lane to where he'd parked his car at the top, and then drove back to Alex.